May 1812

M. M. Bennetts

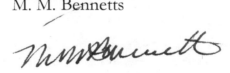

Dragon International Independent Arts

Available from all major online retailers
and available to order through all UK bookshops

Or contact:
Dragon International Independent Arts
Suite 133, 80 High Street
Winchester, Hampshire SO23 9AT
0845 643 6480
books@diiarts.com
www.diiarts.com

Printed in the UK

For the Beloved

Es war, als hätt' der Himmel
Die Erde still geküßt,
Daß sie im Blütenschimmer
Von ihm nur träumen müßt'...

By the same author

Of Honest Fame
(to be published by diiarts in 2010)

Unstable dream, according to the place,
  Be steadfast once; or else at least be true;
  By tasted sweetness make me not to rue
  The sudden loss of thy false feignèd grace.
By good respect in such a dangerous case
  Thou broughtest not her into this tossing mew,
  But madest my sprite live my care to renew,
  My body in tempest her succor to embrace.
The body dead, the sprite had his desire;
  Painless was th'one, th'other in delight.
  Why then, alas, did it not keep it right,
Returning to leap into the fire,
  And where it was at wish it could not remain?
  Such mocks of dreams they turn to deadly pain.

Sir Thomas Wyatt (c.1503-1542)

London

Unstable dream, according to the place,
Be steadfast once; or else at least be true;

1

The last of the evening's bottles lay empty on the floor beside his chair as he sat in the pristine silence that was night melting into early morning. Before him, the breakfast table was covered with pages of dog-eared letters and intercepted dispatches, with copies of more letters and more dispatches, strewn and in stacks, and each page covered in lines of numbers, all of them written in the Grand Chiffre, as they called it. Streaks of paly flame burned upward from the wax stubs in a single candelabra, five stripes of light against the curtained gloom, while about their bases the liquid wax pooled or eked over to drip, stippling the table with dark dull rounds on the polished mahogany surface. His coat he had removed and discarded, flinging it onto a side chair where it hung uneasily on the handle of a spare driving whip left there some days ago.

Myddelton swallowed the last of his coffee and briefly looked up at the green walls of the eating parlour, crammed with an array of engravings and portraits of his father's favourite hunters.

"20.14.59.29."

The coffee was cold. His eyes were red-rimmed and about his throat his neckcloth hung limp and dishevelled as if he'd spent the night whoring in some King Street bordello. He hadn't.

"20.14.59.29?"

Again he scanned the most recent letter, which he'd copied with ample space between each of its lines for translation. *"Ah, mon ami, il ne peut pas dissimuler qu'il 20.14.59.29 le 36.49.1.12.63.14.17 de 6.28.27.30.31..."*

Was *20.14.59.29.* the sequence for *était*? 'Struth, it must be. For no other word would complete the sentence properly. Yet with so many symbols for letters, one of them could be a bigram.

And breaking the silence in that clockless room with the muted scraping of Metallic pencil upon paper, Myddelton drew brackets under the numbers. And noted the probable bigrams below each. And studied the table of bigrams and syllables he had compiled: *E* was the most commonly used letter in French, so code-numbers one through twenty might well equal *e* and its combinations.

Then, studying the lines of code in another recent dispatch, he searched for the recurrence of 20.14.59.29. And then for 14.59.29.

Because if 20 equalled *et,* then 14 was *a,* 59 was *i* and 29 was *t.* And if that was so, then he had cracked one of the most commonly used verbs.

Suddenly sure of it, he smiled. "Got you, Froggie bastard!"

And with a new rushing energy of intellectual pleasure to banish his fatigue, Myddelton began once more, methodically searching out all instances of the repeated numbers on the several pages before him, segmenting off the coded sequence wherever he found it. And shifting the piles of ragged-edged and smudged pages, at the top of another page, a sentence caught his attention—for there too were words amongst the code, several words in fact.

"Dans la lettre de 16ème mars, 1207 annonçait que 516.1264 donnait 703.1328 le commandement de 409.1327.1333.210.249.523, mais faisait 1165.1060.1238.820. Votre Excellence..."

And translating, he read it again: "In the letter of the 16th March, 1207 announced that 516.1264 gave 703.1328 command of..." And smiled again.

For 1207 had to be a proper name. As did 516.1264. Thus 1264 was the surname, and 516 a title or rank.

"Ha!" His smile grew. "Got you again..."

But what if the whole code was broken into sections? Two sections? Or even more? Piss in the wind, Frenchie lobcock.

Marking his place with his finger, rapidly he compared the placement of the numbers above 1200 with those below. It *was* possible...

Without knocking, oblivious, Myddelton's private secretary and cousin, Mr. Thomas Broke, entered carrying a tray with the morning's newspaper and post upon it. The correspondence he had sorted already:

invitations were opened and laid out chronologically; letters of estate business had also been opened; private or official letters he had left, their many coloured seals intact, in a neat pile.

"Good morning, my lord."

Myddelton put up his hand to still any further conversation as he scribbled notes along the margin of the second letter. "What is it, Tom?" he murmured without looking up.

Broke hesitated, then glanced warily at his employer. "It's…" He swallowed. "…morning," he said. "I've brought the post."

Blinking, Myddelton raised his eyes. "Go away, Tom. Just go away."

And his finger upon the phrase of numbers he was attempting to decipher, Myddelton blew out a long breath of satisfaction. Hell and all its angels, he had it. He'd broken into the bastard. He looked across at the slices of light penetrating the half-shut draperies. It was morning. He had been here all night.

Uncertain, Broke hovered like a young peahen transfixed by a hunter's boots.

Myddelton sat back in his seat to stare at the ceiling roundel, mercifully unenhanced by the frolicking presence of naked Roman deities with attendant nymphs. His legs were stiff from sitting too long. "All right," he sighed, giving way. His eyes ached with the light, the fatigue. 'Struth, if he shut them, he'd be asleep where he sat. "Right…" he said absently. "What have you got there? Anything from Hinton?"

Relieved, Broke set the tray down in front of his employer, his great and handsome cousin. "Yes. He writes that he has cleared the pasture down by Gander Bottom, just like you said, and has moved the two mares in there, and that seems to have solved the problem. And Morley writes that Mrs. Fred is breeding again and he expects the litter before midsummer."

Dragging his mind away from the French and their pestilential codes, Myddelton tried to summon some enthusiasm. He rubbed at his forehead. "Excellent. Tell him to put aside a bitch for Pemberton, will you? Any word yet on the new stable block?"

"No, my lord, not yet." Mr. Broke paused. He shifted his weight

13

from one foot to the other. "Ehm, I'm afraid that there is another letter from Ruttridge here though." A small missive lay open, its red seal cracked and broken, beside the invitations on the tray. "Sent by special messenger. He seems quite insistent this time, almost adamant, really, upon an interview." Broke's eyelashes fluttered nervously. "I have checked *all* the files, though I can find nothing to demand your immediate attention. But, ehm, he has been requesting an interview f...for over six months, so perhaps...I suppose it could conceivably be about the will..."

Myddelton regarded his earnest young cousin and gave a whisper of a laugh. "Ruttridge, eh? 'Struth, he is a prosy old fossil. I'll have to see him, won't I?" He gazed down upon the pages yet undecoded. He might be here for another six months altogether without cracking the whole. Still. "'Struth, if you say there is nothing, then, I have no doubt it will prove to be so...Tom, you exhaust me with your thoroughness...But, ehm, while I'm thinking on it..." His concentration now well and truly broken, Myddelton poked at the invitations, then perused the letter from the persistent Ruttridge. "Go by Weston's today, will you, and order yourself a new coat. The cuffs on that one are threadbare."

Mr. Broke gave a worried glance to his cuffs.

"Yes, Tom, they are. And I'd not like it said that Myddelton is too clench-fisted to clothe his private secretary, you know. Particularly as it ain't true. Have Weston send the bill to me." Carelessly Myddelton broke open the seal of a letter from a cousin and read: *My gout has improved; I should be glad of a gun dog out of your Mrs. Fred when next she is in pup. Yours, etc.*

"Truly, it's not necessary," Mr. Broke protested.

Myddelton looked up from the letter, regarding Broke as an elder sibling regards his awkward, underfed stripling of a younger brother. "'Pon my soul, Tom, it is. Indulge in your morbid fondness for funereal black, that's as you wish, but you will order a new coat. No, make it two. We are agreed?

"Oh, and tell Morley he's to put aside one of the dogs for Fitzjohn, will you?" Myddelton yawned. He reached for his snuff-box and again picked up the note from his solicitor. And reread the contents.

"Adamant, I think you said? Agitated, certainly, the old devil. It will have to be Monday, though. I'm meant to have this lot cracked by last week." He shook his head. If he were to go up now, he could sleep for what? Four hours perhaps. "Send a note off. Make it for three." He glanced out of the window. "Is that the sun come out? 'Struth, I hardly recognise it after all this time."

And supporting his chin against his knuckles, Myddelton lifted a page from underneath the others in order to start again, to match it against the columns of numbers and the corresponding words he'd assembled. And laid it alongside the list of bigrams. Damned Frenchies. "Thank you, Tom. You're a prince. That'll be all... *Dans la lettre de 16ème mars, 1207 annonçait que 516.1264 donnait...*"

Broke fidgeted. He drew a sharp breath. "Perhaps, sir, if you was to sleep more, you'd find it easier..." he ventured.

"Yes, Tom, yes..." Myddelton agreed idly. "Have Kettering send in a fresh pot of coffee, will you? And a tankard of ale..."

"Yes, my lord." Broke bowed, and withdrew, muttering under his breath, "I'm sure even Napoleon sleeps...even if it is just two hours a night, as they say..."

❧

They were late.

"Remind me why we're here," Myddelton said doubtfully.

Beside him, Pemberton stood a near mirror image. "Because you like your cousin and it's her party," came his careless reply.

"Ah. Yes. I suppose I must do," Myddelton agreed. He paused to polish the quizzing glass he wore on a ribbon about his neck, then raised it to survey the crowded room, to look out over the collections of turbanned dowagers and middle-aged matrons in subdued silks seated against the four walls, the knots of young and not-so-young gentlemen clustered about the various beauties, and saw tucked away in the corners the cliques of the politically-active, oblivious to the gossip and flirtation. From the open door beyond came the strains of a popular dance tune. The evening's hostess was nowhere in sight and the cacophony was murderous.

"The things one endures for family…" he concluded. "Do you mean to go on to White's later? Then I shall join you. Come find me…" Persistently and patiently, stopping every two or three steps to speak with a friend or nod to an acquaintance, he began to shoulder his way into the room.

"Myddelton!" Sir Miles Northcote, the husband of the cousin whom Myddelton liked, greeted him with a clap upon the shoulder. "Do you know, I hoped you would favour us with your presence. Though I must say, I wasn't counting on it. When Anne said she expected you, I told her there wasn't a chance—said you was likely to be holed up with Planta until well past midnight."

"Evening, Northcote. Don't tell them I've slipped the lead, will you?" As it happened, Myddelton liked his cousin's husband equally well.

Northcote's eyes gleamed with amusement. He lowered his voice. "No, no. Not a word. But come, allow me to fetch you a glass of something," he said, leading the way through the maze of guests toward the dining room where a cold buffet supper was being laid out. "One hears all variety of rumours about the goings-on in the Foreign Office, but I do not suppose you can confirm or deny any of 'em, can you?" he said as they sidled past two ancient ladies and their even more aged companions who were observing the dancing.

"No." Myddelton said dampeningly. Then: "Well…Perhaps. I dare say it depends on what you've heard."

"Ah…Hmn.…Here we are, champagne?" Northcote helped himself to two glasses from the tray of a passing footman without ever entering the dining room and handed one to Myddelton.

"Thank you."

Shrewdly, Northcote waited while Myddelton tasted his champagne. A balding, round-faced gentleman of middle years, he was possessed of an affable nature and a wry sense of humour. "Any word from the Americans since the Prime Minister announced the repeal of the Orders in Council?"

"No." In the ballroom beyond, one dance had finished and another commenced.

"Not a word? But that's good, isn't it?" Northcote pressed.

Myddelton frowned and drank the full glass of champagne down. "We've written to Barlow, the American ambassador in Paris to let him know that we intend to revoke the dashed Orders. From all I've heard he's a decent enough fellow—so we may expect plain dealing from him. And as the Orders were the source of American grievances, I should hope that'll be an end to it. At least as far as we're concerned." It was their one success in this long winter of war…

"You don't sound convinced," Northcote observed.

"No, no," Myddelton demurred. "'Struth, Miles, it's all dragged on for too long and I for one am happy to see an end to it. The Hawks in the American Congress shan't be pleased, I dare say. From all I heard, they were hoping to use a small war as an excuse for a land grab in Canada…"

"Bally colonials!" Miles exclaimed. "They want teaching a lesson."

Myddelton laughed. "Perhaps. Perhaps. Still, I am content that with a fair wind our letters and dispatches will get to Washington as soon as may be."

"But?" Sir Miles prompted.

Myddelton paused, then said with a trifle more heat than he perhaps intended, "Upon my word, Miles, the Frogs have been playing a double game from the outset—setting us off against each other like schoolboys and we should have known better. Even if the Americans are too naive to see it. We should have known."

"Still…still, we have fulfilled our side of the bargain and that should be an end to it," Myddelton said with finality, then drew out a neat gold snuffbox, etched, and incurved to nestle in the palm of his hand. Absently he regarded the lid before flicking open the box with his thumb.

"Will it satisfy Napoleon and the damned French, do you suppose?"

Myddelton touched the edge of his thumbnail to the finely ground tobacco, snapped the box shut and brought his hand up so that he might inhale the grains of snuff from off his nail into each nostril, then slipped the box back into his pocket and dusted off his fingertip. And sniffed hard to inhale. "No. That vainglorious little Corsican upstart has marched his armies from one end of the Continent to the other, slaughtering God knows how many innocent souls, removing legitimate rulers willy-nilly and replacing 'em with one member after another of his pestilential family—each of 'em more feckless and debauched than the last—and he must be stopped."

Sir Miles refused to be flustered—Myddelton was not the only Foreign Office hothead he knew. And he was very well acquainted with his cousin-by-marriage and had had this conversation (or one remarkably like it) before. Though for once Myddelton was remaining almost calm. Northcote signalled to a footman for another glass to be brought.

Myddelton changed his empty glass for a full. "The French are naught but a country of butchers and madmen—and the Americans are fools if they think they can negotiate with 'em. There is not a single treaty to which Napoleon has put his name that he has not broken. Not one. And we are all paying the price of French ambition. All of us."

"I know you see a great deal more than most of us are allowed to know..." Northcote murmured. "I do wonder that you can sleep at night..."

"Good lord, Miles," Myddelton said with a wry half-smile. "There's far too much work to allow for sleeping." He gazed about the room, upon the milling guests, caught the eye of someone from across the room and nodded a greeting.

"Is that so? That's Castlereagh's idea of remuneration, is it? No sleep?" Northcote quipped, diverted. "But what of our Peninsular Allies—the Spanish? What of them?"

"Ha! The Spanish!" Myddelton exclaimed, beginning upon a recitation he could repeat in his sleep. "Do not talk to me about the Spanish, Miles. Upon my word, Wellington reckons that they are the most incapable of all nations, the most vain and at the same time, the most ignorant—lacking decency, honesty or even common spirit. And his brother agrees with him. Nevertheless, every dashed letter I translate from 'em is the same—they rail in the vilest terms against our presence anywhere near their precious American colonies, they abuse us for every military defeat they suffer at the hands of the French, even though their generals are little but overfed cretins, and their army is half-naked and lacks even basic military training. Do you know," he demanded, his voice rising. "Do you know, Wellesley says he wouldn't even trust the protection of a favourite dog to that pack of rabble? Meanwhile, that mob of humbugs and mushrooms they call the *junta* sits in that bally *cortes* of theirs, not—as you would have thought—discussing the war effort or addressing themselves to anything as commonplace as paying their troops' wages. No. No, they're debating whether or not they want the Inquisition any longer. And then, then, they demand a further increase to the subsidy we're paying 'em!" Belatedly, most belatedly, Myddelton looked up and caught the gleam in Northcote's eye, the twitching at the corners of his mouth. He stopped cold, drew breath, then gave a rueful laugh. "You're roasting me now, ain't you? You're practising on me, you unconscionable coxcomb…"

Northcote's smile grew. "Forgive me. The temptation is too great."

For an instant, Myddelton clamped his jaw tight and rolled his eyes toward the ceiling. Then, with a laugh: "Miles, you are the most unpardonable devil…And one of these days, one of these days…" He shook his head, before looking up. "Ah," he murmured, his mind now in two (or three) places…*1207 annonçait que 516.1264…annonçait que ce…*516 must equal *ce* or *cet.* "'Struth, Miles, you must pardon me, I believe I am engaged for this waltz." And still chuckling over Northcote's well-aimed raillery, he waved his farewell, and went in search of his partner.

It was much later, after he had danced, and spoken again to Northcote, that Myddelton left the ball with Pemberton. The night air had cooled, and he smiled as they made their way from Berkeley Square toward Piccadilly and St. James's Street, thinking of the unquestionable charms of Miss Wythenshaw—the young lady whom he had partnered. 'Struth, with that raven black hair and bow-like red mouth, she might have been the prototype for Schneewittchen had she been born twenty years earlier and German. Nor did her physical perfections end with her face.

"I still don't see why you thought I should come tonight…" Myddelton commented at last. Then with a sideways glance at Pemberton, he added, "All that about being sick to death of seeing every female under the age of sixty swooning over that poxy charlatan Byron, and wanting some sensible company was hornswoggle, wasn't it?"

"Not a bit of it!" Pemberton protested. "He wasn't there, praise

God."

"You know, one of these days, I shall kill you," Myddelton said pleasantly. "You, Dunphail, Alvanley, and Northcote. Together or separately, I don't much mind which...No, on second thought, separately. You shall be last. And *I* shall enjoy every painful minute."

Tall, yet Myddelton was the taller, the darker, and broader in the chest, they had been friends since school and for much of that time inseparable if not indistinguishable. However since joining the Foreign Secretary's staff, a measure of sobriety had crept into both Myddelton's demeanour and dress so that now he favoured the statesman's choice of black and white for evening. The younger by six weeks, he had outgrown the follies of his extravagant taste sooner than his friend. Though Pemberton had at last, at the age of eight and twenty, outgrown that lankiness which often accompanies height in a man.

Pemberton laughed. "So what did you and Northcote have such a go about, back there?"

Myddelton shrugged. "The Repeal of the Orders in Council..."

Pemberton digested this. "By my life, do you Foreign Office chappies think of nothing else?"

Myddelton stopped to consider the question, then with an aggravating lightness said, "Yes. Occasionally... Occasionally, Castle-reagh thinks about his 'cello. Occasionally, I think about going to sleep." And then because it was Pemberton, he admitted, "Or better still, getting myself shagged senseless, and then going to sleep."

Which gained him an unsympathetic chuckle. "You're just still testy because of Ianthe's defection."

"Acquit me, if you please," Myddelton sniffed. "She was tedium personified. She had only *one* talent." Lud, she'd been a lively one, her eagerness unrivalled by any, before or since. "No. No, I wrong her. *Two* talents. That, and pouting. Her acquisitiveness had also become a trifle wearing, shall we say? She still writes to me now and again, you know..."

Pemberton slanted a glance at his friend. "I hadn't realised she could write. Or read, come to that..."

Coolly: "Oh yes. Upon my soul, she was most, ah, enterprising in all matters of education. Particularly after she came across a couple of old

20

books detailing the various means and methods of heightening physical pleasure, don't you know." He ignored Pemberton's raised eyebrow. And smoothly explained, "Apparently, the greater the physical gratification for the female, the greater the chance of conception..."

"What?" Pemberton yelped.

"Ah! Did you not know that? Well, neither had I..."

"Ha! I'll wager you wasn't slow in learning though..." Pemberton mocked. "And had to practise a great deal, did you?" he added mildly.

The recollection earned him a wide smile. "One must never disappoint a lady. Though as to her letter...With the greatest regret, I have had to reply that the house in Kensington was being refurbished prior to being sold."

"Refurbished?" Pemberton said, still reeling from the previous revelation. "What? Not again."

"Yes. I felt the pink and gilt putti cavorting in the bed chamber a trifle *de trop* for most tastes. Including mine."

"Pink and gilt putti *cavorting* in the bed chamber?" Pemberton echoed. "They'll love that at Jackson's."

"Thank you, Pem. It is such a blessing to know one may rely on the discretion of one's friends."

They continued to stroll down Berkeley Street in silence, past the elegant, now darkened rows of houses and beneath the softened shadows of the mist-enshrouded street lamps toward the traffic and early morning bustle of Piccadilly. But eventually, Pemberton ventured: "So then...you wasn't planning to offer for the Wythenshaw chit?"

Myddelton regarded him in surprise. "Od's my life, you cannot seriously be asking me that. 'Struth, I'd be more than happy to mount her. But marry her? Pem, do I look to you like a man about to slip my neck in the noose?" He stopped dead in the street so that Pemberton was forced to survey him.

Pemberton grinned. "Never can be sure with you. You're so dashed deep."

Myddelton laughed and started walking again. "Ha!"

"But in case you'd not noticed," Pemberton continued, "She has her eye in your direction. Though sweet Christ, she'd be a handful from the moment you popped the question."

"My sentiments entirely. But where you got the idea that I was thinking of making her an offer…" Myddelton shook his head.

"You was holding her a bit closer than necessary."

"Ha! Had you ever waltzed with her, you would know why. She holds her hips here…" Myddelton laid his hands against his own hips. 'Struth, she was a pleasurable handful. And it was pleasant to tease the senses. *Quite* pleasant… "And leans the top half of her body away, while managing somehow to keep her chin lowered, so that all you see are those great eyes of hers…Believe me, you have to hold her close if she ain't to go spinning off across the floor."

Pemberton nodded. "And I expect the proximity of her hips has nothing to do with it," he said, the beginnings of a leer on his face.

"Oh she's cockish, all right. But I ain't such a flat as to be trapped like that, I can assure you. When I choose to marry, you shall be the first to know, my word on it…In any event, I fancy Ned has interests there."

"Myddelton!" A voice hailed him from across the way. A gentleman waited for a hackney carriage to pass, clattering on the empty cobbled street, then crossed the street toward them, raising his cane in salute.

"Verdon! Where are you off to? White's?" Myddelton said, recognising the approaching figure.

"Evening, Pemberton." Mr. Verdon joined them and answered Myddelton's question with a nod as he began to walk with them.

"I say, Verdon, ain't you on Liverpool's staff at the War Office now?" Pemberton asked. He pushed his hat further back on his head with the knob of his cane and yawned. "Lud, it must be later than I thought. What o'clock is it, Myddelton?"

"Gone two. Or three," Myddelton replied, without looking at his watch. His eyes were beginning to ache again.

"I've been with Liverpool since September," said Verdon. He was a serious young man, modest, well-connected. "But recently…" He paused, glancing at Pemberton.

Myddelton, interpreting the look, countered, "In spite of appearances, he can be trusted, Verdon. I have it on excellent authority that he not only listens to the speeches and debates in the Commons, he actually understands them."

"Who said that about me?" Pemberton demanded, straightening.

"Miles Northcote, if you want the unhappy truth."

"Never believe it, Myddelton. Northcote's going soft in the brain," Pemberton declared.

Myddelton ignored him. "…You were saying, Verdon?"

"Yes, well, perhaps I oughtn't to mention it, because I don't know how deeply the Foreign Office is involved, nor when the Commons will be receiving a full report, but…"

"Is it the casualty lists? From Badajoz?" Myddelton asked.

"Well, yes, actually." Verdon drew a breath. "It's all pretty grisly, I can tell you," he said wetting his bottom lip.

"May one ask, unofficially, of course," said Pemberton, pretending to gaze at the fog-blurred moon. "How many did we lose?"

"At Badajoz? Well," Verdon stalled. "Well…At least four thousand casualties. We believe. Possibly more. There are so many still missing, do you see? We cannot be certain."

"Four thousand?" Pemberton repeated, open-mouthed. "Four thousand?"

Verdon blinked once. "Yes. Yes, that's right. But, do you see, it's worse that that! For at least two thousand fell in the first two hours. In a space of less than a hundred yards."

"What?" Pemberton whispered. "Two thousand men fell in the first *two* hours? In less than a hundred yards? Why, that's only from here across the street!" he protested, scanning the short distance of it, first once, then a second and a third time. And fell silent as he tried, and failed, to encompass, to digest this. "Anyone we know?" he asked, looking at Myddelton. His levity had quite deserted him.

Myddelton nodded. "Yes. Quite a few." He paused, recalling names on the lists. It was like roll call at school. Only this wasn't school any longer. But at least he did not weep. As he had when first he'd seen the lists. "Ridge. Gray. Both the younger Ormesbys…Kit Hatherill… Young Ruthven. Little Jack Henderson. That young Smith—that just married Mary Worthing. Old Picton was wounded."

"The 74th lost sixteen officers," Verdon added bitterly.

"Od's my life…You're joking," Pemberton whispered as the three of them stepped into White's well-lit vestibule. For what else was there to be said?

With a bow, Verdon excused himself.

"It's war, Pem," Myddelton said softly, earnestly, clear-eyed despite his nagging fatigue. "Soldiers die. They fight, and they die. D'you know, Napoleon had more than ten thousand casualties at Austerlitz—to me an inconceivable number. Yet he called it the Greatest Victory." Then, needing to change the subject, he spotted a waistcoat he recognised at the far end of the Morning Room. "There's Hardy! What shall it be? Piquet or whist?"

2

For Myddelton, leaving the Foreign Office with his desk still covered in untranslated, undecyphered reports and uncracked codes, his mid-afternoon departure was out of all proportion pleasant. And he paused without the shadow of Whitehall to feel nothing more than the breeze fresh upon his face while his groom brought up his carriage.

It had been a day like any other. Reports from the Peninsula, from Canada, from Swabia, reports from everywhere had poured in and onto his desk all morning. Or perhaps they just multiplied rapidly like rabbits. Or rats. But whatever the case, they were there and he was not. And it was out of all proportion pleasant.

He climbed into his waiting curricle, took up the reins, and flicked the whip over their heads to prompt the horses into action, while Kester, his small-statured groom, ran to swing onto his perch at the rear of the carriage. And though the drive through the narrow crowded streets of the city of London proper was nothing out of the ordinary, the afternoon was fine and pleasanter still, the horses were fresh.

Eventually, drawing up before a tall early Georgian building of once red, now soot-blacked brick, he looped the reins and stepped down from the carriage. "Walk 'em, Kester," he instructed the tiger. And ducking to avoid the low door-head, went through the portals of his lawyer's chambers.

The main office of Ruttridge and Chart was large, with walls that were a combination of wainscot and unadorned whitewash. The bare floor was liberally strewn with scrolls and sheaves of paper and leather-bound volumes. While in the centre of the room stood several high desks where the ink-smirched copyists sat, heads down, scribbling away, with frequent recourse to their communal inkhorns.

The senior clerk, a man of austere and sterile appearance with cropped thinning grey hair and an incongruous little nose, came forward as Myddelton shut the door. And bowed. "Lord Myddelton," he pronounced in the voice of one who was not tone-deaf but wished to be. "Mr. Ruttridge is expecting you." And deferentially, he took Myddelton's hat, gloves and driving coat to pass them to the junior who had materialised just behind him. "If you would be so good as to step this way, my lord."

And with his head down to avoid the low overhead beams, Myddelton followed the clerk up the narrow wooden staircase to the partners' private chambers. The clerk knocked discreetly on one of the doors. Upon the stentorian "Enter," he opened the door, then bowed before withdrawing into the shadow.

"Come in, my lord, do come in…" Mr. Ezekiel Ruttridge, tall, broad, etiolated, and still wearing the style and wig of the previous century, emerged from behind a paper-strewn partners' desk to bow and to usher Myddelton in. "Well, well. Good afternoon to you, my lord…"

"'Afternoon, Ruttridge…"

"I trust I find you in good health, my lord. And all well at Great Myddelton? Good, very good…" The solicitor indicated one of two armchairs of faded green Moroccan which directly faced the desk. "Please, my lord, will you not be seated? Do you care for some refreshment?" He gestured toward the door, beyond which the clerk hovered, awaiting an order for brandy or wine.

"No, no, nothing for me, thank you." Myddelton gave a polite smile, and cautiously lowered himself into the appointed seat. As he remembered, it was a chair that had been constructed with something other than comfort in mind. Puritanical thrift or parsimony probably. And glancing about at the neutral shade of drab above the wainscot, at the print of Whitehall hanging above the mantelpiece, at the banks of built-in bookcases and the worn carpet, he felt sure that nothing had been altered in the four years since last he had sat here. Not even the dust.

"I must say, I am most thankful that you have finally granted this interview, my lord…" The solicitor reseated himself behind the cluttered desk and folded his hands across his stomach. "Though it is unfortunate that you were unable so to do before now. I hasten to add, my lord, that the situation *is* unusual or I should never have presumed..." He pursed his lips and looked down at the papers before him, then, briefly trained his speculative glance upon Myddelton.

His lips tightening, Myddelton stretched out his long legs and shifted on the lumpy seat. The chair creaked ominously.

"Ehem. Shall we to business then?" Ruttridge permitted himself an inconsequential half-smile and sat up to his desk. And adjusting the papers laid out there, he lifted one to place it neatly beside the others. "Forgive the impertinence, but did my lord, the late Earl, your father, ever mention the name of Heron to you?"

Myddelton shook his head. "No. Not that I can recall."

"No," Ruttridge confirmed. "I see. And you have never come across that surname in any of your business affairs or in any of the estate papers?"

"'Struth, I do not think so," Myddelton said. For despite the early onset of unqualified boredom—even Tom found Ruttridge a dead bore— he was determined to remain courteous. But what had this to do with the will? It wasn't some annuity he was meant to be paying, was it? "My steward, Hinton, or my private secretary may have done, but if so, they have said nothing to me. Though since my father's death was unexpected, it is not surprising that he may have neglected to inform me of some things—which in the normal way he would have done." Which surely Ruttridge must know.

"Ah. Ah, yes. Yes, I see. Just as you say, my lord, just as you say." Ruttridge performed his perfunctory smile. "Well now, some years ago, your father had a friend, a Colonel James Heron by name. I was given to understand that they had been up at Oxford together. Perhaps they had also attended Eton together, I do not know. Certainly, they were briefly members of the same military regiment. That would be before your father inherited the title and sold out, and Captain Heron, as he was then, went off to serve in India."

Myddelton nodded encouragingly.

"Despite the inevitable peripatetic nature of Captain Heron's military career, they remained close, and some years later, this Colonel Heron, as he had by then become, lent your father a considerable sum of money. For the payment of your uncle's debts, I believe it was. And because of the vastness of that sum, the late Earl, your father, deemed it proper to furnish some sort of security for the loan."

All of which was about as interesting as a pile of grass clippings. Or dead leaves. And made as much sense. "Yes?" Myddelton prompted, for clearly some response was merited—Ruttridge had glanced up with an expectant look on his old sturgeon's face. But, Od's teeth, his uncle? The uncle he dimly remembered, having met him but once or twice? His backside was tingling with discomfort. 'Struth, he ought to have a new pair of chairs bought for Ruttridge and never mind the expense, if he were to visit here often.

Ruttridge paused, sucking in his bottom lip, and pressed his fingertips together. "At that time, the Colonel's wife had just died, leaving him with a small daughter. At your father's request, this document was drawn up concerning the infant." He tapped at the parchment page with one bony finger.

Narrowing his eyes, Myddelton raised his quizzing glass to peer at the document. A bequest for the daughter then. It had to be. But why in Heaven's name drag him here to tell him that? Surely the prosy old fossil could have written.

Unless…? And assailed by a brevet of doubt, Myddelton frowned. What if? No. Smoothly: "'Pon my life, Ruttridge, I hardly feel that anyone as wise as my father would have set me up as, ehm…" He hesitated, balking at the word. "*Guardian* to a child."

"No, no," agreed Ruttridge. "Absolutely not. He would never have been so foolish."

Taken aback by the discourtesy and its unflattering implication, Myddelton straightened. "I beg your pardon?"

"No…" Ruttridge continued. "No. The provision made by your father was that you will marry her. By her eighteenth birthday."

"What?" Myddelton blurted. "What's that?"

And distinctly enunciating each word so there could be no misunderstanding, Ruttridge repeated: "The provision made by your father and agreed to by Colonel Heron was that you will marry the girl. By her eighteenth birthday, as I said."

Myddelton sat stock still, stupefied and stared blankly. As if struck from behind, hard, between the shoulders, he sat, his breath seizing in his throat and his mind flailing against the bald announcement. Sat, stunned as his world slipped from its axis, slipped, slid and tumbled arsy varsey from its known orbit and into total chaos.

Beneath the white muslin of his starched cravat, the vein in his throat was throbbing erratically. And his heart suddenly pounding wildly, he drew a necessary and painful breath. Had Ruttridge really said his father had arranged a marriage? Was that possible? Red hell and bloody death. His father? His father would never have done such a thing. No. Nunquam!

"Is this a joke, Ruttridge?" he gasped. And the stranglehold that had been clutching at his throat and lungs loosened its fearful grip. "You're practising upon me, Ruttridge, ain't you?" he murmured, his heart still thumping hard as he breathed again. "'Pon my soul, Ruttridge, which of those jackanapes—Pemberton or Dunphail—was it who put you up to this? Or was it Northcote, that mumping devil? 'Struth, I shall have their baubles off 'em…"

Orotund and irascible, like a blade Ruttridge's voice sliced though that growing laughter. "I beg leave to inform you, my lord, that this is no *joke*." He spoke the word as if it were an abomination to him. It was. "I do not indulge in schoolboy pranks."

"What? Your pardon?" And his throat contracting once more, Myddelton started forward in the chair, the laughter, the air choked out of him. "Are you? Can you…be telling me…" He could not say it. His lungs were collapsing. "…that my father arranged a marriage for me?"

"That is the case," the solicitor affirmed.

"I beg your pardon?" Myddelton stammered. "What?" Floundering, he put a hand to his temple, seeking some rational thought in the dizzying riptide of instant outrage. And found none. "'Fore God…'Afore God, I never heard of such a thing."

"I am very sorry, my lord, but it is the truth."

"Do you say? Do you say that I am to believe this then?" Myddelton demanded, his voice breaking. "You ain't practising upon me, then?"

Abruptly he rose to clench and unclench his fists on the chair back. He could marshal neither himself nor the rioting melee of his sentiments. "Do you say this in all honesty?" he demanded, his voice rising. "That I am to... *marry*?" He whispered the word. "And that my father arranged this...*marriage* for me?"

"Yes. Yes, indeed," Ruttridge affirmed.

Suddenly, like a burst of unexplained, unexpected fireworks, Myddelton strode forward, looming over the solicitor. "Well I am damned if I will! I am damned if I will! This..." He thrust a finger at the document. The muscles in his jaw quivered and flexed. "This is clearly lunacy, and I can assure you, I have no intention of abiding by whatever idiotish maggot my father may have had lurking in his benighted brain. This ain't the Middle Ages! And I ain't some damned Frenchie neither." His gaze darted over Ruttridge as an asp's tongue flickers at its victim. "Break that infernal thing, whatever it is, Ruttridge, because I tell you this...I tell you this: I ain't bringing home to wife some brass-faced chit of a bloody social-climbing Nabob! I don't care who or what she is. And I don't care who arranged it neither! D'you hear me?"

It would be too much to say that Mr. Ruttridge did not approve of those clients who believed, erroneously, that they might threaten him. It was not his place to approve. Habitually he dismissed or ignored those reactions he designated as 'ill-behaved posturings', just as he would dismiss or ignore inclement weather or the tantrums of an indulged child. And secure in his professional superiority, his impunity, his serenity remained unimpaired, while his voice grew softer. Softer and more measured and implacable. "I regret to inform you, my lord, that your wishes in this matter are of little consequence."

"What?" Myddelton snapped. "What's that? Do you presume to dictate to me, sir?" he bristled. "Well, a pox take you!" He paced toward the window, his back to the solicitor. "Upon my soul, I shall not do it. Buy her off!"

Ruttridge, his nostrils pinched with peevishness and contempt, paid no heed: "Had you heeded my summons six months ago...but that is neither here nor there, now. I have, I can assure you, explored every possible legal means of breaking the terms of this contract already, feeling that it was my duty to you, my lord. But this document precludes all such action. It is unbreakable. Your father, as you may yourself attest, was no man's fool, and he instructed the lawyers to set down such terms as to render it wholly binding..."

"What?" Myddelton ground out.

Ruttridge pressed on: "Nothing short of your demise, my lord, or that of the young lady will nullify this agreement. Indeed, it is stipulated that should you attempt to break any of the conditions found herein..."

Dear God, was there no end to this torrential gabbling?

"The *entirety* of your inherited properties shall be liquidated, and the monies used, first to compensate the lady, and latterly to build and maintain foundling homes throughout the country."

A second-time stunned, his breath once again sucked from him, Myddelton turned. "He did what? My father did what?"

With each pronouncement, the distance between that which he had expected his life to be and that which had been predetermined was gaping wider, until now, now the gulf was a chasm which could never be bridged and beyond which he could not even imagine. And it was all, all barely credible.

"What did you say?" he whispered. And nearly unmanned by the sudden tears that pricked against his eyelids, his heart hammering against his ribcage like a prisoner against the bars of his prison window, Myddelton fumbled for words: "This is monstrous. Do you say he has practically disinherited me? For what cause?" he protested. "For mercy's sake, what about the entail?"

"The entail applies solely to the house at Great Myddelton, as you know, and the adjacent properties—which are..." Ruttridge sniffed. "...If I may venture an opinion, hardly enough to maintain the house."

"But why?" Myddelton demanded, flailing again. "Why did he do this?" He tried to frame a sentence but found that he could not. "Hell and confound it, am I...am I not his son? And...And if I had come here six months ago?" He ran his fingers through his hair, catching at a handful to steady himself. S'life, where had he been six months ago? Hunting in Melton Mowbray? In Kent, at North Cray with Castlereagh?

"You were to have made the young lady's acquaintance and established an amicable friendship," Ruttridge said shortly. "In effect, you were to have wooed her."

It was too much. "What?" Myddelton burst out and again came to face the lawyer over the desk. "What?" And brows gathered, his eyes wild, his agitation unchecked and uncheckable: "Do you tell me that I was to go a-wooing some money-grubber's brat? And then what? Beg her to marry me for my own inheritance? For what is already mine?"

Repelled by the hideousness of such a prospect, recoiling, and caught in the cascading of such disjointed emotions that he could neither contain it nor disentangle himself, Myddelton returned to the window. He stared out through the soot-stained glass upon the row of houses opposite washed bright by the afternoon sun, trying to focus, and saw nothing. He was to be tied to the inconsequential offspring of some half-pay Captain. Tied for life. Bound over like an indentured servant, with a life's sentence. Sweet Christ!

And striving to think clearly, to extract some glimmer of hope or respite, anything, from amongst the welter of conflicting passions, he groped in his pocket for his snuff-box. And finding it, he opened and closed and opened and closed it. Eventually he turned to say softly, "Could it, perhaps...could it not be broken with a plea of mental incompetency?"

"I do assure you, my lord, I did investigate that," Ruttridge answered carefully, his detachment and precision unmoved by Myddelton's distress. "Such action would, however, bring into question the terms of his will. In addition, there would be the entirety of his very large acquaintance to be dealt with, as well as finding a medical practitioner who might attest to it." He spread his hands. "You may, of course, wish to consult with another solicitor, my lord. But should you challenge the legality of this document, I fear it will prove a costly mistake, and none but an unscrupulous pettifogger would counsel in favour of such action. And that is Mr. Chart's opinion, as well as my own. I am sorry, my lord." Then, as an offering, a consolation: "The sum was not inconsiderable, my lord. In excess of thirty thousand pounds, it was."

Myddelton looked away, swallowing hard on the rising bile as the blood rushed wildly to his head. "Thirty thousand pounds?" he faltered. It was a final body blow—a swift, finishing, incapacitating punch to the sternum, aimed to leave him winded and broken. If he had fancied he might buy his way to freedom, that foolishness was now wrenched from him. His own income was only somewhere…in the region of eighteen thousand, provided the harvests were good, which they hadn't been for some years. Were he to sell everything but the shirt off his back, he could not hope to raise such a sum. "You say 'in excess of'. Does that mean it was more?" He felt himself growing lightheaded.

"Yes, my lord. Much more."

Dazed with incomprehension, Myddelton remained where he was, his mind struggling to absorb or to understand. There would be no recovery. Not now, not ever. And it was not a joke.

In a strangled voice, his expression bleak, he began: "How long till I…" And found that the words dried in his mouth, that the atmosphere in the chamber was stifling and nearly suffocating him. He stopped, then clumsily, he tried again: "When will…when does this girl turn eighteen?"

"This Friday, my lord. The first of May."

"The first of April would have been more appropriate, don't you think?" he snarled. Blindly he stared out of the grimy window pane as he sought to quell the spasmodic churning of his stomach, the tears, and the violent rage buffeting him. He must be wed as soon as practicable. Within the week, or he would be stripped of everything. Stripped, with nothing left but his title, and Great Myddelton. And without the land to support it, he would be forced to mortgage or sell even that—Great Myddelton, his house, his home. He had been robbed of his right, this most basic and fundamental right—this right to choose a wife—and by his own father. And quietly now: "For pity's sake, you do know that I work for the Foreign Office, Ruttridge. I can't just disappear…I have duties to fulfil, obligations…"

"Of a certainty, my lord, you may choose to ignore the information I have imparted to you today," Ruttridge said curtly. "Indeed, you may feel your other commitments nullify those arranged by your father. I can do nothing about that. But I would advise against it."

So there would be no quarter given. Not even for King and country.

Myddelton forced down the incipient panic. "Where shall I find this…" He paused, for when it had been mentioned he had not been paying close attention. He shook his head to clear it. "…Miss Heron, is it? And her father?" S'life, to be cheated of his right to choose his own wife! And instead, instead to be spliced to some commoner's brat, some female of whom he knew nothing. Whether she was chaste or clapped, handsome or bracket-faced, amiable or shrew. What chance for happiness or amity had he now?

"Colonel Heron was a military hero, killed at Marengo, where he was serving as a diplomatic aide to the Austrians. Miss Heron resides, as she has always done, with her uncle, Sir Charles Heron, in Oxfordshire." Ruttridge could only guess at the young man's thoughts; it would be a damnable match.

Myddelton drew a ragged breath, her father's heroism registering not at all. At last, he left the window and came toward the solicitor's desk. If he were not to disgrace himself, he must quit the confines of this office. "Is there anything else I should know?"

"No, my lord, no. I have apprised you of all the pertinent facts."

Pertinent, sweet Jesu! "Then I had best be off to make the necessary arrangements…If I am to have a leg-shackle fitted by Friday…" His bitterness had become a palpable thing, hanging over the room like the unwholesome stink of scorched linen or burning flesh. "That document, can you put it into a folio, so that I might take it with me, or does it remain here?"

"No, my lord, there were four copies made at the time it was drawn up, so you may take this with you…And all of the other related papers." Ruttridge gathered up the documents and placed them inside a brown leather case. "Here they are. I have copies in my files. May I hope that all turns out better than…"

"Yes. Yes, thank you for that," Myddelton said viciously as he reached for the dossier. "And good afternoon to you, sir." And without bowing, he quitted the room and descended the stairs, taking his coat and hat from the junior clerk as he rushed out.

Yet as the senior clerk closed the door behind him, Myddelton paused, and stood to lean his head against the doorjamb, to draw breath and inhale through his parched and aching throat as deeply as he might, to feel the remnant sun upon his face and air cool and kind upon his forehead. "Oh damn me..." he murmured, fighting back the grief. To have been bought and sold. Bound over and shackled like this. "Damn me..."

Kester was still walking the horses around the square. Seeing his master emerge, he attempted to bring horses and curricle to a decorous halt but before he could stop the carriage, Myddelton had hauled himself up, settled, and unwound the reins. And taking the whip, he cracked it violently over the horses' heads. Unruffled, Kester released the leader's halter and scrambled around onto his perch. "What's bit 'im, then?" he grumbled, flicking an oat from off his sleeve.

A long drive over sound roads, through a countryside bathed in sunlight, the air fresh with the scents of newly mown grass, blossoming fruit trees, primroses and bluebells, might be counted upon to restore the equanimity of one who had lately sustained an unpleasant shock or a severe financial setback, particularly if the individual had passed a significant portion of his life in just such a setting. But a drive through London, over poorly maintained streets and narrow lanes crammed with tradesmen's drays, job horses, hired chaises and hackney carriages, the acrid smells of rotting manure, decayed kitchen refuse, and unwashed humanity filling one's nostrils, the ubiquitous grey fog closing in and a shower beginning, could be guaranteed to have just the opposite effect. Indeed, such a drive could overset the most placid of temperaments.

By the time Myddelton reached St. James's Square, his being had been overtaken by a punishing turmoil of self-loathing and invidious loss. Rounding a corner, he slackened his grip on the reins and cracked the whip, causing the horses to quicken and the carriage to career dangerously. He swore. And drew sharply on the reins to halt the curricle, before stepping down, leaving Kester to run and grab hold of the sweating horses before they bolted.

Warily, Kester eyed him from under the horses' heads and made clucking noises as he stroked the jumpy animals' necks. He had heard such expletives during the return journey as to make a gunner blush. With a baleful glare for his employer, he patted the nearest horse, then led the animals off toward the stable mews.

Given the rage now enveloping him, it might have afforded Myddelton some degree of release to put his fist through the front door. But the habits and temperament of a lifetime are rarely undone in a moment, even a moment of such extremity. Then a footman opened the door to him and deprived him of the opportunity.

Tossing his hat and gloves upon the nearest table, Myddelton stalked through the foyer to the library and kicked the door shut behind him. He threw the folio onto the library table, crossed to a small sideboard and poured himself a large brandy. And downed the contents of the glass, before dashing it against the bricks of the fireplace to send a shower of crystal over the grate. It improved nothing.

He poured and drank another glassful.

Then another.

And finally, staring at the golden liquid in the greying afternoon light, concluded that it was a deuced good thing the girl was not to hand. Had she been, Heaven alone knew what he might have done to her. "S'death, what an infernal disaster..." he mumbled, disgusted, and refilled his glass.

He had intended to drink himself blind, to drown every perception or lingering sentiment. But those too long hours spent in the Foreign Office and the interminable late sittings in the Upper House conspired against him. Closing his eyes briefly, he fell asleep. And the remains of the afternoon crept away with him slumped in a chair, dreaming fitfully of thousands of horses being transported to somewhere by a river he did not recognise, and cyphers he could not break.

Evening slid her blue-grey fingers through the open curtains, enshrouding both the room and the slumbering man with her blanket of glimmering half-light. A footman came in, carrying a lit taper. Seeing his lordship thus—his cravat loosened, his head leaning heavily against the wing of the chair and his eyes shut—he lit only the candelabra at the edges of the room. He walked softly to avoid waking him, then hurried out, closing the door behind him with exaggerated care.

It was some noise in the outer hall a while later which finally roused him. Waking, Myddelton cursed himself for sleeping in a chair. "A plague on it...always gives me a stiff neck," he muttered and stood up to stretch.

Then he remembered. And felt again the stab of outrage and piercing betrayal. He pressed a hand against his forehead as his eyes began to smart.

He was to marry. Dear God in heaven, he must marry. Knowing nothing of her people, still less of her. Within the week—a day or less would make no difference. And she would be a stranger. Without liking, or even acquaintance. Without affection. 'Struth, she might turn out to be a frowzy, unwashed trull—another Caroline of Brunswick—but still he must wed her. It had been arranged, ordained, by his father. Yet in all that time he had never taken it upon himself to tell him. Sweet Christ, what must she be like?

Silently, through the haze of unregulated bitterness and aching numbness, he contemplated it, the future-blighting sheaf of papers upon the library table. He crossed to pick up the brief and pulled out the documents to peruse the one on top. Then, half-sitting, half-leaning against the oak table, he studied the marriage contract, that devil's bargain, that unbreakable damning and damnable life sentence handed down by his father. He gave a snort of hollow laughter. S'life, it was lucid as a summer's day at Great Myddelton. There were, as Ruttridge had said, no loopholes. If he did not marry her by Friday, by Saturday he would be ruined.

Her name was Jane Caroline Sophia Heron. She lived near a village called Britwell St. Luke, Oxoniensis. And he had been betrothed to her since he was twelve.

He could always leave…go to Ireland. Or marry her, then buy himself a commission in the army.

And closing his eyes, he cast about for those elements of his life which remained intact. Were there any? None but his work with the Foreign Office. His work. "O hell and damnation…sod it, sod it, sod it…" he murmured, holding his eyes closed with his fingertips. Sweet Christ, if she were anything, anything at all, like Prinny's misbegotten arranged bride—that lumping gobblecock—she must never be permitted to set foot in Great Myddelton. Not ever. He must see to that. And tasted the bile as it rose in his throat.

Underneath was the marriage settlement, naming the figure of her dowry. "Twenty thousand pounds? Twenty thousand…" Giddy, he read on. And it had been paid in full these fifteen years. Red hell, he was not even to have the right to that. But such a sum! "Od's blood, Father, why hobble me like this?"

And beneath that, her father's will. "Dear God in heaven…her father was a frigging Croesus!" And the properties to be settled upon her, and… And there, there at the bottom of each page, his father's signature as witness, his signature and seal—the seal from the ring he now wore on the small finger of his right hand. Myddelton ran a disarranging hand through his hair.

"Christ's wounds, Father, why did you never tell me? Did we really need the money so badly? What in God's holy name can have brought this about?"

The door opened to reveal Kettering, Myddelton's starchy hawk-faced butler.

"Yes?" Myddelton barked, though he had not meant to. More mildly: "Yes, what is it, Kettering?"

"Good evening, my lord. Will you be dining in this evening?"

"No, Kettering. Not tonight."

"Very good, my lord." Kettering bowed and turned to leave.

And now, the first steps in performing this duty, his duty. To the stranger. To his father. Myddelton closed his eyes, swallowed hard and clenched his jaw. Christ, could he bear to even speak of it, this forced marriage? Did he have a choice? No. No choice. "Kettering? What state are m'mother's rooms in? Are they fit for habitation?"

His face betrayed nothing, neither interest nor curiosity. "Mrs. Pinch sees to them, my lord. With the removal of the Holland covers and a thorough cleaning, they would be fit, my lord."

"See to it then, will you? And my mother's personal effects—if *anything* of hers remains, have it removed as well."

"I shall see to it personally, my lord."

"Good." Myddelton drew a shuddering breath, momentarily overpowered. "I shall be bringing home a bride by Friday, so see that it's done before then, will you?"

"Yes, my lord. Very good, my lord." Still, Kettering's face was expressionless. As Myddelton had known it would be. "Will that be all, my lord?"

"No. No." He paused, finding the words. "You will impress upon the staff that my marriage is not a matter for their discussion, and I would not appreciate word of it getting about before I insert the notice in the papers." Amazing that he could speak of it all. He felt like retching.

"Certainly, my lord."

"Thank you. That will be all."

"My lord." Kettering bowed and quitted the room.

In stolid wretchedness Myddelton sank into a chair to wait as his pulse stilled and his stomach quieted. And stayed thus, head in hands, still, thinking nothing, still stunned by the forfeiture of his rights and his future—that future he had never really contemplated, had always taken on trust, recognising it only now by its irredeemable loss. He glanced over at the papers upon the table once more. Od's death, there was no help for any of it.

And locked in a vice of inaction and the inconceivable hopelessness of raw despair, he remained, still—while outside darkness fell and linkboys ran, shouting their 'make ways', and the lamplighters with their torches and ladders and spills went from lantern to lantern, from street to square and back again—still dazed, still unable to see beyond the fog of disbelief, unable to comprehend, still thinking nothing, wholly abject in his obedience to his father, in his submission to his duty. And only finally, much later, he roused himself and left the room to dress for the evening.

It was past nine o'clock when Myddelton, now in formal black and white evening clothes, wandered into the estate room to find Mr. Broke hard at work. Broke looked up distractedly. Myddelton pulled out his watch and checked the time.

"I believe, Tom, that it is customary, at least in Town, to eat one's dinner at this hour."

"Yes, my lord." Mr. Broke rose hastily from his desk. "I was just finishing this letter to Morley and then I ..."

A footman entered bearing a covered tray. "Your dinner, Mr. Broke, sir." He set the tray on a table, and bowed to both gentlemen. "My lord."

And quitted the room.

Myddelton raised his quizzing glass to survey the tray. "You were saying, Tom?" He let the glass fall and smiled expectantly.

Mr. Broke began to stammer a reply.

Myddelton continued to smile as he held up one hand to silence his secretary. "And did you find time to drop by Weston's?"

"Yes, my lord. Yes, I did. And ordered two coats, just as you said. One black, and one blue." He thought Myddelton would be pleased.

"Blue? Good. Excellent. Blue, you say? Now make sure you find the time to eat your dinner."

"Yes. Yes, my lord."

There were those who held that Myddelton treated his secretary and cousin badly, teasing him when he was so painfully shy, and, because of his position of dependency, unable to respond in kind. But Tom Broke did not think so. With two overbearing older sisters and one boisterous younger sister at home, he thought his life at Myddelton House quite a haven of tranquillity. He had a natural aptitude for numbers and order, and he found he liked his work very well. And, as for Myddelton's gentle raillery, he did not mind it in the least, for it told him that Myddelton saw him as an equal and not as a servant.

Myddelton twirled his quizzing glass on its velvet ribbon. "And Tom..." He paused and drew a breath, hoping to still any quaver. None in the household must suspect that today his life, somehow, had become a nightmare—a carriage suddenly swung out of control, the reins lost, the coupling strap broke and the horses plunging. None must suspect, not even for a moment. Not even Tom. Especially not Tom. "Will you send a note 'round to the Archbishop? I shall be wanting a special licence by tomorrow afternoon, so send a draft on my bank along with it, will you?"

Mr. Broke blinked. "M'my lord?"

A shuttered look came over Myddelton's features. He felt increasingly ill, but his voice remained light and teasing. It must. "Yes? 'Struth, you needn't look so like a startled sheep, Tom. It's quite usual for men in my position to marry, you know." He studied the gilt filigree edge of his quizzing glass. He must remain calm. "Send that note 'round now, will you? Ask him if I may wait upon him in the morning."

"Yes. Yes, of course," said Thomas, striving to mask his surprise and awe.

Myddelton took his handkerchief and polished his glass. "And send a note off to Rundell as well, will you? Request a private interview. Tell him to have a suitable selection of wedding bands on hand."

"Yes, my lord. Anything else?"

"Ehm, yes. Find Britwell St. Luke—Oxfordshire—on a map for me. It must be near Britwell Salome, I should imagine. Somewhere..." Myddelton shrugged and affected not to see his cousin's eyes widen—yet again—in surprise. "Thank you, Tom. That is all. I shall now leave you to your dinner. I hope it hasn't grown cold on my account." He nodded and left the room quietly.

He had meant to go to White's—was engaged for dinner there—but instead Myddelton found himself walking in the direction of the Foreign Office. His life's hopes, unarticulated, but no less genuine for all that, were yet tumbling through the hollowness of his mind as down through some darkened and dry well. Splintering and breaking as they collided with the stone walls of his father's will, before they sank in that barren emptiness which had once been clear and sweet water. He stopped to draw in a breath and to feel nothing. And sighed—surely for the hundredth time. Would he always feel thus? Dumbfounded? Numb? Bereft? Or was the nausea and flashes of blinding fury merely the result of his surprise, or of mawkish Romantic sensibility? Several of his friends' marriages had been arranged, hadn't they? "But why could he never bring himself to tell me?" he asked of no one. "It don't make sense. Can he truly have thought I would disobey him?"

His work. The Foreign Office. That one remote, untainted island of sanctuary now left him: the reports of troop movements and maps which ask no questions, the cyphers and translations which give nothing away—nothing, until that moment when one word, one letter would yield to his painstaking, teasing understanding, and with that, the whole chimerical structure would begin to disclose its secrets. And it was there, finally, there among those cerebral, companionable companions, in the quiet emptiness of his small room as the candles burned and dripped, that at last he found some solace, some measure of friendly oblivion in the work and hope, that real hope of defeating the rapacious, insatiable plunderer, Napoleon.

3

Like a searing sudden burst of bright artillery, the mid-morning sunlight which filtered into the bedroom struck the sleeper in the old-fashioned four poster bed as painfully blinding, and nothing like an agreeable brightness designed to entice one into the new day. He raised a hand to shield his eyes, groaned, and rolled over, pulling the feather bolster over his head. And felt himself drifting, spinning, sinking back into cavernous oblivion. Yet at the back of his consciousness, an ill-defined something nagged, and kept him from settling again. Wearily, his eyes pricking with lack of sleep, he shoved the pillow onto the floor.

And peered reproachfully at the obstreperous morning light. "A plague carry you off, Stamp, what the devil d'you think you're doing?"

"Good morning, my lord." Myddelton's valet greeted him with his habitual undertaker's expression. "Preparing your bath, my lord."

Myddelton squeezed his eyes shut. Pestilential nit-squeezer. His head pounded and his mouth was desert-dry. He rubbed his face.

"What would your lordship wish me to do with the guineas now littering the floor?" Stamp asked patiently.

Myddelton lay still. "Leave 'em," he mumbled. What guineas? And disregarding his aching head, tried to recall the events of the previous evening. He'd gone to the Foreign Office to work at the Grand Chiffre and French troop movements, finally using coloured corks for regiments on the map of Prussia. And then he'd gone to White's sometime after two. And then? Oh lord, what then? Wherever it was, he'd been there with Dunphail. Was it a knocking shop? Could he have been so drunk that he didn't remember? No. 'Twas Watier's! That was it. He'd gone to Watier's with Dunphail, where they'd played faro...But why had Stamp wakened him so early, after what must have been, even to Stamp's poxy, jaundiced way of thinking, a late night?

"Very good, my lord. Your bath awaits."

Myddelton blinked several times, his mind groggy still. His bath? What had he to do this morning? The Archbishop. God's truth, he had to see the Archbishop! He had to see the Archbishop for a special licence. He sank back, feeling sick. For the wedding he did not want, to the bride he did not know. "Oh Christ!" And clenching his jaw against the nausea and flinging the bedclothes away, he stumbled from the bed, smashing his head against the oak bedpost.

"Oh fuck me!" He reeled back onto the bed, clutching his forehead. "Od's death…"

"Is there something amiss, my lord?" Stamp reappeared in the doorway of the dressing room.

"The bath, Stamp. Get me into the deuced bath…Damnation… Ow…'Struth! And fix whatever that revolting concoction of yours is."

"Was it a sticking plaster for your head, or a cure for cropsickness that you required, my lord?"

Insolent hell-born bastard. "Both, damn you." Myddelton closed his eyes and sank back against the pillows. His head pounded. "Hell and confound it…"

"My lord. My lord…If you would care to drink this, my lord."

Waking again, Myddelton regarded Stamp balefully. Through the glass bottom of the tankard, he could see the raw egg skulking in the depths of Stamp's liquid cure-all. He struggled to sit upright and took the tankard. He knew better than to smell the contents. Shutting his eyes, he drank the mixture down without a pause.

"If we were to brush your hair slightly forward, my lord, the bump would not be so noticeable…" Stamp commented, some three quarters of an hour later.

Myddelton sniffed irritably. "Fine."

He glanced at the clock and grimaced at his reflection in the mirror. He was late. Very late. And his cravat, that which was meant to be an elegant arrangement of stiff white muslin with a discreet knot at the base of his throat, looked more like a wadded bandage tied in the dark by someone wearing woollen mittens.

"Stamp! Where are you, you insolent…"

"Yes, my lord. If you would allow me the privilege of arranging your neckcloth this morning, my lord…" Stamp soothed.

"Make it quick."

"Yes, my lord."

❧

Beneath the long barrel-vaulted ceiling of White's coffee room, the tables were crowded with members enjoying the various courses of their dinners, filling the air with the chink, scrape and clatter of cutlery, with the mingled aromas of roasted mutton, pork and beef, varied sauces and fruit compotes, and a masculine drone of conversation unmarred by female shrillness, with the single exception of one unfortunate gentleman's regrettable trill of high-pitched laughter. More regrettable still, the gentleman laughed frequently. It was an opulent room, reflecting the wealth and status of the club's members, with red brocaded wallpaper and hundreds of blazing candles lining the walls. Pemberton and Myddelton occupied a small table in one corner of the large room, the remains of an unexceptional meal still before them.

Pemberton took another sip from his half-emptied glass of port. "Saw Ianthe in the Park today."

Myddelton said nothing. He had passed the day feeling exceedingly nauseous, a sensation he knew to be completely unrelated to a morning hangover. But, by late afternoon, all had been accomplished: he'd been granted a few days' leave from the Foreign Office, the special licence lay on his dressing table at Myddelton House, as did three gemmed wedding bands. He had meant only to choose two. But in the end, an even smaller and plainer band had caught his fancy, the Lord only knew why, so he had taken that as well. 'Struth, if only he knew what she looked like.

"I heard about your winnings at Watier's last night," Pemberton said as Myddelton pulled out his snuff box. "Hardy says you cleaned him out for the quarter," he continued. Having shared a study with Myddelton when they had been at school, and having lived on the same staircase when they had been up at Oxford, he was in no way discomfited by

Myddelton's taciturn moods.   Indeed, mostly he ignored them.   Of course, the worst had been when Myddelton's mother died.   The moods still occurred now and again, particularly since Myddelton had joined Castlereagh's staff, but still...

"He says that every time he loses," Myddelton replied, taking a pinch of snuff and sniffing hard.

Pemberton regarded him closely.   "'Struth, what happened to your head?   You've a lump the size of a goose's egg.   S'purple, too."

"I am aware of both its size and colour, thank you."

A grin pulled at the corners of Pemberton's mouth.   "Some doxy's bed chamber you ain't familiar with?"

Myddelton's glance was withering.   "No.   My *own* bedpost."

Pemberton exploded into laughter, drawing the attention of those at the neighbouring tables.   Unchastened by Myddelton's fulminating look, he finished the contents of his glass.   "Was you planning to stay here for th'evening or do you care to come along to Jersey's?"

Holding the stem between his thumb and forefinger, Myddelton twirled his wineglass on the table.   "Where are Hardy and Dunphail this evening?"   He could stay.

"Hardy's dining with your Guvnor...He took his violin with him. Dare say they're playing duets or trios or some such..."

Or join Dunphail.

"And Dunphail's off wenching..."

Or go home.   Or...Od's life!   Anything to take his mind off it.   "I fancy I shall join you."

By the time they reached the Jersey townhouse, situated like that of Myddelton's cousin, in Berkeley Square, it had begun to mist lightly, giving the house a soft, warm appearance and melding the outlines of the torches into the dark.   Entering the foyer, they gave their chapeaux bras into the keeping of a footman and went up to the ballroom.   Lady Jersey was waiting at the top of the stairs, to welcome and receive her guests.

"Ma'am, y'r obedient."   Myddelton bowed over her hand.

Lady Jersey spoke in paragraphs, never sentences.   "My dear Myddelton," she exclaimed.   "How utterly divine of you to come.   I am delighted you could, you know, because, of course, since I haven't seen you at all recently, I did rather wonder whether in fact you were even in Town. But then, of course, Anne-dear reminded me that you were rather tied up at the Foreign Office, not that I know anything at all about those sorts of affairs, but then I recalled Emily telling me that you had joined Castlereagh's staff—such an amiable man—so I knew that I must send you an invite and simply *hope* for the best. *So* good of you to come to my little party...

"And Pemberton, my dear..." She laughed, her blonde curls shaking beneath her evening blue silk turban, when Pemberton reached for her hand and kissed it lingeringly.

"One waltz, dearest Sal, is all I ask," he murmured.

"Pemberton!" she said, rapping his shoulder with her closed fan. "How can you even suggest such a thing. My reputation would be in tatters," she declared with a ripple of laughter. "Waltzing with a dashing and unmarried gentleman like you! What would darling Jersey have to say, I ask you?" She gave another trill of laughter. "How wicked you are. No, not another word. Myddelton, do take him away. He is a most dissolute influence and I cannot think how I came to invite him," she protested. "Oh, take him away, do!"

Pemberton laughed and bowed again, then together, he and Myddelton began the gentle push through the crush of guests blocking the doorway toward the ballroom. Absently Myddelton raised his quizzing glass. "Excuse me, I see someone I need to speak to..."

If three dances were judged by Society to be only acceptable between an affianced couple, two were deemed to signify a Serious Intent on the part of the gentleman who had requested that pleasure twice from an unmarried lady. And the lady who granted the privilege of two dances in one evening to the same gentleman was understood to be accepting the compliment. Thus, those who were close observers of such niceties—the matrons, the dowagers, the gossips—were more than a little titillated by the sight of Myddelton dancing twice with Miss Wythenshaw. Her determined interest had been acknowledged for some time. His, previously, had not. But now...However, such polite gossip grew less and less fulsome as Myddelton was later seen to dance twice with Miss Charlotte Nuttall, twice with Lady Anne Fyvie, and twice with Miss

Cassandra Staines-Smythe.

At last, having left the ballroom floor, Myddelton was leaning against a pilaster in an attitude of idle negligence, sipping at one in a series of glasses of champagne. Alone.

Pemberton approached him without a smile. "Hell and confound it," he whispered furiously. "What *is* the matter with you? Are you gone daft? What the deuce are you doing?"

Myddelton studied with apparent fascination the bubbles rising to the champagne's surface. Pemberton's was not a question about his sobriety. Or lack of it. He drew a breath; his heart lurched and began to pound. "Teasing."

"What?" Pemberton snapped.

"Teasing." Myddelton narrowed his eyes and looked about the ballroom, at the courting couples, the flirting, the matrons—all of Society who mattered in fact—then drank down the contents of his glass. He had known it would have to come out. Had known that it would have to be sooner rather than later. But how did one find the words and frame the phrases to describe the incomprehensible, the previously unthinkable? However much he had drunk that evening, it wasn't enough. "Or put another way...I was, ah, comparing charms...and contemplating a future of wedded bliss." There. It was out. And if he had not been able to keep the anger from his voice, at least half a dozen glasses of champagne ensured that the anguish was well-concealed.

Pemberton's eyelids flickered. "I beg your pardon?"

Myddelton looked away again, his jaw tightening.

Pemberton regarded him knowingly. "To be sure, you need not tell me if you do not wish to, but do me the favour of not talking Greek. In any event, you ain't about to slip your neck in the noose. You told me so yourself t'other night, when you wasn't three sheets to the wind."

"Ah, yes. So I did." Myddelton replaced his empty glass with a full one from off the tray of a passing footman. And despite the wine-induced haze which softened and slurred everything, he felt the breath go out of him, and the rage and wretchedness and now familiar cold roiling nausea churning in his stomach. "That was before I paid an overdue visit to the family solicitor. And learned that m'father had the foresight, shall we call it, for want of any better term, to arrange a marriage for me." He took a long drink of champagne.

"I beg your pardon?"

"M'father, in his infinite wisdom and perspicacity, er, arranged a marriage for me."

"He did what?" Pemberton exclaimed, feeling suddenly completely and utterly at sea.

"I confess, at first I thought it was one of your little practical jokes," Myddelton admitted.

"What?"

"Yes, that's right. However, it wasn't. I learned of the arrangement yesterday. I am off on the morrow to make the acquaintance of my bride and to tie the knot." He felt the cold sweat breaking out on his chest and back and gave a sardonic smile.

A pair of female chaperones of uncertain age regarded Myddelton sourly, then turned away. He did not notice.

"I beg your pardon?" Pemberton demanded yet again.

"You may well stare! S'life, imagine my reaction. The thing has been settled since I was twelve and no one deigned to tell me of it before now." The resentment in his voice was unmistakable.

"What?"

"'Struth, I think you'd better have the quack look at your ears. Your hearing's gone decidedly sidledywry."

Pemberton, ignoring the jibe, shook his head. "No...no. That is...I mean to say, who?"

"Whom am I to marry? Or who told me?"

"Both," said Pemberton in a strangled voice. "I don't believe this," he muttered.

"It was Ruttridge who very kindly informed me of the arrangements. But as to who the chit is...Upon my word, I have never heard of the family and I never heard of her neither. The whole thing was set up with me as security for some deuced loan."

"I beg your pardon? What? Security for a loan? When?" Pemberton asked more quietly, struggling still to grasp the facts.

Myddelton stared blindly ahead. "Some fellow apparently lent my

49

father a considerable sum." He clenched his teeth together and fought back the rising wave of bile. "To pay some gambling debts..." Od's life, to be deemed of no greater value than as payment for a loan. Robbed, cheated, betrayed—it was a litany now. "The wedding is to be this week. I leave in the morning." Christ, still to know nothing, nothing of her, nothing of her people, nothing of anything beyond the morrow. It was beyond bearing.

Pemberton's forehead creased with concentration. "Dash it, Myddelton, the whole thing defies belief. Are you sure it ain't some hoax?"

"I told you, I thought you'd set it up..."

"Wish I had," Pemberton countered, in comfort.

"However, seeing the marriage settlements with m'father's signature and seal upon 'em dispelled any sanguine hopes I may have held, I can assure you."

"No...There ain't some way you could wriggle out of it, is there? Pay her off?"

"I believe my immediate demise would answer. But, short of that, no. My father saw to it that there would be no routes of escape." Myddelton favoured him with a grim smile.

With a leisurely calm he did not feel, Pemberton polished his quizzing glass and returned his handkerchief to his pocket. Casually, he surveyed the room—the dancing couples, the dowagers, the small orchestra industriously playing away, the few red-coated officers, the ostentatious dandies—and wished angrily for something helpful to say. And could think of nothing. There was nothing, really. Finally, he drew a deep breath: "Well...I dare say it could have been worse."

"'Struth, I fail to see how," Myddelton exclaimed.

"...It may not be as bad as all that," Pemberton continued hopefully. "To be sure, she might turn out to be a beauty." Unlikely.

Myddelton snorted in disbelief.

"Well yes, I dare say that's too much to hope for." Bemused and confounded, Pemberton lapsed into silence. He eyed the company without enthusiasm.

Myddelton sighed heavily, knowing himself to be sinking into self-pity. He'd be sick before the night was out.

"I say, you'll not go leaving Town without telling me, will you?" Pemberton said finally.

"I told you, I'm off in the morning. First thing."

"Oh yes. Right. I'd forgot…Avery, if there is anything I can do, you have only to ask. You know that. I shall come with you, if you like. For moral support. After all, you and I thrashed Harrow together, didn't we? And Cambridge. I reckon we could manage a quick wedding…"

A fleeting smile caught at the corners of Myddelton's mouth. "So we did. With a century each…" Lud, he could see the wedding now. Both of them drunk as emperors, capsizing…How would the jumped-up Miss Heron and her fleecing uncle fancy that? No, no, it was not to be thought of. He shrugged. "Look, I think I'd best be off…"

"Yes," Pemberton nodded, then watched him go. Watched him thread his way (steadily and with barely a waver) around the crowded perimeter of the dance floor. Watched as ladies glanced and stared from behind open fans. Watched as gentlemen nodded cool farewells. None gave him a direct cut. He was, after all, still the Earl of Myddelton, even if he did dance twice with four separate young ladies, the madman. And anyway, they should have known better than to accept two dances with a single gentleman.

"You are, though I dare say you have forgot, supposed to be dancing this set with me," said Lady Anne Northcote quizzically as she tapped upon Pemberton's shoulder with her folded fan.

Pemberton turned to face her. "Lud, am I? 'Struth, I am. My apologies, Anne. How long have you been standing here?"

"Not so very long…" she replied, tucking her hand through his arm. "I do not suppose you would care to tell me…What has Myddelton looking so defiantly handsome and behaving with such…" She paused, selecting her words as one selects a choice peach from a bowl. "…unwonted indelicacy?" She averted her gaze to ostensibly study the toe of her satin slipper.

"No."

"We could go and sit on that settee in the corner and I could pretend you were flirting wildly with me," she coaxed.

"No."

"Pem, he is my cousin and I give you my word, I shan't tell a soul. Not even Miles."

"Oh you can tell Miles. He's tighter than a clam."

She smiled fondly. "He is at that...Pem! What is it? Tell me."

Pemberton frowned with indecision, then began to lead her toward the unoccupied corner settee. "He's getting spliced."

She sat down with an ungraceful thump. "What? Myddelton? To whom?"

"Keep your voice down," Pemberton admonished as he sat down beside her. "No one we know. It's to some chit he ain't even met. His father arranged the match. Old Ruttridge told him yesterday."

"Lud." Her eyes widened.

"He's off in the morning to do the thing, and as you may imagine, he ain't well pleased."

"Good heavens, no. Oh, my word. You're not teasing, are you? One saw that he was boosey, but...Oh, my word."

They sat in silence for some time before Anne, considering the whole, shook her head sadly and murmured, "...the poor child."

Pemberton's expression was surly. "Struth, Anne, whatever else you may call Myddelton, and I know there's plenty, you can hardly call him a poor child," he exclaimed.

"I did not mean Myddelton" she said patiently. "I meant the child he is to marry."

"What has she to do with anything?" Pemberton demanded.

"A very great deal, it would seem. Or do I need to explain the facts of marriage to you? Such as, it takes two...And *he* shall hardly behave like a model husband."

"Well dash it all, Anne, what do you expect? She's some ill-bred pasty-faced little sow who ain't fit to wash his linen! This ain't a love match—like you and Miles—or even a match between consenting parties. And even then, well...But this don't even have the merit of being a suitable match. It's just been arranged, that's all. He don't owe the poxy female anything."

"Oh really? That is as may be," she replied wisely. "However, he shall take the fact that the marriage was arranged without his consent and fullest heigh-ho as an excuse to go on exactly as he has always done."

"And what's wrong with that?" Pemberton bristled. "Any number of decent fellows do so."

"Aside from the fact that it is a sure receipt for misery, nothing. Why, you have seen his behaviour here this evening. Imagine what he shall be in five years' time—if he carries on in this manner." Her smile was regretful and she sighed. "A wife for whom he cared deeply might have checked that...and I had always hoped he would...oh, how can I say...fall desperately in love with some delightful girl, someone with whom he had a great deal in common, with whom he could talk, with whom he could laugh, in whose company he would be blissfully happy..." She gave her head a little shake.

"'Struth, Anne, we all wish for that. But it ain't generally the way it falls out, is it? Look about you. To be sure, the Jerseys are still keen. But who else? Show me. The William Lambs? The Cowpers? If Myddelton ever did have a chance for that, then this...this arrangement has put an end to it. For better or worse, he's to be leg-shackled to some whey-faced doxy with the manners of a fishwife and the scent of a stable lad."

Anne gave a snort of annoyance. "Pem! And if she is not, as you so charmingly phrase it, a whey-faced doxy? Not that I am meant to know about such things," she reproved, then continued: "Myddelton's father was no loose screw, you know, who would arrange an unsuitable alliance for his only son and heir! It is only natural that he should have done every thing in his power to promote the happiness and prosperity of his family. What gentleman would not? And he had but one son. It would have been more surprising had he done nothing at all. And you remember him. High in the instep don't do him justice."

Pemberton chuckled. "'Struth, yes." He pulled a face. "Lud, if you could have seen the look he gave me and m'sister Gussie when we..." He stopped short, and shook his head. "No. Never mind."

Anne smiled broadly. "My point exactly. So just because her marriage was arranged for her does not mean this girl, whoever she may be, is physically or morally deformed. It is not automatical. And given Myddelton's father, she is hardly likely to be anything other than supremely suitable."

Pemberton gave a reluctant laugh, then paused. "No." He toyed with his quizzing glass, examining the filigree handle, the knotted velvet ribbon which held it, the glass surface for fingerprints or dust, then said, "It's odd, you know…a childhood friend of mine is in the same case. Her parents arranged a match when she was small…to protect her. She's worth as much as half this room put together, I reckon. I should have known nothing about it, except that some of her family's property marches on that of m'grandfather, and he it was who proposed a match between us—thought it would be a good thing. It would not have been bad. I had no objection. But, when he inquired of her family, it turned out as I told you."

"And your friend, is she in any way objectionable? Or disfigured?"

Pemberton shook his head and laughed. "'Struth, no! Just the opposite. But we ain't talking about her." he said, his temper flaring again. "We're talking about Myddelton being spliced to some pudding-faced little nobody who…"

"I cannot believe what I am hearing!" Anne declared. "No sooner do you admit that…"

There was a flurry of steps and a rustle of silk near them. "What can the pair of you be arguing about?" Lady Jersey demanded without preamble. "I have been watching you for the past half hour. And at my party too! It is bad enough that Myddelton got himself drunk as an emperor and then played the loose fish, dancing twice with four separate girls in one evening and then left, with no apologies to me, I might add, for causing an uproar. I vow I was ready to scream with vexation. Not that I particularly minded him giving the Wythenshaw chit and that odious grasping mama of hers a set-down. Heaven knows I have been wanting to do it myself this age. The way she waltzes is nothing short of indecent. But that is beside the point. Why did he have to choose Anne Fyvie and little Cassa Staines-Smythe? Of all people? If the Drummond-Burrell creature don't make an issue of it, I shall count it a miracle. And now this! Naturally, one wishes to have one's do's talked about by all and sundry, but not because of the indiscretions committed by one's friends while they were there. So what, if I may ask, is of such vital importance that it has the two of you at each other's throats? Could it not have waited until you were private? Lud. Why did it have to be at my ball? Of all places? Well?"

Anne gave her the most innocent of gazes. "Napoleon's troop movements, Sally. What else could it be?"

By tasted sweetness make me not to rue
The sudden loss of thy false feignèd grace.

4

There is a subtle yet unmistakable difference between half-sober and half-drunk, but it was unclear which of these described Myddelton as he left London for Oxfordshire early that morning. For notwithstanding his best efforts, he had failed to achieve anything like the sense-sodden equability he desired, yet another reason for his grim, foul humour.

He had been travelling north and west for some time and the City was far behind. Now, on either side of the road, beyond hedgerows of briar, livestock—cow and calf, horse and foal, sheep and young lambs—grazed on fallow land overrun with primrose and cowslip, and orchards of fruit trees were in blossom, and in the fields, furrows of brown earth were split and speckled with the fresh green blades of corn, and all punctuated with the occasional blinding white of a blackthorn in bloom among the hedges. Myddelton saw none of it.

Kester, clutching the tiger's metal bar as the carriage careened wantonly at a curve in the road, swore to himself—and to his Maker—that he would attend church on Sunday next if he came away from this ride in one piece.

But Myddelton, bereft, and in a rage of his own or perhaps his parent's making, remained as oblivious to this as to everything except the seething resentment he felt. Spurred by something akin to self-hatred, unmoved by the pleasure of the wind in his face or the steady rhythm of the horses' hooves, he drove without his customary precision or skill, all the while wishing that he might never arrive at his destination.

By midday, they had passed through Britwell St Luke—a dab of a rural hamlet with little more than a smithy, a baker's and a public house called the Blue Boar lining one side of the road. Beyond—about a mile

out, Mr. Broke had said, tracing the route on the map with his finger—
would be the main gate of Britwell Park. And there it was.

A pair of large, wrought-iron gates stood open between two solid
pillars of yellow Cotswold stone. Myddelton slowed the horses and
turned in. The gatehouse, with its neat garden plot, was unattended.
Beyond, a raked gravel drive led up a gentle incline under a thick canopy
of new green, of oak and yew and holly. Beneath the trees, the ground
was densely covered with evergreen, lilac, wild garlic, forget-me-nots and
late primroses, their scents mingling, sweet and sharp. Here and there, a
shaft of sunlight broke through the interlaced branches and foliage to
dapple the earth with patches of light, illuming the motes of dust that
hung in the still air.

Suddenly uncertain, Myddelton allowed the reins to fall slack,
overcome by an intense weariness, the combined effects of too much
anxiety and anger and brandy, too many translations and troop reports,
too much turning and tossing and too little sleep. He had arrived and
nothing might stay this meeting any longer. He paused to readjust his hat
and to flex his shoulders. Then, he slapped the reins; and the horses
started up the drive.

Ahead, the drive stretched through the wood without a discernible
end, tunnelling through the trees, a refuge of deep shade and midday
hush. Once, twice, three times, cart tracks crossed the drive, but he saw
no one. Gradually he lost all sense of time, though he noticed that the
incline had become a hill. Whilst at the back of his thoughts, an
unwonted hope had begun to glimmer that by some miracle, some act of
Providence, without fuss or discord or further dismay, life might
somehow be made normal again.

The horses, spent by their long drive, strained at the poles to drag
the carriage over a final rise. And there, startlingly, the wood gave way to
a vast lawn surrounding a large house of mellowed Cotswold stone which
seemed to glow in the sunlight. Myddelton blinked in surprise. What he
had been imagining since Monday, anticipating with contempt and
disdain, he could not precisely say. But it was surely not this.

Had he possessed a travellers' guide book to Oxfordshire, it might
have told him that Britwell Park was a fine house built during the early

years of the Restoration. That it had been constructed like those houses from an earlier generation, on an H-shape plan, with a central block flanked by projecting cross wings. Yet unlike those earlier buildings, this had a hipped roof with gables and symmetrically placed transom windows, and that chief among other Italianate features was a graceful pedimented Ionic portico. But Myddelton had no guidebook, so he was struck, not by any architectural innovation, but by the quiet dignity, the sense of security and continuity, the still beauty and harmonious symmetry of this supremely quiet place.

He climbed down from the driver's seat and stood staring at the front of the house. The polished surfaces of the glazed windowpanes glinted in the sunlight. To the right of the house, a large formal garden (a knot garden perhaps? a parterre?) was just coming into bloom within meticulously clipped hedges of box and rue. To the left, another lawn fanned out to meet a grove of trees in the distance. Still dazed, he rose on tiptoe to stretch the backs of his legs, then shook his head in disbelief. Had he mistaken the way and taken a wrong turning? One of the horses snorted, jangling the harness. Could this be the right place? Was it possible?

Into the silence erupted the ripple of a child's laughter and the resonant barking of a large dog, followed by more laughter. Myddelton hesitated, then stepped toward the sound. Then he checked himself, unbuttoned the top buttons of his driving coat and resolutely started for the portico.

Another ripple of that laughter cascaded into the quiet. Myddelton paused. From the side lawn, it was.

Kester, standing weakly alongside the horses, ran an idle hand over the leader's nose and watched without seeming to do so. And was startled when Myddelton turned sharply on his heel and walked away from the portico toward the lawn. "Well, bugger me blue! Touched in 'is upperworks..." he muttered. He patted the leader's head reassuringly. "Too much French brandy."

Myddelton stepped around the great fragrant lilac at the corner of the house. Before him stretched a wide lawn. At the centre of it, in a flurry of white lace and petticoats, lay a girl, laughing. Near her feet, a large yellow-coloured dog growled in play as he gnawed at something held tenaciously between his front paws. The girl rolled onto her side, giving Myddelton a brief glimpse of fair curls, and studied the dog. Then, snatching the dog's trophy, she jumped to her feet and started running, the prize—a sash of bright blue—swirling out behind her like the tail of a kite. The dog bounded to his feet to give chase, leaping and snapping at the sash as it fluttered in the air over his head. He lunged into the air, his hind legs swinging free as he snapped at the ribbon's end and caught it. He landed and jerked the ribbon free.

Like a triumphant soldier having taken enemy colours, the dog tore away, the end of the ribbon held tightly between his bared teeth. Laughing, the girl stumbled after him, always laughing. Until finally, she tumbled to the ground and lay on her back, laughing helplessly, just as she had done when Myddelton had first seen her.

Such unaffected delight disarmed him. And in spite of himself, Myddelton smiled.

The dog trotted over to the girl and dropped the sash at her head. He nuzzled her hair and her cheek and began licking her face.

She broke into fresh laughter. "Lotto, stop it." Her voice was clear. "Stop it! It tickles! Lotto, stop!" Her voice quavered and she began to laugh again. And pushing ineffectually at his nose, she rolled over to envelop his head in a hug. The dog emitted a series of snorting grunts.

Reluctantly, Myddelton turned to walk back to the front of the house.

A breeze ruffled the leaves in the nearby stand of trees. Sniffing the air, the dog pulled free, barked once and stiffened. Certain that the animal had caught his stranger's scent, Myddelton stopped.

The girl sat up, and stroking his head, spoke quietly to the dog. And then she too saw Myddelton—a tall stranger, very tall, wearing a high-crowned beaver and a long drab driving coat, unbuttoned against the heat, his face obscured by the brim of his hat—standing at the edge of the lawn.

With the grace of a wild creature which has known no fetters, she rose to her feet and shook out her rumpled skirts, then bent to pick up her bedraggled sash, the dog's prize. Then, with neither hurry nor concern, and her dog as sentinel at her side, she approached.

She was small and delicately built and too young to be his Miss Heron. But, dear God, she was a beauty. 'Struth! Was she a daughter of the house? A cousin, perhaps?

Appraising the wreckage of her former sash, she subjected the retriever to a baleful look and said pointedly, "You are a horrid dog. No one loves you as much as I do, so you may believe me when I tell you you are a horrid dog. And I'm covered in dog-lick!"

Od's life, her eyes were a startling blue. Like fireworks, they were. Even at this distance, Myddelton could see that. And the ivory skin, still flushed from play, caressed her cheekbone before sloping into her gently curved chin like a carving by Cellini or della Robbia. 'Je ne vis onques la pareille de vous ma gracieuse dame...' *I have never seen the equal of you, my gracious lady*...Was it Hardy who'd been singing that? Had to have been. Who else? And it was true of her. Dear heaven, it was true of her. Was it possible that her cousin, his Miss Heron, looked anything, anything at all, like her?

Myddelton sketched a bow and tipped his hat. "I am Myddelton."

She curtsied, but said nothing.

Her silence took him aback. "Forgive my unpardonable intrusion. I...ah...heard your laughter from the front of the house and could not resist the desire to locate its source."

"Oh yes." Her expression told him nothing.

He could not help staring. "Perhaps you would be so kind as to direct me to Sir Charles Heron. My business is with him." Close up, she was achingly beautiful though her head came up only as far as his shoulder.

She studied his face for a long moment, then smiled. Her teeth were white and even. "Please, come this way. I shall take you to him." The pitch of her voice was lower than he had expected. She turned toward the house. "Lotto. Come."

Disconcerted by her composure (or was it a signal lack of interest?), shaken by her beauty, and lightheaded from the sun and a lack of sleep, Myddelton followed her into the house through an open side door and into a long hallway hung with oil paintings—landscapes and a few small portraits—with Persian carpets scattered over the parquet floor. And from there into the main hall.

Like many great houses, the main hall of Britwell Park had linenfold panelling and a barrel-vaulted ceiling of moulded plaster. But here there was also the benefit of windows facing both south and north, so that the room was washed with light. Involuntarily, Myddelton stood to admire the ceiling's intricate pattern of flower-filled quarterfoils, rectangles and heraldic devices. Nothing was as he had imagined it. Nothing. Near the large hearth that dominated one side of the room were two wing chairs and a small sofa. Portraits by Hoppner, Aikman and Reynolds adorned the walls, including one of a young red-coated officer, already with a chest full of medals. The young James Heron perhaps? And at the centre of the hall, an ancient round table supported an enormous copper bowl filled to bursting with cabbage roses.

Ignoring him, the girl tugged on a bell-pull. A footman appeared to receive Myddelton's hat and gloves and to help him off with his dust-caked driving coat. And still she said nothing, but crossed to a double set of doors, knocked, then slipped inside. Then reemerged a moment later.

"Sir Charles will see you now," she announced in her soft musical way.

Myddelton's stomach tightened. She indicated the open door. He reached into his pocket and gripped hard on his snuff-box. She curtsied as he passed and he gave her a final wondering look, then she closed the door firmly behind him.

"Myddelton! My dear young man," exclaimed a voice. And the warmth of recognition in that voice caught him by surprise.

Then: "By my life, you do resemble your father! B'Gad, you've the look of him." From the shadows of one corner of the book-lined room, emerged a face and figure to match the voice—small, wiry and robust, the very image of a country gentleman at ease with himself. Welcome and geniality were etched in the smile lines of his face. He paused for a moment, legs astride and hands on hips, to consider Myddelton with intelligent eyes.

"You're taller though. A good deal taller though, ain't you?" He sighed. "'Struth, he was ever a handsome devil! I was very sorry to hear of his death. Very sorry, indeed. A sad business, that." The gentleman crossed the Indian carpet, stepping lightly, without that sense of burden which passing years add to many shoulders and belying the silver hair which had lately begun to thin. "I am Charles Heron." He extended a hand and began pumping Myddelton's with enthusiasm. "Damme, you do have the look of him! Od's fish," he exclaimed in delight. "I can scarce credit it." Sir Charles stepped—hopped really—to the bell-pull. "Sit down, do. Some refreshment? Drove up from London this morning, did you? Did you stop on the road?"

A manservant, bearing a tray of cold meats, cheeses and fruit, entered the room.

"Ah Jenner, you anticipate my every desire." Sir Charles rubbed his hands together. "Show Lord Myddelton up to the east wing, will you? There's a room ready, is there? Yes, good…He'll be wanting hot water, I dare say…"

The pepper-haired butler, taller than his master and with a much greater air of consequence, held open the door for Myddelton and bowed. "Yes, sir."

Sir Charles smiled. "Don't know why I bother giving the orders. You're always well beforehand. Thank you, Jenner."

Bemused by the warmth of Sir Charles' welcome, by the house, by everything—and still curious about the girl—Myddelton bowed, mumbled a 'thank you' and followed the butler into the hall and up the carved oak staircase. The condescension and pride of consequence with which he had been prepared to wither and crush the pretensions of the upstart Herons had no place here. 'Struth, if anyone was to do the crushing, it would be the dashed butler.

Some time later as he sat in the library opposite Sir Charles, Myddelton, now washed, refreshed and well-fed, felt, as the requisite conversation on the state of the pike roads and the weather reached its natural end, that unwelcome return of awkwardness clutching at his shoulders, and the fear pulsing in his stomach, even as his eyes yearned to close in sleep.

Sir Charles, silently observing him, took a clay pipe from the desk and began systematically to fill it. "Now, young man, how may I be of service?"

Myddelton's eyes flickered open and he swallowed the tightness in his throat. He looked down upon his boots and then up again. The purpose of his business now baldly before him, he felt detached, exhausted, unwell. "Ehm...A certain document has been brought to my attention, concerning m'self and your niece, Sir Charles. Miss Jane Heron?"

Concentrating on his pipe, Sir Charles tapped again at the tobacco in the bowl and fussed with lighting it. "Ah yes. Yes, indeed. And a very peculiar document it is." His eyes twinkled as if in appreciation of some private joke. "Would you not agree?"

"Then..." S'life, did he have to make this more difficult then it already was? "...I expect you know my purpose in coming here today."

His eyes bright, Sir Charles nodded. "Oh yes. Yes, I do." His eyes narrowed to slits. "And here I sit, not making a single effort to help you out, in a situation which is already deuced awkward. How very churlish in me." He watched as some of the strain abated from Myddelton's face. "In truth, I had been wondering when you would arrive. More wine?"

His ease, like that of the girl, was disconcerting, though Myddelton could not have said why. "Yes...No, no, thank you...I would have come sooner, but, you see, I only just learned of the arrangements the day before yesterday."

"The day before yesterday?" Sir Charles repeated with some feeling. "The day before yesterday? That's leaving things rather late, ain't it, even for Old Ruttridge!"

Further discomfited, Myddelton began, "To be sure, he may have meant to tell me sooner...but although for the past several months, he has been writing to request an interview, he never gave any indication of urgency, until the other day."

"Hmph," snorted Sir Charles. "And you are not at all content with the arrangements, I make no doubt."

Nettled, Myddelton straightened. How could Sir Charles have known? And with such accuracy? "Sir, I..." he began in protest.

"No," Sir Charles silenced him. "No, do not deny it. It is written in your face. You forget, I knew your father. Rather well, as it happens."

He drew a long breath, while his eyes never left Myddelton's face, watching as the indignation diffused to be followed by what? "Hmn. Shall I tell you how this difficult business came about and what I know of it? You should know the whole." And more to himself, he added, "You ought to have been told years ago..." He frowned. "I cannot imagine Ruttridge gave you the full story, if indeed he knew it. An excellent lawyer and an astute man of business—so James always believed—but a deuced cold fish." He took his pipe from his mouth. "I warn you though, the tale is not a pretty one, and I fancy it will only serve to anger you. But still, you shall know it." He held the bowl of his pipe in his hand and pondered it, then glancing at Myddelton, pondered how much of this sequence of events he should be forced to hear.

"Do you remember your uncle St. Maur, Lord Maundrel that was?"

"Very little," Myddelton admitted, now sobered and wary with anticipation. "Ruttridge mentioned him, as well. As a boy, I was called down to shake his hand once or twice, I believe, but that was without question the extent of our acquaintance."

"Very wise," Sir Charles commented. "Very wise. Though hardly surprising really. Well...As you are perhaps not aware—for I cannot imagine your father, God rest his soul, speaking so plainly—the fellow was a damned loose screw. He had the reputation of a libertine. Well-deserved, I do assure you. He was a man of vicious propensities, rather like that young poet, Byron...Passed his time with the hangers-on of the Devonshire set or with Mohocks..." He shook his head. "In any event...it would have been in the autumn of '95...yes, that's right... that he took it into his head to seduce your mother."

Unprepared and recoiling, Myddelton started from his chair, as a bolt of outrage shot through him. "What?"

Sir Charles, reading the revulsion behind the tightening of Myddelton's lips, stopped. "You are shocked," he said gently. "Forgive me for distressing you. I ought to have prepared you..."

Blenching and stony-faced, a stern alertness having banished all fatigue, Myddelton resumed his seat, but did not, could not settle. "No," he said. "Please, continue...My mother, sir? What happened?"

"You may rest easy," Sir Charles said. "He did not succeed."

Myddelton exhaled hard, dispelling a degree of tension.

"Perhaps she was a challenge to him?" Sir Charles continued. "Saw him for what he was and treated him accordingly? I cannot say. I was never in his confidence. Though she was, I can assure you, unlike his usual female acquaintances." Sir Charles paused in recollection. "Hmn. Your father was away at the time—in the North, it may have been. So it was my brother, James, who caught him at it. Forcing himself on her, as it were. He heard her crying out, do you see, and came to find her struggling and in great distress. And as your father was away from Town, James called him out." Sir Charles stopped and drew a deep breath. Reading the anger and profound disquiet writ on Myddelton's face, he frowned again. Was it indeed possible that he had known of none of this? Not any of it? He shook his head and sighed. "The damn'd fellow did not even have the grace to delope. Winged James."

Sir Charles paused again, choosing his words and his presentation as would a fine lawyer or a scholar. "The surgeon and James' second both assured me that James did not shoot to kill that morning. He intended only to wound. Indeed, I understood him to have arranged for your uncle to be pressed soon after their meeting, for it was James' conviction that the Navy would either make a gentleman of St. Maur or kill him…" Seeing Myddelton again start with rebellious indignation, he added, "Again, I have shocked you. You think it a harsh sentence. But can you not see, either way, your family would have been saved any further embarrassment and that must outweigh all other considerations?"

Wholly discountenanced and now battered by such a storm of disgust and disquiet, Myddelton felt, for the hundredth time in the last days, the unwelcome presence of new tears pricking at his eyelids. But these were unlike those previous. These were the pricking of repugnance and remorse, of regret, of futile solicitude for his dead parents. And he wished suddenly that he were back at home where he might contend with such sentiments in private.

Sir Charles regarded him compassionately. "But it goes without saying that St. Maur was drunk for his dawn meeting, and swayed at just the wrong instant. Though I dare say he would have preferred such an end to the sponging house, or life on board, if it comes to that. He was buried, not in your family's vault—your father would not countenance it after all that he had done—but in the churchyard near the inn where he died.

"There was no scandal and few questions. James had arranged matters well. St. Maur's second disappeared from sight too—I fancy in the absence of St. Maur he was pressed. And that appeared to be the end of that. Until over the next few months, it became clear that St. Maur was indebted to nearly everyone in the country. Gaming debts, in the main. Ilchester was another one such, you know—owed nearly forty thousand pounds when he died. The family nearly had to sell up. People thought Charles James Fox lost a great deal at the tables…Ha ha! But those chappies are all the same, and his losses, I can assure you, seemed a pittance by comparison to St. Maur's. At least to your father…Whigs, humph!

"It was about that time that your father was getting the estates back on their feet after your grandfather's excesses. You look surprised. Did no one tell you about him neither?"

"No…" Myddelton admitted dazedly, his confidence and self-regard undermined by Sir Charles' sordid revelations. He shifted uneasily in his chair.

"Ah," Sir Charles said gently. "Well, a bad run at the tables as I understand it. However, that's as may be. The gist is, your father had only just cleared the mortgage on Great Myddelton. Things were beginning to look up for him and he was in despair when he learned of it.

"James, bless him, was something of a Nabob—money meant nothing to him—do you see? He'd gone to India, discovered quite by accident that he had a knack for making money, and amassed a fortune. And there was all his prize money as well. So he insisted on clearing St. Maur's debts, declaring that it was his *duty* as it had been his shot that had brought the duns to the door, so to speak. Which was a nonsense—but, knowing James it was no less than one would have expected. And, it was then that this match was arranged." Sir Charles relit his pipe.

"I strongly disagreed with the arrangement. The amount hardly dented James' fortune. But your father felt he owed James so much. It was not just the debts. It was your mama as well. And rightly or

69

wrongly, your father believed that this arrangement was the only acceptable thanks he could offer. Particularly as James' wife was only recently dead."

Sir Charles emitted a great puff of smoke which twirled into a fading wreath about his head. "I did my utmost to dissuade the pair of them. But there was no reasoning with either of them. James was posted to Vienna shortly thereafter. As a diplomatic and military aide. He was killed at Marengo, in June 1800." Sir Charles sat quietly for a moment, thinking of his dead brother, and perhaps of the small child he had left behind, but never alone.

He resumed: "Your father did repay it all, you know. To the last guinea. He was a good man, your father. But then, James was killed and…well, I have always believed that is the reason that rather mediaeval document was never torn up and consigned to the fire. It was all of it hushed up at the time, of course. But it was a terrible business, from first to last." There was, perhaps, a great deal else he might have added.

"My niece has lived here all her life." Sir Charles smiled sadly. Then, as if he'd been too long dwelling on the sins of the past, too long inactive and could no longer be still, he rose and walked to the window to throw it open. "There now." He strode back to the desk. "And where does that leave us?" He frowned. "With the inevitable present, no doubt…However, perhaps you can now see your way clear to detaching the blame from her."

Myddelton, still beset by such repulsion, looked up, stung that his sentiments had again been so easily perceived. "I beg your pardon?"

"My dear young man," Sir Charles said levelly. "I could hardly have failed to apprehend your feelings. Particularly as you left matters so late." He drew himself up, then leaned forward and placed his hands on his knees—as if to address a child. "You should have gone to bed last night, instead of sitting up drinking at your club."

For the past few days, Myddelton had been conscious of nothing so much as his superiority on every level to these upstart Herons, had known with solid conviction that he was the wronged party in this singularly ill-judged affair. But now, inarticulate with dismay, and facing the inescapable conclusion that all blame must fall upon his own family, upon the profligacy, the venery of his uncle, that these Herons had saved his parents and himself from moral opprobrium and financial ruin, that his own behaviour richly deserved the implicit rebuke issued with such quiet authority and more beside, what remained of his self-possession and much-prized sangfroid deserted him. The Master at Eton had never quashed his pretensions so effectively. Nor the Senior Censer of the House.

"No," he began, fumbling for words. "No, I…that is, you are quite right, sir. I…ehm…" He swallowed tightly, keenly, uncomfortably aware of his own inadequacies, the arrogant pride, the self-importance and impudence of rank, the misplaced self-righteousness. "To be sure, had I known what I now know, I would have behaved very differently. Though whether that would have been of any avail…However, ehm, however, I trust that now…now that I have been made aware of the circumstances surrounding the arrangement, I shall behave as honourably as my father would have wished. My word on it." He groped in his fob-pocket for his snuff-box.

"I have brought a special licence with me. Your niece and I…we can be married as soon as you think fit. If that meets with your approval."

"Insofar as none of this business has ever met with my approval, that meets with it!" Sir Charles retorted. "These sorts of arrangements are the height of idiocy! I can see by the gleam in your eye that you think so too. But, regrettably, it is not up to us. And because of the requirements laid down, an immediate wedding will have to do, if you are not to lose your estates." He harrumphed, clearing his throat.

"I shall speak to Jane. She knows nothing of this." Sir Charles shook his head. "Utter folly…

"I have kept a close eye on your career over the years. Do not be surprised. I may live retired, but I am not entirely unconnected at Whitehall. Nor at Christ Church, come to that…Your Greats tutor and I was up together…" he recalled fondly. "I thought those Latin verses of yours quite, ehm…" He paused, searching for a word, while Myddelton suffered the further unpleasant shock of realising that Sir Charles must be well-connected indeed to know of that episode.

"...Remarkable, when they was shown me. The rhyming schemes in particular were most felicitous." Sir Charles smiled sunnily, then his tone took on that edge of honed steel again. "I have tried to see that my niece learn all the necessary things. She is a fine girl. I only hope you deserve her." He stood up and stretched his back.

"But now, I see you are falling asleep. Forgive me. Here you are, ready to drop, and first I burden you with a tale of such wickedness, and now all I do is preach at you! Come. Upstairs with you and have a rest. We cannot have you falling asleep over the proposal."

Sir Charles' tone was so light, so amicable, that Myddelton wondered if he'd imagined the earlier severity, even as he began to squirm inwardly at this new thought. S'life, he wasn't expected to propose too, was he? "I had thought I would stay at the inn..." he stammered.

Sir Charles laughed. "Oh my dear Myddelton, you cannot do that! Good lord, the innkeeper would rob you blind inside an hour." He chuckled again. "Your sentiments no doubt do you great credit, but fancy, staying at the Blue Boar. No, no, you must stay here." He tugged on the bell-pull. "I insist upon it. The Blue Boar, indeed. I shouldn't mind the dirt, if they was at least respectable. They tell me you can catch the pox from the sheets there, dear boy...

"Ah Jenner, there you are. Show his lordship up to a room, will you? He shall be staying for a few days. And send Miss Jane to me. In half an hour..." Sir Charles smiled warmly and watched as Jenner held the door for Myddelton. Turning to face his master, Jenner bowed and shut the door.

5

Sir Charles stood, facing out upon the garden through the large sash window thrown open to admit the fine afternoon air, a stark silhouette against a rectangular background of broad day. On either side of him, the book-lined walls of the library were deep in shadow despite the hour, the colourful leather spines and gold lettering of the rowed volumes muted and dulled by the blocking of the light.

"Uncle?" Miss Jane Heron slipped into the room, held the door open for a long moment, then quietly closed it. "You wished to see me?" She leaned against it, hesitating. Her firecracker blue eyes had turned grave and unaccountably dark.

Sir Charles turned, looking up from the book he had not been reading. "Yes...Yes, Janey. Come in and sit."

Miss Heron left the door and seated herself on a long sofa near her uncle. Her fair hair had been brushed into a semblance of order and she had changed her rumpled muslin for a gown of tamboured organdy, its hem deep in lace.

"How is that disobedient animal of yours today?"

A smile broke through her gravity as she regarded the yellow furred head which appeared on her knee whenever she sat down. "What you mean to say, sir, is 'how many of your grouse and pheasant chicks has he startled today?'" Gently, she began to stroke the dog behind the ears. "The answer is none at all. He has been a paragon of canine virtue all morning and Sanders even told me he thinks he should be trained as a gun dog for you."

She paused. "But you did not send for me so that you could ask after Lotto," she reproved mildly.

Sir Charles gave her a measuring look. She was far too perceptive, this child. She always had been. "No." He had been bracing himself for this moment for the past six months. Had been rehearsing what he must say for the past half hour. "You observed the arrival of the young Earl of Myddelton today?"

"Having eyes, I see. He has a great bruise on his forehead," she stated dispassionately.

"Has he?" asked Sir Charles, much surprised. She noticed everything, this girl.

"Yes. He has." Then: "He is come for me, isn't he?" Her look was direct, unflinching.

Sir Charles' fine and sensitively phrased speech evaporated. "I beg your pardon? How did you know?"

She paused, and drew a deep breath. "It had to be him, really, didn't it? You have been training me and drilling me almost without ceasing since I was twelve. Dancing lessons until my performance was perfect, comportment, lessons on the fortepiano, drawing, painting, French, Italian—indeed everything requisite to ensure that I would be a most accomplished young lady, ready to take my place in Society. Only you never mentioned a Season in London. Not even when the Misses Greenwood and their mama—whom you admit to liking very much—rattled on and on about it, even going so far as to suggest that I might accompany them if you did not like to undertake the Season yourself." There was no rebuke in her speech, only the highest regard for the facts.

Sir Charles pursed his lips and eyed her shrewdly. "Ah."

"For a time I was convinced you intended me for Lord Pemberton."

"Young Pemberton?"

"Yes, dearest," she answered softly. "Indeed, half the county still think it."

"Do they?" he said.

"Perhaps not now. But until Lord Choate came calling…"

"How did you know about that?" Sir Charles exclaimed, startled.

Miss Heron ignored the question. "Miss Unthank…"

"Who?"

"Miss Unthank," she repeated patiently. "Lady Choate's cousin and companion, has spent the larger portion of her time thinking up names

74

for our unborn children."

Sir Charles snorted. "Silly female."

She did not laugh. "But that came to nothing. Still, none of the young gentlemen who danced with me at the Oxford assemblies ever came courting. All were held at arm's length, as if there were some sort of barrier between me and them. And gradually, I became aware of the gossip." She saw his look of patent disbelief, perhaps discomfort. "Yes, dearest, the gossip. Just because you do not gossip does not mean that the rest of the parish so abstains. And I could hardly fail to overhear Mrs. Sayer telling her daughter that she needn't worry about me stealing her admirers—my family were marrying me off to a peer of the realm on account of my fortune. Indeed, anyone within six miles of Carfax could have heard her."

"Repellent woman!" Sir Charles growled.

"Yes," Miss Heron agreed prosaically. "She is rather...So really, it would have been impossible for me not to have twigged. And since then, I have been waiting. Then, when I went round to the stables, I saw the crest on his carriage." She bowed her head so that the curls falling around her forehead obscured her face from view. "It is the same as that which Mademoiselle has had me stitch on countless sheets and linens, only she told me she had made up the pattern of laurels herself. I cannot think why I believed her."

"Yes. I see..." And he did. All too clearly. "Janey, I'm sorry."

She did not, would not, cry. "Is it for my fortune?"

"Yes. No. Not really." Sir Charles drew a long breath. Those carefully thought-out speeches, those bracing words of cheer and courage, now the moment had come, dried upon his tongue. "To be sure, it all happened a long time ago," he said, beginning the tale he had told already once that day. "Your father and his father..."

"My father!" she exclaimed, roused from apparent placidity. "My father? What has he to say to anything? He never looked at me above twice in his life."

"Janey, that's not true."

"Yes, it is," she insisted. "He wanted a son. A son to follow him into the army and die—gloriously, no doubt—just like him."

"Janey! That is not what happened. Neither does it have any bearing on your marriage to Myddelton."

"Then what has?" she asked, a wise quiescence replacing the brief show of spirit.

"The Fourth Earl of Myddelton—you will remember him—this Myddelton's father? He was always used to visit once or twice a year, you'll recall. Well, he and your father were the greatest of friends. Had been since their school days and as young men, they joined the same regiment. Myddelton sold out eventually, of course, and your father went off to India. Later, when he came back, he married your mother and you were born..."

"And she died..."

"Yes." Sir Charles rose and took a turn about the room. There was no way to wrap it up in clean linen. "Yes. Yes, well...This Myddelton had a brother, Lord Maundrel St. Maur, he was called." Nor was it likely that she would be fobbed off with half-truths and innuendo. "A thoroughly bad lot...It happened all such a long time ago now...As I said, St. Maur was anything but a gentleman. He was a scoundrel and a knave, without a single redeeming quality that I could ever find out. In any event, he came upon Lady Myddelton alone one morning and attempted to seduce her..."

"Uncle!"

Sir Charles regarded her crossly. "Don't be missish, Janey."

"I am not," she insisted. "But you must confess, sir, this is a tale even the Minerva Press would have qualms about printing."

Bristling and distracted, unhappy with his role as the bearer of tales—this tale in particular—Sir Charles retorted: "You shouldn't be so well-read."

"You shouldn't have taught me..." She exhaled. "Do go on. I shall not commit the crime of missishness again, you may be sure."

And silently, conscientiously, she listened. Listened to the history of his uncle's wickedness and her father's honour and his kindness to his friend; listened to how two men had arranged for her future while she was still in her cradle, neither of them knowing whether she would survive childhood; listened to how her father had gone off to Austria and

76

had never returned.

"...It was intended that young Myddelton should have come here—to woo you—six months ago, as I understood it. But there appears to have been a mix-up somewhere. No doubt if your father, or his, had been alive, their plan would have gone off smoothly enough. As it is..." Sir Charles finished, now finding himself at an unaccustomed loss.

"When?" She hesitated over the words. "When must I marry him?"

He felt like a judge handing down a sentence he knew to be unjust. "Tomorrow."

"Tomorrow?" She exclaimed, looking up, glaring at him with blazing eyes, a furious flush mounting in her cheeks. She had not been angry until now. "Tomorrow? So soon? Why so soon? I don't even know him!" Her arm tightened about her dog's neck and she slid onto the floor to kneel beside him. "Why?" she demanded. "How could you not have told me? Why did his father never say anything? Why?"

Sir Charles had never seen her so angry. Flustered, he declared: "Janey, I was forbid it! I fancy his father expected to tell you—to ask you—himself...Indeed, I believe he meant to effect the introduction himself...and once an amicable friendship was established, only then to propose the match." So much had gone awry. Too much. "But, of course, he died so suddenly, quite unexpectedly, it was...and I heard nothing, and did not know what to do for the best...As for young Myddelton—he must marry you before your eighteenth birthday or he shall lose the greater part of his estates. Do you not see? Oh, my dearest angel. He has no choice! His father arranged everything, as he believed, for your sole benefit, do you see? He believed he owed everything to your father and he arranged it all for you!" And if there was more to be said than that, now was not the time for such things.

He gathered her into his arms to hold her close, and looked out over her head upon the fine spring afternoon, upon the garden beyond, and the sunlight on the fresh green of the young leaves. And knew he should never have permitted this to happen to her. And within the circle of that loving embrace, her jaw quivered as the exigencies of Myddelton's situation punctured the fine self-righteousness of her rage and diffused it. They, none of them, had any choice.

Sir Charles stepped away, taking her hand to cradle it in his own, as he had done all her life. "Janey, my dearest girl, I know that this is not—cannot be—what you have dreamed of, but you shall do it and you shall do it well. I have, as you have said, trained you for it. I have done all in my power to see that you was prepared." What did they call those army fellows who led the assaults on fortresses? The forlorn hope? They were not the only ones.

She did not give way to the threatening tears; she would not. Struggling, she blinked and nodded. "Shall I like him, do you think?" she said simply.

What did the attempted lightness in her voice cost her? Sir Charles pulled himself up to answer with equal lightness: "'Struth, he is such a handsome young devil, I should have thought you'd fallen head over heels in love with him already."

"I did not ask if I should love him," she responded. And Sir Charles felt the tender sting. For that, surely, was too much to hope for, too much even to dream.

He gestured helplessly. "How can I possibly say, my dear? I wish I knew." He halted, unhappy with his own inadequacy. "He is on the whole, I believe, an honourable young man. He will, he *must*, treat you kindly." He looked down on her small smooth hand tucked, in all trust and confidence, in his own.

"Janey, I am so desperately sorry. If I knew a way out for you, you must believe I would have taken it. But I do not. There ain't one. Your father and his father—well-meaning dunderheads both of them—saw to it." He stood beside her as she huddled on the carpet beside her dog, her blessèd overgrown puppy of a dog. "He is a lucky man. And Od's death, I shall miss you sorely." He must give her up, his bright shining girl. How would he bear it?

Reading his thoughts, she bit hard on her lip. "I had best go upstairs then, sir. To begin packing." There were tears in her voice.

"Yes." Sir Charles left her side to gaze out the window at the knot garden she had designed and planted three springs ago.

"Must I?" Her voice quavered and broke.

He could not look at her and he thought his heart would break.

"Yes, you must."

She stood up and shook out her skirts. Lotto followed her to the door. "When shall I meet him?"

"At tea, I should imagine. Janey…" he said suddenly stern. "I shall expect you to do this as you have done everything else."

She nodded. "Yes," she said, her voice thin. "I shall not disgrace you." The tears filled her eyelashes. "I shall never disgrace you, sir." For an instant she stood with her head bowed, motionless. Then, raising it, she left the room with the quiet dignity of a decorated soldier.

It was to be expected that after receiving such news, Miss Heron would have sought sanctuary in the garden, her garden. Most particularly in the rose garden, on the south side of the house, away from that part in which *he,* their guest, was lodged. And it was there that Mlle Célie de Resnay found her, seated on a bench, half hidden by a climber, at the end of the walk. The air was fragrant with the scent of wallflowers, of sweet william and late tulips, and that particular tang of drying earth, though as yet, the roses, her roses, were only just covered with a complement of tiny sprigs and even tinier tight green and grey-green leaves still enfolded upon themselves. It would be a month at least before the flowers came.

Mlle de Resnay had come to Britwell Park some four years earlier as companion to Miss Heron. When he had engaged her, Sir Charles had explained that her role was not that of a governess. Rather, she was to be a friend and companion to the young Miss Heron; she was to ensure that Miss Heron's manners were perfection itself, that she would be as comfortable at court as on horseback, that her carriage was as graceful as any swan's, that her taste in clothing and furnishings was exquisite. Mlle herself was elegant rather than beautiful, her English was adequate and her French flawless, and over time her charge had grown both to like and to admire her very much.

Miss Heron had been crying, but was no longer. Mlle regarded her with some concern, then came to sit beside her.

"Je crois que c'est une affaire un petit peu difficile, n'est-ce pas? Et toi, tu es un peu stupéfaite, peut-être, ma chérie, non? And…upset also, I think?"

Miss Heron's expression remained blank, blank and perfect. "Yes. But, no, I am not upset, Célie," she corrected. "I am angry." She continued to stare into the far distance.

Feeling her way, Mlle began as ever with the practicalities: "But why is this? It is not as though your papa, he arrange a match beneath you...And you shall be mistress of a fine house, non?"

"I am mistress of a fine house now," Miss Heron said in a flat, even voice.

Mlle leaned her head to one side. A small crease appeared in her otherwise smooth brow. She paused delicately to consider. Then, trying another tack, she said, judiciously as she thought, "Perhaps your papa, he arrange this marriage because he love your maman, and he love his friend, and he think, eh voilà, tous seront heureux, n'est-ce pas?"

"If he were so devoted to my happiness, if that is so, why place me at such a disadvantage?" Miss Heron asked reasonably. "For it is plain the Earl sees this as nothing more than a financial exchange which enables him to retain his estates."

Mlle caught her breath. Such plain speaking was not the response she had anticipated. "Enfin...Voyons...perhaps this is so," she conceded. "I cannot say. I have not made the acquaintance. But..." She drew breath, seeking a way forward, a way to comfort yet to steel her pupil. "But, you know, and I know, that it is a woman's lot to be a wife."

"And I do not question that it is a woman's lot to be a wife," Miss Heron stated equably. "...That I must marry, and marry well. I have never," she continued with some feeling, "...doubted that it was my lot in life to be someone's wife. The only question was whose? But now I find I have not the liberty of choice. I, who have everything, lack that. And I never did have it. Although of course, I did not know it. In my ignorance, I believed I should have some say in the matter. If not whom, then at least when." She made a moué. "Why, even the chambermaid at the Blue Boar has more choice than I!"

Surprised and not a little shocked, Mlle exclaimed: "What do you know of the chambermaid at the Blue Boar?"

Jane shook her head as if to say, 'never mind what I know', then said earnestly: "Only that she is five months gone with someone's child." She ignored Mlle's raised eyebrows. "She says it is William Kendall's. But now, Henry Brown has said it is his. And last week, George Long said it was his." And likewise the patent astonishment in Mlle's expression. "So you see, even Betsy may make her choice."

Her tone softened and she fretted: "I do not know that she will choose wisely. But at least she—five months enceinte and with nothing to recommend her but her winning smile and happy ways—she may choose for herself. While I, I, with all the wealth a gentleman could desire, a house, property, I have not that freedom. And I never had. So she is richer than I, is she not?"

Confounded, and unable to think, not just of an appropriate response, but of any response at all, Mlle folded her hands and looked upon the plum coloured geranium, spilling like a splashing of ink among the mottled claret and rose of the sweet william.

She had always found this facet of Miss Heron's character difficult. Had she been of a Romantic turn of mind, full of her own conceits and refinements, with that Mlle could have dealt admirably. But this unflinching honesty, this rational intelligence, this she found impossible—for it was usually inarguable and, generally, irrefutable. She nibbled at her top lip, then ventured, "But you will have fine children…"

"I may have fine children. Or I may not." And with more emotion than was her wont: "I might have had fine children with any number of men. All I know is that he is a stranger. Yes, all right, I will grant you, a very fine and handsome stranger." Miss Heron smiled briefly, sadly. "But without any fondness…or indeed, without the veriest acquaintance?" She shook her head and turned away, overcome by the folly of those two fathers who had bound her thus, unable still to contemplate the injustice of that which they had arranged and the surrender they required of her without tears.

Mlle hesitated—those who believed that the admirable self-control and dispassionate application of logic as displayed by Miss Heron must indicate a want of feeling much mistook the matter. Just because she did not wear her heart upon her sleeve did not mean that she had not the heart to wear. Quite the contrary. Mlle placed her hand upon Miss

Heron's and waited while Miss Heron blew her nose and recovered herself. And finally, gently probed: "Alors, qu'est-ce que tu feras? Will you not marry him, then?"

"Can you truly believe that I am so vindictive, Célie? So full of my own importance? Of course I must marry him. And tomorrow," Jane declared passionately. "How can I not? How could I, in justice, strip him of all that is his because his father was as foolish and feeble-minded as my own? He did not learn of the arrangement until two days ago. I can hardly fault him for that!"

Mlle heard the strain of despair in that clear voice and found herself wishing to cry as well. But did not. Instead, tenderly placing her arm about Miss Heron's shoulders, she drew her close as Miss Heron gave way to that which she had been determined to avoid, that which she wished none to witness, and wept again.

Slowly, gently, Myddelton came awake and, savouring the complete relaxation that left his limbs heavy and peaceful, looked about. It was not his own bed. Nor his own bedchamber. He was at Britwell Park.

He had not believed, in the wake of Sir Charles' damning disclosures, that he could sleep. But sleep he had. For those questions which had most vexed him, nagging, gnawing at him night and morning, had at last been answered by Sir Charles' recitation of infamy and honour. Myddelton drew a deep breath and found that the too-familiar clutch of anxiety did not return. With a rush of energy, he swung his legs over the side of the bed. Time to rise. Time to meet her. He gave a swift tug to the bell pull.

He told himself as he bathed and dressed that having met Sir Charles and having found him all that was considerate and amiable that he no longer had anything to fear—that if Miss Heron was anything at all like her uncle, they would manage to rub along tolerably well. But he did not convince himself. He knew of too many families where the parents were perfectly affable and their daughters were vain, shallow and grasping. To be sure, he knew of plenty of perfectly charming people whose parents he wouldn't wish on Attila the Hun. He drew a deep breath and finished buttoning his waistcoat. And now he was meant to meet her, and regardless of liking or disliking, to propose to her. He adjusted his waistcoat with dissatisfaction. It ought to have been a patterned waistcoat—a copper engraved silk perhaps—to propose in. Or that's what Hardy would have said. It was too late to do anything about it now.

He was still seeking to reassure himself as he came downstairs. Surely a girl brought up in such circumstances of wealth and respectability, her family intimately acquainted with those at the pinnacles of political power and academic erudition, surely such a girl must be suitable in every way. But then, so surely ought Caroline Lamb to have been suitable in every way... and Lord knew her behaviour defied description, though suitable was one word that did not apply.

The Morning Room doors were shut. She was on the other side of those doors. Drawing a deep breath, Myddelton paused to take a pinch of snuff.

Just at that moment, Jenner emerged, and seeing Myddelton, he bowed and stepped back to allow him to enter. "My lord."

She wasn't there.

"Ah Myddelton, good man, there you are..." Smiling, Sir Charles set down his cup and rose from his seat. "Jenner, where is my niece?"

"Miss Heron desired me to say that she has gone to the brook to paint and will not be taking tea this afternoon."

"She said that?"

"She did, sir. Will there be anything else, sir?"

Sir Charles pursed his lips in annoyance. Had he been alone he would have favoured Jenner with a selection from his large though generally unused vocabulary of expletives. However, he was not alone.

"If I might..." Myddelton found himself saying. "That is to say, might not I go to discover her there?" Better surely to meet her privately, without the anxious or prying eyes of relatives or servants to gauge or guess at his hopes or disappointment. Of a surety, it would be far, far better to propose without witnesses. 'Struth, what a thought!

"My dear fellow, that is kind of you, but..." Sir Charles began, vacillating. "I had meant to effect the introduction myself...But..."

"No, I do assure you," Myddelton said. "If someone could but

point me in the right direction, I should be happy for the exercise."
Infinitely better to meet without witnesses.

"You are certain? Right, then…" Sir Charles said, more relieved
than he cared to admit. He had not been looking forward to making this
introduction. He had not liked the resignation with which Janey had
accepted this arranged marriage. Neither had he liked the pricking in his
eyes when she left the library. "It's quite simple, really." He led
Myddelton to a rear facing window. "Along the far edge of the wood,
there is a path…do you see? You simply follow it to its natural
conclusion. That's it. You are sure about this? I can show you if you
like. No? Fine, good. I confess, I have some letters to catch up on…"

Myddelton told himself that, having been reared in the country, the
walk would do him good. But as he strode through the wood, he knew
this to be yet another ploy to summon up his courage. It was true, he
had noticed that the land of Britwell Park was in good heart. Indeed, he
had seen that the gardens were extensive and well kept and the ancient
wood through which he now walked was clear of choking undergrowth,
the trees ivyless. And he knew he ought to feel encouraged. But he
found it impossible, given that his stomach continued to tick with dread,
an unvanquished fear, all arguments as to the suitability and possible
beauty of his unmet-intended notwithstanding. Somewhere a nest of
baby blackbirds was singing with raucous abandon, clearly convinced that
their extraordinary volume more than compensated for what they lacked
of their parents' musicality.

He saw her before she saw him. Seated on a fallen tree at the side of
a small clearing, with her back to him. Beside her lay the yellow dog.
Myddelton slowed his steps. All at once, he heard the soft plash and
gurgle of the brook. In a moment, she would hear him and turn. Still,
amidst the tension that gripped at his stomach and throat, he could well
understand why she had chosen to come here rather than remain in the
house.

The brook was spattered with shards of light which shone through
the intertwining branches overhead and the surrounding wood was
similarly chequered with streams and splotches of blinding brightness.
Around her small clearing, the wood encroached thickly, a live palisade of

oak and yew. She was still, except for the precise movement of her right hand, in which she held a paintbrush, shading and perfecting a painting in watercolour, filling in the shore with quick light strokes, touching the brush to her paints, delineating and refining a clump of leaves.

Beside her, the dog slumbered on, his dream of a plentiful rabbit pie unmarred by unknown strangers and their city-scent.

Myddelton stopped. She turned. Great glorious God, it was the beauty. *Je ne vis onques la pareille de vous...* And then she smiled, sweetly, and Myddelton no longer knew what he felt.

"Have they sent you to find me out?" Unfazed by his sudden appearance, her composure unmarred, she dropped her brush into a jar of water beside her.

"Miss Heron?" Surely, it could not be she.

"Yes. I am Miss Heron."

"Miss Jane Heron?" The beauty was his Miss Heron. She with her della Robbia face and those firecracker blue eyes so bright with lively and eager intelligence.

"Yes. And you are the Earl of Myddelton," she said easily, completing the introduction. She kept her voice even. If there had been tears this afternoon, there was no trace of them now. Her self-possession, her self-control, was absolute. She eyed her painting critically—it was still too wet to cover.

He came closer. The dog stirred, stretched and yawned, then ambled over to sniff at Myddelton's boots. Instinctively, Myddelton smoothed the dog's muzzle, ears and head before she said, "Lotto, come."

With obedience born of rigorous training, the dog left the kindness of Myddelton's hand and lay down again at her feet.

His emotions fluctuating wildly between relief and the tongue-tied stupidity he associated with extreme youth, Myddelton drew a deep breath and wished he knew why it seemed his London polish had so summarily deserted him. She was nothing like those visions of nightmarish vulgarity which had peopled his waking moments during the past few days. She was beautiful, beautiful beyond belief, even if she was only the veriest child from the schoolroom. Then, catching sight of her painting, he began to study it, comparing the fusion of colour and shadow and line of her work with the woodland which lay beyond the brook.

"You are an accomplished artist, Miss Heron." He hadn't meant to compliment her. It had slipped out.

She smiled and her face was transformed with that bright timelessness which had captivated him before, when he had first seen her playing with her dog. "Thank you."

She glanced at him, her eyes still gauging and measuring, studying his face as if to draw it. "I should ask you to sit but there are no other chairs. And I am not at all convinced that the ground is dry. But perhaps you are wishing to return to the house…" At her feet was a leather satchel which she now opened and into which she carefully inserted the watercolour. Efficiently, she collected her brushes, emptied out her water pot, closed up her paints.

Her ease disconcerted him. And it was too soon. He knew it was too soon. He had only just met her. Too soon and too bald. But it had to be now. He had no choice. None at all. He did not kneel down. His pulse was racing, the words jamming in his mouth. "Miss Heron? Miss Heron, did your uncle…did Sir Charles tell you why I have come?"

She hesitated for an instant in fastening the buckles of her satchel. "Yes. He did."

"He explained the arrangements that were made concerning us?"

She nodded and stood to face him. He thought he saw annoyance or distress in her face, though it might have been something quite different.

"Miss Heron…"

She stared resolutely at the ground, willing herself calm.

"…I should count myself the most fortunate of men, should you honour me with your hand in marriage." There. It was done. He had said it.

She said nothing. Her dog stretched and sat up beside her, ready for her command.

"I assure you, I shall do all in my power to see that you are comfortable, and lack for nothing. And I sincerely hope that you shall

86

suffer no disappointment through this match—that I am breaking in on no previous attachment…" He was wittering. He knew he was wittering. Why did she say nothing?

She shook her head. "No. There are no previous attachments." She did not smile.

"May I hope that you do not, at least, dislike the match?" He had promised to behave honourably, had given his word. "That if, perhaps, this ain't what you would have chosen for yourself, that it ain't displeasing to you?"

Even as one part of her mind was clamouring to point out the choice was not hers, that it did not matter what she thought, she was reaching her hand toward him in a gesture which her uncle would have recognised and found hopeful, a gesture which she unintentionally reserved for those dearest to her. She touched his sleeve. "No, it is not displeasing to me," she said. "I should deem it a great honour to accept your kind offer."

She smiled sketchily and her eyes searched out a glimpse of sky through the treetops, before she looked at him again. "I hope I shall not be a burden to you…that is to say, this cannot be what you had planned for yourself, and if there were a way for me to do so without injury to yourself, I should release you. But I cannot, and I am so sorry. So very sorry. I shall try never to be a burden to you. If you would prefer it, I shall remain here, or at one of your country houses—I am very fond of the country." Her eyelids fluttered with uncertainty as she gazed at him.

Myddelton drew himself up. "I had not realised that my person was repugnant or…"

She reached out desperately, again touching his sleeve. "Oh no. No. How could you think it? I only meant to spare you my presence, should you wish to…or not wish to…"

Myddelton took her hand, holding it tighter than he intended. "Jane." It was odd to use her name. Odd and vulnerable. "Miss Heron, this may not be the match of your choice, but I ain't such an ogre as all that, I do assure you." He drew a deep breath. "And I ain't planning to banish you to the country. Should you wish to live in the country, then assuredly you shall. But I shall never tell you to go. You have my word on it."

"I am sorry. I had the impression that all this was distasteful to you and I thought..."

"Miss Heron, please..." He paused. The worst surely was now over. He had proposed. She had accepted. She had said yes. The firecrackers had gone out. "I, ehm, I brought a special licence with me. Your uncle has agreed that we may be married on the morrow. To be sure, I know this is sudden...but I did not know what else to do," he finished, realising with a shock that this was shabby treatment indeed.

"No," she agreed. "How could you?" She gathered up her satchel of watercolours, brushes and paintings.

Was she always so compliant?

"And then? London?" she asked. She had banished any whisper of uncertainty from her voice.

"Yes." The worst wasn't over. "It's the Foreign Office, d'you see." He smiled awkwardly. It was the poorest of excuses and he knew it. Castlereagh would certainly have given him more leave had he known. Hell's bells, what an infernal cock-up.

Seeking a neutral topic for conversation (Were there any? Any at all?) Myddelton drew out his snuff-box, then returned it to his pocket unopened. "My, er, tiger, Kester, tells me that you have a stable full of prime horseflesh." Anything. Anything to restore that elusive semblance of comfortable normality. Christ's wounds, where were his wits?

Her relief was patent. The shadow of bleakness receded from her eyes. "Does he so?" Together they began to walk back in the direction of the house. "My uncle would be pleased to hear that. It is his only claim to extravagance...except perhaps for his books. Shall I show you?" She smiled suddenly. "The stables, that is...not the library."

Myddelton offered her his arm and she took it, though she continued to keep her head down, her gaze averted, as they returned toward the house. It seemed the right—the appropriate—thing to do, a gesture to cover the inadequacies of the moment.

She wished vaguely that she had the gift of inconsequential interrogatory chatter. But how could she enquire 'Are you musical? Do you prefer whist to piquet? Do you farm your land or leave it to your agents? Do you hunt all the winter, or merely in the autumn?' of the man she was to marry the next day? These were things she ought to know already. Only, she did not. She knew nothing. And had no notion where or how to begin. He was a stranger. As unfamiliar to her as an Iroquois-speaking native of the Americas.

The stables were located to the left of the house, partially hidden by a stand of trees. In silence, they passed the lawn where Myddelton had first seen her. A stable lad was sitting in a pool of light just outside the main stable entrance, polishing tack. As they approached, he rose and tugged at his forelock. His cheeks were flushed from the sun.

"Aft'noon Miss, milor'."

"'Afternoon, Sam. Minding the shop, are you?"

The boy's smile was radiant, guileless. "Yes, miss."

Miss Heron led Myddelton inside. "There was a terrible fire in my grandfather's time...no horses were hurt, I believe, but the previous building was utterly destroyed. So he had it rebuilt to his own specifications." She gestured at the vaulted wooden ceiling, the overlarge box stalls, the ample feed stores, the elegant sash windows placed high up, the several wide doors which stood open letting in light and air.

The animals, scenting a stranger, stirred in their stalls and poked their noses out over the half-doors into the wide passageway. A large black whinnied importunately.

Myddelton smiled. "Devoted to his horses, was he?"

She returned the smile. "My uncle says everyone in the neighbourhood thought him foolish, or mad. But I believe, after one or two of them also suffered fires, they copied several of his improvements." She reached into a grimy bag suspended from a nail in the wall and pulled out two very large carrots.

As she approached the stall which housed a great black, Miss Heron snapped the carrots into bits. "I am sorry, no ride today ..." she said, smoothing the animal's long nose. The horse gobbled the carrot from the flat of her palm, then nuzzled her hand and wrist in search of another.

Myddelton raised his quizzing glass and stared. S'life, surely, she did not ride that beast. Surely not. The horse stood a clear sixteen hands.

And she…well, her head barely reached the top of his shoulder.

She continued stroking the horse's nose while she fed him the second carrot. "You are perfectly right to feel neglected for I ought to have taken you out this morning. I am only surprised you did not send Sam to fetch me out to you…"

Myddelton let fall his glass and came to stand beside her. "Never say this is your mount, Miss Heron…"

Her face flushed with pleasure. "Oh. But, he is. Indeed, he is." She smiled and turned toward Myddelton. "He is the very sweetest goer. And the dearest fellow imaginable. Always a gentleman." She drew a breath, obviously toying with whether to impart more. Then rubbing his nose, she admitted: "Patroklos dislikes hedgehogs, though…and pheasants, don't you, boy."

Myddelton stared. She knew the Iliad? And read Greek? Was that Sir Charles' notion of training? "Please, do forgive my asking…Where was he bred?"

The smile she gave him was apologetic. "I've no idea, really. My uncle bought the mare in foal. The owner had been away and met with an accident, so the estate was being sold off…and Sir Charles liked the look of the mare."

"Ah. Of course. 'Struth, I should love to see him in action."

"Then, of course, you shall."

"I confess I have been doing a little breeding myself at Great Myddelton…"

"Have you? And have you large stables there?" she asked over her shoulder as she returned to the carrot bag before proceeding to the opposite end of the stable block, where Myddelton's bays were temporarily housed.

She broke up another handful of carrots as she approached the stalls at the end of the row. "Yes, you are a beauty," she said, addressing the bay directly as she held out the carrot. "Rumour did not lie, did she? No, indeed." The bay snuffled at her hand, mouthed her fingers, then gobbled the carrot. "And you know it too, don't you? Just look at you…" She rubbed the muzzle of the second bay as it prodded and nosed at her shoulder.

Having assessed the points of Miss Heron's fine black, Myddelton wandered down the centre aisle toward her, running an eye over each of the horses as he passed it—the riding hacks and the carriage horses, the shires, the one old pony. Then stopped dead. For ahead at the far end of the row, *she* was nuzzling and petting two of the jumpiest carriage horses in London. His horses. Stroking their noses, rubbing their manes, fondling their ears…Usually they allowed no one but Kester or himself near them.

"Miss Heron!"

"Oh, my lord, they are beautiful! And such lambs. What are they called?" She was radiant with delight. For it appeared that they had, after all, some thing in common, a basis, perhaps, for friendship even.

Carefully Myddelton tucked his quizzing glass back inside his waistcoat and reached into his fob pocket for his snuff-box. He glanced up. "Lightskirts…and Ladybird." He flicked open the box with his thumbnail and took a pinch of snuff.

For an instant, a brief, unlikely minim of time, her eyes blazed at him. Then they went dead and the look she gave him was expressionless, unreadable, and her voice tremorless: "I must go." She went to the door and collected her painting satchel. "My uncle does not change for dinner, so you need not trouble yourself neither.

"If you cannot find your way back to the house, Sam will be happy to direct you.

"Lotto, come." The dog, who had spent his time in the stable poking his nose into dark corners searching for mice and sniffing at bits of manure, quitted this pleasant pastime to follow his mistress out into the stableyard toward the house.

Myddelton waited until she was out of sight before giving way to a thunderous snuff-sneeze. Red hell, what was the matter with him? Sighing inwardly, he blew his nose hard and stuffed his handkerchief back into his pocket. The fellows at White's had thought it a famous joke when he'd first named the horses. But it was, perhaps, a joke which had not worn well.

6

The Large Drawing Room at Britwell Park was well-proportioned, and amply furnished with an eclectic selection of chairs, sofas and small tables, an embodiment of the Herons' changing tastes over the last century. Testament too that the prevailing fashion for massive sphinxes and other exotica picked out in gold leaf had passed them by entirely. A three-quarter length portrait of Miss Heron's mother hung over the mantel. A fire had been lit in the grate to dispel the chill that was as inevitable in April as the thought that spring evenings were meant to be pleasant and warm, though they seldom lived up to expectation.

Dinner was finally over. An interminable meal. The gentlemen were still in the Library, with their port and politicks.

"And long may they remain," Miss Heron was heard to murmur as she adjusted the candelabrum before sitting to play the fortepiano.

Nearer the fire, Mlle de Resnay was searching through her silks in an effort to match an elusive green for her petit point. Presently, she spoke: "That is not very cheerful music for the eve of your wedding, chérie. What is she called?"

"'She' is called 'Funeral music for Queen Mary', by Henry Purcell," Miss Heron said evenly, continuing to play. "And I am not feeling particularly cheerful."

"Perhaps not. But you do not think that a dirge is a trifle in excess, n'est-ce pas?" There was an edge of amusement underlying Mlle de Resnay's voice.

Jane stopped, drew a breath and closed the folio of music, and replacing it on the stand with another folio, resumed playing.

Mlle listened for a while. "And this one, what is she called?" she asked.

"'O Let Me Weep', from *The Fairy Queen*. Also by Mr. Purcell."

Mlle emitted a very French "Pho!" Then: "And still, you do not think a dirge un petit peu de trop?"

"It is not a dirge. It is a lament. Or, if you wish to be pedantic, a plaint."

"Of course. Just as you say." Mlle raised an eyebrow but continued to sort through her silks. "And what, I wonder, shall milor' think when he enters le salon and discovers that his bride, she is playing a dirge?"

Jane paused. "Well, he wasn't behaving particularly loverlike himself, was he?" She played a few more bars.

Mlle laughed. "And what would you have? You wish that he will fall at your feet and declare his grande passion? If he were to do so, you would know him for a—what is the word? Un menteur, non?"

"A liar," supplied Miss Heron. "True. But he could have been a little less obvious in his distaste."

Mlle was unimpressed. "And you? You were all warmth and affection, non?"

Jane drew a deep breath. It was meant to have calmed her. It did not.

"Chérie, be reasonable. Think what all this must be to him. You spent the afternoon weeping in the garden…"

"That was for the roses. For I shall not be here in June to see them," Jane said.

"Of course. You weep for your roses. Comme l'Impératrice Joséphine…" Mlle nodded sagely. "So ask yourself, what must this be to him? Perhaps it is better, perhaps it is worse. You do not know. Perhaps he was tout à fait amoureux de quelqu'une and wished to marry. You do not know. So what must this marriage be to him but a duty, hein? "

Jane remained silent, considering. Then closed the sheaf of Purcell. "I think I shall retire early. Make my excuses, will you, Célie?" She rose from the fortepiano.

"No, I shall not. How can you ever expect him to respect you, comme sa vrai femme, if you run away every time he approaches? If you run away, so, I shall very much think he will have little but the contempt." Mlle squinted while she slid a thread through the eye of her needle. "He will think, bah, she is a rabbit that one."

Jane rolled her eyes. "And if I do not 'run away,' as you so charmingly put it?"

"Mutual respect, of course. Which is absolument nécessaire, je t'assure."

Jane paused in her perusal of the sheaves of music that littered the lid of the fortepiano. "I do not want mutual respect," she said softly, almost to herself.

Mlle heard. "Alors, of course you do. You have no idea of what you speak. If he were fat and horrible, alors, ça sera impossible...but he is not. And even then. But he, he is a very fine gentleman..."

"Fine gentleman or no, I do not want mutual respect."

"But he is very handsome, non?"

"Oh yes," Miss Heron concurred. "Very. And he knows it."

Mlle de Resnay gave her young companion a long, measuring look. "Alors, you are bien éprise, n'est-ce pas?"

"How can I be?" Jane was remarkably clear-eyed. "I have scarce spoke three words to him. But when first I saw him...When first I saw him, I thought, let it be him...let him be the one." She stopped, remembering that first moment, that first imprint upon her senses, when she had seen him, the tall and elegant stranger whose air must mark him out wherever he was, standing at the edge of the sun-washed lawn. And then he had spoken and she had heard his voice, that deep, well-modulated voice. Then: "But Célie, do you know what he calls his horses? His matched bays? Well, I shall tell you: Lightskirts and Ladybird!"

Célie stared at her, then burst out laughing.

"It is not funny!" Jane said hotly.

"But no, it is not funny, it is absurd." Mlle shook her head, as over the antics of a child. "Ma foi, les hommes..." In an entirely different voice, she said, "Ma chére, do you care for a bit of advice? Oui? Alors, you must be certain that you are not so easily shocked. It is not as though you are in ignorance of these things. Your uncle, he has seen to that. One would not choose to appear forward, certainement, but perhaps Lord Myddelton, he is not used to such modesty as is considered proper here." Carefully, she poked her needle through the stretched linen she was embroidering. "You and I, and Sir Charles most of all, we have laughed over certain passages in Molière, or you in your Ovid. So it is not as though you are not acquainted with these things. Eh bien…since he is to be your husband, perhaps if you were not so easily shocked, yes? Perhaps, even to jest at an appropriate moment. But above all, to take it very lightly, non?" She held her needle mid-stitch and smiled kindly.

Jane looked up from the pile of music. "You, of course, are right. I shall not forget next time. Since there will undoubtedly be a next time." She chose a folio of music and placed it open on the music stand.

"D'accord," Mlle agreed. "Moi, je pense qu'il est un gentilhomme qui avait beaucoup de maîtresses, n'est-ce pas?"

"Célie!" Was that meant to comfort her? To encourage her in the belief that hers would be a happy union or to foster the required nonchalance?

The door opened to admit Myddelton and Sir Charles. Jane began to play the opening bars of a favourite sonata by Herr Haydn.

"We have come to join you, my dears," Sir Charles announced brightly. And with a shrewd look at his niece, he added, "But what has Mlle de Resnay been telling you that has so shocked you that you cry out, 'Célie', hmn?"

Mlle laughed delightedly and bent her head to her needlework.

"Whatever makes you think she has shocked me, dearest of all uncles?" Miss Heron replied, still accurate to the note.

Myddelton regarded her curiously. Was there more to her than he had originally suspected? A sense of humour, even?

"Ha! Perhaps I'm ubiquitous," Sir Charles said, settling into his favourite armchair across the room from his niece. From here, he could see her as she played—frowning in concentration or with a private half-smile on those rare occasions when she was pleased with her performance. "But don't try this 'dearest of all uncles' business with me, Janey. It won't wash, because I happen to know I am your only uncle."

She flashed him a blinding smile.

"Ah, Myddelton, you see how she smiles. Janey, you are

incorrigible."

"If I am, sir, it will be laid in your dish, for you had the bringing up of me."

Definitely, a sense of humour. Myddelton had not expected that.

"A lowering thought, to be sure. Still, I dare say I shall bear up under the ignominy of it." Sir Charles watched her play for a moment more. "Myddelton, may I interest you in a game of chess? I feel sure you can give me some real competition."

Bowing her head, Miss Heron hid her smile at this blatant exercise in the combined skills of twisting the facts and luring an unsuspecting victim to the chessboard.

Had Myddelton asked his affianced bride whether she would prefer him to turn the pages of her music for her or to play chess with her uncle, she might have taken pity on him and agreed to the former, thus sparing him the intellectual humiliation of several early checkmates. As he did not ask, she did not offer, but left him to the mercy—a quality in very short supply when chess-men were involved—of her uncle.

For a while, the occupants of the room continued thus, intent on their several activities: Miss Heron finished the sonata by Herr Haydn and began another, Mlle found another fugitive strand of green silk so as to complete an entire leaf, and the gentlemen pored over the chessboard or reassembled the pieces on the board after Myddelton repeatedly fell prey to Sir Charles' cunning.

"I say! 'Struth, you have beaten me again!" Myddelton exclaimed. It was the nth checkmate in a very short space of time. Mercy had been notable only for its absence.

"Now there is a surprise. One might even call it a 'shock'," Miss Heron murmured in an undertone audible only to Mlle de Resnay.

Sir Charles smiled. "Very slovenly about guarding your queen, ain't you? It's a mistake, you know...The queen is the king's greatest asset... Janey, where's the tea tray? Myddelton, here, is in dire need of a bit of revivification."

She stopped playing. "Oh is he? And why would that be, I must wonder? It is a good thing no one ever thought to build you a bottleneck dungeon or give you a pair of thumbscrews, Uncle..." She shook her head in mock censure. She closed the lid of her instrument and went to ring for the tea tray. She had meant to come and stand beside her uncle, but instead found herself standing at Myddelton's shoulder. She made a moué. "Did he beat you very badly?"

Her solicitude surprised him. He looked up at her. He looked at the chessboard which showed a nearly full complement of black pieces, while the number of white chessmen had been substantially reduced. And those which remained had been rendered ineffective. "Very badly," he admitted.

She nodded. Placatingly, she added, "It is his worst fault, you know. You'll know better next time." Her smile was so sweet, so kind, that suddenly Myddelton wished he had not come here to marry her so abruptly.

~Θ

30 April 1812

The parish church of Britwell St. Luke had been built during the reign of Henry VII, stripped during the dissolution of the monasteries under Henry VIII, and rebuilt after the Restoration, following the depredations of Oliver Cromwell and his Levelling Puritans—an eventful history for a small church which had never housed any holy relics or items of particular popishness and, when packed to the rafters, could hold not more than an hundred people, including the choir. During these frequent changes in the fortunes of their local church, the parishioners had done their best to safeguard its few treasures. The gold communion plate had miraculously disappeared in 1538 and reappeared, equally miraculously, some fifteen years later. As had a fine late mediaeval triptych of the Virgin and Child with St. Luke. Even more wonderful were the carved choir stalls which dated from the incumbency of the Reverend Geoffrey Choate in 1610 and which had—along with various altar cloths and the finely carved pulpit—curiously enough, passed the years of Puritan rule in an inaccessible corner of a local grain barn. That its survival was largely due to their fidelity had only strengthened the parishioners' affection for their church, and they minded not at all that its fabric was a cobbled together version of ecclesiastical style and local craftsmanship over four centuries.

Alone, Myddelton stood outside the church, staring up at the grey stone bell tower. He had not slept well. In between the bouts of fitful dozing, he'd passed the night rehearsing his words to her in the stable and seeing that frozen look on her face. And then came the morning. Well, that the morning had proved no more than awkward spoke volumes for the excellence of Sir Charles' manners, and those of his servants.

It was meant to be a joyous occasion, marriage. A household was meant to be buzzing with excitement—the kitchen alive with the preparations for the wedding breakfast, the maids giggling on the stairs, the stable lads busy plaiting ribbons into the manes of the carriage horses. Miss Heron had not appeared. At least he had not been allowed sight of her, but her several trunks were corded and ready in the hall, a reminder to all that their dear Miss was to be taken from them as part of this business transaction, for it was nothing more. It might have been more. It might have at least been an amicable arrangement. Had he perceived what sort of a family she came from. But he hadn't, and it wasn't.

Soberly, he passed through the porch and entered the church. The great wooden door thudded closed behind him. The church was empty. He paused, breathing in the silence, and studied the stained glass windows and the memorial plaques below. His father would not be proud of him today. After a while, he started up the aisle, his leather heels sounding on the stone floor, to sit in the front pew. The flowers at the altar were fresh. How could he have so misjudged the situation?

"Ah, there you are, my lord," exclaimed the Reverend Mr. James with unwelcome cheer as he came through from the vestry, still adjusting his surplice. He wore no wig. "I do apologise for being late. Parish duties kept me longer than they were meant to, I'm afraid. It's always happening…Did Miss Heron not accompany you? Oh no, that's right, Sir Charles said in his note that they would be arriving separately."

The rector was a young man, younger than Myddelton had been expecting, and he found himself staring hard at the young cleric. For he reminded him forcibly of…whom? It was the eyes—behind the small gold spectacles—and the easy smile. 'Struth, he knew that face, but from where?

"Perhaps we should take up our positions?" Mr. James suggested, in no way daunted by the grim expression on Myddelton's face. Mr. James stood with his back to the altar, his prayer book open in readiness.

Myddelton took his appointed place and tugged at his waistcoat. It was dove grey, and subtly patterned—appropriate for a wedding. The sun came out for a brief moment to shine through the stained glass windows. He felt hollow.

The church door swung open. Sir Charles appeared in the doorway and held out his hand, drawing his niece into the church. She was dressed in white with a shawl of white gossamer covering her shoulders and head. Myddelton sensed her hesitation rather than saw it, and then he saw her face, saw that all her laughter, all her joy was extinguished, and in her eyes, the firecrackers had gone out. Mlle de Resnay entered the church behind Miss Heron and gingerly shut the church door. A draught of air caught at the fabric of Miss Heron's gown, causing it to float and linger in the air behind her as she approached the altar.

Pleasantly, Mr. James began the service and Myddelton listened as he outlined the sacred nature of marriage: "...signifying unto us the mystical union that is betwixt Christ and his Church...is commended of St. Paul to be honourable among all men: and therefore is not by any to be enterprized, nor taken in hand, unadvisedly, lightly, or wantonly to satisfy men's carnal lusts and appetites, like brute beasts that have no understanding..."

Myddelton glanced down at her. Her face was expressionless, bleak, as if she had exiled all emotion.

"...but reverently, discreetly, advisedly, soberly and in the fear of God, duly considering the causes for which Matrimony was ordained...for the procreation of children, to be brought up in the fear and nurture of the Lord...for a remedy against sin, and to avoid fornication...for the mutual society, help, and comfort which the one ought to have of the other, both in prosperity and adversity..."

And for the bride's money, Myddelton added to himself. To keep the groom's estates intact. Od's life, she must despise me. And with all good cause. He swallowed bitterly and stared straight ahead.

Afterwards, Myddelton would think that the ceremony had been over in an indecently short time, for something that lasts forever. But as he stood before the altar, listening and not listening to Mr. James' mild voice threading its way around the carvings of the church, he felt that all time and reality had been suspended.

"...Wilt thou have this woman to thy wedded wife...wilt thou love her, comfort her, honour, and keep her...forsaking all other, keep only unto her, so long as ye both shall live?"   The vows. How could he vow to love and cherish this girl—this child—whom he had met only yesterday? He did not love her. 'Struth, he barely knew her. How could he vow to keep only unto her? How could his voice suddenly and inexplicably not be his own? Oh, he had been practised upon, all right... "I will." He felt ill.

"If you will take her right hand in your own, my lord, and repeat after me..." Mr. James said, still irritatingly cheerful.

Myddelton had never touched her before. Her hand was small, and cold as snow. Had she trembled, he could have borne it better.

"Now repeat after me. I, Avery George Charles..."

He glanced at her. She would not look at him.

"...take thee Jane Caroline Sophia to my wedded wife, to have and to hold from this day forward... to love and to cherish, till death do us part."

She spoke her vows with a stillness that reproached his uneasiness. If she were hesitant, ill at ease, disconsolate, it was well hidden. Her uncle's idea of training had seen to that. "...in sickness and in health, to love, cherish, and to obey, till death do us part, according to God's holy ordinance; and thereto I give thee my troth..."

Mr. James asked for the ring, laid it on his prayer-book and then returned it to Myddelton with a radiant smile.

Myddelton felt a moment's quailing as he slid the smallest of the wedding bands over her third finger. It fit. He exhaled. "With this ring I thee wed, with my body I thee worship, and with all my worldly goods I thee endow..." Then, she did look at him and he fancied he saw fear in her eyes, but then it was gone and he thought he must have imagined it.

He couldn't know that she was shaken by a knell which kept proclaiming: 'He owns me now. He has whatever rights he chooses to take.'

Still beaming with unassailable good will, Mr. James pronounced them man and wife and led them to the vestry to sign the register.

As ready as she would ever be for the inevitable parting, the new Lady Myddelton stood on the steps, talking quietly to Mlle, unable still to articulate her fears. She must leave her home, her dear uncle, all that was precious and familiar…to go with a man of whose character she knew little. (And what little she did know hardly inspired confidence. For, indeed, he might take after his uncle…) To live as his wife, in a place she had never seen. Had she been of a dramatic turn of mind, she might have clasped her hands at her breast and wept, or clung to her uncle and wailed piteously. But she was not, and it brought a momentary smile to her lips to reflect that however much she might have liked to indulge in such melodramatic displays, she was far too prosaic to do so with any real conviction.

The only hint of her unease had been given in her quiet protest to Mlle that she had no caps and how should she go on without at least one, now that she was married. Mlle had understood more than was apparent and had insisted she take two of her best lace caps, including the one Jane had given her for her last birthday, saying that Jane might replace it at a later date.

The wedding breakfast—a morose and uncomfortable meal—was now over. Kester had brought Myddelton's carriage to the front of the house; Lightskirts and Ladybird were twitching and fretting with impatience. Her uncle's own coachman, John Bright, sat on the box of Sir Charles' well-sprung travelling coach, behind a team of carriage horses as calm as they were large.

Sir Charles had not liked the idea of his niece travelling to London in an open carriage, no matter how excellent the horses, or the driver. It was too long a journey. Myddelton had not liked the idea of Kester driving his matched bays unsupervised on such a long journey. Sir Charles had insisted: his niece must travel to London in his carriage;

Myddelton could go on ahead, driving himself. Of a certainty, her journey would take longer—a travelling coach was necessarily slower than a carriage built for racing—but that was how it must be.

And still the air of hesitation and reticence marked her. Myddelton, engaged in the spurious exercise of convincing himself that his life need not change because of the morning's events, for she was a well brought up girl and she would know her place, was relieved to see his horses looking disagreeably tetchy. No one—certainly not Sir Charles, the owner of such fine cattle—would expect him to hang about making overlong farewells, while leaving his horses standing and growing less manageable by the minute.

Sir Charles frowned, watching the young man, now his nephew, then came forward to shake his hand. "Farewell, young man. I am trusting you to look after her as she deserves, but you shall have to earn her affection."

Her affection interested Myddelton not at all. He took refuge in formality and bowed politely. "She shall lack for nothing, sir. I give you my word." He shook Sir Charles' hand. "Goodbye."

Sir Charles, dissatisfied with Myddelton's too glib reply, watched him mount the step of his carriage, then came to stand beside his niece. Mlle went back into the house.

"My dearest girl..." Sir Charles said, placing his arm about his niece's shoulders. "You will look after yourself..." It was a question, not a statement.

"Yes."

"I am not at all happy about this, my dear. I should have done more to stop it. I..." Sir Charles began.

"Hush," she said mildly. "Do not say it. It will only make matters worse to think that way, you know. When I am settled, perhaps you shall come to visit?"

"Yes," he raised his hand in salute as Myddelton wheeled his horses about and started down the drive. Together, they watched him go.

If he had sent her away to a ladies' seminary to be educated, would this parting have been easier? Sir Charles doubted that it would. He disliked her leaving. Whatever training he had given her, it was inadequate. "My dear, you must go too." He kissed her forehead, kissed it as though he were parting with all joy, then helped her into his travelling carriage.

She did not cry, but held tightly onto his hand. She wished she might ask how long she must remain with Myddelton, but that implied failure or maltreatment. "Uncle?"

Mlle de Resnay hurried down the steps of the house, a large covered basket over one arm. "Chérie. An offering from the kitchen to make your journey more bearable, non?" She handed the basket to the maid to stow in the carriage.

"Courage, ma petite," Mlle whispered, taking Lady Myddelton's hands in her own. "One is always stronger than one believes, of this I am certain. But now, it is the time when you will find what is it you are made of, non?" Her smile was reassuring. She kissed her former charge on both cheeks. "Adieu, chérie. Write to me often. It will be good for my English."

"Your English is beyond my poor talents, Célie, even if I was to write to you every day," Lady Myddelton said firmly. Then: "Farewell. Thank you for all you have taught me. I shall not forget."

Sir Charles shut the carriage door.

Lotto, who had been sniffing at the carriage wheels, saw the door close and barked in protest. Sir Charles rapped on the side of the coach. At his signal, John Bright flicked the reins. Crunching the gravel beneath their hooves, the horses drew the carriage away from the front steps.

As the carriage started slowly down the drive, Lotto, confused at having been left behind—for he never had been before—began to race frantically between the carriage and Sir Charles. But when the coach continued down the drive heedless of his requirement that it stop immediately and admit him, he paused to give Sir Charles a final look, then tore after it, barking as he ran.

Since she had first learned of Myddelton's purpose in coming to her home, the new Countess had been allowed not one moment of reflection and no chance to ponder or consider those changes to her state which marriage must inevitably bring. Nor had she had time to learn from Myddelton the practicalities of her new station. But now, she could do nothing to escape that litany of unanswered questions: Did he live in Town or in the country most of the year? Where was his principal seat? Did he like it or did he spend most of his time elsewhere? Was it a mouldering ruin or newly built? Was his London house large or small? Did he even have one?

And what did he expect of her as his wife? What were her freedoms? Her duties? Would she be allowed to come and go as she pleased? To visit Britwell Park as she chose? And tonight, her wedding night? Would he be kind and patient with her ignorance? Or would he expect to get his heir on her and then pursue his pleasures elsewhere? Would he allow her time to accustom herself to their marital relations or did he regard her with indifference or even contempt, deserving only the roughest of use? She had no experience in these matters. Would he even know to be kind? Or would he shun her, judging her not for her own qualities, but prejudicially, because she had not been his choice and he did not care for her? Indeed, would he publicly flaunt his mistress? Or a succession of mistresses?

She had never believed in the much vaunted advice that a 'good cry' was beneficial in some way. Crying solved nothing. And it could not mitigate the distress of this unwanted marriage to a man she barely knew. Nor would it return her to her uncle's house and protection. But as she watched the familiar line of trees and the stone statue of a youth—she and her uncle had so often disputed whether it was meant to be Hermes, Adonis, or even Paris—pass by her window, with the uncertainty of her situation plaguing her more and more, her logic and stoicism deserted her. Tears clustered in her eyelashes and washed over her face. And she could not stop them.

Her maid, a quiet young woman with several younger sisters, watched her mistress unhappily. Had it been her sister, she could have offered comfort, a shoulder to cry on. But none could comfort a countess except a member of her own family, or an old servant—Mlle or her nurse, perhaps.

A glance out the window confirmed that they were nearing the gate lodge. Bereft and unprepared, the Countess turned away, unable to watch as the outposts of her home slipped away from her. It was ironic really, she had always assumed she would be married from her home, assumed her wedding would be held in the tiny parish church. And it had been. But the neighbouring families had not been invited as guests. Not Lord and Lady Choate. Not the Greenwoods. Not to the church. Not to a wedding breakfast afterward. For her, there had been no rose petals thrown in her path, there had been no attendants drawn from her acquaintance. There had been no wedding hoops to walk beneath. For all that they spoke of the enlightenment of the age, she had had no more control over her future—immediate or distant—than had she been a woman in ancient Rome. Like them, she had had no choice, only duty. Like them, she was chattel. Myddelton's chattel. And he might do with her as he chose.

Yet even as she wished—with her head—to laugh at her own morose hyperbole, she realised that there was no one to laugh with anymore. And overcome by the prospect of such loneliness, she succumbed to a fresh bout of tears, even as she despised herself for her weakness.

John Bright was a kindly man, with a genuine fondness for animals, and several times he wished to halt the carriage so that the dog might be sent home. Small wonder the dog followed her, she'd raised it from a pup—but with her crying so, she wouldn't know the dog was following. Still, so long as the horses kept to a gentle pace, and they were on Heron land, it didn't much matter. But at last, they came to the gate lodge and John Bright reckoned it was time for the dog to be taken home by one of the lads, so he halted the coach and climbed down from the box.

Lady Myddelton scrubbed her face with her handkerchief in a ruthless effort to obliterate all trace of her tears, then put down the window. "What is it, John Bright?" Her throat was swollen and her voice sounded thin and painful.

John Bright pushed his low-crowned hat back on his head and approached the window. "It's your dog, Ma'am. The young scamp won't go home. He'll not leave you."

She frowned and sniffed and covered her mouth with her hand. "Where is he?" Miserably, she looked round.

The object of the conversation trotted into sight, greeting her with an indignant woof.

"Oh Lotto." She swallowed painfully. She was not meant to cry. She knew she must not. She sniffed and wiped at her eyes with the back of her glove.

John Bright had never seen that look on her face before; but still, he knew what to do. "Why do you not take him with you, milady?"

"Oh." She hesitated, weighing the consequences: What would Myddelton think? What would he do? Would it anger him? Did he have dogs of his own? How would she live without Lotto? Without her dog? "You say he will not go home?"

"No, ma'am."

She gave him a watery smile. "Oh." She drew several short breaths. "Then you are right, John. He must come with me." She opened the door hasp. "Lotto, come." Jubilant, the dog clambered into the carriage, his tail beating a bruising tattoo against everything within its radius. She hugged him close and smiled, although her tears hadn't stopped. He wriggled and licked her face wet. The maid settled into the back-facing seat.

"You must send one of the children to tell my uncle…so he does not worry. And then you may drive on, John Bright," she said, sounding almost like herself. A dog could comfort a countess.

"Yes, ma'am." Relieved, John Bright closed the coach door, issued his instructions to the small lad from the gate lodge and remounted the box for the drive to London.

By good respect in such a dangerous case
  Thou broughtest not her into this tossing mew...

7

L ondon.

The carriage had been bumping over the capital's gravel and clay streets for just over half an hour, and outside the carriage window, dusk was beginning to fall, bathing the buildings and squares with a diffuse wash of rose shadows and apricot and amber light. In such a light, the monotonous grime-stained brick or stone houses of old London could appear every bit as welcoming as the neatly-kept mansions which flanked the elegant squares of St. James's and Mayfair.

It was all much as Jane had expected it would be. Larger than Oxford, certainly. There were more people of course. And the houses were bigger, and there was more traffic. There were no students either, rushing between lectures or lounging on street corners in their academic gowns and trencher caps; but everywhere there were soldiers, militiamen, in ones or twos or threes, patrolling or just walking together. There was more noise too, infinitely more noise—a clamouring, clanking, grinding, clip-clopping cacophony. And it smelled—of coal smoke and horses and ordure. And everything was shrouded and damped and muffled by fog— a footpad's paradise. The famous London fog, that heavy blanket of fixed grey mist which draped over the city each evening—she had never truly believed in it before now. And looking away from the scenes outside the window, Jane sighed as if to summon her courage. What now?

She had not meant to sleep on the journey. But like Odysseus and his fellows, she had found refuge from grief in sleep, while the waking hours of the journey she had passed in a state of unhappy numbness, already missing her home and all that was familiar, all the time assuring herself that whatever might be in store for her, she could withstand it.

And tonight, her wedding night with a stranger, she could, would, endure this too.

She had her uncle's word for it that Myddelton would not mistreat her—whatever that might mean. And certainly, she knew she was better placed than many of her contemporaries to face the marriage bed, for often they entered it in ignorance. She at least knew in theory what to expect. She sighed again, raggedly. When does dread listen to logic?

Lotto half-licked her cheek. He disliked the tension he sensed building in his mistress.

The carriage swayed and lurched as it turned into St. James's Square, drawing up before a double-fronted townhouse of pale sandstone wedged in a corner against another of blackened brick. On either side of the door, flambeaux had been lit against the lingering approach of night. A liveried footman came to open the door of the coach and put down the step. She was expected.

The footman extended a hand to help her from the carriage. Steeling herself, Jane smoothed Lotto's head, wetted her lip, and took the proffered hand to descend.

Impatient with her hesitation, Lotto flounced down the step ahead of her to wait expectantly.

With the unpleasant thud of trepidation pounding in her stomach, Jane groped for the carriage step, even as she looked anxiously at the rows of windows in the classical facade before her. She caught her breath and stepped down onto the pavement.

"Welcome to Myddelton House, my lady." The footman bowed.

She smiled. Automatically. And inclined her head. Graciously. "Thank you. And you are?" Whatever her sentiments, the training had been impeccable.

"William, my lady." William blushed and bowed a second time.

Belowstairs, they had not known what to expect. They had talked of nothing else—when Mr. Kettering was absent, that was—and the speculation grew wilder even as her arrival drew nearer. But one glance at her neat half-boot, and another at the fine lace edging upon her petticoat and at her cuffs provided the answer. They had not expected a lady. For who would wed a lady in such haste or secrecy?

She smiled again. "Thank you, William."

She was perfect. His heart was won.

"William, will you see to my maid, Haseley? She is just coming."

Moreover, a lady who looked after her dependents.

"…She has rather more boxes than she can reasonably carry. And a basket that needs most particular care."

Again that smile—reserved, sincere, gracious. He was her slave. "Yes, my lady."

Wishing with every breath that she might return to the carriage to be taken home, quaking for she could not, unable to tear her eyes from the imposing front of Myddelton House, she crossed the pavement until her view narrowed to include only the sandstone porch with its Corinthian columns and the heavy oak front door, now thrown open to her.

There was no one to carry her over the threshold. She did not expect it. Those were country manners. Her uncle would have disliked the determination and courage in her eyes; he would have preferred that she never have need of such strength; her father would have been proud of it.

And bracing herself against this future without friends or familiar faces, this future of solitary pursuits, she stepped into an entrance hall of graceful proportions and Corinthian pilasters with an archway decorated with classical scrolling and motifs picked out in gold and dark blue, a polished white marble floor and a domed plasterwork ceiling. She caught a quick breath, taking it in a single glance. Lotto remained at her heel.

Then a tall man, with gleaming white hair and a hawklike nose, stepped forward and bowed deeply. "Welcome to Myddelton House, my lady. I am Kettering. On behalf of the entire staff, may I wish you every happiness."

He would have recognised her anywhere, would have known her to be the daughter of Colonel Heron, the late Earl's dearest friend, had he met her in a country lane in China.

"Thank you, Kettering." Her outward calm did not waver. And the smile for the butler must be nearly imperceptible. She began to draw off her gloves. "Lotto, my dog, will be wishing to examine the garden and the stable mews. When he has done so, will you have him brought to me in my room?" A life with strange servants, not those who had known her—nor her father and uncle—since birth.

"Yes, my lady," he replied solemnly. A dog. His lordship had said nothing of that. But the Herons always kept pets.

Kettering eyed the animal sitting at attention beside his mistress. A well-trained dog, too. A descendant of the late Colonel's Shandy—a very well behaved animal, that—by the look of him.

Jane held out her hand to Haseley. The handle of the basket was placed in it. "And here is my cat. Kettle." She lifted the lid and peered inside. "He is, I regret, rather the worse for wear..."

Kettering did not blink. A cat had certainly never been mentioned. But had he known that 'the lady' was Miss Heron of Britwell Park, he would have expected it. "Yes, my lady."

Had they been close enough to hear, those underservants who had been trained to fear Mr. Kettering would have been amazed and bemused at the warmth in his voice.

"The cat was fed milk, heavily laced with brandy—or perhaps brandy laced with milk would describe it better—before setting out, in the belief that he would travel easier." Jane paused delicately. "So, if he could be placed in a chair near the fire in the kitchen while he sleeps it off. And make sure that he doesn't go prowling until he has been given something to eat and is..." She hesitated over her choice of words, "Completely sober again, if you would be so kind. He is a fine mouser..." she smiled deprecatingly. "When he's not foxed."

Kettering took the basket she held out to him. Its occupant was snoring gently. "Yes, my lady."

Without ceremony, Myddelton erupted into the hall. "Oh good. You've arrived." He was already dressed in his evening clothes.

She winced and hid it well. "Only just this instant. There had been an accident just beyond Hyde Park Corner, I believe," she said pleasantly. She had forgot how handsome he was. And how the dark colour of his coat emphasised his great height and the breadth of his shoulders. She swallowed, suddenly very afraid. She was sticky and travel-stained and her stomach had begun to thump again.

"There always is." Myddelton consulted his watch. "Dinner will be in half an hour."

Seemingly unfazed, she smiled—the perfect guest, the equally perfect hostess. "Of course. Kettering will show me to my room and I shall be with you presently." Was that all by way of a welcome? Just 'Oh good, you've arrived'? She smiled again vaguely and wondered how one could ache so much and still give no indication of it.

Kettering paused to have a quiet word with William—several quiet ordering and don't stand about gawping words in fact—and to bestow the basket of sozzled cat upon him, then said: "If you will follow me, my lady..." before leading the way up the curving stair that defined one wall of the entrance hall.

And torn by a need to look everywhere at once, to see all that she could of her new home, anxious lest she drop behind or not mark the route and afterward get lost on her way to dinner, Jane followed him, pausing only once, halfway up the stairs, to look down over the rotunda of a hall and at the ornate plasterwork of the ceiling dome. The stairwell was hung with portraits—the St. Maurs and their relations, she supposed. No. No, there was one of Lady Hamilton. Not all relations, then.

The suite of rooms to which Kettering showed her was a fine apartment, consisting of a large bedroom with its own sitting and dressing rooms, located on the first floor, with the bedroom at the back of the house. At least she would not be troubled by the cries and calls of early morning hawkers. And after standing in the doorway, regarding the bedroom from floor to ceiling, she went in to walk from room to room, surveying the panelled walls, painted with swags and flowers, the rosewood furnishings, the, the heavy Aubusson carpets. Everything spoke of wealth and taste. She looked at the tester bed with its blue silk hangings and looked away again. "Thank you, Kettering. The rooms are lovely."

"Thank you, my lady."

"The panelling? Can you tell me, was it painted by Miss Kaufmann?"

"Yes, my lady." Kettering's expression softened in approval, though she did not know him well enough to notice.

"I was very sorry to hear of the deaths of Colonel and Mrs. Heron, my lady."

Jane caught her breath, blinking in surprise. "Thank you, Kettering." There was puzzlement in her voice. "Were you acquainted with them, then?"

"Yes, my lady." Again, that warmth. "I had recently taken on the role of butler to his lordship's father, when Colonel Heron returned from India…"

"Ah." Perhaps not all strangers then. She hesitated over the choice of words. "You…no doubt, knew my father better than I, then, for I never met him but twice in my life. And I do not remember him, for I was too little."

"Yes, my lady."

It was extraordinary how he managed to convey such warmth and condolence in those four syllables. He might as well have said, I will serve you to the death, for that was what he meant, she was certain of it.

"And Sir Charles Heron, if I may be so bold?" Kettering continued. "I trust he enjoys his customary good health."

She smiled broadly, now sure of the message. "Yes. Yes, my uncle continues to be in excellent health, thank you, Kettering."

"Thank you, my lady." Kettering crossed to indicate a door in the panelling. "His lordship's apartments are through here. Dinner will be served when you are ready." He bowed, again deeply, and left her.

Washed, changed into a fresh gown—though perhaps not a gown appropriate either for evening wear in London or for her status as a Countess—and restored to some measure of her customary equanimity by the application of soap and warm water, she found her way back to the staircase and down to the ground floor, then stood in the front hall, eyeing the several doors which opened onto…what? Would not Myddelton be in the Drawing Room? And where, she would have asked had anybody been present, might that be?

Kettering appeared at her elbow. "His lordship is in the Library. This way, my lady." He went across the hall and opened a door—the door through which Myddelton had erupted upon her arrival.

"Thank you, Kettering." Her relief was genuine. The library. The door at the rear of the hall. Of course.

It was an oval room with columns and pilasters of black marble, a rich room—rich in colour and full of a rich man's pleasures. The walls were lined with glass-fronted bookcases which were filled with row upon row of books with tooled leather bindings—reds and golds, browns and greens. There were heavy Indian carpets on the floor, their patterns formed in those same colours, and the chairs were large and Moroccan-covered. Gentlemen's chairs.

She did not see Myddelton at first. And then she did, leaning over a table, studying some papers. "Have I kept you waiting long?" The whiteness of his high cravat and collarpoints emphasised and outlined the strong line of his jaw.

He straightened. "Miss Her..." The word died in his mouth; he smiled at his faux. "Not Miss Heron."

She returned the smile to cover the awkwardness and retreated inside herself. A silly slip, surely. She must not allow herself to reflect upon it. "No, not Miss Heron. Not any longer."

He came forward to greet her, took her hand and sketched a polite bow over it. "M'dear, forgive me. I was rude earlier and have now compounded the offence. Shall we go through?" He led her out and through the hall toward the rear of the house.

"I trust you find your rooms to your liking," he said, drawing out his snuffbox. "They were m'mother's rooms, but I've not been in there in years."

"Yes, thank you. They are lovely, and most comfortable." A conversation between strangers.

"Good, good. The, ehm, panels in the walls in there are rather first-rate...painted by Angelica Kaufmann. M'father commissioned her to do them after he'd seen the Drawing Room at Broadlands."

Without seeming to do so, she watched as carelessly he took a pinch of snuff, one-handed, an exquisite feat of dexterity she had never witnessed before his arrival at Britwell Park. Then he sneezed rather more violently than he was meant to as he ushered her into the Dining Room. And there too, she watched him, afraid and alert as she had never before been in her life. Watched as he ate, smiled, paused, cut his food, drank his wine. And he was, by turns, taciturn and charming during the course of the meal. Had she been a friend or dinner guest, rather than a newly acquired but superfluous wife, he must have made a delightful host. There were those rare glimpses of his understated wit and superior intellect which piqued her interest, and she found herself wishing—so very much—that she might have met him previously, and known him as an equal, without the tension which their preordained relationship must include.

He asked after her journey; she admired his library. He extolled the virtues of the pike roads; she admitted to never having visited London before. Unconsciously her eyes wandered over the Dining Room draperies, while she paused to consider whether daylight would show the silk to have faded unevenly. Experimentally, she fingered the corner of her seat cushion and felt a frayed edge of fabric. For all that they were dining in state, the room had that peculiar air of having been used infrequently. Perhaps Myddelton entertained only rarely? Or not at all? Should she ask?

Recalled to his manners by her straying attention, Myddelton glanced about the room. "'Struth, I had not given it any thought, but of course, you must feel free to redecorate or change things as it pleases you. This is, ehm, your home now. And I dare say, I dare say several of the rooms could do with some attention." His smile was affable, noncommittal.

"Thank you. I shall be happy to undertake whatever may need doing." The compliant wife. She would check the silk draperies in the morning light. And the seat covers.

He waved for Kettering to lay the second remove. And sniffed hard. "I should warn you though, I ain't at all partial to the Egyptian stuff with all that gold leaf, or the porpoises littering up the Trafalgar stuff, neither."

Kettering placed a bowl of early strawberries on the table in front of her. Delicately, she chose one and then another and then a third. "Well, in that case, I shall endeavour to curb my natural tendencies toward the vulgar and ostentatious."

He had forgotten that unexpected sense of humour. Intuitively he savoured the irony in her reply, but waited until the servants had withdrawn, to look squarely upon her and to say with a quirk drawing his mouth into a smile, "Humbug."

"Not at all," she countered. "How are you to know how my tastes run? For all you know, I may thrive on gold porpoises and sphinxes."

His smile broadened. "And my horse is going to win the Derby."

"Is it? How delightful!" she replied, diverted.

The smile grew to a grin. "I've only entered at Newmarket this year for the first time."

"Ah. How disappointing." Ignoring the smile in his eyes, she chose three more strawberries.

Surreptitiously now, he observed her, his wife. 'Struth, she was a beauty. A diamond of the first water. Or she would be. When she grew up. "Which reminds me…at the risk of offending you and being thought a great boor, I'm off in the morning to Newmarket."

"Your horses?" She would have concealed the irony in her voice if she could.

He ignored it. "Yes, that's it. I have little expectation of winning anything, but the thing is, I arranged this months ago. I would offer to bring you, but the company at Newmarket tends to be a little…"

"Rough?"

"Yes," he confirmed with surprising relief. He had not, following his previous indelicacy, known how to describe the sort of women to be found there. And why did horses cause him to be indiscreet, he wondered. "I should return by Thursday, at the latest."

"I wish you the greatest of good luck." So, having just arrived in a new and strange city, knowing no one but her maid, and now, the butler, she was to be abandoned. Delightful. Why could he not have left her at Britwell Park, if that was what he meant to do?

He misread the expression on her face. She was, just as he had reminded himself earlier, a well-brought up girl. She would know how to behave, to be a credit to him. "Ehm, for the sake of the servants, and I dare say for my friends as well, I trust you'll not find it too difficult to call me by my Christian name. They will expect it to slip out. At least occasionally."

"Yes. Yes, of course," she assured him as she studied the remaining strawberries before choosing one of remarkable plumpness. She did not look up. "And which of the Christian names which festooned our wedding service would you prefer me to use? Silvius?"

He slanted a glance at her. Did she always notice those things one preferred left unnoticed? "Ah, no. A conceit of m'mother's, that."

"Of course," she agreed, compliant still. He would learn to distrust that particular compliant sweetness. Sir Charles had done so for donkey's years.

"I prefer Avery."

"Avery, then," she repeated softly, almost to herself.

He said nothing further until he'd finished his wine. Then, noticing by accident the beginnings of shadows beneath her eyes: "Upon my word, you must be exhausted..."

She stilled to a perfect breathless silence. It had come. The moment had arrived. And she looked up at his face and felt ill with apprehension even as she acknowledged that there must be dozens of women eager for the intimacies which he now meant to bestow upon her. Did a man being a practised lover make it better or worse? At least he had not grabbed her. And her breath now shallow, she swallowed and willed herself calm. "Yes," she admitted, telling herself she must be grateful for his solicitude or courtesy in allowing her to retire first. "I shall leave you to your wine and go up to bed, if you do not object," she said, committing herself to acquiescence. In the dark, none would see if she cried. Her fingers were trembling nonetheless.

"Mmn. A sound idea..." He rose from the table in concert with her.

How long before he would join her?

"I fancy I shall have a look-in at my club," he said, reaching into his pocket for his snuff-box. "And see you again when I return on Thursday." He smiled, oblivious to all her turmoil and expectation.

Had he doused her in cold water, she could have stood it better. Angry now, she smiled. Politely. Pleasantly. The perfect guest. Why did he not leave her at Britwell Park? "Good night, then. Safe journey." She did not curtsy—but paused to bow her head merely—the days of curtsying to him were over. He was her husband now.

And exiting the room as she had been taught, gracefully, waiting while the footman opened the door for her, she proceeded with dignity down the hall. She paused by the staircase to admire the roses on the half-moon table. Stirred by the movement of her breath, two petals dropped and lay like splashes of white, supine and soft, marring the perfect marquetry surface.

❧

The evening traffic was still heavy, the streets busy with private carriages, torch-bearing linkboys and hackneys. Myddelton was strolling down King Street and over St. James's, enjoying the cool night air with its slight edge of dampness, when it came upon him, growing from its antithesis, like the suffusion of colour that is dawn to sunrise, beginning gradually and unnoticed, then moment by moment until completion. It had crept up, step by step, and at last wholly overtaken him as he'd entered White's familiar portals, pausing to acknowledge the doorman's "Good evening, m'lord." It was relief and well-being and satisfaction together. For he had done it. He had married the girl and nothing had changed. His lands and properties, rents and income, he'd managed to save it all. Dinner hadn't been the easiest of meals, but no matter—he rarely dined in. Yes. Despite all the odds, he had done it. And the sordid history which had precipitated this peremptory alliance, well, all that was over and done and gone. He had married her and nothing had changed.

Myddelton handed his hat and gloves to the footman, "Evening, Barker. Lord Castlereagh, has he come in yet?"

"Good evening, my lord. M'lord Castlereagh came in some hours ago, but whether he is still at table, I regret I cannot say, sir."

Myddelton nodded, and feeling for his snuff-box, stepped into the Morning Room. No friends in sight, just nodding acquaintances. Brummell's wing chair in the bow window stood empty; he was still at the theatre, no doubt. Myddelton turned to mount the great winding staircase for which the club was justifiably famous, and passing the long mirror at the first landing, took the left turning to continue on until he reached the Game Room.

119

The Game Room, with its low ceiling and Doric columns, was neither as large as other clubs' gaming rooms, nor were the stakes for which gentlemen played here as high as those which were common at Watier's or Brooks's. It was filled with tables, some large and round for hazard, with a cutout portion for the dealer, and some small and square, for those who might prefer whist or piquet, but it being only just this side of eleven, the room was only half-filled and there were several gentlemen roaming between tables, trying to fix their fancy for the evening. Castlereagh wasn't there.

A loud whoop echoed through the hush. Like wheat rippled by a breeze, the occupants stirred and turned.

"I say, Myddelton!" Pemberton rose from his chair, and excused himself to his partners. Quickly crossing the room, he grabbed Myddelton by the elbow and steered him out through the doorway toward the stairs. "Back so soon? Was it all a hum or what?"

"'Struth, delighted to see you too," Myddelton returned, genial in this newfound contentment. "Looking fit as ever, I see. Yes, I would like that brandy, now that you mention it. Kind of you to offer. And what was the meaning of that tantwivy?"

Pemberton threw back his head and laughed. Then, in a rush: "But I say, what news? What's she like? Tell me the worst. Is she as bad as you feared?"

"I beg your pardon?" They started down the stairs.

"The girl, Myddelton, the girl! Damnation! Must you always be so obtuse?" Pemberton exclaimed.

Myddelton stopped, drew a deep breath and contemplated the snuff-box in his hand. No need for the rising nausea anymore. It was done. He had married her. Brought her home, come to that. And all was as it had ever been. Nothing had changed. "She is…" He stopped to consider, and noted with interest that detachment had replaced the discomfort. "She is…ehm…an untouched gem, I think." He took a thoughtful pinch of snuff. "Yes. That's it." He smiled and started down the next flight of steps.

"So, when are you tying the knot?" Pemberton demanded, hurrying behind him.

"We was married this morning. By special licence."

"What?" Pemberton exploded. "'Struth, where is she then? You never left her at home! Not on your wedding night, Avery! You ain't *here* on your wedding night!"

"Yes," Myddelton said. "She is, even now, back at Myddelton House. In bed, I fancy."

A sideways glance and a leer replaced the surprise. "Ha ha! You're never keeping her waiting! Ain't like you, Myddelton. Ain't like you at all."

Myddelton's brows drew together with a certain impatience. "She was rather exhausted after all the travelling," he said dampeningly as they stepped into the Morning Room. S'life, how to shut Pemberton up?

"Travelling? 'Struth, is that what you're calling it these days?" Pemberton shouted with laughter, drawing the attention of all those present. "Travelling! I like that." Creasing with laughter, he doubled up over the back of a wing chair.

Myddelton frowned, the meaning of Pemberton's words eluding him, then angry that a bald statement of fact might be so transformed by innuendo. "What?"

Brimming with laughter, Pemberton sidestepped him, bellowing: "I say, gents, what's the odds that Myddelton's got an heir for himself at the first go?" His voice, famed for hallooing over the hunting field, carried easily through the adjoining rooms and up the stairs.

The tall Scot, Dunphail, with his cousin, Mr. Hardy, rushed into the Morning room to be joined by others from the Coffeeroom who had heard the commotion.

"S'death, Pemberton, whatever has been said of me, forcing myself on virgins has never been in my line." Myddelton's voice was tight with fury.

Laughing, Pemberton patted his cheek. "Lord love you, Myddelton, she ain't a virgin now! George, break out the champagne, will you?" he called. "Must toast the bride and groom."

Pemberton's voice having carried—not just into the Coffeeroom, but also up to the Game Room—within moments, there was a thundering of footsteps on the stairs as a mob of gentlemen hurried

121

down to raise a toast to a fellow member, to slap him on the back, to shake his hand and drink his health, to share in the traditional ribaldry, to secure the best odds on the date of the heir's arrival. And from the rooms beyond, came another surge of members, all eager to join the crush, jostling Myddelton, adding their voices to the celebrations. Corks began popping and glasses clinked against bottles as the fizz spilled and splashed into the glasses and onto the floor.

Bemused and disconcerted, Myddelton began shaking the hands thrust at him, nodding and smiling awkwardly as he received the congratulations and the hearty back-slapping, baffled by the unexpected, exuberant jollity.

"Married? And nary a word? Ain't you the sly dog!" Mr. Hardy exclaimed, all pleasant surprise, clapping Myddelton on the shoulder.

"Where's that betting book?" Pemberton called over the rising din. "Ten to one on an heir within the ninemonth!"

"You've done the job properly, have ye, Myddelton?" Dunphail teased.

"Only ten to one, Pem? Give me better odds than that!" Mr. Hardy declared.

"Aye, this bucko's worth more than that!" Dunphail pronounced with the air of an expert horse coper. He stepped back and looked Myddelton up and down, as if he were inspecting a stallion, then went round the back of him, clapping him firmly on the back and shoulders. "There's prime blood here. 'Spect he breeds true." He bent down and lifted the tails of Myddelton's coat. "Aye, look at those quarters. And his legs. I should ha' said he's worth twenty to one at least."

Beside his cousin, Mr. Hardy doubled over with laughter.

Dunphail went round, peering at Myddelton's waistcoated chest and stomach. "Shall we have a look at his tackle, gents? See if he's all he's cracked up to be?" he called, reaching for the buttons of Myddelton's breeches. "Reckon his cock's still got a touch of the cherry red?"

"Put fifty guineas down for me!" cackled one bewigged ancient.

"You can bugger off, Dunphail!" Myddelton bristled, brushing him aside.

"Gentlemen!" Pemberton shouted, lifting his glass high in the air.

The roomful of men subsided into silence, scores of glasses were raised in the air.

"I give you the Earl of Myddelton and his bride!" Pemberton proclaimed.

"Myddelton and his bride!" the members repeated solemnly and drank down the contents of their glasses.

Waiters scurried about, refilling the glasses.

Dunphail raised his glass. "Gentlemen. I give you the heir."

"Hear, hear…The heir!" The cry went up.

"With his reputation for performance, Dunphail, who's to say it won't be nine months from tonight? Heh, heh, Myddelton?" Lord Alvanley said, winking and lifting his glass. "What date would you make that, Hardy?"

"The thirtieth of January, Alvanley…But it could come early, you know," Mr. Hardy posited wisely. "Ten to one it comes before the 30th, what do you say?"

"Upon my life, was it necessary to make me the butt of every vulgar and lewd joke by announcing my marriage here?" Myddelton whispered, scowling.

Pemberton looked up sharply as Myddelton's voice hissed in his ear. "I say, steady on…" Pemberton soothed, his good humour wholly unimpaired.

"…D'you think it amusing to hear someone's name bandied about in terms appropriate for the stables, without any prior knowledge of her character?" Lud, to think he now needed to defend her. The bride he wanted none of. He'd as soon watch a lamb be savaged as not.

"You ain't the one to talk," Pemberton snorted. "Who was it led the roasting when Sudlow got spliced? And whose name is entered in the betting book with odds on Dunstan getting his heir at the first go?"

Northcote appeared at Myddelton's elbow, an amused tolerance on his face. "Do not fret, cousin. It'll be over in a flash, I can assure you. And you will survive. I did." He studied the contents of his glass. "As I recall, a certain gentleman's comments—a relation, he was—were particularly difficult to swallow…but what of that?" His smile was affable and kind. "I dare say your powers of recollection are far superior to mine…"

Recalling instantly the mock-scurrilous commentary on his cousin's wedding celebrations, Myddelton gave him a grudging smile. The tension drained from his shoulders.

"Just so," Northcote murmured, seeing the light of understanding in Myddelton's expression. "Just so." He lifted his glass in salutation.

Practising his patience, Myddelton took a cool pinch of snuff, then glanced over Northcote's shoulder: "'Struth Hardy, that waistcoat is an offence. Don't let the Beau see it—he'll be laid up for a week. Where is he, by the by? Watier's?"

Mr. Hardy, who was wearing a buff and lavender-patterned waistcoat and derived much pleasure from the exotic colours and patterns found in his collection of waistcoats, took instant umbrage. "Envy, that's what it is. 'Struth, you just won't admit it."

Dunphail sank into a chair still laughing. Their bets laid, the toasts drunk, the pack of members began to dissipate, some returning to the Game Room, others to the Coffeeroom and their now cold meals.

Myddelton eyed Pemberton as he came to stand beside him. "By God, I cannot fathom why I put up with you."

Pemberton grinned, viewing this as an high accolade.

"You ain't seen Castlereagh, have you? He is the real reason I came out," Myddelton said, a grudging good humour returning.

"In the Coffeeroom, I expect," Pemberton said carelessly. "With the Prime Minister."

Myddelton closed his eyes briefly, stilling the frustration. S'life, he might have avoided this whole debacle. "Thank you."

Pemberton chuckled with unholy glee. "You still off to Newmarket in the morning?"

"I leave at eight," Myddelton confirmed.

"Pull 'round my lodgings, then. I'll be waiting."

Myddelton nodded in salutation and agreement, then made his way to the Coffeeroom.

And there they were, together and alone, undisturbed by the recent commotion, two of the most powerful and respected men in Britain, the pair of them. Just as Pemberton had said. Viscount Castlereagh, the

Secretary of State for Foreign Affairs, Pitt's successor as chief instigator of the efforts to bring down Napoleon, and architect of Wellington's stellar career and the Peninsular campaign; and the Prime Minister, the one man, many said, who commanded enough respect to hold together a government in these troubled times of war, inflation, wheat shortages and monarchical crisis, the man King George called 'the most straightforward man I have ever known'. Dressed in his habitual black, Sir Spencer Perceval was a Cambridge man with a distaste for intrigue, and, like his Foreign Secretary, a modest man, devoted to his wife and children. Though he had risen to the position of Prime Minister and Chancellor, he had retained that thoughtful, deliberate and penetrative air of his original profession of a barrister.

Like him, Lord Castlereagh was a man of modest habits, a man of dignity, courageous, calm, and considerately tolerant of difference of opinion. A shrewd man of good humour and affability, admired and revered by his friends, respected by his political opponents. A handsome man of middle years with a marked preference for plum-coloured coats, he had a strongly aquiline nose and dark eyes, beneath a head of cropped greying hair that looked like it might have a will of its own, if given half a chance.

Myddelton approached and bowed to Sir Spencer. "Prime Minister." And to the Foreign Secretary. "Sir."

"Ah Myddelton, you are here…" Castlereagh smiled warmly. "Was you not meant to be at Newmarket? Oh no, that's not for another day, is it? Sit down, do," he invited, pushing away from the table. "Was your ears burning just now? For I was just this instant mentioning some of your thoughts to the Prime Minister, you know, about the unrest over on the Continent and the latest intelligence you've been translating for me…but perhaps you would care to…" He shot him a glance of veiled complicity, wry, amused even.

Myddelton, in the act of extracting his snuff-box from his pocket, stopped, and let the box slip back into recesses of his coattail. "Why yes. Yes, sir," he said, instantly shutting away all thought of the day's events, the emotion of even a moment ago, everything beyond those constant companions, the codes and reports he translated and read. Careers were made in moments such as this.

Sir Spencer regarded him expectantly.

They none of them noticed that the room had begun to refill.

"Ehm, yes," Myddelton began. "Well, Prime Minister, there can be little doubt that whatever popular support Bonaparte may have enjoyed, across the entire Continent, that support has been steadily eroded these last years. He ain't seen as the great liberator any longer. He—and all Frenchies—are the oppressors. The Spanish may be the loudest and most active in their opposition. But they ain't alone. Everywhere it is the same picture of resentment and discontent, with the causes just piling up, one on top of another.

"The costs of war are huge. And Bonaparte has bled the Continent dry to feed his lust for glory and conquest. Any region he has marched through has been stripped bare by his troops' foraging—the horses all requisitioned, the livestock all slaughtered to feed his army, and whole harvests destroyed. If that were all, perhaps, just perhaps he might manage to keep a lid on it. But it ain't. It's only the start. For now, the shortages of what you might call everyday goods are grim—because of his infernal Blockade. There is no tea to be had, sir. No coffee neither. Nor sugar nor chocolate. Not anywhere. There is no cotton cloth, and certainly no silk.

"Here and there, the shortages are so desperate, there's been rioting. Depending on the summer and whether the harvest is good, it may spread. But two of Napoleon's brothers—Jerome in Westphalia and Louis in Holland—have already taken to openly defying the Blockade—if only to keep the peace—so dire are the shortages there.

"Prussia is the worst affected. The heavy indemnities they pay to France, and the widespread official looting haven't helped. And by all accounts they've had some hundred thousand or more French troops quartered on them for the past five years. But even there, it's the shortages of the common everyday goods that are the real source of grievance. Things have eased slightly since Russia reopened her ports to us back in '10. I have it on good authority that half of all our exports to Russia now slip across the border into Prussia. But even so, even when, or if, there are goods to be had, few can afford 'em. Any industry which relied on imports of raw materials is closed down. Most men are out of work. The shipyards have shut, the mills and factories have all closed."

He paused. "D'you know, sir, out of the four-hundred sugar factories in Hamburg at the beginning of the war, there are only three remaining?"

"Three? Out of *four hundred!*" Perceval repeated in disbelief. "Dear God…"

"That's in Hamburg, is it?" Castlereagh suppressed his smile. "Myddelton, your capacity for recalling such details of apparent insignificance never ceases to astound me."

Myddelton stopped short. "I hope that was meant as a compliment, sir…" he said, blinking with misgiving.

"Oh it was, it was," Castlereagh hurried to reassure him—though he did not try to expunge the affection which creased the corners of his eyes. "My word on it!"

"Thank you, sir." His colour heightened, Myddelton drew a deep breath. "But in any event, Prime Minister, Westphalia and Holland are openly encouraging smuggling now, as are Sweden and Prussia, and so…so, our sources are saying that Napoleon is having to redouble the efforts to control his allies and his conquests across Europe. Which he— or his minister of police—is doing with terror…"

"What!" the Prime Minister barked. "What's that?" He straightened. "With terror, you say? Good God!" he exclaimed with distaste. "I've read of the shortages, of course. Young Flint has mentioned them frequently. But using terror?" He shook his head. "Though it should not surprise us. Not at all." He snorted in disgust. "Brutality—it's what they always fall back on, don't they, the damn'd Frogs…Have they sent in troops?"

"Other than in Pomerania? Not to my knowledge, sir," Myddelton replied. "Not if by that you mean the Infernal Columns, such as were sent to the Vendée, to slaughter and burn. No. They're relying on the local militias to do the job for them. Though it don't seem to be working…"

"And civilian casualties?" Sir Spencer demanded.

"Of a certainty, sir," Myddelton said. "Anywhere they have resisted

French overrule. Spain is the worst. But Italy is not far behind, I fear. And Germany has had its share too."

"By God, he sickens me," Perceval said quietly, pressing his fist to his mouth. "He is a veritable anti-Christ! The Tsar is right on that score at least."

Perceval turned to his Foreign Secretary. "I trust we are in a position to exploit this disaffection, and build on it—particularly in Prussia? We have agents in Berlin, do we?"

"Oh yes," Castlereagh said, nodding. "Yes. Our agents are well placed to make the most of the situation. Wouldn't you say, Myddelton?"

"Yes, sir. Though to be sure, Bonaparte's doing a great deal of their work for 'em... Though I cannot believe he had the veriest notion of what life would be like under a full naval blockade when he instituted the Continental System. Perhaps he reckoned that everyone would enjoy the privations which his army seems to thrive on?"

Perceval gave a sudden dry laugh. "Wellington don't reckon they're *thriving* on it in Spain. Says they're nought but a ragtag mob much of the time."

Lord Castlereagh rested his chin in his left hand, his eyes brightening expectantly. And smiled to himself, waiting. Myddelton had spoken as he had hoped, as he had known he would—passionately, expertly, persuasively. He trusted that he would not leave it there.

"But, with respect, sir," Myddelton continued, without looking at his mentor. "I fear we shall be unable to, er, exploit these events—if we cannot stave off this war with the United States." He swallowed. This was rough ground. Very rough ground, and he knew it. It had been Perceval himself who had drafted the Orders in Council, five years since. But Sir Spencer had not stiffened. And Castlereagh intended him to press ahead, that he knew.

Perceval put up his hand. "I know. I know. You are going to tell me that to enter into war against the Americans will stretch our naval powers grievously, well beyond their capacity. You are going to tell me that there is not a well-informed naval man who would wish to go into action against any Yankee-built ship...That they are fine sailors and their ships are fast, they manoeuvre well, and are very nearly impregnable."

"Yes, sir," Myddelton agreed meekly, and lowered his gaze. "It's due to the design of the hull and this new wood they've been using... Live oak, it's called..." His brows drew together. "Though, I must confess...I do not completely understand what that means..."

Again Castlereagh smiled to himself. Myddelton and details...

An officer, wearing the short-tailed blue jacket with scarlet facings and gold lace of the Horse Guards, his bicorne tucked under his arm, paused at the entrance to the Coffeeroom. Then, sighting his quarry, he wound his way amongst the tables to stop before the Prime Minister and make his obedience. "Sir," he said first to the Prime Minister. And turning to face Lord Castlereagh, he added, "My lord." He handed the Foreign Secretary a sealed missive.

Myddelton, falling silent, watched. His audience was finished.

Castlereagh cracked open the red wax seal, and unfolding the page, read its contents, then handed it to Sir Spencer. The Prime Minister read and returned the folded paper .

"Tell him I shall be along in an hour, if you would. Thank you," Castlereagh said to the officer, who again made his obedience and left.

Sir Spencer tapped one finger against the table as he thought. "Thank you, Myddelton, thank you. That is excellent work. And I assure you, I shall bear all of it in mind. It must all be thought through. But I should like it in writing...when you have a moment."

"Myddelton," Lord Castlereagh interrupted smoothly. "There are more reports from Spain awaiting your attention back at the Office— again, when you have a moment—but the Prime Minister and I, we did wonder whether you could find the time to look them over with a view to addressing the Upper House on Tuesday?" It was not in fact a request.

"Yes," Myddelton said instantly, rethinking. Not staying in Newmarket till Thursday, after all. Returning first thing on Tuesday. Pem could find his own way home. "Yes, to be sure. Will there be a debate?"

The Prime Minister's expression was touched with good humour. "I spoke to Liverpool earlier today. He expected that Holland would have something germane to say..."

"Hasn't he always?" Castlereagh murmured.

The Prime Minister emitted a snort of laughter. "...But Liverpool says Tuesday would be best."

"I shall come prepared, sir," Myddelton affirmed.

"Thank you, Myddelton. I knew we could rely on you. I shall speak to you on the matter on Tuesday and..." Lord Castlereagh halted, apparently thinking better of it. Then: "But you have horses running this week at Newmarket, do you not? How many are you running? Two? Three? Hoping to give Lord Kerry's stables a good run, are you?"

8

The first of May. Her birthday. Her eighteenth birthday. She awoke still and quiet and long before Haseley came with her morning tea. Awoke in an unfamiliar bed to the unfamiliar noise from the next room. Yet awoke the same as she had ever been. Awoke alone. And lying still, she allowed her gaze to wander over the pattern of pale pleated and ruched silk which lined the canopy of her bed, then looked out upon the room, upon the decorative panels, the paintings upon the walls, the fireplace, the floral silk of the counterpane, upon all that would be hers for as long as she would live. But she was unchanged. A wedding and a birthday had brought no alteration.

She had been persuaded she would be unable to settle. Too much had occurred in too short a time for her to rest in comfort, she was certain. But the bed had proven too welcoming, the linen sheets smooth and warmed, the pillows a gentle cushion for her head: she had been asleep within the instant. Nor had anyone come in to disturb her.

Lotto, dozing on the foot of the bed, stirred and yawned and sighed.

From the yard beneath her window, she heard the jingle and clop of horses being put to a carriage. She arose, wrapped herself in a shawl and went to the window to see a tan and green sporting phaeton being made ready. Then, she went through to the sitting room, and perching on the window seat, watched from behind the lace curtain as the carriage was brought round to the front of the house, and a footman—William, was it?—secured Myddelton's bag onto the back of it while a groom made a final check of the bays' harness. Belatedly, Lotto came to join her.

Myddelton stepped from the house, his drab driving coat swinging about his ankles, his face obscured by the brim of his tall beaver hat. Barking an order at someone, he sprang into the driver's seat. He did not look up. Calmly he possessed himself of the whip and the reins, and gave a nod. The groom stepped away from the horses. Myddelton flicked the whip over the bays' heads and the vehicle pulled away from the house.

Jane watched until he turned the corner out of sight.

So, having performed his duty, having married her and brought her to London, he was now gone, and she was alone. In a strange house. In a strange city. Perhaps he did have a mistress.

Lotto began to lick one paw. If Haseley did not come soon, he would begin scratching at the door to go out. Jane rubbed his head and ears.

"My lady?"

Lotto trotted to the bedroom door and barked once.

"My lady?" Haseley put her head round the corner of the door. "There you are, my lady. Did you wish for your tea in here? I'll just let the dog out."

Her birthday. And none but Haseley knew of it. "I shall come through."

A small fire had been lit in the bedroom grate. It might be the first of May, but no one had yet managed to convince the weather that a balmy breeze from the south was what was called for, not a chilling east wind and a murky sky. Jane returned to the warmth and security of the bed, and poured out her tea.

A frantic barking, followed by a cat's hiss, which was routine rather than threatening or defensive, announced the return of both Lotto and her cat. Kettle demonstrated his mastery of the situation, his supreme indifference to his mistress or any presumed canine threat, by rolling on his back in the centre of the carpet and commencing to wash with immodest abandon.

Moments later, Haseley appeared bearing several small wrapped parcels and a large leather jewel case. "Sir Charles bade me give you these for him, with his kindest wishes for the day, my lady." She laid the gifts on the bed beside the tea tray. "And on behalf of the staff, may I wish you many happy returns of the day..." Her voice trailed off.

"Thank you, Haseley." Not entirely alone then. Nor entirely forgot. "Thank you very much."

Haseley curtsied and went off to ready the bath, as her mistress untied string and unwrapped parcels.

From Lady Choate, there were two volumes of poetry. ("Choate would have chosen sermons for you, my dear, but I thought you would prefer Wordsworth. I certainly should.") Reading the inscription, Jane smiled. "How clever of you…"

From Mlle de Resnay, a delicate confection of lace and ribbons, which in exclusive circles would be called a cap. Twirling it about on her hand, Jane smiled. A less utilitarian garment had yet to be fashioned.

And unwrapping as she tore the paper from the final parcel, her hand went to her mouth to stifle her cry. For from her uncle there were three miniatures: her mother, her father, and himself. Those of her parents, she knew, had always been his favourites. But that of him was recently painted. Yet how had he ever managed to sit for the limner and conceal it from her? He was hopeless at keeping secrets. Soberly she regarded the three small paintings in their etched gilt frames, but mostly she studied that of her uncle. He had kept the secret of her marriage all these years. She wished he were here now. Downstairs, pottering in the library.

And keeping his picture by her, she prised open the clasp of the large jewel case. They were all there, and one by one she held them up: her mother's jewels, her grandmother's jewels, the large stones in their exotic settings which her father had brought back from India, her great-grandmother's jewels with their elaborate Restoration filigree. All were newly cleaned. In the morning light, they winkled and sparkled garishly, sending light-shadows gambolling over the walls. Rubies and diamonds, emeralds, sapphires and pearls together. Kettle, roused from his native indolence, began pursuing the coloured light patches with a frenzied zest comprehensible only to other felines. Impassive, Jane lifted out a necklace of pearls and small diamonds—her mother's necklace for her presentation at court. It was in the portrait at Britwell Park. She laid it back on its satin bed and closed the lid. No surprises, then.

"Haseley," she called. There was no putting it off. "Haseley, I shall need to look decorous and elegant today." And there must be no shrinking. Whatever unwelcome surprises lay ahead today. And at least

Myddelton would not be present to witness her early mistakes or contemn her schemes of refurbishment.

Haseley appeared in the doorway from the dressing room. "Decorous and elegant, my lady?"

"Yes. For I must tour the house. And we both know that everyone—even the tweeny, if there is one—will discover some reason to be in position to command a fine view."

Haseley dimpled. "Ah. Decorous and elegant, my lady," she nodded.

It was not the province of a butler to usher a lady about her own house. By rights, the privilege and onus of conducting that first tour belonged to the housekeeper. To her belonged that duty of explanation and justification of all things domestic, customary, done, or left undone. Particularly in an establishment of the size and prestige of Myddelton House. But upon this occasion Kettering had no intention of adhering to either precedent or rank. Indeed, he had brooked no opposition to his plan, and (fortunately, for the harmony of the servants' hall) Mrs. Pinch, the motherly but excellent housekeeper, had no wish to oppose him in anything. Certainly not in this.

They had begun their tour in the front foyer—an admirable introduction to Myddelton House, to be sure. And from thence to the Library which proved as ample in its furnishings as the contents of its shelves were erudite. But now they had passed through to the Dining Room.

Jane eyed the silk hung walls. Last evening, in the candlelight, she had not seen the dark patches on the walls where pictures once had hung, revealing the original colour to have been aquamarine, not the dulled grey which was now predominant. "These walls need new silk, Kettering," she remarked dispassionately. The chairs required new seat covers, and upon inspection, the curtains had proven as fragile in the morning light as she had suspected they might. "And the curtains want replacing as well. The sun has all but destroyed these, so we should have voile as well or even Venetian blinds to protect the new, do you not think?"

"Yes, my lady."

And it was to be the same, or worse, in every room they entered, barring the library, the entrance foyer and the comfortable eating parlour at the rear of the house. For the decades of gambling debts, retrenchment and grief had left their mark everywhere. Room upon redundant room, deserted, stripped and sterile. Below elaborate plasterwork ceilings and heavily carved cornices, within walls which needed patching, fresh paper or paint, a melange of furnishings— exquisite, comfortable, ill-fitting or all three—partially and awkwardly filled the large cold rooms. What should have been straw coloured satin had become mottled tan. The parquet floors with the remaining Indian or Aubusson carpets appeared incongruous, as if they belonged in a different house altogether, their rich or soft colours and textures emphasising the inadequacies of the rooms they were meant to grace.

From Kettering she learned that following the third earl's demise, his son had stripped the mansion bare, auctioning off as many of the fitments as he could find buyers for in order to pay the debts. He had intended to sell the house too, but had been persuaded against it by a close friend, Kettering had thought. She had no need to ask the friend's name. With careful investment, the family fortunes had recovered— hence the refitting of the library, the foyer, her apartments. But Lord Maundrel's death, followed shortly thereafter that of Lady Myddelton had ended the proposed refurbishment. And the grieving husband had retreated to the country, leaving his London house for good.

And Myddelton? Was he a gamester like his grandfather and uncle? Was that why her money had been left so tied up? Yet according to Kettering, he rarely ventured beyond the library, the eating parlour, and his bedroom. Presumably then, although he might have continued the renovation had he so wished, it was impossible to gauge whether he was acquainted with the true state of things. Or had he become so used to the situation that he noticed none of it? Or did not care? Jane sighed inwardly.

Kettering led her through a small salon and into the Drawing Room. The shutters had been opened to admit daylight for the first time in months. Again, the walls were marked, the silk—once green, now awkward blue—was beginning to shred, and the unhappy blend of chairs and sofas gave a haphazard look to what ought to have been a most elegant chamber. The ceiling was in good order though—painted like the entrance hall and the panels of her bedchamber with swags, medallions and other classical emblems—and several of the chairs required nothing but fresh upholstery. Pulling her shawl more closely about her, Jane asked finally, "How frequently are the chimneys swept?"

"Once a year, my lady, in the autumn before my lord returns from the country."

"And fires lit?"

"At least once a season, my lady." Which was neither sufficient nor wise. At least in Kettering's opinion.

Jane wished she possessed Mlle de Resnay's unflappable character, wished indeed that Mlle was even now beside her. "Well..." she faltered, sinking into a chair, faint-hearted at the task which clearly lay before her. At Britwell Park, she had never felt thus. But that, that had been her home. There must be no shrinking, no balking. No quailing. And setting her face, she rose. "Well, that must change instantly if we are to dispel this cold. I shall want to see fires lit in all the grates in the public rooms every day, or these rooms shall never dry out." She drew a deep breath. "Is there no fortepiano in the house?"

"There was used to be, my lady...in the boxroom."

"Ah." She had a very clear idea of what that meant. Idly, she wandered from chair to sofa to chair, trailing her fingers over the worn fabrics and the fraying trimmings. The mantel was bare of ornaments. "Are all the rooms like this, Kettering?" None of it was as she had anticipated. Another young lady, one less prosaic than herself, would have resorted to strong hysterics by now, she was sure.

"Yes, my lady. My lord, since he inherited the title, has preferred to keep to the Library and the eating parlour..."

"And he does not entertain?"

"No, my lady, my lord has never been known to entertain here." Kettering paused, weighing honesty against diplomacy. Honesty triumphed. "It should be added that some of the bedchambers on the second floor lack furnishings altogether."

136

"Really? Do they?" No flinching, she admonished herself. "I see. Yes…Well…" She craned her head back to study the painted swags. And eventually, as she looked over the room once again, said softly, almost in echo of Mlle: "Well, some of it is salvageable surely." She shook her head, as if to ward off the dismals. "Will you kindly ring the bell for Haseley, Kettering. Tell her to find my housekeeping notebook and bring it me." There were still a few fine paintings on the walls.

No tantrums. Nor visible dismay. Kettering felt a whisper of hope. "Yes, my lady."

She wished she possessed Mlle's sangfroid. "Ah Haseley, there you are. You have my notebook? Good. Thank you." She drew a deep breath. "We had best make a start then, Kettering." And softly, almost to herself: "It wants a small army thrown at it!"

Kettering heard. "Yes, my lady," he agreed, and permitted himself the luxury of a smile. Jane was not to know it was in relief.

She bit at the corner of her mouth. Myddelton had said she was to redecorate as pleased her. And it was her money.

"So…to begin, we shall need to engage several painters and plasterers. Engage only the best, Kettering. Shall you need to hire another two or three maids as well? These ceilings shall need particular care and they must not be ruined by incompetent workmen. Will you see to that right away? If they were to begin the work this afternoon, or no later than in the morning, some of the plastering and patching could be started, surely, and whatever else it is they do before painting…They should begin in here—the ceiling wants a good thorough clean before anything else is begun. If Mrs. Pinch does not have a recipe for a gentle cleaning solution, Haseley will provide her with mine."

"Yes, my lady. I shall see to it at once…" He had hoped, from the moment of first seeing her, that this was how it would be. That like her father…

"And seamstresses. Mrs. Pinch must know of several. We shall need at least a dozen, I should imagine. Lord Myddelton has said he shall be away until Thursday, so we must accomplish as much as can be before he returns—for gentlemen do not like their house in disarray…at least Sir Charles never did," she confided with a wry smile.

"No, my lady," Kettering agreed.

"...I shall visit the drapers' this afternoon—but you shall have to tell me to which I should bring my custom. I shall postpone making my decisions upon colours for the walls until after I've seen what can be had at the drapers'. And I shall require the direction of Clementi's showrooms as well."

"Yes, my lady." That like her father, she would prove indefatigable.

She opened the notebook and found the first empty page. Looking about her measuringly, she began a rough sketch, jotting notes as she drew. "These windows face which direction? And these are eleven foot ceilings, are they not?" She directed the first of many inquiring looks at Kettering. "So that's, let's see, one two, three four, five six, seven eight ells of fabric for the curtains." She turned the page and began writing again. "Have these walls always been hung with silk, do you know? Perhaps it is time for a change...How many ells for a valance? Heavens, I don't know. I dare say the drapers shall advise me...And these floors, they shall all want dry scrubbing, but I dare say if we were to wait until the painting is done and then scrub them with green herbs, it would be much better."

"Yes, my lady." Had she been the son Colonel Heron had professed to want, she would by now be one of those superior sorts of aides Wellington collected about himself, directing the ordering of men and provisions, rather than households and fitments and furnishings, making it all run smoothly, like clockwork. Just as her father had done with that unfortunate mountain of debts.

"How long since these carpets have been turned for cleaning? That must be seen to at once. And how many of the upstairs chambers are empty? We may wish to hire a cabinet maker at some point. But that must be secondary...If we were to hire a person to upholster and mend the chairs, surely it would be sensible if he was to set up a workshop in one of those unused bedchambers, do you not you think? Shall you see to that as well? Yes? By my count, all the chairs in here require some attention.

"My uncle recently had a pair of book cabinets from one John McLean, here in London, and they were of excellent quality, so I shall pay him a visit. But not today.

"And, when I return from the drapers, I shall expect the woodwork beneath the dado to have been washed in here and the carpet to have been turned onto a light sprinkling of wet sand under the dust sheets— can that be done? And I shall also want William, that we may begin shifting the furniture. I shall look in on the eating parlour again, and then I must go up and change. You must tell Mrs. Pinch that the trunks with my dower linens should arrive sometime this afternoon and we will go through those together."

❧

4 May 1812

Tired already, Myddelton returned from Newmarket to find his house in chaos. Her ladyship considered it a fine bustling chaos, one ordered and overseen by the ever-watchful Kettering and Mrs. Pinch.

Myddelton's view was rather different: From the moment he entered through the partially opened front door, he was forced to cleave to the wall by workmen manoeuvring a long ladder through the foyer to the hallway ("To me...to you...Mind the paintwork, Jem...to me...Mornin' Guv...") while Kettering observed their cautious progress. "Hell's teeth, it stinks in here," he muttered, finally able to leave his flattened position beside the door. "Kettering!" he yelled. "Oh, there you are. What the devil is going on?" He stamped across the foyer in the direction of the library, his driving coat dust-caked, and as ever flapping about his ankles. His nostrils were pinched against the pervasive acrid smell of drying paint.

"The painters have been in during your absence," Kettering said calmly.

"S'life, who ordered that? It's bloody awful!"

Kettering's gaze remained curiously blank. "Lady Myddelton," he said with a courteous half-bow.

Myddelton scowled, his brows drawn together; Kettering's countenance did not invite a response. "Did the pouch from the Foreign Office arrive yet?"

139

"Yes, my lord. I have placed it on your desk in the library."

Myddelton disappeared through the library doors for a moment. He returned an instant later. "What in the blazes is that thing doing in my library?" he demanded.

"I beg your pardon, my lord?"

Nodding irritably in the direction of the library windows, Myddelton exclaimed, in rising decibels: "The forte-whatsit? Where the devil did that come from?"

"The fortepiano, my lord? It arrived from Mr. Clementi's showroom on Saturday afternoon, my lord," Kettering replied pacifically.

"Red hell and bloody death!" Myddelton dashed into the library and reappeared with the leather pouch. "If anyone wants me, I shall be at the Foreign Office. Or at White's." He started out of the front door. "Tell Stamp to send me a change of clothes."

Kettering's own nostrils pinched with disapproval; he had grown used to the smell of paint yesterday. "Very good, my lord," he said, closing the door with such an air of elegant imperturbability.

Jane, engaged in choosing wall covering for the Morning Room, heard the commotion in the hall and thought to come through. But even as was she stepping over and around the unfurled rolls of printed Chinese silk and wallpapers bestrewn with flowers and exotic bird life, the anger she heard in Myddelton's voice made her hesitate. A moment later, she heard him explode, "Red hell and bloody...Foreign Office...White's..." And then he was gone. She bit her lips together. Lotto yawned and went back to licking his paw. Kettle—thoroughly persuaded of his own courage and perspicacity—dived under a sheet of wallpaper to battle an imagined enemy.

She perched on the edge of a low chair and puffed out her cheeks, then exhaled a sough of air. "I told you gentlemen dislike having their houses in disarray," she said finally, directing her remark to the cat. Who ignored her. "Though perhaps Myddelton dislikes it rather more than does Sir Charles."

She looked about her at the floor crowded with rolls of painted paper, at the ells of fabric unfurled over the back of the sofa and every chair. "So, having now married me and brought me to London, he shuns me. How charming." She picked up the sprigged paper, rescuing it from Kettle's claws. "Stop it, Kettle." She held it away from her to reconsider. "Still, I wish I knew what he thought of some of these." A sudden low chuckle escaped her. "...When he's not swearing. What do you think of this one? Rather garish, don't you think? With all these unlikely birds of paradise? Do you suppose it will fade?"

9

"Who is this...What is her name?" Lady Jersey demanded, peering once again at the newspaper in her hand. "Miss Heron? I do not know any Herons, do you, Emily? In any event, I thought Heron was a gypsy name. My mother could tell us, of course, but she is not here. But that is beside the point. Why has he not brought this Heron creature into company? Performed her introductions? Is she not presentable? Is she expecting, do you think? You do not suppose she's some tradesman's brat, do you? His father was rather rolled up a few years back, you know, but...Is there more tea in that pot, Anne?" She reached for another little cake off the plate at her elbow. "I should not eat so many of these. I shall grow quite stout if I continue." She nibbled appreciatively. "Lemon and apricot? Perhaps your cook could give me the receipt. They really are too..."

The morning room, at the rear of the Northcotes' townhouse, was comfortably and tastefully furnished. It was late afternoon—but, in London, so near to the summer equinox as early May, dusk does not fall early, and late afternoon may tarry over several long gilded hours. Three married ladies of wealth and breeding whose custom it was to reign over society were gathered in this small chamber. They had known each other since childhood, these three, and could recall with varying degrees of accuracy each others' worst and best traits, and had no need to ask, 'One lump or two?' of each other, for these were the small details with which they were as familiar as with their own gloves.

Sally continued: "If he did not wish to offer for the Wythenshaw chit—and who would, with a mother like that—all well and good. But he need not have gone to such lengths. He hadn't compromised her. Though to all appearances, she has done her utmost to compromise him.

So I cannot understand it. Is it longstanding, this relationship? I will not believe in Myddelton experiencing a *coup de foudre*. That, I declare, is an impossibility..."

If it bothered her that the subject of her friend's strictures was her cousin, Lady Anne Northcote did not say so. For she had long accepted such outspoken criticism as a necessary, even integral element of friendship with Sally Jersey. "Well, Northcote told me at breakfast that he has known for days," she said, breaking in on her friend's soliloquising. Belatedly, she looked into the teapot—for it was her morning room and thus her tea service—and found it half full. "He said they toasted Myddelton at White's last Thursday evening." She dumped the residue from Sally's cup into the slop bowl and poured her a fresh cup, adding a dash of milk.

"And no one said a word?" Lady Emily Cowper gawped.

"The curious thing is..." Anne pursed her lips together. "I knew all about it, only I forgot!"

"You did what? You forgot about it?" Sally demanded.

"Pem told me. At your ball, Sally. After Myddelton had danced with..."

"Miss Nuttall, Lady Anne Fyvie, and twice with little Cassa Staines-Smythe," Sally ground out. "I remember it far too clearly, thank you. I should have liked to have murdered him for that! But you!" she said accusingly. "You told me you were discussing Bonaparte's troop movements!"

Emily laughed. "Anne, you never did..."

"I did. I am terribly sorry, my dear, but he bound me to silence."

"Ha!"

"Hush, Sally," Emily said. "What did he say, Anne...These *are* good cakes..."

"Nothing definite. You know Pem," Anne lamented. "He did say that it was an arranged marriage and that Myddelton had just learned of the details from the family solicitor. It had been arranged by his father, some years ago..." Discreetly, she omitted the other less savoury details. Myddelton was, after all, her cousin.

"By his father?" Sally echoed, for once content with only a phrase.

"How very feudal…"

"What else did he say?" Emily asked.

"Nothing."

"Nothing? Nothing at all?" Emily demanded, getting up to pour herself another cup of tea. "Not anything?"

"No. Nothing. He just kept ranting…in a misogynist fashion. You know what he can be at times. The way he was talking, she is some moneylender's daughter. Myddelton had not yet met her and, like us, had never even heard of the family," Anne said.

"He's probably jolly right," Sally declared. Her expression hardened. "And I shall tell you all this now: If Myddelton has contracted a mésalliance with some *low* creature, I, for one, shall not receive her. I am sorry, Anne, I do not care if he is your cousin! And as for vouchers…" She shook her head dramatically.

"Oh come, Sally, you remember Myddelton's father," Anne protested, unswayed. "She cannot be a moneylender's daughter. My uncle would never have contracted a mésalliance for his only son and heir!" She rooted with the unfolded newspaper. "Where is that notice? Here. Listen. 'Miss Jane Caroline Sophia Heron. Daughter of the late Colonel James Heron, ADC, MC…Niece to Sir Charles Heron, Bart. of Britwell Park, Oxon.' That is not the direction of a moneylender, Sally."

"'Tisn't," Emily agreed. "But why the secrecy, then? And why has he not brought her round to meet us? Or even you, Anne? Because he ought to have done that at the very least! You don't suppose she is ill? Or as Sally says, expecting?"

"That direction tells us nothing," Sally pronounced. "It could be a ramshackle barn in the middle of nowhere for all we know. And a baronetcy does not confer good breeding—we have all—and more often than one would care to admit—met baronets whose families are full of nothing but hoydens and…"

"You do not think he has married her and left her in the country, do you?" Emily broke in, suddenly intent. "No! Wait. I saw a young woman getting out of a carriage and going into Myddelton House last week. Friday, it was. I know because I had just been for a fitting with Fanchon. And that was Friday afternoon. So it must have been her! It must have been! I think we should call on her."

"What did she look like?" Anne asked instantly.

"No!" Sally insisted. "Why has she not called on us? Why has Myddelton not brought her round to conduct a proper bride visit? No! If anyone should call, it must be Anne!"

"Oh, you're all here!" exclaimed Lady Derham as she burst through the door, the morning newspaper clutched in her hand. She shut the door behind her and waved the paper in the air. "Have you seen today's paper? About Myddelton?" She sounded as though she had raced up the stairs two at a time.

"Sophy," Emily said. "Do take off your wraps. Anne will pour you tea…"

"Of course we've seen it," Sally declared. "It positively leapt from the page this morning."

Sophy, Lady Derham, did as she was bid and laid aside her hat, and absently patted the neat row of brown curls over her forehead. The eldest of the four women, she had been their favourite 'older girl' at school. "You will never believe this. I cannot believe it myself."

"Sophy, your tea," said Anne. "What?"

"Georgina Wythenshaw, that is what," Sophy replied.

"What has Miss Wythenshaw to say to anything—the foolish child?" enquired Sally.

"Well," Sophy began, "I shewed the notice to Alice this morning—not that she had any interest in Myddelton, for she hadn't. But later she walked to Hookham's with Georgina and told her about it, and Georgina, well, Georgina became quite indignant."

"I beg your pardon?" Anne said blankly.

"Indignant, why?" Emily said at the same time.

"Apparently," Sophy continued, still as mystified as when her daughter had first confided this information to her. "…the Wythenshaws were under the impression that Myddelton was about to declare himself. Or Georgina was. And that the matter was as good as settled."

"I told you, Emily, did I not, that that Wythenshaw chit had her eye in that direction all Season?" Sally proclaimed, shaking her finger. "I told you…"

145

"Hush, Sally," said Emily. "What else did Alice say?"

"Well, she said that Georgina has said that if the notice turns out to be true...and why would it not?...then she will marry another, but that Myddelton is her 'great love', and that after she has done her 'duty' she and Myddelton will set up house together...or some such thing."

"I beg your pardon?" Sally Jersey's cup rattled in its saucer as she set it clumsily on the table. "That girl has read too many gothic novels from the Minerva Press!"

"If all else fails, she could make a career writing the silly things," Emily added in an undertone.

Anne placed a calming hand to her throat. "She cannot know what she is saying. What did you say?"

"What could I say?" Sophy enquired. "I hardly knew where to look. But Alice was so shocked and distressed by it all, I knew she must be telling the truth. Her imagination is not that original. And she was quite definite about what Georgina had said. Is it possible, do you suppose, that Myddelton has led the girl on? Anne, I am so sorry, I know he is your cousin..." She shook her head apologetically. And frowned in concentration. "And...I know you will all tell me I am fretting unnecessarily, but I cannot stop thinking of Myddelton's bride—whoever she is. London is a vast place and without any friends or acquaintances..." She trailed off. "But Society can be so very cruel if you do not know your way about. And...that is, it seems to me...that is, I am afraid that Georgina may be capable of great spite..."

"I shall spite her," Sally said, a martial look in her eyes.

"Sally," Emily's mouth puckered into a mock frown. "How unlike you."

Sally's smile was reluctant. "It's that mama of hers. I cannot abide her. No, I cannot! She drinks, I'm certain of it! And as for putting such notions in that child's head. No wonder the foolish girl always looks like she's half ready to swoon and half ready to commit some indiscretion. From the moment she laid eyes on Myddelton, she set her cap for him. And he knew it. But until the other night at my ball, he took the greatest care not to give her any undue notice. I would swear to it! Yes, I would! But I also told you, Emily, didn't I, that that foolish girl would not believe anything she did not wish to believe. I told you, you know I did. And you have seen how she waltzes. Throwing herself hither and yon, clinging to her partner as if she were…"

"Sally, we have all seen how she waltzes," Anne murmured. "But I agree with you. I cannot believe that Myddelton would have led her on. For I never saw him do so…and Miles has never said anything to that effect. Which he would have done…"

"You do not think he's been seeing her in secret, do you?" Emily asked. And as the others shook their heads, continued flatly: "No, nor do I. Well, why would he? And last week at your rout, Anne, was the first time I had seen him in…well, it must be months…"

Sally, the authority, shrugged. "No one has seen him since joined Castlereagh's staff at the Foreign Office! And that was when? February? Early March?"

Anne, now listening with half an ear, sighed and reread the newspaper notice once more. "I shall call on the new Lady Myddelton tomorrow, in the morning. Who knows? She may prove delightful."

"You only say that because you have a tender spot for *him*," Emily teased. "Come and see me after you've been." She rose. "And now I must get home, or I shall never be dressed in time for dinner."

Myddelton paused under the portico of White's Club and yawned. Another day nearly over. He had spent the afternoon at his desk in the Foreign Office, and just as he had finished the final translation in the file, Planta, Castlereagh's secretary, had arrived, looking cheeky as a sparrow, with the pouch of intercepted dispatches, all written in that diabolical Grand Chiffre. But at least the unaccompanied walk from there to here had allowed him to stretch his legs and think about nothing in particular. Which made for a pleasant change. It was still light—perhaps he should go for a ride in the Park…no, that would involve calling round at Myddelton House. He stepped inside and felt in his pocket for his snuff-box. Perhaps he should ride down to Great Myddelton in the morning. He handed his hat and gloves to the footman on the door. And by the time he returned on Monday, perhaps Myddelton House would no longer reek of paint fumes. Though she would be there. He inhaled the grains of snuff. Was it simpler to stay away altogether?

"I say Myddelton, what has you looking so cheerful?" Pemberton demanded, coming down the stairs.

"God knows. 'Struth, you look like death."

Pemberton grinned, yawned and threw his arm about Myddelton's shoulder. "I dare say. Only just got up, you know. I say, have you a minute?"

"Yes, what is it?" He allowed Pemberton to draw him into the Morning Room, unoccupied but for a pair of otiose flies.

"Bring us a bottle of claret, George, there's a good fellow," Pemberton called, settling into a wing chair in the far corner and stretching his legs out in front of him. He dug his hands into his breeches' pockets. "The thing is," he began. "The thing is…There's beginning to be some talk, do you see? In the Coffee Room. Over breakfast. That sort of thing. I know you don't care for gossip. But Brummell mentioned it. And the fact is these things don't take long to spread." He paused tactfully. "Hope you won't be offended at what I'm about to say."

"What could you possibly say that would offend me? That you haven't already said at some time or other?"

Pemberton yawned again and grinned. "You ain't heard it yet."

"Ha!" said Myddelton, pouring out two glasses of claret.

"Well, it's about your wife." Pemberton stopped to fortify himself with a sip of wine. "The fact is, it don't look good. You come in here, announce you've got leg-shackled, but there ain't a bride. Or at least, not that anybody's seen…"

"I suppose you are referring to the announcement that appeared this morning," Myddelton said coldly.

"What? 'Struth, how could I be? I ain't seen a paper all day. I told you I've only just finished my breakfast." He took a gulp of claret, then placed his glass on the table and stared at it. "Still, it don't look good, Myddelton."

"I fail to see how my actions concerning my wife are the business of anyone else."

"'Pon my word, Avery!" Pemberton exclaimed in exasperation. "You slept here last night. And the night before that. What would you think if you was standing in Alvanley and Brummell's shoes?"

"The house stinks of paint. My bride," Myddelton ground the word out. "Is having painters in…and heaven alone knows what else."

Pemberton sighed. "In any other circumstances, you could say that and it would go down a treat. But not now," he declared with more animation than discretion. "You just got married, idiot. S'life, we toast you Thursday, you leave for Newmarket on Friday. All well and good. You had horses running. But to spend the night here, less than a week after you've been spliced, tells Alvanley one story and one alone. If you ain't careful, you shall have the mother and father of a scandal on your hands," he declared. Then added gently, "And you would hate that. You know you would."

His previous pleasure in the afternoon effectively dampened, Myddelton stared out the window at the pedestrians and carriages for some little time. "And what do you suggest I do, O sage?"

Pemberton ran his hands through his hair and wondered for the millionth time since they'd been at school together how Myddelton could be so provoking. He frowned. "She is presentable, ain't she?"

"Oh yes," Myddelton nodded.

Pemberton puzzled over this apparent approval for a moment, then said, "Well, take her about a little then. It don't have to be for long. Only until she's met some people and knows enough to go on by herself, if you ain't interested in playing the lover…But make damn'd sure you sleep at home for the first three months at least. After that…" he shrugged eloquently.

Myddelton stood up, ill at ease. "Any suggestions for this evening?"

Pemberton scratched his nose and thought. "Maria Sefton's throwing a ball this evening… dare say your invite's sitting at home. But I ain't going." He glanced out the window. "It looks a fine evening, what about Vauxhall?"

Myddelton finished the last of the claret in his glass. "Good claret, this. Vauxhall it shall be. And my word upon it, I shall sleep at home. Pem." He gave a brusque nod and headed for the door.

10

In any event, Myddelton did not reach home until well after seven, significantly later than he intended, and by that time all he wanted was his bath and his dinner. For upon leaving White's, he found himself cornered by an ancient General, an acquaintance of his grandfather's he rather thought, waving the morning paper, and saying, "Jolly good, jolly good, ye young scamp." This, he assumed, in the absence of anything more concrete, was intended to signify approval to his marriage. The old man then dragged him off to partake of a celebratory bottle or three, the consumption of which served as a backdrop for a lengthy recital of a foreign campaign—possibly conducted in India or Canada, Myddelton never did learn which—punctuated by numerous "Heh heh, ye young scamps", descriptions of the General's gouty foot, and rheumy coughing fits. During this campaign, wherever it was, the General had been accompanied by someone who had, apparently, impressed him greatly. Again, Myddelton tried in vain to discover who, but ended up wondering if it hadn't been Colonel Heron, though this seemed improbable, given the General's age. He finally escaped by pleading Parliamentary duties, to which the old man exclaimed, "Well done, well done, lad. Go to her. Well done, ye young rascal," before lapsing into another coughing fit.

Myddelton let himself in and sniffed; the smell of paint had dissipated. The candles in the wall sconces had been lit, but the house was still. Were it up to him, dinner would be followed by a quiet evening in the company of a good book. Regrettably, it was not up to him. Pemberton—to save him from the odium of the chattering classes—had decreed Vauxhall. Thus Vauxhall it must be. Still, there was no sign of workmen or chaos. Which was an improvement. Unaccountably cheered, he went directly upstairs.

Bathed and fed, and his conscience tweaked by Pemberton's tacit charge of neglect, he dressed with deliberate care. No, not that waistcoat. The other one. No, not that coat, the new one of blue superfine.

"Thank you, Stamp." Myddelton gave his waistcoat a final tug and pressed at a fold in his cravat. "Kettering, ehm…Lady Myddelton is still at dinner, is she?"

Myddelton's own dinner tray in hand, Kettering replied: "No, my lord. Her ladyship may be found in the Library at this hour. My lady does not keep town hours. Will that be all, my lord?"

Only Stamp discerned the stiffening of Kettering's spine, the lifting of his chin, the thread of disapproval in his voice.

Descending the stairs to the ground floor, still Myddelton detected no evidence of the fresh paint, no change to the hallway. Yet there was a new unmistakable sense of order, an air of expectancy even.

And she was, as Kettering had said, in the Library. Standing over the library table, engaged in sorting through stacks of papers or folios of music or whatever it was. Lotto, dozing by the fireplace, stirred, lifting his head at the sound of the latch. Then stern aloft, he stretched, and ambled to Myddelton's side to sniff his shoes and nudge at his fingers. Belatedly, smiling slightly, she looked up. Upon seeing Myddelton, not a servant, she stilled, her hand poised mid-air.

"Lotto appears to have settled in well," Myddelton observed, regarding the dog who having received his proper tribute now returned to his spot by the fire.

At that, she chuckled low in her throat. "Yes. Oh yes," she agreed drily, thinking of the coy flirtations he had been conducting with the chef, the housekeeper, the head groom, the tweeny…Revolting animal. Without preamble, she continued: "Your horses, did they do well then?"

It was as if he had only parted from her an hour ago. And was nothing like what he had expected. He had fancied there might be a scene. Or at least an awkwardness; she possessed, it seemed, the art of dispelling awkwardness with the prosaic. Surprised, but pleasantly, he answered, "Yes, they did. A second and a third. Which came as something of a shock, I must confess. It was more than I hoped for, certainly."

Her smile broadened. "Congratulations." Then: "You wish for your library. I shall leave you."

"No. No, not at all. I had just thought..." Her self-possession, her ease within a place he had always regarded as his own disconcerted him.

"You are certain? Because I cannot believe I am making any headway whatsoever here, so I would be quite content to abandon the effort..." She gestured vaguely at the disorganised piles on the table. "For the moment."

"No. No, I just thought that you might wish to go out for the evening. Since it looks to be a fine night, I had thought you might like to visit Vauxhall." For all his experience he felt inadequate to the moment.

She stopped and for an instant regarded him quizzically. Then delight lit her eyes and she smiled. "How very kind in you! I should love to," she exclaimed. Then stopped again. And while her smile remained, something in her expression clouded over. "Only... Only, I am so sorry, but I must refuse your kind invitation. For as you see, I have not changed for the evening." She looked down at the crumpled mull she was wearing with an apologetic smile.

Neither was this what he expected. "I shall wait while you change."

She made a moué. She did not know him in this obliging mood. But determined to meet it with composure. "No," she said firmly. "You are very kind. But still I must say no..." She shook her head.

"You are unwell?" Her response was too unexpected, too puzzling. An odd thing for him to be asking surely. "Oh no, I am perfectly well, thank you."

"Then why..."

She opened her mouth to begin, and closed it. Then paused, as if searching in her mind for an acceptable phrase or word. And again, drew a breath as if to start a sentence, then did not. Dear Heavens, to be inarticulate to the point of stupidity. "Well," she faltered. And finally plumped for impeccable honesty. "Well, because, I expect it will sound very foolish indeed..." She blinked rapidly. "But you see, over the last few days, I have become aware of how very provincial I must appear. Here, that is, in Town. And while, it may not matter quite so much

152

during the day, because, in the general way of things, I do not go to fashionable places...And of course, no one knows me. But in the evening...and in your company, it would matter. And I would not wish to cause you any degree of embarrassment. So you see, that is the reason I must say no," she finished brightly. "But I do thank you for your kind invitation..."

Her candour amid the exquisite courtesy of her answer disarmed him. "What?" Women were not as a rule so frank. At least he'd not previously found them so.

She shook her head. How could he not understand? "I have nothing to wear."

She was lying; she must be. Sudden impatience made him snap: "'Struth, women are always saying that." Assuredly, Ianthe always had. "Besides, I make no doubt you have been shopping for days."

"Yes. Yes, but not for gowns," she agreed, her openness quite unmarred by his brief display of temper. "And certainly not for evening gowns." Sighing, frowning, she wandered over to stand at the keyboard of the pianoforte. Involuntarily, she began to scan the music open on the stand and silently to finger the keys. "No, actually, that's distinctly untrue," she admitted, honest to the last. "I haven't been shopping for days, because I've already spent most of my pin money until the end of the quarter." And inexplicably her eyes, those firecracker blue eyes, were bright with pleasure.

Her calm disregard incensed him. "What? You can't have! 'Struth, that's impossible! Your pin money is more than..." Was she some sort of inveterate gambler? "By my life, what can you have spent it on?" He stopped. He was arguing with her. S'death, he was arguing with her! They'd only been married a week. And about pin money.

She began to play a tune, slowly, with one hand. Then she paused, looked up and smiled.

It was an intimate smile, a smile shared as a secret, as if between partners in a game of charades or whist, inviting him to read the answer in her thoughts. Myddelton blinked uncomprehendingly. "What the devil..."

Slowly, she replayed the tune.

And bemused, staring, he drew a deep breath, for in that instant he knew the answer. "You spent it on the fortepiano? All of it?"

"Oh no! Not all," she clarified. "Because I did have some left over from last quarter." Gently, she closed the lid and ran a caressing hand over it. "But it was the only way," she explained. "It has all the latest improvements, you see—a deeper box which makes for greater sonority. And it's better than the one I have at home...I mean at Britwell Park. It was meant to be delivered to someone else on Monday, but Mr. Field demonstrated it for me anyway. But, you see, I would have to have waited for at least a month..." She made it sound an eternity. "While they built another, so I..."

He was amused despite himself. "So you bribed them with a roll of soft..." he finished. It was a perfectly underhanded thing to do and she had done it, quite cheerfully, it would seem.

"Not *bribed*, exactly," she stated. "I simply offered payment on the spot. Whereas the person who had ordered it had done so on credit and few businesses these days can afford to let a roll of soft, as you call it, walk out of the door..." Then she sobered. "I am sorry. I should have thought and taken myself off to the dressmakers. But, you see, I didn't. I assumed...wrongly, that I did not need..." she halted, her forehead creased with concern.

None of this was anything like what he had intended or imagined. And it was all of it, too far beyond his realm. And for a moment he regarded her as if she were an alien creature. 'Struth, she was less like a female than any of his acquaintance. "'Faith, for all that I am male, and therefore expected to be ignorant of such matters, I do understand enough to know that you have nothing but the best of everything."

"Yes," she replied unequivocally. "To be sure, my uncle and Mademoiselle have always seen to that. But it is the best of everything for an unmarried and unattached young lady, do you not see? In a country neighbourhood. A young lady not yet out. And I am persuaded it would not reflect well upon you, were I to appear as I am." Her smile was penitent, contrite.

What made him say it, he didn't know. But suddenly the prospect of an evening spent in her company was no hardship, no chore, perhaps even a pleasure. "Come out anyway," he said. "It's of no great matter, I promise you. You will enjoy it. Wear what you wore…'Struth, I don't know…at dinner at Britwell Park…Go on. I'll wait."

❧

She had not been out at dusk since her arrival in Town, a sennight past. Nor had she ever been in such a confined space as a closed carriage with him before. It might have proven distinctly uncomfortable, unhappily, distressingly close. But Myddelton seemed determined to please her, pointing to the great white stone edifices of the Admiralty and Horse Guards as they drove past. And then, waiting beside her as they stood on Westminster Bridge while she took in the great width of the Thames, the barges and boats—open, canopied, for pleasure and for trade—their lanterns glowing in the evening light and fog, and along each shore the wide allées or the jostle of buildings up to the water's edge, the endless huddles of red tiled roofs punctuated by the thin, rising spires of parish churches. And high above all, overshadowing all, the lantern and great dome of St. Paul's. And as the oarsman rowed them across the river and downstream, and Myddelton leaned against the seat of the scull, a lazy smile never far from his lips and his eyes, he again pointed out the sights to her—Lambeth Palace, the Houses of Parliament, the two great square stone towers of Westminster Abbey dominating—all the while recounting a wildly and purposefully inaccurate history of the city and its denizens which made her laugh. The water lapped against the sides of the boat. And though she knew that he might ignore her tomorrow, and knew also that the river was used as a sort of open sewer and would stink in high summer, nothing could spoil her happiness, her thankfulness for his kind affability, her delight in seeing the city and the river in the evening light, the flickering lamps and torches, soft in the mist.

And then she caught sight of it. "Oh. Oh. Is that it?"

Even from a distance, Vauxhall Gardens on the south bank of the Thames appeared marvellous. The thousands upon thousands of tiny coloured glass lanterns which illuminated the gardens seemed unconnected to anything below or above, little blobs of red, blue, green and yellow light shifting in the breeze, possibly the work of an elf with a sense of humour. And as they drew nearer, she caught glimpses of the groves, the dome of the grand pavilion, the rotunda and ornamental temples above the clipped hedges. The Misses Greenwood had told her all about it, but she had thought them prone to hyperbole and had disregarded half of their glowing report. Now she realised that, if anything, they had erred on the side of restraint.

But then, they debarked and Myddelton escorted her to the entrance and all thought or word was banished from her mind, for it was splendid beyond description, splendid beyond anything she could have imagined. Double rows of the coloured lanterns festooned the pillars of the entrance, while above, hundreds more had been hung in the concave arch of the long passageway, so that the whole resembled the heavens on a starry night. And then, then they were walking down the Great Walk, and it was bordered with tall elms, flowering shrubs and box hedges— and all had been hung with these tiny lamps, some in marvellous patterns even, so that the whole place was lit by a flood of golden and many-coloured brightness. To one side was one of two great semicircles of supper boxes, each filled with half a dozen guests dining, and each of the boxes lit like the trees. In the distance was a triumphal arch, while off this way or that, narrower paths led to grottoes or temples or walks adorned with statues and fountains or pillars and with illuminated paintings and secluded benches. And everywhere, before and behind them, on either side and at every turning, the Gardens were filled with hundreds of others—courting couples in their finery, with or without chaperones, loud parties, and rowdy, jostling groups of officers in dress regimentals, though she felt little sense of crowding. She said nothing, though Myddelton could hear her small gasps of wonder and the delight like a current running through her. He saw few acquaintances; presumably the socially inclined had descended upon the Seftons' for the evening.

"Should you care to sit and listen to the orchestra?"

The smile she beamed him was answer enough.

With that facility born and nurtured by years of town living, he led her through the gathering crowd into the fanciful Gothic temple that served as the orchestra, and steered her to the far side and two unoccupied chairs. "Some champagne, I think. I shan't be above a minute," he said, and dashed off in search of one of the Park's Attendants.

The orchestra was very good. Mrs. Greenwood had assured her that the music here was superior to anything, but again she had not believed her. But it was. Far better indeed than the collection of musicians got up as orchestras which played in country neighbourhoods—even one like Britwell St. Luke, so close to a centre of learning and commerce such as Oxford. They were part-way through that perennial favourite, Handel's Water Music, which she had heard, but never performed so well. Enchanted, transported even, by every thing, happier than she would have believed possible, she sat listening as she gazed idly up at the ornamental Moorish tracery of the vaulted ceiling.

"Od's my life! Jane! Janey Heron!"

Startled, catching her breath, she jerked to attention. The voice was as familiar as home. And searching everywhere among the throng of faces about her, at last she saw him. And involuntarily rose to her feet. "Pem?"

He would have broken into a run—that she should be here, of all places—but had to be content with long strides as he stepped around and about to avoid those who separated them. At last reaching her, he snatched up her hands. "Janey. What in Heaven's name? What are you doing here? 'Struth, who are you with? Where is Sir Charles? Is he ill? What..."

She blinked. A number of curious onlookers had turned to stare.

"By all that's wonderful, why did no one tell me you was to be in Town?"

She swallowed tightly. "Pem! I...I am here with Lord Myddelton. He is...I...We are..."

Pemberton quieted. "Angel, what is it? You're here with Myddelton, did you say?"

She nodded. "Do you know him?" Unwelcome tears sprang into her eyes.

The colour drained from his face. Still, he held her hands in that vice-like grip and studied her familiar-since-childhood face, but words had—for the moment—abandoned him. Finally: "'Struth, he never said it was you. I swear he never said it was you." He threw his head back for a moment to clear it, then returned that intent gaze to her face. "'Struth, I hardly know what to say." Then, he raised her hands to his lips and kissed them. "I wish you every happiness, Angel. He is the luckiest of men."

"Thank you," she whispered. Of all Lord Choate's grandsons, he had always been her favourite.

"But when...No. I know the answer to that. Last week. But was you married from Britwell Park? And who..."

"Mr. James, of course." And at that she could smile.

"Toby? Toby? That poxy little weed! He never said a word..."

"Jane!"

As one, she and Pemberton turned at the sound of her name.

"Pem?" Myddelton's voice held only confusion now.

"'Struth Avery, why did you never tell me it was Janey? Deuce take it man, I would have stood up at the wedding." He might have silenced the hurt in his voice had it occurred to him.

"I had not realised you were acquainted..." Myddelton answered, attempting to extract himself from the mess into which he had unwittingly wandered.

"And Janey tells me that young Toby married the two of you," Pemberton exclaimed.

"Young Toby?" Myddelton repeated, bewildered. The extrication was not going according to plan. "Your champagne, m'dear." He handed the glass to Jane.

"What are you giving her champagne for?" Pemberton demanded, in the manner of a protective sibling. "She loathes the stuff. Never drinks it...You know my weedy young cousin, Toby James!"

Bright colour had flooded Jane's cheeks. Myddelton gave her a quizzical look. "I'm afraid I didn't give her the chance to tell me. About the champagne, that is." Floundering, he groped, "...Or your cousin, if it comes to that. S'life, was that young James? I thought I recognised him, but could not place him."

"Here Janey, give it to me," Pemberton said.

"Thank you for the champagne," she said to Myddelton, recovering. "But Pem is right, I do not often drink it. Shall you mind?" Her concern was unfeigned. She handed the glass to Pemberton. "Pem and I, we have known each other since I was in the nursery." She saw the tightness leave Myddelton's jaw. She took his arm.

Together, they began to move away from the orchestra stand and out onto the South Walk. Then, suddenly, Pemberton began to laugh. "Lud, Myddelton, remember that Candlemas we collected all the frog-spawn from the pond in order to serve it up to m'sisters as foaming water? Gad Janey, fancy you marrying Myddelton!" He looked down at her and smiled broadly. "And then Toby fell down—because he was laughing so hard—and dropped the jug just when I had convinced m'sisters…"

"You lying toad, Bertie Pemberton!" she exclaimed with all the conviction of one who had known him since her earliest days.

Myddelton began to chuckle. How pleasant to watch Pemberton receive his just due, for once. And yet, he felt the curious stirrings of a new unease. She was, it seemed, not entirely unconnected nor unchampioned in his world.

Shaking her head, she continued: "I had the whole story from Gussie and Marianne. The spilling of the frog-spawn—Heavens, you are repellent—was entirely your fault. Not that they were ever for an instant taken in by your dubious tale of 'foaming water'."

Pemberton, well-acquainted with the differences between his sisters' perception of the truth and his own, laughed. "And how is Sir Charles keeping these days?"

"Oh, as ever," she laughed. "He invited Myddelton to play chess with him, and Myddelton, knowing no better, succumbed to his blandishments."

Pemberton gave Myddelton an amused look.

"And checkmated him several times in a row, I believe," she finished, smiling as she glanced at Myddelton for confirmation. "But, he did suffer quite a reverse a fortnight or so ago, for Lord Choate repiqued and capotted him, so I dare say it all works out evenly."

They had wandered away from the orchestra, past an Octagonal

Rotunda and down the so-called Hermit's Walk, talking and talking of the comfortable nothings of every day. It had grown darker, making the coloured lanterns appear even brighter. The fireworks display was not far off. They came to the Lilac Walk, and Jane paused to smell a fragrant bough, while Myddelton and Pemberton stood paces away watching her in companionable silence.

Presently Pemberton said, without his customary humour: "M'grandsire adores that girl. Always has. As does m'grandmother."

"I never met her when I visited you..." It was an implicit question.

"'Struth, no! Sir Charles kept her sacrosanct. No one was allowed within a mile..."

"You were."

"No, not really. I don't count. 'Struth, I was never more than Gussie and Marianne's elder brother..." Then, his voice full of its usual insouciance: "I say, she didn't bring that wretched dog to Town with her, did she?"

She had turned. Her smile grew. "Indeed, I did."

Pemberton laughed. "How is the incorrigible brute?"

"Wait till you see him!" she declared. "He has grown far bigger than we thought he would. He's even bigger than Shandy! And very well behaved now."

"Ha! In your dreams, Janey. D'you know, Myddelton..."

Having come to a cul-de-sac with only a shaded bench for two, they turned back.

"...D'you know, one time when I was visiting in Britwell Salome, that animal crept into the Hall and chewed right through one of my riding boots. Chewed the tassel off one of my Hessians too. 'Pon my soul, I could have shot him!"

Jane was laughing. Lord Choate had thought it 'devilish amusing' at the time. In spite of himself, Myddelton too had begun to laugh.

Nearby, a newly commissioned officer in dress regimentals stumbled on the gravel. Full of swagger and arrack punch confidence, and so young that the down moustache which shadowed his upper lip had only rarely met with a razor, he'd been separated from his fellows by a call of nature. He staggered for a few feet, reached out to right himself with a handful of the shrubbery, then fell awkwardly into Myddelton's arms.

"Ouf! I do beg y'r pardon. You mus' 'scuse me. 'Do beg y'r pardon..." His face flushed and sweating, the young man pulled himself into an impression of uprightness, but was so obviously drunk that Myddelton, risking the sick which was assuredly not far off, reached out again to steady him. The young officer shook his head to regain some of his punch-sodden senses. "I thank you...Good sir." He belched loudly. He would have sketched a military bow to his saviour, but found that manoeuvre quite beyond him. A vacuous beatific grin split his face.

Myddelton exchanged a knowing look with Pemberton. These boy officers were one of the risks of Vauxhall, and all of them long on barracks' boasting and pitifully short on any experience. Too young, they were all too young. At their age, his head had been filled with bawdy Latin verses, and playing cricket.

The young officer peered at Pemberton out of bloodshot eyes. "'Pon m'soul, I do 'pologise again, good sirs. If you mus' know, I am off to Spain on th'morrow, an' the celebrashuns..." He burped softly and stopped, blinking in confusion.

Listening to the drunken ramblings with half an ear and a false smile to mask the boredom, Myddelton exchanged another significant look with Pemberton.

"...have been magnifishent, I c'n tell you," the soldier finished proudly. "'Pon m'life, I 'ave never had rack punch b'fore, d'you know ..." he confided, waggling his head in what he clearly meant to be a sagacious nod. Though the effect was rather different. "But you gennelmen c'n be sure I c'n hold my rum...an' my aim is as sure as...as..." He blinked and smiled vacantly, himself having lost the thread of his simile.

"I do not doubt you shall bring great honour upon your regiment," Myddelton broke in. He wished to end the conversation. "But you must not let us keep you." It was not to be.

"Aye, you c'n be sure, we shall show ol' Boney an' his Fro...Frogs wha'...wha' proper Br'tsh officers c'n do," the young man continued, thrilled to have stumbled upon a receptive audience for his tales of intended exploits of bravery and honour. "Aye, we shall show 'em...We

161

shall thrash 'em an' thrash 'em…" His voice trailed off.

Without knowing why she did so, Jane stepped closer to Myddelton, tucking her hand firmly into the crook of his arm. And tried not to feel uneasy. Why did they not move off? Was there no way to extract themselves?

Noticing her at last, the young officer wobbled in his boots. "'Pon m'soul, by all tha's wunnerful! Whatsis?" He tried to focus on Jane, wobbled again, and waved an unsteady finger at Myddelton. "A lady, 'pon m'soul. Out fr'a pleasure stroll, wha'?"

Recoiling, her uneasiness growing, Jane looked up at Myddelton. He did not notice—he was gazing off into space. Neither did the young man notice. He hiccoughed.

"Whash'er name, li'l one?" he leered—rather foolishly, given his years—and leaned unsteadily toward her so that his face and fetid breath were only inches from hers.

He sketched a clownish bow in Myddelton's direction, and as if he were both gallant and sober, he offered his arm to Jane. "'Suredly, sir, 'suredly, you gemmen will not be so unpatr'otic as to d'ny an officer an' fellow gemman—off to fight the Frenchies th'opportunity to sample the charms…"

Myddelton refocused his attention on the young officer. What was he on about now? He didn't see the protective wariness creeping into Pemberton's eyes. He had been watching the crowds flocking towards the best vantage points for the fireworks display.

Too late, Pemberton perceived the direction of the young man's speech, and broke out in a sweat.

"F'r good luck, don't ye know…to sample the undoubted charms o' this charmin', charmin' ladybird?"

"What?" Myddelton said. He was all attention now. And his astonishment at hearing that word 'ladybird', was swiftly followed by dismay, amazement, revulsion, and an instant unparalleled anger.

Oblivious and undaunted, the officer answered. "I was sayin', tha' I should like t'sample…"

"What did you say?" Myddelton spat, suddenly lunging to grab the soldier's collar. "'Struth, that's my wife, you bloody coxcomb. That's

Lady Myddelton, you insolent whelp!"

The officer was too drunk to know fear. Or perhaps he had not heard correctly. He giggled. "She looks a charmin' li'l piece t'me."

Glancing at Jane, Pemberton saw her confusion and distress. Saw— even in the unreliable half-light of the coloured lanterns—that she was retreating, backing away from the incipient, inevitable clash, from the hateful violence being thrust upon her. She had paled to ash. A muscle quivered uncontrollably below her cheekbone. 'Struth, a disaster, this. Instinctively, he placed his arm between Myddelton and the boy, and said reasonably: "No, Myddelton. Leave it. He's slewed."

Myddelton pushed him away. "Stay out of it, Pem. It ain't your affair."

"No, Myddelton, don't!" Pemberton exclaimed, again pulling at Myddelton's free shoulder.

Myddelton shoved at him. And tightened his grip on the officer's collar. "You'll not sully her name, you pestilential scrub, by speaking of her. You'll eat your words, you poxy little coxcomb..."

Pemberton thrust himself between them, knocking Myddelton clear.

Unaccountably, the young officer began to laugh foolishly, and ineffectually to struggle. Perhaps he mistook Myddelton's rough handling for barracks' wrestling. Or believed his own boasting. Fumbling with the buttons at his waist, he continued raucously, "A'ready a buttered bun, is she? Nev'mind. I'll show her wha'an officer does wif' his cock." He giggled, hiccoughed, belched. "Com'ere, miss, so I c'n stuff y'proper, like..." he leered, lunging for her.

Pemberton tried again to drive Myddelton back. "Avery, don't."

But it was too late. Pulsing with rage, Myddelton slammed his fist into the officer's face, knocking his head sideways and back. Blood spurted from the boy's nose and spread from the side of his mouth. "Wha..." he cried..

Behind them, pressed against the box hedge, Jane had begun to tremble. Even as she sought to back still farther away.

"S'death, no, Avery!" Pemberton cried, launching himself between Myddelton and the young man once more.

Overhead, the fireworks boomed, hissed and snapped, casting

coloured shadows.

"I shall kill him!" Myddelton ground out, and punched the soldier again.

The boy's nose spurted again. Blood streamed from a cut below his eye. "You will not speak of her again!" Myddelton roared, ramming home another blow—a face-breaker. "Ever!"

Pemberton caught Myddelton's arm as it descended a fourth time. "For Christ's sake, Avery! He's only a lad!" he shouted, throwing all of his weight against him, dragging, hauling him off.

Sobered by the explosion of pain in his face and broken nose, the young officer had begun to writhe and to cry. And to retch. Moaning and sobbing, clutching at his face, he fell to the ground and was sick on the path and all over the knees of his dress uniform.

Nearly weeping himself—in anger or frustration—Pemberton looked up and saw that Jane had not moved. But was pressing her hands to her cheeks, to stop the quaking, to hold herself close against the degrading violence and the horror of it. "Good God, Avery!" he begged. "Forget the boy! Take her home. Take Janey home."

He had forgot her. Seething with blood lust, thinking only of beating the insolent scrub within an inch of his worthless life, Myddelton regarded the boy contemptuously, now covered in his own blood and vomit. Then looked up to see her, shivering and stricken and quailing, her breath coming in short gasps as helplessly she looked from him to the young officer to Pemberton and back again.

"Quickly, man. Now!" Pemberton insisted.

Stunned, drained and still furious, Myddelton obeyed. He snatched up her hand to draw her away. White-faced and shuddering, she staggered after him, tears streaming down her face.

The fireworks display continued, lighting the sky, while the onlookers shouted and sighed with delight. Yet many turned to stare at the precipitate departure from their ranks and thought they understood well the scene: An arrogant toff, probably a lord, with an innocent from the country, a seduction gone rough and badly awry. And serve him right too. He ought to have stuck to those who understood the rules of the game.

Dragging her along even as she wept, Myddelton headed for the entrance. She tripped and nearly fell, but his arm encircled her, steadying her on her feet. Yet he never stopped walking. She stumbled again and clutched at her side.

Myddelton looked down on the crown of her bowed head. Her arms were pressing flat against her chest as if she had been stripped naked before a crowd.

"I am sorry," he said tightly. It was all he could manage. She did not raise her head.

His arm about her still as they reached the entrance, Myddelton called for an Attendant to summon his carriage. He could feel her trembling and the sobs wracking her, but whether from cold or shock, he did not know and would not enquire.

Something of the vehemence of his demand must have been communicated by Attendant to coachman, for the crested town carriage was extracted from its position in the Carriage Field and brought up to the entrance without the usual delays or the chorus of expletives from the other coachmen. Without ceremony, Myddelton bundled her into the carriage and flung himself onto the seat opposite, pulling the door shut hard behind him.

She pressed herself into the corner of the seat. A trickle of perspiration slid down over her temple. Her cheeks were hot and prickling with tears. Biting hard on her lip, she struggled to regain control of herself.

Enraged, his breathing shallow and his neckcloth too tight, Myddelton turned from her to look out the window. Great God, he had thought he knew the face of his own anger before now. The years at Eton and Oxford had taught him certainly how to measure his patience, how to hold his tongue even when his thoughts proved less governable. And indeed, he had felt himself regaining his equanimity since returning from Oxfordshire. But now, as he sat stiff and furious across from her, he felt his heart and head pounding together—like the beat to quarters— with the violence of his reaction to the insult. To himself. To his *wife*. Od's death, the word made him seethe. But why? Why did it rankle? For she was his wife. Though he wanted none of her and she was *no* wife. Was it not her very existence? Without her, there would have been no insult.

Yet there had been, and the emotion which engulfed him was far beyond the rage he had felt when first he learned of her. Only a day ago he would have vowed that he wanted nothing from her but separation. But now...now, he saw that neither intellect nor sentiment would ever, could ever, vitiate the vigour of enraged pride: her honour was now his honour. An imputation upon her honour belonged doubly to him. A slight upon her virtue was a stain upon his manhood, his family name, upon his very being.

Across the coach, huddled in her corner, she was silent, her head bowed, her despondency absolute.

She summoned a shard of courage. It was long in coming. "Please, let me go home."

"No," he said. It came out emphatically.

She drew a breath and wiped her cheek dry with the palm of her hand. "Please. You do not want me here," she whispered. "Let me go. Please..." She was begging.

It was exactly what he had wanted—her absence. Now, it would only advertise his failures. "No."

She had few defences. Against brutality and crudeness, she had none. She did not even know where to begin. She had never needed any before. "Please..." Her voice was soft in the darkness. Would he strike her too? Beat her? And suddenly afraid, and cowering before the thought, she felt new tears welling up. "Please...He was drunk. Even I could see that. Sober, he would never have...Indeed," she said, grasping for some shred of reason. "Indeed, it might have happened to anyone. And I dare say...I dare say in the morning, that young man will not even know how he came by his hurts. So it cannot matter. Not really."

Then she recalled something and her voice hardened slightly—her uncle would have noticed instantly. Myddelton did not. Nor does intelligence render one defenceless. She tried for lightness and failed: "And I dare say in a year, or two—if he survives the war—you may meet with him in your club and even play piquet with him..."

Upon the white silk of her gown there was a smearing of blood.

And crumbling inside, for that instant, dazedly, she regarded it. Blood, come from the back of Myddelton's hand, from his fist, from his grazed knuckles, wiped there by accident. Covering it, she pressed her fingers against it as if it might thus be erased.

"But what of me? I have been called a ladybird…And by a soldier." The unwanted tears trickled down her face and caught at her throat. He could not begin to comprehend her hurt. She drew her arms hard against her chest, her hands against her face, and looked upon the smear until she could bear it no longer, and there was a bleakness in her voice which would have frightened her uncle: "…Just like your horses." Her voice cracked. She began to sob in earnest. He would assuredly beat her. What had her father been about, marrying her to this violent brawling…

Myddelton stared out of the window as if he were ignoring her. He wasn't. But anger and shame had become so intermingled that he no longer knew where one began and the other finished. The rage he felt toward that lobcock of an officer had expanded to include her: that she should dare censure him. He should have called the scrub out. Even though he was a boy. He had called his wife a doxy, a ladybird, and for far less, he should have called the scrub out, and hang Castlereagh and his ban upon duelling. He pulled and loosened the knot of his cravat and swallowed tightly. And wished that he too were drunk.

Finally: "Jane…" S'life, how he hated the forced intimacy of using her name. "I regret that you were witness to such an event as took place…this evening. Please, accept my apology for what must have been a most unpleasant experience." It was not enough. It should have been enough. But he could think of nothing to add. Christ, why had he married her? He fumbled in his pocket for his snuff-box, but could not locate it.

"As you have rightly said, that young officer was drunk as an emperor." He hesitated. "And he never would have behaved like that had he been sober. At least I should bloody well hope not." He ran his tongue over his teeth but it didn't help. "'Struth, I should call him out…"

"What?" She sounded so far away. "Like my father did? He killed your uncle. But it is against the law now."

167

That stung. "I should call him out," Myddelton restated harshly. "My word, I should very much like to! It's no less than he deserves." He stopped, furious that he had admitted as much to her. "But I can't, don't you see? Because, 'fore God, it's forbidden to those of us in Government circles. Castlereagh'd have me on a spit! And it would also be murder since I doubt that *boy* can hit a barn door from the inside. Which would make it a hanging offence," he finished, shaking with the force of his self-loathing and rage.

"No," she agreed distantly. "I do see that." Abject, she said: "It needn't be Britwell Park. I could go to Great Myddelton, couldn't I? Then no one would say..." She was crying again. Silently.

"No."

"As you wish." He could barely hear her.

The coach slowed and stopped. A footman swung open the door and let down the steps. Swiftly and without a backward glance, she alighted and went into the house.

Myddelton, close on her heels, meant to follow her. Then he caught sight of his hand prints, smudged in blood upon the back and side of her white muslin gown, glimpsed too her ashen face as she paused to thank Kettering for something; read the concern on Kettering's face. And sickening, his mind flailing, he lost all heart to pursue the matter.

He watched her as she approached the staircase, stepping past a bowl of roses that had begun to brown at the edges. Watched while she stooped to gather up her cat who had been waiting motionless and solitary on the first step. And noticed there were purple smudges beneath her eyes as if she too had been struck. And felt ill.

"Oh, sod it. Sod everything," he whispered, and shutting himself inside the Library, determined to drink himself insensate.

11

The desk where Lady Anne Northcote wrote her letters was in the morning room, and it was there that she was often to be found, though, as a rule, no callers were admitted before eleven. This was the time she dedicated to reading and correspondence—an exalted description for writing to her sisters and aunts—and she preferred that nothing disturb her. However, this fogbound morning, as she was finishing a letter to her sister-in-law, Kempis intruded upon her quiet, bearing a salver with a card upon it. She read the name on the card and was perplexed. "It is very early for him to be calling, Kempis, don't you think?"

"Yes, my lady," the elderly Kempis said gravely. "But if I may be permitted to say, my lady, his lordship appears to be in a state of considerable agitation."

"Agitation? Does he? How very singular." She sighed and resigned herself to the unavoidable. "You had better show him up, then." She laid aside her pen and closed the standish.

The sound of someone coming up the stairs rapidly and two at a time informed them that there would be no need. Kempis went to the door to open it just as the gentleman was about to enter. "Lord Pemberton, my lady," Kempis announced, then exited and shut the door behind him.

"Pem. My dear." His appearance took her aback, for Kempis was right: Lord Pemberton did not look well. Though he was freshly shaven and a comb of some description had been dragged through his hair, clearly it had not been done by his exacting valet. Yet it was his air of passionate fury which she found more unsettling. "It is very early for you, is it not?" She raised her face so that he might kiss her cheek.

Lord Pemberton rendered the kiss in silence. And, still unspeaking, went to the window, twitched at the curtain and stared out at the mews in a bid to regain his composure. Which failed. Then he began pacing, prowling the room like some wild creature, to the mantel and back, as if he had forgotten her presence altogether.

Her curiosity greatly aroused, Anne watched and waited. That he was in the grip of strong emotion, she perceived, but...

Abruptly, he rounded on her: "Do you know who she is? Do you know? And what he's done? Do you have any idea what that good-for-nought cretin has done?"

There was no disguising the fact that he had caught her off guard. She toyed with the idea of appearing to know precisely to whom he referred, but discarded it. She regarded him warily and shook her head.

"'Struth, how could he? How could he? I tell you I simply cannot comprehend how anyone could be such an unconscionable coxcomb. Or that he could be so infernally buffle-headed that he does not know who she is. Od's my life, I thought I knew him." He was prowling again, his volume rising. "Do you know...do you know he hasn't the veriest grain of simple kindness or proper feeling in his entire body? That he married her and *abandoned* her? *Left* her? Night after night?"

Slowly, Anne shook her head again. With each question, she felt herself growing less wise and cast about in her mind for who, of their mutual acquaintance, could have done all this? Could have behaved so abominably as to have precipitated this exceptional outburst? For Pemberton was not an angry man. Not like some. No, he was affable and amusing, of the most equable temper...

"Did you know that he *rips up at her* for looking after that mouldering barracks of his, when if she did not it would fall about his stupid ears before long? And me..."

The look of contempt and detestation upon his face shocked her. How had he become embroiled in this, whatever it was? For she could make sense of none of it.

"How could I have stood by and done *nothing*? 'Struth, do you know I waited up until five this morning for him, expecting him to turn up and ask me to second him?" He rested his elbow on the mantel, briefly covering his eyes with his hand, then added in a voice rich in repugnance: "Dash it all, I would have seconded him when she was the one who was grossly insulted. I would have seconded that rag-mannered, care-for-nothing brute! I should shoot him for this. I really should. *I* ought to call him out. And if m'grandfather ever comes to hear of it—or her uncle—they *will* call him out. If they don't suffer apoplexy first." He ought never to have mentioned this to her. Manners, honour, society, all forbade it. But something had snapped in him, and the emotion that was washing over and through him had rendered him oblivious or uncaring of those niceties which before he had observed so punctiliously.

Anne had begun to feel headachy and alarmed. She did not like scenes. She did not liked being yelled at. Even as now when it was clearly not directed at her. And she did not like violence either. She wished Miles were home. She broke in: "Pem. Dearest...Perhaps you might sit down in that nice chair over there and tell me about this, calmly, rather than pacing about the room and making threats which I can neither condone nor comprehend."

In surprise, Pemberton looked at her. As if he had only just realised where he was. And went and flung himself into the nice chair.

"Thank you." She pressed her fingers to her temple. "Forgive me for being so stupid, dearest, but...what is this about?"

He blinked rapidly. "Myddelton. Of course."

"Myddelton," she echoed. "My cousin, Myddelton." She paused, no wiser. Instead it had added to her absolute confusion. "And," she hesitated, wondering if she dared to ask her next question or whether that would merely inflame his rage. "And, dearest, forgive me, but what is it exactly that he is meant to have done?"

"What? Do you mean you don't know?" he exclaimed, off again. "Can it be that you really don't know? You do not know who she is? Whom he has married?"

"I read the announcement in the paper, only..."

"Janey Heron. Miss Jane Heron, of Britwell Park."

"Ah," she said, as if all had been made plain. Only it hadn't. "Should I know her? Have I met her?" Then, with growing dismay: "Do you know her?"

Pemberton expelled a great breath and rolled his eyes. "Know her? 'Struth, I've known her all her life. *She* was the girl I told you about. The one m'grandfather Choate wanted me to marry." Any remaining vestige of calm was destroyed.

Anne looked stunned. "She is? Oh my dear. Oh, this is too awful. When did you discover…"

"Yesterday," he said bleakly, trying to compose himself, though her ignorance had temporarily, briefly, deflated his passion. "I discovered yesterday. At Vauxhall…You see, I met up with Myddelton at White's and told him what I'd heard, that there had been some talk because although we'd roasted him about getting spliced, no one had seen the bride."

"Yes?"

"He got a bit shirty, but eventually agreed to show her about a bit and said he'd take her to Vauxhall for the evening. So I toddled along to Vauxhall…"

"Yes?"

"And then I saw her. Upon my life, I couldn't believe my eyes. 'Struth, I didn't know what to say." He shook his head, almost as if he were on the point of tears. "She'd been sitting alone. Myddelton had gone off in search of champagne. And he was dashed amazed to return and find me there with her…" Pemberton frowned and eyed the reflection in his boot. "But we got over the initial awkwardness of Myddelton finding me talking to her…And my amazement that my cousin, Toby James, had married 'em, with never a word to me…And we was strolling down the Lilac Walk. And up comes this baby of an officer. You know the sort of thing—parents nagged into purchasing a pair of colours, and what's a little white lie about his age…"

"Yes, I know." Her disapproval was patent. "What happened?"

Pemberton looked miserable and savage at once. "Well, the boy was three sheets to the wind. Lord knows how much rack punch he'd had. And he comes stumbling down the Lilac Walk and sort of falls into Myddelton…"

"Yes?" Anne could feel a nagging consternation growing in the depths of her stomach.

Pemberton drew a deep breath and exhaled. "So he apologised. Profusely. And then he noticed Janey, and took her for a..." He could sit no longer. He rose abruptly from his chair and strode to the window. Outside, the fog still had not lifted. He drew another deep breath. It did not improve matters.

"Yes?"

"'Sdeath, he took her for...for a...ladybird." He could hardly bear to have the word in his mouth.

"What?"

Pemberton appeared not to have heard. He was reliving his dismay. "And a piece. And started blabbing about sampling her charms..."

"Dear Heaven. What did Myddelton do?" Anne demanded, anticipating the worst.

"Went mad. Went absolutely mad. Janey just froze. You see, one minute, Myddelton and I was just standing there, listening to this...drunken lout...and the next minute, Myddelton had him by the collar and was punching his daylights out. But not before the scrub had insulted her in every way possible.

"'Struth, I hardly knew what to do. I tried to separate them. But even so, Myddelton broke the lad's nose. There was blood all over. And then the stupid boy shot the cat all over his regimentals. And there she stood, as if she'd been turned to marble, clutching her hands to her cheeks with this look of horror on her face. And all the time, this drunken ensign was shouting obscenities, tellin' her...Your pardon, I shan't repeat what he said." He paused, so unhappy that he could not imagine how he might contain it.

"Finally I told Myddelton to get her away. So he did. But not the way he should have done. Not at all as he should have done. 'Struth, he just dragged her off as if she was a...a...And left me to sort things out...It was all too much. He'd been behaving all along as though she's nobody, as though...D'you know, when I first saw her, she was sitting alone, while he'd gone off to fetch champagne." He had begun pacing again. Anne did not try to stop him. "He left her alone in that place. Upon my life, what if that officer had come up then? Or a whole gaggle of them? And the things he said! I should never speak to anyone like that…"

"I see."

"To be sure, he was right to get her away, I do see that, but not in that way. Not dragging her off. Had you seen her face, Anne, her angelic little face…" He broke off. Honesty had riven the dam of his reserve and it was now well and truly breached. "I thought he'd be 'round later, don't you know, wanting me to second him. But he never turned up. Her uncle…her uncle will kill him if he ever finds out."

Anne drew a deep breath and said with finality, "Then you must make sure he never does."

Pemberton looked obstinate. "Dash it all, Anne, I thought Myddelton could be trusted." He rolled his eyes. "I didn't know what to do for the best. 'Pon my soul, I did not. Eventually, I went off in search of one of the Park attendants and told him that this scrub couldn't carry his liquor and had insulted a peer of the realm and his wife. 'Struth, Anne, I thought Myddelton could be trusted to look after her, whoever she was. But now, I don't even know…"

"No," she agreed. "And after this, will she want his looking after?"

"Upon my soul, I would lay down my life for that girl. She is the most," he paused, searching his mind for the word. "Upon my soul, she is the most perfect creature I ever knew. And I would lay down my life for her. And if Myddelton don't…if Myddelton don't…" He could not formulate the thought. "Cousin or no cousin, Anne, I shall call him out!" Then after a moment's pause, he added, "Forgive me. I should never have said that."

She bit her lips together and nodded. His story had distressed her beyond words. And she did not doubt that he meant this last. Measuredly, she asked: "But where would you go after that?" It was not an idle question. Pemberton, amusing, affable, equable Pemberton, was among the finest marksmen in England. If he called her cousin out, he would do so in order to free his childhood friend from a detested husband, and he would not miss his mark.

Levelly—for he had in some detached way thought it all through—he said, "America. Perhaps. Or I could always join Wellington's little mob, and shoot Frenchies in Spain."

She placed her fingers against her lips in unhappy contemplation and thought and did not think. "I had planned to call there this afternoon. But perhaps, perhaps it might be better if I went now. What do you think? Are you all right?"

Relieved, unburdened, still unhappy, Pemberton smiled blearily. "A bit groggy. But that'll mend."

She nodded. "I shall go around there now then."

He strode over and took her hand and held it. "Do something for her, will you? Anything. Look after her, Anne. You must look after her. Please?"

She nodded. Like her husband, she thought Pemberton the best of the Choate horde. And she did not like the idea of him living so far away, in America. Or dead, on some mountainside in Spain. "I shall do what I can."

"Bless you, Anne." He kissed her hand. "Bless you."

Myddelton pushed away his plate of half-eaten gammon and eggs then took a long drink of ale. He did not have a hangover. Nor had he drunk himself legless. Instead, he had ended up as he always did, measuring out the hours with glasses of brandy and pots of coffee, while he pitted his wits against the Grand Chiffre, struggling to break it down. And later, too, as he sorted through the files on the much disputed Orders in Council—on which the Prime Minister urgently required a full report, as the Commons debate on them was scheduled for Monday. Until first light, when at last he made his way upstairs to bed. Still, it was better than thinking. And far better than reliving the infernal balls-up he'd made of the evening, damning by damnable minute. Though it did nothing to resolve or mitigate the now-surfaced tensions. Nor did it dispel the air of veiled malaise in the house. Though he had never before experienced malaise in his household, veiled or otherwise, he found he disliked it intensely. Particularly at breakfast.

He took another long drink of ale and pondered his now emptied tankard. He should speak to her before he left for Lombard Street. And say what? What could he say that would begin to repair the sorry mess he had made of things and this present...what? Buggeration? 'Struth, if there was a word to describe this peculiar variety of self-induced domestic disaster, he didn't know it. He pressed the heels of his hands against his eyes. "Lady Myddelton, is she upstairs, Kettering?"

"Yes, my lord." Kettering checked the sideboard for her teacup and saucer. They were there and ready. "Did you wish me to call her for you?"

"No. I'll go m'self, thank you."

Unhappy with the thought of Myddelton going up to her, Kettering followed him into the foyer. Though no one had furnished him with the details, he had a very clear idea of what had occurred at Vauxhall Gardens. He had not been the de facto head of three households for twenty years without learning something of how young women reacted when they had been assaulted. It had been he who had ordered the heating of the dozen cans of hot water at that ungodly hour so that Haseley might bathe her. He who—when Haseley had insisted that *she* wouldn't drink the recommended brandy, *she* did not like it—had prepared her tea, himself, and brought it up to her after Haseley had put her to bed. Concerned, Kettering watched Myddelton start up the staircase and would have followed him, but the door knocker went. Scowling, he went to answer it.

"Good morning, Kettering. Is my cousin at home?" Lady Anne stepped into the hall and looked briskly about her. "My word, you have been busy with the painters, haven't you? It looks very well in here. Very well, indeed. It must do your heart good to have it looking so splendid again."

Kettering liked Lady Anne Northcote. Though it was not his place to say so. Or even to hold an opinion. "Yes, my lady. Thank you, my lady. If you will follow me to the Library, I shall see if his lordship is in."

"Of course."

Upstairs, Myddelton had knocked on the door to *her* sitting room and upon hearing her muffled 'Come...' had entered. She was seated by the window, with her dog and her cat, playing chess. The white king was in check.

Myddelton could not know that she had been playing herself to a

176

draw since first light—it made thinking easier: To go? Or to stay? If she went, would he come after her?

She appeared pale and drawn—her fatigued silence a rebuke—and starkly virginal in white tamboured muslin, yet still exquisite, apparently unmoved and untouched by anything that might or might not have happened. And now that he was here, Myddelton was sure he did not know what to say to her or even if he should have come.

She remained silent, and her deep reserve made her appear composed, though she knew she was not.

"I thought you would wish to know…I wrote to your uncle to ask him to send your horse down. Patroklos. So that you could ride in the Park."

"Thank you." As if she would care to ride in the Park. He did not mean to let her go then. Did it matter? Chattel. She would not cry. To save herself that exposure, that embarrassment, she studied the chessboard, considering how and if the white king might be saved. Or was his case hopeless?

The moments stretched out like a unrolling carpet between them. The mantel clock ticked. Noisily and relentlessly. Myddelton began to wish he had not come, though he knew, with the certainty of death and taxes, that an abject apology was requisite. But how to frame the words for behaviour so shameful, so appalling that he could not comprehend how it had come to pass? Or how he had become embroiled in it? How could he have behaved in such an odious fashion, that any civilised observer passing judgment must assuredly say the fellow who acted like that deserved to be whipped?

"My lord," Kettering said quietly from behind.

Kettering, the welcome interruption.

"…Lady Anne Northcote has called to see you. I have put her in the Library."

A reprieve. Praise God! "I shall be down in a moment." To Jane: "Excuse me." He bowed and thankfully left her.

When Myddelton entered the Library (once his private sanctum, but no longer), Anne was peering knowledgeably at the music on the fortepiano.

"Anne." He came across and kissed her.

"Myddelton." She chose a sofa, sat down and began drawing off her gloves. She was prepared to be patient.

"What a delightful surprise. Have you come to..."

"I have called to meet your bride," she said facilely.

"Ah. My bride."

"Of course. As your cousin, I am eager to make her acquaintance. I am certain I shall love her as a sister."

There was something about the clearness of her eyes, some hint of knowledge, which disturbed him. But how could she know? Or, contrariwise, how did one begin to tell what had happened? There was no way to wrap it up in clean linen. "Ehm. Yes. I am not at all certain...That is to say, ehm, I do not know that..." He felt his collar growing tight and hot. Perhaps honesty was the only course open to him. "The thing is, Anne...I, ehm, took her to Vauxhall last evening and..."

"Yes. I know."

"What? How can you know?" Good God, it was out already. Who had been there and seen them? Christ!

She was determined not to become shrill. And wished that she had even half of her grandmother's air of consequence. She looked him full in the face. "Pem was 'round, this morning, to tell me."

Momentarily distracted: "What? This morning? Pem?" Myddelton glanced at the mantel clock to reassure himself. "'Struth, it ain't even eleven."

"This morning," she repeated.

"Then you know what happened."

"Yes," she affirmed. She was not going to make it easy for him.

"She wants to go to the country. Home or to Great Myddelton."

"I do not blame her."

He did not like her answer. Did not like the clarity of her gaze upon him either. "I was meaning to spend the morning here." But would he have spent it with her? Undoubtedly not. Though he knew he should. "But Castlereagh needs me to prepare a report for the Prime Minister..."

"Of course he does." She knew about Ministers and Parliament. They always required fullest attention at the moment a domestic crisis was to be resolved. She said easily, "On the Orders in Council? Yes, Miles told me that he believes they will be repealed soon. Perhaps then war may be averted.

"Have you apologised to her yet? I can see from the expression on your face that you have not." She refused to be daunted by the fact that he had turned from her.

"No, I have not," he admitted finally.

"Avery, this is a most appalling mess you have landed yourself in. I trust you understand that much at least. You have treated a gently-reared girl with all the civility normally reserved for a fishwife. Or a doxy." She paused to choose her next words. "As I understand it, last night, you took her to Vauxhall—hardly the wisest choice—and once there, you behaved with all the courtesy of an illiterate tenant farmer with a jealous temper and a fondness for drink. Or perhaps I am being unjust to tenant farmers. But the result of this extraordinary and disgraceful breach of manners is that if you do not mend your ways, and mend them quickly, you will find yourself laid out on a field some dawn with your brains shot out. And I do not exaggerate."

"What?"

"Good gracious, who did you think this girl was? What maggot did you take into your foolish head that you thought that normal standards of propriety did not apply to you? What madness overcame you? Were you aware that none other than Lord Choate had sought the hand of this girl for his grandson and heir? And you may be sure that if Choate was trying to contract a marriage there, that her family, her reputation, her breeding, and her fortune are so far superior to ours as to make us appear entirely insignificant…"

"For Pem?" He turned to face her.

"For Pem," she confirmed.

"Good God!" And turned away again.

"And his attachment to her is longstanding. He is beside himself with grief and rage. Grief, that one so dear to him has been so shamefully used—berated for her efforts to restore your house and fortune…have I got that right? And rage that you, his closest friend and companion of all these years, should have brought such misery upon her." She could not see, but she could feel his dejection, and continued: "You have been married to her for less than a fortnight and already you have brought yourself and her to the brink of ruin. Avery, this marriage is not some schoolboy's lark, you know."

He spun about to confront her. "Do you think I do not know it? Dear God, it confronts me each morning and every night, whichever way I turn. Every time I go into a room in this house that I was used to avoid because of the rotting walls and the unmatched sticks of furniture—you should see the Drawing Room—and now, it's ordered and beautiful and clean, and it's as it was in my mother's day. 'Struth, do you think I don't know that Kettering now serves her, not me? Do you think I am somehow unaware that I hardly know what she looks like or that I haven't spoken above five words to her since the day we married? But every time I turn around these days, there's Planta with another pile of translations or another report to be written, and some soldier's life depends on me getting that information translated into English and into Castlereagh or Liverpool's hands as soon as I can. But last night, last night, I swear to you, Anne, I was trying to make amends." He stopped to contemplate for a moment the snuffbox in his hand, then returned it to his pocket. "But I don't know what happened. How can I explain? I, obviously, was not...No, let me begin again...I acknowledge that I have behaved abominably. Indeed, I acknowledge all that you say. But, 'struth, Anne, the fact is that until a fortnight ago, I had never even heard of her." He came and sat down near her. "But you must believe me when I tell you that I had intended to mend all that. You must believe me. And when I saw her last night, standing with Pem, I believe I saw her for the first time. But then this young ensign came upon us, and I..."

Anne saw the despair on his face and wished very much to comfort him, but would not. "...set to like a publican in an ale-house brawl?" she snapped.

Myddelton flashed her an angry look. "No!" Then fighting back his temper, he tried again: "Yes. You see, I didn't think...that is, I have never been there with anyone that I...that is to say, I have only ever been to Vauxhall..."

"With Ianthe Dacre," Anne said drily.

"How can you know about her?"

"Myddelton, everyone knows about her. Infants in swaddling clothes know about her. We're not stupid."

"Ah…" He still had the grace to feel embarrassed, and to his cousin's relief, turned a shade pink. He drew himself together. "Well…well, then you will understand how I might not have been prepared to escort a gently-bred girl, which is what Jane is, about Vauxhall. Nor was I, in any way, prepared for the jealousy and rage which came over me when that officer insulted her. I had assumed, wrongly as it now appears, that my marriage had changed nothing, and that I was completely indifferent to her."

"And so you punched his daylights out, as Pem so delicately phrased it."

"Yes."

"And exposed a gently-reared girl to prize-fight violence and then dragged her away as if she were a misbehaved schoolboy when she failed to appreciate your pugilistic prowess. And left your closest friend to sort out the young officer, and once he had done that, to wait in his rooms for you to arrive and request that he should second you in a duel against this officer."

He sat dully silent for a long moment as the unpleasant honesty of her account settled over him. "Yes."

"How edifying. Were you drunk?"

"No," he said bitterly. "No, I cannot even claim that excuse."

She made no effort to mitigate the effect of her carefully chosen words.

"I shall have to apologise to Pem."

"That would seem wise."

"And to her."

"That would appear equally wise."

"What if she still wishes to leave?"

"Then you must convince her, by your exquisite courtesy, your tenderness, your unfailing concern, that your previous behaviour has been an aberration."

"Will you…will you talk to her? Add your weight to my efforts?"

She stiffened her jaw. She ought to let him reap what he had sown. But he had never requested her help in anything before. Not really. Not in anything that mattered. "Only if you go and apologise now. And leave her in no doubt that such gross misconduct will never ever recur."

He eyed her levelly. Since they were children, she had not minced her words. He opened his snuff-box and took a took a few grains. And sneezed. "Yes. All right. And then…Ehm, shall I fetch her down to you?"

"Please."

He did not bound up the stairs as had been his wont. But felt something of that nagging unease he had known as a young scholar on his way to the proctor for a wigging when those bawdy Latin verses had been discovered. And with each step he tried to compose his apology, but reaching her door, felt no more fluent than when he had started.

Without knocking, he went in and found she was standing still, pondering her chessboard, sombre. Few white pieces remained; the black queen, bishop and king were on the offence; the white king was still in check, his position all but lost. Myddelton's presence seemed not to affect her.

"Madam."

She rested her faded blue gaze upon him. Her fear had become so overwhelming that it now appeared as courage or stoicism.

He came and stood before her. "Jane." His voice lost the tightness. He took her hand, and repeating his cousin's choice of words, continued: "I owe you the most abject of apologies."

She looked down on her hand in his, then up into his face and saw honesty there, and nearly cried.

"I am so deeply sorry, and so heartily ashamed…I behaved abominably and disgracefully. But I give you my word, I shall never behave so again. Never."

In all her life, she had never been able to view the suffering of another creature with equanimity. She could not begin now. Involuntarily, her eyes full of tears, she reached up to brush the words from his lips, resting her fingers upon his mouth as briefly as thistledown on the wind. And he could remember no one else who had touched him with such gentleness. And he recalled to his further shame the arrogance of his proposal to her.

"It is forgot," she whispered.

His breath came in a short gasp, and he bowed over her hand to hide his dismay at her kindness. "Thank you." There was no mockery in his gaze when he straightened. He had never been so honest with another creature before. Nor received such compassion in return. He should have taken her into his arms, but he did not know how to. "We have a caller. Someone I believe you will like. A cousin. Come and meet her."

She decided that whoever the visitor was, she had a beneficial effect upon him. "Yes. Of course." But, still fragile, wished she need not meet her. She paused, surprisingly, to take the black bishop with the white queen. The king was in check no longer. And followed Myddelton to the Library.

Jane gained a brief impression of a slender woman with dark hair, exquisitely gowned, who upon hearing her name, turned, her expression radiating delight. Jane performed her curtsy.

"Oh Myddelton, she is lovely!" Then, with a wry smile for her cousin: "Far more so than you deserve."

He smiled awkwardly. Definitely, a beneficial effect.

Advancing toward Jane with her hands held out in welcome, she said, "My dear, I am Anne Northcote. How happy I am to meet you at last." She embraced her and kissed her on both cheeks, reminding her of Mlle.

Ruthlessly Jane quashed an impulse to cry.

"I have so been looking forward to making your acquaintance. Now Myddelton, do go away. I am convinced that Castlereagh was expecting you hours ago. And one must never keep a Minister of State waiting, I'm sure."

He smiled and bowed. "My dear. Anne." A beneficent effect, even. Might this be a truer measure of his character than...

Jane found her voice as he closed the door. "Will you not be seated, ma'am?"

Anne turned and surveyed the room. "Thank you. Yes." She chose a small sofa. "I see you have had the painters in. I applaud you for it. Myddelton's mama died so long ago, you know, and I am perfectly positive nothing has been done since then. It must have been dreadful."

Jane seated herself a polite distance away. "No. Not dreadful. Tired perhaps. But scrupulously clean. And the staff is excellent."

Anne smiled. The wall of reserve was higher than Pemberton could have anticipated. He should have warned her—but how could he know, never having seen it?—what a wall of reserve exquisite breeding and intelligence might build? "Still, I should imagine your work was cut out for you." She paused, then said, "I cannot tell you how pleased I am to make your acquaintance and to find you thus. One always wishes the best for one's friends and favourite relations and if they do not find it, one is invariably disheartened.

"But tell me, how are you adjusting to Town life?"

"I have had little experience of it. Still, I believe I shall soon return to the country."

An impenetrable wall, perhaps? Anne rose and crossed to the sofa where Jane was seated. "My dear, please, do not run from him." She sat down, hesitated, then, risking all, said, "Pem told me what occurred last night…" She watched the shadow fall over the young Lady Myddelton's features, the hurt now unmasked in her eyes. "I make no doubt you must be feeling shocked and dismayed, and perhaps only time will ease that. I do not know. I only ask that you will not judge Myddelton on the basis of that one encounter. Young men such as insulted you last evening are not among those you would find at most places, I do assure you. I should not speak ill of Myddelton—he is my cousin and I hold him in the greatest affection—but had he done the thing properly and introduced you as he ought, this would not have happened."

Jane stared down at her hands, folded neatly as ever in her lap.

"Please stay. At least give him the opportunity to redeem himself. If you leave now, it will only prove harder for you both. He needs you to stay." It was an impassioned plea.

Jane looked up at her, surprised, disliking the conflict she now felt. "I very much doubt that." Her chin quavered but there were no tears. Then, giving way to a confidence she would have withheld: "Certainly he cares for his good name—as does any gentleman—so he will wish me to remain until he is convinced that no lasting damage has been done. But that is all."

Anne paused, afraid in her heart that the young Countess was right. She nearly wept herself. "Yes. That is so. But you know, gentlemen do require affection. Every bit as much as we do. Hunting, gaming, their clubs..." She spread her hands helplessly. "These are their diversions, but are rarely enough to satisfy. I have known Myddelton all my life. I know he is as devoted to his friends as anyone, and I know he worshipped his mama as did his father. And that he did not recover lightly from her death. So I believe that he has a great capacity for affection."

Silently, Jane had begun to weep. And though she hardly dared do so, gently, Anne put her arm about her shoulders.

"For years I had hoped to see him married that he might have a centre for this undoubted capacity. But he has not appeared even vaguely interested. I cannot blame him. He has far too many points against him. No, do not look surprised. He is titled, wealthy and...not unhandsome. Until that announcement appeared, he was considered amongst the greatest of catches. Little wonder that he chose the safe confines of the Foreign Office over the dangers of society gatherings and match-making females. So please, do not leave. He needs you to stay."

"I wish I could believe that."

"Truly, do you doubt it?" Suddenly, Anne laughed, dispelling tension. "I believe, from what he has said to me, that he wants you to stay."

Jane continued to appear unconvinced. "You are very kind."

"No, I am not. I only wish I were. Now. Tomorrow evening I am holding a small rout. Say that you and Myddelton will come. Because you know, staying at home, by yourself, your feelings will only prey upon you, and that cannot be good."

"No. That is...no. I do see that." Jane dried her face. "But as to your kind invitation, I must refuse, at least for myself. It is as I told Myddelton when I tried to refuse him his invitation, last evening..." She glanced up at the ceiling, searching for words, struggling to regain her self-possession. Why was it that trifles, mere nothings, reduced one to the point of tears? "I have no gowns suitable!" she cried, now angry with herself. "Not for my position as his wife, as a countess. I know I must sound like some stupid, stupid creature, but it is perfectly true. I have the best of everything. I always have had—for an unmarried girl in the country, but not...and I am persuaded that is why I was mistaken for a..."

"Now that is quite enough of that!" Anne declared firmly, rather as if she had been speaking to her eldest and most adventurous son. "Come. We shall visit the dressmakers instantly. It will do you good. Give you something to distract your thoughts...And as for Myddelton...Have no fear!" She smoothed her glove and her eyes narrowed. "I shall send my husband after him, and he too shall come. Now, go and fetch a bonnet and gloves while I admire the fortepiano."

"Miles," called his wife as she fussed with the pillows behind her head. It was well past two in the morning. She had not seen him all day. Or evening. Only in the last quarter hour had she heard his tread on the floorboards outside her door and the familiar rattle and slide of his wardrobe doors as he changed his clothes in the next room.

Northcote appeared in the doorway which connected their bedchambers, his dressing gown hanging open over his nightshirt. "Yes m'dear? Very fetching nightcap you have there." A tender smile lit his eyes. "What is it you have on your mind?"

Anne smiled at his unerring faculty of perception, then frowned. "I disobeyed you today. I interfered in a marriage."

Miles frowned in mock sobriety. "This sounds truly terrifying." She watched as he snuffed out the candles in the sconce by the fireplace, then settled in the seat by her dressing table. "Tell all."

"Well Pem came 'round this morning..." she began.

"I've spoken to Pem today, yes. What did he have to say? Anything of import?"

"At his request, I went to see Myddelton and his bride."

A smile appeared on Sir Miles' modestly good-looking face. "Did

186

you, by Jove? Splendid! Nice girl, is she?"

"Miles, you are not taking this as you ought!" Anne complained. "I tell you I've interfered against your strictest dictum and you settle down for a comfortable coze and cheerfully ask, 'Nice girl, is she?'"

"Truly unforgivable, I admit. My sincere apologies, m'dear. I promise to behave...Now, where were we?" His expression had grown serious though his eyes were still merry. "Ah yes, you were confessing that you had paid a morning call upon Myddelton and his bride because Pem had come 'round breathing fire and it seemed the best solution at the time. Do go on."

"Then you know already!" she exclaimed. "And here you've let me ramble on like some overdramatic peagoose." Then, she admitted frankly: "She is perfectly lovely. Only Myddelton," she began, then broke off. "How do you know all this?"

"I told you I've spoken to Pem as well today. Or perhaps I should say I listened to Pem, as well, today."

"And was he still breathing fire when you saw him?" she asked.

"Oh yes," Miles reassured her. "He was suitably incandescent on the subject of Myddelton and his rag-mannered treatment of his bride. He was also concerned lest his visit to you and your subsequent visit to Myddelton House might have caused a rift between us." Miles rose from the chair and removed his dressing gown. His nightshirt was without the usual adornments of lace or ruffles. "I told him, 'Nothing of the sort'. Do you care for some company tonight?"

For answer, Anne smiled seraphically and moved to the centre of the bed, then threw back the quilt. Miles climbed in beside his wife and kissed her gently.

"You're not cross?" she asked softly.

"Good lord, no." Miles leaned back against the pillows and thought. "Your cousin Myddelton has got himself into a fine mess," he said in his measured way. "Acting as he has. This girl he has married is not without protection. As Pem tells it, the young lady is looked upon as one of the family by Lord and Lady Choate. And her uncle, Sir Charles Heron, is their nearest neighbour and dear friend. One can only assume that they belong to the Choate inner circle. Their closest friends include

Portland...Liverpool...and the Prime Minister, you know. Should she return home to her uncle, Myddelton may well find himself at the centre of sexual scandal that will ruin any hope of a political career he may have. What people do not know, they invent. His speeches to his peers will be used as opportunities for harassment of the most scurrilous nature, I do assure you. And Heaven only knows what the cartoonists will make of it—with old Rowlandson leading the pack."

"I see." Anne bit her lip. "I hadn't thought that far ahead. I only thought..."

"No. Quite. It could prove very unpleasant. Still, tell me what you have accomplished." He regarded her fondly.

"The rout we're holding...tomorrow evening. Tonight," she said between kisses. "I have invited her. And Myddelton, of course. But she believes he shan't come."

"Why wouldn't he come?"

"Miles," she reproved. "How often do you see Myddelton at a private function? Or with his fingers unstained from working all hours at the Foreign Office? Nor has her previous experience been such as to encourage her in the belief that he will lift a finger for her," Anne declared acidly. "Even though he has promised to behave. But you know how it is—he'll bury himself at the Foreign Office or hole up with whatever committee he's got himself appointed to or he'll be working away and forget the time or... Lud, I don't know."

"I take your point," her husband conceded and kissed her hand. "But you have invited the Castlereaghs, have you not? And they have accepted? And Liverpool? And he has accepted? Myddelton'll come."

"I shall murder him if he does not."

Miles smiled. "I shall warn him."

"Miles," Anne added, determined to keep nothing back. "I also took her shopping."

"Good. Excellent," Miles approved. "Now, are you genuinely partial to the light of this candle or do you agree it is a superfluity without which we could do quite nicely?"

But madest my sprite live my care to renew,
My body in tempest her succor to embrace.

12

Every candle in her dressing room was lit. Resolutely Jane stood before the looking glass. Frowning, she turned this way. And that. Inspecting every inch of herself in the dense, warm light, head to toe, cap-à-pie, as if she were both her father and his troops. For tonight, she must be parade perfect. Nothing less would do.

Anne had insisted they visit the shop of a French dressmaker—a Madame Fanchon's—who could be relied upon for exquisite taste and for speed, both of which were of the essence. The modiste—all shrewd dark eyes and pomaded black curls beneath an ornate lace cap—had treated Madame la Comtesse with all due deference and wasted no time. She ushered them to a private salon fitted out in the French manner. Then she had produced this gown of palest blue silk, trimmed with Brussels lace and seed pearls and slashed elbow-length sleeves. But yes, certainement it would be ready for Madame la Comtesse by the next afternoon. She, Fanchon, had said it. And what else did Madame require in the way of gowns? For walking in the Park? For the morning? Pour le soir?

Jane turned again to face the long mirror. She pressed at her bodice neckline. The silk of her petticoat and gown slipped and whispered about her waist and legs. Encircling her throat, almost as an amulet, was her mama's diamond and pearl necklace.

Yet was it enough? For tonight, she must be as her Uncle expected and Mlle had trained her; tonight, for her introduction to Society, her first appearance as Myddelton's bride, she must be *perfect*.

Or was it too much? Most brides in her position had at least the benefit of one Season's experience behind them. That which was pardonable in a debutante would be inexcusable in one of her new station.

She bit at her bottom lip. Was it enough? Meticulously she studied the gown, her jewels, the pearl strands woven into her hair, the rosettes on her slippers once more. Was it perfect? Or would she be marked out as a thrusting heiress, moneyed and underbred? Lud, who could tell what the spiteful old cats would think? She sighed. At least she was unlikely to be mistaken for Myddelton's mistress.

She pinched her cheeks and began to draw on her long gloves. And smiled. And in that instant, she hardly knew why, she felt a bubble of elusive and effervescent confidence buoying her up, lifting her spirits, and banishing the spectre of nervous anticipation and dread, the residue of her evening at Vauxhall.

"I shall have my cloak now, Haseley."

It was to be expected that she was ready before he was. So, patiently, equably, she stood by the fortepiano, perusing the pages of music as she waited, humming this bar, fingering that—she had, after all, been raised by a bachelor uncle who habitually mislaid his black kneebreeches whenever they were meant to attend an assembly in Oxford.

"Ah, there you are," Myddelton said as he came through from the hall. And halted just inside the room to bow to her, presenting himself as her escort. "Forgive me for being so late." The peal Anne had rung over his head was sounding still, reverberating and echoing, and he was determined to fulfil his promise to the letter. To her and to Anne.

She looked up at the sound of his voice. And did not add, 'It is of no matter,' for at the sight of him, as he bowed—his hair still damp from the bath—her voice stuck in her throat. And for that moment, she faltered, his elegance in his evening clothes, his physical presence near overpowering her, his easy polish a stark contrast to her uncertainties.

He reached into his pocket to assure himself of his snuff-box and gave her an appraising glance. She did not recognise a glint of approval in his eyes. He smiled. Then, after a little thought, he added: "I, ehm, trust you ain't damped your petticoats under that cloak of yours..." Already he was certain of the answer.

"I beg your pardon?" she said. Why was he asking her such a thing?

"I should say not," she answered lightly. "Mademoiselle would never have countenanced such a thing."

Mischief danced in his eyes. Mischief...or was he suffering from a sudden pride of possession? "A sound woman, your Mademoiselle. It's one thing I disapprove of—dampened petticoats, that is...You'd catch your death. Shall we be off?"

Myddelton himself assisted her into the town carriage. "I apologise for keeping you waiting," he said again. He settled in his seat and drew out the ubiquitous snuff-box. "I had meant to get away hours earlier, but every time I got to the bottom of one file of translations, Castlereagh'd send in another..."

"Is that what you do for the Foreign Office? Translations?" That, she had never suspected. He had spoken of the Foreign Office once before, only she'd had little idea of what he had meant. But translations?

"Mostly. Yes," he said carelessly. He stretched out his legs. "French, obviously. German. Some Italian, Spanish, and a bit of Portuguese." He omitted the cypher work. Nor did he specify what it was he translated.

Little wonder he was never to home. "Sir Charles said you were a learned man..."

"Did he?" Myddelton asked in real amazement. "'Struth, I gained the distinct impression that he thought me a jumped up dissolute with little breeding and less manners."

She chuckled, enjoying this avuncular view of Myddelton. "Did you?" And chuckled again. "Well he would hardly have said as much to me, you know, even if he did think it..."

He narrowed his eyes, enjoying her smiles. "Was that kind remark intended to reassure me? Because if it was, I feel I should tell you, it failed miserably."

Her low chortle comforted him even less. "I do assure you, Sir Charles said nothing to your discredit. Ever. Upon my honour."

He glanced sideways at her. She was smiling. "'Struth, he may have said nothing to my discredit, but his looks spoke volumes."

This was too much. She laughed. "My uncle wouldn't know how to give a black look if his life depended on it!"

"Ha! 'Struth, if that's what you think, my girl, you've been sadly misguided." The carriage lurched in and out of a small lake disguised as a pothole left by workmen. "Still, tomorrow, when I'm sitting in my crabby little office translating letters from some overwrought Spanish hidalgo, I dare say I shall find it comforting…"

She sobered and was quiet for a moment as she digested this. "I did not know you had a crabby little office…"

"Yes. Upon my word, it's perfectly dismal. But then, the whole Foreign Office is. 'Struth, we get flooded out every time it rains."

"Do you? Ugh." Her compassion surprised him.

Myddelton smiled, suddenly relaxed. "Very nearly. Which is why, occasionally, I'm forced to bring the lot of it home."

The carriage swayed as it was negotiated around the corner, and slowed, coming to a halt in front of the Northcote residence. And again, it was Myddelton who assisted her down the steps. Odd of him. "You'll not be bothered by all the quizzes who will have come to look at you, will you?" He meant it kindly. She was, after all, from a tiny hamlet in Oxfordshire.

"No," she affirmed. "I shouldn't think so." She smiled, her composure immutable now that they had arrived. This was, after all, what she had been trained for.

Puzzled, he paused to consider the novelty of this less-than-diffident aspect of her nature, then followed her up the red carpet which had been rolled out over the front steps and onto the pavement. If one hadn't known better, one would have thought it was *she* who had the years of town bronze which gave such countenance.

Unaware of Myddelton's incipient confusion, she allowed him to help her off with her cloak. Now, without the camouflaging garment, he looked her over again. She did not see the appreciation kindle in his eyes. He was too astounded to know it was there. "Confound it, you might have warned me," he murmured, the merest shadow of a self-mocking smile softening the corners of his mouth. How could she, this merest slip of a girl, suddenly appear looking like that? Elegant. Beautiful. No, ravishing. But how? And when? Dear God!

Jane looked up. "I beg your pardon? Warned you?" Surely…surely, that was never admiration in his gaze. His smile was an enigma. It would be pleasant to be admired by a gentleman like him…

His breath had shortened and something else again was clutching at his diaphragm. He placed his hand at the small of her back to propel her toward the staircase. "You ain't damped your petticoats, but by Jove, those who have this evening will find their efforts have been wasted."

She treated him to a quizzical look over her shoulder. Had he really thought her *such* an antidote? Apparently. How lowering. Never mind. She glanced at the ceiling—by Adam or was it Wyatt's work? And then Pemberton, dear Pemberton, was rushing down the stairs to greet her.

"Janey." Pemberton took her hand, kissed it and tucked it through his arm. "You look divine…'Evening Myddelton." Myddelton's apology to him had been sincere, succinct, and accepted. "Now, don't dawdle over your neckcloth, m'boy. Come along."

Jane chuckled, pleased. "Dearest. I did not know you were to be here."

"'Struth, I shouldn't have missed it for the world, Angel. Besides, Gussie and Marianne will want a full report. I warn you though, Anne has a full assembly of august personages waiting for you up there. Half of 'em ain't been out of dry storage in a decade." He schooled his features into a look of grave foreboding.

"Has she? How terrifying." Her eyes were fearless. Pemberton gave a crack of laughter. "Witness my trepidation." She smiled broadly.

If he had been discomfited by her appearance this evening, and heaven knew he was, at least, by virtue of entering the Drawing Room behind her, Myddelton was in the unique position to witness her composed entry. For word of her had spread. And in that first moment, as the guests turned to survey the newcomer in their midst, the silence and astonishment it caused. Had they too been misled into believing she was the obscure offspring of some county squire turned soldier? Her equanimity remained unruffled, her smile—that spontaneous expression of pleasure which came to her so easily, defined her even—remained unaltered. (Though she might be scarcely acquainted with her own husband, this, this she knew how to do.) And then, before the silence of a large room full of guests all staring at one slight and very beautiful young woman had turned to awkwardness, Lady Anne surged forward, Sally Jersey in tow, to whisk her away for that ordeal known as trial by introduction.

"As usual, Anne-dear, you had it all wrong," Sally exclaimed, as Jane executed the smallest requisite curtsy. Sally took her by the hand. "She told me you were lovely; she failed to say you are dazzling. Myddelton certainly is looking dazzled. I am very pleased to have made your acquaintance. Did he really marry you out of hand? Then I declare it is the first sensible thing he has done in years. But I really cannot forgive you, Anne, for keeping her to yourself until this evening and not bringing her 'round to meet me. It really was most inconsiderate. I should have to excuse it in Myddelton, I dare say—for after all..." She glanced coyly at Jane and then at Myddelton as she allowed her voice to trail off in insinuation. "I am sure it would be impossible to deny him anything."

So this is Silence, Jane thought, but replied quite cheerfully, "Oh no, ma'am, you must not blame Lady Anne. Truly. I have been engaged in putting Myddelton House to rights, you know, and could not allow myself the distraction of enlivening company."

Lady Jersey cast a curious look in Myddelton's direction. "Is that what he gave you for a honeymoon? The opportunity to put his house in order for him?"

"Indeed. But surely you knew, ma'am," Jane began, deflecting the question behind the question. "He favours the novel approach in most instances."

Underneath her satin turban, Lady Jersey's features sharpened as she scrutinised Jane's face. For she had not yet finished her probing. Nor was she to be gainsaid by a chit just turned eighteen and newly arrived from the country. "You sound almost complacent, my dear. Surely you were as shocked and unprepared as Myddelton to be launched so precipitately into an arranged marriage and to a gentleman with whom you were unacquainted?"

Anne's eyes widened with indignation even as she gasped, wordless in the face of Sally's determined bid to put her guest out of countenance.

But she had not the benefit of Mlle's formidable training. Quelling, even before it became evident, all hint of a martial gleam in her eye, Jane smiled with regret. "Our fathers were the dearest of friends, ma'am..." She paused delicately. "Indeed, after my own father was killed at Marengo, the Fourth Earl continued to be a frequent visitor to Britwell Park until shortly before he died. I knew him and he knew me, quite well. So why should either of us have found it surprising or, as you intimate, distressing, when we knew our union to be our fathers' dearest wish?" And if that does not halt you in your steps, Lady Jersey...

"Sally, you will forgive me for taking her from you, I know," Anne broke in, determined now to draw Jane away.

"Yes, yes, I know you must present her, Anne-dear," Sally answered with single-minded vibrancy. Yet determined to test the newcomer still further, tried another tack: "But first she must tell me how long she has been acquainted with Pemberton. From the look of his greeting to you, my dear, you must be old friends indeed."

Jane smiled. Now to parry. "Oh, I have known Lord Pemberton all my life, ma'am. The Marquis of Choate is my uncle's nearest neighbour, if you must know. So Pem is quite one of the family, and we, together with his sisters and cousins, are old playfellows."

"Tell me I do not err in detecting a note of past romance between the pair of you?"

Jane smiled her perfect smile. Then, pleasantly, lightly: "Ma'am, I should find it very difficult indeed to entertain even the vaguest hint of a tendre for someone who, on more than one occasion, tried to push me into the frog pond. Particularly during tadpole season."

Without warning, Lady Jersey gave way to laughter. "Horrid boy!"

"Do excuse us, Sally," Anne said, tucking her arm about Jane to lead her away. Sotto voce she said, "Did that loathsome wretch really try to push you in the frog pond?"

"Constantly," Jane replied.

"What a revolting boy he was!" And lowering her voice still further, "I apologise for that. Sally is rarely the most polite of guests, but I did not imagine she would be quite so rude...Lord Castlereagh, will you allow me to name the Countess of Myddelton, my cousin's bride."

Bemused, listening with half an ear to Pemberton, and feeling as though his world had once again suddenly and inexplicably lurched out of its orbit, Myddelton could only watch as this unknown creature, his wife, chatted and charmed her way about the room. Now she was talking with Castlereagh...now they'd been joined by Hardy and Dunphail. Now by...'Struth, where had Anne come by this collection? Debrett's Peerage? The full listing? And at the centre of it all, still smiling, talking, laughing, radiant with happiness and ease, was his wife. His. If it had been any other girl, he thought, it would have been sick-making. But she, she never fawned, never fluttered, never lowered her eyes in false humility. Perhaps she didn't know how. Instead, she was treated by them all as an equal. Dear Christ, what a thought. Great God, surely that was never Liverpool with her now? Yes, it was. He would recognise that voice which daily boomed through the Upper House anywhere.

"Little Janey," declared the Earl of Liverpool. "My dearest girl. Well, bless me, I'm dashed. What are you doing here? And where is Sir Charles? Never say he has allowed his Angel to come to Town without him? Northcote said to me that Myddelton was bringing his bride along this evening, but I never suspected, not for a moment..."

Myddelton exhaled slowly. Not only was it Liverpool. To judge by the greeting they exchanged—no curtsying, no bowing, instead the Minister for War held her hands and kissed her warmly on both cheeks— he'd known her from her cradle. And now, the formal and austere, the hawkish Liverpool, the bane of all peace-brokering Whigs, had tucked her hand through his arm and was exchanging gossip, or jokes, for they were both laughing heartily. Dear God in heaven...

"I say Myddelton, why'd you not tell me?" Mr. Hardy exclaimed with excitement. His jacquard waistcoat featured aquamarine and yellow tulips.

"Tell you what, Hardy? That your waistcoat would make a blind man..."

For once, Hardy swept on, regardless of the provocation: "Your bride, Idiot, Lady Myddelton, had lessons on the fortepiano by none other than Maestro Clementi!"

Myddelton felt his smile freeze in place. How could he tell what he had not known?

"I trust you know enough, Vandal, to know what that means? I cannot believe you did not tell me something that extraordinary and...profound. 'Pon my word, I am in awe. In ecstasy. She says she will play for me. With me. Does she mean it? Truly mean it?"

The smile remained fixed. "I dare say." Taught by Clementi. Of course. Nothing and no one but the best. Why hadn't he guessed?

"Myddelton, my sincerest congratulations," Castlereagh said, shaking him warmly by the hand. "My dear fellow, you could not have found a better wife and companion for yourself had you searched the country over. Look at her!"

Hardy drifted off to talk to Pemberton. She was still arm in arm with Liverpool. Northcote was there too. And the Prime Minister.

"She is a delight, a pure delight. And such a beauty..." the Foreign Minister continued. "And connected. There, you have chosen very wisely. Very wisely, indeed. With a wife like that at your side, you shall go far...An interesting family, you know, the Oxfordshire Herons. There was a time, of course, when everyone expected them to be the next political dynasty...Pitt—yes, Pitt was friendly with Sir Charles, don't you know? Well, yes. Indeed, Charles Heron was one of those rare few whom Pitt considered a friend...he was ever after him to stand for Parliament—promised him a ministry, according to Liverpool. And James...well, had James lived, I should think he would have taken over from Moore in Portugal, not Wellington. Though I dare say he might have been running Horse Guards by now instead—would have made a better fist of it, no doubt about that...I never met James. But I clearly recall Pitt presenting me to Sir Charles. Clear as day. An extraordinary family, the Herons. But then, of course, you know, Mrs. Heron died, and James was killed—blown to bits by a French cannonball...oh, did you not know? No, how should you? I shouldn't have imagined Sir Charles would wish to repeat that. It was, I am sure, most difficult for them. Then, of course, Charles simply retreated to Britwell Park to raise the child...And now you have married her. Well done, my dear fellow. Many congratulations. 'Struth, she is a lovely girl...And such a fine musician. I am so looking forward to playing trios with her—she knows the Haydn trios very well indeed...I dare say once you are settled, Sir Charles will join you here...perhaps Pitt shall have his way after all.

Wouldn't that be a thing?"

Bewildered—how could he have been so pigheadedly blind? An altogether misplaced confidence in the correctness of his own conclusions?—Myddelton watched her. She was with Liverpool still, speaking to him with such affection in her every gesture and expression. Lady Perceval, and her husband, too, were looking charmed. Palmerston and Dunphail were there as well.

Castlereagh was in the right of it. She was beautiful. Alluringly so. Intoxicatingly so. He drew a deep breath and felt the air sharp in his nostrils. *Je ne vis onques la pareille de vous ma gracieuse dame*...His wife...She whom he was to have and to hold. His. And he knew in that instant that although he had never held her, he wanted to; and not to watch from a distance across the breadth of a crowded salon as other men admired and courted her. Determinedly, he searched out his cousin.

"Anne, you did say there would be dancing, didn't you?" Myddelton murmured against his cousin's ear.

Anne gave him a shrewd and measuring look. She had seen her cousin in hot pursuit before. "No. I did not. Why?" She asked the last artlessly. How pleasant to tease one's bear of a cousin.

He didn't notice. "But the ballroom. Surely it's a little thing to move the orchestra in there and roll up the carpets." He wanted his bride in his arms. Now.

Anne smiled seraphically. "Well, I don't know..."

"Anne..."

She pretended not to hear the warning edge in his voice. Very pleasant, indeed. "It is not a little thing to move the orchestra and roll up the carpets," she declared roundly. Then, seeing the look in his eye, she relented. "Oh, all right. Give me half an hour..."

"Open the dancing with a waltz."

She gave a little laugh. "A waltz? Are you mad?" He was. And didn't care. "Oh, all right! I shall make sure Sally's on hand to lend you countenance, you daft creature." Then: "Myddelton, be gentle with her..."

He didn't hear. Already, he was going to join the coterie about the new Countess Myddelton, to stand beside her, his wife. To await the moment when Anne announced that dancing would begin in the ballroom.

The announcement came. Myddelton bent low toward her ear and possessed himself of her free hand. "The waltzes all belong to me."

She felt his fingers close about hers. His breath was warm, intimate against her temple and throat. He smelled of bergamot, orange blossom and cloves. A hint of confusion troubled her clear gaze. What was this intended to mean? "But I mayn't waltz," she said firmly and softly for him only, and caught her breath. That protected world at Britwell Park had admitted none like him. He was too powerful, too polished, standing out even in a room full of London gentlemen. Or was she just partial? Impossible. For he had not a care for her. Impossible, and foolish. "I have never been to Almack's, so I cannot have received either the approval or the approbation to waltz in public."

Myddelton smiled, undismayed by her oblique refusal, and replied, still in her ear, "M'dear, I hardly think even that ominous-looking female in the scarlet turban, otherwise known as Mrs. Drummond-Burrell, th'one standing over there beside Sal Jersey..."

Jane looked and identified same.

"...would have the balls to deny a husband the right to waltz with his wife. And Sal shall be on hand should official sanction be necessary."

The vulgarity did not unsettle her—though he should not have used such language in her hearing. Certainly not in a salon full of other ladies. But she hardly noted it. She was far too surprised and flattered by his determination that she should waltz with him. Was this for public show? She wished it were not so. It would be pleasant for it not to be so. Tentatively, she ventured, "I have never waltzed in public, you know. Still, I shall be honoured..." Inwardly she quailed, her composure crumbling. His hand was firm about hers, firm and large. He made it impossible to resist him, impossible to bar him access to her emotions.

Did she mean it? Or was it only her impeccable politeness speaking? He did not care. It was unimportant. Again he drew a deep breath and caught the perfume of her hair. Noticed too the curve of her throat, the tendrils curling against the nape of her neck. And did not release her hand. But waited while Liverpool made his fond farewells, then led her toward the ballroom which was well filled with guests, most particularly, female guests.

Lady Jersey stood nearby, smiling and nodding benignly, as Myddelton took Jane into his arms.

The act itself was a shock. She had never been in a gentleman's arms before—only her uncle's—and certainly that had never felt like this. And now, beginning to waltz with Myddelton, she was too too aware of his hand, pressing against the small of her back, and the brush of his thigh against hers as they stepped in time together. For one who had been denied any such physical contact, it was unmanning. His scent of spiced orange blossom and snuff caught at her senses. His smile, the intent unreadable look in his eyes as he gazed upon her, the warmth of his hand through the silk of her gown, the feel of his broad chest hard and so close to hers, all combined to overwhelm. She caught her breath, her self-possession dissipating. And she knew in that instant that despite an admirable attempt at self-control and that shadow which was her fear of him and his temper, she was not, could never be, indifferent to him.

Pleased, a half-smile played about the corners of Myddelton's eyes and mouth. She was in his arms where he had wanted her. He could smell her, feel her contour—exquisitely lissome, gently feminine—and the warmth of her skin through her gown. He traced his thumb against her side as he guided her past the other dancers. "You are very quiet, m'dear."

She had not expected that he would dance so expertly and was determined he should not know the effect he was having on her. "I am minding my steps," she replied, intent on maintaining her public face. "I told you I have never waltzed in public before."

"What, never? Surely not." Pleasant. Very pleasant. Only this wasn't teasing. This was his wife. And he was holding her. "Surely, you have waltzed at least with Pem?"

She shook her head, grateful for the distraction of conversation. "No. He did once try to tempt me. But I refused."

Executing a back step to bring her to his side, Myddelton placed his hand more closely about her waist. "'Struth, it must have been the first time in his life that a woman refused him anything."

She laughed easily, in spite of the hand, his hand, pressed about her waist, drawing her closer.

Nonplussed, he said, "What is there in that to set you off?"

"It's just the thought of not refusing Pem. I am sure I never heard anything quite so absurd in my life," she declared.

Carefully, deftly, Myddelton formulated his answer: "Then certainly you must be the first woman to refuse the requests of one whom you hold in greatest affection."

"I beg your pardon?" She paused. And smiled. "Are you implying that I must have said yes to Pem's request that I waltz with him, because I was..." She hesitated. "'In love' with him?" She was unaware of how closely he was watching her, how much her answer mattered. He was unable to gauge it.

Following his lead, she came about again, and chuckled, all tension released. "Now who is being absurd? In theory, I would have liked to have had a dreadful crush on him when I was fourteen. But reality always intruded: he was a dreadful tease. And such a coxcomb about his clothes."

This made Myddelton smile. He had forgot Pemberton's youthful taste.

She continued: "And most disgusting of all, he was worshipped by a 'young female', as Sir Charles would say, called Miss Sayer. And I positively refused to have anything in common with the likes of her, even the object of my affection. So it was no trouble to refuse him when he asked me to waltz. Anyway. He knew I would refuse. Gussie and Marianne had told him so."

He liked her answer so much. "Ah."

She drew a quick breath. He was a danger in this mood. But just as she determined to deflect him, the music finished. She buried the relief she felt at not having succumbed to whatever it was about him that was so unnerving.

Still holding her hand, he escorted her from the floor. "'Struth, I expect there is a queue of gentlemen anxiously awaiting you somewhere..." He scanned the collection of on-lookers ringing the dancefloor. "There they are: Pemberton. Hardy. And...Dunphail! I shall leave you then."

Astonishingly, holding her hand tightly, he bowed over it and kissed it. Most definitely a danger.

She did not dance with him again for no more waltzes were performed. A blessing, however mixed. And they were both silent during the ride home. She was exhausted, and relieved. And he, well, though slouched in the corner, he did not appear to have drunk too much, but she found it impossible to know.

Within the dim interior of the coach, lit only by the paly flame of a single carriage lantern, Myddelton was profoundly aware of her, of everything about her, and pondering. Had she been some other female, he most assuredly would have continued his wooing that night. Would have pressed home every advantage of her inexperience and his desire. But the dilemma: she was no other female. She was his wife. And a very well-connected wife she had turned out to be. All of which altered the equation beyond recognition. A nameless female, to whom he might or might not offer the use of his Kensington house, was disposable. If she displeased him, or he her, it mattered little; he need never see that nameless her again. But his bride, his wife, Jane, was neither nameless nor unknown. Should he offend her, should he be too rough or go too fast, for Heaven only knew what she understood of country matters, her unhappiness would be marked. She might even return home. Which was an idea he found he was liking less and less. As well as now clearly being an unique form of social and political suicide. Awkward. Deuced awkward.

But even had he resolved to woo and, should she prove willing (welcoming was surely too much to hope for), to bed her—it was not even two, the night was still young enough for that—such thoughts were banished from his mind, for Kettering met them at the door. An altogether unusual occurrence, for Myddelton did not encourage the servants to wait up for him. Not ever.

"My lord. My lady."

"Good evening, Kettering," she said softly.

"My lord. A runner arrived earlier this evening with a packet from Sir Charles Flint at the Irish Office. I have put it on the table in the

Library."

Myddelton blinked and snorted in resignation. "Ah. A large pot of coffee, I think, Kettering. Thank you."

She hesitated, then touched his sleeve. "I shall leave you then. It was a lovely evening. Good night." And smiling her affectionate smile, she started up the stairs.

And watching her, Myddelton could only regret that he might not go with her.

13

11 May 1812

"Heavens, will you look at them all?" Jane faltered, looking upon the collection of invitations on her breakfast tray, organised into neat rows like bedding plants or parade ground soldiers, crowding the tea and toast. Engraved ivory boards requesting her presence at this musical evening or that ball, this dinner or that soirée, and punctiliously phrased letters including her in previously issued invitations. All as a result of her presentation to the Northcotes' circle of friends two evenings previous. And too morning-muddled still for self-satisfaction or pride of status, she added, "Lud!"

She took a first sip of tea—the best and favourite of the day. Then meticulously, with one finger, she lifted the corner of an ornately scripted affair to scan the opening lines: *Dear Lady Myddelton, it would afford us the greatest pleasure*...She expelled a large breath, closed her eyes and expelled a second breath. "It would appear I am a Success," she observed drily.

She drank her tea. Then suddenly exclaimed, "Oh bother!" envisioning, with some alarm, the hours and days of shopping it would entail. For again, she had nothing to wear. Or wouldn't have after two more parties. Always assuming that Myddelton would choose for them to attend any of these events.

Without enthusiasm she flicked through the cards again—ridottos, al fresco luncheons, routs and balls—and noted belatedly the Almack's vouchers nestled in amongst the rest. For she had meant to spend the day occupied with the refitting of the Yellow Saloon, or dirty-buff as it had become over time—overseeing the stripping of the old silk and the arrival of the new, consulting with the upholsterer. Not standing at the dressmakers, her body immobilised by pin-sticking, needle-wielding assistants. "Oh bother..."

This she had not expected. For it had not happened at Britwell Park. But there, she had never needed any kind of presentation—everyone knew her, had always known her. And sometime after her sixteenth birthday the invitations which arrived for her uncle had included her as well. Britwell Park...She felt the tug of longing and bit on her bottom lip. She must not think about home or her uncle.

No, she had not anticipated this. Not any of it. For one thing, country life never provided so many competing diversions. Rarely had she attended more than a single party of an evening there. If for no other reason than the distances between the houses prevented it. And of course, there, she had had the luxury of wearing the same gown twice. But she was in Town now. And to be in Town was to be on display. In all places and at all times. Too many scurrilous reports masquerading as news filled the Society pages of the daily gazettes with the details of everyone's appearances. For many, they provided the one spot of brightness in the diet of otherwise bleak reading of war, inflation and corn shortages—to that she could testify. And wearing the same gown twice would undoubtedly, rightly or wrongly, be considered by the gossip-greedy public as proof of parsimony or financial instability.

She shook her head. "...There's nothing for it, is there?" And choosing one of the ivory boards, she eyed it with misgiving. She gave an unexpected laugh. "Though I must confess, I find that I cannot picture Myddelton at a *ridotto*. Can you?" she said, addressing her dozing cat. Who did not wake. "Well, let me know if you think it likely..." she murmured, still amused at the thought.

And wishing that she might draw upon the companionship and good taste of Mlle, she determined to call upon Lady Anne Northcote—and hoped she was not presuming either upon their tenuous relationship nor upon Lady Anne's kindness.

Anne was happily and easily persuaded to accompany Lady Myddelton; she liked her cousin and she had discovered she liked her cousin's young wife. And together they set about to accomplish in one day a fortnight's preparation for a London Season, first spending the morning at Grafton House, the treasure trove for the financially prudent and sartorially wise, then descending upon Madame Fanchon.

Madame greeted them with great courtesy. And, settling them again in that exclusive salon which she reserved for her preferred customers, she surrounded them with fashionable periodicals which they might peruse, and more fabrics from which they might make further choices.

❧

For once, the ill-lit hall which snaked about Westminster's warren of chambers and rooms was uncluttered, empty of even that usual collection of clerks, secretaries, errand boys and honourable members who daily clogged its narrow precincts. A miracle, thought Myddelton gratefully, albeit a minor one. Or testament to the importance of the afternoon's debate on the conduct of the Peninsular Campaign? Still, it might mean that instead of being button-held by whichever member was canvassing for votes, or wishing to discuss his recent marriage, or his horses' performance at Newmarket, with a bit of luck, he could be home before nine. For once. He stopped to consult his watch. Nearly five. And snapped it shut, before absently returning it to his pocket. Surely they should have finished by now? Oughtn't they? And he had only two more members of the Select Committee to see before the debate on the Orders in Council. Which was next. If he then spoke to Castlereagh…And did not allow himself to be sucked into a discussion with Planta…It was possible, just possible, that he might be home by seven. Though earlier would be preferable. Curlee had returned yesterday from Britwell Park with her horse. Perhaps if he ducked his meeting with Castlereagh—he had, after all, spent the morning reviewing those plagued reports from Spain and America with the Foreign Secretary—he might even be home in time to…No. No, that would never work.

But there they were now, pouring out into the lobby through the thrown-open doors, a chattering, jostling tide of the country's honourable members. First out—Northcote, looking jolly pleased to see him—the Whigs must have been rabbiting on then. And Smith (M.P. for Norwich?) and General Gascoyne. And just ahead, emerging from the Lower Chamber through the side door which stood adjacent to the stone stairs, was the Prime Minister, deep in conversation with Osborne.

Still, it might be possible to be home by eight. Certainly, it was worth an effort.

"Myddelton!"

"'Afternoon, Northcote." Myddelton nodded to Smith and Osborne. Then stopped briefly to bow: "Prime Minister."

"'Afternoon, Myddelton," acknowledged Sir Spencer, and resumed his discussion with Lord Osborne, remaining still in the doorway to the Lower Chamber.

"Good lord, Myddelton, you look done to death. Even for you," Northcote exclaimed as he came to stand beside him. "What can you have been doing? Not gaming your nights away at Watier's, I trust."

Had it been anyone else—Lord Castlereagh, for instance—Myddelton would have demurred. He gave a tired smile. "S'life, I don't know, Miles...I dare say it's those deuced reports on the Orders in Council. There are reams of 'em, you know. 'Struth, I've spent my nights with 'em. And my days. I do assure you, I've never transcribed and translated so much in all my days." He managed a soft laugh. "And then, of course, when I've a minute, there are my friends, the Spanish..."

A compassionate twinkle had appeared in Northcote's eyes. "Calling 'em your friends now, are you?"

"I know, I know..." Myddelton said, rolling his eyes. "In some ways, you know, they're all the same. Once you've read one of their damned importuning letters, you've read 'em all...All that varies is the intemperance of the language!" And lowering his voice, for it was only Northcote, he confided: "And then, when I've finished those off, there's this code the Frenchies have concocted that Castlereagh is ever after me to crack—though I've virtually nothing to go on. A more diabolical conflation of numbers and bits of words, I have yet to encounter..." He rubbed his forehead. "S'life, when I think on those bliss-filled nights at Watier's when I was used to sit up till four and sleep past noon..."

"Never think it, Myddelton. Never think it. Put it behind you," Northcote advised genially. "Because Castlereagh is never going to allow you within a stone's throw of the place again. He'd never be so foolish."

"Ha!" Myddelton laughed. "That's what I'm afraid of..."

An explosion like a thunderclap boomed through the swell of

conversation. Boomed and shook the lobby walls. Shook the floor beneath Myddelton's feet. Echoed and reverberated.

Stopped, silenced, deafened, Myddelton froze. His throat gripped with apprehension. His breath caught. And he remained thus, his stomach and legs quaking. And unable to hear anything, felt rather than knew that he was unhurt. And smelled powder. Burnt powder. As from a musket. A flintlock. A breechloader. But...it couldn't be. Not here. It wasn't possible. But the smell, the smell close by, was that of scorched powder. Was that of a pistol just fired off. At close range. But it wasn't possible.

Chaos descended. Someone was shouting. Yelling.

"Oh..." cried a voice. The voice of one in great pain.

And implicit peril sharpening his senses and his heart pounding, Myddelton began searching, looking everywhere at once. But for what? Northcote? No, there he was—still beside him. Thank God! And he too was unhurt. And Smith? Where was he? And Osborne? And Gasgoyne? And...

"...I am murdered."

Who'd said that? Who was it?

A man—Christ, who was it? Black coat, pale breeches. Sweet Christ, who was it? Clutching at a gush of crimson beginning to spread over his chest as he swayed and crumpled at Smith's feet.

Smith, quailing and ashen, stooped to help the man, the fallen man. Sweat broke out on his forehead, as terrified, he struggled with the weight of him. Struggled, and with Osborne's help, finally turned him face up.

"Oh my God! It's the Prime Minister!"

In stunned horror, Myddelton stared. Shuddered and stared. Felt ill. Paralysed. And shaking, trembling, began impulsively to pull and rip at his cravat, tugging to remove it, as he rushed forward, pushing Miles to one side and dropped to his knees by the fallen Perceval. Christ, the bleeding! "Where's he been hit?"

His chest was awash in blood. 'Struth, he was bleeding everywhere. And it must be stopped. The bleeding must be stanched. But already, the blood—garish, mesmerising, in rivulets—was dripping onto the stone floor. It seeped from beneath Smith's and Perceval's fingers, spread across the breadth of Perceval's chest, soaking the torn fabric of his shirt and waistcoat and coat. Myddelton felt his own breath painful in his throat, his mouth parching, as he tore the neckcloth free and wadded it, pressing it to Perceval's breast. Od's death, there was so much blood. So much. Hell's wounds, where was it all coming from? Seized by dread, holding the wadded muslin against the wound, gently, carefully, Myddelton slid his fingers beneath Perceval's head, lifting it so gently to cradle it. Perceval's eyes flickered, and shut.

"*Someone fetch a doctor!*"

"Shut the doors! Let no one out!"

"Hold fast, sir...It will be all right..."

In anguished silence, like figures frozen in a tableau, neither Smith nor Myddelton dared move, but held the Prime Minister, pressing the wadded, blood-stained cravat against his chest.

"We must move him..."

"It won't be long now, sir. Just you hold fast..."

"Have ye shut the doors, damn ye? It's the damned French! It's a conspiracy!"

And still the wound bled. Ceaselessly. And Perceval's blood, now sticky and sluggish, stained their hands and cuffs and sleeves, saturated the wadded linen of Myddelton's neckcloth, and soaked their waistcoats and breeches, and dripped and pooled on the flagstones beneath them.

"Seal off the doors!"

"We must move him. Osborne, get his legs. Smith, at the count of three..."

A trickle of blood slipped from the corner of Perceval's mouth. Insensibly, Smith began to weep, the tears streaming down his cheeks and over his chin unheeded.

"It'll be all right, sir. Hold fast..."

"One, two, three..." And struggling and straining, mute and alert, their arms beneath Perceval's shoulders like pallbearers, they lifted as one, and began to inch forward, step by shuffling step through the gathering ranks of wide-eyed members—an agony of a journey—to carry him to the closest chamber, the office of the Speaker's Secretary, and there, gently, gently, they lowered him onto the sofa. A trail of blood followed them.

"There you are, sir. Hold fast now..."

And still they held him, pressing the sodden linen wad to his chest. Held him as his breath shuddered painfully, and faded. Held him close, smoothing his hair from his forehead, cleaving to him, just as all over Portugal and Spain, on the battlefields and in tents, in the open, and among the rubble of besieged buildings, soldiers cradled the heads and bodies of their stricken comrades, praying and pleading with their God that all danger might pass and another precious life might not be yielded.

And they were there still...Dear God, how long had it been?...unmoved and unmovable when the black-coated doctor from Great-George street arrived, running. Was it minutes? Hours? Who had called for him? Myddelton would never even know to ask.

Submissively, anxiously, they watched as he searched for Perceval's pulse or other glimpse of hope. Watched him in terror, dread and shock. Watched as he felt at his throat and wrist and temple. And as through a mist heard him pronounce what they already knew: "It is too late, gentlemen. I am sorry, he is dead."

Dead. Just like that. His lifeblood drained away; his spirit gone.

It was as if the structures of life had been taken down and abandoned. And Myddelton felt that he had somehow passed into this distant shadow of phantasy which was both less and more vivid than reality. Tears ran down his face. And no one noticed that he too was covered in the Prime Minister's blood. They all were.

And suddenly someone cried: "Where's the rascal that fired?"

Blinking, disoriented, Myddelton looked up. The fellow from the Commons Vote Office, was it? Or Dowling? And yes, who? Who had fired that fatal life-robbing shot? Dazed, bereft, bloodied, Myddelton stood, just stood helpless, and then, finally, bestowed a final long look upon his Prime Minister and better. *He was dead. Just like that. Dead.* And, his mind reeling and stricken, he bowed, deeply, closing his eyes upon this unimaginable.

And at last returned to the hallway where now—as the news spread—everyone was beginning to congregate. And there, from out the shadow of the stone staircase, an insignificant little nothing of a man with a grey face, a balding creature shrouded in an old brown greatcoat, was emerging, proclaiming loudly, "I am the unfortunate man!"

Was he mad?

~

In a city as vast as London, the largest by far in Europe, with a population of nearly one million souls, news of whatever nature will travel slowly or quickly, depending primarily upon whom one knows. Those who lived in the shadow of Westminster Palace learned of the afternoon's dreadful event soon after it occurred, for the doctor from Great-George street was not slow to relate all he had seen and heard. And there may have been those who, out for a pleasure stroll in St. James's Park, heard but did not understand the wailing and weeping emanating from 10 Downing Street as Lady Perceval and her many children received word of their grievous loss. But those in the boroughs far removed from Westminster would not learn of it for hours or even days, for word of mouth can be an unreliable informant. Certainly, the news did not penetrate that bastion of ladies' fashion, Fanchon's, while Jane was there. For who would bear such a report to such a place? A blood-stained member of Parliament perhaps, or one of the unkempt running boys?

Thus, at half past six, Lady Myddelton's thoughts were fixed on a matter of small domestic significance, rather than on any event of political or national import or security—she was weighing the merits of inviting or not inviting her husband's cousin into Myddelton House for a refreshing cup of tea. Because, of course, she had not mentioned the one subject about which she craved advice. She had asked obliquely as much as she dared. And felt churlish for it. But how could she be direct without revealing the true state of things?

William stood waiting beside the carriage, ready to assist them in alighting.

Anne, though uncertain as to the cause of Lady Myddelton's hesitation, could empathise: she *was* in the awkwardest position. And Myddelton going about like a leopard ready to pounce. Nor was she in any hurry to go. For as much as Jane wished to learn about Myddelton,

213

Anne wished to discover the extent and success of *his* attempts to woo his wife. She told herself it was because he was her cousin. And said kindly: "You are convinced I shall disapprove of any and all changes you have made. But I promise you, I shall not. I shall approve with my whole heart." She laughed, then sobered. "I only saw most of it once, you know, and it was the saddest house. And, there is something I most particularly wished to say...but not where we might be overheard. Has my cousin given you the Myddelton jewels, yet?"

Jane's interest was piqued. "No. I did not know there were any...Of course you must come in. I am being foolish. William, will you kindly fetch in the bandboxes?"

There was about William an air of rigorous pride these days, and it was this, as well as his absurd deference as he handed her from the carriage, which bolstered Lady Myddelton's spirits, inspiring confidence where moments ago there had been only diffidence.

Anne followed her up the steps and into the house. "Oh yes. The coronet in particular used to be quite famous, I believe. And I do not believe they were sold off during that bad patch...I could be mistaken though.

"May I have a look at the Drawing Room? I've been so longing to see it...Oh, you have been busy. My word, what a transformation. It was used to be so grim."

Anne, true to her word, praised all there was to be admired, and there was much, as, for no little time, Jane showed her about the restored rooms. The Morning Room she found light and genial; the Dining room infinitely improved; the Drawing room a perfect combination of ease and elegance, and the addition of several fine paintings in the Drawing and Dining rooms laudable. But she gave no hint of the promised confidence and instead, to Jane's growing impatience, she held her peace until they were seated in Jane's small sitting room, Kettering having brought the tea and cakes and withdrawn.

Anne accepted a cup of tea and looked about her, noting with interest the three miniatures in pride of place upon the mantel, the books, which despite Haseley's best efforts never remained for long on their shelves, the chessboard where a game was in play. A most comfortable room, light and altogether pleasant, even now, with the curtains half-drawn and the candles lit. It told her a great deal. Did Myddelton ever venture in here, he would have felt at ease. "You will have noticed, I am sure...Indeed, how could you have failed to...the young lady, who, would have, with her mama, intruded upon us at Fanchon's this afternoon..."

Jane sipped at her tea then set the cup down so that she might rub Lotto's ear. "I'm sorry, I didn't see her. Madame was far too quick for me. But her name was Miss Wythenshaw, I think you said."

Anne frowned as if vexed. "Yes. That's it. How shall I put this? Well. Along with several other girls this Season, she set her cap for Myddelton, and, as I understand it, believed that she had succeeded in engaging his affections." She hesitated and considered the tea in her cup. "In any event, when she did learn of your marriage to him, she vowed...well, I hardly know how to say this, for it is quite beyond anything...she vowed to take him as her lover."

Jane's hand stilled on Lotto's head. She looked up. "I beg your pardon?"

Anne frowned again. When Emily and Sally had insisted she bear this tale, it had all seemed quite straightforward. Lud. "It would appear that she considers theirs a lasting passion ..."

"What?" Deeply embarrassed, Jane paused. "Why...why do you tell me this?" she asked softly. A frightening and unpleasant tingling began in the pit of her stomach. Was she in danger of mistaking his easy manners and affability for a measure of affection?

Anne did not like this position of informant. "Because, we—that is to say, Emily Cowper, Sally Jersey and I—wanted you to be on your guard. For she may intend mischief." Seeing the distrust forming in Jane's level gaze, she tried again: "My dear...Jane..." she said, drawing herself together. "It goes without saying that Myddelton had formed no connection there. You must believe me! It is nothing more than fancy. But Miss Wythenshaw is one of those spoilt young girls who have come to believe that whatever they wish for must be theirs, as if by right. She set her cap at Myddelton. They all do—or did—for his title. And it seems—though I am certain it is no more than talk—she does not feel bound by the conventions of marriage."

It was too much. Feeling naive and ill, Jane clutched vaguely at Lotto. "I beg your pardon..." she repeated unhappily.

Her reaction was not what Anne had envisioned. And now clutching at straws, and most anxious to reassure her new young cousin (Whatever had Sally and Emily been thinking?) she ventured, "It may be that she has been reading that wicked Wollstonecraft creature?"

Without warning, the door was thrown open. And Myddelton, his face like chalk, his cravat gone and his clothes all bloodied and askew, stood on the threshold.

Taking in the state of him, Jane felt as though her heart had stopped. "Myddelton! Oh dear God!" And terrified, she was on her feet running to him—to support him, to help him, to staunch his bleeding, to do whatever must be done that he might live. "What has happened?"

Unconscious of his appearance and the fears it must raise, Myddelton blinked at the light. "The Prime Minister. He is dead. Shot. He's been killed." His voice was as the croak of a chough. "Outside the Commons..."

Jane had taken his hand and was clutching it to her breast. His cuff was still wet. His eyes were clouded with shock. Inexplicably, she burst into tears. He was safe.

Tears starting in her eyes, Anne pressed her hand against her cheek and breathed one word: "Miles?"

"Miles?" Myddelton blinked again, as if his mind had ceased its functioning. "Miles is...fine. He is fine. He...was with me."

She did not know what to do. Still holding his hand to her heart, Jane swallowed hard. Involuntarily her arm had gone about him—to hold him close—and his around her, and intuitively, for reason had been abandoned so many minutes ago it equalled an eternity, they moved farther into the room still entwined for consolation against the present. "Come," she whispered. "Come, you must sit down..."

He followed, seeing nothing. "We did not know—it was impossible to tell in that narrow hall—where the shot came from. I did not even know that anyone had been hit. And then...then, Smith was yelling that it was...that it was the Prime Minister..."

He did not see that Jane was weeping, for the Prime Minister and the country now, not for him. He only saw with his mind's eye what he had been seeing for hours—the fallen Perceval, the drenching blood everywhere. Slowly, Jane disengaged herself and went to tug on the bellpull for Kettering, then returned to Myddelton's side.

"I must go," Anne murmured. "I must go…" She had gathered herself together and was rising, her tears unstopped. "Miles will be coming home and will expect to find me there…" She brushed at her cheek with the back of her hand as she hurried from the room.

Myddelton hardly noticed. "We, none of us, even thought to look for who had fired, don't you know…it was only afterwards, after he had…after he had…" He stopped, unable to form or speak the terrible words. And rocking ever so slightly, drew several sharp breaths. "…After we had moved him to the Speaker's Drawing Room. And someone…I…I, I don't know who, was yelling that it was a conspiracy and who would be next…so some of the fellows went searching for his accomplice… and had the doors sealed off.

"But the chap, Bellingham his name is, he did not try to escape. He did not even struggle when we seized him…he just came with us and we just put him on this bench and he…he just stayed there…Quiet as anything."

Myddelton glanced about the room—hopelessly, searchingly, fearfully—and drew a short breath, almost a sob, before beginning again. "There wasn't an accomplice though. At least not one they could find. They didn't find anyone else. And this fellow, he just said, 'My name is Bellingham…it is a private injury. I know what I have done. It was a denial of justice on the part of the Government.' No one could credit it…No one could believe he said it. 'Want of redress and denial of justice,' that's what he said. And he did not understand what he had done. He shot the Prime Minister! What sort of man shoots the Prime Minister in cold blood? What sort, I ask you?" he demanded of no one. And shuddered violently. Then, ran a hand through his hair.

"He's mad. Barking mad. I heard some of his confession in the prison room. He blamed Perceval—Perceval of all men—for the failure of his business in Russia or wherever it was. He told us over and over again how he'd planned it all. How he was used to come every day and sit in the gallery while he planned it." He looked at her. "Smith was sick in the corner." Then looked away. "Finally, Castlereagh had to shut him up..." He shuddered again. "When we searched him, he had another loaded pistol...A short screw barrel, it was. And an opera glass. And letters. Bundles of letters. But they was all nonsense. And the gun was still loaded."

Outside, the fog was descending like a murky blanket of mottled white and grey. By late evening, one would be able to see only as far as the next house.

Kettering, having assisted the weeping Lady Anne into a carriage and seen her off with William as escort, appeared in the doorway. "My lady?"

"Oh Kettering." It was a sigh. "Good, you are here." She half rose and then did not, for Myddelton's arm had tightened about her as if he would not be parted from the warmth of this other living being. She looked distractedly at him for a moment, then regathered what remained of her senses. "Bring some brandy. And...tell Stamp to heat the water for a bath." She bit her lips together in a bid to regain some measure of composure. "The Prime Minister was murdered this afternoon. Assassinated."

Kettering remained still, blenching as he absorbed the news, the state of his master, his mistress. Then, his features set like stone, he bowed and left.

Myddelton raised his eyes to the ceiling and beheld nothing. He had taken her hand and his grip on it was painfully tight. Then his eyes fixed, he began again, reliving it: "We took him to the Bar in the Commons then. And, almost...almost at once, the Bar was full of Members...and Peers...and fellows no one had ever seen before. 'Struth, it was like a mob. Like Paris...during the Terror. And the Speaker was banging and banging away with his gavel, trying to get everyone's attention, but no one noticed. They was shouting. They was all shouting. And fighting with each other to get to the murderer. Everyone was shouting. Demanding justice. And going out into the hall to see the spot...to see the blood... for there was a pool of it, where he had...where he'd..." He stopped, unable to continue, still incapable of articulating the dread words. "Then, then they all came back and was pointing at me and Smith and Osborne. Because we was covered...we was covered in his blood...It was on our hands. And our clothes...

"We took him away to the prison room by a private passage. One I didn't even know existed. But we had to. The Speaker insisted on it. Once everyone had seen what had happened, they wanted to hang him, there and then. Or have him shot. But the Speaker insisted." He looked down upon his right hand where Perceval's blood had stained the grain of his fingertips and dried to a crust beneath his nails. "I could have killed him myself," he half-whispered intently. "With my bare hands." He paused, staring into space. "So we took him. Castlereagh and a Sergeant and Osborne and me...I don't know who else..."

"The brandy, my lady."

She tried to smile her thanks. And fighting back the tears, failed. She had no smiles. "Set it there, Kettering." She pointed to a side table. "Will you pour it?"

Tremorless, Kettering unstopped the decanter and filled a glass.

Myddelton had sunk back against the cushions of the day bed, his eyes closed. She held his hand. Only now was his breath beginning to slow.

"My lord?"

She waited while Myddelton opened his eyes, took the glass from Kettering, drained its contents and returned it to the near table.

"He shall be here when his bath is ready, Kettering. See that it is hot."

"My lady." His bow was as that for royalty, and silently he shut the door behind him as he left.

Myddelton sank back against the cushions once again. She brought his hand to her lips and kissed it and held it and kissed it.

Finally, his voice torn with despair, his tears beginning again, Myddelton said: "Upon my life, I tried everything I could think of...God knows I tried...but the bullet must have gone straight through his heart. That's all I can think. He was dead almost instantly, you know. I tried to stop it. But I could not. I couldn't stop it. I could not stop the blood...I could do nothing to stop it!"

She ignored the tears she wished to shed and clasped his hand against her cheek, cleaving unto him, wishing she might but unable to ignore his coat and breeches dyed red with the Prime Minister's blood, fearfully aware that it might have been his own. Nor did she know whether she would weep for Perceval and his now-bereft wife and children, or for the stain his murder had left on Myddelton.

Stamp, grim and stiff, appeared at the connecting door. "Your bath awaits, my lord," he announced and withdrew.

Myddelton caught his breath on a sob and dragged his free hand across his face, smearing the tears. "I must go..." he murmured. And rose unsteadily onto legs weak with accumulated strain. He did not release her hand, but drew her up and to the door with him. His gaze upon her was anguished, his voice breaking as he spoke: "I shall need to go back...after I have changed...for news...Bellingham's before the magistrates now, I expect. And a Cabinet Council's been called for later. Castlereagh will want me on hand. And I must return to the Foreign Office after that..." Soberly, he contemplated her hand in his. "I don't know when I shall be back."

Then with gravest intent, he said: "They've called out the militia already—they're in the streets now. But there's no telling what will happen next. It may be a conspiracy, do you see? And there may be rioting...I don't know. I shall send word as soon as I can, but I want you to stay indoors. Have the servants put up the shutters against looters."

"Yes," she nodded. "Yes, of course." She searched his face, his eyes. Had the fear, the shock lessened? Or did she just wish it to be so? And if there were riots, or God-forbid, a coup—like in Naples—would he be safe? "Will you be all right?"

He regarded her closely. "I shall survive," he said. And after another moment, added: "Tom Broke's a fair shot. Should you need him. Though you'd not know it to look at him. But he is." He lifted her hand and brushed a kiss on it. "I shall be back when I can...Stay indoors." He bowed, then disappeared into his own chambers, pausing only to shut the door behind him.

Nursing that hand, she returned to sit—dry-eyed and pensive or weeping and overcome—at the window. She listened to the thumping march of the soldiers patrolling the streets, and looked out across the Square through the mist at number 16, Lord Castlereagh's residence. Who was also safe. And, finally, much later, she came to her desk and, opening her standish, chose a quill, dipped it, and wrote: "My dearest Uncle, This news, I know, will shock and distress you. Indeed, I can hardly bear to write of it, such is my grief and dismay…"

14

The violence which had erupted across Europe, rupturing societies, spreading like a cancer for the past twenty years from its source in Paris where it had devoured some forty thousand souls, to the Peninsula where even now it stalked the countryside, that violence had at last fetched up here, in this green and civil land. And it was as if a bell jar had been placed over the city. The assassination of the Prime Minister—though he had not been universally loved—had changed everything. Everything and nothing.

During Monday's long evening hours while the Cabinet Council met, Myddelton had sat, a glorified clerk, as the Ministers argued and fretted and shouted their way to emergency measures, that panic might not engulf the city: All mails stopped from that instant until instructions were prepared to secure tranquillity throughout the land; the Household Cavalry guarding the King, the Queen and the Prince Regent, was to be trebled; the militias called out and at the ready to keep the peace, and all those in the Thames Police Office were placed on alert to guard the waterway and its environs. It was even mooted that the King be taken secretly to Wheedon and there kept from harm. And his fingers cramping about the quill, Myddelton, leaden-eyed and his mind empty of all but a grim concentration upon each sentence as he wrote it, copied the instructions over and again that they might be distributed throughout the counties by the armed messengers now thronging the lobby.

But already, in the shops, in the streets, in the houses, a mood of general hysteria threatened or prevailed. People spoke of little else. And revelling in gruesome detail, they decried the fiendish depravity of the assassin, while adding their own masterful touches, so that hourly, fresh rumours circulated of Jacobin assassins creating new Reigns of Terror or

Guy Fawkes-like plots to blow up Parliament, all, all begetting new suspicions, new frissons of terror, and a palpable insecurity.

The penny broadsides were full of it: Was it a conspiracy? Who would be next? Was it a coup, like when Tsar Paul had been murdered? Or in Spain, where the king had been imprisoned and made to abdicate? Or Portugal, where the whole Royal family had fled? Was dear Farmer George, the mad old King, still safe at Windsor? Were they all safe? Or were there French spies on every corner, awaiting a signal from Paris that they might rise up?

Eventually, the interminable Cabinet Council finished. And Myddelton watched as at last, under a strong military escort of the Light Horse, Bellingham, still outwardly calm though his hands were manacled, was marched from the building to be taken to Newgate Prison. And only then did Myddelton make his way through the once-quiet streets, now thronging with uniformed militiamen and bands of torch-carrying citizens—a city at war—to the Foreign Office. And from thence to the Irish Office. Where he found the Resident Secretary, the measured and deceptively mild Sir Charles Flint, behaving like a man possessed, his chosen agents scouring London, running the length and breadth of the land to bring in reports on the locations and activities of every Frenchman known to them. And drawn into this secret world, a world far removed from his daily routine of translations and cyphers, Myddelton pored over the files of all those with treasonable associations, seeking any hint, any clue of a general conspiracy. And found none. And so kept searching. For every desperate hour was punctuated by the nagging fear of 'what did Bonaparte know'? Was his eastern build-up a feint? Or did he have another lightning force poised to strike, waiting for a signal of general chaos? Were they already all-unknowing fighting a rear-guard action?

He came home but once, early Tuesday morning, for a change of linen, before the inquest. And after giving his evidence, he returned to his desk at the Foreign Office, where he continued to copy the orders Castlereagh dictated and copy them again and again, as before.

At Westminster, business had proceeded almost as usual, but hushed, always hushed. The horror was too fresh for that scurrilous and ebullient name-calling which was the preferred mode of communication there. And several members had spoken out in favour of some form of police force—to protect their persons, if nothing else. The Commons, achieving unprecedented accord, voted Lady Perceval a handsome annuity in recognition of her husband's sacrifice and his contribution to the stability of the country. And the Government—though ostensibly rudderless—laboured on. Castlereagh and Liverpool, convinced that the tide of war was at last turning in Britain's favour, beetled ahead with their plans for summer offensives against the French.

And through that afternoon and night, unable to think or to sleep or to breathe without a litany of cries—*Oh, I am murdered* and *It's the Prime Minister...it's the Prime Minister*—his thoughts a disarray of images of the dying man, of blood he could not stanch, Myddelton remained at his desk, attempting to shift the great mounds of paperwork that resided like an archipelago around the perimeter of his desk. Though often, too often, he found himself sitting, the heels of his hands pressed against his eyes, pressed against the rage and futility and tears, just sitting, without any idea how long he had thus sat. Until toward dawn he awoke, dry-mouthed, disoriented and alone, face down upon a stack of Spanish letters. And blinking at the light, he rubbed his face, took up his quill and began again.

And in truth he wished he were there still, translating the contents of the afternoon's dispatch pouch, or alone in the detached concentration of chiffre-cracking. Or in the measured safety of the Lord Castlereagh's company. Not at home, not preparing for a public assembly at Almack's, Society's most exclusive club, and dreading it—resenting and dreading it all: the crowded rooms, the false affability, or even worse, the morbid curiosity cloaked beneath displays of sympathy. But the Foreign Secretary's genially posed query, "Shall you be joining us later at Almack's this evening?" had been an order and no question. And the words which followed it were an avowal of defiance, of sangfroid, in the face of whatever might threaten. Still, Almack's?

"S'blood, a more infernal place was never thought of..." Myddelton swore. And the candles on the dressing table guttered briefly with the force of his words. 'Struth, he would rather be anywhere else and doing anything, anything at all other than fastening the buttons at the waist of his knee breeches—a required element of a gentleman's Almack's uniform.

Stamp, in the act of producing a choice of waistcoats, hesitated. He understood perfectly to what his lordship referred. "My lord? Did you desire to change the knee breeches for a pair of inexpressibles, then, my lord?"

Myddelton knew—from Kettering—that Jane had remained home at his order since that day. And had seen no one. Not Anne. Not Emily. Not Sally Jersey. Not even Pemberton. She had been alone. Nor had she the universal panacea of ceaseless mind-numbing Spanish translations in which to seek solace.

He frowned. It was too bad. "No," he conceded. "Where's m'waistcoat? No, not that one. The pale grey—th'one with the narrow gold stripe. Yes, that's it."

And his brows drawn together, he buttoned himself into the waistcoat. He ought to have stayed on at the Foreign Office where Liverpool was closeted with Castlereagh to confer upon Napoleon's latest withdrawal of troops from the Peninsula. He ought to have asked Pemberton (or Hardy...or anyone...) to escort her to the deuced place and a pox take all gossips! Though that would be unjust. For her kindness that night had provided the only hope, the only respite he had known in all this. He could still smell the blood. He twitched at the knot in his cravat, finished the last of the brandy in his glass and slipped his snuff-box into his pocket. "'Faith, it will have to do."

From the ground floor came the distant music of the fortepiano. And coming downstairs, Myddelton followed the sound to the Drawing Room, not the Library. (So she'd had it moved, had she? Or bought another one. Surely not even she...) And let himself into the now cleaned, painted and refurbished chamber, and paused to look upon it all, noting that it smelled curiously fresh, as if of crushed herbs.

She was seated facing away from him. S'death, from the back, she looked no more than a child. A slim, yellow-haired girl. Great God, what had possessed him, when was it? Was it only the other night? S'life, had he truly felt desire for this...this child? Had he truly abandoned the security of his work-laden desk to escort this *child* to Almack's? 'Struth, what he needed was the comfort of a woman. A proper woman. Not this mish mash of a marriage, neither one thing nor t'other. And it was too soon for him to seek out another...

"Damn, damn and damn."

She turned at the sound, which she heard only indistinctly, and brightened at the sight of him. "Oh!" she exclaimed. "Have I kept you waiting?" she asked, rising from her seat.

No, most definitely not a child. That white silk might give the appearance of the virginal, but her femininity vanquished his every sense, banishing any thoughts of 'child' or 'ought to have stayed at the Foreign Office'. The cloth of her gown clung, and nestled in the fabric at her breast was a large emerald-cut sapphire surrounded by pearls and amethysts. It must have cost someone a king's ransom, that brooch.

Myddelton drew a deep breath and felt again her kindness. "No," he rushed to assure her. "I have only just this minute come in."

"Oh good." She picked up one of her long gloves and began to draw it on. "I was not certain for I do not always hear everything when I'm practising." She snatched up the other glove and her shawl and came across the room toward him. "Thank you so much for returning to take me to Almack's...I am certain you must be wishing yourself anywhere but here, if even half the stories I've heard about it are true." She saw that his face was pale with fatigue and grief, and his eyes had faded from blue to grey. Gently, delicately, she touched his arm. "You look so tired. Are you sure you wish to go? We do not have to, you know. I shall not be disappointed, I promise you." And smiled.

That kindness, her kindness, wholly disarmed him. The cutting retort which had been hovering at the back of his mouth ready to leap to his lips died, unspoken. Her smile, he reflected, could lead a rational man to...well, spend the evening at Almack's. 'Struth, her smile could lead a one-armed soldier with a wooden leg to attempt the waltz. "Not at all. Well... that would depend upon which stories you may have heard, I should think..." he said, attempting to lighten any impression of gloom. "You're wearing your hair differently...it's good." It was true, but he hadn't meant to say it.

"Thank you." She didn't just smile, she glowed.

He was lost.

And taking his arm, she resolved to wear her hair just as it was now—whatever Haseley might say. "Mr. Hardy called today, apologising profusely for having done so without permission. And at the same time apologising for not having called earlier…"

At least someone possessed an ounce of courtesy. Thank Christ for Ned Hardy.

"…And brought me sheaves and sheaves of music…"

Myddelton's eyebrows rose. "Any of it worth hearing?"

She laughed. "Oh yes, all of it…well," she admitted. "Most of it. Provided I practise a great deal."

Had she always been this engaging? This direct? This restful?

"…Though to be fair, much of what he brought was songs by Herr Mozart. He hopes, that is, he has asked if I will accompany him next week at this musical evening—at Lady Romford's, is it? I have assured him I shall do my best but that I can make no promises…" She shook her head. "Does he often choose music that's not worth hearing?" she asked as they went out to where the town carriage stood waiting.

She had resolved that nothing he should say or do would mar her composure, not even if he behaved as he had at Anne's the other evening, not even if *he* insisted on helping her into the carriage—as he was now doing with his hands firmly planted about her waist—rather than allowing William to hand her decorously up. She could hardly know what comfort he found in having his hands about her waist, even briefly.

"Dunphail says so," Myddelton said. "But then according to Dunphail—who's his cousin, by the by—he spends half his time playing the most extraordinary things—crashing chords or discords or…He says it sounds 'driven' or impassioned or something. I don't know m'self. I've not heard him."

She paused to consider, before venturing. "I should think that will be the music of Herr Beethoven." And diffidently: "I rather like him. But…I haven't always the strength or the speed to play his music well."

Myddelton waited until they were seated and the carriage in motion before he took a careful pinch of snuff, inhaling hard, and returned the box to his pocket. "Why do you not play for Hardy? He told me that you were taught by Clementi—which I hadn't known..." He intended it as neither a compliment nor a rebuke, only as a statement of fact. "...and that you are superb." He perceived rather than saw that she was blushing.

"What?" It came out as a squeak. "He said that? Well," she began, "Well, I was taught by Signore Clementi...for a while, but...he said that?"

He smiled, refreshed by her bewildered modesty.

She calmed, laughed a little, and tried to recover. "I'm all very well at sonatas...or variations. But then, I've been playing those since I was a child, so it's nothing wonderful. But, as I have never been much good at accompaniment, I have always leaned toward the solo repertoire, do you see? It's lack of practice, more than anything, I dare say. And a song—to be performed well—is more like playing quartets or trios...or even in an orchestra. All the performers must work together—must listen and breathe and count entirely as one—in order to create that single moment of beauty." She drew a deep breath. "But since I have not had the practice, I do not know that I have the knack of it or that I can do it at all well."

None of which he had known or even considered. "Surely you played for others at your uncle's."

She shook her head. "No. No, not really. Gussie and Marianne would have been the obvious choices for that, but...well, neither of them ever sat still for long enough to learn an instrument. And certainly not to practice it."

Amused by such forthrightness, Myddelton chuckled. "No," he agreed. Then: "Lud, it must have been fairly, ehm, exuberant, having those two for close neighbours."

That low chortle began in her throat—the one that was not the product of a ladies' private finishing school. "Oh, it was. But occasionally, you know, they did go home to Somerset, allowing us the unutterable bliss and luxury of restorative tedium."

He laughed out loud at this.

And was still laughing to himself as they stepped through Almack's famed front doors, past the footmen who zealously guarded their prerogative of turning away underdressed gentlemen and late-comers, and into the main hall. Myddelton eyed the room—the white pilasters, the shell pink walls, the odd flake of peeling paint, the clusters of well-bred, anxious females here to catch a husband, the dandies—and again wished passionately that he were anywhere but here. Through clenched teeth, he said: "Smile, m'dear, and savour this moment. For you and I are making history."

Obediently, brightly, she smiled. He felt her tuck her hand just that much more firmly about his arm (which he found oddly soothing) while she too surveyed the room and its many occupants dressed and overdressed in their finery. "History?"

"Od's death, I had forgot just how much I dislike this place. Indeed. History. I've not been here in...oh, it must be two years. And now..." His features hardened slightly. "Now, I have reappeared in the company of m'lady wife." He watched as news of their presence spread and head after head turned to ogle them. He nodded to several of his acquaintances across the room.

"Two years? Can it be that you have only been snoring away in the Lords' chamber for two years? From the way everyone behaves, I had assumed you to be a permanent fixture there—rather like the benches." Her smile was particularly sweet—her uncle would have been instantly wary at the sight of it.

Myddelton was learning to be. "Ah no. Before that I contained my frivolity so that it did not spill over into the chambers of government." And nodded again to a dowager who had known his parents and her unmarried granddaughter.

"Oh, I see. And what can have caused you to allow it to spill over so abandonedly?"

She saw that the bleakness was back, had come with the suddenness of night falling as in the west, where the sun, there bright one minute, then gone in an instant as it drops beyond the mountains and into the sea. Around his mouth there appeared a white line of strain as he tightened his jaw against a welling up of incapacitating rage and misery. "A cousin of mine became French cannon fodder," he said. "And, although he was considered the black sheep of the family, I had been fond of him." He wanted to shout.

"Oh Myddelton, I am so sorry." Her voice was soft, laced with the unhappy knowledge that she had exacerbated his grief. "Forgive me, I had not realised…"

"What? That I had a cousin?" he snapped. He had not meant to, but everything—every emotion and reaction—seemed so beyond his control. "Or that I could be fond of someone?" Why had he come here?

She refused, positively refused, to be intimidated. She blinked rapidly against incipient tears, telling herself this was not the place for a display of emotion, and said with deceptive lightness: "Oh no. No, nothing like that. It's just that I had assumed *you* must be the black sheep of the family."

It was too unexpected. Laying hold once more on that elusive equanimity he laughed, though it sounded more like a croaking bark than laughter. Once more, heads turned to watch them. "Oh no, m'dear." Had they been anywhere else, he would have cleaved to her. "'Struth, I can assure you, in comparison, I am merely a nondescript grey."

There was that low chuckle again. She scrutinised his face and his eyes which were losing their bleakness, then nodded sagaciously. "Of course. I see it now. My mistake."

They had reached the ballroom. A quadrille was finishing. "Do you really mean to bar me from waltzing with everyone but you?" she asked with a calmness she did not feel.

In honesty, he had not thought. But knew suddenly he was damned if he would allow any other man to have his arms about her. And was sure of it as he gazed round the room at the dandified town tulips, the scarlet-coated officers, the other eager young whipsters. "Yes."

She paused. Her perfect smile hid her surprise. "But surely, it will cause a great deal of talk, will it not?" Which did not disguise her puzzlement. Why should he be doing this? Out of grief or loss? Inconceivable, surely. Then what?

"Perhaps." He would not be drawn. "Yes, I dare say."

This did confuse her. She was not accustomed to the oblique. "But why?"

"Why what? Why should I restrict you? Or why will it cause talk? I should have thought the answers to both those questions were obvious." A sudden whimsical smile transformed his features.

She hadn't an answer. He *was* in that dangerous mood. Or one very similar.

Lady Jersey, bejewelled and resplendent, was bearing down on them with a look of immense superiority.

"Ah Sally, good evening." Myddelton's smile was distant. He hoped she would not prove solicitous on this occasion; he was fine as long as no one offered him sympathy or enquired after him.

"Myddelton, my dear, you have returned to us at last," Lady Jersey began. "Your dear little bride must be the reason for that. Good evening, my dear. How perfectly lovely you are looking. Myddelton always was one of the best dancers, you know, and I for one considered it nothing short of tragic when he stopped coming to our little assemblies. Gentlemen who dance as well as he have no business making themselves scarce on such occasions as these," she declared, rapping the air with her closed fan. "No one performs Mr. Beveridge's Maggot better than Myddelton. No one. Not even Mr. Brummell, though I beg you shall not tell him I say so. But Myddelton has such a sense of elegance...and style. Myddelton, I trust you will behave yourself and not squirrel yourself away—as you have done so often in the past—in the cardroom after you have danced with your wife. Because Pemberton is here... somewhere..." She waved a hand vaguely in the direction of the card room. "And I trust I know what the two of you can be like when you're together. Myddelton, you must present your lovely bride to the Princess Esterhazy, because I know she is most anxious to make her acquaintance and...Oh, there is Emily. You must excuse me, dear ones, because I simply must speak to her..." Her tongue still in full spate, she drifted away.

"Ah Silence," Myddelton murmured.

Jane suppressed a giggle.

A waltz was beginning. Myddelton turned himself toward her, and with a composure he would not have imagined possible three minutes ago, bowed formally and solicited the hand of his wife. Which she—with a wistful half-smile—bestowed upon him that he might lead her to the centre of the floor before taking her in his arms.

As Miss Heron, she had not been reared for danger. Certainly not for the emotional danger which Myddelton embodied. But the residue of uncertainty or fear or resentment which had coloured each instance they had been together, had been diluted and dissolved in the aftermath of Perceval's death. She had been in Myddelton's arms before, when he had smelled of orange blossom and when he had smelled of blood and fear. She had felt the hardness of his chest against her cheek, had felt her hand dwarfed and surrounded in his, had felt him warm, unthreatening, protective, safe, alive. And was finding, to her surprise and even confusion, that she liked it and liked it very well. She drew in a deep breath of him—snuff and spiced orange blossom—and strove to match his steps.

And Myddelton, having found in her a comfort he craved (was it only two days since?) found again—despite the anger, the distress, the fatigue, the grief—that comfort, felt again the pleasure he had known three nights previously when he had so wanted her in his arms. Her. His wife. This lissome, beautiful girl. Owned, belonging, and quiescent against a background of well-performed music. For the first time in days, he remembered and felt the unequalled frictionless contentment of normality.

"Myddelton," she began. "Myddelton," she repeated after completing a turn. He saw that she was looking perplexed. "There is a young man staring at us."

"Nonsense. There is a young man staring at you." His eyes had lost their bereft-ness and there was almost a hint of his former smile somewhere to be found.

"All right then," she agreed. "A young man staring at me."

"'Struth, every fellow in the room is staring at you."

Was that a compliment? "No," she laughed. "This one is really staring at me." She craned her neck—just a little—to see him better. Yes, there he was, still standing, gawping, beside the pillar.

"Perhaps he is fixated by your fancy garters? You did wear them, did you not?" he enquired, enjoying her blushes.

232

"I did." She refused to be affronted. Or embarrassed.

"Pity I can't see 'em."

"You should have thought of that earlier. Had you said something in the carriage…"

So she did know how to flirt. Delectable. "You make me envy the wallflowers."

"Such a compliment to my dancing!" she declared, making him smile again. She did like it when he smiled. "Do you not see him? He is standing over there. He has been staring at me since we came in. He is wearing a pale blue cravat."

Myddelton narrowed his eyes against the too incipient pleasure and protested, drawling broadly, "'Pon my soul, I positively refuse to look upon anything so unsettling as a fellow sporting a pale blue cravat. Even for you." Her chuckle grew. "Just think how it might affect m'digestion. Even if he has tied it in an Osbaldstone knot…" And drew her a fraction closer. *His* wife. "Fancy appearing in the Osbaldstone at Almack's…" he continued piously. "'Struth, I'm flummoxed they didn't turn him away at the door…"

By the time the waltz had finished, Pemberton had emerged from the card room and stood near the edge of the dancefloor, ready to claim her as his partner for the next dance, whatever it might be. Mr. Hardy succeeded him, and remained with her long after their dance had finished to discuss the music he had left with her: Did she not think *Abendempfindung* sublime? And what of *Dans un bois solitaire*? And did she not feel *Trennungslied*, with its unadorned left hand—to be sure, like a portent of doom—was quite unlike anything else Mozart had written? But perhaps not when one recalled the opening of the C Major Quartet, which was so dark and despairing…More indeed like the Requiem… And would it be convenient if he were to pay her a visit that they might practice together before the Musicale on Monday next? Then sighting Lady Anne Northcote, with whom Jane hoped to speak, across the crowded room and—still talking of music—they began the winding journey toward her through the cliques and couples crowding the perimeter of the dancefloor.

"My dears," Lady Anne exclaimed as they approached. She paused while Hardy kissed the air above her hand, and she leaned forward to kiss the air beside Jane's cheek. "You did come. I am so glad. Mr. Hardy, how do you do? No, don't tell me, I can see. You have been discussing music with Lady Myddelton, I have no doubt, and are enjoying yourself beyond measure. Am I not right?"

His obvious pleasure in her company was answer enough. Mr. Hardy bowed and excused himself.

Anne tucked her arm about Jane's and said quietly and seriously, "Now tell me—though this is hardly the place—how is it? How has my cousin been?"

"He is still much shocked …and grieving, I believe," Jane said after careful thought, searching the room for a glimpse of him. "I would say he is not himself…but I hardly know what that means. That is, I have only known him a fortnight… but he seems…angry. He remains at the Foreign Office. I do not see him…"

Anne listened in silence. Then something caught her eye and she murmured, "Oh no, not him."

Jane stopped. "I beg your pardon?"

She expelled a peevish breath. "Oh lud, he is coming this way, determined to be presented to you, I make no doubt…Jane. My dear, you will not thank me for this, but I cannot see how I may avoid performing the introduction. Therefore, I shall beg your forgiveness now…" she said pointedly, regarding the him in question. "Before you have met. Because afterward, I know of a certainty, that you shall not grant it."

"What?" Bewildered, it was all Jane could manage. Then she saw. The pale blue cravat. "Oh. He cannot be as bad as that, can he?"

"I regret to say, he is worse. Much much worse," Anne muttered. "And how do you do, Mr. Pickering-Stone?" She bestowed one of her best and most gracious smiles. "I trust you are well?"

Surreptitiously, Jane eyed the young Mr. Pickering-Stone. His face might have been called divine by his admirers, and she had no doubt he had many. It was dominated by his very large, very pale blue eyes, heavily lashed. His nose was straight and his mouth, soft and beautifully curved. He looked, Jane thought, with his perfectly disordered fair curls, like a model for some Renaissance master's angel. His coat was well enough cut, but, unusually, was of a delicate shade of pale blue-grey and his knee breeches were of a dark grey, instead of the preferred black. And there was that pale blue cravat.

He swept a low bow. "I am in alt, Lady. To be in the presence of such beauty as is present here this eve is to dine with Orpheus." His gaze did not waver from Jane's face. "Say that you will present me to this, the fairest of Olympia's offspring."

The merest trace of a frown creased Anne's brow. "But of course, Mr. Pickering-Stone. Jane, my dear, you will allow me to name Mr. Pickering-Stone to you." She stopped, briefly held her breath, then said, completing the introduction: "Mr. Pickering-Stone, the Countess of Myddelton."

Mr. Pickering-Stone placed a reverent kiss upon Jane's extended hand. "I am abased before such perfection." He spoke as if in a trance. "Aphrodite must stand in awe. 'Did my heart love till now? Forswear it, sight! For I ne'er saw true beauty till this night.'" And kissed her hand again.

Jane looked blankly. An eccentric. How perfect. Or was he merely inebriated? Hard to say. She produced an automatic smile. Pemberton became, according to his sisters, wholly stupid (as opposed to mostly stupid) when he drank too much. And Myddelton became, well, morose, she rather thought. Perhaps this Pickering-Stone spouted poetry when squiffy. It was possible. And glanced quickly at Anne for some guidance, but saw that Anne was looking away, carefully not giving way to laughter. "How kind of you to say so, Mr. Pickering-Stone. I perceive you are a student of Shakes…"

"Say not that, fair Aurora!" protested Mr. Pickering-Stone. "'Tis but the meagre offering of a mortal to a goddess. Say only that you will deliver me from the depths of woe by bestowing upon me the privilege of breathing the aura of your immortality."

"I beg your pardon?" Mlle had not trained her for this. And then she caught sight of Myddelton, standing at the far side of the room, talking with Lord Castlereagh.

Suddenly Anne spoke: "How kind in you to ask Lady Myddelton to dance, Mr. Pickering-Stone." She ignored the look of mute protest from her cousin's wife. "I am sure she will find it edifying beyond words." Then, whispering in Jane's ear, she added, "It rendered me speechless."

Again Jane glanced across at where Myddelton was. Then firmly, she said: "It is an honour that I dream not of."

But Mr. Pickering-Stone did not recognise the answer to be no. Instead, he bowed lower than he had previously and grasped her hand to draw her toward the dancefloor.

Had there been any way in which she might extract herself, she would have taken it. But there was not. Not without creating at least a demi-scene. So reluctantly, she allowed him to lead her to a place in the line for the cotillion which was forming.

Initially, blessedly, Pickering-Stone was silent and the movements of the dance separated them. And she imagined that he would not be an undesirable partner, for he did move most gracefully, if only he would cease staring at her face with such patent admiration.

But when he reached for her hand to complete the final section of the dance, Pickering-Stone began, bowing his head with reverence, "'If I profane with my unworthiest hand this holy shrine, the gentle sin is this…'"

She recognised that his memory of Shakespeare's verse was excellent, but surely, he must know how inappropriate…

"'My lips, two blushing pilgrims, ready stand…'"

He did not realise. Or did not care. She looked about, panicking that someone might overhear.

"'To smooth that rough touch with a tender ki…'"

He meant it. Lifting her heel, Jane caught her hem. The sound of ripping fabric was unmistakable. "Dear me, I have ripped my hem!" She hoped she sounded suitably dismayed, and knew she did not. "You must pardon me, Mr. Pickering-Stone, but I must go and have it repaired." With an apologetic smile to the other dancers, she hurried from the dancefloor toward the ladies' tiring room.

Where she remained for long after the attendant had basted up the hem of her gown, sipping at a glass of water until she was certain she had no other dances free.

"Anne," Pemberton said softly, sometime later as he joined her on a small sofa, where she had been sitting, happily alone for some minutes. "Have you seen Janey?"

"Not recently, no. But I do know where she is."

"Where? Because she is meant to be dancing with me. Or was. I dare say the set is nearly finished by now."

"Well, you cannot dance with her, because she is in the ladies' having her hem seen to. And I rather think Myddelton is expecting to dance with her next, because he has been waiting for her this age."

Pemberton looked across the room at Myddelton who was now leaning against a pillar which faced the corridor that led to the ladies chamber. And watched as Jane emerged and Myddelton started toward her with the intentness of a serpent coiling to strike. And feeling suddenly far more cheerful, he grinned. "S'life would you look at him. He looks ready to swoop down an' bear her off!" he marvelled. "'Pon my soul, I didn't know he had that much energy in his whole body,"

"Hmn," Anne agreed.

"I say, did you know that he has barred her from waltzing with anyone but himself?"

"Has he? Good heavens, how very extreme."

Pemberton chuckled. "'Struth, would you look at him! When was the last time you saw Myddelton whisper in anyone's ear?"

"I'm sure I couldn't say. Pem, dearest, I am utterly parched. Do you suppose we might leave my cousin in the throes of first love or whatever it is, and go search out some refreshment?" Anne said, certain of the answer.

"My poor darling," Pemberton teased, kissing her hand to remove any sting. "We shall not keep you waiting a moment more...You don't really believe it's first love, do you? Heaven preserve me, Myddelton in love! That'll take some getting used to..."

As Jane emerged finally into the assembly room, Myddelton caught his snuff-box, with which he'd been toying, in his fist and dropped it his pocket, before springing to life and crossing that expanse of floor which separated him from his wife. He took her hand without preliminary greeting and tucked it through his arm.

She might have demurred or looked askance had she noticed, but she did not: she was too relieved that he was not Pickering-Stone. "How was the card room?"

"A dead bore," he admitted in her ear. Then, his mood shifting once again: "Will you mind terribly if we leave now? I shall see you home and then return to the Foreign Office."

Would he never sleep? Never rest? "Yes. No, of course, I do not mind…But, you look so tired. Will you not come home and lie down, even for a little…and sleep?"

He had escorted her out into the pleasant cool of the night. Their carriage was second in the queue. A small detachment of the militia stood guard at the corner of the street. "I can't sleep." He declared it baldly.

Finally: "No." What solace could she offer? None. Never mind. And she thought, as the carriage wobbled over the cobblestones, that she would have liked to thank him for this evening, that she wished she could offer him some escape from that scene of mayhem which must torment him, but he seemed so lost or forbidding as he slouched there in the corner of the seat.

"I understand you had the pleasure of dancing with this Season's Adonis," he said, after a long silence.

"I beg your pardon?" Why did he always disconcert her? And what had he heard?

"Pickering-Stone," he clarified.

Jane flushed a deep red. What had he heard? Surely not that Pickering-Stone had been reciting…This must be stopped. "I cannot think why people suppose Adonis to have been fair. For I have always assumed him to have been dark. It is, perhaps, my preference. But, after all, Adonis was a Greek, and they are rarely fair."

He could not see her furious blushes. But neither could she see the interest in the look he gave her.

"Might one look for a compliment in that?" he ventured.

She hesitated, unsure how to answer, uncertain what the real question was. "One might," she conceded.

She could not tell if he were smiling. She rather thought he was not.

"Jolly good," he murmured. "I must warn Dunphail that he's not a hope of winning your affection," he said, determined to deflect.

For once, she was not fooled. "Yes, you must," she agreed airily. "For he hasn't."

He paused, wanting to ask more. Wanting the comfort and surety of knowledge. And yet...surely it was enough that she was his wife. So, lightly, as if it were of no consequence: "Might one ask who has?"

She felt as if she had been playing a game in which the stakes had suddenly, inexplicably, become too high. And knew herself to be in danger. She swallowed and met his insouciance without flinching. "You may, of course, ask whatever you wish. But equally, I may not choose to answer." Then honesty compelled her to add (Why could she never manage to be coy like other young ladies? Why?): "Particularly if I do not know the answer."

As ever, it was unexpected and almost made him laugh. But such shadows still clouded his every thought, blanketing like heavy fog each glimmer of joy or hope. And when the carriage stopped in front of Myddelton House he could not bring himself to come inside with her.

15

"William, if you were to move that chair a few inches to the right..." She had already been out that morning to Schomberg House, to Harding & Howell's. And had returned, bearing ells of rich heavy fabrics, fabrics she intended for use in the Library, where she now stood, scrutinising and considering the various appointments. "Yes, like that. Perfect. Thank you, William."

Then, softly: "Kettering." She paused and turned to face him, her butler, her ally. "Kettering, did Lord Myddelton return home last night?" She could wish that Kettering did not look so grave—but then, everyone was looking troubled these days. The trial of Perceval's assassin was set to begin next morning.

"His lordship returned for a change of clothes this morning. And left again."

She nodded. And sighed. "Yes. I thought I had heard him...Kettering, I did think that if we were to put a day bed...there, perhaps." She indicated the place made available by William's furniture shifting. It was a spot just away from the windows and direct light, where one might lie down briefly, if one were so inclined. Not to sleep, of course, though that might follow if conditions—such as comfortable upholstery and an available rug—were conducive. And she was determined that they should be conducive. Most conducive.

Kettering appeared to frown and consider. Though he did not need to. "A very wise choice, my lady, if I may be permitted to say." Kettering understood her fully. She had known he would.

"There is, is there not, a day bed or chaise longue awaiting the upholsterer's attentions abovestairs?"

"I could not say for certain, my lady. Shall I enquire?"

"Yes. And if there is not, one must be procured instantly. It must be completed by this evening. There is the fabric for the covers." She indicated a heavy damask. "And you will ensure it is well padded. Very well padded. With a proper bolster, Kettering."

He believed he saw a glimmer of hope for his master. Or a glimmer of sleep. He had been concerned by the purple and grey shadows beneath his lordship's eyes this morning. Neither had he liked the greyish tinge to his countenance. "Yes, my lady. I shall see to it." He bowed and went off to find the soon-to-be-most-busily-occupied upholsterer.

Half an hour later, she was on her knees beside Haseley, before an open trunk in the box room, searching for a rather fine cashmere shawl which her father had brought back from India; it had proved far too voluminous for wearing, whatever the Empress Josephine might designate 'fashionable'. Which she felt might serve as the required 'rug', were it draped artlessly over the back of the day bed.

Having found her at last, Kettering gave a discreet cough.

She rocked back on her heels. "Ah, Kettering, the day bed? Will it be finished? Oh Haseley, you've found it. Well done. Oh, are there two? Oh, there are three... Kettering, do you not think one of these will answer?"

He paused for a moment, recalling with certain pride why he served her with such loyalty. "Mr. Dawkins has assured me that the day bed will be completed to your specifications by this evening. If I may be permitted to say, my lady, I believe the shawls will admirably serve the purpose for which you intend them."

She noticed the tray in his hand.

"You have a caller, my lady." He held out the tray with the card upon it.

She took the card. *The Hon. Mr. Pickering-Stone* was engraved upon it in ornate script. How odd. She had not given him leave to call. She looked closely at Kettering and was relieved to see that he did not approve. "Where have you put him?" She reached behind herself to untie her apron.

"In the Morning Room, my lady."

"Perfect. Have some tea sent in, will you? I am ready for it, even if

241

he is not." She reached up to check her hair and felt the curls tight at the nape of her neck. It was beyond help, the humidity saw to that. "Thank you, Kettering." Beginning to remove her apron, she smiled and made her way downstairs to meet the rag-mannered Mr. Pickering-Stone.

Her first impulse upon seeing him was to turn and leave. Her second, also suppressed, was to laugh. Mr. Pickering-Stone had dressed for the occasion in what she assumed was his idea of the poetical: his shirt was open at the neck and his velvet jacket resembled a doublet more than anything else, being loosely laced across his chest, and the sleeves of which were slashed to reveal flourishes of blue silk. With dark velvet breeches and soft boots of black kid, he looked ready for a fancy-dress ball or the stage or a well-costumed game of charades. And quelling the laughter which was welling up, she thought unhelpfully and irrepressibly, 'Lord Hamlet, with his doublet all unbraced, no hat upon his head, his stockings fouled, ungartered, and down-gyved to the ankle...'

"Mr. Pickering-Stone. How unexpected." She advanced into the room. She was determined not to extend her hand that he might kiss or fondle it. She waited while he bowed, deeply, hyperbolically even, then said: "Will you not be seated?"

Mr. Pickering-Stone began as he apparently meant to go on—by staring like a mooncalf at her face. And instead of seating himself, he rushed forward to fling himself on his knees before her and reached to take the hem of her gown and kiss it.

Quickly, she took a step backward.

"Fairest flower that e'er breathed Olympia's air, I pray you, accept my tribute, the first fruit of this season, as the commencement of the praise which shall never from my lips cease, henceforth." He rummaged in his cuff and produced a folded sheet of paper, which he kissed and held out for her.

Gingerly, hesitantly, deliberately ignoring the kissing bit, Jane took the paper—thank heaven he hadn't stored it next to his heart. In the light of day, he appeared much younger than he had last evening, scarce older than herself. "Do, pray, rise and be seated, Mr. Pickering-Stone. I am certain you will find it much more comfortable than the floor." She smiled, indicating the seat opposite for a second time. Perhaps if she

242

were seated he would follow suit? She perched on the edge of the nearest chair; no, it made no difference. And with certain reluctance unfolded the paper. A pucker appeared between her brows as she exhaled in surprise, and read:

A Sonnet

by E.H.R. Pickering-Stone

The fairest lily ne'er had eyes so blue,
Nor cheek that ever did so semble rose.
As fresh as grass that is bedamped with dew
As dawn breaks forth, thy countenance so shows.
The goddesses of yore thou puts to shame
And leavest all the demoiselles in tears.
Upon thy beauty none hast any claim;
Thou shalt be timeless, unassailed by years.
Would that I could but worship from afar!
Yet still thy beauty draws me ever near
Although I am close blinded by this star
Of Beauty such as thine. Thou art too dear
For use upon this earthly mortal sphere.
Be but my muse—may I but worship here.

She exhaled again. And swallowed. "Mr. Pickering-Stone, I greatly fear that you have outdone yourself. I scarcely know what to say…"

"Say nothing, Gracious Font of Inspiration, but that I may abase myself before you with profoundest adoration."

She opened her mouth to reply, then closed it. Believing Pickering-Stone an eccentric with poetic and Romantic pretensions had been too generous. Or if this was the effect of drink, he had started very early. But somehow she thought not. A pity, really. "Will you take tea?" She went to the bellpull and tugged.

"To partake of any refreshment in your gracious presence is to sup upon Olympia's summit."

Definitely far too generous. And how would Mlle have handled

243

this? With unforgivable élan, no doubt. She turned and began again, with a sweetness which could not last. "Why do you not sit down, Mr. Pickering-Stone? I am convinced you will find it infinitely easier to take a dish of tea if you are sitting down."

Moments later, for he had been waiting for her summons, Kettering appeared. "Tea, my lady."

"Oh thank you, Kettering. That is most welcome news. Put it here, thank you." Her gratitude was far too heartfelt and she knew it. 'One must never appear panicked before one's servants'...whoever had said that clearly had never had to cope with the like of young Pickering-Stone, the addlepate poet with an alleged love of Olympia. Though she was sure his understanding of such a place was nominal.

"Very good, my lady. Will that be all?"

"Thank you, yes," she said, giving him a look which affirmed the opposite.

Kettering bowed and was gone, leaving her once again in the company of Mr. Pickering-Stone, who had at last seated himself in the chair opposite.

"Mr. Pickering-Stone, do you take milk or sugar?"

"Whatever thy nymphlike hand shall deign to bestow upon me shall be my choice above all things and forever."

She smiled perfectly, masking all real emotion. "Ah."

To administer tea to one guest or many is no great matter. Certainly, as Miss Heron, she had done so on countless occasions. But this, she was finding, was entirely different.

She poured out. Ought she to add milk? Or sugar? Or both? No. He could have it black. And she very much hoped he preferred nursery tea—pale and sickly sweet.

Mr. Pickering-Stone rose from his seat to take the cup.

She froze, praying he would not go down on his knees again.

He did not. But with an obsequious bow, he received the cup and saucer, murmured fulsome thanks and returned to his appointed chair.

She tried to remain calm. Yet even as she busied herself with pouring out her own tea, she could hear the mantel clock ticking away, and wondered how many minutes until Mr. Pickering-Stone's half-hour visit would be at an end? He would be polite and observe the etiquette regarding social calls, wouldn't he?

"Have you always been interested in poetry, Mr. Pickering-Stone?" she asked at last. And immediately wished she hadn't.

With surprising grace, he set his teacup on the nearest table. "Dearest Lady, with such inspiration as your omnibeauteous self…"

Lud. Why hadn't she the wit to ask his opinion on Coke of Norfolk's farming techniques?

"…And from my youth, Wordsworth's preface to the Lyrical Ballads has been my Bible, leading me ever upward toward the summit of true poetical vision and voice…"

Or the much-debated reform of the 1598 Apprentice Acts?

"…And now having found you, I know that my star is at last in the ascendant. I have been praying Olympia to send me a sign. And last eve, upon glimpsing the handiwork of Venus in the roseate glow of your cheek and the ivory of your brow, I knew that my supplications had not been in vain…"

"I beg your pardon, my lady…"

She turned instantly. "Oh Kettering!" She ought not to have let her relief sound.

Kettering appeared not to have noticed. Nor did he seem aware that his presence had caused the poetical spate to dry up and parch. "Forgive me for disturbing you, my lady, but this missive has just arrived and the messenger has been instructed to await your reply." He held out a tray with a sealed letter upon it.

"Excuse me, Mr. Pickering-Stone," she said, taking the letter and prizing the seal open. It was an invitation to join the Northcotes in their box at the Opera House that evening, the which, Lady Anne wrote, Myddelton had already accepted for himself. "Kettering, please to inform the messenger that Lady Myddelton accepts the invitation with gratitude."

"Very good, my lady."

She glanced at the clock. Pickering-Stone had been there for twenty-four minutes. Which surely was more than anyone should bear. She rose from her seat. "Mr. Pickering-Stone, I really must not take up any more of your time."

She ignored his look of surprise and dismay as he stood up; did she not know that he had planned to declaim a ballad which he was composing upon the subject of Aurora threading her rosy light fingers through Lady Myddelton's fair tresses? Nor did she know (a blessing, surely) that during the night as he had dreamed, and poetised his rapturous paeans, he addressed her more familiarly. Obviously, she did not yet comprehend or appreciate the depth of his passion and of his devotion to her.

"Thank you so much for calling. And for the sonnet." She extended her hand for him to salute, but snatched it away as soon as he had touched her fingers. "Kettering, Mr. Pickering-Stone is just leaving."

Scuppered, the poet swept her the lowest, most elegant, most 'immolated upon the altar of courtly passion' bow.

"Goodbye, Mr. Pickering-Stone." She smiled again and hurried from the room. Perhaps she was beginning to understand more than he reckoned on; certainly it would be well if she did.

The King's Theatre, Haymarket: It was not as Jane had anticipated it would be. Not at all. They arrived late, during the first interval. And Madame Angelica Catalani of the 'prodigiously beautiful voice' was not singing. She said she had a sore throat. Rumour said she'd had a spat with the manager. Neither was the Irish tenor, Michael Kelly, of the powerful and amazing legato, singing in the evening's performance. Nor was it a much-anticipated premiere of one of Herr Mozart's operas. That too would have to wait. She had missed the opening of *Cosi Fan Tutte*…And knew that *Le Nozze di Figaro* would not be performed until June. Still, it was the King's Theatre and she was there.

Ornate gilded plasterwork adorned the ceiling and the fronts of the boxes, most of which were filled with well-dressed and overdressed ladies, not-ladies and gentlemen. The glass chandeliers glimmered and winkled, as did the jewels adorning the ladies' and the not-ladies' hair, throats and wrists. And the orchestra was said to be very fine. Very fine indeed. Though she knew from the Greenwood sisters that few would listen to the entr'actes, or to anything else, for that matter.

They had been seated for some minutes, had been seen and acknowledged and observed with interest, when Sir Miles had volunteered to go in search of refreshments, or a servant to procure same or both. Myddelton was delayed which was to have been expected.

"I do assure you, I have never been so rude in all my life," Jane declared, now that there was no one to overhear. "I never knew I could be that ruthless. I dare say I never had cause before, but all the same…"

Lady Anne was pressing her gloved fist against her lips to stifle her laughter. It wasn't working.

"It was not funny! Well, actually, it was…" Lady Myddelton too began to laugh, though reluctantly at first. "I hardly knew where to look. And when he persisted in kneeling and tried to kiss the hem of my gown, I could not think what to do!"

"Kicked him, I should have thought…"

Jane laughed. "And he kissed the paper most tenderly before he gave it me! It was too revolting. Really it was." She smoothed the fingers of her glove.

Undignified it might be, but the thought of Mr. Pickering-Stone in fancy dress, on his knees, delivering a poem, gave Lady Anne Northcote the giggles. "Did you bring it?"

"I could hardly leave it at home to be found by a servant, even Kettering." Jane opened her reticule. "Here it is…It is meant to be a sonnet. That is to say, it is in sonnet form." She gave the folded paper to Anne. "And don't you dare laugh out loud."

Meticulously, Anne unfolded the paper, and composed her features. "A sonnet. By E.H.R. Pickering-Stone." She read it. "Dear me…" And reread it. She did not mean to, but she began to giggle again. Eventually she refolded the paper to return it, remarking only: "I had not realised that lilies had eyes at all…let alone *blue* eyes."

Jane risked a glance at her. "No," she agreed. And replaced the paper in her reticule. She shook her head. "Lud…I shall have to tell Kettering to deny me, I think…" She smoothed the ecru silk of her gown. And wished that Myddelton might come soon.

Which he did, as if on cue, looking tired, the fingers of his writing hand badly ink-stained, and taking in all of her in one long look.

"Myddelton, you did manage to escape at last. Well done," Anne declared as he appeared in the doorway to their box. "And here is Miles, right behind you, with the champagne. What could be better timed?"

He greeted his cousin and her husband with fond familiarity. And thought with a mixture of ruefulness and possessive pride that *she* was looking particularly beautiful. And was pleasantly surprised to realise that it no longer shocked or angered him to think of her as his wife. Then, he found he could think of no greeting which was either adequate or appropriate under the so many circumstances, so said, as he took her hand to kiss and hold, "M'dear. I should have thought of bringing you to the opera sooner." And felt immediately that that too was inadequate.

"I am happy to be here now. And I shall hold you to that, next month, for the premiere of *Le Nozze di Figaro*," she answered, deeply glad that he had come.

"A subversive opera, one understands, from an even more subversive play," he teased, content and at ease.

"Myddelton, do sit and have some champagne."

"No, no, I mustn't," Myddelton said, seating himself toward the rear of the box. "I've not had a moment to dine. One glass and I'll be drunk as a monk."

"Good God," Northcote exclaimed. "My dear fellow, you really must learn to call a halt or Castlereagh'll work you to death. I know I've said it before, but whatever it is that comes in in that dispatch pouch at eight o'clock in the evening can wait, at least until the next morning. I know you Foreign Office chappies find that hard to believe…"

Tired, but surprisingly content, Myddelton laughed. "I know, I know. But on this occasion, it honestly could not wait."

Northcote smiled. "I suppose one can only be grateful the Admiralty never learned of your linguistic talents. Had they, I make no doubt but that you would have been shipped off as private secretary to some crusty old Rear Admiral and never see dry land, let alone your wife, for years while you patrolled the Mediterranean on a leaky man-o'-war."

The second act of the opera was beginning. Jane and Anne moved forward to the very front of the box to listen and watch.

Northcote slid a glance at his cousin by marriage and said genially,

"And how are the Spaniards these days…"

A smile twitched at the corners of his mouth, but Myddelton did not rise to the bait. For once. "The same. The same," he said, his affability not at all ruffled. "Idle…vain… unscrupulous, venal…They denounce Wellington for not feeding and clothing their army, they blame him because at least half the Spanish army has deserted because they're starving, poor blighters…Cuesta whines because Wellington don't let him dictate the campaign, and then they denounce us for not increasing their subsidy…When all the while we know perfectly well that not a ha'penny of the tens of thousands we're paying 'em has ever reached the troops for whom it was intended…" He laughed a little. "D'you know, Miles, I sometimes think reading their letters is going to send Castlereagh off in a fit of apoplexy—damned if I don't. Still…"

Then, he dropped his voice so that only Northcote might hear—for Northcote was one of those few who had a shrewd idea of what his work in the Foreign Office entailed—and continued: "But this afternoon… this afternoon, it was yet another set of intelligence reports, d'you see, all confirming a French withdrawal from the Peninsula of some proportion." He rocked his chair back on its hind legs and balanced comfortably. "The estimates vary, depending on the writer—where he is, where he has been, that sort of thing—but it would seem that we probably looking at a withdrawal of some five to seven thousand French troops."

"What? You don't say." Despite his surprise, Northcote too kept his voice lowered.

"I do assure you…"

"But why, Myddelton? Why on earth would Bonaparte do such a thing? Why take such a risk? Already, Wellington has beat the French out of Portugal, and now they're losing ground in Spain too! And to withdraw troops in the face of our victories…One would have thought Boney'd want to go there himself, not…"

"Wellington has been expecting him to come any time this past nine months! He writes so to Liverpool every week," Myddelton cut in. "As have we all! It has been our greatest concern. But Boney ain't stirred from Paris. And now, I've even got one Spaniard who's talking about a combined pull-out of ten thousand French troops," he said, stopping, and would not say more. Then, conscious that he must hew a careful line between the acceptable exchange of news between friends and a dishonourable and dangerous breach of confidence, he added: "Though, I must confess, that does seem a trifle excessive...So, you see, it was, on this occasion, rather important that I wade through it all and get some sort of a report over to Liverpool. He was expecting to answer questions on the Peninsula later this evening and Castlereagh reckoned he could do to have these reports up his sleeve."

"Well I never...Ten thousand troops?" Northcote repeated in certain awe. "Ten thousand? What would that leave? A band of skirmishers or two?" And drew a deep breath. "That would leave Wellington a clear field to do as he likes. There would be no stopping him. Bonaparte would be finished. Certainly in Spain and Portugal..."

"Finished...Is it too much to hope for?" Myddelton said lightly. Then, his voice darkening: "Not if the Government falls, and Prinny hands power to his old friends, the Whigs. Because the first thing they'll do is pursue their imbecilic policy of appeasement. In which case, I'll be blunt, we're sunk. And not only us. All of Europe."

"Good lord, yes." Frowning over the potential crisis of government, Northcote fell silent.

Myddelton leaned his chair further onto its back legs and watched *her* watching the opera. S'life, why could he not have met and married her in peacetime? It might have made so many more things possible. But when had there been peace? Not in his lifetime. Not really. Not unless one included that brief spell of fourteen months back in '02 when he was what? Eighteen? Which would have made her eight. Anyway, that *peace* had proved to be nothing more than another of Napoleon's feints during which he had rearmed his men and assembled a fleet for the sole purpose of invading England. Which only Nelson had stopped.

The third act of the opera finished and the audience applauded, though not enthusiastically; Jane was delighted, but not entranced.

Myddelton and Northcote had resumed their conversation, though it had moved from foreign to domestic affairs: "...Northcote, that trial tomorrow is going to be a damned farce. You know it is. Bellingham is as mad as that old coot who, year after year, builds her nest just downstream from Folly Bridge and takes on all comers, up to and including the swans and the punts...Or mayhap it's generations of mad coots...But that's beside the point. You should have heard his testimony to the Magistrates th'other night. No matter what was asked, he denied any personal enmity toward Perceval and in fact expressed the greatest sorrow for his death. And then he insisted that he hadn't injured the individual, though he had taken away the life of the Chancellor...If you can work that out..."

"What?" Sir Miles exclaimed.

"Myddelton," Lady Anne interrupted, after watching her cousin's wife watching her cousin for a long silent moment. "Myddelton, when do you intend to take Jane down to Great Myddelton? To show her about, and allow her to become acquainted with her new home? Your tenants and neighbours must be longing to know her."

Quite surprised, Jane looked first at Anne and then back to Myddelton. He was still leaning back on his chair, balancing on the balls of his feet. He looked so handsome to her—so elegantly dressed, his cravat so beautifully starched and knotted—so unattainable.

"'Struth, I don't know. To be sure, I've not had the time." As a general policy, he disliked being managed by his cousin, but found to his surprise that in this instance, he had not the slightest objection. He smiled at Jane. "I'm sorry. D'you mind very much?"

"I..." she began, but got no further.

"You could leave after the trial. Tomorrow," Northcote put in. "For quite honestly, Myddelton, Castlereagh will work you to death if you ain't careful. All with the best will in the world, of course. Obviously, you must be at the trial, you've got to give evidence, I know, but it should all be over in a trice."

"Unless Bellingham confesses to more than Perceval's murder," Myddelton said.

Northcote sighed and agreed: "Yes. Well, that is to be expected. But I trust we have his measure by now. And we have his signed confession, so I should think..."

"It sounds a very good plan to me," Lady Anne said, determined to

251

bring the conversation back to the proposed visit to Hampshire. For she had detected the kindling of hope in Lady Myddelton's eyes.

Myddelton regarded Jane steadily. "Would you enjoy that? It ain't a long drive. Just under four hours. We could be there in time for dinner."

She could hardly believe it. It was too wonderful, too much to have hoped for. "Yes. Yes, I would enjoy that very much."

"It's settled then. We'll leave in th'afternoon." He rocked back and forth. "'Pon my word, it will be pleasant to be away for a day or two."

Did she imagine it, or had a certain unlooked for tranquillity settled over him at the thought of being at his home? Nor could she quash the burgeoning anticipation, hope and excitement which now began to fill her thoughts.

The orchestra had retuned and the conductor returned, with his violin, to stand before them. He tapped out the count in the air with his bow. The music began; the velvet curtains swished open for the fourth and final act. Jane barely heard. She could only think that she would be with him. They would be away from London and all the responsibilities which dominated his existence. She would not be afraid. Not at all like when he had come to her home, when he had come to claim her.

"Lord Myddelton?" A footman in dark livery had entered the box. "My lord?" He squinted anxiously first at Sir Miles and then at Myddelton.

"Yes, what is it?" Myddelton lowered his chair back onto its front legs and took the sealed letter. Opening it, he scanned the contents. "'Sdeath."

Jane noticed a muscle had begun to quiver in his cheek, and did not like to see it. "What is it?"

He swallowed tightly. "M'dear. Anne, please excuse me. I must go. I'm needed and required elsewhere." He rose and took his wife's hand. "I'm truly sorry, but after the trial I must accompany Lord Castlereagh to North Cray..."

Miles exchanged glances with his wife. This sudden invitation to North Cray meant one thing only: Myddelton was being launched into the innermost circle of the Foreign Office, into that small band of Castlereagh's most trusted allies. He could not refuse.

"...so I shall have to take you to Great Myddelton another time. Sooner, rather than later, though." And for the first time, Myddelton found that he was angry that he must leave her, found himself hating the new tears which he believed he saw collecting unshed in her clear eyes.

"What's this?" Pemberton slid past the footman and into the box. "'Evening all."

"The Foreign Office..." Myddelton explained.

Narrowing his eyes, for he recognised that tone in Myddelton's voice—it did not ever augur well—and he did not like hearing it there, Pemberton looked to Jane, gauging her reaction. Her command of herself was total. Or would have appeared so to one who did not know her well. But he did know her. "Ehm, shall I see Janey home for you then, old dear?" He moved to stand beside her chair and laid a fraternal arm across her shoulders.

"Would you?" Myddelton relaxed slightly.

Jane, teetering between despair and relief, smiled her gratitude. "Thank you."

Myddelton, making his farewells, took her hand to kiss. "I shall look to see you when I return. On Monday."

"Not to worry, old thing," Pemberton chimed in, insouciant as ever. "I shall look after her. See if I don't."

Myddelton laughed. "Northcote, I shall see you at the trial. Anne. Pem." Myddelton bowed and left the box, attended by the footman.

Pemberton watched them go, then settled himself on the chair beside Janey and leaned toward her. "Now Angel, tell me all of the things you've been longing to do since you came up to Town, but ain't had the chance to do yet..."

16

Miss Heron of Britwell Park had not been schooled for a life of elegant uselessness and vapid pleasure-seeking. Instead, she had been reared as a gentlewoman. That is to say, from her childhood she had been raised to expect that she would oversee and manage a large household, that she would compute and pay the taxes, tips, and weekly wages, that she would hire and retain housemaids, that she would cut and sew her husband's shirts, as well as bed-linens, direct the polishing of silver and copper and furniture, and that, should she be so blessed, she would supervise her children's education—and, regardless of domestic provocation, would always appear a gracious lady of leisure.

It had been Lady Choate who had insisted upon Miss Heron's twelfth birthday that she begin to keep a notebook of household œconomy in which she must record all the necessary information. And so she had. And what a compendium of knowledge that was to become under the Marchioness' tutelage! For as everyone knew, a gentleman hadn't the least idea about managing a household, or as Lady Choate had pithily expressed it only recently, "Show me an ill-run household and I will show you a household that wants a mistress…If the housemaids run off, then you may depend upon it, a man will sleep between dirty sheets. And probably never even notice!" For who had not suffered the decampment of one or several housemaids and sometimes the cook each time a regiment marched through the county, and what man could cope with this? "And it's no good…" Lady Choate had continued, now on a subject close to her thoughts, if not her heart. "…telling the silly girls that they won't enjoy being camp followers in Spain—the weather's dreadful, for one thing—or that these lads have a 'wife' in every county they pass through, because the foolish creatures never listen. Believe me, my dear, it is a waste of breath…But what I particularly resent is the thought of that young scalawag Wellington getting all my well-trained girls to do the washing and ironing for that army of his. He is a delightful boy, and I love him dearly, but I still resent it…"

Therefore, utterly untutored as the new Lady Myddelton was in the undoubted benefits of indolence, she had found Myddelton's lack of interest or guidance as to her position or duties an insuperable trial. But the realisation, scrupulously nurtured by Kettering, that Myddelton House stood in need of much attention had allowed her the scope to do that for which she had been reared.

Initially, the staff had found her energy and determination bewildering, if not extra-ordinary. However, under Kettering's exacting eye, they were now coming to appreciate her orderly campaign of cleaning and refurbishment and the subsequent tranquil discipline of their new mistress's regime.

Nor had it come as a surprise to Kettering upon answering her late summons, after her return from the opera with the Northcotes, to learn that the painters, paperers and the tireless Mr. Dawkins were required on the morrow—for they were to refurbish and renew all the appointments in his lordship's bedchamber during his absence over the weekend. And they were to begin work the instant he left the house.

Indeed, Kettering had been awaiting this sequence of events— though he had given no indication of these private sentiments to anyone—for it was he who had initially showed the new Lady Myddelton my lord's rooms. Yet whether it had been the faded, disintegrating hangings, or the chairs' upholstery sagging upon the threadbare carpets, which had decided her that a spot of timely intervention was requisite at the earliest possible opportunity, he did not venture to think. She had said so little—simply, "Ah!" and "Thank you for showing me, Kettering." And since then, he had never doubted that restoration and refurbishment would speedily take place; he had merely wondered how and when she would effect it.

Hence, as she required, a small, efficient army of workmen was assembled in the kitchen before eight, ready to begin work upon my lord's quitting the house. And with only one false start—caused by my lord's return moments after his departure to retrieve some indispensable sheaf of papers, during which time the workmen hovered, silent and wary, on the backstairs—just after ten, they had begun removing the rotted silk of the old curtains and hangings, shrouding the furnishings and floors in paint-spattered canvas and stripping and cleaning the dado, infill and frieze, ready for my lady's further instructions.

Lady Myddelton breakfasted early and alone. And departed while Myddelton was still in his bath for Messrs. Harding and Howell's emporium, whence to immerse herself ('once more into the breach') in the vexatious questions of which fabrics for the bed hangings and draperies, and which papers for the walls, and did Myddelton prefer blue or green: "This newest arrival from India is very fine, my lady. Or perhaps you would prefer a more subdued pattern? In green, perhaps? Though this Chinese red is magnificent, is it not?" And eventually, she returned home, the carriage seat laden with choices for her to examine at her leisure. Only she hadn't any leisure. Not this time.

By now, Myddelton appeared to have left for good, and Kettering was waiting to inform her that the workmen had discovered, under obscuring layers of soot, a painted cornice and frieze decoration, similar to that in her rooms and the Drawing Room and did she wish them to clean and restore it or paint over it? Clean and restore. And leaving William to transport the ells of fabric and the rolls of paper upstairs, and Mrs. Pinch to oversee the removal of Myddelton's old wool mattress and much diminished featherbed, she sought the services of the reticent Mr. Broke.

Mr. Broke had, thus far, managed to evade any participation in the restoration of Myddelton House, his happy quiet existence unmarred by workmen or paint fumes or the placement of fortepianos. He continued, undisturbed and unruffled, drafting Myddelton's speeches, corresponding with the tenants and overseers who farmed Myddelton's lands, scanning the newspapers for items of interest to his lordship.

This halcyon state of affairs could not last. They never do. Lady Myddelton had heard rumours that Lord D_____ and a certain baronet had each played the tables recklessly once too often, and were wanting to sell all they could of their London furnishings before the bailiffs arrived.

Thus she had steeled herself to insist that Mr. Broke visit the aforementioned households, despite his inherent shyness, and his protestations that he knew absolutely nothing of art or fine paintings—that he wouldn't recognise one if it kicked him in the toe—with what Broke considered to be an obscenely fat roll of banknotes with which he might negotiate and purchase some French or Netherlandish (she was most definite on that point) seascapes or still lifes. These, she felt sure, could more usefully be employed adorning the vast tracts of empty walls in Myddelton's bedchamber than stacked in the corner of some bailiff's warehouse. When Mr. Broke continued to demur, she bit hard on her lip, and offered him a running boy to bring her word if he had any doubts about the desirability of a given artist or painting. And restated her admonition that he should negotiate solely with the mistress of the household, who would guard such monies, and not the master, who would in all likelihood squander his gains at the gaming tables, leaving his family as much in the lurch as ever.

With Mr. Broke reluctantly on his way, she returned to the perilous task of choosing for Myddelton. And did so with the same uneasy sensation as that of riding a horse too strong and unschooled for her to handle. Should the horse behave, then well and good, but one false start, however small, would land her such a fall as from which she might never recover. She knew little of Myddelton's taste or preferences, except that he disliked the gold leaf lions and porpoises. She had never feared to offend her uncle. And her notebook of household œconomy had no word of wisdom to offer on the subject. All might so easily end in tears. And she knew she had not the courage for that.

She was still embroiled in this domestic dilemma, this decorating disputa—paint or paper, blue or green, sprigged or Chinese—when Lord Pemberton arrived.

He was greeted at the front door by William. Then, after learning that 'Milady is in the Morning Room', he assured the footman that there was no need to announce him and made his way toward the back of the house, noting with a shrewd eye that the old place was looking better than he'd seen it for some time, even taking on something of the atmosphere of Britwell Park, for it reminded him of that. He opened the door to the Morning Room, and taking in the scene—the light, the real elegance and harmony of the new appointments, and the chaos of papers and fabrics strewn about the floor—said, by way of a greeting: "I say, you have made a pig's breakfast of this, haven't you, Angel? What is all this rubbish?"

She had known him for too long to be offended. "Oh, it's you. What are you doing here?" She held up two different unrolled sheets of wallpaper. "Blue or green?" And saw that he was dressed for riding.

"What?"

"Blue or green?" she repeated, and prodded Kettle, who was as ever envisioning mortal enemies under every roll of paper and responding to that threat with the various martial skills at his command. The cat ignored her and pounced on a corner of paper.

"I'm very well, thank you," Pemberton replied cheerfully, equally unperturbed by the absence of greeting, though he hadn't a clue why she kept asking 'blue or green'. Not that it bothered him. "Kind of you to enquire…"

She frowned and looked from one roll of paper to the other. "It's really very important."

"What are you talking about?" he demanded, and wondered how it was that these Myddeltons always managed to confound him.

"Wallpaper. For Myddelton's bedchamber. Does he prefer blue or green?"

Pemberton blinked. "Lud, I don't know. Blue, I dare say. No, green. He likes green."

She examined the predominantly green sprigged paper. "Green it is, then. And if he does not like it, I shall blame it on you," she said seriously. "Did you want something?"

He pondered the blue sprigged paper, then the green. "Aye, the green. It's good, that. Where'd you come by it? What? Oh, yes. Came to take you for a ride in the Park." What he did not add was that he had been busy on her account—arranging all manner of entertainments with the same care he would have taken for a favourite younger sibling or cousin.

Delighted, she smiled. "Did you? Really?"

He regarded her with curiosity. "I said so, didn't I? Wouldn't have asked you if I didn't mean it." And eyed her gown with a friendly degree of disfavour. "I'll wait while you change." Then, as she vanished down the hall: "And bring that wretched dog along with you. He could probably use a good run after being cooped up with you…Perhaps we'll meet Brummell—he likes dogs…"

⁂

It had been, Jane thought, giving a final dissatisfied prod to her hair, the most delightful two days since her arrival a fortnight past. Last evening Pemberton had taken her to three successive balls where she had danced with him and Dunphail and Mr. Hardy. And they had ridden in the Park again today. And now, Pemberton was below, waiting to escort her to Drury Lane to a play, with private supper at Grillon's afterward.

It was not so much what they had done or seen which had made it all so pleasant. No, it was the comfortable informality of it all. Pemberton made her laugh. He teased her, talked of their mutual friends and neighbours in Oxfordshire, and spoke to her as he had always done, as an old and trusted friend. With him at her side, she had remembered herself.

Then too, there was the additional pleasure of learning to accompany Mr. Hardy. Of learning to listen to him, to breathe with him as he sang, to give him that fraction of space he needed to extend a beautiful note or to accelerate that little bit so that he would not run out of breath, to—with him—be in total submission to the composer's vision. And the songs, those he had chosen, were so beautiful and tender. It was hard work, but she loved it.

Which left only her faithful admirer, Mr. Pickering-Stone. She paused, regarding with disfavour his latest poetic offering which lay upon her dressing table. It was all very well to say that she had been trained, that Mlle had seen to everything. But that assumed that everyone followed the same rule book. Only they didn't. Or at least, he hadn't. For he constantly strayed over the line of what was acceptable, not just occasionally, but almost as if he did not know there was such a line. Or that to do so was a breach of such discourtesy. He said and did things which she did not foresee, could not prevent, and which continually placed her in an awkward position. Yet he seemed not to notice. Or if he did, not to care that his behaviour caused her disquiet. At home such uneasy situations did not arise—or at least they had not arisen in her vicinity. For who was brave enough to call twice a day at Britwell Park and so risk the gentle mockery or censure of Sir Charles? Or to tag along after a married lady? It would never have been tolerated. But in Town, things were different. She knew that. A married lady was meant to have admirers, it signified her desirability, was proof of her status and beauty. She knew this. And Pickering-Stone was welcomed everywhere. He was even courted. All the patronesses at Almack's thought him charming, if a little foolish, yet so handsome. So, what to do? His admiration seemed excessive. No, in truth it made her squirm. But did she, a stranger to London Society, dare exclude him from Myddelton House and so risk being gossiped about or thought countrified? For whatever she might choose to do or not do, it would reflect upon Myddelton.

As she descended the stairs, Pemberton, who had been rifling through the calling cards left on the hall table, looked up at the sound and smiled. "Hallo, Angel. Are you finally ready?"

She returned the smile. "Well, I could return upstairs and change my gown again if you'd prefer to wait longer."

He grinned, and looking her over approvingly, said, "No. I reckon you'll do. Just."

Then he added: "I say, what's that Pickering-Stone doing calling here?"

Repressively: "I do not wish to discuss it." But, after they were settled in the coach and on their way, she said hopefully, "Should he not be calling?"

"What? Who?"

"Pickering-Stone."

Pemberton paused. "Ehm, well, I shouldn't have thought that Myddelton would fancy it much. I know very little about him, but he has always struck me as a bit of an odd bod. He ain't precisely a dirty set of dishes, but definitely an odd bod.”

“Ah.”

Pemberton peered knowledgeably at her in the carriage’s half-light. “Why ‘ah’, Angel?”

She sighed. “Well…well…” This was difficult even with him. “The thing is he doesn’t just call…”

“What?”

“Pem, no. Good gracious! Nothing like that! It’s just that he…He’s been…Well, he writes me poetry.”

“Poetry? What?”

Now started, she could not stop, and continued: “I think he imagines that this is a *grande passion* or something.” She ignored Pemberton’s ever more frantic ‘whats?’ “It has been horribly awkward and I haven’t known what to do. He calls twice every day, even though I’ve left instructions that I am never at home to him. He writes me poetry. Passionate poetry. Execrable poetry!” Mercilessly, she pulled at the strings of her reticule and dug out the folded sheaf of paper. “Here. This is this afternoon’s.”

Hesitantly, as if the paper had been contaminated by some unspecified contagious disease, Pemberton took the page she’d tossed at him and unfolded it. And held it to the uncertain light to read:

O, thou incomparable nymph of dreams
From my heart love flows as from a stream
Eternal, constant, pure and true
Your radiant presence to bedew.
Carried away in Lethe’s arms
My thoughts fly thou-ward, laced with such charms
As will beguile thy very soul
And bind our spirits into one whole.

Then like the summer’s zephyr fair
Which sweeps caressing through thine hair,
And o’er earth’s bower bringst to bloom
Winter’s once-entombèd womb

261

That far and near, the earth enflowers
With beauty all our laughing hours,
Thy twice lovely tender smile
Enflames my passions more the while.

Each thought of thine enchanting gaze
Kindles my longings into blaze,
The which consume my every part,
And still more contrary, feed my heart,
Until I with passion near expire,
Yet still live I in tremulous desire.

Finishing, Pemberton stared blankly at the page. "Dear God..." Inexplicably, he began to laugh. And could not stop. "'Fore God, Angel, this is gruesome."

"It is not funny," she said sharply.

"Yes it is," Pemberton returned maddeningly, unable to sober. And still laughing: "Myddelton'll go mad. Absolutely mad! I say, there ain't more of these, is there?"

"No!" she retorted. "I burn them."

Pemberton straightened. "Good." He handed the paper back to her. "Burn this one too. If you want someone to write you poetry, get Myddelton to do it. He was used to win all the Latin and Greek verse competitions—his Latin sonnets won every term. His epigrams was always clever too. He's famous for 'em." He did not tell her about the folios of Latin bawdy verse which had had quite the opposite effect on the masters, at least in public.

"I didn't know Myddelton wrote poetry. Or epigrams." Then: "But what am I to do about Pickering-Stone?"

A hardened look came over Pemberton's features. One she did not know. "Leave it to me. I'll see to it."

"What will you do?"

"'Struth, I don't know," he admitted. "I haven't thought. But I'll see to it for you. So forget it."

Relief swept over her. But his sudden protectiveness made her ask that which she had meant never to mention: "Pem? Were you very surprised to find me married to Myddelton?"

He paused to consider. "Not very surprised, no. But surprised, yes. M'grandfather had wanted me to marry you, only then he discovered you was already spoken for. So I knew you was betrothed to someone. But even when Myddelton told me he was to marry—that his pater had arranged the match years earlier—I never put it together with what I knew of your circumstances."

She looked carefully at the beading upon her reticule. "And would you have?"

"Would I have what?"

"Married me?"

He eyed her intelligently. 'Ssuredly, there was no need for her to ask. "Angel, you know I would."

His honesty silenced her. Eventually though, she spoke: "Do you ever regret it?"

He did not flinch, but looked away through the carriage window. "'Struth, I don't know. But that's neither here nor there. You're married to Myddelton. You're his wife."

"I know." And unexpectedly, she chuckled. "You know, sometimes I wonder how all of this could have happened to me. It is all so far-fetched, so gothick, and I am anything but that."

He smiled. She had always possessed the keenest eye for the ridiculous and the absurd.

She continued: "Like at our wedding dinner..."

Lud! He could well imagine it. Particularly as he had seen Myddelton shortly thereafter and would have, were he of a charitable turn of mind, described Myddelton's temper as a touch testy. "'Struth, I'll wager that was a charming meal. Sorry I missed it. The height of compatibility, was it?" He did not anticipate the bluntness of her response.

"It was," she said frankly, "quite simply, the worst evening of my entire life." She paused, not seeing his expression, then corrected herself. "No, the second worst evening of my entire life."

Pemberton looked at her sharply. He could guess which was the first. And cagily speculated on what it was about that second which gave it such distinction.

Not noticing that narrowing of his eyes, she added, "I have never been so mortified, I think, nor made to feel so inadequate and out of place. After I went up to bed, I cried myself to sleep, which is something I'd never done before." It did not matter if she confided in Pemberton; he would tell no one. She knew from experience that he never had and never would. "Myddelton said he was going to his club. And the next morning he left for Newmarket... Pem, did he really go to his club, do you think?"

He frowned. She should not be asking this. "I know he did. And I know because I was there with him. I—that is to say, we—all the fellows toasted him. And his bride. And the future heir." He exhaled slowly as if it were almost painful.

"What else?" she asked, knowing there must be more. There always was.

He rolled his eyes eloquently. Why had he never learned to lie to her? "And a great many wagers were laid on his getting an heir at the first go..."

"Oh Pem, no..." she began.

"Do not tell me!" he exclaimed. "For I do not wish to know." A wry smile began at the corners of his mouth. How was it that she always managed to expose him? He sighed. "'Struth, I feel the perfect fool. For it was me that led the toasting, you know."

She had been watching him with wide eyes, her mouth open in amazement. Then wisely, she added, "And led the betting too, didn't you?" A chuckle began in her throat. "It serves you right, you know," she said with cheerful ruthlessness.

"Serves me right? How d'you figure that?" he demanded, sitting bolt upright. "Serves me right for what? For having a bit of fun with my dearest friend? The best of all fellows I've ever known? A fellow I've seen in action enough to know that he..." He broke off, appalled at his own indiscretion.

Her eyes were laughing. "You were saying?"

"Nothing."

Her smile so lacked malice, was a smile of such friendship. And she added, gently, fondly: "Indeed, it does serve you right, you know. Wagering on something about which you knew absolutely nothing."

In that instant, it was as it had always been. Janey—occasionally abetted by his repellent younger sisters—provoking him, and then having, in the nicest possible way, the final word. He eyed her with a rueful combination of affection and displeasure. 'Struth, perhaps it was better that she had married Myddelton. Because, perhaps, she was too much a sister—the sister he would have liked to have had, rather than the ones with whom Providence had seen fit to furnish him—to ever have been the wife he might have wished her to be. Had he married her, that is.

Then, breaking the long silence which was growing, he exclaimed, "Oh look, we're here. At last. 'Pon my word, the traffic in this town gets worse every year..."

Not all the world had decided to attend the theatre at Drury Lane that evening for the militia were still out in numbers on the streets against the threat of the mob. Still, there were enough to give the appearance, if not the takings, of a full house. The benches in the pit were full of young men, and the boxes were mostly occupied, some by a single gentleman, others by at least a small party of ladies and gentlemen, or not-ladies and their escorts. But, as Jane had observed at Covent Garden, the audience paid only desultory attention to the stage.

And to anyone just taking their seats, the reason was plain enough. The play, a poor production of *Two Gentlemen of Verona*, had been chosen solely as a vehicle for displaying the charms of the two leading ladies, and could boast few of the technical refinements or engaging dramatics that sophisticated London theatregoers had come to expect. Still, the first act kept many amused by its very awfulness. For in addition to its other deficiencies, it was woefully under-rehearsed. Then, in the second act, the actor playing Speed began to describe the lover—occasionally losing his place and apologising with unflappable good humour to the pit for his lapses. With the rest of the audience, Jane found herself laughing, before whispering that this must be where Pickering-Stone had got his ideas.

"No, no, no, Janey," Pemberton replied, his eyes still on the stage where the action was rapidly turning into a full fledged farce. "He has private lessons from that fellow playing what's-his-name...Valentine, that's it."

"Who has private lessons?" demanded Mr. Hardy, who with Dunphail had joined them in the box at the interval.

"Pickering-Stone," answered Pemberton.

"'Struth, I shouldn't have thought he's had private lessons in anything except how to keep his hair looking like that!" declared Dunphail. "Or perhaps in tying his cravat," he added with disdain. "It takes a certain *je ne sais quoi* to achieve such a ruin day after day."

"Oh no," Jane laughed, relieved that the whole situation was now known by Someone and would be Dealt With. "You mistake, Lord Dunphail. Mr. Pickering-Stone sees himself as a Romantic and a Poet, and therefore cannot be expected to behave as other mere mortals."

"Or so he believes..." added Pemberton in an undertone.

"Is that his excuse? I always did wonder," exclaimed Mr. Hardy with an ingenuity that made even his cousin, Dunphail, regard him with bemusement.

At the interval, Pemberton and Dunphail left Jane and Hardy discussing the songs for the Romford musicale while they went off to fetch refreshments. Though before quitting the box, Dunphail added: "I expect the lady to still be breathing when I return, Ned, so mind you don't let her see that waistcoat. And don't bore her to death neither..."

"I assure you, Mr. Hardy," continued Jane, dismissing Dunphail's teasing with a wave of her hand. "...it is not that I dislike *Trennungslied*. Never that. On the contrary. But it is so heart-wrenching and..."

"Well..." began Mr. Hardy earnestly. "Well, if that's how you feel, we certainly shan't perform it. We could, I suppose, instead, do that other we rehearsed, *Mit einem gemalten Band*—the Beethoven, you know...I have been doing a great deal of thinking, you know, and I was wondering if you'd be interested in performing a piano concerto or two." This evening, Mr. Hardy's waistcoat was a subtle (subtle as defined by him, not his friends) brocade of gold, aquamarine, silver and white. "You see, last summer, I got together a bit of a scratch orchestra—you know the sort of thing. Castlereagh came down to St. Cross for a few days and brought his 'cello. Prinny was meant to come with his, but could not get away as it happened. But we had a superb time. Myddelton and Pemberton both came...One needs an audience, you know...and Great Myddelton is under an hour's drive from St. Cross, so I was thinking perhaps if you was interested in doing one of the Beethoven Concertos, perhaps the third or...Oh, Pickering-Stone."

Mr. Pickering-Stone stood stiffly against the back wall of the box, then came forward and bowed. "Mr. Hardy."

Jane drew a deep breath, and vaguely wishing for Pemberton, extended her hand.

Abruptly Pickering-Stone rushed forward and grasping that inadvisedly extended hand, began, "Oh fair nymph, you grace us with your divinity once more..."

Instantly agog, Mr. Hardy tried to swallow his laughter and incredulity.

"To see you is to fall upon my face to worship..."

Jane felt a hot flush creeping over her cheeks.

Then turning dramatically to face Hardy, Pickering-Stone proclaimed so loudly that those in the neighbouring boxes might hear each word quite distinctly: "'O she doth teach the torches to burn bright! It seems she hangs upon the cheek of night...'"

"Please, Mr. Pickering-Stone," Jane said, now blushing furiously. "I do not believe that Mr. Hardy wishes to hear you recite Shakespeare."

Mr. Hardy lapsed into fitful coughing and dared not catch her eye.

But Mr. Pickering-Stone was not to be gainsaid; he was not to be dissuaded from performing those courtesies which his selfish or frenzied and naive sense of adoration informed him were obligatory. He gave the object of his affection a look of reverence and fell to his knees before her. "Divine, most precious lady..." he began.

Jane could feel the perspiration prickling on the back of her neck. And almost as palpably, the ripples of amused or malicious chatter breaking out in the nearest boxes, as well as the scores of heads turning toward them, fascinated to witness this unexpected and interesting facet to the young Lady Myddelton's character. And torn between wishing that Pemberton might return instantly and—or—that the floor might open and swallow her up, said urgently, "Please Mr. Pickering-Stone, get up. Please! You are making me the cynosure of everyone in…"

Mr. Pickering-Stone's breath came harder as if from great exertion. Having worked himself to the sticking point, he was determined to speak, regardless of her protestations. For she could not possibly be in earnest. "Blessed demoiselle, I must know the happiness of your divine caress…"

Mr. Hardy, his amusement transformed into a quake of dismay, sat rooted to his chair, his voice unable to function, to say what he surely knew he should be saying.

Pickering-Stone was holding her hand so tightly that it hurt. "Together, we two may worship at Aphrodite's altar. Say that you will come to me this very evening."

"Stop this!" Jane cried. "Stop it at once!"

But there was no stopping him. "…Or that I may come to you. Do not bar your door against our perfect and eternal love, but say that tonight we shall consummate the immortal glory of our passion in the fire of…"

"How dare you!" she broke in. And no longer caring for her dignity, she wrenched her hand free as fury replaced mortification.

Then, laughing at some quip, a glass of lemonade in his hand, Pemberton stepped into the box. "I say, Janey…" he began. And taking in the scene, he broke off, his laughter ceased. And his features hardening, deliberately and with a languid ease, he raised his quizzing glass to his eye to study Pickering-Stone as if he were some repulsive and rare specimen of insect.

Pickering-Stone had prepared himself for many things, but neither the remorseless glare nor the chilling hauteur of the Viscount Pemberton, heir to one of the oldest titles in the land, was among them. A dark red stained his cheeks. And for the first time, he felt the foolishness of his position.

Spiteful or witty whispers were breaking out in the neighbouring boxes and there were those now peering up from the pit, eager to see, as well.

Relentlessly, cruelly, Pemberton continued to stare, noting every detail of Pickering-Stone's poetic attire, the flushes of now-acute embarrassment colouring his face. And at last, lowering the glass, he drawled: "Upon my word, Pickering-Stone, I do not believe the lady wishes for your attentions. So I shall ask you to leave..."

A flood of intense fear washed over Pickering-Stone, drowning all amorous intentions, all poetic inclinations. Suddenly awkward, he struggled to his feet and without another word, bolted past Pemberton and Dunphail to escape into the corridor.

"Pem!" Jane whispered as he came to sit beside her, tears starting in her eyes. "Thank Heaven you came,"

"Never mind, my love," he said quietly. "Tell me about it later...Now take your lemonade and smile. Yes, smile. And laugh. As if I'm telling you the most amazing joke ever. Like the time you and Gussie and Marianne used my hat for target practice with the acorn-shooter..."

It was very late in the evening. And although the gaming tables were still moderately full, the temperate of White's membership had long since gone home. Those who remained were the dedicated gamblers and the younger members of society who saw no reason to seek their beds at any time before dawn. And it had reached that hour of the morning when the accumulation of an evening's wine might be counted upon to make the more inexperienced less discreet than may have been wise.

"I say," drawled one young exquisite, whose collar-points made it impossible for him to turn his head. "Have ye heard the latest on-dit?"

"Whassit?" slurred his gaming companion as he stared aimlessly at the flame of a candle which was guttering at the end of the wick. He had lost heavily to his companion that evening. Very heavily indeed.

"The Viscount Pemberton an' the Countess of Myddelton, that is what, m'dear Reding," replied the first young man, adjusting himself so that he might see his companion more clearly.

"You don't say," replied the morose Mr. Reding.

"Really?" interrupted a Mr. Wystan-Hyte. "I saw them together at the theatre this evening, but Lord Dunphail an' Mr. Hardy was with them too...all of Myddelton's set was there. Except for him, of course. But Pemberton was merely her escort. After all..."

"No, no!" cackled Mr. Stansgate, straining to lift his head above his shirtpoints so that he might enjoy the astonishment on their faces when he told them the next. "Much more to it than that! They was at Grillon's together afterwards, for a private supper, if you must know…" He smiled condescendingly. "An' if it ain't happened yet, it's only a matter of time. Why else would Pemberton go to such lengths to cut out Pickering-Stone? Pickering-Stone was competition—only this afternoon he was crowin' that she was on the point of sayin' yes, that it was only a matter of time between 'em!"

Mr. Reding, chuckling lewdly, grew more flushed. "Damme, but she's a tasty bite o' jam. Wouldn't object to a bit of rumpy-pumpy wi' her m'self."

"Perhaps you may have your wish one day, m'dear Reding. Who knows? She ain't been at all discreet. But what else can one expect from a cockish country gel?" Stansgate sniffed. "A tumble in the hayloft is no doubt her custom."

Reding's chuckle became a guffaw. "Who would ha' thought it? What wi' Myddelton havin' such a reputation wi' the ladies an' all. But how long till he finds out, eh? How long till he finds out?" The thought of another's misfortune pleased him mightily, facing as he was the loss of five thousand pounds as the result of one evening's play.

"'Struth, I think you must be coming down with brain-fever!" muttered Mr. Wystan-Hyte. "If you cannot talk sense, I am going home to bed," he declared, rising from his seat.

"Ten-to-one, I'm right," sneered Stansgate.

"Don't be daft," declared Wystan-Hyte.

"Done!" exclaimed Reding. "Waiter! You there! Bring the betting book!"

Mr. Wystan-Hyte eyed both his companions and shook his head, suddenly disgusted with himself. How could he have spent so much time with these malicious tattle-mongers? Beside which, it was clear that Stansgate was only playing with Reding in order to fleece him. With a polite bow, he took his leave, and wandered out of White's to begin his walk home, vowing that on the morrow, he would seek out a new circle of acquaintances.

17

She did not wish to speak of it. Indeed, she wished only to put it from her mind. Permanently. Thus it had taken Pemberton more than a little coaxing to prise from her the details of Pickering-Stone's conversation. Patiently, tenderly, he had begun again: "Angel, truly, you must tell me what happened."

But again she had shaken her head in denial. For how could she tell him that she had been treated as a creature of no virtue whatever?

At last though, she had been persuaded. So, after a private supper at Grillon's accompanied by Dunphail and Mr. Hardy, in the carriage's kindly half-light, in half sentences, punctuated by embarrassed pauses, Jane had revealed the essence of Pickering-Stone's speech. Had revealed also her fear that the public manner of his proposal must bring notoriety upon her. Revealed too her dread of an unfaithful union—she knew, of course, of those homes where infidelity was as common to the husband as to the wife and this had brought only wretchedness to all. She had always hoped for a marriage born of mutual affection, but everyone must know she slept alone. All servants talk, it is the way of things. Why else would Pickering-Stone have so presumed? And she had not the protection of a husband as she ought. So how could she now be expected to cope?

Pemberton's response had been straightforward and perhaps predictable—he had assured her he would take care of the matter. And she had been content with that.

And it had been still later as he had sat in the library of his rooms in Stephen's Hotel, sharing with Dunphail and Hardy a bottle of vintage brandy, and discussing the matter, that they had all agreed something must be done and Pemberton must do it. He was, after all, her escort.

But how? And what?

In the end, it had been Hardy who had resolved that little conundrum: "It's simple really. You warn him off."

It had been Hardy too—to Dunphail's astonishment—who had known how to create just such an opportunity. "He comes into White's Coffeeroom nearly every morning, you know," he said. "Eats his breakfast there…"

"How d'you know that?" Dunphail had demanded.

Hardy had shrugged at his cousin's indignation. "I often pop 'round there m'self. If you was ever up at a civilised hour, you'd know too."

And so it had been decided: Dunphail would go 'round to White's in the morning and invite Pickering-Stone to share his table for breakfast, and Pemberton would join them there. And the rest would follow. It was, as Hardy said, quite simple.

Dunphail found Pickering-Stone, just as Hardy said he would, alighting from a hackney carriage in front of White's. And keeping to himself the reflections that he'd never understand how the fellow got in, and how amazing that Hardy of all people should have known where to find him of a morning, called out affably, "Pickering-Stone! Well met! Come inside, do." And added after a glance at the slate-coloured sky, "'Struth, I reckon we're in for a wetting, do not you?"

For an instant, Mr. Pickering-Stone had stared at Dunphail without recognition. Then he remembered himself, and a dull flush spread over his cheeks. But it was too late for that, for already Dunphail was saying, "Do join me for breakfast, won't you?" as he draped a casual arm about Pickering-Stone's shoulders to herd him inside.

Following Saturday evening's debacle at Drury Lane, Mr. Pickering-Stone, the indulged only son of a cossetting mama and absent father, had kept to his rooms, wallowing in a satisfying morass of dramatically thwarted passion and an uneasy dread of reprisal. Certainly, his pride had been more than stung, it had been swatted by Pemberton's summary dismissal. Yet in some dim recess of his fertile imagination, Pickering-Stone had known a glimmering of salutary mortification, or perhaps reprieve, that his intended affaire had come to nothing. But the self-important and self-centred rarely indulge in self-knowledge for long, so that soothed by Dunphail's easy manner and charming camaraderie, he began quickly to reassess, and realised that his proposition to Lady Myddelton had at last placed him on an equal footing to such men of address and feminine conquest as Dunphail and Pemberton. And after all, was it not his due? For was he not the next great Romantic poet?

This happy burgeoning of manly pride was checked, however, by the sight of Pemberton, already seated at table in the half-empty Coffeeroom. And Pickering-Stone, who was not actually as stupid as he seemed, hesitated, fearing another nasty set-down.

But Pemberton did nothing in fact to indicate that he recognised in Pickering-Stone the creature he had expelled from his box at Drury Lane. Had Pemberton been drunk and had no recollection of the incident? Mr. Pickering-Stone felt a happy relief and seated himself as Pemberton nodded and murmured some indeterminate greeting.

Upon Dunphail's appearance in the Coffeeroom, a waiter had brought a trio of tankards of ale, placing them centrally on the table before Pemberton. These were shortly followed by three plates, and platters of ham, grilled kidneys, eggs and streaky rashers from which the gentlemen were liberally served by a waiter they called George.

Their plates now laden, that certain silence fell over their end of the table as Pemberton and Dunphail set to. Mr. Pickering-Stone availed himself with rather more restraint. He did not wish to overstep the boundary of what might be pleasing to his companions and so risk his unlooked-for good fortune, for it would do his reputation no little good to be seen with such gentlemen as Pemberton and Dunphail. And of course, the delicacy of his stomach and his pocket, dictated that he partook of no more than toast and a boiled egg at this hour of the morning.

His first course done, Dunphail settled back into his seat and began to enquire into Pickering-Stone's sentiments on such topics as pugilism and curricle racing. This however elicited little response: Mr. Pickering-Stone knew little and cared less. Following the hounds? Shooting? No, again. Music? Better. But still Mr. Pickering-Stone appeared either particularly diffident or perhaps just ignorant. Then neatly, so neatly that Pemberton nearly choked on his ale, Dunphail introduced the subject of poetry. And ignoring Pemberton, asked knowledgeably for Pickering-Stone's opinion of the Romantic Movement. Did he think it burnt out? Had he heard of Sir Walter Scott? Did he admire Byron?

This was Mr. Pickering-Stone's element and his vanity rose nobly to the occasion. And the display of such emotion as he felt on this most quintessential of subjects could only enhance the beauty of its messenger. Sadly for Pickering-Stone, neither Pemberton nor Dunphail were admirers of masculine beauty, unless it had been carved by some classical sculptor on a plinth or frieze and liberated from its native soil by an English or Scots gentleman while on the Grand Tour.

But before Mr. Pickering-Stone had fully outlined for his listeners the strengths and pitfalls of those Romantics who had gone before, the unimaginable vicissitudes faced by the new generation of Romantic poets, and his perception of the differences between the true Romantic who was enslaved by the beauties of his Muse and the mere dilettante or jobbing writer who feigned his raptures, Dunphail had interjected, "But where does the poet find such inspiration?"

Pemberton, who during Pickering-Stone's relentless soliloquising had nearly dozed off, glared across the table.

"Everywhere!" uttered Mr. Pickering-Stone with misplaced fervour. "It greets the enraptured sensibility at every turn: The sublime grandeur of Nature in all her myriad humours, the transcendent sadness of a rose beginning to fade and fall, the sudden, swift ecstasy of one's first and only eternal true love..."

Dunphail, having witnessed a fair share of ecstatic first eternal true loves, and second, and even third, eternal true loves, chose discretion over reality and said, "Well yes, I can appreciate that to a certain point...To be sure, I find the countryside around my home beautiful and I think on it often. And I'm deeply attached to the, ehm, fairer sex..." The affectionate glow in his eyes would have been familiar to several ladies and not-ladies of his acquaintance. "But, ehm, do you not worry about jealous husbands and that kind of thing?"

Dunphail's genial smile was one Pemberton knew well, for it was to be seen when he had been dealt a particularly nice hand at cards, and Pemberton had learned to be pleased or wary at its appearance, depending on whether he was partnering Dunphail or no. Mr. Pickering-Stone was unfamiliar with it. And quelling his amazement at the facility of Dunphail's blather, and wondering if Pickering-Stone was really so dim-witted that he didn't perceive this to be a set-up, Pemberton entered the conversation for the first time: "'Struth, I think I'd be concerned about jealous husbands if it was me writing the stuff. You can never tell when a fellow is going to get the wrong idea…And not everyone is as tolerant as Lamb. Take m'friend Myddelton, for example…"

At this a vague suspicion did trouble Mr. Pickering-Stone, and had he been less convinced of his own superior understanding, and less self-satisfied, there is no question that this perceptive inkling might have taken hold. But he was not and it did not.

"Lady Myddelton is an angel, an absolute angel …" And, with an inward apology to Myddelton for the gross misrepresentation he was about to utter, Pemberton continued, "But I trust I know Myddelton well enough to say that he is among the most jealous of men, and when his temper is upon him, which happens more frequently than it might, he don't think." The last at least was true.

"That's perfectly true," agreed Dunphail as if astonished. "D'you know, I once heard him say that if anyone so much as looked at Lady Myddelton, he would horsewhip 'em."

Pemberton shook his head. "Well, Myddelton can be a bit of a barbarian in some ways. But did he really say he'd horsewhip 'em, Dunphail? Ugh!" He shuddered. "Leaves dreadful scars, don't it?"

For days Mr. Pickering-Stone had been ardently imagining himself a martyr to the cause of Romantic passion and envisaging the affecting engraving of himself, languid and languishing in his tristesse, which would adorn the frontispiece of his volume of posthumously published verse. But this, this ghastly vision of himself, disfigured and racked with pain, cringing and begging for mercy while the fiend Myddelton raised his whip over and over again, was too terrible to contemplate. Unable to suppress his quavering, he blanched and ran a finger along the inside of his collar.

"Do things like that never worry you, then?" asked Dunphail, again at his most affable and charming.

"Me, I should prefer a bullet," stated Pemberton emphatically. "Generally speaking, you have an even chance with a bullet." And with a schoolboy's relish for the truly revolting, continued: "Or at least if a vital part is hit, death is instant. Whereas, with horsewhipping, one might linger on for days, in agony…And hell only knows what the sawbones would do. I dare say he might try to stitch the welts. Or cauterise 'em with brandy and a red-hot poker. But if putrefaction set in…"

Mr. Pickering-Stone whitened further and felt himself struggling for air.

"Or gangrene…" added Dunphail helpfully.

"But he couldn't amputate one's back or chest though, if they was infected, could he?" enquired Pemberton.

"Shouldn't think so," said Dunphail. Then he sighed deeply, feelingly. "Still, I don't think Myddelton would actually shoot to kill, Pem. Be more inclined to wound, wouldn't he? Terribly bad ton to kill." And with a frown took a drink of ale.

Mr. Pickering-Stone had never been to school; he had been educated at home, else he would have recognised those telltale signs of hyperbolic indulgence in the crude and repulsive which particularly afflict adolescent boys. Thus by the end of Dunphail and Pemberton's little recitation, he was feeling decidedly ill. And that inchoate dread of reprisal which had previously created such a delicious frisson within his breast had turned to solid conviction that Myddelton, about whom he actually knew very little, was shortly to seek him out and in an inhuman and maniacal rage whip him to death. Which premonition was now causing his breakfast to churn in an ominous manner. But, he considered feverishly, if he were to leave Town immediately, this very morning in fact, perhaps he might avoid Myddelton and the excesses of his jealous and barbaric fury.

Pemberton noted Pickering-Stone's pallor with satisfaction. And said, pushing his plate away, "Regret to say, gentlemen, but I must be off. I've an appointment with the gunsmith. Devilish glad to have seen you, Pickering-Stone." He rose from the table, and nodded, "Dunphail."

"Must come along too," Dunphail said, equally contented with their morning's work. "Pickering-Stone, it has been a pleasure." Again, he produced that charming smile. Then he rose and accompanied

Pemberton out of the Coffeeroom.

In their wake, the waiter called George came to remove the remains of their meal. And Mr. Pickering-Stone, now bereft of his poetic bravado, waited only until they had left before hurrying from the Coffeeroom, and from White's, so that he might quit Town just as soon as his packing was done.

❧

That staple of English conversation and novels, the weather, was up to her usual May-games: The exquisitely bright sunlight had early been obliterated by clouds—massive and dark—and the rain, brief pelting cloud-bursts which continued for five or five and thirty minutes depending upon the whim of the winds, had become a relentless downpour.

Myddelton, driving home from the Foreign Office in an open curricle, felt the moisture progressing down the back of his neck, even as the wind drove the rain directly into his face and soaked his collar and cravat. With growing impatience he manœuvred through another congested city lane, easing the horses and carriage in and out of yet another mud-filled pothole. In the end, he decided to stop at White's. It was closer.

"Take 'em home and rub 'em down well, Kester." He brought the curricle to a halt near the club entrance and stepped down. "I'll get a hackney later."

"You're rather late..." Northcote began as Myddelton crossed the threshold into the Morning Room. And added, as Myddelton struggled out of his driving coat and mopped at his face with his handkerchief, "By heaven, Myddelton, you're soaked through. George! A rum toddy, instantly."

The servant called George paused to catch Myddelton's eye—to his certain knowledge the Earl of Myddelton did not drink rum toddies—and Myddelton smiled.

"No George, the usual brandy if you please..." He searched his pockets for his snuff-box.

"I expect Castlereagh is glad this business with Bellingham is over,"

Northcote said, accompanying Myddelton to stand near the fire which had been lit against the chill weather.

"Well, it ain't over yet, Northcote. Not by any stretch. The hanging is over, thank God. But, 'struth, we're in a deuced awkward position. No Prime Minister. No Chancellor. The Whigs shifting about like a pack of hounds waiting to be let out of kennel. And Castlereagh is up to his collar points in it."

The waiter arrived with Myddelton's brandy. Myddelton took the glass and swallowed the contents in one. "Another, if you please.

"As for the hanging, I could have done very well without it. I drove back from Kent this morning, you know. And when all those damned fool women started crying out, 'God bless you! God bless you!' as though Bellingham was some sort of infernal folk hero," he said bitterly. "…I swear I could have throttled the lot of 'em."

"Yes, quite," Northcote agreed. "I confess I found the behaviour of the crowd somewhat unsettling."

The palest glimmer of amusement appeared in Myddelton's eyes. "Miles," he drawled, "And you a magistrate."

"I may be a magistrate, but in my district, the worst we see is disorderly conduct on the part of the blacksmith if he fails to win the hammer toss at the Midsummer Fete! But to change the subject entirely—what do you think of Hurst's chances against Alvanley in the upcoming race? Even Anne, bless her, says Hurst hasn't a chance."

Myddelton paused. A race. The blissful normality of it. "Is Alvanley racing the greys?"

"He is," confirmed Dunphail stepping up from behind. "Greetings to you, Myddelton. Are you just back?"

Myddelton nodded. "I stopped off at the Foreign Office."

Dunphail nodded his comprehension. "Aye, well, Hurst is determined he shall beat Alvanley." He paused to take a pinch of snuff. "Which is, doubtless, a noble ambition. But he ain't got a hope. Not with those bays, he hasn't. The leader's fast, but he's got wind-galls!" He flicked at a speck of snuff that had fallen onto his cuff. "However, if you want to wager, I've no doubt that Hardy will give you odds."

"With the greatest affection in the world for your cousin, Dunphail,

Hardy don't know one end of a horse from t'other! Where is he?...Hardy!" Myddelton hailed his friend who was seated in the bow window with Brummell and Alvanley. "Dunphail tells me you'll give me odds on this race with Alvanley. Are you gone mad?"

Hardy's equanimity appeared unruffled—he was after all wearing his favourite rose and lemon patterned twill waistcoat. "Alvanley could lose, you know. It could happen..." he insisted against the ripples of laughter issuing from his companions. "No, truly. Listen! All it would take is a loose wheel or one faulty turn, inclement weather—of which we've had plenty—whatever...I know you don't believe me. But one of these days, there'll be a better team or a better driver or the luck will be with the other chap, and Alvanley shan't win. And I shall be laughing all the way to the bank."

Dunphail, who had been listening to his cousin with a tolerant amusement, said in Myddelton's ear, "He don't need to know one end of a horse from t'other, for he's right, of course." And louder, to his cousin, "You're just greedy, that's what it is. You just want another one of those Italian violins you're forever looking out for...What is it you call 'em?"

Hardy smiled broadly and rolled his eyes. "Stradivarius or Amati." Brummell and Alvanley laughed harder.

"George, bring the betting book...All right then, Ned," Myddelton agreed cheerfully. "What odds will you give me this time?"

Hardy rubbed his chin. "Hmmn...Fifteen to one should do it, I think...It's the law of averages, you know. One day I shall win."

Myddelton reached for the betting book to sign his name, while adding over his shoulder, "Well, all right then, Ned. But only for a pony, because it goes against the grain to fleece a friend too often!

"Alvanley, how much do you expect to beat Hurst by?" Myddelton demanded.

"A healthy five minutes at the very least!" declared Alvanley.

Myddelton laughed as Alvanley sniffed at Northcote's suggestion that it might be a closer race than that. And bending to scrawl his name, saw an entry on the opposite page. An entry about his wife. His wife and Pemberton. And in the brief few seconds it took to read that wager, felt both an inability to take such a thing in and a frightening mixture of disbelief and nausea, revulsion and shock take him over. Then a new word entered his head. A snaking vile unmanning word. The most soul-destroying word in the language: 'Cuckold'. Paled, he straightened without signing.

And Northcote, standing nearest, saw the colour in his cheeks turn from tan to tallow, said, "Myddelton, what is it?"

"...You ain't going to be playing that fiendish violin sonata, or whatever it is you call it, this evening, is you?" Dunphail was asking Hardy. The conversation had moved from horses to the Romfords' musicale. "Because if you are, I shall think about going elsewhere..."

"Is that a warning to us?" Brummell said archly. The others laughed.

Myddelton did not laugh. A rage, still as ice, had replaced all other emotion. Cuckolded. He closed his eyes briefly against a rage so desperate it took his breath away. Then, without a word, he pushed the betting book across the table.

Northcote picked it up and perused the entries until he found it. "Utter nonsense!" he breathed, setting the book back on the table. "Absolute tosh."

"Is it?" Myddelton asked. They laughed at cuckolds. Everyone laughed at cuckolds. Within hours, everyone would know. If they didn't already.

"Dunphail, you was with Pemberton all the weekend...Tell Myddelton that this wager ain't worth heeding," Northcote said, handing the book to Dunphail.

Dunphail frowned and read. "What? Myddelton, m'dear fellow, this is a nonsense. Stansgate and Reding? 'Struth, I shouldn't take their word for the colour of my horse."

"They ain't talking about your horse," Myddelton said tightly.

Hardy had come to peer over his cousin's shoulder, and reading, exclaimed: "Good God, you can't be serious, Myddelton! Don't be an ass. It's grub-street-news, that. They're rascals, both of 'em."

"Myddelton," Dunphail said earnestly. He had seen where Myddelton's thoughts had taken him. "They must ha' been foxed. 'Struth, man, I was with Lady Myddelton and Pem most of the time. As was Hardy, here. And nothing occurred. Nothing. I'd stake my life on it," he added, striving to keep the agitation out of his voice. "S'life, Myddelton, you cannot pay attention to cawkers like that!"

But Myddelton had done listening. Had done thinking. For his imagination was now running riot and each fresh image of his wife and his friend together wracked him anew with the nausea of betrayal and fury and loss. Cuckolded. Dear God, how could he have been so blind? And how long had it been going on? Dear God...He pushed through his friends. "Not to worry. I don't shoot infants." And without a farewell, strode to the door, snatched his coat from a servant and left the Club.

"But where does that leave Pem?" said Dunphail, helplessly watching him go.

"Or Lady Myddelton?" added Hardy a moment later. "Or Lady Myddelton?"

❧

She had practised at the fortepiano until her shoulders ached; Mr. Hardy might be convinced of her innate superiority upon the instrument, but she was not so sanguine. And told herself firmly it would not do to work oneself into a pother over it. So she retired to the Morning Room and was determinedly not thinking about the evening's performance. Instead, she was considering the colours of the needlepoint she had been working, and wondering, if she were to change the brown in the pattern to green, if it would not suit Myddelton's bedchamber very well? For the painters, paper-hangers and the inestimable Mr. Dawkins, bless him, had worked the clock 'round and had performed miracles and the rooms were ready—even the old wool mattress and featherbed had been replaced, and the floor green-scrubbed under the new carpets. But still...

She did not hear Myddelton until he had opened the door. At the click of the latch she turned, expectant. But the expression on his face made her freeze with an unknown dread. She had never seen anyone so angry—not even him, at Vauxhall. And in that brief instant, cast about in her mind to discover some cause and found nothing, and panic overtook her.

He slammed the door behind him. "What in the name of God do you think you're playing at, Madam?" His voice was deceptively soft, clipped, cutting. "I am gone for three days…three days for Almighty God's sake! And I return to find you and your indiscretions a byword! 'Struth, I know this marriage was not of your choosing—God knows I did not want it neither—but could you not have waited? Waited until at least the line was secure to cuckold me?"

"What?" she whispered. Had he struck her she would not have been more shocked.

"The commonest harlot would have done as much! Or was you and Pemberton just picking up where you'd left off?"

Tears had started in her eyes and she had begun to shudder with the violent force of his rage. "What?" she mouthed, lost.

"No wonder he was so damned surprised to find you married to me! Red hell and bloody death, you and your damnable show of innocence. I expect you and Pemberton have been having a good laugh up your sleeves, haven't you? Hell and damnation!" he roared. "Have neither of you ever heard of discretion? Or honour?"

Like some player having come in on the rehearsal of the wrong play, she could only stare at him in utter confusion. In her lap, her hands had begun to shake.

"Even if you think so little of me…" His voice had become soft again, like a lash before the whip and sting. "Was it necessary to drag the name of Myddelton through the mire? And how did you intend to explain it? 'Struth, did you really think I'm such a flat that I would not know the difference between you and an unspoiled virgin? That I wouldn't be able to tell that you was damaged goods? Or are you already carrying his bastard and just waiting till I'm nicely ginned up some evening to slip between the sheets and pass it off as mine?"

Suddenly, the sense of betrayal so overwhelmed him, he stopped. He wanted to weep and scream and beat his fists against the walls. And still that word, 'cuckolded', sneered at him, shrivelling, shredding all self-esteem or sense of self-worth, flooding him, drowning him with disgust and revulsion and contempt. Striving to regain some or any vestige of control or composure, he strode to the mantel and laid his fist against the pristine paintwork. And the Morning room, so airy and light and pleasant even on such a grey day, came into focus. He breathed heavily, but composure was desperately far beyond him. He tried again.

"And this house! I gave you leave to redecorate. I did not say raze it and start over! Or is all this just your idea of the proper setting in which to conduct your amours? How could you do this to me? And with Pemberton, my dearest friend?" he bellowed. And clutched at the mantle to still his own shaking. "S'death, you sicken me!"

When he spoke again, his voice had quieted with a brittle irony. "Do you know, when I went into my bedchamber just now, to change out of my wet clothes, I thought I had opened the wrong door by mistake. So I stepped out again, only to find that it was the right door. It ain't even the same room now that you have…"

Weeping, she had not known how to defend herself against the onslaught. It was too far beyond anything in her experience. But this, this she could dispute. And a professional soldier's calm came over her, numbing her fear and she rose in dignity, scattering her skeins of wool upon the floor where they lay like the beginnings of a many coloured coat.

She did not shout. She did not need to: "Stop this. Stop it right now. I do not know where you might have heard such things of me, nor do I care to know. Clearly, you judge everyone, even me, by your own sordid and immoral standards of conduct. You assume that because you are no respecter of virtue, that I must be like you. Well, I am not. I never was, and I never shall be. As for this house and its fittings, I have spent a fortune—my own fortune—in making it fit for habitation. As to your bedchamber, I ordered its refurbishment because everything was worn through. The rugs, the draperies, everything. Just like everything in this house before I came. Which you would have known, if you had ever bothered to notice anything beyond your own conceit and arrogant pride!"

Her accusations were unanswerable and her self-defence antagonised him more than her silence. "The Myddelton bedchamber has always been kept like that!"

"I can well believe it," she snapped, having learned anger herself. "And I dare say those were the original hangings and carpets, were they?" The cool-headed retort was back. "Still, if you wish it, the rag and bone man might be persuaded to return them."

Stung, he turned on her. She had gone too far. "Damn you, you sanctimonious trollop. Damn you to hell!" What he recognised as her innate innocence and honesty enraged him beyond all reasoning. He strode toward her, his hand raised to strike.

Involuntarily, she backed away. But her fear was vanquished, routed by that fine intelligence which had rebelled against his unspeakable slanders. "Don't you touch me," she enunciated with a strength and quiet fury that stopped him cold. "Don't you *ever* touch me." And turning, she ran to the door and wrenched it open. Then, looking back at him for an instant, she said, "How greatly you wrong me!" before disappearing down the hall.

Her battle-courage lasted only until she had reached the sanctuary of her private sitting room. She closed the door and rested against it for a long moment, then went to stand near her own prettily carved mantel upon which rested the miniatures of her mother, father and uncle. Leaning against a chair to steady herself, she tried to regain her equanimity, to blot out the twin stains of Myddelton's venomous allegations and her vituperative response. But it was impossible. And faint-headed, she sank to the floor and gave way to the tears and racking sobs which seemed to epitomise all that this marriage had brought her.

Pemberton considered the pair of side arm pistols in their case on the desk, then lifted them out, cradling one in each hand, weighing them up. The inlaid rosewood hilts were comfortable and smooth against his palms and fingers. He held one up and then the other, examining the length of cannon barrel, setting his sight, and squeezing the triggers. 'Struth, they were the sweetest pair ever, throwing neither right nor left. A perfect marriage of mechanics and artistry, these. And not too heavy to carry in the pocket neither. He exhaled with a singular contentment and returned them to their case. Now to the serious and pleasant business of cleaning and priming.

Methodically, he got out the requisite oil and polish, his rags and ramrod, laying them on the desk beside the pistols.

"Mr. Wystan-Hyte to see you, milord," said Willetts, Pemberton's factotum-cum-valet, entering the library.

"Hmn? What's that, Willetts?" He lifted a pistol once more, just to cradle it, and peer down the straight line of its barrel, then laid it tenderly in its case again.

"A Mr. Wystan-Hyte to see you, milord," Willetts repeated.

"Oh. Show him in then, Willetts." Pemberton closed the pistol case and fastened the latch.

Willetts bowed and allowed Mr. Wystan-Hyte to pass into the room. "Mr. Wystan-Hyte, milord."

Mr. Wystan-Hyte gazed about him in frank interest as he entered. He hadn't known what to expect—everyone said Pemberton and his family were well-heeled—but Lord Pemberton kept a suite of rooms in Stephen's Hotel rather than living in the family townhouse. What he had not expected was the lack of affectation, the signs of wealth but without any hint of opulence. And this library, or was it a gun room, for there were surely as many guns as books to be seen... He began baldly, even before Willetts had closed the door behind him, and he looked distinctly ill-at-ease—because he was: "I hope you will forgive me, my lord, for intruding upon you in this manner."

He was barely acquainted with Lord Pemberton. True, he thought Pemberton and his close set of friends, with their strict code of honour and sportsmanship, top of the trees. But he had never aspired to the dizzying heights of rubbing shoulders with them; he was quite content to admire from afar. But then Stansgate had started spreading that nasty little story and he had found himself suddenly aware that those gentlemen, who had seemed very tonnish when he'd first made their acquaintances, did not in fact belong to the first circles. And worse still, he was astonished to discover that he had principles—and that spreading unfounded and malicious rumours did not sit well with them.

"...But, you see, something occurred the other evening that has left me feeling not a little uncomfortable. And as it concerns yourself, my lord, I felt I must speak to you about it. I am only thankful that I found you at home."

Pemberton eyed Mr. Wystan-Hyte with curiosity: he was acting a little too like one of his brothers caught out in a prank. "Won't you sit down? Have a glass of something?" He gestured vaguely toward a well-stocked sideboard.

"No. Thank you, but no—to both your kind offers. I shall be brief."

Pemberton's curiosity increased.

"My business is this: While I was at White's the other evening—Saturday, that would have been—in the company of Messrs. Reding and Stansgate..." He dropped his gaze to the floor momentarily. "Well, it so happened that Stansgate mentioned that there was a new on-dit going about and that it concerned your escort of the Countess of Myddelton." Wystan-Hyte drew a sharp breath for courage. "With the implication that there was rather more to it than that.

"I tried very much to discourage him from making such remarks, but he and Reding took no notice. And before I left them, they were calling for the betting book and Reding was offering ten-to-one odds that..."

"That what? I am Lady Myddelton's lover?" finished Pemberton.

"Yes," affirmed Wystan-Hyte, much surprised. "Then you know?"

Pemberton shrugged. "It wouldn't take much to guess if that lot were telling the tale." The smile did not reach his eyes. "I shouldn't let it worry you though...I ain't, you know."

"I never believed for an instant that you was!" Mr. Wystan-Hyte burst out, then reddened and tried again. "That is to say, I never thought..."

Pemberton gave a lop-sided grin. "Thank you for your trouble."

"It was no trouble at all, I do assure you. After all, I felt responsible."

"S'life, it ain't your responsibility." And added with uncharacteristic grimness: "Both Stansgate and Reding are hangers-on, you know. That fellow Reding is a knight and barrow pig, and Stansgate's a little rodent with the tongue of a viper...Why does a young lad like you bother with 'em? I don't mean to pry, but 'struth..."

Mr. Wystan-Hyte smiled despite his obvious discomfort. "Well, I don't mean to continue, I can tell you. Thank you for seeing me, my lord. No, don't ring for your man, I can find my own way out." He gave an awkward, relieved bow and hurried from the room.

"Pleasure..." Pemberton said to the air. And turning back to the desk, reopened the case before him and uncorked the bottle of oil to clean and prime his splendid new pistols.

And he had just finished when the knock he was expecting came.

"Lord Myddelton to see you, milord."

With such care, Pemberton laid the second pistol down. And heard rather than saw Myddelton burst into the room. "'Struth, I was wondering how long it would be before you came charging in here."

"You are here!" Myddelton exclaimed at the same time. "What the hell d'you think you are playing at? I return home after three days to discover that you've cuckolded me—with my wife of a fortnight. You! My oldest and dearest friend! So how long has it been going on then, eh? Tell me! How long? No wonder you turned pea green when you found her married to me. For God's sake, Pem, how could you? How could you do that to me?"

Quietly, Pemberton turned to face Myddelton. The usual insouciance and sparkle were gone. "I didn't," he declared flatly.

"I don't believe you," spat Myddelton.

"No, you wouldn't," Pemberton confirmed wisely.

"You shall pay for this," Myddelton said with such contempt.

"I ain't going to fight you, you know, though God knows you need something to knock some sense into that obstinate head of yours. But it won't be me. So if that's what you came for, you can save yourself the trouble..."

"You know damned well that's what I came for."

"Well, sorry. Your luck's out this week, Myddelton. I ain't in a fighting mood." Dismissively, he turned back to the desk and his pistols, to tidy away the bottles and rags he'd been using.

"Od's death, you and she make a pretty pair—my wife and my best friend—a dell and a coward."

Suddenly, Pemberton swivelled around, the pistol in his hand. His voice lowered with the anger he had been determined to avoid. "Is that what you think? 'Struth, Avery, you're an ass-head. A bloody obstinate ass-head."

Myddelton stared furiously.

"Can you truly believe that I would ever do anything to harm you? Or her? You've known me for how long? And you believe that?"

"I hardly know what to believe!"

"You know better than that. Od's my life, Myddelton, how can you even think it? You know that I wouldn't. And if you ever bothered to talk to her, you'd know that she wouldn't."

"She didn't deny it."

"What?"

"She didn't deny it," Myddelton repeated harshly.

Pemberton's eyelids fluttered with incredulity. "Do you mean to say you have accused her?" And then he was furious, and his grip tightened on the pistol hilt. "You ass-head, Myddelton. You bloody ass. That girl worships you. She'd do anything for you. Good God, you're the air she breathes. You don't believe me? Then go. Go and find out for yourself. Take her to bed, and then you'll know, for good and all, that you're the first and only in that field!"

"I can hardly pluck the flower of a wanton. Especially as you've already had that pleasure. Was she worth it? Maybe I should have a go—you haven't given her anything, have you, like the clap? Or a brat?"

"What the devil? What did you say? What did you call her?" Pemberton said quietly and lowering the pistol, took aim.

And for Myddelton, suddenly the game had changed. Nor was it a game. And the face looking at him from behind the pistol was no more that of a friend—it was the set, still features, the clear, cold eyes of a marksman—the man who would never miss his target, the man who shot with equal accuracy using either hand and either eye. And suddenly, Myddelton began to wonder what could have happened to him to bring him to this. And knew, too, that whatever the truth of the matter, he had lost. And if it was all nothing but a scurrilous slander, then he had destroyed all and lost all for a lie. Detached and numbed, he watched, and waited for the shot.

Still aiming at Myddelton's heart, Pemberton rose from his seat. "I should shoot you for that. Whether you believe it or no, I have never touched her. Nor would I ever. Not only because you were my dearest friend, but because of the highest esteem in which I hold Sir Charles. Nor has she ever indicated by so much as a look that such attentions would be welcome. But there have been times, Myddelton, times like these, when 'struth, I wished she were mine, so that I could keep her from mawworms like you." He raised the pistol ceilingward and tugged at the bellpull. "Now get out, Myddelton! Get out and take your ill phantasies with you.

"Willetts, Lord Myddelton is leaving now...See to it that I am not disturbed again." Pemberton turned away and listened to the closing of the door and the heavy tread of footsteps retreating down the hallway. He laid the pistol in its case and covering his face with his hand, said to no one: "Oh God, Janey."

18

The air inside the vaulted hall of Jackson's Boxing Saloon was heavy and sour with the smell of sweat. At the centre of the whitewashed room, men with rapiers and metal face guards practised sword play, their buttoned foils clanging and screeching as they thrust, parried and engaged, the floorboards resounding with the thudding of their rapidly moving feet. From one corner came the creak and jiggle of a large balance, in the weighing tray of which was seated a gentleman of substantial proportion, his feet dangling, while an attendant added a progression of brass counterweights to the other tray. And from another corner came the dull smacking of bandaged fists battering at hard-muscled flesh and the grunts of exertion which signalled a bout.

When the fight in the corner began, no one paid much heed, for they were a regular feature of the daily routine. But now, unusually, a crowd had gathered, surrounding the pair, following each move, calling out advice, cheering each hit—for this was no ordinary bout.

Of the two combatants, Jackson was a professional fighter of eminence whose experience was apparent as he danced and defended himself with astonishing ease and skill. Yet what his amateur opponent lacked in science, he made up for in strength, determination and passion. Battering away, first with his right, then with his left, then unexpectedly with his left again, he slipped under the other's guard and hit Jackson hard on the jaw.

The crowd cheered and stamped their feet with surprise and approval.

But that blow startled the inimitable Jackson, sobering him, and he lashed back with punishing blows to the stomach and chest and shoulders. Myddelton, now panting and furious, defended himself gamely, planting body blows whenever the opportunity arose until the bell was rung, and the two men stepped away from each other.

Heaving with exertion, his throat stiff and parching, Myddelton bowed to Gentleman Jackson, and murmured his thanks. Then, after listening to his tutor's criticisms, he broke through the ring of congratulatory onlookers to head for the changing rooms. They were emptying as he entered. Wearily, he sat and slumped on a bench while his breath returned. His chest, shoulders and arms all ached and stung where he'd taken the pummelling blows; those who had never sparred with Jackson had little notion of how hard he could hit. Yet after all that had happened, he drew a certain comfort in the physical pain, for it seemed fitting somehow. Eventually though, the solitude became too much, so he rose, and finding the water in the ewer was still warm, poured it out and began to wash and dry himself.

A moment or so later, Mr. Hardy appeared and, choosing a chair, draped himself backwards over it and said: "I say, Myddelton, you are showing to advantage today."

"Thanks, Ned." Myddelton said quietly. Had he forgotten already the contretemps at White's? Did he not yet know of the quarrel with Pemberton?

Mr. Hardy looked him over measuringly. "I've never seen you fight like that before...Fancy, slipping under Jackson's guard and planting him a facer! I should never have the skill to do that, not in a thousand years."

"Ned, as you've never even stepped inside the ring once in your life, it cannot possibly come as a surprise that you have no skill at it." The best he could produce was a grim half-smile.

Mr. Hardy smiled broadly, but said: "I did, you know. I did once. At school. It was horrible." Then, seriously: "You *are* coming to Lady Rom's musicale, this evening, ain't you?"

The shuttered, wary look returned. Then he didn't yet know. "No. I'm otherwise engaged for th'evening."

"A pity, that." Mr. Hardy shook his head. "I had rather hoped you'd be there." He paused, carefully choosing his words—he had not forgotten this morning's contretemps. "Lady Myddelton will be playing, you know. Accompanying me, as it happens. But then, I dare say you know that. Still, I rather think, that is to say, I'm hoping, that tonight will be magnificent. She said she was a bit off her stride, yesterday, but I dare say she's feeling more at ease now, knowing that Pemberton and Dunphail have warned Pickering-Stone off, and that's all done and dusted..."

He did not want to listen to Hardy wittering on about her. He'd been doing his best to ignore it. But what was this about Pickering-Stone? "I beg your pardon?"

Hardy eyed him with undisguised curiosity. "Didn't Pem tell you?"

"Tell me what?" Myddelton pulled his shirt on over his head.

Hardy drew breath, feeling that he had suddenly—and he didn't know how—stepped into dangerous territory. He gave Myddelton a hard look. "Well...you did know that Pickering-Stone had been calling on her and writing her poetry, didn't you?" he began. "No? Ah. Well, I expect she must have been too embarrassed to tell you. I should have been—if what Pem quoted me is any sample."

Myddelton had stopped dressing and was listening intently. "He wrote her poetry?"

Hardy nodded. "Pem said it redefined the concept of awful. Sent her two or three every day. And called on her twice a day until finally she told old Kettering to deny her. But even that didn't stop him." He paused to study Myddelton's reaction, but could read little beyond a certain guardedness in the set lines of his face. "Then, the whole business came to a head at Drury Lane on Saturday evening—Pem and Dunphail had gone to fetch champagne and lemonade, while I remained behind. And Pickering-Stone just burst into the box and threw himself on his knees before her."

"What?" Myddelton exclaimed in total surprise. "He threw himself at her? In the theatre?" This was incredible. Why had no one mentioned this? Why did no one think he needed to know about it? Christ, he was such an ass. No, make that a complete booberkin.

"Aye. He made a dashed cake of himself, I can tell you. Made one of me, too, for I should have known what to do," he admitted, with Hardy-esque chagrin. "But the fact is, I've never seen anyone behave like that before in all m'life, and I couldn't think what to do!" he explained with a certain frustration. "Anyway, it turned out that he was making improper suggestions to her, the coxcomb...Blabbing on about worshipping at Aphrodite's altar, and who knows what else..."

"What?" Myddelton faltered.

"Everyone was staring. It was dreadful. Like a circus, really. He had latched onto her hand and she was desperately trying to wrest it from him and growing more embarrassed by the moment. And I just sat there like some stupid frozen dolt..." Hardy blinked with remembered mortification.

Myddelton had dropped onto the opposite bench and appeared no longer to be listening as Hardy continued: "Then, finally, Pem came back, and cool as you please, raised his quizzing glass to stare Pickering-Stone out of countenance, and said, 'I believe the lady does not wish for your attentions.' It was brilliant! And then, Pickering-Stone jumped up and tore out of the box...I say, you're looking a bit funny, Myddelton. Are you all right?"

"What? Yes. Perfectly." No, he wasn't. He felt completely ill and aghast and disgusted by his own self-justifying arrogance. "What happened then?"

"Oh. Ah. Well. Lady Myddelton didn't wish to speak of it...who would? But eventually Pem found out what Pickering-Stone had been up to. So this morning, Dunphail and Pem met up with him at White's and told him you was a jealous husband and that you'd horsewhip anyone who so much as came near her. Dunphail said Pickering-Stone turned the most glorious shade of greeny-white!" Mr. Hardy recounted with glee.

"You wasn't there?" Myddelton asked.

"No," Hardy admitted. "No. I was engaged for this morning, seeing a fellow about some music..." Which, if one knew Mr. Hardy at all, explained everything. "I wish I had been though. Dunphail says he reckons Pickering-Stone will never so much as look at her again." Mr. Hardy paused and eyed Myddelton thoughtfully. "Did you not know of this?"

Myddelton had risen and was now taking refuge in the delicate task of rebuttoning the small pearl buttons of his waistcoat. "No." He could think of any number of reasons why this might be so. None of them gave him comfort. Quite the opposite.

"Not any of it?"

"No."

"That's peculiar." Then: "Still, it's a pity you can't come to Lady Rom's this evening. What have you got on that's so pressing? I didn't know anyone had anything to conflict with the Romford do."

Hardy's kindliness proved too much. Unable to keep the tightness out of his voice, he said: "Actually Ned, I had thought to spend half the evening at the Daffy club, drinking blue ruin till I'm legless. And the other half, at Watier's, gambling away a fortune." Simple and effective escapism. Perhaps he should make a start now.

Mr. Hardy sat forward while he thought on this. "Don't do that, Myddelton. I expect it's Bellingham's nubbing that has you blue-devilled. You never was one for a good ottomising. I'm not, m'self. Or mayhap it's those poxy rodents, Stansgate and Reding. But it ain't worth it, Myddelton. You know it ain't. Come to Lady Rom's. Castlereagh'll be there. And Lady Myddelton shall be looking to see you there. I know it."

He was so temperate, so modest, that Myddelton wished that he might be convinced. Or convince himself. But, of course, Hardy knew nothing about this afternoon. Nothing about his soon-to-be-known-by-everyone rupture with Pemberton. Nothing about his surely inevitable and soon-to-be-gossiped-about-incessantly separation from his bride of a fortnight. Indeed, all things considered, he rather thought that his presence was the last thing Jane would want. Ever. 'Don't touch me,' she had said. 'Don't ever touch me.' No, Lady Romford's musicale was the very last place he'd think of showing his face on this or any other evening. "I'll think about it," he lied.

"Good man," Hardy approved. "Which way was you heading? White's? No, well, perhaps I shall see you this evening then."

Determined to resist that unavoidable moment of facing up to the fiasco that was now his life, Myddelton turned away and did not watch Hardy go, but set about to think of nothing and no one. Which was doomed to fail. For there was no escaping the unhappy fact that today he had destroyed life as he knew it. He'd accused the closest thing he had to a brother of cuckolding him. And charged his own wife with being a lightskirts and a wanton. How could he have done so? These…these were the gravest accusations, and honour would never allow such offences to be lightly forgotten or forgiven—though they were not true and he knew it. Whether Jane would speak of it, or when and to whom, he didn't know. Perhaps to her uncle? Probably to her uncle. Which would eventually and undoubtedly lead to an annulment—certainly, it's what he would seek, if she were his. And then, he'd lose everything. But before even that, everyone would learn of the row with Pemberton. And when that was known, the cuts direct would begin. And soon, which of his acquaintance would still be speaking to him? Very few, he reckoned. Very few, indeed.

He finished dressing and left the premises quietly. What was there left for him now? Would his career in the Foreign Office survive? Would Castlereagh stand by him? Perhaps. Perhaps if he asked, Castlereagh would post him abroad. But now he knew too, that even before all of this had blown up, she had been too afraid of him to tell him that she was being pestered by that randy little twiddlepoop, Pickering-Stone, and what did that say? About his temper? Or the fact that he was never to home, but for all intents and purposes lived at the Foreign Office…Christ, what an appalling mess. What a botched bloody cowhanded mess he'd made of it all. 'Struth, Pemberton was right, he was an asshead.

Jane paused in the doorway of the Romfords' large gilt-encrusted drawing room and looked bleakly at the rows of spindly-legged Louis XVI chairs and the grand fortepiano and harp at the far end of the room. And wondered why she had come here. The cream of society were present too, a gathering crush of guests—gentlemen dandies with their pomaded curls, exaggerated coats and satin waistcoats all hung with gold seals and fobs, debutantes in pastel-pale evening gowns, the dowagers and matrons, the Corinthian set in sombre well-cut evening clothes—all standing or sitting together in groups of four or five or six, and all talking, talking, talking. It was just the sort of event in which her uncle had trained her to shine—all the music lessons with Maestro Clementi, the deportment with Mlle de Resnay, the subtle lessons in the art of conversation with Lady Choate, all were designed for such an end.

"Well, what d'you think, Ma'am? Quite an Event, ain't it?" Mr. Hardy said brightly.

Jane swallowed and tightened her grip on his arm as a wave of cold dread swept over her. No, she did not want to be here. "I am only surprised Lady Romford did not have a dais built."

Mr. Hardy chuckled. "Oh she did—three years ago. But the fact is, Lord Romford tripped over it and sprained his gouty ankle. End of dais!"

She smiled weakly. She should not have come.

It had been Haseley who had found her asleep on the floor, and informed Kettering and Mrs. Pinch. And like the excellent upperservants they were, they had united about her to shield and protect her, to ensure that though her private world might have descended into a nightmare of discontent and recrimination, none but they should ever know of it. It had been Haseley and Mrs. Pinch who had awakened her, undressed her, and bathed her as if she were their cherished and overtired child. Kettering had brought her dinner on a tray and Haseley had gently fussed over her, urging her to eat a little of that, a bite more of this. Then Haseley had dressed her for the evening with meticulous care in embroidered silk as if she were a milliner's porcelain doll. And all the while, dazed and dozy, compliant and shocked, she had wanted to say that she could not come out tonight, she could not bear it, but even that had been beyond her.

So when Mr. Hardy had arrived to escort her, she was ready, and it was to him she tried to make those stammering apologies. And though his face was full of the tenderest concern, still he could not hide his dismay: "Are you sure you cannot, Ma'am?" he had asked. "I would say nothing, but...well, you see, this evening was to have been a sort of debut, so to speak. For you see, I have been having lessons with Mr. Kelly—the tenor at Covent Garden, you know. Only no one has heard me—only Dunphail, and being my cousin, he don't listen—and I've said nothing to anyone, so tonight..."

But if she had thought she could not bear to go into company after

296

all that had happened, no more could she bear to disappoint the kind Mr. Hardy, and her will broken, she had said, "No, of course I shall accompany you. It will be a pleasure. I had not realised..." Though now, gazing at all these people, she knew she had been mistaken and feared she would disgrace herself by being sick.

"Do you care to go up and examine the fortepiano, ma'am?" Mr. Hardy was saying, leaning solicitously toward her. "It is a splendid instrument. Made by Broadwoods to a design by Mr. Sheraton, you know. I know you shall enjoy playing it...It has the most luscious sonority and..."

Across the room, Pemberton detached himself from a group of acquaintances to make his way towards them. And she knew from his unsmiling and clouded expression that Myddelton had charged him with adulterous relations as well and that their easy friendship must now be severed. Knew that now she was to be denied even the familiar joy and comfort of his teasing companionship. That the venomous allegations which had damned her had damned him also. And she felt the hollow numbness and terrible melancholy renew their hold of her and tears pricked at her eyelids.

Knowing her as he did, Pemberton could only watch as the unmitigated bleakness of their situation registered. He saw the traces of her hour of weeping, the translucent skin, the pale blue smudges beneath those eyes which had darkened almost to black. And because he knew more of the world than she, he knew also that to protect her reputation, no one must ever suspect that Myddelton had linked their names. That he must never, under any circumstances, be alone with her again, and that no one—not even Dunphail and Hardy—must ever guess that this was the case. And now, seeing this girl whom he had never kissed, never held in his arms, loved but never longed for, and bowing to her, he felt the clutch of an angry despair eliminate all other emotion.

"Janey," he said with false cheer. "And Hardy." He took her hand and held it tightly, though he kissed only the air above it. "You look exquisite, Angel," he said and spoke the truth. Still gripping her hand in an innate and unconscious rejection of Myddelton's calumny, he added: "Shall we go and find some seats? Hardy? Toward the front, don't you think? I rather think Lady Rom is wishing to begin."

They found seats close to an aisle and settled themselves with Jane in the middle. Disoriented, inwardly quaking with unhappiness and impending loss, she laid her hand, for this last time, upon her dearest friend's arm. Dunphail came and sat beside his cousin. Lady Emily Cowper flitted over for a moment before returning to her seat beside Lord Palmerston and Lady Jersey. The facade was in place.

Now, Lady Romford, a small motherly figure in striped tabby silk, made her way slowly to the front of the room, pausing here, to squeeze the hand of a close friend, there, to kiss the cheek of another. When she attained the front, she cleared her throat, blushed a little, and began: "Welcome again to you all." And clasping her hands tightly at her waist, for she was not a natural public figure, she began: "I shall not say more than that, because we've so many friends here this evening...So shall we just begin by welcoming..."

The first young lady played a brief but charming piece on the harp. She was followed by two sisters who sang a trio of English folk songs. Another pair of sisters played a duet for piano and harp. And the audience, because these were of their own circle and not paid entertainers, applauded when each of the performers had finished and admiringly discussed their efforts.

After the sisters finished their duet, Pemberton said, with a knowing gleam in his eye: "I say, that wasn't half bad, eh Hardy?" It could not fail.

"No, Philistine, it wasn't. Half bad, my eye..." Mr. Hardy retorted. "It was dashed good, and you..." Seeing that gleam, he gave a snort of laughter. "I don't know why I put up with you. 'Pon my soul, I don't. Philistine!"

And slowly, slowly, Jane began to feel less disconsolate, began to think that perhaps she would not be sick. That protected by the phalanx of these three, with their polished manners and easy address, their social standing and many graces, she might yet find some small measure of equanimity. And that would be enough. Indeed, it would have to be.

"And now, dear friends, we have a most particular treat, which I know many of you have been anticipating..." Lady Romford was saying.

"The charming and talented Miss Wythenshaw shall perform for us on the harp."

There was a smattering of applause. Unnoticed, Mr. Hardy folded his arms across the apricot and silver silk jacquard of his waistcoat. Beside him, Jane tilted her head, the better to see the young woman of whom she'd heard so much.

She was stunningly beautiful. Tall, amply endowed with a gentleman's favourite attributes and raven-haired, and gowned as if she were royalty, Miss Wythenshaw made her graceful way to the front of the room, enjoying every moment of her procession down the length of the room. She knew she looked well, knew she outshone every other woman. Her selection was full of rapid arpeggios and delicately interwoven contrapuntal melodies too, cleverly chosen to ensure that her supremacy over all other performers. But where those arpeggios might have descended in graceful and ordered rapidity, Miss Wythenshaw produced a romantic torrent of notes, losing the interlinked melodies in fits of passionate phrasing and ill-chosen emphases. Still, to the non-musicians in the audience, it was most impressive.

Mr. Hardy did not react well to such musical blunderings though. He frowned, tapping his fingers restlessly, and stared hard at the floor or fingered an imaginary accompaniment for the violin.

And when eventually, the becomingly flushed Miss Wythenshaw finished, her performance was greeted with enthusiastic applause and repeated calls for an encore from her court of admirers. Artfully, she tucked her chin and shook her head modestly in refusal.

"Well, thank Heaven for that at least!" Mr. Hardy declared. "By my life, I could not have borne much more of that, I can tell you. Whose jingle-brained idea was it to let her loose on Scarlatti? 'Struth, you'd think with him she'd pay a bit more attention to the music and stop thinking about that face of hers, wouldn't you? Posing her head this way and that to create the perfect picture or some such nonsense! S'life, why cannot she stick to the fortepiano? Her performance on the harp—as just witnessed—is nothing short of torture—to the instrument and the audience." His features settled into an obstinate grimace.

Pemberton stared in amazement.

"What's with you?" Dunphail protested.

"What?" Hardy seemed surprised by the question. "Nothing. I just hate to hear fine music desecrated by the foolish airs and vanity of an inconsequential chit like the Wythenshaw. Musical greatness is something one labours one's whole life to achieve. And to be forced to listen, while some stupid flirt of a girl violates every musical principle, choosing an instrument as some sort of accessory—like a pair of gloves or a clip for her hair—not because of any innate feeling for that instrument, but because she thinks it makes her look more beautiful than some other poor girl, or because she thinks it'll land her a title or a richer husband, and then treating it like it's no more than a…"

"Ned!" exclaimed Dunphail. "What are you on about?"

Throughout, Jane had sat undisturbed and quiet, distant even, her hand still resting upon Pemberton's sleeve, gazing off into nowhere, unaffected by Mr. Hardy's vehement denunciations. Yet now, unconsciously, she looked up and saw the object of those pronouncements passing quite close to them, saw an inexplicable flashing of outrage, quickly suppressed, ignite in Miss Wythenshaw's eyes. And turning to face her companion, said composedly, "I think she heard you, Mr. Hardy."

For Myddelton, the late afternoon and early evening had passed in a kind of dream. From hour to hour, he had been anticipating the beginnings of ostracism, had kept expecting that first cut—direct or indirect or even sublime. But nothing happened. No one turned their back to him and nothing seemed to have changed. Brummell and Alvanley greeted him much as always. And in the office, Planta cheekily presented him with the usual overflowing dispatch pouch 'with the Foreign Secretary's compliments'. It was true he was dining alone, but that was by design and the other members had all greeted him when he strolled into the Coffeeroom. Was it possible that Pemberton had said nothing? Such a thing defied reason. Yet, how else could he explain it? Frowning over it, he took a pinch of snuff.

"Ah Myddelton! There you are," Lord Castlereagh declared as he approached the table. "I had hoped I should find you here. Say I am not disturbing your dinner."

Immediately, Myddelton placed his knife and fork together on the plate before him to signal that he had finished his meal. "No, no. Please, sir, will you not sit..." he invited, even as the Foreign Secretary was availing himself of the remaining seat.

"Thank you, I will, yes." And without further preamble, the Foreign Secretary reached into his breast pocket and produced several sheets of paper, dirtied and dog-eared, folded together. "Now tell me...here, have a look at this, will you?" he lowered his voice significantly as he spread the letters before Myddelton. "What d'you make of these, eh?"

Myddelton opened flat the first, glanced over it, then made the mental adjustment from English to French and read.

"Well, what d'you make of it all?" Castlereagh said again. "They were intercepted by one of Flint's lads, you see. And I wanted your reading of 'em. Now tell me what you think. Honestly. I rely on you."

Myddelton frowned, unfolding, then looking over the further two letters. Three letters, three different authors but all telling the same tale. He raised his head and looked about. No one at any of the near tables was paying them the slightest heed. Indeed, the cacophony of so many eating, drinking and talking together precluded even the possibility of eavesdropping on another's private conversation.

"Well, sir, this one...written just under a month ago...who's it from? Colonel... Umn, can't read the signature..." He paused, scanning the page. "This one confirms the rumours of a large withdrawal of French troops from Spain." He began slowly to read aloud, translating as he read: "'My noble Emperor...I cannot write too strongly against this loss of troops. The English'...No, make that 'the damnable English skirmishers and sharpshooters are everywhere. They sit in the hills and prey upon us like wolves. And now, now, my beloved Emperor, I learn that you have said that you must take ten thousand of the best men away, for a campaign of glory against our enemies in the East. Nom de dieu. Can you not see that this, this shall leave us with nothing to defend Spain, nothing to defend our empire and...'"

"So, it's true then? It says that?" Castlereagh interrupted, with the smallest glint of excitement in his eye. "A firm withdrawal of ten thousand troops and all for a...a...what d'you think? Can he mean Russia? Can it possibly be Russia? Can it be that Boney's taken the bait?"

"Yes," Myddelton agreed. "To be sure, it could be. But can he have looked at the map, do you think, sir?"

"Well..." Castlereagh began, rubbing his hands together. "Well now, it has been clear for some little time that he has no grasp of the situation on the Peninsula. We know from Bourrienne that he don't read the dispatches from Spain—puts 'em into his pocket unread." He frowned. "How much do we pay Bourrienne's manservant? Do you suppose it's enough?" He exhaled heavily, then continued: "Nor should I imagine he has appreciated our efforts to reconcile the Turks and the Russians..."

Myddelton hesitated. Then, cautiously, diffidently even: "It could be the campaign you have been working to bring about, sir. It could be the campaign against Russia. I know everyone believes I've lost my reason when I say so, but I've thought and thought and I can arrive at no other conclusion." He shook his head.

"Od's my life, I do pray you are right. But tell me, why do *you* say so, Myddelton? I have hoped, and obviously worked for this end, but...Of a certainty Tsar Alexander's refusal to abide by his Continental System don't please Napoleon—upon my word, I expected war when Alexander reopened all the Russian ports to English trade early last year," Castlereagh said firmly. "But nothing came of it."

"I know, sir. I know. But, I'm certain of it. This time, it is different. I am convinced that it is!" Myddelton said, reviewing it all in his mind. Emptying his thoughts of all but his work for the Foreign Office, banishing his emotions and the day's and week's wretchedness to the nether-regions of his consciousness. And going over the details of his knowledge as puzzle pieces in a too-large jigsaw, as he had done for weeks, nay months.

And preparing to listen, his eyes narrowing shrewdly, the Foreign Minister propped his left elbow on the table and cupped his chin in his hand, pleased to have drawn Myddelton out—for in the office, he said little and confided less, deferring to the others, and always working, working, working, always at his translations and code books, his maps and dispatches.

Myddelton contemplated the lid of his snuffbox, laid upon the table before him, then said: "It has been evident for some while, Napoleon intends a large campaign, bigger than anything we've seen before. Europe is crawling with French troops on the move—it ain't just the ten thousand men to be recalled from Spain…For months now, there's been a massive build-up of stores of rice, wheat and fodder in Danzig…He has an army in training on the Vistula—it could be as many as fifty or sixty thousand men there, French and French allies—Germans, Poles, Dutch, Swiss. And the troops in Italy were mobilised under his step-son, Eugène—I don't have their number yet. There are also regiments training in Croatia. So, there can be little doubt he's planning something.

"The obvious arena would have been Spain and Portugal. But if it were to be the Peninsula, then one would expect the army to be concentrated in France, specifically southern France. But that is exactly where it ain't. It's all in the East. And all through the winter and early spring, Boney himself barely stirred from Saint Cloud.

"I know our information is at least a fortnight, if not several weeks, old—even the new cyphers which have come in from Paris…Equally, I know that Boney can move a massive army across Europe at lightning speed…and I have wondered if he just don't want the army in France as it'd be too costly. Nor can I tell you as much as I could wish about the Russian situation, because I don't have Russian…" he apologised. Then added as an afterthought: "Though I have been thinking I should give it a go one of these days—it ain't that different from Greek…"

Castlereagh smiled indulgently—that vaguely bemused and wary smile which is reserved by monoglots for those who pick up languages as easily as another picks up a glove.

"But you see, sir, now there's this business of the clerk in the French War Administration who's been selling information to the Russians, which *le Moniteur* is calling a Russian abuse of trust…an excuse for hostilities, if you will…" Myddelton paused. "And the cyphers I was working on today…I've not finished them yet, but they was from Bayard in Paris. And one of them was about Savary—you know, the new Minister of Police...Well, Bayard says that Savary has been rounding up political suspects and chucking them in prison...But also, he believes that the age of conscription may have been lowered again. To the age of fourteen."

Castlereagh straightened. "To the age of fourteen? Do you say Bonaparte's conscripting boys as young as fourteen now?" he repeated in disbelief. He drew a long breath and folded his hands tightly together. "By my life, I tell you he is a tyrant and a madman and a despot. 'Afore God, it'll be a damned slaughter of innocents...Wherever it happens!"

"Yes..." Myddelton agreed, now glancing over the letter again, and finding himself suddenly caught up in Castlereagh's fierce enthusiasm. "But wait, sir. Ehm...This confirms it. Listen: 'I have heard from my dear family that the army is again recruiting in our beautiful France and that boys—children?—are joining this Nouvelle Armée. Beloved Emperor, do not send these poor infants to war. We have enough glory. The Russian artillery will scatter their loyal French hearts to the wind...' or something. The ink has blotted...You see, sir?"

Castlereagh was silent now, contemplating this new grief Bonaparte would inflict on France, measuring and weighing this new shred of evidence. "Yes. Yes, I do see." His tone hardened. "Well, if Bonaparte in his infatuated mushroom arrogance thinks that he shall invade Russia and bring about another Austerlitz, then he is much mistaken! Because it won't happen. By my life, not this time. Di Borgo and Armfelt have worked it all out! The Russians will just fade away, d'you see, burning their fields behind them..."

"Like the lines of Torres Vedras?" Myddelton demanded.

"Yes! Yes, exactly. And the French will find themselves drawn farther and farther into Russia until there is no escape..." Castlereagh stopped. Then refocusing his attention on the letter: "But it definitely says 'the Russian artillery' though, does it? 'Struth, they'll do just that. Hmn." Then rousing himself, said: "Well...well, this is good news for us, ain't it? Liverpool and Wellington will be very pleased, no doubt about that." And envisioning a new alliance which would wipe the old enemy off the stage of Europe, his eyes began to glow with a hint of speculative triumph: "Oh, we'll have him! By God, we'll have him! Unless..." He came down to earth with a thump and sighed, giving way, unusually, to bluntness: "Unless that bufflehead Alexander takes fright and and scuppers the lot with some shameful peace treaty! Just like the last time! I tell you, Myddelton, the man has no backbone! Upon my word, he is prey to such fancies—it's like negotiating with quicksand.

"We must write to Di Borgo in St. Petersburg immediately. He must keep Alexander to the sticking point! And we must inform Wellington, too. When is high tide? I shall need you to write all this up as soon as possible, you know..." But then, his enthusiasm plummeting, he said, "This is very good news indeed. And heaven knows, we need it...I shall tell you this now, you'll hear it all on the morrow in any event." He frowned, the deep lines of his brow drawing tightly together.

"What is it, sir?"

"Those damnable French, Myddelton. We've been double-crossed and I have only just learnt of it. When Barlow—you know, the American—went to the French Foreign Office, the infernal French rogue put on a fine performance, and calm as you please told him that they'd revoked the Berlin and Milan Decrees a year ago. April last. And then he produced a decree from his records and said he couldn't think how it was that they hadn't received it!"

Myddelton stared. "What?"

Castlereagh's scowl was growing deeper by the moment. "Yes. I tell you this, it's a damnable forgery. I am convinced of it. 'Struth, it has to be. And of recent date. Because if that oily Corsican maggot could have found a way to shoehorn us into war with the Americans sooner, you may be certain he would have done, and we would have heard of it! He would have been trumpeting it all over Europe." He blew out a breath of air. "So I fancy it was written sometime in the past fortnight, just as soon as they heard that we intended to repeal the Orders in Council."

Myddelton blinked, trying to comprehend, to see and to understand all the ramifications of this new twist all at once, his mind now a whirl of troop numbers, ships, supply lines. "So...are you saying we must prepare for a second front opening up, sir? Surely, the Americans ain't so naive to be taken in by such a ruse?"

"I pray it is not so. But, yes, I fear it may be." Lord Castlereagh nodded and took the letters back, folding them carefully and returning them to his pocket. "Come 'round first thing in the morning, will you, and we'll get a dispatch off to Di Borgo. And then I shall need full translations of these letters…I haven't yet spoken to Liverpool about this mess in Paris." He rubbed at his chin, then smiled amiably. "And tomorrow afternoon, perhaps you can give me a full report on those troop movements across Europe? Good." He paused. "There now, I do can nothing about it all tonight, and neither can you, so I shall be off to enjoy some music. I am promised to Lady Romford, you know, dare not be late."

"Do you perform then, this evening, sir?"

"Yes. Most assuredly, yes. A charming little duet by Haydn, with young Hardy. I have been looking forward to it for weeks now. It is a sheer delight to play, you know. Such a beautiful interplay of melodies between the two instruments…And so very tender, I find." Happy at the thought, he rose. "Thank you for that." He patted his breast pocket. "Shall you be joining us at the Romfords'? No? Ah well. I shall say good night, then."

Myddelton watched as the Foreign Secretary threaded his way through the maze of tables, chairs and members, then stared moodily into the dregs in the bottom of his wineglass, the inward calm of rigorous intellectual challenge abandoning him once more to bleakness. Pemberton had not yet told anyone, but at some point, he would. And in the morning or afternoon, whenever he finally returned from the Foreign Office, she would be gone. And in the meantime, there was nothing for him but war, the pressing need to reinforce the North Atlantic fleet and send troops to Canada—troops they'd need to raise, troops they didn't have. And suddenly he was filled with a kind of hopelessness such as he had never known.

"I say, Myddelton, mind if I have a sit-down?"

Myddelton looked up to see the young Harry Shuster towering over him. He braced himself inwardly for a spate of unending and inconsequential sporting babble, smiled and said, "No, help yourself." And raised his quizzing glass to survey the inelegant mess about Shuster's

306

throat—a spotted Belcher handkerchief knotted about an unironed shirt collar. "It must take some effort to achieve results like that, Harry," he commented, lowering the glass.

Harry grinned, slouched into the chair and stretched out his too long legs. "Aye, you should see me. Sometimes, I take my shirt and throw it on the floor and walk on it, in order to get it right. It's meant to look like I slept in it. Though of course I didn't."

"Really..." What else did one say? Myddelton returned his snuff-box to his fob pocket.

Unusually, Harry looked quite serious. "Ehm, Myddelton, you're with Castlereagh's staff now, ain't you?"

"I am." Where was the obligatory recital of someone's latest escapade on the hunting fields? "Why?"

Harry laughed. "Well, the thing is, you see, it's about m'brother Georgie. You remember Georgie..."

Myddelton smiled. "How could one forget him?" At school it had been none other than George Shuster who had, one day, decided he'd had enough of being beaten for his many and varied misdemeanours and so, in assuming 'the position', had clenched his buttocks as hard as he could. When the stick had descended upon this now rock-hard object, it had broken loudly and unmistakably in half—to the fury of the Master and the delight of the boys.

Harry grinned. "Aye. Well then, you know he's with Wellington. But the thing is, we ain't heard from him in a bit, d'you see? I ain't sayin' he writes a lot, but he always writes to say that he's all right."

Myddelton shook his head. No news usually meant one thing. "That's Liverpool's department or Horse Guards. I'd ask Liverpool if I was you, or Palmerston. Or even Verdon."

Harry shook his head. "Don't know Verdon or Palmerston at all well. And I don't think Liverpool's too fond o'me."

"Ah! Well," Myddelton said, weighing the options. Honesty was out. "Is Georgie one of Wellington's own staff or..."

Harry nodded happily. "Aye. Ain't that amazin'? Georgie!"

"Well, if he's on Wellington's staff, then if anything has happened to him, it'll be the Duke himself who writes. But Wellington's had them on the march for a month or two now…so Georgie's probably just too busy."

Shuster nodded, a serious expression in his rogue's eyes. "Aye, that'll be it then. I'll tell m'mother that she would have heard if anythin' was wrong. But you know her—she's convinced I'm touched in the upperworks."

"With you dressing like that, Harry, it's no surprise!" Myddelton said.

"Ha! Well, at least I ain't a twiddlepoop like Pickering-Stone!" He failed to notice the sudden tightening of Myddelton's expression. "Devil take me, Myddelton, I never laughed so hard in my life as this morning when I heard Dunphail pitchin' that rum lay about you horsewhippin' him. It nearly killed me to keep from laughin' in his face."

"I gather you was present." Myddelton's calm disinterest fooled no one. Horsewhipping, now that was a satisfying concept.

"Aye. Sitting just there, at th'other end of that table." He nodded in the direction of the long table near the centre of the room. "Jesuadon was with me." He laughed. "And then, Pemberton starts talkin' about the scars you get from bein' horsewhipped and gangrene settin' in and oozin' pus…God's garters, it was brilliant!"

"Harry!" Yes, and though Pickering-Stone no doubt deserved it, Myddelton rather thought he'd prefer to begin with Stansgate and Reding. Together, or separately. It didn't much matter.

Unrepentant, Harry continued to laugh. "It wasn't me that said it!" he protested. "'Struth, Myddelton, they're your friends, not mine! But then, wait for it, I saw him, Pickering-Stone I mean, about two hours later. He was leavin' Town in a post chaise. I even stopped him and asked where he was off to. He nearly died o' fright. You should ha' seen him!" Harry tried to sober himself. "Od's my life, you should have seen the expression on his face! And he was shakin' like a deuced rabbit." He shook himself out of his hilarity, then narrowing his gaze, said shrewdly, "I say, Myddelton, while I'm thinkin' on it…Has you ever caught anyone cheatin' at cards?"

"Not here," Myddelton replied. "And I make a point of staying away from those hells where cheating is, ehm, allowed."

Harry nodded. "Aye," he agreed. "I wouldn't say this to anyone, y'know, but I have my suspicions about someone. Stansgate it is…" He saw that Myddelton had a frozen, wary look about him, but continued. "I ain't so clear about Reding, neither. But I think…I think Stansgate is fleecin' him too. I've never played with 'em, myself. But Jesuadon, you know Jesuadon, don't you, well, he was stripped naked by 'em t'other night, playin' faro."

Ignoring the anger and anguish he felt, Myddelton said evenly, "Faro is hardly the safest game, Harry…"

"You don't know Thos Jesuadon, then. He has the damn'dest memory. He can remember every card, d'you see? And this particular night, he said he was certain that Stansgate had already turned up the ace of hearts!"

Myddelton was quiet, digesting this. Stansgate was the last person he wanted to discuss. Ever. "Well, there are two things one can do—challenge him, or wait and see if it happens again."

"Well the fact is, Myddelton, I'm in a devilish spot. Stansgate's mother is a friend of m'mother's. But he always was a spiteful little toad and he was used to get us in more trouble with his sneaking little lies…"

"I hadn't realised he was prone to lying." Myddelton tried and failed to sound distant. This cut too close. But there was no point in pretence. "What about his wagering?"

"D'you mean the one about your wife and Pemberton?" Harry said with the brutal candour of youth.

It was so bald and sudden and hit Myddelton so hard that it knocked the breath out of him. He turned away and stared about the room. Most of the other diners were finished and departing. "Yes."

When Harry answered, there was none of the boyish in either his speech or his look. It was as if he knew exactly the damage that had been done. Levelly, he began: "Stansgate would tell you your mother was a dog-fox if he thought there was winnings to be had. He's as spiteful as you can stare and he has the mind of a piss pot." He flexed his shoulders. "The last I heard is that he nearly killed one of the girls down at Madame Lucille's nug-house. I was there for a party a couple of nights later and they was all still talkin' about it."

Myddelton gave Harry a long look. Whatever might be said of the

Shuster brothers, and there was a great deal, they were not shammers. They had certainly spent as much time being thrashed at school as they had in lessons, but neither had ever been a bully or a liar, nor had they ever acted out of malice or spite. Pensively, Myddelton toyed with his snuff-box. "Stansgate ain't a Peep o' Day boy, is he?" Myddelton asked quietly.

"No." Harry shook his head, then winked. "Doubt they'd have him. They've got their reputations to think of, you know."

In spite of himself and his fiasco of a life, Myddelton chuckled.

"Ah well, must push off." Harry rose ungracefully to his feet. "Thanks for that, Myddelton. I'll tell m'mother that there's nothin' to worry about." He nodded his leave taking and lurched out of the Coffeeroom.

Myddelton sat back in his chair and did not pour another glass of wine. How could have been so infernally blind? Stupid? Jealous? Assheaded? And tomorrow, she would be gone. Od's life, it was too damned much to be borne! But…but he still had tonight. It was only gone ten. He still had tonight.

Abruptly he stood up. He knew she was expected to perform with Hardy at the Romfords'. If he were to hurry, he might just be in time to hear her. And if he were there, if she saw him applauding…surely then, he could manoeuvre it so that he—not Hardy or Dunphail or Pemberton—escorted her home. And that…that would give him the chance to at least begin to apologise…

19

Myddelton was not the only late arrival at the Romfords'. He was but one among many who were neither musically nor matrimonially inclined, who wished to be seen attending but who had arranged to arrive late and quit early. A trio of gentlemen had left their scores at home and were just now returning, music in hand. Several ladies and gentlemen who had dined elsewhere had also just arrived. All of whom were delighted to see him and to exchange the civilities and inconsequential little nothings which are the stock in trade of Society. Clearly, Pemberton had said nothing and to no one. And when at length he entered the Drawing Room he found it full, with little space for latecomers. And the previous self-assurance which he had so long taken for granted having deserted him, he remained stuck at the rear of the room, scanning the backs of heads for a glimpse of her. A baritone was singing, but he could not see him and did not recognise the voice. Finally, a gentleman noticed him and courteously moved to one side so that he might progress farther into the room. Though through the forest of fine head-dresses he could see little.

Patiently he pressed forward and sideways and worked his way toward a side aisle till he came to a clearing. And…Sweet Christ, that was Hardy singing! But where had that voice—smooth, strong, and deep, lustrous even—come from? Heaven knew Ned had always sung, but he had never sounded like that before.

And there…at the fortepiano, there *she* was. Graceful and composed, intent upon the music, but every now and again glancing up at Hardy with a smile upon her face.

Hardy was singing: "Wie ich dich liebe mit warmen Blut, Die du mir Jugend und Freud und Mut Zu neuen Liedern und Tänzen gibst. Sei ewig glücklich, Wie du liebst."

Goethe, wasn't it? *How I love you passionately—you who give me youth and joy and spirit for fresh songs and dances. Be always happy as you love me...*

Myddelton's breath caught in his throat. The music wreathed about his brain. She played the final chord and beamed a smile at Hardy. Myddelton felt a burst of possessive pride and joy and something else again. 'Struth, she was lovely...

The applause began. Myddelton joined in with pleasure and delight.

"My dear Lord Myddelton!" a voice beside him purred.

Not Miss Wythenshaw.

But yes, la Wythenshaw.

"It has been too too long since we have met..." she continued, laying her hand upon his arm and ducking her chin. "Where can you have been hiding yourself, my lord?"

Not this. Anything, anything but this, please, Myddelton thought with a stab of desperation. He inclined his head. "Miss Wythenshaw," he drawled even as he took in the charms of her person as revealed by her decolletage. He straightened and did not smile. "I have been away from Town a good deal lately." Pointedly he returned his attention to the front of the room where Hardy was waiting while Jane resumed her seat at the fortepiano.

The audience quieted.

"Well it has been our loss, I must say." Miss Wythenshaw tucked her other hand intimately about his arm, and leaned her head toward his, so that her dark, exquisite curls brushed his shoulder. "So many of the ton parties would be nothing other than insipid if it were not for the good company. And when the good company leaves Town..."

Instinctively, Myddelton distrusted her. Nor did he like what he hoped was not a suggestion of ardour in her gaze. That was all he needed. "I fear you flatter me, Miss Wythenshaw. I appear too infrequently at parties to be accounted as any kind of company at all."

Unperturbed, Miss Wythenshaw bestowed a silky smile. "They do say that distance lends enchantment to the view. Or is it 'distance makes the heart grow fonder'? Something like that..." Her face was nearly brushing against his lapel.

'Struth, he needed to extricate himself from this. Now. This was not what he had come here for. And she wasn't intending to talk through Hardy's performance, was she?

But she was. She most certainly was. For the alluring Miss Wythenshaw had a score, or several, to settle. And she was nothing if not tenacious in her affections and desires.

About them, all were still, expectant. At the front, Mr. Hardy was composing himself, drawing himself up and together. And at the fortepiano, Jane waited upon him, her hands poised upon the keys, her whole being attuned to him, listening for his first breath, his first note, unconscious of all else.

"I do think …" Miss Wythenshaw began.

Was there no way to extract himself? "Our conversation is drawing attention, Miss Wythenshaw. Can it not wait until Hardy and my wife have finished their performance?"

Tentative as the first breath of summer, his hand placed unaffectedly over his heart, Mr. Hardy began: "Ich liebe dich…" *I love you…*

And matching him, softly, Jane joined in with the accompaniment of broken chords.

"…So wie du mich, am Abend und am Morgen,"

…as you do me, in the evening and the morning.

"Noch war kein Tag, wo du und ich nicht teilten uns're Sorgen…"

Yet there was no day where you and I did not share our sorrows.

"Auch waren sie für dich und mich Geteilt leicht zu ertragen; Du tröstetest im Kummer mich, Ich weint in deine Klagen, in deine Klagen."

Shared, they were easy to bear for you and me; you comforted me in my sorrow, I wept in your lamenting. Overcome, Myddelton thought such music, lilting and soaring yet infinitely tender, must bring him to tears. For these words conjured up the image of that which he desired above all else.

"D'rum Gottes Segen über dir, Du meines Lebens Freude…"

Therefore, God's blessing on you, you my life's joy…

"Gott schütze dich, erhalt dich mir, schütz und erhalt uns beide, erhalt uns beide, erhalt uns beide." *God keep and protect you for me, protect and keep us both.*

With a rousing flourish Jane finished the song. And there followed

313

that rare moment of hush, while the audience held its breath at such beauty, and then released, remembering as one to breathe again and applaud. Rapt, Myddelton exhaled slowly. Warmed, seduced even by this much-longed-for but never acknowledged union of sympathy with affection, he came to himself only gradually, then he too began to clap.

Ever courteous and considerate, Mr. Hardy turned, paying no heed to the audience, nor to the applause for which he had laboured so long, until he had taken Lady Myddelton by the hand and brought her forward to share in the acclaim. Smiling and laughing together, they took their bows.

Whoever it had been who said Beethoven's music was full of crashing chords and discords—a sign of his passionate anger and loneliness in his deafness—was surely wrong. This was so very pure, so achingly gentle upon the ear and heart. And surely such sublime delicacy, such melismatic perfection as this could only have been written by one who loved deeply and well, whatever Herr Beethoven's critics might aver. Nor was Myddelton the only one touched by this frictionless melding of concord and poetry. For the audience was now on its feet, the gentlemen shouting 'Bravo' and the ladies clapping enthusiastically, their rigid decorum and fashionable boredom momentarily forgotten. Still applauding, Myddelton watched his wife, *his*, and Hardy, both triumphant and humble, take another bow.

A voice from the audience called for an encore, then another, and again. Hardy bent to say something in her ear; sparkling and happy, she laughed.

Miss Wythenshaw did not applaud. She tightened her hold on Myddelton's arm. "I have wished to ask for some time, my lord, do you spend the summer in Brighton or shall you leave us bereft of your company over the summer too?" she said, twitching at his sleeve.

Myddelton hardly heard. He so wanted to be there before her, his wife, so that she might see how the music had touched him, so that she would know, despite every appearance to the contrary, how this idyll of truly requited affection rejoiced his tired soul. Thus with his eyes still on his wife and Hardy, Myddelton inclined his head toward the splendid Miss Wythenshaw, that he might better hear her question. "I beg your pardon?"

A brilliant smile lighting her face—she had not anticipated such a reception—Jane raised her eyes to scan the audience and saw. Saw at the rear of the crowded room, her husband and a young woman—the sumptuous Miss Wythenshaw, it was—with their heads together in intimate conversation. And knew in that instant, with what was almost physical pain, that she had been wrong. There was nowhere safe from him. Nor was there any phalanx powerful enough to spare her or protect her from the spectacle of his licentiousness. And felt a return of that dreadful invidious emptiness.

Bemused, Pemberton watched her expression change from pleasure to dismay. And turning, he followed the line of her vision until he saw. "Oh Lord," he whispered to no one, though Dunphail heard. "I don't believe it."

Mr. Hardy had felt her hand stiffen in his and looked for the cause. Then he too saw.

Had she been able, Jane might have noticed Hardy's sudden pallor or the bleakness in his eyes. But she did not, could not, see it. His hands clenching and unclenching at his sides, Hardy paused for a moment, then bent to say in her ear, "I do not suppose you brought the music for *Trennungslied*, ma'am? Though not to your taste perhaps, can you play it for me?"

Her eyes and her response were both clear. "Yes. Yes, I can." She swallowed, unhappy. And committed herself: "Of course, I can play it."

Miss Wythenshaw smiled broadly and repeated her question. Though Myddelton's reply hardly mattered now.

And Myddelton, trapped by manners, misunderstandings and malice, watched as his wife misread the situation, watched as her equanimity and smiles turned to betrayal, and could do nothing. Then she returned to the fortepiano and the audience returned to their seats and became quiet.

Standing beside her, Mr. Hardy was still. Then, with searing simplicity, he sang: "Die Engel Gottes weinen..."

The angels of God weep...Gone was the poetic vision of solicitude, of felicity in unity. This was rage. Searing melodic rage. Then Jane began to play the dark, driven accompaniment. And Myddelton knew that she

315

played from the heart.

...when lovers part. How will I be able to live, O maiden, without you? A stranger from all joys, I now live in sorrow. And you? And you? Perhaps Luisa will forget me forever... Listening, hearing, Myddelton felt a kind of trembling, for this was, surely, her answer to him, to the abuse to which he had subjected her. *Awake or dreaming, I will name Luisa: to speak her name is divine service for me; I will even name her and praise her before God above. And you? And you? Perhaps Luisa will forget me forever...*

Like enraged horses galloping headlong into some vortex of hell, the music, agitato, discordant and impassioned, thundered on. And Hardy's resonant voice was transformed into the voice of all despairing. And Myddelton could see in Jane's face, that mirror of her thoughts, such distress and grief as she played—now pianissimo, now fortissimo—even as her performance demonstrated her mastery of the instrument and her technique.

I cannot forget her; at every turn I am haunted by the touch of love from her hands. I tremble to embrace her and find myself forsaken....Forgetfulness steals in hours that which love created over years. Like the wave of a hand, so hearts turn away. If new tributes were to displace her memory of me, O God! She will forget me forever... But this was not her song. Not really. Such desperate rage and desolation did not belong to her. She might be angry and deeply hurt, but this...

O think of our parting! This tearless silence, this relentless pounding of the heart, may it weigh on you like the harsh appearing of a ghost if you should think of another, if you should forget me, if God and you forget... He, he would be the forgotten one, not her.

O think of our parting! May this memorial, bitten onto my mouth with kisses, may it judge me and you... Just as he would never know the touch of her mouth on his, never know how sweetly she might return his kiss, nor hold her in his arms. His would be the void. She would forget him. *With this memorial engraved on my mouth I arrive at the bewitching hour, at the fateful knowledge that Luisa has forgotten me, she has forgotten me...* And he did not know how he would bear it. *She has forgotten me...*

And as Hardy held the final note and let it fade, she performed the final chords which tolled, sonorous and awful as a death knell. And

Myddelton could see that she was white and struggling not to weep. And nearly wept himself.

Uncertain, the audience remained still. For all that many might indulge in the raptures and pathos of Romantic sensibility in private, such terrible passion did not belong to the Drawing Room. For this had been such a plumbing of anguished depths as audiences associated with Herr Beethoven. But this was Mozart, and anyone hearing it must have concluded that his had been more than a passing flirtation with bitterness and heart-ache. And it was not what they expected. And who among them would have guessed that the amiable Mr. Hardy might harbour such emotion as this? Who might be the cause of it? For someone must have known if his addresses had been rebuffed in such a way as to cause him such unhappiness. But there was no one, no name to be linked to a rejection so heartless. And anyway, what girl would be so foolish?

A single gentleman began to applaud, then others now reminded of their duty joined in. And soon that second round of applause matched the first for, truly, it had been a tour de force.

Separation. Was that miserable half-life all that was left them? Shying from it, watching her, hollow with despair, Myddelton feared that it was.

Pemberton came to stand at Jane's side and, with Hardy, led her to face the audience. She curtsied and did not cry. Drawn, she looked to the rear of the room and saw that Myddelton was still with Miss Wythenshaw. She shuddered violently. Nothing had altered.

Scowling with unspoken disapproval and anger, Pemberton tucked her hand through his arm and said reassuringly, "It's all right, Angel, I'll see you home now. Well done."

Bereft, knowing that he had lost her and all, Myddelton watched her go. Watched Pemberton escort her through the farthest door, and felt it was his life and all hope departing. He had lost. He had gambled and had lost.

Miss Wythenshaw noticed nothing. Ignorant and vain, she bestowed her most dazzling smile upon him. "I cannot think why Mr. Hardy should have chosen such a song as an encore, can you, my lord? Indeed, I do not believe Lady Jersey or Mrs. Drummond-Burrell are looking very amused. It was hardly appropriate for such a place and amongst such a gathering as this and I think…"

"What?" Myddelton snapped, looking down upon her with a sudden intense dislike. "What do you know about it? What do you know about anything?"

"I…" she faltered, surprised and stellar no longer. Bewildered, she took a step back.

And seeing in his mind's eye the hunted look upon Jane's face when she had seen him with this girl, and the unhappiness and tears which surely had followed as Pemberton had escorted her away, said brutally, "Do you have any idea, any idea at all, what you have done?" And with a barely civil bow, he left her standing alone and solitary.

His hopes of reconciliation now cheated, civility abandoned, and in the grip of a savage fury, Myddelton strode from the Romford establishment and down Berkeley Street toward St. James's, heading for nowhere. For where could house such anger, such grief?

A slight-figured cutpurse lingering in a shadowed alley listened to the sound of Myddelton's shoes as he marched down the street and thought his luck must be in. From the light sound of the tread, the boy recognised a well-heeled pair of shoes—probably from Hoby, the Quality's bootmaker. And the steps belonged to a solitary gentleman—perfect for surprise and confusion. Licking his lips, the boy prepared to dash out and accidentally collide with his intended victim. But a glance a Myddelton's face as he passed under a street lamp stopped the child. There was murder in that face.

Warily, he retreated into the shadows and watched as Myddelton stalked past. "'E'd split yer open as soon as look at yer, that'un," he muttered to himself.

Myddelton paused at the corner of King Street. He could still go home. She would be there, certainly. And beg her forgiveness. But would she believe him? Would she trust him now? Overwrought—what had he done?—he ran a disarranging hand through his hair. Why had he not gone to the front of that damned Drawing Room? Then at least he would have avoided this latest debacle with that pestilential Wythenshaw female. 'Struth, he would have done better to have gone to Daffy's and drunk himself insensate. If only that weasel Stansgate had not...

Stansgate.

The name echoed in Myddelton's head. Stansgate. 'Struth, he should wring his poxy little neck. Or spit his worthless carcass on the tip of a rapier for having started this whole pack of lies. Or better still, blow his head off. Yes, that would afford infinite satisfaction. Abruptly, he turned. He would go to White's. What he had to do there could not wait.

He stopped in the club's foyer to catch his breath, then started up the curving staircase, paused at the entrance to the gaming room and in the far corner, sighted his quarry.

Forcing himself to breathe slowly and evenly, Myddelton made his way toward the rear table, nodding to friends and acquaintances as he passed them. When he reached the far table, the two card players were tallying the points of a rubber of piquet.

"I have rubiconned you, Reding! B'Gad, I have!" Stansgate crowed, his habitual sneer giving way to a less pleasant expression.

Myddelton's jaw tightened. S'life, he wanted to blow a hole through Stansgate's pox-ridden vitals. Ruthlessly, he quashed the desire and thought. As a member of the Government, duelling was forbidden him. Castlereagh would, must, dismiss him for it.

"Messrs. Stansgate and Reding. How very fortunate..." His tone was bored. His stomach was heaving. Myddelton forced himself to smile lazily as befitted a gentleman.

"Evenin', Myddelton," Stansgate replied.

Mr. Reding muttered a good evening, but his face had begun to take on a reddish hue which ill-matched the burgundy colour of his coat.

"I know you will forgive the impropriety of my breaking in on your game..." Myddelton paused to study his fingernails. Lud, this was hard. "But the matter of a certain wager has come to my attention. Which I feel sure must have come about as a consequence of a grave misconception on the part of the, ehm, wagerers."

Reding's eyes had begun to bulge in their sockets—he had heard stories about Myddelton and his aim with pistols and shot. Stansgate idly shuffled the cards.

"A misconception. Or perhaps several misconceptions…" Myddelton drawled.

Reding reached up and tugged at his too tight neckcloth. Was this the prelude to a duel? For all he was on his fourth bottle, he did not like the tone in Myddelton's voice. Nor the look in his eye. And if Myddelton meant to fight, both he and Stansgate would come out corpses, be it sword or shot. He would apologise and that'd be an end to it. It had been a bit of foolery spoken when he was foxed and that was all…

"Should such misconceptions ever so cloud your judgment again, I shall be pleased, at the first opportunity following such a lapse, to thrash you both. It being…" Myddelton reached into his pocket with what appeared to be ease for his snuff-box. "…Against my principles to fight my inferiors." He opened the box and took a few grains from off his thumbnail. "Do I make myself clear?"

Reding heaved a sigh of relief. "Pleased to oblige you in anythin', my lord. Y'r most obedient…A bit of drink-fuddled foolery that. Never meant to imply that Lady…"

"Indeed," Myddelton interrupted, "It might be better if you refrained from mentioning the lady's name ever again." He dusted an imagined grain of snuff off his sleeve. "Perhaps that may keep you from falling into the way of temptation."

Mr. Stansgate now craned his neck and lifted his chin about the mammoth pile of starched linen which he affected as a neckcloth that he might look directly at Myddelton. "'Pon my life, my lord, I am sure I should be delighted to do all in my power," he began. "Still, it may prove devilish difficult t'oblige you if we was ever to be presented to the lady, don't you think, Myddelton?" he sneered.

He had gone too far. Myddelton grabbed the collar of Stansgate's coat and hauled him half out of his chair. "Look, you little blaggart, if I ever hear that you have so much as mentioned my wife's name again—in any context whatsoever—I'll set a press gang on you and give orders to have you flogged 'round the Fleet. Do I make myself clear?"

Reding, who had a cousin in the Navy, blenched.

Stansgate was not so wise. Two spots of colour had appeared on his cheekbones, but when he spoke his voice still retained that thread of insouciance. "I am sure I cannot think what you are referrin' to, Myddelton. Still, anythin' to humour you. My solemn vow on't."

Myddelton released his hold on Stansgate's collar. Stansgate sank back into his chair. "But you know," he continued, blandly adjusting his waistcoat and cuffs, "You really ought to be directin' your spleen towards Reding, here. It was he who introduced the disreputable wager, if you must know." His slack mouth stretched into a sneering grin.

Myddelton held his breath. The blood pounded in his temples and chest. Reding was shaking his head in mute denial. Myddelton looked from one to the other. "I am sure we need not quibble over points, Stansgate. You and I and Reding here all know the score. Remember what I said. They do say a flogging 'round the Fleet can take days." He gave the merest sketch of a bow. "Good evening, gentlemen."

He would have preferred to be drunk. Exceedingly drunk, with every sense awash in a sea of blue ruin. He had tried. 'Struth, how he had tried.

He had gone to Daffy's and sat himself down at a table with a glass and a bottle of strip-me-naked, instructing the waiter to keep the bottles coming. But it hadn't worked. He'd drunk one glassful and poured himself a refill, and then, found himself staring and staring into the clear liquid, rehearsing the events of that awful day, and ruminating. And had discovered too that he could find no solace either in the gin or in what he had always considered the congenial atmosphere of Daffy's. Had it been the noise? The argument in the corner between two pot-valiant soldiers? The overweening aspirant young Bloods crowing over who'd had the greatest triumphs on the hunting field? The roisterous bawdy songs coming from the next room? Or the unforgiving litany of his own thoughts? But abruptly he had realised he could not stand it a moment longer, and setting the glass down, had quitted the place.

And now, here he was, not drunk, at half past one, standing at Pemberton's door, while Willetts, dear Willetts, temporised: "I assure you, my lord, my master is not at home."

"I'll wait," he insisted.

Poor Willetts.

"I do not believe that would be wise, my lord. That is to say, I do not know when Lord Pemberton will return…and, your parting from him, my lord, if you'll forgive me, was not of the most amicable. So, perhaps it would be better…"

"No Willetts. I shall wait. If I have to wait all night, I'll wait. I must speak to him."

Dear Willetts, caught on the horns of such a dilemma. For he had known Lord Myddelton for as long as he had been employed by Lord Pemberton, and was devoted to them both. Indeed, he had always thought the Earl of Myddelton the best of all young gentlemen, excepting, of course, his master. Willetts sighed. "I am not at all convinced, my lord. But as you wish. He may not see you though."

"He must, Willetts. He must."

Willetts pursed his lips together. He had never seen the Earl so determined. Sighing again, he admitted him and led the way to the library.

Where Myddelton waited. Watching the candles burn down in this most familiar of rooms. Anticipating the worst. Staring morosely into the guttering flames of the fire. Reflecting upon the day's and weeks' misdeeds and mistakes and thinking longingly on how he might have avoided them.

Until finally, a good hour later, from the outer hall: "No Willetts! Get rid of him. I'm in no mood…"

Myddelton closed his eyes against the bleakness of this final despair. For how could he break this impasse into which he had brought them all?

"I am sorry, my lord. But his lordship is adamant. He will not see you," Willetts said from the doorway.

"Go to bed, Willetts," Pemberton said finally, absolving his manservant, sending him away. Then, ruthlessly: "Get out, Myddelton. Go home." It was the voice of a stranger. "By my life, I cannot think why you came here. For I do not think there is anything which you could possibly have to say to me now."

Myddelton stood and faced his former companion, his closest and dearest, and wished in his wretchedness that Pemberton had fired that shot. Then softly, painfully, knowing there was no hope, said: "I could apologise. I could beg your pardon." He wanted to weep at the wanton loss of everything. "I could ask you if you know of any way I might keep my wife from leaving me."

For the longest time, Pemberton said nothing and did not move from his spot by the door. For Myddelton had violated every principle of friendship and honour. Yet how did one turn one's back on the habit and devotion of a lifetime? Or upon that friend who needed one, now, in his utmost distress? No one knew Myddelton as he did. He knew him as well as his own face. And understood the depths of that anguish which had brought him here. He knew too what that apology must have cost. And seeing before him the man who as a boy in their last year at Eton had wept in his arms upon learning that his mother was dead, scowled and sighed heavily. "Dear God, Avery, what have you done?" And came into the room to face his still-dearest friend.

"I do not know," Myddelton answered truthfully and without self-pity, and sat down to hold his head in his hands. Eventually, from his heart he said: "But I do know that every time I try to behave as a proper husband to her—as I know I ought, as I should have done from the first instant I met her—or to prove to her that I am not some sort of curst loose fish, it turns into an infernal cock-up and I make everything worse, much much worse. And I do not know how it happens or why it happens. And I don't know what to do."

Pemberton went to the sideboard and poured out two brandies. Silently, he offered one to Myddelton, then sat down near the fire.

And knowing he should not ask such a thing, for surely he knew the answer and should not embarrass Pemberton with maudlin sentiment, Myddelton said, "Why did you not shoot me this afternoon?"

Pemberton eyed him. Should he tell the unflattering truth? Why not? And said drily: "The gun wasn't loaded." And seeing the chagrin, discomfiture, shock and self-mockery as they flitted across Myddelton's features in rapid succession, he began, unfeelingly, to laugh.

Myddelton may not have known how to manage his domestic affairs with any great success, but he did possess considerable experience of

Pemberton laughing at him. And as ever, it dispelled all preponderance toward the melodramatic. And at this moment, Pemberton's unstoppable laughter had such a quality of normality about it that Myddelton, for all his distress and chagrin, positively welcomed it—and even, surprisingly, saw the humour himself.

Pemberton did not stop laughing until he lay back against the sofa with his sides hurting. Still chuckling, he loosened his cravat and finished his brandy.

At last, Myddelton said: "Obviously, I know better than to have paid any attention whatsoever to the gossip or slander of bleaters like Stansgate and Reding." He paused, searching for reason and shook his head. "But I'm damned if I can explain it. I saw that wager written in the betting book and I went mad. And I'm sorrier than you'll ever know…"

Pemberton regarded him steadily. "Is it the war?"

"What would that have to do with it?"

"For Christ's sake, Myddelton, you can't be that obtuse. You don't even have time to…" He broke off. And cleared his throat. Lud, this was a pretty situation. He wasn't meant to know about *that*. Neither could he say that he knew precisely why Myddelton had gone mad at the idea of being cuckolded—he was panting to bed her. 'Struth, he knew what would cure Myddelton of this madness, but he assuredly was not going to be the one to tell him. Gently, carefully, he began again: "Perhaps you should go home to Great Myddelton for a while. Take Janey with you. She'll love it there. Give yourselves some time together…Let Planta do some work for once. Tell Castlereagh to find himself another code breaker for a month or…"

"How can you know about that?" Myddelton demanded, suddenly alert.

Surprised (was this dangerous water too?), Pemberton recovered and said: "What? 'Struth, Myddelton, you speak how many languages fluently? Six? And who's that mad poet you love, the one who writes in all those different languages in each bally poem?"

"Skelton. John Skelton," Myddelton said repressively.

"Christ, how stupid do you think I am? I've known you for how long? I know you better than my own brothers—which given what I know of Harry and Bobbin can only be a good thing... Of course you're his code breaker. You probably read him all the foreign newspapers as well."

Thoughtfully, reassessingly—indeed, how stupid did he think Pemberton was?—Myddelton began, "I can't leave immediately. I might manage it in a month or so. After we're found ourselves a new Prime Minister and Chancellor. But..." He was back where he had started. There was no disguising it. Again, bleakly: "Will she leave me, do you think?"

Pemberton didn't answer at once. He shrugged. "I don't know," he admitted. "She didn't say..." He looked at Myddelton and seeing the answer written on Myddelton's face, continued: "I take it you don't want her to leave...Well...well, then, if I was you, I'd start buying her presents. Smartish." And added in disgust: "And stop those little tête à têtes with other females, like the Wythenshaw."

"Her!" Myddelton exclaimed. "Why do you think I came tonight? I came for the express purpose of seeing my wife and then, that bloody female cornered me and started rabbiting on about ton parties and God knows what all."

Pemberton was unimpressed. "I told you she'd be trouble."

"Well, you were right...Will she forgive me, do you think?"

There was something different in the way Myddelton asked this, some hint of emotion that Pemberton had suspected, but never before heard. And it was equally clear that Myddelton, the great idiot, was as yet unaware of it. Blankly, Pemberton shook his head. "How should I know? She was...Well, she was fairly, ehm..." Pemberton paused, searching for a word that would wound as little as possible. And finally settled on, "Unhappy, after the Romford do."

"You mean she was crying."

"Yes...well, yes," Pemberton confirmed. "But it's as I said—presents. Start buying 'em for her. Soon. Like first thing in the morning. Only don't buy her jewellery."

That was a surprise. "Why?"

"Because she ain't Ianthe!" Pemberton ignored Myddelton's sudden bristling and went on, "And...because her father brought back a king's ransom in jewels from India. And she reckons they're vulgar and won't wear 'em. Says they give her a fit of the sillies…But you had better beg her forgiveness first though. And I mean *beg*."

"Yes." Myddelton got up and rubbed his face. "Yes." And prepared to leave.

"Hardy says you planted a facer on Jackson this afternoon," Pemberton said idly.

"Hardy talks too much."

Pemberton grinned. So it was true. And was quiet for a time. Yes, he had a very clear idea what was ailing Myddelton and a crystal clear notion of what would cure it. Had it been Dunphail, he would have told him to go and get himself rogered senseless. But one didn't say that to a newly married man. Nor could one say to Myddelton, 'Go and tell her you love her, you great idiot.' Instead: "You could always write her poetry, you know. I rather think she'd like some Latin verse."

"Ha! Poetry! Hardy says you warned Pickering-Stone off for me this morning."

"Pickering-Stone—that snivelling little freak of nature!"

Myddelton was not deflected. "Hardy said you told him *I* was a jealous husband!"

"You *are* a jealous husband, idiot. But if you try to horsewhip me, I'll kick your teeth in," Pemberton said affably.

Which threat left Myddelton feeling absurdly and immeasurably cheered. At the door, he paused: "Thank you."

"Go home, Myddelton," Pemberton said gently, without looking up. "Go home."

20

It is one of those peculiarities that glib remarks, thoughtlessly made, often contain the most truth and are what are remembered long after the intricacies of profound discussion have slipped from thought. Dawn was a smear of light above the rooftops to the east when at last Myddelton returned to Myddelton House, let himself in, and lit a candle to make his way upstairs. He had walked, as did Castlereagh so many nights, for miles, thinking. Thinking about his work for the Foreign Office and what he knew about the situation on the Continent. Thinking about Perceval's murder and where that left the Government and the country. Thinking about Jane. And considering the truth of Pemberton's avowal that he *was* a jealous husband and wondering how that had come to be, for he could not deny it. But he was still very far from certain on what he might say to Jane or how to apologise.

He opened the door on his bedroom. As in all else, he was now prepared to be wrong about this. There was no fire in the grate, but those candles that Stamp always left burning threw a soft curtain of light over the room. And holding his candle high, he looked about, regarding the bed hangings, draperies and new arrangements. And found that he rather liked it. For it looked a dashed sight better than that faded and tatty red had—even in this poor light. Unconsciously, his gaze wandered over the green sprigged papered walls to scan the ceiling and he saw that it was painted with swags as in the adjoining room where Jane slept. Unbelievable that he'd never seen it before now. And over there, were those not new, those two small paintings? He went to peer at them in the half-light. There was a new carpet underfoot too. Had she chosen these two still-lifes herself? For if she had, she had chosen well—especially the one with a teapot, grapes and apple. He shook his head in regret—such a unbelievably confounded balls-up he'd made—and sighed, and sat down at his desk to compose his apology to her.

Some time and several drafts later, he went to the connecting door and opened it. Her room was bathed in the sombre light of early morning. The bed curtains were not drawn, and she, like a child in a too big bed, lay asleep with one hand flung out onto the pillow by her cheek and her cat curled up in the crook of her knees. Lotto, sensing Myddelton, woke, stretched and came to sniff.

She was so lovely, this girl, his wife. Engaging too, but without airs. Perhaps, probably, he should have talked himself round when first they'd wed. She was very beautiful. And infinitely desirable. It would have been no task to bed her. And yet...no...No, he wanted no cold-blooded coupling. Nor did he believe he could use her as he would have done another, visiting her when the mood struck him to satisfy himself on her and depart. He wanted none of these convenient marriages such as several of his friends had.

She turned in her sleep and stretched her hand out on the pillow. What he wanted...What he wanted was...not only to wrap himself in her arms each night, but to find, when he awoke, that her fingers were still entwined with his. What he wanted was for her to be there, warm and dozy and trusting and familiar, when he arrived home late after a debate in the Upper House. And if she was not with him at breakfast, he wanted to know it was because she was still upstairs asleep in *his* bed. And if that made him a jealous husband, well then...What he wanted was for her to awaken, right now, and opening her arms to him, to welcome him that he might erase all memory of his folly, atoning for each misdeed with the tenderest of kisses, redeeming himself with even gentler lovemaking.

But she did not wake.

The servants, led by the doughty Kettering, adored her. And he, for all his starch, positively worshipped her. That much had been very clear when, the other day in answer to some flippant remark about her dog, Kettering had replied in that tone he reserved for crushing the pretensions of encroaching relatives: "I believe him to be the offspring of the late Colonel's Shandy, my lord. A very fine animal that, if I may be permitted to say so." Myddelton rubbed Lotto's ear and muzzle. "He put me in my place, didn't he, boy?

"Don't let her leave me, will you?" he said softly. And gingerly, carefully, tucked the note he had written into her outstretched hand. Tenderly, he reached to touch a curl of her hair. Though she had told him never to touch her, surely he was allowed that. It was soft as he knew it would be. "Don't leave, Janey," he whispered. But would she forgive him? He bent to kiss her fingers. He would beg if he had to. She stirred, and settled. He wished he had the courage to push the cat from her bed and lie down beside her, that he might fall asleep with her soft hair brushing against his cheek. But she would hardly welcome that now, would she?

What had Sir Charles said? That he hoped he deserved her? Well, he didn't. He didn't at all. Quelled and aching, he returned to his own room.

She came awake slowly, reluctantly, and late—for the strong mid-morning sun was penetrating through even the heavy drawn curtains—to an overwhelming sense of malaise. And disliking the sunlight, unwilling to face the now inevitable bleak vision of life that was to be hers, wanting only to delay that unhappy moment and hour and day, she turned her head away, and lay still, closing her eyes that she might drift back into unconsciousness. And drifting thus, noted in her hand the presence of something…which was vaguely puzzling. She opened her eyes again. It was a paper? Folded. Dozy and incurious, she looked at it and held it up to uncertain examination.

Please forgive me. There can be no words to express either my regret at my unspeakable folly or my hope for your forbearance. Please, do not leave me. Myddelton

She blinked, feeling stupid, rubbed at the sleep in her eye and struggled to raise herself onto one elbow to read again. *Please forgive me. There can be no words to express either my regret at my unspeakable folly or my hope for your forbearance. Please, do not leave me. Myddelton*

For this, she could not wake quickly enough. And unable to comprehend or to understand, feeling as though she had walked in on the final act of a play without knowing all that had gone before, she fell back against the pillow, trying desperately to gather her senses, and read again...*Please forgive me*...Now awake, she held the page flat against her chest to breathe heavily and deeply. Forgive him? How could she? After the things he had said? Calling her damaged goods. Implying that common harlots behaved better than she...Had he not broken all bonds of charity in maligning her, in thinking her capable of such treachery, such treachery as adultery? Tears smarted in her eyes and she wished they would stop, but of course they did not. Forgive him? Striving to remain calm, she felt herself beginning to quaver. Surely, surely, she had wept enough. "I don't want to cry any more," she exclaimed.

'Forgive us our debts as we forgive our debtors.' One said it so easily each Sunday, but the doing of it rarely came with such facility. Forgive him. Could she truly close the door on all that he had said and all that he had done and not done and never think on it again? Never resent him or it, nor bring it to mind? Neither to reproach nor reprove? He asked much.

There can be no words to express either my regret at my unspeakable folly or my hope for your forbearance. And yet? *Please, do not leave me.* She stilled, cradling her cheek in her hand. Had he truly expected her to leave him? How came he to think such a thing? For that, surely, was sheer foolishness.

She lay back against the pillows, sniffing, and smiled wistfully at herself. But was it so far-fetched? Certainly she had wanted to return to Britwell Park often and often...Or, alternatively, to retire to his house at Great Myddelton. And heaven knew, she had reason enough. Although, recently, she had thought, had come to believe, that separation was not what she desired. And though there was still too much left unsaid and undone...yet she had felt there was cause for a justified hope. Then, yesterday, out of nowhere had come that savage attack. She shook her head, unable to make sense of it. But...surely, he could not believe that she had meant to quit this house without a word.

Then, practical and irrefutably honest to the end, she half-smiled again. This was all such nonsense and she knew it. She wiped her tears away with the palm of her hand. She had all the will of a spineless sea-sponge when faced with contrition. And she was a fool if she believed or pretended otherwise: Were he to walk through that door right now and apologise to her, she would forgive him instantly. She would reach out to touch him—his arm, or his face—as she had done from the first. As she would always do.

"Why am I so will-less?" she murmured unhappily. And rang the bell for Haseley.

Who was waiting for her summons.

Thoughtfully, Jane regarded the connecting door to Myddelton's room, beyond which he was or probably was not sleeping. Poor Myddelton, did he ever sleep? And thought that at some time during the night he had come into her room, not to disturb nor to harm, but to place this letter in her hand and leave again. *Please forgive me. There can be no words to express either my regret at my unspeakable folly or my hope for your forbearance. Please, do not leave me. Myddelton*

She wished there were someone to whom she might talk—Mlle de Resnay would have done very well—for there was too much she did not understand. Was she to behave as if nothing had occurred? Would Myddelton speak of it further? And what of Pemberton? Was her friendship with him to be as it always had been or...

"Good morning, my lady," Haseley said, full of smiles. For she was expecting to find that same grieving and unhappy child as she had put, weeping, to bed. "You've slept ever so late."

"Good morning, Haseley. Lord Myddelton, is he still in?"

Haseley checked briefly. That was an odd question for Her to be asking. Especially in that voice. And placing my lady's tray on the bed, she poured out the tea. "No, my lady." And though she could not say why she thought she should mention it, nor was she given to gossiping and had never been encouraged in it, began, "But..." And receiving no look of rebuke for speaking out of turn, continued: "Mr. Stamp is most concerned, for my lord did come in last night and did come up to his rooms, but he did not sleep there. He slept on a sofa in the library...And after changing his clothes went off early this morning. I thought it might still be fumes from the paint."

Jane knew it from memory now. *Please forgive me. There can be no words to express either my regret at my unspeakable folly or my hope for your forbearance.*

331

Please, do not leave me. Myddelton It was not the fumes from the paint.

"And begging your pardon, my lady, but there is another puzzlement. This morning, when he wanted to be let out, your dog was scratching at that door..." Haseley gestured to the connecting door. "Not, as he usually does, at the door that leads into the hall."

Suddenly, inexplicably, Jane felt quite calm, and happy even. "Did he?" Lotto had never done that before.

Somehow, remarkably, much had changed: He had entered her room to place this letter in her hand and Lotto had welcomed him. And because he was who he was, Myddelton had rubbed Lotto's ears and muzzle before he departed. So Lotto had designated that door as friendly. And unaware that her half-smile was causing Haseley to feel no little perturbation, she smiled again. How would Myddelton have behaved at that late hour had she wakened? And where was he now? In his crabby little room in the Foreign Office? Poor Myddelton.

❧

Myddelton, poor or no, was nowhere near the Foreign Office, though he'd been there earlier; he was on Bond Street. And was finding that Bond Street was relatively empty at that hour of the morning. Only those who devoutly worshipped at the shrine of fashion were abroad, peering critically or enthusiastically through shop windows, religiously visiting each and every emporium in pursuit of the greatest bargain, the latest import. Myddelton saw few he recognised. Not that it mattered, for he was on a mission—that rather quintessential mission of finding and choosing a gift for his wife. And it was no easy task. And he must not get it wrong, though he had no experience in it, and neither was there any book of advice on how to get it right.

He had slowed to study the varied offerings—shawls and slippers, gowns and caps, bonnets and boots—in shop windows as he passed. Would she like this? Would she prefer that? He paused in front of Fanchon's window where a gown of seafoam green was draped on a dressmaker's figure. And struck by a distinctly pleasant and alternate thought, he smiled. A negligee? Yes, that he would definitely like to give her. And not just one. More than one. Many. Lud, what would she make of that? No. Definitely no. 'Struth, she'd think him the worst kind of libertine, if she didn't already. A pity, for there were some jolly attractive negligees to be had, if one knew where to look.

He raised his quizzing glass to peruse the display in a milliner's window—poke bonnets and chip straw cottager hats festooned with ribbons, silk flowers, and feathers. No, she did not favour the ostentatious. And even if she had, he felt...he felt, rather than knew, that while it might be perfectly acceptable—expected even—to choose gowns or bonnets (or nether garments) for one's mistress, such a gift would surely not be as appropriate for a wife. His wife. His wife whom he held in great esteem. For such a gift, like the fancy which bred those liaisons, denoted the ephemeral and the fleeting. Which left jewellery. And Pemberton had said 'no jewellery.' Which did make things awkward.

He walked on.

A horse? She had horses. Fine horses. Beautiful horses.

A lady's curricle? He could teach her to drive. Had she wanted one, assuredly her uncle would have bought it for her. But perhaps she would like to learn to drive?

What about books? She loved books.

And then suddenly, he knew what she would value more than any other thing. What would give her the greatest pleasure and demonstrate both his admiration and his respect for her. And hailing a hackney, he directed the driver to take him to a place he had never thought to visit: Clementi's showrooms. Where he startled the proprietor by demanding to purchase, on the spot, an instrument such as had been chosen by his wife some weeks previous, with all those latest improvements of which she'd been so proud, such as a deeper box for greater sonority—whatever that meant. And after having used that same purchasing policy as had been successfully employed by her—the roll of soft—he gave instructions for Signore Clementi's finest to be transported that very day to Great Myddelton. And left the proprietor to write to the now twice-disappointed client, explaining that he was sorry, it would take a few more days before his instrument was finished, for it was terribly difficult to obtain the best seasoned wood and to engineer the perfect placement of all the hammers...

And this Myddelton knew was right. And, emerging an hour later, pleased and satisfied, he stood on the street: to take a pinch of snuff, to glance idly in either direction, to savour this nascent sense of well-being.

Out of the corner of his eye, he noticed a box—of tulipwood? Or possibly satinwood? —in the window of the adjacent Book and Curio Seller. He polished his quizzing glass and stepped closer to the window to study the box. It was carved, and inlaid with an intertwining pattern of garlands on the sides and lid. Another worthy gift? Perhaps. And twirling his quizzing glass on its ribbon, he went down the three steps and entered the shop, ducking his head as he passed under the lintel.

The light in the shop was dim and the walls of bookcases were half-hidden in the gloom. Myddelton strolled between the display tables and cases, eyeing the many artfully displayed curios, examining a book here, a fob or bibelot there.

The owner appeared through a doorway at the rear of the shop. He was a small man, and bent, and he greeted Myddelton in heavily accented English and with a deferential bowing of his head.

After acknowledging the greeting with equalled politeness, Myddelton gestured toward the display window. "The box, it is Italian?"

The little man bowed reverently.

"Venetian perhaps?" Myddelton inquired.

"Florentine, monsignore."

Myddelton approached the window, stuck his cane under one arm and carefully lifted the box to inspect it. It was lighter than he had expected. He tested the silver latchet and peered through his quizzing glass at the top and four sides, looking for scratches or hairline cracks. There were none. It was perfect.

"It is a case for the music, monsignore. Not for the letters. As it you open, you will see the wooden layers with the hinges. This is for the musician to keep the sheaves of his music separated." The old man's voice crackled like crushed dried flowers.

Gently, Myddelton set the box on a table and opened it, finding the thin wooden layers, as the signore had said. The dividers swung open easily, stationed as they were, at different levels of the box's inner walls, and designed so that they would lie flat, one on top of the other. He closed the lid again and tapped at it with his finger. "When would this have been made?"

"In the last century, my lord." The old man's eyes were shrewd and bright and assessing.

Myddelton ran a hand over the carving and liked the feel of it, the smoothness of the wood's patina. "How much d'you want for it?"

The proprietor's thin mouth drew into a considering frown. "I cannot let him go for less than thirty guineas."

Myddelton paused and ran his fingers over it again, tracing the garlands on the top and sides. "Fine," he nodded. He and Hardy had seen a similar box in Paris, during the peace, a decade ago now; it had not been for sale at any price. He carried it over to a table upon which sheaves of music were laid.

"Have you anything by, ehm, Mozart, I think?"

The Italian bookseller shuffled over to the table and adjusted his spectacles. "But of a certainty. Let me see here…" He lifted the various sheaves and peered at the frontispieces. "I have the sonata…"

Myddelton shook his head. "No. No, I should think she has all of those."

The old man inclined his head. "Then perhaps a…what is the word…ah… transcription of one of his operas? Uhn?"

Myddelton hesitated, wishing he could speak of her with confidence, but of course, he couldn't. He did not even know if she were still there. "I don't know."

"I have here the transcription (he said it proudly) of *Le Nozze di Figaro*. She will not have. This…" he gestured with the music. "This, she is new to me, yes?"

A smile softened Myddelton's face. "Yes. Can you put it inside the box?" He placed the box on the counter. "And, ehm, can you have someone deliver it to Myddelton House in St. James's Square. It is to Lady Myddelton."

An expression—beatific, enraptured, delighted—lit the old man's face and he lifted his hands in the air. "And you, you are the Lord Myddelton, yes?"

Such a transformation was unprecedented in Myddelton's

experience, but then he had never travelled in Italy. "I am."

"Ah!" The Italian bookseller drew the syllable out and folded his hands at his breast tightly as if in sincerest prayer. "Maestro Hardy, he tell me all about la bella contessa, your wife." He radiated pleasure. "He tell me all about how she play at the musical evening." His chest expanded with importance.

This was all so new and unexpected, that Myddelton found himself, not responding with aplomb, but blurting out: "Hardy comes here?"

Signore Agnello threw his hands in the air. "But yes. Every week. He is the best of all my fine customers. I find the signed copies of the music for him—the originals, you understand. And he come here yesterday, and he tell me that she play the Mozart better than anyone he ever have hear. She will like *Le Nozze di Figaro*, yes?"

"I don't know," Myddelton confessed, too nonplussed to be anything but honest. And recognised the paradox of his desires: To want everything and to know nothing.

The signore folded his hands again at his breast. "She will like." Then, he smiled. "But wait. I know just the thing." He went to the door leading to the back room of the shop and called: "Giancarlo. Giancarlo."

A small boy appeared and the signore, producing a coin from his pocket, bent to speak to him in Italian.

Myddelton caught only a few words—*piccolo angelo, rosa, por favore*—which without context meant little to him. He removed one of his cards from his case. "Have you pen and ink?"

A smile broke the signore's face into a mosaic of wrinkles. He retrieved an ink stand and quill from a nearby shelf. "Just here."

The boy darted away.

Myddelton dipped the pen in the ink, and paused. Then: *My dear, Signore Clementi assures me that his beautiful fortepiano, with the deeper box for greater sonority, will arrive at Great Myddelton by tomorrow evening, none the worse for the journey, and that he shall have it tuned and ready for you there.* And turning the card over, he continued: *I believe somewhere in the country there is a now twice-disappointed customer who shall be forced to wait yet a bit longer for his new instrument. Myddelton* He waited while the ink dried, then placed the card in the open box.

The little boy, Giancarlo, deeply out of breath, with his face flushed pink from exertion, emerged through the back doorway, triumphantly brandishing the purpose of his errand—a single, full-blown, red rose. His grandfather took it from him and patted his cheek. "Good boy." With a tender smile, he proffered the rose to Myddelton, and gestured toward the box; the signore had lived long and knew much.

"Thank you," Myddelton said. "Thank you."

Her spirits recovering, Jane had taken her horse and her dog for a run in the Park. But this pleasant exercise had been cut short by a singularly squally downpour which had arrived in the wake of a cold north-westerly. So now, gowned and still warm from the bath, she was reflecting with some asperity that wretched weather, though never welcome, was particularly intolerable, if all too usual, in May—when it ought to be fine. She was considering too this latest turn of events with Myddelton—the letter was in her pocket—and playing an unequal game of chess in which the white king was sweeping all before him. And drawing her shawl closer about her shoulders, she went to perch on the opposite chair in order to better contemplate the white king's advantage, when Kettering entered her sitting room bearing a large parcel.

"Yes, Kettering, what is it?"

"My lady." All his pleasure at seeing her restored was in those three syllables. They were all he was allowed. "This parcel has arrived for you."

"Is it from my uncle?" She did not look up, but considered the fate of the one remaining black pawn, before the white bishop took him.

"I do not believe so, my lady. The boy who delivered it was most certainly London born and bred."

"Ah." Smiling now, she looked up, and rose and went to the console table to regard the parcel which Kettering had placed upon it. She did not recognise the hand which had written the direction. Outside, the sun had broken through the clouds for an instant, briefly illuming the room with bright light, then the rain began again, like a burst of pebbles thrown against the window.

"Will that be all, my lady?"

"Yes, Kettering. Thank you." She smiled and waited for him to depart. And turned to Lotto. "Now, what do you suppose this is?"

The dog cocked his yellow head attentively and helpfully wagged his tail.

"And who, do you suppose, sent it?" Neither the brown paper, nor the cribbed writing revealed anything.

Lotto cocked his head to the other side.

"You're not much help!" she declared, beginning to untie the string and unwrap the layers of protective paper, of which there was a great deal. And with increasing and intense curiosity, she tore through to the final layer and ripped that away. And saw the honey-coloured wood, the carved and inlaid intertwining garlands, and gave a small gasp.

"Oh." Gently, tentatively, she ran her fingers over the laurels on the lid.

"Oh," she breathed again. And pushed the paper away from the sides, bending to look at them, to touch them. "Oh, it's beautiful."

She slid one finger under the hasp and opened it and saw the rose, the red rose, and gasped again, covering her mouth with her hand. And beneath it, Myddelton's card.

And in a rush of panic and excitement and giddy anticipation, lifted the card to read: *My dear, Signore Clementi assures me that his beautiful fortepiano, with the deeper box for greater sonority, will arrive at Great Myddelton by tomorrow evening, none the worse for the journey, and that he shall have it tuned and ready for you there. I believe somewhere in the country there is a now twice-disappointed customer who shall be forced to wait yet a bit longer for his new instrument. Myddelton*

Her breath was now coming heavily and fast. Confused and rejoicing, she laughed and began to cry.

"Oh my word, he has bought me a fortepiano. Oh, Lotto, he's bought me a fortepiano. And had it sent to Great Myddelton! Can you credit such a thing?" Tenderly she rested her fingers against the petals of the rose. "And sent me a rose…A red rose." Did he know that red roses signify true love?

She sniffed hard, and groped in her pocket for a handkerchief, and drawing it out to wipe her nose and eyes, pulled out his letter as well. And dabbing at her nose, still bemused with surprise and amazement, trying to make sense of the so many conflicting emotions and messages of the past four and twenty hours, reread his letter, then his card and, thoughtful, sat down.

Admittedly, she had little experience of extravagant gifts, or of rowing and making up, and knew Myddelton still less, yet she felt that this was neither. For, a fortepiano surely was more than a whim or pacifier. For did it not speak of knowledge and understanding? Indeed, he had even repeated her boast of it having "a deeper box for greater sonority…" And to have had it sent to Great Myddelton? Did that not signify that contrary to what he had said only yesterday, that he wanted none of this marriage, did this not say that he expected her to live as his wife? As mistress of his principal seat? For why else send a fortepiano there? And, pensive, she went to gaze upon the carved and inlaid box once more, to open and close it and trace the pattern of garlands with her finger. And noticed a corner of an edge of something peeping out from beneath the top dividing layer. Gingerly, she ran an exploring finger along the blue velvet lining, then lifted the divider and found the sheets of music.

"Oh Myddelton," she breathed, growing bright with delight and awe. "*Le Nozze di Figaro!*" Reverently, she lifted the music and, like any true musician, opened it, and taking in the lines of music, drew a breath of deep satisfaction and pleasure at the challenge of it. And her eyes sparkled and she grinned, first cheekily, then softening as she thought on Myddelton and wished she knew where to find him now. Right now.

And then, because she had an inquisitive and retentive mind, she looked again at Myddelton's card, and drew out his letter to study his hand. For, though it was impossible surely, she would swear she had seen his writing before. But where?

❧

Myddelton stepped into his box at the Opera House, and glancing about the horse-shoe shaped theatre at the assembled array of friends, acquaintances, political foes and nobodies, sat down near the front. No sign of her. Rocking his chair onto its hind legs, he settled back, quizzing glass to eye, to survey the nearest of the five tiers of boxed seats—or more specifically, to survey the incumbents of those boxes and their guests or hangers-on.

Directly across from him, a coterie of demi-reps was holding gossip-grabbing court. A flashy brunette of their sisterhood noticed him and leaned forward to bestow an enticing glimpse of her ample cleavage and a tantalising smile upon him—enough so that he would know she would abundantly reward his advances, but not enough to draw the attention of her current protector, who was seated, drinking, beside her.

Myddelton frowned. Lud, that was all he needed. To be seen with the likes of Lydia Ransome—voluptuous convenient of the rich, randy and indiscriminate—making 'come hither' eyes at him. Everyone would think he had initiated it, too. Pointedly, he looked elsewhere. Alvanley was there, but no Brummell... Emily was (Gad, could it be true?) with her husband...the Derhams and young Verdon...Ah, there she was. Four boxes away, seated close beside Lord Liverpool, laughing. 'Struth, she looked beautiful.

And there was Pemberton too, standing behind her chair, laughing as well. At something Liverpool was saying. Odd, for one didn't think of Liverpool as any sort of chucklemeister.

Straightening, Pemberton saw him, pulled a face, bent to excuse himself to Jane and Liverpool, and quitted the box. Still, she didn't look up, didn't see him. Liverpool bent his head close to hers again—it must have been quite some story—and her smiles continued.

"Thought you said you wasn't coming tonight," Pemberton said as he closed the door behind him, and sat down, backwards, upon a chair.

"I wasn't. But I find I can only listen to Greville blathering on about the war for so long. S'life, he talks pigswill! So I decided I could either go home to bed or come here, so I came here." Aside from the single glance of friendly greeting at Pemberton, he had not taken his eyes from her; she was still laughing. Giggling now, really. Which made him smile.

Pemberton regarded him with frank curiosity. "Janey says you bought her a fortepiano and had it sent to Great Myddelton."

"I did."

Observing that hint of wary and repressed tension in Myddelton's still features, Pemberton smiled to himself and took pity. "You scored quite a hit there, you know...She's been full of it ever since." When this too failed to elicit an immediate response, he added: "She said you'd given her something else as well, but refused to say what it was..."

Myddelton had not realised the full measure of his anxiety until the joy he felt at hearing Pemberton's summation of her response washed over him. He had been right in choosing the fortepiano. Thank God! And a burgeoning of promise, gratitude and quiet hope welled up within him.

"I take it your apology was accepted then..." said Pemberton, still probing.

"So it would seem." He drew a deep private breath of relief.

"Grovelled, did you?" No response. Then: "You wouldn't like to tell me what the other thing was..."

"No." Maddeningly, Myddelton shook his head. "I wouldn't."

Pemberton watched him for a moment and saw the transformation. "Why don't you just go over there to her?"

"Oh yes? And have the first encounter with my wife, since I most shamefully vilified her and wrongly accused her of adultery, with the entire company of the Opera House looking on, and under the nose of Liverpool, her uncle's dearest friend and my Governor's close political ally? I think not. If I am going to make a complete fool of myself, I would prefer to do it in the privacy of my own home, and not for the edification and delight of the assembled masses. Surely, even you can see that."

Pemberton grinned and chuckled. "...You ain't really a mawworm, you know."

Myddelton glanced at Pemberton and raised an eyebrow. "Thank you for the vote of confidence."

Pemberton laughed.

Content, for the moment, merely to admire her from a safe distance, Myddelton said: "What is Liverpool telling her?"

Pemberton had begun eyeing up the talent on stage. "What? Oh,

341

about Sir Charles' monkey." He lifted his quizzing glass to observe the three rows of scantily clad milkmaids—at least he supposed they were meant to be milkmaids, they were carrying pails—who had come, skipping, onto the stage.

"What?" Myddelton brought the front legs of his chair back to the ground with a thump. "A monkey?" Pemberton had his full attention now. "What monkey?"

"Sir Charles' monkey, Young Jenkinson," Pemberton said absently. The girl in the second row of dancers was new. She was a pretty little thing.

If there was any hint of "struth, you are stupid' in Pemberton's voice, Myddelton didn't notice it. "He has a monkey called Young Jenkinson? He named his monkey after Liverpool and called it Young Jenkinson? I didn't meet any monkey there."

Pemberton turned. "No, of course you didn't. He's been dead for years. Buried in the family vault."

"They buried a monkey in the family vault?"

Now the look and tone were unmistakable. "Of course they did," Pemberton said. "He was part of the family. Everyone knows that."

"Well, I didn't know it," Myddelton exclaimed. Though Kettering did, no doubt. But now that it had been mentioned, there had been a portrait of a monkey in the room where he'd slept. "But why is Liverpool telling her, then? And what is so amusing about it?"

Pemberton had returned his attention to the stage—perhaps he should pop 'round to the Green room after the interval to meet her. Always assuming someone, Lamb for instance, hadn't got there before him. "What? 'Struth, he's not telling her about that. Young Jenks was still alive when she was tiny. Even I remember him. What he's telling her…" Pemberton grinned. "What he's telling her is what they got up to when Sir Charles and he and Young Jenks was up at Christ Church."

"He had him when he was up?" Good Lord. That did present opportunities for mischief. Probably better than Latin verse.

"He did," Pemberton confirmed. "And this one night, when they'd been out, Young Jenkinson had been partaking rather freely—though frankly I should think there was little to choose between the three of 'em.

Anyway, on their way back to college, who'd they meet but the Proggins, coming up St. Aldate's."

Myddelton chuckled. "I don't suppose it was after hours…" It had to have been. It always was. Was it eight times or nine during their undergraduate years that he and Pemberton had been caught by the Proctor, and hauled up before the Junior Censor?

"Aye. Of course it was. So they tried to run for it, and the monkey got away up a drainpipe, but the Proggins collared Sir Charles, so sadly, that seemed to be that. But Young Jenks, being an intelligent little soul, understandably didn't like to see his master in the clutches of authority. So he jumped down onto the Proggins' head. Which was a bit of a shock, because the Proggins hadn't seen him at first, and didn't know what this thing was that had landed on him…"

Myddelton gave a snort of laughter. "Please, do tell me, what is the punishment for jumping onto the Proctor's head?"

Pemberton shrugged. "It gets better, though," he said, grinning. "The Proggins dropped his lantern, of course, and lashed out, because he thought he was being attacked. Which I suppose he was—in a way. But that just drove Young Jenks wild. So he started chattering and cackling insanely, the way monkeys do, you know…So the Proggins was jumping up and down, and flapping his arms about like a mad thing, and young Jenks was grabbing at his ears and his nose and pulling off his wig and jabbering all the time…So the Proggins is getting madder and madder and finally he starts shouting: 'Be off you infernal demons, you Beelzebub…'"

Myddelton, rocking his chair back precariously, had abandoned any effort to stifle his laughter.

"And when it didn't work in English," Pemberton went on, "…old Proggers starts blabbing in Latin! 'Pon which, of course, the inevitable happened, and Young Jenks shot the cat. All over the Proggins' head and down his gown…"

At last, in a foolish attempt at sobriety, Myddelton said: "I suppose since the monkey wasn't a member of the University, the Statutes didn't apply…and he could hardly be sent down for it…"

Still laughing, Pemberton continued: "…By which time of course,

Liverpool and Sir Charles had legged it down the street and was safely inside College, thanks to a friend who hauled them in through a ground floor window. So Young Jenks, feeling much better for having shot himself of a gallon or two of puke, gave a final cackle and scampered off back up the drainpipe to Sir Charles' rooms with the Proggins' mortarboard."

It took some time to recover from this.

Finally: "So what happened?"

"Nothing," said Pemberton blandly.

"What d'you mean 'nothing'?"

Pemberton shook his head. "Nothing," he confirmed. "There was a couple of rumours going 'round the next day—one said that the Proggins had been set upon by a huge number of ruffians, who'd broken his arm or his leg or some such, so he was going off to rusticate for the rest of the term. The other," he continued after pausing to catch his breath. "Was that he swore he'd been attacked by demons, and the University had sent him away to Canterbury, or somewhere pious like that, to visit an exorcist...I mean, no one was going to admit he'd been sicked up on by a monkey, now was they?

"Though 'pon my life I should have loved to hear him explaining it to his scout...And Liverpool and Sir Charles didn't say anything, but it must have got out, because Young Jenks was the toast of the College— and of every public house within six miles of Carfax—for weeks afterwards..."

Which made Myddelton laugh even more.

"But wait, wait," Pemberton protested. "The best of it is that the Proggins at the time was that old goat, _____."

Which image proved too much for any restraint whatever.

And when, at last, he and Pemberton sobered, he found that his wife and a great many others besides were watching them and not the farce onstage—she with a smile in her eyes from behind her fan, as if she knew and fully understood his laughter. Because she did. Or at least, she had a fair idea.

And still feeling slightly giddy, Myddelton stood, and politely— though it had more of honour and reverence and intentness, if a bow could be said to be intent, than mere courtesy—bowed to her. And saw from her eyes that behind the fan her smile had grown, as graciously, she inclined her head in acknowledgement. Then, with the farce in full flow onstage, Liverpool bent to say something to her, and ever the perfect guest, she turned to listen, the expression on her face shifting between smiles and half-smiles.

An image of her as he had first seen her flashed through Myddelton's mind: she had been laughing. Indeed, it had been that ebullient laughter which had lured him round to the side of the house at Britwell Park. Myddelton smiled to himself. She had laughed with unquenchable joy as that repellent hound, Lotto, licked her face, laughed as she ran in circles on the lawn—her legs and petticoats flying—laughed as Lotto caught at the ribbon she trailed behind her. 'Struth, she was intoxicating.

Raucous applause greeted the end of the milkmaids' dance, startling Myddelton from his reverie. The dancers, playing to the pit, fluttered their eyelashes and performed a number of coy curtsies.

Myddelton looked back at her. She was giggling now, pressing her gloved fingers to her mouth to stifle it, though her shoulders continued to shake. Liverpool smiled in response to her amusement, but when he began to speak again, she sobered. And Myddelton wondered what he must be saying to elicit that delicate half-smile that hovered about her mouth. For she had smiled like that when he had asked her to marry him. She had smiled like that when she had asked him to forgive her for accepting his offer. Forgive her? What had she ever done that required his forgiveness?

Shrieks from the stage snapped his attention back to the present. A bull—or rather, two actors in a bull's costume—was running about the stage, charging at the milkmaids who shrieked and scurried away. The audience in the pit was shrieking as well—with hilarity—and yelling out lewd advice to the bull, which, of course, had the unwanted effect of setting Myddelton's blood racing.

He groaned inwardly. S'life, the Opera House was hardly the appropriate venue for lusting after one's wife. Particularly when she was seated several boxes away. Nor was it a comfortable setting in which to suffer the pangs of unrequitedness.

The bull finally succeeded in 'goring' one of the milkmaids. The pit came to its feet, roaring with laughter, as one of the bull's horns came out red.

She, Myddelton noted, had been the watching the proceedings, but her laughter had nothing to do with the ribald amusement of the pit. For as she smiled and laughed, she leaned closer to Liverpool in the sharing of some private joke between them. Lud, it was anguish to watch her. He jerked his chair back onto its front feet and stood up. "S'life, I don't know why I maintain a box here. There ain't a damned thing worth seeing on this stage."

Pemberton, who had rather been enjoying the farce, looked up. "Aye," he agreed noncommittally. "Are you off then?"

"Yes." And wanted nothing more than to go over to Liverpool's box, claim her and get her into the nearest coach so that he could start kissing her. "Where are Dunphail and Hardy this evening?"

Pemberton yawned and arched his back to stretch it. "Hardy said White's." The Green Room and the milkmaid would have to wait. Pity.

Quashing his impulses, Myddelton said with a calm that was the very antithesis of his sentiments, "I was hoping for a hand or two of whist before I go back to the House for the vote. Care to join me?"

From Liverpool's box, she looked at him, a question in her eyes. But he did not know the question and doubted she was ready for his answer. And feeling undone by his own inadequacy and longing, he bowed to her again, while Pemberton stood up and also bowed before following Myddelton out of the box.

White's was exceedingly crowded when they arrived. The Morning Room was fully occupied, and upstairs, the gaming tables were all in use. They found Dunphail and Hardy at the faro table, but since Hardy was going down badly, there was little difficulty in persuading him or Dunphail to leave the game. And when, eventually, two gentlemen quitted a small table toward the rear of the room, Pemberton hurried over to claim it.

They had just settled in to play—Pemberton was dealing—when someone from the front of the room yelled, "Cheat!" And everything and everyone seemed to freeze. Then, all eyes turned in the direction from which the voice had come and necks craned for a better view. And Myddelton saw Thos Jesuadon, his lanky form taut, standing over someone, yanking him out of his seat by the wrist even as he held that arm up for everyone to see. It wasn't Stansgate he had there, was it? Merciful heavens, it was.

Jesuadon pulled Stansgate's wrist toward him and reached into the cuff to pull out three cards. No one in the room moved. Jesuadon threw the cards onto the table. "I should call you out for this, Stansgate!" he bellowed. "But it would be a bloody waste of a good bullet." He released Stansgate's wrist.

Bewildered and amazed, Stansgate stood staring at him.

"Get out, cheat!" Jesuadon commanded. "Get out before I throw you out—through the window."

Shamelessly, Stansgate turned to the table and bent to take up his substantial winnings. But Jesuadon caught him by the shoulder. "Oh no you don't, you sharping bastard!" And shoved him hard onto the floor. Then he started toward Stansgate, raising his foot to kick the downed man.

For a long moment, Stansgate seemed mesmerised by the raised boot of Thos Jesuadon. Unbelieving, he stared at it. Then, his senses jarred back into action; he scurried to his feet and ran to the door, nearly tumbling down the stairs in his haste to be gone.

Then with a hauteur born of his extra-ordinary intelligence, Jesuadon sat back down at the table and calmly called for a fresh deck of playing cards.

A wild scramble of conversation broke out at every other table.

Dunphail frowned. "Damned if I know how he thought he could get away with it."

"It's been suspicioned for some time now," Mr. Hardy replied, perusing the cards in his hand. He had tried to tame his musician's hair for the evening, but with limited success.

"What?" exclaimed his cousin. "Don't tell me you knew. And never told me? I might have played with him!"

"I didn't let you, did I?" Hardy retorted. "And when he tried to wangle an invite to our card party last month, I told him there wasn't room at table, remember?"

"Aye, well, so you did…But you might have told me," Dunphail complained.

"I didn't wish to go voicing such a thing about. I mean, what if it hadn't been true. I might have done immeasurable damage, don't you see?" Hardy said earnestly.

"Have you two finished resolving your domestic differences?" Pemberton said amicably. "Or shall Myddelton and I take a turn about the room while you discuss the new upstairs maid's dusting technique?"

Dunphail looked abashed. Hardy flushed.

"I dare say you've known about it all along, Myddelton," Dunphail murmured as he picked up his cards and arranged them in his hand.

"It had been mentioned to me, yes."

Suddenly Dunphail grinned. "But not before yesterday morning, I'll wager."

It was Myddelton's turn to flush. "As you say, Dunphail. I wouldn't have behaved like every kind of an ass if I had known, now would I?"

"Oh, I should think that's debatable," Pemberton drawled. "Your call, Myddelton."

The body dead, the sprite had his desire;
Painless was th'one, th'other in delight.

21

The Royal Chapel of St. Stephen, the long narrow chamber where the House of Commons met, was unusually full for a Thursday, or for any other day of the week for that matter. The tiered wooden benches that faced each other along the length of the room were filled, their dark cushions hidden beneath some four hundred of the most ordinary men—elderly Members in bag wigs and knee breeches, younger Members in riding clothes with their hats cocked awry—all of them packed in together, as they lolled on the benches or on the steps, or crowded near the doorways. And above the benches, the balconies that stood like canopies, their weight supported by spindly blue and gold columns—against which more Members leaned—these were crowded too. Journalists, cartoonists and artists from Fleet Street leaned over the railings or scribbled on precariously balanced note pads, their ink stained fingers like mottled hummingbirds that darted and pointed and jotted. A thin light filtered through three grimy arched windows at the end of the chamber and fell uncertainly on the centrally placed Speaker's seat and the Speaker in his ceremonial robes and 17th century wig. And above all, a din of voices, coughing, whispering, raised in argument or passionate discussion filled the air, echoing above the rows where regularly attending Members were squeezed and jostled by those who were present only because their patrons and benefactors required their votes today.

"D'you mind, Northcote?" Pemberton inquired as he cautiously extended his long legs along the second row of Tory benches, forcing Sir Miles to tuck his feet beneath his seat.

"Not at all."

"'Struth, one would think Prinny was about to come in and settle his debts this afternoon. I didn't know this chamber could hold so many,"

Pemberton said, yawning.

"It can't," Northcote answered tersely, glancing behind at a cluster of Tory backbenchers more familiar to the proprietors of gaming hells than to their fellow legislators. He sat up straighter, folding his arms across his chest.

"Where d'you reckon they all come from?"

Northcote shifted on his lumpy cushion and eyed the balcony. "Where they come from is painfully obvious, I should have thought. As to the others, I assume they are all Members. Though as to the Honourable, I find myself unable to comment." He regarded a particularly malignant looking dandy and his friends on the Opposition back benches with disfavour. "God is my witness, I would swear I've never seen half of 'em before in my life."

Pemberton shrugged. "Devonshire's pocket boroughs, do you not think?"

"Yes," Northcote agreed. "Perhaps." He grimaced and folded his arms more tightly across his chest. "D'you suppose they have any idea of the folly they are about to commit?"

"What?"

"It's a disaster, this!" Northcote exclaimed, giving vent at last to his growing irritation. "It's the worst kind of disaster too. Self-inflicted. And what the deuce was all that pother that Wortley was spouting? '...that the administration which was now upon the eve of being formed was inadequate to meet the exigencies of the times...' What the devil did he mean by that? Eh? It's the very same fellows who have been running the country for the last several months and doing a damned fine job of it. What did he mean, eh? '...that the present government was not very strong, even with the aid of Mr. Perceval's great talents...and that they were certainly worse than weak without them.' Certainly worse than weak? Does he know nothing?"

"Miles..." Pemberton soothed. And got no further.

"Upon my life, he's a spoiler, that's what he is!" Northcote declared testily. "And he has no idea of what he speaks! We have enjoyed the greatest security this country has known for more than two decades, during the last few months. We are at last free from the threat of invasion, we have turned the tables on that poxy little Corsican and his troops, our trade is flourishing, the Regent is in place and the King, bless him, is being looked after properly. And that pestilential little spoiler would throw it all to the dogs! And to call this Government worse than weak..."

"Wortley only said that because he don't like 'em," Pemberton said bluntly, now abandoning any effort to calm his friend. "No doubt he thinks he'd make a better fist of it himself."

"Well, he wouldn't!" Northcote snapped. "He don't have the brain for it...Nor the application..."

A clerk in a rusty black coat entered the chamber by a far door, proclaiming, "Lord Castlereagh to speak! Lord Castlereagh to speak!"

A great buzz of conversation broke out. A few more MPs hurried to squeeze into the odd available inch on either side of the chamber.

"I pray God he will put an end to this farce, once and for all!" Northcote muttered.

A moment later, Lord Castlereagh entered looking sharp-eyed and affable, his grey hair turned silver by the plum colour of his coat. He nodded to his acquaintances, paused to speak briefly with the Tory front bench, then approached the podium.

And shaking his head as if over the difficulties in which they found themselves, began: "Mr. Speaker, and Honourable Members of Parliament." He paused thoughtfully, then raised his voice. "At no period of our history was it more necessary that a Government should be formed of the united talent and honour of the nation..."

Lord Castlereagh had never claimed to be Parliament's greatest orator. Yet his intelligent grasp of the events and their consequences— the grave consequences of not meeting the French threat of European domination and subjugation, his shrewd understanding of domestic political reality and his good sense, gave his listeners much to ponder, much to answer. Still, there were those, such as Northcote, who had felt a certain alarm at the packing of the Opposition benches, and an equal measure of misgiving at the more than usual unruliness of those back benches.

Castlereagh paused dramatically in his speech, then turned to the question of Catholic emancipation in Ireland.

Northcote frowned mightily. Not this! This was too divisive a subject, awakening too many long-held prejudices. The catcalls and cheers grew louder. Of course, Castlereagh was right, Catholic emancipation was necessary and proper. But why bring it up now? When anyone with a grain of sense—and that included Castlereagh—knew that as long as mad old George who had violently opposed it was alive, it would never pass; so it must not be allowed to cloud the issues of the day. Heaven knew Prinny would never agree to it, if only out of belated devotion to his father. And there were so many other vital issues which must needs be resolved, and instanter! To be sure, what a muddle. And now, without Perceval here to keep tempers measured and cool...

Pemberton, listening soberly, viewed the tassels on his boots with disfavour.

"...I am, myself, ready to resign," Castlereagh stated emphatically.

Pemberton straightened. A roar of protest went up from the Tory benches. And shouts and cries of "Get on with it, then," from the Opposition.

Unmoved, Castlereagh raised his voice and continued: "I have, in point of fact, already tendered my resignation to the Prince Regent."

The booing escalated.

"But for the moment..." Castlereagh's sharp-eyed glance raked both sides of the House, quelling them. The Members quieted. And the Foreign Secretary lifted his voice, saying, "But for the moment, the whole attention of the administration should be bent to the *great* difficulties in which the country is placed, and, *above all*, to conducting the war on the Peninsula on the largest possible scale."

A great cry of approval rose up and many "Hear, hears" from both sides of the House. Castlereagh returned to his seat.

Pemberton leaned close to Northcote. "Does he mean it? He's resigned?" he demanded.

"Yes. Yes, he does," Northcote ground out. "He hasn't a choice really. Not with that silly ass Wortley demanding this vote of confidence in the Government. It should never have come to this! Still, I should think, that is to say, I trust the Government will survive. Though, God knows, another Prime Minister does need to be found. And soon."

Pemberton nodded. It was what Myddelton had said too. But 'struth, if Castlereagh resigned from the Foreign Office there'd be chaos. He was such a firm hand on the reins. Though it might mean that Myddelton would be freed up. Or would he? And did that mean that Liverpool had resigned from the War Office as well? Pemberton twirled his quizzing glass nervously and gazed about. And where would that leave all the lads fighting with Wellington on the Peninsula?

From the row behind, a middle-aged squire leaned his head between Pemberton and Northcote's shoulders and declared, "A fine speech, that. Shouldn't think that Wortley's motion has a chance. Not after a fine speech like that."

Northcote pursed his lips. "I suspect it will be much closer than you think, Mr. Smith. The Whigs will grab at any opportunity to gain office, you know. And I shouldn't count on Tory unity too much neither, for there are those among us who would be more than pleased to see Castlereagh given his congé."

"Damme, who would be so unpatriotic. We have a duty to our nation…"

"Mr. Canning and his supporters," Northcote said mildly.

"I'll tell ye plain, Sir Miles, I've never liked that man," Mr. Smith stated. "He always struck me as a smooth-talking here and thereian, if you don't mind my plain speaking…"

The Speaker, rapping with his gavel, demanded order, and then announced that the voting would now commence. All those in favour of Mr. Wortley's motion of 'no confidence' in His Majesty's Government were to exit to the left. Those who opposed the motion must file out to the right.

Pemberton remained seated, watching and counting as his fellow Members left their seats and headed for one or other of the doors. Smith bounded down the steps only to add to the already lengthy queue of those wishing to exit through the right hand door. The dandies from the Opposition benches filed out to the left.

Eventually, still glaring at those filing out to the left, Northcote rose. "Are you ready?"

"Yes," Pemberton replied grimly. He'd tallied the numbers and did not like the result. He stood and stretched, then sauntered down the steps behind Northcote and out through the right doorway.

❧

"Od's fish, Janey, what is the matter with you?" Pemberton protested. He slowed the horses as the curricle lurched in and out of a newly created series of ruts and potholes in Rotten Row. So much for cutting a dash.

"Nothing!" Jane assured him. The weather, though still grey and dank, was at least dry—that is to say, not bucketing it down—and it was bliss to be out of the house. Though the Park was hardly crowded; perhaps too many thought more rain imminent?

"Then why, in the name of all that's holy, do you wish me to take you home? We have only just…" The strain of the afternoon's vote of 'no confidence' had exacted a price—his equanimity.

"I don't," she declared, giving the opposite side of the Park a searching look.

Pemberton turned to her. "Well then, you can stop looking for Myddelton, because he ain't here. Nor is likely to be."

She jerked about to face him. "How do you know?"

Grim-faced and tight-lipped, he said, "I know because I just left him hanging about outside the doors of the Commons, that's how. There's been a vote of 'no confidence' and the Government has fallen. All right?"

"Why weren't you there?" she demanded.

"I was!" he ground out. "'Struth, I've just come from there, haven't I? I was there. Northcote was there. Everyone was there. But the motion was carried by a majority of four. All right?"

Suddenly, finally, she noticed the absence of insouciant laughter, the gravity. "Oh Pem, I am sorry. I didn't mean to snap…It is very bad, isn't it?" she said soberly.

"Yes, it's a bally disaster. The middle of a war ain't the moment for a change of Government! And after the way Castlereagh and Liverpool have devoted themselves to office, working all hours of the day and night...Well, I don't have to tell you that..." He sighed. "It's a bally disaster," he repeated. "And a shabby way to act, that's all I can say. Still, Castlereagh was a gentleman about it. As always. Unlike some. Talked about forming a Government of the united talent and honour of the Nation."

"Will that mean Myddelton, do you think?"

He exhaled heavily. "Lord love you, Janey, I don't know. Perhaps. It all depends on Prinny now and whether he'll keep his promises to his old friends or not.

"'Afternoon, Brummell...yes, it's true. The Government has fallen...No, I left before old Sayer tossed his wig in the air. Happy about it, was he? I say, you couldn't talk some sense into Prinny's head, could you, and get him to ask Liverpool or Sidmouth to form a Cabinet smartish? No? Well, it was worth a try..."

Pemberton waited until Lord Alvanley's carriage, carrying both himself and Mr. Brummell, had passed before continuing: "Angel, I know how you must feel, but could you kindly not spend all the time you're out with me, craning your neck to see Myddelton? He ain't here and my self-esteem can't bear it."

She tucked her hand about his arm and smiled penitently. "I am sorry. It's just that I have not seen him," she confessed. "Not since Tuesday evening..."

"What, at the Opera House?" He sighed. It wasn't just the government that was a bear's breakfast. "S'life...Well, in that case, we'll overlook it for now. Just don't let it happen again."

"I shan't," she chuckled. "I promise...Did he say anything?"

"Who? Now there's a turn-up for the books: Sally Jersey and Clementina Drummond-Burrell in the same carriage for a second day running...What's that all about, do you suppose?"

She ignored the comment and said anxiously, "Myddelton, you jingle brains!" And gave Pemberton's arm a gentle squeeze.

"Did he say anything for you, d'you mean? No. He had that fanatical gleam in his eye, though. And that stern look on his phiz. You know the one I mean. And if you don't now, you'd better soon. The one that says he'll be holed up with Castlereagh all night, and probably most of tomorrow, too."

"Oh." She had tried not to sound dejected. And failed. "That look."

They had completed their tour of Hyde Park, had seen and been seen, and the rain, which had politely declined to fall on Lady Myddelton, now signalled—through the concerted gathering of black clouds—its intention of abandoning this congenial behaviour in favour of drenching everything within a ten-mile radius.

Pemberton manoeuvred the curricle out through the Park gates, then grinned at her. "I call it his 'official business phiz.' Emily was having some do, this evening. But all the Cavendishes and Ponsonbys are likely to be there, and I'd lief as not be in a company full of Whigs tonight, if you don't mind. So, I'll have a look at all the other invites and call for you after nine, shall I?"

"That would be lovely, yes. Thank you." She smiled earnestly at him, and at his care of her.

Pemberton nodded as they pulled up before Myddelton House. "Just after nine, then."

❧

And by evening, she knew that Pemberton had spoken only the truth: the Government had fallen and Myddelton would spend his evening in the company of former Cabinet ministers, political allies and other influential Tories. He would not be home for dinner; he might not be home till dawn.

She prodded at a jelly on her plate. It did not tempt her appetite as the chef had imagined it might. Perhaps she ought to have chosen one from the many invitations which sat upon the mantel and dined in company. Pemberton would have acted as escort, certainly. But that would not have answered. For it was not company she craved, lacking it, but the undemanding companionship of her uncle or Mlle or Lady Choate, the comfortable silences and easy conversation. She took a final desultory mouthful, then crumpled her napkin, threw it on the table. (Tomorrow evening, she would ask for a tray in her sitting room and read a book while she dined.) And bored or peevish, and missing her home, she went up to the Drawing Room. It was the pattern now.

Resigned, she went and opened the fortepiano. Beside it on a table was the carved music case, his gift to her. And though there was none to see it, her smile was winsome as she traced the pattern of laurels with her finger.

"I should have been named Penelope," she complained. "Perhaps I should take up weaving…" And was at once cross with herself for being so mopish. And moving the candelabrum closer to the music stand, took her place at her instrument.

Mr. Hardy, ever pursuing his own musical entertainment and delight, had kindly sent her a copy of a piano concerto by Herr Beethoven, newly arrived from a publisher on the Continent, which he hoped she would wish to play. Which was generous, or purely selfish, depending on one's point of view. But wishing to oblige such a considerate individual, she dutifully opened and sight-read the first few pages, and the adagio, before abandoning it in favour of a sonata, also provided by Mr. Hardy, also from the pen of Herr Beethoven. And turned to the less-than-a-doddle Allegro movement, which she began tentatively, tapping out the time with her foot.

"One, two, three. One, two, three. One, two, three." Striving for accuracy and to learn it properly and well, she played slowly, for there was none to hear her or be dazzled by her virtuosity. Then after counting for a few bars, she started to hum the haunting melody. And turning the page, launched into the Minore segment of rapid or not quite as rapid as they ought to be arpeggios—but dismayed by the dissonance, she stopped to peer quizzically at the key signature. And exclaimed, "When did you become six flats? Oh. I see. At the top of the page. Of course. Stupid!" And began again.

Then, from out the corner of her eye, she noticed a movement in the doorway which was not Kettering. She stopped and turned.

Myddelton stood, leaning with his back against the door, dressed for the evening in his favoured black and white, inhaling a pinch of snuff.

"Myddelton!" She always forgot how tall he was, how broad-chested. And how elegant. "I did not expect to see you this evening. Pem told me…"

"'Pon my word," he interrupted, "I didn't think you ever made mistakes. Or had to practise." Myddelton, who had been there for nearly five minutes, wiped his nose with his handkerchief, then straightened and came toward her.

Her eyes widened. "I beg your pardon?" she said blankly. Lud, this was not how she had imagined their next meeting. "Oh. Do you mean this?" She nodded toward the music. How could she sound so idiotic? So utterly brainless? "Of course I practise. For hours...sometimes."

Myddelton replaced his snuff-box in his pocket. "'Struth, I never suspected." And noted how beautifully she moved, how the colour of her gown complimented her firecracker blue eyes and set off the pale skin of her throat and the bloom in her cheek. And thought too that he had left her too much alone and uncompanioned, that he should have been there with her, at dinner and breakfast and in between and after.

About to say one thing, about to demur, she hesitated, then said that which she felt must come before all else. "I must thank you for the music case. It is exquisite, and I love it." Then, more diffidently, for this was a greater matter: "And I must also thank you for the fortepiano...It was the most thoughtful gift I have ever received, and I think there are not words..."

And suddenly, he was there right before her, taking her hand in his and holding it so tightly. "No, you're right, there ain't," he said baldly. "There are no words, not to express my shame nor to encompass the revulsion I feel for the injustices I have done you. And any apology I make will only sound lame or insincere...given my previous conduct..."

Shocked, for she had not anticipated this, she began shaking her head in dissent, to silence him, but he insisted, "No. Janey, you must let me speak..."

And clasping her hands at his breast, he drew her closer and regarded her seriously. "Can you forgive me? Will you forgive me? I have behaved appallingly toward you. And I am fully aware of the great wrongs I have done you. I have maligned you, misjudged you, and in my folly, and my unspeakable arrogance, I have accused you of unchaste and light behaviour. And I know to my shame that I have caused you untold misery and wretchedness." He paused, drew breath, and continued:

"...but I swear to you, Jane...I promise you, it shall never happen again. Not ever. And from this day, upon my honour, I shall do all in my power to right those wrongs...Upon my life.

"As for the fortepiano, it was mere gesture. But I'm glad to have pleased you." And then, because he had said what he knew he must say, because he feared her answer for so much depended upon it, an awkwardness came over him, and when she did not instantly reply, he began to babble: "To tell you the truth, I do not believe there is a fortepiano at Great Myddelton, or that there ever was one. At least not one that I remember seeing, for m'mother was not at all musical..." Which was not at all what he wished to say, so he halted, tried to gather or reassemble his thoughts, failed, and would have begun again, but she hushed him, placing her fingers softly upon his mouth.

And she, sweetly, gently said, "Please...Enough."

Still gripped by that awkwardness or uncertainty, convinced that still some explanation or further admission of guilt must be required, he said, "Pem says I'm a jealous husband."

She regarded him steadily. "And are you?"

Surprised, but when did she ever say the expected, he said bluntly, "'Struth, I think I must be...why else would I behave like a madman at the thought of...that is to say, every time someone says anything that..." And he would have kept talking, prating and prattling, but the look in her eyes was so trusting that instead he checked, bent, hesitated, searched for rejection or refusal and seeing none, bent closer, and like a brief stirring, soft as a fall of apple blossom on the first breeze at dawn, touched his mouth to hers, tenderly, lingeringly.

Then, in the midst, he pulled slightly away. "Oh Christ, forgive me. I'm sorry. You said I was never..."

"What?" she broke in, confused, still with that look in her eyes which banished his fears. For it was not as she had expected. And she did not wish him to stop. For he had kissed her and...

"Nothing," he breathed, and bent to kiss her again, gently now as the touch of down upon a gosling's breast—once, twice, thrice—until at last he kissed her as he had wanted to kiss her for so long, but had never acknowledged even to himself until this instant. And would have gone on kissing her, kissing and kissing her all night, forgetting all the paraphernalia of her engagements and his...for if at first she had been trusting and not unwilling, he had then felt her tentative answer...but Kettering had knocked and entered, so Myddelton drew away.

"Lord Pemberton is waiting for you, my lady. In the Library."

"Oh. Yes. Thank you Kettering." She put a habitual exploratory hand to her hair as Kettering withdrew. "I shall be with him directly."

"I haven't mussed it, I promise," Myddelton whispered, bending near to her ear.

She smiled, broadly, winningly, as much as to say she didn't care if he had mussed it. She could smell the lingering scent of orange blossom, cloves and bergamot that was used in his bath water and perfumed his soap.

He possessed himself of her hands once more, and contemplating them, small, held between his own, said: "I dare say you will have heard that the Government has fallen? Then you will not be surprised to learn that I am obliged to take my seat tonight...and then go on to the Foreign Office when the debate's finished in the Upper House. I've heard it said that Prinny's asked Wellesley to form a Government, though I do not know the truth of that. But if that is the case, then Wellesley will of a certainty ask Canning to serve. And since Canning has said he will never serve in a Cabinet alongside Castlereagh, things are in a right muddle. That's the short and the long of it. So Castlereagh wishes me to join him for the weekend down at Broadlands with Palmerston and a few others and to leave in the morning..." And he found himself kissing her hands, one then the other, which was altogether unlike him, but which had become, somehow, entirely appropriate and proper. "Which ain't precisely what I'd had in mind...But I thought...ehm, I thought, perhaps, you might like to visit Great Myddelton this weekend. I want you to see Great Myddelton. I believe you'll like it there. At least the fortepiano. I hope you'll like it. And it ain't that far from Broadlands, do you see—a little under two hours' ride—and I thought I'd just ride over on Saturday, before luncheon...And that way, I could show you the gallery and we could spend the afternoon...together." Babbling again. Why didn't she say something? Stop him? For she had been gazing at him so intently.

"I'd like that," she murmured. And smiled tentatively. "I should like that…"

"Good." Such relief. "Splendid. That's excellent, then. Take Lotto with you."

"Yes," she nodded, her mind very far away from her dog or Myddelton's country seat. "Will they offer you a post in the new Cabinet?"

"'Pon my word, I should be very much surprised if they did!"

"But why?" Stupid to ask really, for she wished only for him to kiss her again, to begin again this beginning of wedded affection.

Myddelton dropped another kiss onto the back of her hand. "Well, for one thing, I am hardly a senior member of Parliament, so I am far too new at this game to have any kind of a reputation for it. And, ehm, for another, my ehm…" 'Struth this was difficult. "Ehm, morals have not been as strict as they would like…"

"Your morals?" she queried. Then with a low chuckle in her voice: "Your morals?"

Myddelton flushed. Yes, those years of acquired town bronze had deserted him, once and for all. "Ehm, yes. My morals. That is to say…ehm…there was a time, long since…it seems like years ago now…though I swear to you I have never been like Dunphail…" He flushed brightly again. Then, emphatically: "You do know that I was not encouraging the Wythenshaw chit t'other night!"

Smiling broadly, she nodded.

"Oh good. 'Struth, that's a relief…As for a ministerial post, I assure you, I have more than enough worries of my own, without adding the problems of the country to 'em." He gave a crack of embarrassed laughter. "'Struth, the life of Castlereagh ain't for me." He hesitated. "Oh Janey." He slid his hand up to cradle her cheek, to study that angelic face for a brief instant, then lowered his head to kiss her again.

She remained still, fully trusting, compliant and yielding, savouring now the taste of his kiss, the warmth of his breath, the soft hardness of his mouth on hers. Then, she freed her hands and reached up to clutch at his lapel. It was all the invitation—all the forgiveness—he could ever have wanted or sought. And his arm went round her, pressing her, moulding her to him: to give, to want, to accept, to atone. When finally, he lifted his head from hers, pulling away slightly, he saw that her eyes shone. His breath caught in his throat.

"Pem is waiting for you," he reminded her, instantly knowing from her look that she did not care if the Prince Regent awaited her in the Library. So he kissed her again, this time trying to control that ecstatic wash of desire to taste her, cherish her, discover her, know her. "I shan't see you in the morning. Castlereagh wishes to leave at six. But I shall see you at Great Myddelton." And kissed her as though he would not see her for months.

"At Great Myddelton, then," she whispered, willing him to kiss her again.

"Yes." Myddelton dropped a light kiss onto her mouth and another onto her brow. "Pem is waiting."

Silently, he escorted her to the Library doors. Once there though, he hesitated, glancing about the hall. And finding it empty of servants or attendants or friends, he placed his hands about her waist, crumpling her 'uncrushable' muslin gown, drawing her to him, to kiss her roughly and passionately—to kiss her breathless—while she clung to him, twining her arms about his neck. Eventually, reluctantly, he released her. She reached to check the pearls secured in her hair.

"I only mussed it a little. Truly." His grin was unrepentant, insouciant.

She smiled, blushing rosily. Myddelton opened a Library door and pushed her inside, whispering, "At Great Myddelton!" as he closed the door behind her, and leaned against it while he recovered himself, and gained some control over the burst of tender elation which now possessed him. Then, he turned and ran up the stairs, taking them two at a time.

"Pem!" Jane exclaimed brightly as the door shut behind her. Her cheeks were flushed and her smile heady. "Forgive me. I have kept you waiting," she said, advancing toward him with her hands extended. She smiled again, trying to get her bearings—which seemed quite impossible, unnecessary and remote for the moment.

"Angel." Pemberton, noticing her rosy mouth and cheeks, her

distracted giddy elsewhere expression and scintillating happiness, took her hands and kissed them. So that was the sum of things. About time too. "Was that Myddelton I heard? Because we need not go if you had rather not…"

"Oh no," she assured him airily. "He is on his way out now. He has to take his seat this evening, you know…" she said with an assurance Pemberton had not heard before—a peal of triumphant happiness ringing in her head: he has kissed me! "So where are we going? I do hope they have a good buffet laid on. For, do you know, I am completely famished."

Pemberton grinned. 'Struth! "Bowls and bowls of strawberries, d'you mean?" he teased.

She threw him a laughing glance as he held the door for her. "Oh yes. To be sure, that would be perfect!"

22

To those unacquainted with the complexities of it, to take charge of a house and household and its surrounding park, of its domestic staff and groundsmen may not seem a great matter. Particularly if one had been bred to it. Yet to do so in complete ignorance of the size or geography of the property, the number of bedrooms or public rooms, of the essential knowledge of the number of staff, which among them are old and trusted retainers, which are from the local villages, and which are mere incomers? It was, Jane thought, not unlike a newly posted major taking command of a regiment he has never seen, about which he knows nothing, and in a place he has never been— the men judge his every move, condemn his every mistake, ridicule his every insecurity, and his lost position of authority may never be recovered. And she had no Myddelton at her side side to perform the proper introductions.

But as daunting as she found the contemplation of that, it was to be preferred to the conundrum of Myddelton and his hot and cold passions. For how could she hope to comprehend those? From the early days of antipathy and active apathy—a contradiction in terms, but so very apt— to what had seemed, at the time, a thaw in his affections, followed by the harrowing grief he felt over the Prime Minister's death which haunted him still. And then had come the glacial destruction of his misplaced jealous rage. Where in all this could she, who had no experience either of men or of the world, begin to understand? Yet, his subsequent apology had been so abject, so contrite, that she could not but believe him. Nor had he ever before shown her physical affection. Or tenderness. And that must intimate that his sentiments had altered. That his affections were now engaged, where previously they had not been. The prospect overwhelmed her with such giddy elation that she became all smiles and wished never to question again: Was it possible?

Great Myddelton could not be far off. They had been travelling for nearly four hours and had left the pike road already.

She rubbed Lotto's ears and wished she knew what to believe. Wished she were not in danger of throwing herself into Myddelton's arms the moment he appeared and prayed she wasn't about to make a great fool of herself over him. For she suspected she was. But, however foolish, that great well of happiness which had at last been uncovered was now perilously close to obliterating all circumspection, all discretion or intelligent care at the mere thought of him. Truly, it was less worrying to fret about the house.

She came prepared for anything—from a damp and mouldering ruin of hideous proportions, riddled with dry rot, plagued with smoking fireplaces, the sum of generations of architectural folly and extravagance, to an outsized Palladian palace, all large imposing state apartments and endless draughty corridors, punctuated by polished marble columns of vast proportion, with nothing of comfort or intimacy. Indeed, she whiled away much of the journey anticipating the architectural nightmares or wonders awaiting her, confident that it would at least be shabby.

What she did not expect was the reality of it.

At the crest of a hill, the coachman slowed, and through the dust-coated window, she saw it for the first time—the long three-storeyed symmetrical Restoration house of pale limestone, sprawled across the bottom of a deep, wooded valley at the edge of the South Downs, peaceful, golden, serene under the late morning sun. Great Myddelton.

The stately procession of latticed windows glinted their classical refinement at the sun. And beyond the central block with its shallow forward-jutting wings at either end, the faded walls of a pillared and pedimented south wing were half-hidden behind a stand of chestnut and elm, while rising on all sides was a natural park with grassy and wooded hills, and house and landscape and sky blended so effortlessly, so inseparably, that architecture seemed to mirror and marry nature's beauty. And as the carriage approached the house, she knew herself to be guilty of gawping, for the loveliness of it all took her breath away and engendered such hope and joy, for this perfect place was, of course, now hers to call home, and she was its mistress.

No, nothing had prepared her for this.

Nor had she foreseen the welcome she would receive. For she could not know that word of her, of her parentage and gentility, of her energies at proper household œcomony and restoration, would have been passed by Kettering to his second in command in the domestic hierarchy, so that she was greeted with that same degree of deference and devotion by Gossage as she had met with upon her arrival at Myddelton House.

And they were all waiting for her when she arrived. All of them, from Gossage down to the humblest pot boy, all standing in the forecourt, correct and accounted for, all ready to pay their proper respects and pledge their devotion to their new mistress. And she found in those first moments of alighting from her carriage, as William, dear enslaved William, performed his duties with all due ceremony and obeisance, and not a little proprietorial pride, and Gossage approached to perform his bow and begin the introductions, that her part was easier this time. That the correct degrees of familiarity and reticence, of affability, of observation and alertness now came without thinking, for now she had had the benefit of practice under Kettering's watchful eye.

And indeed, as she had anticipated nothing else, so she had not anticipated the spacious elegance of the interiors, for Great Myddelton had suffered none of those depredations which in the name of retrenchment had been inflicted upon the London house. No, this was the delightful home to which Myddelton's father retreated with his wife every summer and which they were loath to leave even for the pleasures of the Season, this the beautiful home where they had raised their son and heir, and this the sanctuary from which the Fourth Earl had rarely stirred after the loss of his beloved wife. And so it had been kept. Here, unlike London, there was nothing for her to do but live in contentment.

24 May 1812

As anyone will understand who has ever been in the grip of that exceedingly powerful emotion known as love, and who has found themselves in that state without knowing how they came to be there, nor having observed in themselves any of the telltale signs of heightened affection, Myddelton was in a state of equal anticipation and uncertainty. He had cudgelled and manipulated his way out of that hectic parade of appearances and duties which is public life in order to snatch just two private hours away with his wife, and had found this a demanding and fraught exercise. He had, of course, prepared a series of ever more elaborate excuses to justify the necessity of his riding home that morning in the event that his first reason—a need to confer with his land agent— had been brushed aside. But no further subterfuge was required. Castlereagh had understood completely. Of a certainty he must ride over for the afternoon, they would see him upon his return. Yet this first easy success and the rush of desire he felt for her—the wife he wanted so desperately—was tempered by his conviction that such gifts as he had bought her had bought him time, not her affection or trust. Those he must begin to earn in these few hard-won precious hours.

Now, baked hard by the late morning sun, the narrow country lane had grown hot and grey with dust. On either side, the long ditch-grasses hummed and stirred with buzzing insects, ground-dwelling birds and other creatures, while early pink foxgloves and sweet rocket bloomed amongst the tall hedgerows, and yellow primroses grew in colonies along the roadside and up the grassy banks. In the shade of a large hawthorn tree, a heavy wooden gate stood half-open, breaking the line of hedge to provide access to a vast acreage of fields, misshapen and square, fallow and cultivated, ripening corn, hay and straw. Beyond, a stand of trees obscured the view of the lush and rolling farmland and the cottages and outbuildings that stood upon it. Myddelton's large bay stood in the dappling shadows of the hawthorn, shaking his head at a persistent fly, while his rider bent low over the gate.

"Plaguey gate! S'life, why didn't I jump it?" Myddelton asked of no one as he leaned precariously far out of the saddle.

He caught at the gate latch with the metal grip of his riding crop and pushed hard. The gelding stirred nervily. "Close, blast you!"

The gate creaked but failed to catch or even budge.

"Damn!"

Sidling the bay closer to the gate, Myddelton removed his foot from the stirrup and gave the gate a hard shove. It moved slightly. "Come on, please, damn you!"

To which, of course, there was no response.

"Stand, Macedon. Stand!" he commanded. And determinedly, he placed his foot flat against the gate, and rammed it shut. The lock shimmied closed with a grating 'ktchk'.

"At last!" Impatient, he groped for his stirrup, and wheeled the horse to the right, flicking it with his crop. It spooked, whinnying and darting sideways, then bolted down the path through the trees. Gradually Myddelton reined in, slowing the horse to a trot, finally relaxing now that he was nearly to home, nearly to her. The pathway, with its canopy of branches and leaves and infrequent patches of light, made a welcome change from the glare and heat of the open country lanes.

In other circumstances, in another lifetime, two hours to be spent with the object of his affections would have meant one thing. Two hours of prone, passionate sport. But Jane was no Ianthe, and his affections had changed and changed him. And while the anticipation of wedded pleasures was never, neither night nor day, far from his thoughts, today, these two blessed dear-bought hours were just that—two hours in which to woo and to court her in private, two hours in which to show her the place he loved best in all the world.

He turned sharply through the main gates to canter up the long drive, then, a curve round a stand of oak and birch, and there it was, his home, Great Myddelton. He halted, suddenly and curiously anxious. Pray God she would love it as he did. That she would wish to raise their children there.

The present house stood upon the site of an earlier Tudor mansion that had been pulled down by the first Earl Myddelton (admittedly, it had been gutted by Cromwell and his Roundheads during the Civil War), and this new house built, he said, in honour of the restored King. (Myddelton's father had maintained that their noble forebear had been honouring none other than himself and his new title with this unprecedented flurry of building. "He didn't go renaming it Great

Charlton, or Great Charles Court, or some such thing, now did he?")

Yes, she would like it. He urged Macedon to a trot.

But she was not in the house when he arrived. Learning from Gossage that she had gone to the lake, (and gathering too that she had been very well-received) he stopped only to wash the dust from his hands and face before stepping out onto the terrace to begin his search of her.

The lake, man-made and strategically placed, was located in the southwest corner of the park. Here it lay, nestled in its own small valley, edged on three sides by a coppice of willow and wild roses, one of the few remaining original features of the property. Pausing just long enough to breathe deeply of that particular home scent—of mown grass, of early perennial flowers and late blooming bulbs, of damp earth drying in the sun and distant farmyards—Myddelton crossed the grassy terrace, descending the double stair to the gravel walk through the garden which gave way to the rolling hills of the Park. He covered the distance with a long, loping stride, hoping that she would not choose to return to the house by some other path, concerned lest she had and already he had missed her.

He came to the crest of a hill and stopped to loosen the handkerchief knotted about his throat. Shading his eyes against the high May sun, he peered in all directions in search of her. In the trees, birds twittered and called. Then, catching sight of her in the distance, he smiled and started down the hill toward her: she was standing near the lake, cool and perfect in white muslin, the obligatory paisley shawl draped over her elbows, her face unshielded by the wide brim of her bonnet—for that was hanging down her back—watching and laughing as Lotto ran to and fro along the edge of the water. It was, unmistakably, her, and the perfect unselfconsciousness of her laughter gave him pause, conjuring up that image of her as he had first seen her at Britwell Park—the fair-haired girl and her dog, playing on the lawn. How beautiful he had first thought her. *Je ne vis onques la pareille de vous, ma gracieuse dame...*

What he meant to do, what he meant to say, were all driven from his mind in that instant. And then she turned, saw him, and as he neared, she smiled. And it was the welcoming smile of a soon-to-be lover, of her delight in him, of her trust and consent.

She came toward him, extending her hand. "Hallo! I did not know when to expect you…"

And taking it, he kissed it. And hesitating only for a fraction of that instant while he studied her face and smile, he drew her closer and bent to kiss her mouth, soft on soft, hers now his.

Lotto, having disturbed as many burrows as he could find, emerged from farther down the bank, and noticing Myddelton, came bounding into and out of the water and raced toward him in a fit of canine exhilaration.

Myddelton lifted his head and placed a kiss on her forehead, then as required, bent to rub the dog's soft ears just there. "'Pon my word, it is a wretched animal, my love."

She smiled fondly. "I know," she agreed, nodding happily. "But the staff think him very fine…for yesterday, he apparently—for no reason I could see—remembered all that he had been taught, and waited until the senior staff had been presented, and then, strutted up the steps and into the house, leading the way as if he were Panjandrum of the united orient and known universe, and I nothing but a mere rani."

"As I said…a wretched animal," Myddelton pronounced, punctuating the statement with kisses on her mouth. And sliding his hand into her hair, he tangled his fingers among her curls where there were neither pearls nor pomade to mar or muss, and as he had before, he lowered his head to kiss her with such sweetness and pleasure and tender delight.

She drew away for an instant, and looking up at him, beheld his smile as it reached into his eyes, and she raised her face to kiss and be kissed again.

Eventually, finally, breathless with her, he draped his arm about her shoulders to walk, unwilling to lose physical contact. "I gather from Gossage you've made quite a hit in the servants' quarters."

"Have I?" she asked, much surprised.

"Turned them up sweet, I should have said, particularly Turnbull."

"The head gardener is that?" she chuckled.

"Yes, and a naggy old tough, he's always been."

"Ah. Yes. Well, he did try it on with me, but I have encountered his sort before…so when I enquired about the creation of a rose

372

garden…you do not mind, do you? Say you do not mind. And he told me that we'd never grow roses on this chalk, I simply remarked that the garden was kept so beautifully that I believed he could grow anything anywhere and I looked to him to point out the most suitable aspect."

Myddelton threw back his head and laughed. "'Struth, I wish I might have seen it. He was used to terrorise me, you know—and my friends—whenever we dared to play on his lawns."

"If those 'friends' included the young Bertie Pemberton, I can well understand his sentiments. He was banished from the garden at Britwell Salome one year after he beheaded all of Lady Choate's prized Dutch hyacinths with his cricket bat."

Still laughing: "Ah yes. That will have been the season his batting improved dramatically…And where has Turnbull decided you may have your rose garden?"

"Near the house. There," she pointed. "On that terraced bit—if you've no objection."

Her very evident happiness at the creation of this garden was as intoxicating as perfume, and Myddelton could not keep himself from kissing her again. And they walked he paused frequently to kiss her and be kissed, finding all pleasing in this simplest, most innocent touch, until at last they found a grassy bank to rest upon.

Lacking chimes or ticking clocks to puncture or punctuate the idyll, time perhaps ceased. Or was forgot. For in the here and now, the pleasure and discovery of pleasure in each embrace, each caress, each smile and each kiss was world and time enough. Each kiss blotting out all past experiences, erasing all past women, all past kisses, until there was only her kiss, and this moment and this feeling of her slight warm figure pressed against the length of him, of her arms twined about his neck and the sun warm on his back. He studied the soft rose of her Madonna's mouth, now flushing bright with his kisses, her firecracker blue eyes alight with her delight in him. He held her closer and bent to kiss her again. Kiss upon kiss, breath upon breath, smile upon smile.

Had she been in the house when he arrived, he would have taken her to their chamber. But here in the open, where any gardener might stumble across them, where he could not protect her maiden modesty…no, he would instigate no such spectacle for the staff, despite his ache for the rapture of the marriage bed. Indeed, he would allow himself no more than the pleasure of kissing her mouth, her face, of the smell of her skin, her scent of rosewater and lavender. And it was much much later when, finding himself reaching to unfasten the buttons of his breeches, Myddelton checked himself, then lay back beside her.

Breathless, he kissed her fingers in their still twined hands, while he regained some measure of composure and his breathing slowed from ragged to merely erratic. "M'dear…"

Awash with a melee of new sensations, then curious, she watched him and smiled. "What is it?"

Raising himself on one elbow to look at her, he smiled ruefully, forcing himself calm. "For all that I am credited with the reputation of a rake—which if I may say is undeserved in the main—treating you no better than a dairy maid and giving you a green gown is one thing I will not do."

Mystified: "I beg your pardon? A green gown? What?" Her eyes widened then, and she reddened. "Oh. Oh, I think I understand…" But then, unexpectedly: "Is that how you treat dairy maids then?"

He noted the sparkle of teasing laughter lurking in her eyes, but protested nonetheless: "No!" And added candidly: "Actually, I don't believe I treat them any way. I doubt if I've ever met one. Except perhaps those in Green Park, but…"

Which made her laugh. She paused delicately, hesitating, before saying—for she had worked out the connection between the writing on his card and that folio of Latin verse which she had seen in the past— "…*tale suave voluptae quam puellas basians*

et genus virides contaminens…"

As amazed recognition and shocked mortification registered on his face, Myddelton sat bolt upright and turned to her. "Good God! Where did you hear that? How on earth can you know about that? I suppose your uncle, or Pem, that little swine, told you…"

For one who had long delighted in teasing her dear friend, Pemberton, his reaction was more than she could have imagined and she began to giggle helplessly, which had the salutary effect of making

Myddelton blush. Which also amused her. She held his hand and kissed it. And at last, she said by way of explanation, "The folio in question was on Sir Charles' desk. And since it was in Latin, naturally I read it. I thought, initially, that it was meant for me—some sort of new translating exercise he had concocted, or something…"

"But you soon found your mistake," Myddelton said, still flushed with that particularly acute embarrassment one feels at the exposure of the more spectacular of one's youthful follies. "Which, I dare say, made it all the more interesting and memorable."

"Well, yes," she admitted, still chuckling.

"And how old were you when this happened?" he asked, adopting a prim expression, trying to regain something of the moral high ground.

"Fifteen, I think."

"Fifteen? Fifteen! 'Pon my soul, when I was fifteen I had never read anything so indecent as those verses!" he exclaimed. He should have known better. Pemberton would have told him she always had the final riposte.

"No," she agreed. "You were writing them!"

To which there was no answer because, of course, she was right. And as she had seen earlier in his eyes, he now saw in hers such unmistakable affection and loving raillery that kissing her was the only reasonable response.

"…We should return to the house. Gossage will wonder what has become of us."

"Must we?" she asked, and he heard the pleading there. But then she smiled, and he found in that expression that which he had never thought or hoped to see there, which he had firmly believed he had forfeited.

"Yes, I regret we must." He stood, and took her hand.

As they returned to the house, slowly, for there were features he wished to point out to her—the rise of the Downs in that direction, this stand of birch, the leaves of which would turn softest yellow in autumn, the beginnings of a Folly over there (and what did she think of it, for it had not been very well thought out), the beech walk from the house—he placed his arm about her waist to keep her close at his side. It was a familiarity with which she was not familiar but found very much to her liking. And wished they might always be so.

Nearing the house, they discovered luncheon awaited them. Gossage, in fine fettle over the appearance of a mistress for Great Myddelton, had reverted to the old customs of the house and ordered a table and chairs to be brought and luncheon laid out under 'the tree'. And after, Myddelton, resuming his stance beside her with his arm about her, began: "I had wanted to show you over the house m'self, but I doubt there's time for that…" It was an apologetic, contented smile he gave her. "Still, I should like to show you the gallery. That is, if you've no objections."

She did like the familiarity. "And shall you point out all the black sheep to me? Or only the nondescript grey ones?"

He grinned. He always seemed to forget her extra-ordinary memory. How was that? "For your information, there are any number of white ones."

"Are there?" she exclaimed in great surprise—genuine or false, Myddelton, enjoying the uncertainty, felt unable to gauge. "How interesting! But this is the first I've heard of it. I have it—on the very best authority, mind you—that…"

"The very best authority ain't told you a thing, my love, and you know it," he laughed. "'Struth, three quarters of the stories are unrepeatable!"

"But what about that great number of little white lambs you were telling me about?"

He noted how she sparkled but did not give way to laughter and he hugged her closer to him as they went inside. "You never did say, is the fortepiano to your liking? And the Music room?"

She nodded happily. "Oh yes. Yes, indeed they are. Perfect, in fact. More than perfect." Then, as they dawdled up the stairs to the gallery: "But were there not some stories you were anxious to tell me…"

Taking her hand as they climbed to the landing, Myddelton chuckled. "You won't catch me out that easily, my girl. I ain't Pem to be blinded by your charming smile or cozened by your sweet words."

"No," she agreed in mock regret. "You know, Pem is a great deal more intelligent than he would wish anyone to know, but he does not count circumspection amongst his many talents."

At which observation, Myddelton could only laugh. "And I don't suffer from this omission?"

Thoughtful, her fingertips against his chest, she stood beside him to regard and admire the gallery—the great length of it, the vaulted ceiling and ornate mouldings, the sequence of windows, punctuated by portraits full and half-length, and exquisite swags of carved woodwork. "No. You may suffer *because* of it—when his tongue starts wagging—but not from it." She frowned, considering. "You know your own intelligence, its capabilities and limitations, and are not, I think, afraid who knows it. Which makes you very much more of a challenge. Like Sir Charles." She did not smile, though he saw her eyes had begun to tease. "Which makes you…rather more difficult to…persuade."

Her now slow smile gave him such thoughts as were not fit for mentioning in polite company. Ruthlessly he pushed them from the forefront of his mind and kissed her hand. "Why do I have this ominous premonition that this won't rest here? That somehow—when or where or how, I hardly know—and despite my alleged circumspection, you shall find a way, and I shall find myself telling you every salacious story I know?"

If he had thought to shock her, he failed. Miserably. "Oh no," she exclaimed. "Surely not every one. Indeed, I could not be less interested in the ones about Pem… Anyway, I probably know all those already. Gussie and Marianne will have told me, do you see—no doubt inventing whatever the facts neglected to reveal."

He had expected to find pleasure in her company, and contentment. What he invariably failed to add to that list of things which delighted him was her blunt honesty, her wry, accurate observations, her fine intelligence. And pleased with such thoughts, he drew her into the room until they stood before the painting of a man in the formal dress and waist-length wig of the Restoration, while on either side of the portrait elaborate carved swags and still-life sculpture hung down the pale walls. "…Here, did you notice these yesterday? When I was a child, I was used to come up here when it rained, because even then it's light. And I would wander about, looking at all the carvings—by Grinling Gibbons they are—trying to count how many different birds there were, or flowers, or fish…Look at this one. It has those absolutely splendid little quails, and at the bottom, a string of trout, d'you see? And this is the first Earl, who built it all, and who was rather more of a…"

"Black sheep?"

Myddelton laughed. "He defined the term," he said, happy to be caught out. "Still, his allegiance to the monarchy and to his king, Charles II, in particular, eventually paid off, so that in the end, he was viewed as the patron saint of the St. Maur family fortunes—a man of foresight and integrity, if you will, and his more infamous exploits were, ehm, sort of…"

"Sheep-dipped?"

Myddelton choked with laughter, and a sudden dizzying happiness. "Yes. Exactly so." And kissing her, like this, like that, here and here, and there, smelling her warmth, tasting her mouth, intoxicated with her, he murmured against her temple, "They had to be, didn't they? Because he accompanied Charles on *all* his wanderings…S'life, you shouldn't encourage me like this."

"Oh." And more from the heart than she wished him to know, she asked, "Then how should I encourage you?" Gently, tenderly, reverently, she reached up and placed her hands about his neck to draw his face close to hers. He closed his eyes. She kissed above his top lip, and on each corner, then soft and full upon his mouth. His arm went about her waist. "Is this better?"

For reply, he kissed her hard and long, clutching her to him.

She turned from him to study the portrait of the thin-faced aristocrat with the haughty, expression, the sleepy eyes and the long curled blond wig. Except for something about the mouth, quirked in the beginnings of a smile, he looked nothing like Myddelton. "You resemble him not at all," she remarked.

"Well no," he admitted, holding her against him. "I take after m'father, who took after his mother…" He steered her across the heavy carpet to the full length portrait of a man, dressed and splendid in the lace and brocaded silk, and powdered wig of 30 years ago. "There he is.

My father." And more softly, "Your father's friend…"

"Yes, I know," she said flatly.

He gave her a surprised look. "You knew him?"

She smiled. "Yes, of course I knew him. He was used to come to Britwell Park to visit with my uncle…Or at least I believed he came to visit with my uncle…" She blinked, feeling suddenly awkward. "And then when…when you came, I felt so stupid for never having wondered…or even suspected…"

He laid his cheek against her hair, silent in rueful remembrance. "It hasn't turned out so badly, has it? Tell me, it hasn't."

She pressed her face into his chest to say in a small voice, "No…Oh no! But…" She stopped. Then determined to continue, to confess all, for she wanted no shadows between them: "But, I couldn't help thinking that you saw yourself as sacrificed upon the altar of family fortunes…"

He took her face in his hands, cradling it, regarding her closely. And did not lie. "Yes, well…I don't think so now." And kissed her.

There were clocks in the gallery, long-cased, two of them, their chimes synchronised to sound together. And sound they did, sonorous, melodious, inevitable.

Myddelton, listening, counting the chimes, said against her hair: "My dearest, I very much regret I must be off. Or Lord Castlereagh will begin to wonder what has become of me." The reverie—which had been very much more than he hoped, as much as he had wished—must end.

Compliant and accepting, she smiled. "I know. I shall walk you to the stables."

"If you do, I may never leave," he said, pulling her back into his arms. "Good God, I really must stop this…" And as, arm in arm, they made their way down the stairs and out, he began, with a new diffidence, for he wished to please her yet did not always know how, "Ehm…I've been thinking…that we should hold a ball, you know…in Town, before the end of the Season."

"I beg your pardon? When? The Season ends officially Thursday week, does it not, with the Carlton House Fete?"

Her response was not the effusive acceptance he had anticipated. "Say Tuesday week, then."

"But that is hardly enough time...And why?" she said, protesting, for she did not see.

Misreading her hesitation, he said, "Do you think no one will come at such short notice? They will, you know. They'll be scrambling for invites, I can assure you."

She shook her head. "No...No, it isn't that...I hadn't even considered that. It's just that I don't understand. Why, all of a sudden, decide to hold a ball? Forgive me, I must be exceptionally dense...and you do not even care for balls, do you?"

"What?" He did not wish to frighten her with the intensity of his sentiment, but thought she must not be allowed to remain unaware of it. "'Struth, no. No, that's not at all what I meant. I rather thought you should be presented to Society as my bride, d'you see, or something like that..." he finished, trying for lightness.

"But I have been..."

"No. Not by me," he declared baldly. And tried again: "'Struth, I have said this badly. I wish to present you as my bride."

And now, perhaps, she understood. She blinked. "Oh! Oh." She smiled, radiant with sudden joy. "What must I do, then?"

"Nothing. Nothing at all, really," he said easily, pleased to have won his point. "I'll send word to Broke; he'll sort the invites. And between Kettering and Mrs. Pinch, I shouldn't think there will be anything to do." (How little he knew.) "Except choose your gown..." And the thought occurred that he would very much like to help her choose it, though he felt that now was not the time to tell her so.

Her smile was that of one who perceived the value of this unlooked-for compliment. "All right, then." And daringly, for she never had so presumed with any man before, she added shyly, "Is there a colour you prefer?"

But this lightly asked so-simple question was not what it seemed and he knew it. He studied her face, all lightness gone, to search there for the answer that mattered so much about that which to another would have been irrelevant or even foolish. "Blue. Wear blue."

He could not have answered better, nor have told her more had he spoken in paragraphs or volumes. "I shall wear blue then," she

380

whispered, telling him as much as he had told her and more. And was kissed by him again.

Then the stable lad brought his horse, and he mounted it and with a wave was off, still with the smell of her, the taste of her in his mouth, the feel of her on his lips.

She watched him until he was no longer in sight, then returned to the park, both giddy and miserable at once, to wait—in dark or dappling shade and brilliant sunlight, walking on paths they had walked together in the gardens that surrounded his home, Great Myddelton, now her home—until that hour when she could return to Town, and to him.

23

S he returned to London in that haze of contented yearning, in her head a litany of phrases garnered from all the poetry, all the songs she had read and learned and loved. From the *Amours* of Ronsard, ...*Vous êtes seule en qui mon cœur respire, Mon œil, mon sang, mon malheur et mon bien*... to her close companion Donne, *I scarce believe my love to be so pure As I had thought it was, Because it doth endure Vicissitude, and season, as the grass; Methinks I lied all winter, when I swore, My love was infinite, if spring make it more*... And the knowledge that she would again be with him filled her with equal parts of happiness and breathless anticipation.

But he was not at Myddelton House when she arrived. Nor had she expected him to be. Though she found that she did not mind. For there were roses waiting for her there. Of purest pink, neatly formed, their blooms just opening to reveal the tightly packed petals, so many that it seemed some tiny hand, unable to fit them all in, had wadded and stuffed them into place. Roses such as they would grow in their garden at Great Myddelton. Roses, and his card which she regarded with that sweet tenderness peculiar to those in a state of blissfully requited affection:

My dearest, I could not be here to greet you as I wished. This, I think, will not surprise you, though I own I regret it sorely. Shall you mind dining with the Castlereaghs tonight before their ball? I should prefer that we dined alone, but that I fear would be open to misinterpretation.   M

And sitting at her dressing table and laying aside her gloves and bonnet, gently she smoothed his note out flat. And smiling at the thought of him, agreed, "No... I should prefer to dine alone too. But I agree, that might be open to misinterpretation." And remained seated, resting her chin in her hand, gazing dreamily at the roses and at nothing, complete in her felicity, and had anyone cared to listen to her heart or head, they would surely have heard traces of Purcell's haunting air of longing, love and music:

> *If music be the food of love, sing on till I am fill'd with joy;*
> *for then my list'ning soul you move with pleasures that can never cloy,*
> *your eyes, your mien, your tongue declare that you are music ev'rywhere.*
> *…Sure I must perish by your charms, unless you save me in your arms.*

And had she been asked, she would certainly have wanted to remain in this honeyed cocoon, dreaming, singing, thinking only of her best and belov'd…or as the bride she was and was to be, then and there to begin her preparations for the night, to choose her petticoat and gown, stockings and garters, to linger over her choice of undergarments or slippers and gloves for this nuptial evening. But she had other duties—those of a wife—to oversee first. For Mr. Dawkins and the painters had begun work on the second floor bedrooms and these must be inspected and the workmen praised or chided. And the linen cupboard must be checked again. And Mrs. Pinch and Kettering must be consulted about the plans for the ball and the decoration of the ballroom, and Mr. Broke about the invitations and acceptances. So that the choosing of wedding clothes, that private hour of placid anticipation and happy aching preparation must be delayed. Though later, the household settled and her choices made at last, like a bride, smiling, she slept, serene in the knowledge that the night was at last nearly upon her, replete with the happiness that was and would be hers.

Myddelton was already waiting in the Library when she, rested, bathed and gowned, descended for the evening. And his gaze upon her, when William, wide-eyed William, opened the door for her but did not announce her, was that of a new husband, proud, doting, smitten. And almost immediately, he was there before her, taking her in his arms, kissing her. And only finally, smiling, resting his forehead against hers for a moment, said, "Hallo…You look very beautiful…"

As a single gentleman, Myddelton had always walked that short distance across the Square to the Foreign Secretary's house. But a wife, a wife moreover wearing dancing slippers, required that all journeys—even such a minute one as this—be made by carriage. And though in the past, Myddelton would have viewed this as an annoyance to be avoided at any price, that too had changed. For now, the darkened interior of a closed carriage, even for this brief interlude, offered that rare and desirable commodity, privacy—to woo, to court, to kiss—and Myddelton had every intention of making the best use of it.

"'Struth, I am sorry about this…" he began once the door had been shut upon them and the carriage—although still technically in front of their own house—nicely stuck in traffic. "I should have preferred to remain at home, but…" He kissed her hand which he held in his own. "I had meant to ask him myself, but did Tom manage to send out the invitations yet?"

"He did. First thing this morning." Her smile was contented. For there was nothing to wait for now, for finally, this long-awaited evening had at last become this moment and Myddelton was beside her, holding her hand and smiling down upon her. She could feel the taut length of him beside her, breathe in his aroma of scented soap and pomade and snuff…

"And I dare say Kettering has sorted out the catering…"

"Ah yes. Well…that required a certain measure of diplomacy," she said and her smile lessened though her eyes sparkled. "Kettering, you see, had felt that Gunter's should do it all. But this did not meet with Philippe's approval, as you will appreciate, and he, in a fit of Gallic temperament and even more Gallic expletives, first packed his bags, and then, having been assured of our great affection and highest esteem for his manifold culinary arts, unbeknownst to Mrs. Pinch who had placed the order, cancelled all but the ices…"

Myddelton had begun to chuckle. He could well imagine the scenes—in the kitchen and elsewhere. And felt no little degree of enjoyment in the settled comfort of this recitation of domestic crises and resolutions.

"However," she continued. "…Kettering has assured and promised me that Philippe is more than equal to providing dinner and a buffet for the hundred and fifty-odd guests, so I must not be concerned…Though I dare say he will keep the kitchen in an uproar for days—before and after."

He laughed and kissed her hand again. "Then, hmn, I had best start looking out a suitable gift for you. Have you any preferences?"

She narrowed her eyes in thought. For he had asked her, not presumed to know. Then, pensively: "Dinner. With you. Every night, for a sennight."

Myddelton drew a deep breath. Her request was like nothing he had anticipated. "I believe that could be arranged," he said steadily.

She smiled broadly. She might have hoped for but had not expected his agreement. "Truly?"

So she meant it. Bliss. What utter bliss. "Yes. Truly." He smiled back. "I shall have Tom cancel all other engagements." And though he meant to kiss her only lightly, briefly, it did not happen that way. Eventually, breathing deeply, his face turned against her hair, he said, "Now that I think on it, you never received a proper birthday gift from me."

Vaguely, for he was beginning to kiss her again, "Did I not?" And kissing was surely more important, more wonderful, than anything else.

"No..."

And looking up at him, taking in his face, his eyes, his mouth, she whispered, "In that case, I should like a fortnight of dinners with you."

Myddelton sat back against the squabs. "Is that all? You're not wanting suppers as well?"

The carriage was crawling, inching along around the square. They neither of them noticed.

She smiled, for this was daring territory and it was heady to be venturing here. "Shall I need suppers, do you think?"

"'Struth, I don't know. That would depend upon how hungry you are, I dare say, or if you've chosen to stay up late dancing or retire early with a book..." And as he realised what he had said, he noticed all at once her widened eyes and his ache of desire, and knew he must change the subject. But didn't, at first. First, he kissed her. Then: "This summer...that is to say, I'd been wondering, would you care to spend the summer at Great Myddelton? Or perhaps go to Scotland in August or September? You see, I had hired a house in Brighton for the summer..."

But amazingly, miraculously—for it had only taken three quarters of an hour to get round the square—the carriage drew to a halt and William was opening the door. And acknowledging or ruing, at least to himself, that this was the last time for some hours that he would be alone in her company, and at the evening's end, he was dashed if they would waste an hour in the carriage, he'd carry her home if she didn't wish to walk, said, "All the waltzes belong to me," and bestowed one final thorough kiss.

"You can't mean to continue with that," she protested, her smile wry.

"Can't I? Watch me," he said affably.

"But it looks so very odd," she declared, chuckling, stepping onto the red carpet which had been rolled out into the street.

"I should also like the supper dance," he requested.

She gave him a sideways look. "And you don't think this will be remarked upon?"

He was finding it difficult not to scoop her up and march back home and up the stairs with her. "I don't really care," he said bluntly.

The square entrance hall, although spacious, was thronged with guests and neither the pattern in the black and white tiled floor, nor the bottom half of the fluted Ionic columns that supported the ceiling could be seen at all. As he guided her without apparent effort through the crowd, his arm twined about her waist, he murmured against her hair, "Despite the undeniable attraction of all this, I should very much prefer to be elsewhere with you."

She twisted to look at him over her shoulder and smiled up at him, and the smile reached up into her eyes, her firecracker blue eyes. "Hush. You shall be overheard and your reputation shall be in shreds."

"My reputation?" he chortled.

"Indeed!" Her eyes flashed at him which sent the blood whistling through his veins (and elsewhere). "You shall never be able to maintain that essential air of unutterable boredom if you go on like this."

He brought his hand round her waist and hugged her hard against him. In the press, no one noticed. "My unutterable boredom has given way to something quite different, I do assure you."

She was not daunted by the passion in his answer. She laughed. "Has it? I know, your neckcloth!" she teased. "You have invented a new way of tying it—your own variation on the Oriental, is it?—and cannot wait to show it off."

Myddelton grinned, undistressed, his contentment growing. "'Struth, had I but known your preference, I should have adopted a Belcher neckerchief on a permanent basis."

This was too close to the truth, but he could not read the look she gave him. Clear-eyed and sober, she began, "I met a gentleman once, an earl of the realm he was, with hair the colour of oak leaves in autumn. He wore a Belcher neckerchief in place of a proper cravat too...I found him positively..."

This was not the place. She was telling him everything he most desired to know—that she had loved him from the very first. But here he could do nothing to show his elation. He waited for her to find the word.

"...Magnetic...the first time I saw him."

"Did you?" he asked, dry-mouthed. "You gave no indication of it."

"How little you know," she murmured.

And holding her hand and kissing it as they started up the stairs to the reception line, he began, "Janey..." He drew a steadying breath. "Janey, I shall make up for every lost or wasted moment." He paused and a smile banished the grave intensity in his regard. "And I shall begin tonight, I swear it." Then, lightly: "I should not, were I you, engage myself for any of the dances following supper..."

And knew from her answering smile that this found favour with her.

"'Evening, Myddelton. Janey!" Pemberton ran lightly up the two remaining steps to join them at the landing and regarded them both with a degree of satisfaction. He had noted how close Myddelton was keeping her, had seen his hand around her waist drawing her closer still. At last. Though not before time. He caught up her hand and dropped a kiss onto it. "You look ravishing, m'dear, simply ravishing! Well Angel, have you any dances left, or has Myddelton claimed them all?"

"No. Only the waltzes and the supper dance."

Pemberton gave a curious look, but said brightly, "'Struth, is that all? You're slipping, m'lad."

"I very much doubt it!" Myddelton said, hugging her that fraction closer.

Lord and Lady Castlereagh were standing at the doorway to the Drawing Room, to welcome their guests, and greeted them with more warmth than mere politeness: "My dears," began Lord Castlereagh, "I am so pleased you found you could join us..." And to Jane, "I have not forgot your promise to play for us one evening. Young Ned Hardy tells me you have been practising duets together—violin sonatas, wasn't it—and that you are a formidable partner. May we hope that you shall play for us together?"

Had she known, at that moment, that his friends all said that Hardy talked too much, she would have agreed with them. "We are not very polished in our performance yet," she demurred. "But with more practice, I dare say..."

"She is pulling your leg, sir," Myddelton cut in. "I have heard them—yes, my love, I have—and I do assure you, they are very, very good."

Lord Castlereagh laughed and looked pleased. "Your secret is out now, ma'am! We shall expect at least one duet...We shall have a musical night in! How does that suit, my dear?" he said turning to his approving wife.

And though now they moved on into the crowded Drawing Room and from thence into the Dining Room to be separated by the length and breadth of the great table, several epergnes and many guests, they found it did not signify. For they had together crossed the boundary into that silken world of requited affection, where to but look upon each other was feasting indeed, each glance a conversation, each smile a volume of intimacy. And in this sanctuary of half-smiles and telling glances, none else mattered nor impinged. Here there was only them, alone and for each other.

They moved from dinner to the ballroom in that same state, and if there were those watching, who were delighted or not so delighted to see that the elusive Myddelton, he who had evaded the charming and well-bred snares of so many, was now well and truly caught, they did not notice. They did not notice the knowing smiles, nor the heads joined together in gossip or ribald amusement.

Pemberton led her off to join a set of country dances, declaring that he'd be the most envied man in the room, although it was all he, her closest and dearest friend, was allowed by *her* jealous husband. Which made her laugh. Myddelton availed himself of a glass of champagne from off a passing footman's laden tray and found himself a vacant column against which to lean. He did not make his way to the card room. If he could not dance all the sets with her himself, at least he should have the pleasure of never losing sight of her.

"Myddelton, Castlereagh said I would find you somewhere…" Sir Miles Northcote began, as ever pleased to see his cousin by marriage. Silently, he followed the direction of Myddelton's gaze and smiled to himself for this choice bit of gossip had been imparted to him already…

"What? Oh, Northcote. Good to see you. Where've you been these past days?"

"Oh, the West Riding, you know…" And ignoring Myddelton's obvious disinterest in conversation, continued, "Some very odd doings back there, I can tell you. We're just close enough to one or two of the smaller mills and weaving areas to have this, what're they calling it? Oh yes, 'industrial action' spilling over. Have you ever heard of it?"

Myddelton looked blankly. "No. Down in Hampshire everyone's far too busy smuggling to have time for that sort of thing. What is it?"

"Well, I can't get to the bottom of it, I assure you. It's something to do with…" Sir Miles spread his hands helplessly. "Well, the weavers apparently are angry that there are these quicker looms being introduced and so gangs of 'em are going about and smashing these looms. Can you credit it?"

"'Struth, it sounds dashed French, if you ask me." Myddelton frowned.

"Well yes, that's what I thought!" exclaimed Sir Miles, with unaccustomed heat. "Because you see, it's all being led by someone they call General Lud…Ludovic? No, Ludd. That's it. General Ludd."

"What?"

"Exactly," Sir Miles agreed. "Exactly." He sighed. "And so I shall tell the Home Secretary or the Prime Minister. As soon as we've got one or t'other." He noted that already Myddelton's attention was straying across to the dancers. "…But perhaps you can fill me in on all the details

389

of whatever I may have missed while I've been up north? The details of the rumoured peace settlement that Napoleon has offered us, for example?"

Myddelton stopped watching his wife, for the set had finished and she was in the midst of the throng departing the dance floor. "Ah, yes, the peace settlement…Be prepared to laugh."

"Why should we be prepared to laugh?" demanded Pemberton, now joining them. "'Evening, Northcote."

Myddelton, at his wife's approach, had straightened, and before she had tucked her hand through his arm, had put his arm about her waist, drawing her closer than was proper. And had anyone observed them together (and there were many to do so now that the ballroom was full, for no one refused an invitation from the Castlereaghs unless they were infected with some contagious disease, or dead…) and not known them as husband and wife, they would surely have marked them out for a pair of lovers. Both Pemberton and Northcote ignored it.

"Is Bonaparte in earnest in offering peace?" Jane asked. Peace. Such a prospect. Myddelton could come home at night. They might even return to Great Myddelton…

But already Myddelton's thoughts were elsewhere. "My dearest, they are opening a waltz. Pem, Northcote, you must excuse us…"

To waltz together. If before it had seemed dangerous, now, it was hardly enough. Though for the moment it would have to do. And if those watching felt that Myddelton was holding his wife rather more closely than etiquette permitted, with his arm nearly encircling her waist, there were others who countered that the Countess was so tiny, he could hardly be expected to do otherwise. And these might also have pointed out that their hostess, Lady Castlereagh, that high stickler, was positively beaming as she watched them together, and heaven knew she would frown if anything of a vaguely improper nature were to occur in her presence. And Myddelton was Castlereagh's aide, after all, and hadn't he always sailed close to the wind anyway? But Myddelton, in the throes of that courtship he had never conducted, only drew his wife still closer as she returned to his arms after performing a pirouette step and she, always happy, now began chuckling.

"Myddelton. Mind yourself." As a reproof, it was particularly stingless.

He sniffed, repressing a smile. "I am. Believe me. Were I not..."

She laughed and a blush rose in her cheek. Was there anything greater than waltzing in his arms?

But out of kindness to himself and to her, Myddelton turned the conversation to the impersonal. "It would appear that Wellesley has failed to form a national government..."

"So he had been asked?"

"Mmn, yes. Prinny asked him last week—on Thursday or Friday— after the vote."

"But if he has failed, what will happen now?"

"Who knows?" He did not add that at this moment he did not care a whit, for it was hardly necessary.

"Prinny could ask you to do it," she teased.

"Ah no! Remember, I'm promised to you for dinner *and* supper, should you require it, for at least a fortnight, so I couldn't possibly spare the time..."

"Yes," she said, smiling tenderly up at him. "I remember..." Dangerous and lovely. Joyful, sweet, heady. Waltzing with him was all of these...*Your eyes, your mien, your tongue declare that you are music ev'rywhere...Sure I must perish by your charms unless you save me in your arms...*And as he gazed down upon her, she thought, breathless, surely, surely we can return home soon...slip away like lovers...and no one will notice...and was certain from the sobering in his look that he read her thought.

❧

Stepping into the ballroom at that late, late moment, the lovely Miss Wythenshaw, gowned beautifully, expensively, with her petticoat seductively dampened and clinging to her person like a second skin, felt like Hera when Zeus had proven faithless: vindictive, enraged, petty. It was bad enough that they were terribly late, but the fact that her tardiness had been caused by her mama's stupid fat pug, who—on account of having been fed too many sweet meats—had been sick all over her mama's evening gown, forcing Mama to change, made it somehow much much worse. It was more than an even-tempered young lady might have borne with equanimity, and Miss Wythenshaw was not known for the placidity of her temperament. They were odiously late. And as her anger translated into spite and recklessness, Miss Wythenshaw assured herself, even as she had listened to her mama's cluckings over 'Poor pug' that it would be all right if only she might spend a few moments in her Myddelton's company. A few moments with him and she would be able to endure even this. She had not seen him in some days, but she knew he would be here tonight and she had been waiting, counting the hours and days, dreaming of him, for he was everything she believed a gentleman should be—and she had given much thought to his great height and sportsman's physique, to the way the light fell on his cheekbones and the clear blue of his eyes as they rested upon her. She had thought also of their next meeting, this tryst tonight when he would apologise for his conduct the other evening and all would be as it had been. But since the moment of her arrival, she had been hearing of nothing but his behaviour, of how the rake was reformed, and how he had not left his wife's side even for an instant. And as if it were sand sliding and draining from a broken hourglass, Miss Wythenshaw felt that the happiness she had promised herself was slipping from her very grasp. And looking over the ballroom, she saw them, there at the very centre of the dance floor, surrounded by thirty or so other couples, there he, there they were. And for an instant she could not control the threatening angry tears, so she opened her eyes as wide as possible and tucked her chin, while discreetly, she daubed at the corner of her eye with her gloved finger.

"Georgina!" hissed her mama. "What are you doing, standing in the doorway like this for, pray? After all the fuss you made, I should have thought your dance card already full..."

"Yes, Mama," Miss Wythenshaw answered obediently.

"I shall be sitting with Mrs. Chamfrey." Mrs Wythenshaw waved her handkerchief at her bosom friend, a plump woman wearing a heavily jewelled pale blue satin turban—which ill became her sallow complexion. "I expect you know how to behave yourself by now. But remember, Lady Castlereagh is a high stickler and one misstep from you will be the end of any hopes we may have! I shall be watching as well."

Miss Wythenshaw drew a deep breath and followed Myddelton's movements with her eyes. Yes, there was that Miss Nobody-chit, his wife, with her arm drawn through his, and a rosy colour in her cheek proclaiming to all that the words he was speaking so close to her ear were words of love. How could he? Such a thin, insipid, passionless, little creature as that. Miss Wythenshaw watched her look up at him, adoringly, and begin to laugh at something he had said. "Yes, Mama. Oh, there is Miss Laurence and her brother...I shall just go and join them...Oh, Lydia, how very glad I am to see you!" she exclaimed, slipping her arm through that of the young lady who had become her closest friend ever since she had fallen out with Alice Derham. "I vow I believed we should never arrive. That stupid pug of my mama's was sick all over her!"

Miss Laurence laughed gaily. "I declare, I cannot believe you have not put out arsenic for that dreadful creature. Ain't that the second time in a sennight?"

"The third!" Miss Wythenshaw ground out, dramatically, mendaciously. "I did not tell you about the first..."

Miss Laurence laughed. "Well you may forget all that now! Jack has been waiting for you all evening..."

"Oh?" Miss Wythenshaw tucked her chin as she cast a quick look in Mr. Laurence's direction. Yes, he was looking eager.

"I declare he never stops speaking of you," continued the loquacious Miss Laurence. "But Georgina, you will not credit it! Do you seen the way Myddelton is hanging on his wife? La, it has practically caused a uproar among the dowager set. And you should have seen them waltzing! I vow, I thought it would turn Lady Castlereagh blue—for you know how pernickitty she is about debutantes waltzing. But she did not even appear to notice. Which is exceeding vexatious, I think..."

Miss Wythenshaw searched the room for a glimpse of them. At the far end of the room, she caught sight of him, first, as he leaned toward his wife who was sipping from a champagne glass; his head was bent so close to hers that at any moment, he might have dropped a kiss onto her face without moving an inch. Pemberton and Dunphail were there too.

And Mr. Hardy. Of course. And then, Lady Emily Cowper strolled up, arm in arm with Palmerston, and chucking Myddelton on the chin, she said something that made Lady Myddelton smile and laugh.

Miss Wythenshaw turned to face her friend. "Well, I know how it appears. But it's so dreadfully sad when couples behave in such a common manner, don't you think? Making such a performance of it? It's so frightfully common. Though, of course, one must never judge a gentleman by his public behaviour—especially not Myddelton." And ignoring the ticking in the pit of her stomach, the exquisite Miss Wythenshaw began to lie: "For I know of a certainty he despises her. Loathes the very sight of her. And who wouldn't? But he is in the Government circle, you know, and ever since..." She lowered her voice to a whisper, for it would not do to be overhead saying this—and she knew this to be true, for her father had spoken of it. "...Lord Castlereagh duelled with Mr. Canning three years ago, there have been exceeding strict rules about not causing scandals!"

Miss Laurence could only gape. "But Georgina," she sputtered, nearly overcome by so much indelicate information. "He is nearly causing a scandal by hanging on her in that vulgar way!" she exclaimed. And stood on tiptoe to observe them. He didn't seem to loathe the very sight of her. Neither did his friends, and as everyone knew, they were connoisseurs and to be noticed by them was notice indeed! She certainly had never been singled out in such a complimentary fashion, although she would have gone to some lengths to gain their attentions. "As if she were his..." She lowered her voice to a whisper, "Mistress."

Miss Wythenshaw smiled compassionately. "Of course, I dare say it is what he must do. It is his way of proving to Society that all is well, that there is nothing amiss..."

"Is there something amiss? How can you know?" demanded Miss Laurence who lacked the imagination of her friend.

Miss Wythenshaw blinked with unspoken meaning, lowered her chin, and continued her fabrication. "Well to be sure there is. We were nearly betrothed, you know. Though I should not be telling anyone, for he swore me to secrecy—but he was forced to marry her, poor man. For her money. Just look at her...Look at that gown!" And looking the

Countess of Myddelton over, eyeing the gown of tissue silk—a rich married lady's gown with its over gown of palest green (the most expensive colour) edged in gold embroidery and pearls, Georgina declared, "Flaunting her wealth which is so very vulgar. And you should have heard her at Fanchon's! She hadn't a notion of how to go on! Yelling like a fishwife, she was, screaming at Fanchon..." she continued, warming to her theme.

"She screamed at Fanchon?" Miss Laurence could do little but boggle.

"I heard her, one day, when Mama and I went for a fitting." She lowered her voice. "I cannot tell you how mortifying it was. Especially as Myddelton and I, we have always had an understanding," she said regretfully. "And affections like that, which run so deep, cannot be easily broken. So he continues to confide in me, even though both of us know it must end." Miss Wythenshaw sighed feelingly, raggedly even. She was quite enjoying being the heroine of her own Romantic vision, the paragon of devoted love and faithfulness sacrificed to duty and possessions. "...But he has promised me—sworn to me if you must know—that theirs is a marriage of convenience only, and he is but biding his time until he may seek an annulment."

"Truly?" asked the stupefied Miss Laurence. Then, for she did not wish to appear naive or lacking in Town bronze, said, though with a certain hesitation, "Well, now that you mention it, it does look exceeding false to me. I expect you are right about her coming from a low background. Certainly, I should never allow any gentleman to treat me as familiarly as she is allowing him to do," she finished, thus demonstrating that she could lie almost as well as the scintillating Miss Wythenshaw.

Miss Wythenshaw shrugged. And feeling infinitely more cheerful for having so thoroughly vilified the character of her rival, she turned the subject. "My word, is that Miss Talbot standing near Lady Jersey? La, she must feel a fool wearing a gown of apricot mull with these red and white decorations..."

"She has to wear that colour," giggled Miss Laurence. "It's the only colour that don't make her look like such a stuffed eel," she said cattily and looked about for another victim.

But Miss Laurence's brother, the dashing-in-his-own-mind Mr. Jack Laurence, approached to beg a dance from the divine Miss Wythenshaw, if it wasn't too late. And in another moment, a select horde of Miss Wythenshaw's other admirers began to make their way over to her for the purpose of securing dances with her. And smug, their hyperbolic compliments soothing away any remaining vestige of spleen, she chatted easily with all of them. And pretended not to notice that Miss Laurence and her brother had broken away from their coterie and that Miss Laurence was earnestly—if inaccurately—reciting all that her dear friend had told her.

Nor could such news be kept to oneself, particularly if one's name was John Laurence, Esquire, so that within an hour, much—in certain circles—was being made of Myddelton's doomed marriage and his ludicrous attempts to disguise the fact...for there had been those rumours about his wife and Pemberton, hadn't there? And remember that business with Ianthe Dacre not so long ago? And where there was smoke, was there not always fire, somewhere?

And satisfied at having achieved so much so easily, Miss Wythenshaw became vivacity itself, smiling, laughing, flirting with her many admirers, both on and off the dancefloor. For she was determined that Myddelton should realise all that he had thrown away, all that was now beyond his grasp by marrying that whey-faced little Miss Nobody.

Why then, alas, did it not keep it right,
Returning to leap into the fire,
And where it was at wish it could not remain?
Such mocks of dreams they turn to deadly pain.

24

Had Myddelton heard the latest on-dit about himself, he would have laughed out loud. For nothing further from the truth could have been imagined. And as he—happy, contented and on the brink of a night of long-awaited nuptial pleasure—led her from the dance floor, following their second waltz of the evening, he was conscious of such a burgeoning of affection for her, that it left him breathless and he wanted nothing more than to enlace her in his arms then and there. Instead, smiling down upon her, he raised her hand and kissed it.

She returned the smile, the volume-speaking smile. "Myddelton, I must go find a ladies' maid and have this hair clip seen to…For if I do not, it shall fall out."

Myddelton continued to smile, incipient laughter making his eyes sparkle. He would happily remove the thing himself, right before tumbling her…"We cannot have that," he agreed. Again he kissed her hand before letting go of it. "Don't be long."

"Where shall I find you?"

Myddelton twirled his quizzing glass about on its black velvet ribbon and paused to reassemble his thoughts. The ballroom had become stiflingly full of guests. "I don't know. Castlereagh has asked for a brief word in his study…but that won't take above a minute, I shouldn't think." He smiled suddenly.

"Janey," Pemberton called, shouldering his way past a foursome of large dowagers, a tall young man in tow. "Janey, will you allow me to name Mr. Thurston to you? Lady Myddelton, Mr. Thurston."

"Good evening, Mr. Thurston," Jane said, extending her hand.

"Lady Myddelton." A broad smile cracked the young man's rosy-cheeked countenance and he gripped her hand tightly in his own, then remembered belatedly that he had not yet kissed it as he ought. Quickly, he raised it to his lips and released it. "My lord." He bowed to Myddelton. Then: "I did hope, ma'am, that you might yet have a dance free, though I am aware it is very late in the evening."

Pemberton gave his closest friend an amused glance. No, Myddelton was still looking entirely satisfied and un-jealous. Well praise Heaven for that.

Jane shook her head. "No. I am sorry." She did not add that since four of the evening's dances had been claimed by her husband, there had been few enough to award even to her friends, though she could see Pemberton thought it.

"Oh. Well. Should any fellow be fool enough to renege this evening, I hope you will not hesitate to call upon me to fill his place," Mr. Thurston said and bowed.

"Another admirer for you, my girl," Myddelton observed as Mr. Thurston went off. He looked down upon her, upon her throat, and the glow of her skin, the curve of her collarbone as it sloped down to her breast. They should leave soon—supper or no supper—for this delightful prelude could easily become an irritating inhibition given the crowd and the heat.

"If you ain't careful Myddelton, the house is likely to be besieged by 'em," Pemberton teased. Though evidently Myddelton was target practice no longer.

"'Struth, it was you who introduced him."

"'Struth, so it was. It's deuced hard being a friend of yours, Janey. Every young sprig in Town wants a favour of me now."

"Oh really?" she chuckled. "Perhaps it will be the saving of your character—teach you not to be so selfish...to do unto others..."

Myddelton's eyes were laughing as he tucked her hand more firmly about his arm. "I say, Pem, could I beg a favour of you..."

"Oh stow it, Myddelton," Pemberton grumbled.

Surreptitiously, Myddelton dropped a kiss onto her hair. "I must go and find Castlereagh, and Janey must go and secure the clip in her hair. Would it be too much to ask you to escort her? I wouldn't want her besieged by all these young sprigs to whom you've so carelessly introduced her." Yes, they should go once he'd seen Castlereagh. And they would walk. Or he'd carry her. He felt a surge of buoyant pleasure at the thought. To home and to bed. To take and to give. To have and to hold. Dear blessèd God, at last. At long bloody last! And he would have walked away whistling had he been anywhere else.

Lord Castlereagh, Myddelton found eventually, was already at the doorway of his study, that small book-lined inner sanctum generally reserved for himself and Planta.

"Ah Myddelton, how good of you. I did hope to have our quiet word before supper was upon us." Lord Castlereagh welcomed Myddelton into the room and closed the door. "I asked you in here..." He began, then paused. "Do you care for a brandy? No? Please, please, do sit down." He took his own seat behind the large desk upon which was his individualised clutter of books, rolled maps, letters, and sheaves of music.

"I shall come straight to the point," he said, shifting effortlessly from his role as host to that which Myddelton knew well, the incisive intellectual, the highly intelligent minister of state, Wellington's ally and co-strategist. "Whilst I have tendered my resignation to the Prince and therefore am no longer the Secretary of State for Foreign Affairs, I remain the caretaker—until such time as a new Foreign Secretary is appointed. You know all this. And regardless of our domestic dilemmas..."—he smiled at the felicity of the alliteration—"...the intelligence information which is so vital to our war effort continues to pour in to the Office—as you know. And earlier today, certain papers came in to us—from Paris—copies of letters the Post Office had intercepted as well as from the Alien Office, you know—which, the more I have considered it, the more I believe that Wellington should see them at the earliest possible moment." He lifted a page of music to peer at the page beneath it, then raising an eyebrow, covered the page again.

And his tone and speech still measured, he continued, "However, with his brother casting about to form a ministry drawn from both the Whigs and the Tories...Not that for a moment I doubt Wellesley's devotion to Wellington or to our troops' safety, don't misunderstand me…But Lord Moira is now in the picture too—oh, did you not know he'd been approached as well? Yes, shuffling about amongst the Whigs—from what I've been told—so things could not be much more awkward." Thoughtful, he paused. "I trust that the next Foreign Secretary will be one who will understand the great dangers in which the country is placed, and who will work with Wellington to defeat the French scourge, but I cannot be sure of it. And there is still much information that I need to pass on to Wellington before I quit this office. For our troops' safety, if nothing else.

"But the sum of Flint's lads are still out combing the countryside for anyone who may have been conspiring with Bellingham…" He shrugged. "Which places me in the damnedest position—for I have no one to send! None I trust in any event." He regarded Myddelton steadily, his dark eyes having taken on that keen sharp-eyed glow. "And then Flint suggested you—for you are well and truly out of the scheming and above all suspicion. And by far our best man with languages. I realise that it is a great deal to ask of you, for you are to all intents and purposes still on your honeymoon. But you must see that I dare not trust anyone else with this. So, I must ask, might you be willing to undertake this little commission for me? The intelligence is absolutely vital. Of that you must be assured. I should not have asked of your time otherwise, you know that. So the question is: Can I persuade you?"

"Why, yes, sir. Yes, of course," Myddelton said instantly. 'Struth, how could Castlereagh even doubt the answer? "I'm at your service."

In great relief, for he had been convinced that Myddelton would refuse outright, Castlereagh brightened. "Oh, that is excellent!" he said in a rush. "Absolutely splendid. Thank you, Myddelton, thank you. You may be sure I shall not forget this!"

Bemused by the measure of Castlereagh's gratitude, Myddelton slanted a glance at him.

"To be sure, I know that it is a great deal to ask, but you see, there is no one else I trust implicitly. You should be gone for no more than three or four days though, I do assure you."

Myddelton frowned. Three or four days? Wait on it. Where was he meant to be going?

"You will ride to Newhaven. There is a Revenue Cutter harboured there, under the command of a Lieutenant Fiske, a most trustworthy fellow, and he will convey you to the Channel Islands—to Guernsey..."

Guernsey? Myddelton's mind tripped on the word. Guernsey? Dear God, what had possessed him? 'Struth, why not make it enemy France and be done with it? And on a Revenue Cutter. Lud, he'd be sick as cat, there and back. Sweet Christ.

But Castlereagh did not notice his silence. "There, you will meet William Semple—he's one of d'Auverne's lads, working for the Channel Island Correspondence. You'll give him the papers, and he shall take them on to Wellington in Spain. You see, it's quite straight-forward."

It was impossible not to detect the note of urgency creeping into Castlereagh's habitually orotund voice, and a new wariness, one that had nothing to do with his fear of the sea or boats, came over him. For Myddelton was no fool. He knew some of the ways of the couriers, the intelligence men, and their codes—cracking and understanding those was his chiefest talent. So what could be of such vital import that it could not be trusted to the normal routes? And if it were so essential that it reach the Commander-in-Chief in the Peninsula without delay, might there not be others also interested in obtaining it? And why not send someone from the War Office? Or even Flint himself? Or his brother? Good God, what had he said yes to? No, he'd be fine. It would be all right. He'd take Jane and they'd go home and in the morning...He swallowed carefully. "When did you want me to leave, sir?" he found himself asking and felt sick at it.

"Well, tonight!" Lord Castlereagh declared. "As soon as may be arranged. Speed is, as ever, of the utmost importance. That is at least one of the reasons I have asked for your assistance."

Dumbly, woodenly, Myddelton sat staring at the lid of his snuff-box, his heart stalling. It was too much to comprehend. He blinked rapidly, feeling as though he'd been culped in the balls. And vainly tried to find his breath. They wanted him to leave her tonight? Tonight? It was unthinkable. He couldn't leave her. Not tonight. But how could he say that? Why not send someone—anyone—from the War Office or the Irish Office, for surely this was more their territory than his. They were

403

the ones who knew all about false passports and safe houses. There must be someone...

He closed his eyes, hearing an echo of himself as he spoke to Pemberton: '...every time I try to behave as a proper husband to her— as I know I ought, as I should have done from the first instant I met her—or to prove to her that I am not some sort of curst loose fish, it turns into an infernal cock-up...' How could he tell her? Tell her what he could not bear to think on himself? That all his hopes, his marriage even, and the proper beginning to their married life was to be postponed? For four days. It seemed forever. And he shrank to almost nothing within himself at the very thought.

And his heart thudding mercilessly in his chest, the words *'No, I cannot'* formed in his mind and mouth. And *'It is not to be thought of. Forgive me. I cannot leave her. Not even for this.'* But the words Myddelton heard himself use were: "Yes. Yes, certainly..." And he wondered at this greatest folly he had just committed, and again at how he would tell her, what words he could possibly find to express his chagrin and remorse at this latest unkindness.

Lord Castlereagh, misinterpreting the expression on Myddelton's face, said firmly, "There is no very great danger attached to this business, so you must not be anxious."

Myddelton stared, then bowed his head, stricken by this new loss, unable to articulate either his concerns or his grief. "Did you wish me to drive or ride?" he faltered.

Castlereagh sucked on his bottom lip, considering. "A single horseman will elude detection in a hundred ways that a driver may not— particularly such a fine driver as you, if I may say so. It would also, no doubt, aid your cause, was you to travel cross-country and to avoid the thorough-fares as much as possible...My dear Myddelton, I cannot thank you enough for taking this on. I am more obliged than I can say..."

And numbed with an aching that now would not be assuaged, and a nagging apprehension, Myddelton tried to swallow. "Think nothing of it, sir," he replied as sincerely, as dismissively as he could, striving to keep the tightness and anger and remorse out of his voice. He failed. And knew he failed. But Castlereagh, engaged in the business of searching out a map of Guernsey from amongst the mess on his desk and floor, equally failed to notice.

❧

It was an undoubted fact of life that if a ball was a crowning success, or to use another term 'a crush', then the rooms set aside for the guests' rest and personal requirements would be twice as crowded as the reception rooms—the air inside them suffocatingly close, stuffy to the point of sickening with the intermingling of too many different clashing perfumes—and the queues leading to them long, winding and hot. So it came as something of a surprise to Jane that the corridor leading to the rooms set aside for ladies' use was miraculously not crowded. Nor were the rooms themselves full to bursting. The first was occupied by several ladies fanning themselves, dozing, exchanging confidences or having their hems quickly resewn by the attendant maids. The second had an equal complement of ladies engaged in much the same thing. And the third was positively, invitingly, empty, save for one little maid seated in a corner, sewing, who, upon seeing a guest, arose and curtsied. And spying a washstand in the far corner, Jane went in, washed her hands and face, and then took a seat near the open window in the far corner: to sit and briefly to savour for just a few tranquil moments the heady pleasure of being and being seen to be Myddelton's beloved...his laughing eyes, his smile...*your eyes, your mien, your tongue declare that you are music ev'rywhere.* The thought of him made her smile. Eventually though, sensing that the time had perhaps passed too quickly, and by now Myddelton would surely be wondering what had become of her, she signalled to the maid and explained the need to have the riband and clip refixed in her hair. And watched in the mirror as two other ladies—a mother and daughter, were they? Or two sisters?—deep in intimate and indiscreet conversation, paused outside the doorway, then entered.

Seeing no one they knew, they continued their tête à tête unreservedly: "Well, what can you expect? Of course it is true, even though the thought of trailing 'round after Byron dressed as his manservant does sound like something from the pages of the Minerva Press...But with an upbringing like that—her father was a violent drunk,

405

you know, and her mother the mistress of how many men...?" The elder of the two, a large woman, who closely resembled a suet pudding dressed up in tabby silk, waddled over to a small sofa and plumped down.

"Wasn't Brinsley Sheridan one of hers? Such a spiteful, horrid man, one cannot think how she could abide him..." The younger was a thick-set woman—short, dark and dressed in a vibrant cherry-coloured silk gown—with the self-assurance of title and wealth.

"I dare say that's the attraction between 'em. His father, Mad Jack Byron, was a violent drunkard, I can tell you...Oh, that is better," said the elder, dabbing at her forehead and nose with a handkerchief.

Idly mapping the pattern of exotic birds over the wallpaper, Jane exhaled softly. Gossips. Surely they must have something—anything—better to talk about than Emily Cowper's sister-in-law, Caro Lamb, and her infatuation with Byron. And listened—for she could not avoid it—while the maid meticulously refastened the ribands. At least her chair was a comfortable one. She could hear the distant strains of The Comical Fellow rising from the ballroom below.

"Well, Lamb was a fool to marry Caro in the first place! He would have done better with almost anyone at all, even one of the Gordon girls. At least they know how to go on. "Still, you mark my words, it will end unhappily for Caro, foolish girl. For despite all the attention she's bringing him, he's passing his nights with her mother-in law..."

Yes, undoubtedly there were Mrs. Sayers in every county, though even Mrs. Sayer had never been either so loud or so indiscreet. Well, at least not in her hearing...

"Do your bunions still pain you, Mama? As for the Prince Regent...the less said about him and his sordid affairs, the better...They do say he's more devoted to the leeches they use to let his blood than to his only daughter and heir!"

Patiently, Jane sat listening, half-listening and wool-gathering whilst the maid went to work on the second clip. And still, the two women wittered on about first one, then another, and another...who could count how many more hapless victims.

"...Mama, he is a rake! A libertine. And he ever has been! I know you have a fondness for the family because his mama was friendly to you when you came out, but he is a disgrace. His behaviour has always been the worst of the whole Tory set. I cannot think why they tolerate him! To be sure, if he were not on such terms of friendship with Brummell and the Castlereaghs and Liverpool, no one would care to know him...Do but recall how he flaunted that unfortunate Ianthe Dacre about!"

"Ianthe Dacre was no better than she should be!" retorted the elder in equally strident tones.

The maid firmly knotted the riband. Jane wondered when the mother and daughter would go away. She did not know them. She did not wish to know them. Nor did she now have the veriest clue about whom they were so tediously and interminably prating. But she knew she would prefer to remain in ignorance.

"You know, I do believe that poultice has made things worse..." Though the ache in her feet did not silence her mouth, for the mama continued: "It is patently obvious that he married that silly chit of a girl for her money. I imagine his gaming debts must be extensive for he plays with Brummell and Alvanley, you know. And I dare say she is some grasping Cit's daughter..."

"Exactly what I say, Mama! Exactly what I say! But I've heard tell that things ain't turned out as he expected, and the miserable chit is such an ill-bred little harridan that he ain't even been able to bear the thought of bedding her..."

Jane's eyes widened. Having been raised by a bachelor uncle whose regard for reason and logic was paramount, she had little understanding of or appreciation for the labyrinthine ways of feminine logic, and unconsciously gave her head a shake.

Briefly the daughter lowered her voice, but not enough. "Though from what one hears, he and Dunphail spend half their time wenching, so I should think it should make no difference to him..."

Instantly Jane grew quite still and breathless. Dunphail? Who was the other he then? It wasn't Pemberton. For Gussie would certainly have known and told her of any romantic entanglements. Or Mr. Hardy. For everyone knew he spent all his evenings playing string quartets, or playing at cards. So that left only...

"This is where the whole story falls apart, Dorothea...I can easily believe his preferring the Dacre creature. That chit he married is such a pale little thing—barely out of the schoolroom, and not to my liking at all. But a man like him don't care what he mounts, you take my word for it..."

"Well it's quite simple, Mama!" pronounced Dorothea. "Indeed, I do wonder at you. He had always wished to marry la Wythenshaw. He made that perfectly clear earlier in the Season when he was dangling after her so obviously—so much so that her parents had to speak to him about it, and learned his intentions then, no doubt..."

Was it possible? Had Myddelton wished to marry Miss Wythenshaw? Or if he had...But Anne had said...Surely this was nothing but idle and spiteful speculation! And Jane should not be hearing it. She knew she should stand and make her presence known, and stare them out of countenance. But she did not. Or could not. But immobilised by sudden fear and apprehension and morbid curiosity even, she remained seated, fixed, hanging on, dreading, the next words. For she had no doubt about whom they were speaking. But how could they know so much, yet have so much wrong? For surely it was wrong...Or had Myddelton been lying? And Pemberton, had he been lying too?

"Has he bedded *her* then?" asked the mama frankly.

"Possibly," replied the daughter to her mama's tsking. "I dare say. You've seen how they waltz together."

Softly, Jane gasped—though only the wide-eyed maid heard. No. Even such a coquette as the Wythenshaw would not consent to...Or had he seduced her? Was that why he had suspected her and Pemberton? And what was Ianthe Dacre to him?

"...But he means to abandon the wife, you know. And will gain an annulment, I dare say, which is so much easier to obtain than a bill of divorcement. All this revolting billing and cooing tonight is nothing more than the flattery of a skilled seducer, designed to camouflage his true intentions."

"But from whom, Dee-dee?" demanded the mother.

Dorothea shrugged, for having exhausted the subject, she no longer cared. "The wife. Or Castlereagh. Who can say? Perhaps he thinks it may secure him a place in the new Cabinet? There's no end to his ambitions, you know…"

It is a chilling thing to hear oneself ill-spoken of. After such an occurrence, such a wallowing in the mire of malicious invention and vicious slander which left her reeling, Jane could only tremble, wondering, "Why do people lie?" Hardly able to breathe, sitting absolutely still and sickening, in the grip of rising nausea, she told herself it should not matter, gossip. It should not have such power to defeat and unman. But it does. It assuredly does. Even when we know it to be nothing but a pack of falsehoods and even mindless spite. Still, it so easily overmasters, crushing out all joy. For it is not just the lie itself, it is the directed and specific and furtive malice which moved the speaker to utter such falsehoods. That is what so thoroughly undermines. And corrodes.

"Upon my word, I am thirsty. Shall I ring for some more ratafia for us? You know Mama, there is a doctor in Harley Street who might be of some use…"

For some moments, she did not know how long, Jane discovered that she had been covering her mouth with her hand—to prevent her from crying out?—as she listened. She felt hollowed and ill, and knew from her reflection in the mirror that she had turned white as wax. She told herself it was all lies. All all lies. Told herself that this is what it feels like to be gossiped about, this is why her uncle would have none of it. Because it is sneaking, evil and soul-destroying. And was repelled that two such women, who knew her not at all, should repeat such slander about her, should vilify her and Myddelton in such coarse and indefensible terms, should say such hateful, harmful things. And found herself wanting to weep. How could someone whom she had never even met hate her so much? What had she ever done to arouse such antipathy? And how many more times, in how many more permutations, by how many more such creatures who had never even made her acquaintance, would this jumble of lies, half-lies, sordid speculation and hyperbole be repeated?

"There now," said the little maid positively, patting a curl into place over the clip. "That's done then, my lady, and need not concern you again this night." She curtsied and moved to attend to the others.

Pausing for a moment, Jane tried desperately to gather her wits about her and waited while a sudden sense of faintness passed. Then rose and fled the room. She must find Myddelton. Must find him at once. Then they could go home. Then they must go home.

❧

Even as he told himself to remain calm, Myddelton listened to Castlereagh with a mounting sense of concern, a growing unease. What had he done in saying 'yes' to this? For it was nothing like the insignificant little commission that had been outlined in the first instance. All must be accomplished in secrecy, with the utmost speed and precision. He must depart discreetly, as soon as possible. And returning to the ballroom, the cyphered letters—Flint's handiwork—already tucked inside his waistcoat, he felt himself at a greater loss than ever. He must find her. There was time for nothing other than the briefest of kisses and farewells. He brushed past a group of young men congregating or cowering in a narrow hallway, evading the onerous exercise of dancing with the wallflowers. But, Heaven of heavens, how would he explain it? How could he explain it? Or would she understand instinctively, for she was a soldier's daughter? And he wished as he had never before in his life wished that he need not put her to this test.

"Oh! Lord Myddelton!" Miss Wythenshaw, swaying a little, placed a steadying hand against the wall.

Od's fish, was she drunk?

"Please…Please, my lord, would you be so kind as to help me to a chair? I find I am feeling quite faint…" Weakly, she raised her hand to her temple.

Myddelton glared at her. S'death, not now! Was there no one else about to help her?

There wasn't.

And denouncing under his breath those rules of polite behaviour which bound him to aid even such a man-bait as her, Myddelton took her arm to help her to the nearest seat. Which appeared to be that in a nearby ante-chamber, where she might rest or regain her composure or

410

whatever it was she was needing. And then he must go.

"Let me send a footman for your mama, Miss Wythenshaw..." He hadn't time for this. Castlereagh wanted him to leave on the double. And he had not yet found Janey.

"Oh please, my lord, do not leave me. I am sure I shall be better directly," Miss Wythenshaw promised with a misty half-smile.

"I really must not..." The seconds were ticking away. Myddelton could feel them as though the minuscule hammer in his pocket watch was placed against his heart. And cursing himself for a flat, and Castlereagh for having placed him in this infernal position, knew he must remain. For he could not rush from the room without arousing comment.

Gripping the carved arm of the sofa to steady herself, Miss Wythenshaw rose. She did not look well. Myddelton stepped forward, extending his hand.

"Please, let me send a footman after your Mama. You are unwell, and should be taken home..."

"Oh, no! Oh no, not that!" Miss Wythenshaw cried, throwing herself upon him so that Myddelton was forced to catch her in his arms were she not to land in a heap.

And wished instantly he hadn't. Knew conclusively that it was a mistake and he should have let her fall to the floor.

Miss Wythenshaw flung her arms about his neck, pulling his head and face toward hers. "Oh Myddelton, do you not know? Can you not feel it? Have you noticed nothing? Do you not know that I love you! I adore you! I would do anything for you."

Myddelton froze. Od's death, she was drunk. And was instantly furious. "What the devil d'you think you're playing at, Miss Wythenshaw? Have you run mad?" He reached up to disengage her hands from about the back of his neck. "S'death, what d'you take me for?"

Jane—haunted, despondent, distressed—descending the staircase, heard his voice, his very dear voice, and followed it like the life-line it was.

Doggedly, Miss Wythenshaw held on, tugging at his head to bring it down to hers, stretching up to meet his mouth. For she was determined to kiss him. Determined too to extinguish all taste of *her* from his mouth. And ignoring all that she did not wish to know or understand, ignoring the loathing that was transforming his face, she cried, "Oh Myddelton, I know what you have suffered. Believe me, I do know! But I swear I shall make it all up to you. We can be together, it does not matter what Society says. For I worship you. I adore you...Oh my dear Myddelton, I can feel your heart beating..."

"Remove your hands from my person, Miss Wythenshaw..." Myddelton's voice was harsh. "Before I break your arm." There could be no denying that he meant it.

His voice—there it was again. And quickening her steps almost to a run, Jane crossed to the antechamber. And saw. And the words that she had been about to call out died in her mouth. For like a mental branding iron, the sight of Myddelton with Miss Wythenshaw in his arms was seared onto her mind's eye.

So it was true. It was not lies. And she became as still and cold as fallen snow.

In the antechamber, with its pale grey woodwork and French toile de jouey wallpaper and its single love seat designed for decorous wooing, his fury was reaching that stage bordering on madness. For Myddelton had seen his wife.

But the exquisite Miss Wythenshaw, enslaved and enraptured by her own fervent Romantic folly, and idle, ignorant daydreams, refused to believe her ears. "Oh Myddelton..." she cooed. Convinced, assured of her incipient triumph, the alluring Miss Wythenshaw laid her head against his chest and sighed. "Where shall we go where we can be together always? Shall we have our own secret love-nest far from London, where..."

With a violent wracking shudder, her throat constricting and her arms crossed over her chest, Jane closed her eyes against the tears. He was a seasoned seducer, and rakehell. Just as they had said. She could have no doubt now. It was true. How had they phrased it? That it was 'nothing more than the flattery of a skilled seducer, designed to camouflage his true intentions.' Dear God, it was true. It was all true. With her fingernails biting through her gloves into the palms of her hands, she forced herself to breathe deeply. And silent, she turned away.

Seeing that look of horror and distress upon his wife's face, the same as that he'd seen at Vauxhall, Myddelton, now enraged beyond measure, had had enough. And taking hold of Miss Wythenshaw's barely gowned shoulders, he thrust her away. Wrenched her hands from about his neck. She staggered backwards, collapsing at the foot of the sofa.

"Get away from me!" Myddelton barked. "Get away from me. And stay away from me, you insufferable, manipulative hellcat! I want none of what you're offering. Upon my soul, I wouldn't have you if you was the last female on offer, d'you hear? And don't go telling yourself I don't mean it!" He strode to the door. "Stay away from my wife too!" And he stood for one brief moment in the doorway, breathing in great gulps of air as he searched the hall in either direction for a glimpse of her.

And there she was. Just a few steps away, pressing herself against the wall, her eyes closed and her face turned from him, silently reciting as a prayer or an incantation of peace, the opening hexameters of the *Æneid*: *"Arma virumque cano, Troiae qui primus ab oris/ Italiam fato profugus Laviniaque venit/ litora, multum ille et terris iactatus et alto/ vi superum…"*

She gave a small cry as he slid his arm about her waist.

"Come." He was shaking. She looked up at him and he saw in her eyes fear and betrayal and loss. And holding her close as a child, he drew her farther down the candlelit hall until they were alone in a place of quiet. His arm tightened about her. But their time had been stolen away. And he paused, hating what he must say, wishing he knew some way to soften it. He closed his eyes to search for words. And in his wretchedness found none. "I cannot explain now," he said. "But I must go…" And took her face between his hands, cradling it. "No, listen to me," he begged. He swallowed hard. "Castlereagh has asked me to do something for him. And I must do it. Do you understand?"

There were tears in her eyes. She had never seen him like this. Not even when Perceval had died. Not even then. "What is it?" she whispered, suddenly afraid.

He raked her face with a glance. Could he tell her? Was he allowed that? He stroked her cheek. "Intelligence," he whispered. "He needs me to carry information. That's all I know. I can't say no. Do you see? But

413

I have to leave tonight. Now. So I need you to throw 'em all off the scent. All of 'em. And say nothing. Not to anyone. Can you do that? Please, will you do that?"

He saw the mute protest in her eyes. She was fighting to keep her face from crumbling. She nodded. "When?" she mouthed.

"Now. There's a Revenue Cutter waiting at Newhaven. I'm to sail with the tide."

Blinking with shock, she nodded. And her tears spilled over onto her cheeks. "It isn't true, is it? What I saw?" she blurted, her voice breaking.

He gave a derisory snort. "No!" And became grave. And despised himself for abandoning her. And with his cheek against her hair, murmured, though the words were ripped from his soul, "I must go…" And bringing his face so close to hers, he kissed her with all tenderness. And cleaving to her, he angled her face just so. And kissed her again roughly. Then put her from him. And clutching her hand, crushing it within his own, he kissed it, then turned and walked away down the corridor.

Lady Myddelton, reentering the ball room, found it was as stuffy and crowded as it had been when she left—one forgets how the heat from the hundreds of candles burning in the chandeliers and wall sconces can easily become overpowering on a warm evening—and that another waltz was beginning. And saw too an answer to her now-predicament standing nearby. "Mr. Thurston." She had wiped away all trace of tears.

"Oh, Lady Myddelton, may I be of service?" Mr. Thurston replied promptly. "May I help you to a chair? You look as though…"

"No, I am quite well, thank you." She paused. Did she dare? And knew that she did. She must. Though the public wearing of their private faces had left her exposed—having revealed so much, it was impossible to lapse back into her public persona, but she had little choice. She must chat inconsequentially, she must not reveal her fear or desperation, she must not even be seen to be missing him. "But I have found that someone has indeed reneged—as you put it earlier—so I should be very pleased to dance with you now, if you still wish it." Forward, risky, foolish even, to put herself forward like this, but she had no choice.

"With the greatest of pleasure, ma'am." Mr. Thurston's smile was infectious as he offered her his arm and led her toward the other couples on the dance floor.

At the threshold of the ballroom, Myddelton paused and drew out his snuff-box in a vain attempt to bring himself under control. Casually, meticulously, attentively even, he inhaled the ground tobacco, returned the box to his pocket and wiped his nose. Almost better.

"I say, are you well?" Pemberton asked, joining him, having recently returned from the card room somewhat poorer than when the evening had begun—Dunphail was playing wisely tonight. So was Hardy.

Myddelton favoured him with a feeling look. "'Struth, you'd never credit it in a hundred years..." He had no time for anything now. He had to leave.

"What? Oh, yes, there's a turn-up for the books," Pemberton began sourly. "When did you give your assent to her waltzing with other fellows? And why wasn't I told?" he demanded curtly, for there was no point in trying to disguise the rancour. Not with Myddelton.

"What?"

"She's there, idiot. Dancing with young Thurston." And saw a new emotion—could it have been despair?—register in his friend's eyes as he searched her out and found her among the other dancers, there, in another man's arms.

Yes, it was despair. More gently: "Oh yes? And what won't I credit? Try me."

"Just now, the Wythenshaw..."

Which prompted that particularly grim 'I told you so' or 'not again' look to come over Pemberton's features. "Oh yes, what's the virago done now?"

"Thrown herself at me and begged me to take her off to a love-nest."

"What?" Incredulity replaced all other emotions for the moment.

Myddelton nodded. "I ain't joking. D'you know that little ante-chamber off the upstairs hall? Well there she was, lying in wait one can only suppose, when I came looking for Jane. Pretends to be faint and asks me to help her to a chair, which flat that I am, I do. Then she flings herself at me and starts blabbing about how she adores me...God in heaven."

"What did you do then?"

"What do you think I did? Told her to remove her arms from my person and when she wouldn't, I threw her off and left." Myddelton shook his head and swallowed hard. There was nothing for it now. And lowering his voice so that it was barely audible above the music and chatter: "Listen Pem, I've got to go, leave Town, tonight. Right now, in fact—for the F.O. For Castlereagh." He took a long hard look across the room at her, and nearly wept. To leave her. The ache for her was nearly crippling him. "Look after her for me. Take care of her, will you? I'll only be gone four days or so. And tell her that I...Tell her I..." He swallowed again. How could he ask Pemberton to tell her what he had not had the courage to speak himself? "Nothing. Just...just tell her I shall be back as soon as I can. And see her home, will you?"

"Anything you like. Are you well?" Pemberton asked again and saw the grief in Myddelton's face, and placed a hand on his shoulder. "You're not, are you? Don't go, Myddelton."

"I must, Pem. It's my duty." Still looking at her, watching as she was swept round the dance floor in Thurston's arms—the music was beautiful, liltingly beautiful—Myddelton paused, striving to quell or deaden his emotions, his longing for her, his love of her. "Put it about that I've gone North after a horse, a matched pair, anything...Take care of her..."

"One minute," Pemberton said, halting his departure. "Is she to know the truth?"

Myddelton hesitated. He wished he knew. "I've told her."

"And this little mission you're running for Castlereagh. How dangerous is it really?"

Myddelton looked sharply at his friend. Why did anyone think Pemberton less than fiendishly acute?

Pemberton smiled serenely. "I like to have all the facts at my disposal before I start telling clankers."

"I hope not." Myddelton frowned unhappily.

"Right. You don't know. I'll take care of it." Pemberton's look was measured, intelligent, impenetrable.

"Thank you...Tell her I shall be home for the ball."

"I'll tell her."

And with a final, now-sorrowing look at her, his dear dear wife, his wife in name only whom he loved as life itself, Myddelton turned, and discreetly left the ballroom and the Castlereagh mansion.

25

From the instant Mr. Thurston took her hand at the opening bar of the waltz, Jane knew it was wrong. Knew it to be a dreadful mistake. And as he took her in his arms, she felt a sudden rising nausea and blind panic—and it was not only because this was too intimate and she felt that none but Myddelton should ever hold her so close. Nor was it that Mr. Thurston vaguely awkward and minding his steps as he led her through one of the group variations and then against took her again in his arms. It was that for all his fine points, he was not her husband. Ruthlessly, she quelled the panic and nausea; this was not the place. Yet all she could think was how much she longed to be with Myddelton and to read in his expression affection and the reassurance that soon they would slip away from this very fine, but increasingly superfluous ball. And she knew that she should have gone with him. That precipitate action all too often leads only to trouble. And at the same time, there were those too vivid spectres of what she had overheard and seen, and she wondered what she should do and how ought she to behave once this waltz had finished. And she wondered how she would endure it. But…had he not sounded angry when she had heard his voice in the passageway? She ought not to have judged him as she did. And there were those vicious, horrible rumours. And even though her faith in him had been buffeted, even one exchange of glances would tell her that none of this mattered a whit, and they would be as they were. She should have gone with him. But she had not seen him standing at the perimeter of the dance floor for some minutes now. She could see Pemberton, but not him.

She did not realise that such the thought of him softened to nothing the frown that had formed deep furrows in her brow, and Mr. Thurston, seeing it, was relieved, for he believed he must in some way have offended, though he did not know how—for she had responded to all of his attempts at conversation with little more than polite monosyllables.

But at last, the waltz, the torment, finished. And Mr. Thurston escorted her toward Pemberton, and she tried to remain calm as she searched the throng for a glimpse of Myddelton. And felt more uneasy and afraid, though she could not say why. Impatient, she waited until Mr. Thurston had thanked her and bowed and left them before she asked the question, "Pem, has he gone?" and was not able to suppress the concern in her voice.

"Ehm, yes," admitted Pemberton. And watching as a sudden despair overcame her, replaced all else, like night falling, obliterating all colour in a moment, Pemberton said, "Janey, are you all right? You look like death."

She paid no attention, though her head had begun to throb. She pressed her fingers against her temple. "Oh…" She did not cry, but felt the tears sting and prick against her eyelids.

"'Struth, Angel, I think we should find a chair for you…There's one over there," he said, taking her arm and weaving a path for them through the cliques and coteries and couples to the vacant seat. And as she was seated, he leaned close: "It'll be all right. He'll be back. It's only for the Foreign Office. For Castlereagh."

She shook her head in denial. "I saw them, you know."

"No, you didn't," Pemberton denied flatly. He had known her too long not to follow her logic. "If you saw anything, then what you saw was the Wythenshaw chit throwing herself at him. Obviously you failed to see him push her away and tell her never to come near him again. Or you."

"What?" she whispered. It was all too much—after the gossip, she could bear no more and she wanted to weep. Why could she not have gone with him?

She did not notice the tightening of Pemberton's easy smile. "Though why Castlereagh, in a rare fit of perspicacity, has sent him off for the Foreign Office just now, I cannot tell you. Obviously, he failed to notice the pair of you courting all over the place…"

She drew a quick breath. She had not really been listening to his blather. "But he might still be at home! If I were to leave now? He will have had to change, won't he…"

"He'll be gone, Angel." He tried to sound soothing, patient, kind. It did not help.

"I must try, Pem. Please, take me home," she begged. "I must see him. We can walk. I'll run. It's just across the Square."

"Angel, he'll be gone…Anyway, I mustn't." And continued gently, "Castlereagh wanted him to leave without anybody noticing. And if you go flying out of here, they'll notice. So you mustn't, Angel." He took her hand and held it. Held it as the tears gathered against her will and the look she gave him was too like that one in the Vauxhall Gardens, too pleading, too trusting, too damaged. He did not add that if Myddelton were still at home, his departure wouldn't be as soon as possible were she to arrive there, it would be some time later. "He said to tell you he'll be home in four days or so and that you must not fret. That he'll be home as soon as he can." Then, asking the impossible: "Don't cry, Janey."

She closed her eyes for a long moment and drew a deep breath. "No." She smiled bleakly. "No, I won't." Then, courageously, composedly: "They are beginning 'Mr. Beveridge's Maggot'. Shall we join them? Though Lady Jersey says Myddelton dances it better than anyone, even Mr. Brummell…"

And as they took their places with the other couples, and joined hands, he saw that she was crying, but there, in that public arena, he could nothing about it. Though most, no doubt, would blame it on the heat.

The two candles in the wall sconce guttered fitfully, their flames wafting, flattening and straightening again as Myddelton moved from wardrobe to table, taking one last shirt to stuff into his saddlebag, then stopped, wondering if he'd need it, wishing Stamp were here to do the packing. There was no point in considering what might have been, what should have been, the reason he'd given Stamp the night off. For that, he required no assistance—not with undressing or anything else, before or after.

Dear God, how dismally wrong he had been. He could hardly bear to think of it. Could hardly bear to think of her, coming home tonight, alone, husbandless. And told himself he must not dwell on it. Yet, how did one resist revisiting such reflections, brooding upon them, like over old wounds that ached so and were slow to heal?

Already, he was dressed for riding in buckskins, boots and an old riding coat. About his neck was a neckerchief—her favourite—he must not draw attention to himself by appearing in the counties as a 'London swell'. That was not what Castlereagh, the master of discretion, wanted. Upon the mantel lay the two small-efficient looking side arm pistols with ebony handles that he'd bought only last March. And beside them, a skean dhu—the neat little double-edged dagger he'd picked up in Inverness when he was last up stalking deer with Dunphail. He tucked the shirt into the saddlebag and buckled it shut. He was about to slide the dagger into his boot top when a discreet knock on the door halted him.

"Come." And fixed the dagger in his boot.

The door opened. Instantly the small chamber was impregnated with the strong scent of horses, muck, hay, and sweat, as Curlee, the wizened head groom, obeyed the summons. "Beggin' your pardon, milord, but you cannot ride Macedon this night."

"Why? What's wrong with him?" Myddelton rapped out. 'Struth, this was all that was needed.

"He's missing his right rear shoe. Like always! Must have kicked it off this afternoon," Curlee stated. That horse went through shoes like a high society female.

"Bloody hell." Myddelton bit at the inside of his cheek and stared at the packed saddlebag. There was no other animal in the stable up to his weight, or strong enough for a long fast journey, except... "Tack up Patroklos then."

Curlee gave him a long measuring look. "My lady's hack? Eeh! And what'll I tell her when she asks for him, tell me that?" he demanded with the authority of one who has been head groom for longer than Myddelton had been alive.

421

Myddelton's nostrils flared. "You tell her that I needed him because Macedon had thrown his shoe, the fidgety bugger!"

Curlee remained unimpressed. "Oh aye, that'll please her, that will."

"You heard me, Curlee. Go tack him up!"

"All right then, I'll tell her…He'll be in the mews, like you said. Milord," Curlee grumbled, grudgingly letting himself—though not his scent—out of the room.

Myddelton stood still for a moment, anxious to regain his composure—a useless and impossible exercise—then bent to fix the skean d'hu more firmly inside his boot. He was liking this mission less and less by the minute. No, that was wrong. He was hating it more and more by the minute. Nor did he much fancy the idea of riding to the coast on a strange horse, even a stallion as powerful and well-schooled as her Patroklos. But that was not what stung and hurt. It was the possible loss of something so dear he had not words to frame it. Again he had broken his promise to her, again he had failed her, again he was not beside her, again he must set aside all yearning. He ran his fingers through his hair, and sat down at his dressing table, to hold his head in his hands. 'Struth, what a wretched mockery it all was. And found himself wanting to yell or curse or weep at the injustice of it. But did not. Od's teeth, he'd not even bid her a proper farewell. Bleakly, he opened his eyes—there was no point in this self-recrimination, not now, he knew that—and was about to rise, when he saw the small volume of poetry he'd been reading earlier in the day and remembered its contents.

Taking it up, he opened to the small poem he'd thought the finest, 'Du bist die Ruh…' *You are tranquillity*… Though he could not be here with her, to hold her, to cherish her, to love her, he could leave her this. Then perhaps she might begin to understand what it was he felt for her, what she meant to him and perhaps forgive him for this latest abandonment—for there was no other word for it.

A few minutes later, the small book left open where she was sure to find it, and his face set in harsh, resolute lines, Myddelton slung the saddlebag over his shoulder, picked up the two pistols and left the house, silently and furtively, by the servants' rear door.

❧

Mr. Hardy, starting for the stairs that would lead him to the supper room, was feeling rather pleased with himself, even though he was well aware that supper was at least half finished by now and that there might be little left. For at last, at last, it appeared that his luck had turned. First, he'd rubiconned Dunphail at piquet, which was altogether the headiest of experiences, being unprecedented, and then he'd won against Thos Jesuadon. Truly, it was an experience to savour—he'd pop 'round to Sr. Agnellino's tomorrow to celebrate; perhaps there would be a new string quartet or violin sonata to be had. He crossed the empty dance floor and walked past two old ladies, deep in conversation. He went out onto the landing and paused to gaze happily at his newest waistcoat—pale celadon with buff stripes, embroidered with posies of daisies, love-in-idleness, roses and lavender, (a lucky waistcoat, to be sure) though you could see very little of it, just the collar and bottom edge beneath his coat—but when he would have started down the steps, the sound of muffled weeping halted him. He paused, hand on the bannister.

No, he must have been mistaken. No one weeps at a ball.

Mr. Hardy hesitated. Then, decisively, turned and made for the small antechamber that adjoined the hallway to the ballroom. Whoever was weeping had to be in there. There was nowhere else.

Mr. Hardy pushed open the door which was slightly ajar, ducking his head around the doorjamb. "Hallo?" he ventured. "I beg your pardon…" He pushed the door farther open. Collapsed on the rug was a young woman, cradling her head in the cushions of the love seat. He stepped quietly into the room and closed the door behind him.

Dutifully, Jane followed those unspoken orders, Castlereagh's orders, and Myddelton's. Followed them as a trained soldier from a crack regiment obeys the word of his commanding officer. To the letter. She laughed, smiled, chatted, danced, drank, ate, sparkled. And it was a stellar performance. One to silence all talk, all gossip, all speculation. And even Pemberton, at her side for much of it, had little concept of what it cost her to maintain the facade and ensure that no one suspected Myddelton's absence for a moment. He did not know that the twin blows of malicious gossip and Myddelton's abrupt departure had been a mere overture to the loss of something far dearer and of greater moment, the consummation so devoutly yearned for that its loss or abeyance made her feel that her heart must cave in with grief. And she wondered, as she laughed and smiled and danced, if this was what it was like to be left waiting at the altar, if this overarching despair was what the poets called a heart breaking. And then she thought not, for if one had been abandoned at the altar, surely there would be no need for a performance of gaiety to cloak the distress of the event.

But by two, she could act no more. She had reached, stretched and overextended the limit of her social endurance, and with her head aching and her spirits numbed, she wandered into the supper room. And finding Pemberton, she rested her hand upon his shoulder, and said, "Pem, dearest, do you think you might see me home now?"

Pemberton, her dearest, in the midst of eating a fine mound of caviar, the spoils of supper, eyed her shrewdly and laid aside his fork. He disliked the glassy-eyed stoicism, and distrusted the static perfection which had marked her demeanour since she had learned that Myddelton was gone. And excusing himself, rose from his seat. "To be sure. Right away, Angel."

And as they waited for her carriage to come to the front of the house to take her home, Pemberton began tentatively, anxious though he could not say why, "Janey, you needn't fear, he'll be back very soon."

She was so still, so distant. "No. I know."

Which made no sense to him. "Then what is it?"

She did not answer at once. "Nothing. It is nothing."

Yet once inside the carriage, even as they made the short journey—for the Square had cleared of much of the earlier traffic—Pemberton could not dispel the sense that something had gone grievously wrong.

Quiet, she sought to set her face against the unhappy knowledge of what was not to be and what had been lost, stolen or sacrificed. And wondered how she would endure this uncertainty and despair or whether indeed she was so tired that she was imagining it all and everything would turn out simply? Whether when Myddelton returned it would be as though nothing had occurred, and he would hold her and kiss her and she would think how foolish she had been? Which would leave only the gossip. But if he held her and kissed her and told her he loved her—and he never had said that, had he?—would the gossip matter? And still her head pounded so that it made her wince.

Again Pemberton asked what was wrong.

And again, she said, "Nothing. It is nothing, I assure you. I am just tired." For she could not say: 'I have been gossiped about, reviled, and slandered. I have seen my husband in the embrace of another. And now I am going home. To Myddelton House, though bereft of Myddelton. Without the kisses and smiles and sighs which I had expected would compose my evening and midnight and morning. This night and every night hereafter. I am going home to silent rooms and a cold lonely bed and prey to such fears as I can neither articulate nor banish. And I do not know that I can bear this final loss. For tonight was to have been my wedding night, *the wedding night for which I dressed as a bride.* With the husband I love so dearly. But now, now it is not. And my dancing has been turned to mourning.'

"Janey, what is it?" he repeated.

She hesitated. No. This burden she could not share. And her shoulders felt weak and quavered at such a thought.

But…But perhaps, surely, she could tell him of the gossip and of what she had seen—for she had to tell someone and it seemed he already knew much of it. Perhaps by the morning she would be able to speak of it…For she did not think she could bear it all alone. "Come 'round tomorrow…I'll tell you then. I am too tired now." And it was the wannest of smiles she gave him.

It was not the answer he wanted, but wisely he left it. "Of course." And seeing her to her door, kissed her hand. "Till tomorrow, then."

But already she had retreated far within herself and it was as if she did not hear or could not feel the warmth of his concern and friendship. And if he found the inured bleakness in her expression hard to bear, there was nothing left that he might do, so unhappy, he left her in Kettering's care.

She heard Kettering shut the door behind her and draw the lock. And so started slowly up the stairs.

"I shall send Mrs. Pinch to you, my lady." Like Stamp, Haseley had been given the night off. And seeing her disconsolate and pale, Kettering would not leave her to the ministrations of an untrained maid.

"No, Kettering, thank you. I want no one." It was as though she could feel the house, the empty house, all vacant and echoing, closing about her, a still tomb for her too many griefs. And solitary, desolate, she came to her own bed chamber and went in. And there, in the unmeasured silence of that lightless room, standing before the bed which she would now not share with her beloved—the marriage bed the happiness of which she would now neither learn nor bestow—and the door to his empty room where he would not be waiting, she remained as though lost and undone. Until sometime later, she found from deep within her came the music of the Nymph's plaint from *the Fairy Queen*— that lament, the summation of all inconsolable grief, thrice heard, and often played, though she knew she had never understood it fully till now: *O let me, o let me weep, for ever, for ever weep...*

And missing Myddelton so badly that it hurt, she hugged herself against this night of wretchedness, of manifold malicious invention and misunderstanding, of sweetest promise and cheated hope, and felt the too long withheld tears finally begin to wash down her face. *I'll hide me from the sight of day, and sigh, and sigh my soul away...He's gone, he's gone, he's gone, his loss deplore...and I shall never never never see him more.*

And she would have wept all night. *O let me weep, for ever weep...*

But Kettering, keeping watch from beyond the door, and listening, at last went to rouse Mrs. Pinch, and sent her in to undress my lady and put her to bed.

Jane did not see the book at first upon her pillow. Did not notice. For still she was awash with tears, overcome by the misery that had beset her as she watched as Mrs. Pinch silently untied the pale blue ribbons of her garters—the ribbons intended for Myddelton's hand, the garters, festooned with roses and lace for this bridal, and chosen with such care for her bridegroom's delight.

She did not see his little book with its tooled leather binding until she would have laid down. And picking it up, meant to put it to one side. For she could not have wanted to leave a book upon her pillow—not tonight—but it was open, and upon the page was Myddelton's writing.

My heart, I shall return to you as soon as ever I may.

And wiping her tears away with her hand, her eyes rested on that sweet message, that single line of consoling hope: *My heart, I shall return to you as soon as ever I may.* And slowly she ran her finger across that line of precious writing, savouring the indentations which his pencil had made upon the page, needing to touch that place which he had touched, their last point of contact. Then, haltingly, for her German was not equal to her Latin or Greek, she began to read and translate the poem which he had left for her to see:

Du bist die Ruh, Der Friede mild,
You are tranquillity, gentle peace.
Die Sehnsucht du, und was sie stillt.
You are longing and what assuages it.
Ich weihe dir voll Lust und Schmerz
I dedicate to you, full of desire and pain,
Zur Wohnung hier mein Aug' und Herz.
as your dwelling here, my eye and heart.

Kehr ein bei mir, und schließe du
Still hinter dir die Pforten zu.
Come in to me and close the door softly behind you.
Treib andern Schmerz aus dieser Brust!
Drive other grief out of this heart—
Voll sei dies Herz von deiner Lust.
May this heart be filled with your joy
Dies Augenzelt, von deinem Glanz allein erhellt, O füll es ganz!
The canopy of my eyes is by your brightness alone illuminated, O fill it wholly!

And crying again, but softly now, for she missed him so terribly, loved him and wanted nothing more than to cleave to him, she held the slender volume, his little book and his farewell message to her, until at last, as the grey light of dawn became stained like a much-used palette with crimson, rose and lavender, gently she slept.

26

At the crest of a hill, the last rise of the Downs before reaching the sea, Patroklos stumbled. To the east, a thread of light was gently widening: dawn.

Myddelton reined in, dismounted and stood, his mind elsewhere or empty or assessing. Finally, he bent down to run an exploratory hand over the horse's sides and legs. 'Struth, if Patroklos had been lamed by this long night's ride, how would he ever tell Janey? But no. There appeared to be no damage, no hurt. Like his rider, he was just tired. Patting him on the neck, Myddelton surveyed the tiny village below that was Newhaven.

"This is a fool's errand, Patroklos." Catching up the reins, he started down the grassy slope toward the village, leading the horse behind.

Myddelton had not found the long midnight ride south invigorating. Nor did he feel heroic—the only danger had been from scuttling hedgehogs, which he'd discovered Patroklos disliked. All he felt was tired. Bone weary. For by now he was inured to the melancholy or discontent that dogged him. And he wanted nothing more than to return home to bed. Initially, regrettably, to sleep.

But as he had considered it over the past few hours—anything to take his mind (and other parts) off what he was missing this night, the more he concluded this whole mission, for want of a better term, was a completely hare-brained scheme. For whom did he know in Newhaven? No one. He had no instructions as to where he might stable a horse, nor yet how he would find this Lieutenant Fiske—a man he knew only by reputation. And why choose him, a thoroughly untrained, uninitiated novice and know-naught? It was all thoroughly cork-brained. And why had he consented to do it? Heaven only knew. And surely, if he needs must ride south, surely it would have made more sense for him to give the letters to Fiske, an experienced intelligencer, and for him to take them on to Guernsey. At least Fiske could be relied upon not to spend the hours aboard spewing his guts out over the side. S'life, it was completely mad from start to finish. Unless, of course, there was some dual purpose in it, the which Castlereagh had not chosen to confide—and God knew what that might be, though Planta, damn him, probably had a fair idea. At least it hadn't rained.

By the time he reached the road into the village, the thread of light had broadened into that band of soft colour upon the eastern horizon, though still there were few awake or astir. Yet within an hour Myddelton supposed the entire village would be up, and by that time he must have Patroklos stabled and himself aboard the Revenue Cutter. So, to stable Patroklos somewhere safe and no doubt inconspicuous to satisfy Castlereagh. Ha! That shouldn't prove difficult—not with a stallion of his size and breeding.

He turned in at the first inn yard he came to, where already a young ostler in a stained leather waistcoat was carrying a large pail of water from the well toward the stable block. The inn itself, half-timbered and white-washed, two-storeyed, well-kept and pleasant, was still quiet.

The ostler, hearing the sound of horseshoes upon the cobblestone, paused and turned his head. "We be full up, Guv…"

Not a local lad then, but one from farther west along the coast. If he ever had been a patient man, or a meek, Myddelton was no longer— the well from which those qualities sprang had run dry some hours or days earlier. He reached into a pocket and pulled out a guinea, secure in the knowledge that if this boy saw so much in a month, it was a rare month indeed. And did not care. The whole of the south coast from Rye to Penzance was smuggler's territory—Revenue Cutters and Riding Officers bedamned—and there were, there must be, safe and quiet stables where Patroklos could be left and tended to.

"He's been ridden a long way," Myddelton said in a hard voice. "He needs a good rubdown, fresh water and hay, and a good rest—preferably in a rear stall where he ain't likely to be noticed."

The boy eyed the gold coin and Myddelton, licked his lip and set down his pail.

"There'll be another golden boy for you when I return—if all's well with him."

The ostler slanted his gaze toward Patroklos and took in the sweating flanks. "'E may need a poultice or summat…"

The sky was beginning to lighten. "As I said, another golden boy when I return." He saw or imagined he saw movement behind the taproom windows.

The lad screwed his face up. "A'right then. I'll see t'him. 'E won't be 'ere though." He nodded his head toward the inn door. "Innkeeper don' like me seein' t'things on me own."

Yes, smuggler's territory, the province of the Gentlemen. "Where then?"

"You take 'im out o' 'ere, turn right an' a th'first close, you turn right again. You keeps on goin' then till you gets to th'end by a little 'ouse. You'll know it's the right'un for it be blue, it do. Th'mews o' the best Gennulmen be there. Second stable on left. T'is nice an' private-like there. You put 'im there. I'll come 'round in five minute, not a moment more, to give 'im a good rub-down an' wat'rin'."

Clearly, miraculously, he, the know-naught, had landed on his feet. Or was it all too easy and would he return to find Jane's fine stallion gone forever, a prize of the Gentlemen? "See that you do." Myddelton flipped the guinea, spinning, through the air.

Deftly the boy caught and pocketed it.

"No harm had better come to him or I shall have your hide. And I do not want him used for midnight runs under the noses of Lieutenant Fiske and the Preventative boys."

The lad grinned, revealing a gap where a front tooth had been broken. "No sir. Didn't reckon you would." And nodding cheerfully: "Reckon 'e'd carry a neat keg or two though, 'e would."

Myddelton almost smiled. Soberly, "I should return for him by Friday." Then, because in spite of the Royal Navy, regardless of Castlereagh's blithe assurances, despite the fact that he was going no farther than Guernsey, to leave these shores was to embark into a world at war, where there could be no real guarantee of safety or certainty,

Myddelton added, "If I am not back by, say, the following Friday, I want you to return him to Myddelton House, in London." And felt the veins in his neck tighten and twist with a fear he had never before experienced nor identified. "Do you understand?"

"Yessir. Myddelton 'ouse, if'n you b'ain't 'ere by Friday week." The ostler gave a brief, intelligent nod, picked up his bucket and headed off toward the stables.

Myddelton turned and led Patroklos from the inn yard. And found, eventually, at the end of the long and winding alley, beside a narrow blue house which leaned drunkenly over a narrow passage, a snug little stable with two large empty box stalls, both mucked out and with clean straw already laid, blankets on the stall gate and fresh water in the buckets. Clearly these Gentlemen valued their cattle.

"Here we are then, lad..." He brought Patroklos into the far side box and closed the gate behind. Then, the stirrups up, he reached under the girth to unbuckle the saddle, as if Curlee were standing behind him saying in his ear, 'You mus' never leave a saddle on a sweatin' horse. Don' matter if you be beggar or lord. If there b'ain't a boy to do the job, you do it yoursel'.' Myddelton took hold of the edges of the saddle and heaved it off, to drop it unceremoniously over the gate. Then, he removed the halter and bit and hung them on the peg in the stable wall. Curlee would not have approved. Curlee would have demanded that he give him a full rub-down and curry after a ride like that. But there wasn't time. Not to rub him down, nor to curry him. Neither to smooth his nose, nor to reflect that when he left this stable and this fine animal—the gift of her uncle and upon which she had bestowed the name of the most honourable of Greek heroes—he would have parted with his last tie to her. Impatiently, he quelled such contemplation—he might tell himself that he was inured to the hurt and the ache, but that did not make it so.

"Behave yourself, lad." Myddelton picked up his saddle bag, threw it over his shoulder and let himself out of the box stall. "I shall be back with you soon." And left the stable to make his way, via the maze of back streets and closes, to the harbour where, in the grey pearl light of early morning, ropes slapped against the swaying masts of rich men's yachts and fishermen's smacks and where the tide lapped at the harbour

431

wall. And where Lieutenant James Fiske and his Revenue Cutter waited.

Mr. Hardy, contrary to what many might have been unobservant enough to believe, was no one's fool. And he knew that his Miss Wythenshaw, his *betrothed*—oh, the unparalleled happiness of those words—had been seen embracing Myddelton by others less discreet, less kind and less forgiving than himself. And if her reputation and Myddelton's were to be salvaged and protected, a measure of friendly, powerful aid was required. Not for long, of course. It didn't need to be for long. Most people were far more interested in the flirtation between Caroline Lamb and Lord Byron. But just until Caro, or Byron, did something, anything, that riveted the attention back on them and such titillating and essentially prurient issues as, 'Were they or weren't they? Or was he rather fonder of…'

Mr. Hardy had known Lady Emily Cowper since childhood. Indeed, there were those who attributed the stability and sweetness of her character in large measure to the frequency of her visits to St. Cross Priory, where she had been known to take refuge from the irregularities of her home life and the tempests of her mother's constant infidelity.

He found Lady Emily as he had known he would, breakfasting at home, enjoying the quiet pleasure of her own company, reading letters as she nibbled on a corner of buttered toast in the small breakfast-cum-morning room. It was an elegant room, charming and feminine—powder blue with white swags and medallions—and quite without frippery. She looked up as he entered unannounced. "Ned! How lovely!" And raised her cheek to be kissed.

He smiled in genuine fondness, kissed her, and stood for a moment to admire her—for she was very, very pretty. Then, uninvited, took the seat beside her.

"What are you doing here so early?" She pushed the letters to one side. "Shall I ring for more tea? You'd rather have coffee, I dare say…" she continued, rearranging the assorted dishes on the table to create a place for him. "You haven't been 'round to see me this age... Though I did wave to you the other evening at the opera. Lud, that was some waistcoat you were wearing! Wherever did you come by it? Even Pam commented upon it..." And then, warily, for he seemed suspiciously cheerful to her: "What have you been up to? You haven't gone and bought another violin, have you?"

Mr. Hardy smiled. Few understood him or loved him quite as well as Lady Emily Cowper. "No. I have not bought another violin. Though I confess I was rather tempted by a lovely little viola the other day. But no."

Emily regarded him shrewdly. "Out with it then. What is it?"

He smiled broadly, for there was no disguising his contentment, nor had he any wish to keep it from her. "I'm engaged. To be married."

He had expected that this announcement would be met with enthusiasm and delight, and was not disappointed—Emily had long made it a habit, in the most non-interfering way, to introduce him to those young ladies with whom she felt he might have common interests. "What? Oh Ned, are you? To whom? Oh this is wonderful news. Tell me to whom. I can hardly bear it! You must tell me everything in an instant," she declared, laughing and clapping her hands.

"Miss Wythenshaw. Georgina Wythenshaw."

Abruptly, her smiles and laughter ceased. "You're joking...Ned, tell me you're joking. You're not joking. Oh Ned, what have you done?" she wailed. And closed her eyes against the smarting of tears of outrage or dismay over this too unequal, too distressing match.

"Oh Emmy, don't take it so hard. I need your help. That's why I've come, Em. Em! I need your help," Mr. Hardy said earnestly.

Lady Emily drew a long breath and unhappily considered her childhood friend. And sighed again. "I dare say you're in love with her," she said finally, ruefully. She was not crying, though this was surely difficult to bear.

"Yes. I am," he acknowledged.

She sighed heavily and shook her head. "You would be. It's just like you..." she exclaimed. "Though I cannot think what you expect me to do." And trying again: "You do know what she got up to last night, don't you?"

"Yes, Em, I rather think I do."

And his clear-eyed honesty concerned her even more than a show of vagueness would have done.

"And that is why I need your help," he admitted.

Thoughtfully, she regarded him. A servant came in with fresh tea and coffee and a rack of slices of warm, freshly toasted bread. Emily waited until the remains of her repast had been cleared away, the coffee and tea had been poured and the servant had left them, before saying, "I fail to see what I can do…"

Mr. Hardy paused, then said, for he had thought it all out most carefully, "If you was to put it about that it was me in the Antechamber with her all the time, do you see? And not Myddelton, me, then…"

Emily rolled her eyes in an expression of astonishment as he spoke, before protesting, "Are you mad? Have you taken complete leave of your senses? She was seen there with him. Seen!"

"Yes, I know! But it can't have been by that many people," Mr. Hardy said intently. "It can't have been! So the rest is nothing but tittle-tattle. So if you was to throw doubt on it, if you was to say you knew for certain it was me the whole time, and not Myddelton—that it made sense that it was me because after all we was now engaged, people would believe it. You know they would, Em. And the whole thing would die down to nothing, don't you see?"

"I can't," Emily declared. "I can't, Ned. It would be lying."

"Emmy, please?" he pleaded. "You know I'd do anything for you. I've always done anything you asked. You know the house is at your disposal for you and Pam, whenever you want it…Please?"

Emily sat back in her chair, her eyes stinging. It was true, he always had done anything she'd asked. And it was equally true that it was due to him, to his discretion and kindness, that no one had an inkling about her and Palmerston. She poured herself another cup of tea. She did not like Miss Georgina Wythenshaw. She had not liked her from the first. And she did not wish to save her from this well-deserved social downfall. But Ned never asked for anything in return for all his many kindnesses. Never. "You really do love her, don't you?" she asked finally.

"Yes, Emmy."

"It won't be easy, you know. Lots of people saw her. Or heard her." She exhaled, then said, "And what about Lady Myddelton? What do you intend to do about her? Because if anyone is a victim in this entire piece, it's Janey Myddelton. I thought you cared for her. And I know you care for Myddelton. So what about them? You did know that in addition to throwing herself at Myddelton, your Miss Wythenshaw started a number of rather nasty rumours about his wife, didn't you?"

Mr. Hardy was silent as he stirred sugar into his coffee. "Well," he began diffidently. "I'faith, no, I didn't know about that. And to be sure, I don't know how that's to be undone. I don't even know what she said," he admitted. "All I can say in her defence is that I truly believe that all of this is no more than...than childish folly. Her father is the coldest fish imaginable, you know. And her mother! Dear God! While I was waiting to see her father just now, I heard the mother yelling at her, and heard her slap her face." He did not stop despite the expression of distaste now on Emily's face. "And given all of that, I expect she was willing to do anything to escape her home life. Even if it meant losing her reputation. Certainly if she was under Myddelton's protection, she would have little to fear from her parents. And I believe she was telling the truth when she said last night that she threw herself at Myddelton's head because she wanted to be dashing and exciting...like Caro..." he finished quietly, well knowing that this reference to Emily's sister-in-law was a risk.

"Like Caro? Like Caro? Why would anyone want to be like Caro?" Emily exclaimed, in sudden distress. "She is the unhappiest creature alive. And I can hardly bear to see William these days..."

"I know that, Emmy," he said gently. "So will you help me?"

Lady Emily Cowper eyed her dear friend with disfavour. "Yes," she agreed. "Of course, I will. You knew that when you came here. But in return, you must go to see Lady Myddelton." She paused, thinking through her plan of campaign and how the object was to be achieved. "If she was to stand by you—not that I think she should, for those were particularly vile rumours, you know—but if Lady Myddelton was to dismiss any rumours of misconduct, if *she* was seen to stand by you and your Miss Wythenshaw, then I should think you may very well escape unscathed.

"I shall, of course, have to see Sally, and convince her not to push for the Wythenshaw's vouchers to be withdrawn. And that will not be easy, because Sally don't like her, or her mother. I shall dismiss all rumours about la Wythenshaw and Myddelton by saying it was you and not him. That, of course, has the added attraction of quashing those rumours about there being trouble between Myddelton and his dear little bride. But beyond that, it's up to you, Ned," she said seriously. "You had better ensure that your affianced bride behaves herself, because one more step over the line and she is finished…"

Mr. Hardy had, of course, begun to smile long before this moment, but now, with this final capitulation and admonition, he was positively beaming. Abruptly he rose from his chair and took hold of her hands to kiss them. "Oh Emmy. Thank you. Thank you, my dearest friend. I knew you would help me. I knew you would understand and help me."

Emily drew back and viewed him with an amused affectionate tolerance. "Oh stop it, Ned," she said as he kissed her hands again. "Ned. Stop it! What would Pam think if he saw us now?"

Still beaming his happiness, Ned sat down. "He would think how clever he is to be in love with the very best, the very kindest woman in the whole world."

And suddenly overwhelmed by the greatness of Mr. Hardy's affection for her and at the thought of her dear Pam thinking such thoughts of her, Emily leaned her cheek upon the back of her hand. "Oh Ned…Silly boy." And sometime later, after he'd gone, she poured herself a final cup of tea and returned to the unread letters on the table. "…I hope that foolish creature knows just what a fine young man she is to marry."

27

Lord Pemberton was blessed with—or suffered from, depending upon one's point of view—a plethora of aunts. And of the seven, there were two of these worthy creatures who felt it their bounden duty to keep their father fully informed as to his grandson and heir apparent's activities, behaviour and friendships. About which, by dint of their large circles of friends and acquaintances, they contrived to know a good deal. Though with varying degrees of accuracy. Naturally, chiefest of these familial pleasures was the relay of tittle-tattle and gossip—damaging or at least titillating being the preferred type—to their mother. To be sure, they insisted that their motives for so-doing were entirely altruistic, that their father might better understand the character of his heir, and provide accordingly. There were, of course, those cynical souls who suspected that the aunts' motives were less magnanimous. Indeed, their suspicions had been confirmed upon learning that young Pemberton had failed to show an appropriate interest—or any interest whatsoever—in his handsome but sow-tempered cousin, Lavinia, the marriageable offspring of one of these aunts.

It was therefore inevitable, by virtue of the ubiquitous grape-vine that was Society, that these ladies learned something of great interest—an extremely muddled version of an argument or a duel or a serious dispute between the Earl of Myddelton and Lord Choate's beloved heir. About which it was only proper that they must apprise their Mama. Over something—Myddelton's wife or his matched bays or a game of whist—though they were in agreement that it had certainly been Myddelton who had been duelling. Or was it fighting at Jackson's? The which Lady Choate had sensibly discounted, for it all appeared rather ludicrous, even by their green-eyed standards.

But she had not felt so sanguine when Lady Castlereagh, a friend of long-standing, also wrote of her concern—and her concerns were rather more personal. For Lady Myddelton was a friend of the Choate family. And Lord Myddelton was her husband's friend and a member of his staff. The disgrace of the Earl of Myddelton, and a duel, would assuredly bring a full measure of scandal, and must damage by association her dearest husband to whom she was devoted. The letter was disjointed, rather like Lady Castlereagh's conversation, and passed from one subject to another without any emphasis to indicate any degree of importance or veracity. And though Lady Choate was well-acquainted with Lady Castlereagh and knew her well enough to know precisely how light-minded she could be, such matters could not be ignored. The ignominy of an affaire, real or rumoured, between their darling Pemberton and sweet little Janey Myddelton, the niece of their closest neighbour and dearest friend, and the unpleasant consequences of a duel between the wronged husband and their grandson, these must be faced.

Initially Lady Choate confided solely in her husband, who dismissed it on first hearing, for he felt it did not ring true. However, eventually, he came to agree with her that their friend and neighbour, Sir Charles, must be apprised of the rumours. To Sir Charles, upon hearing the London gossip, it appeared too possible, and he made up his mind to pay a visit to his niece and her husband, that he might assess the situation for himself. Only then would he know how to act. And with this in mind, he set off for London early in the morning, intending to arrive at Myddelton House sometime after luncheon.

It was not early when Lady Myddelton awoke, silent and alone, to a listless despair. Beside her, breathing raggedly or softly, there was no husband and lover. In his stead on the pillow was the slim volume of German poems, that last singlemost glimmer of the promise of requited affection—*My heart, I shall return to you as soon as ever I may.* She regarded the book with an unequal mixture of yearning and despondency and wondered for how long she could endure this half-giddy, half-wretched longing, this purgatory of tenderness, ignorance, and waiting. And wondered how frequently must her fondest hopes be dashed before despair left a permanent stain upon her spirits? How often could her dreams be trampled underfoot before apathy set in? Indeed, for how long would she be a bride denied her bridal?

And still, the world awaited, the gossiping, busy-body, Paul-prying world, ready to suspect and judge her every move, her every word—spoken or unspoken. And somehow, she must endure it. Must face the loss of her good name, the suspicions about her marital status or impending lack of it, the quizzing, the speculation, the innuendo and perhaps even insolent questioning, and all without Myddelton. Myddelton, whose very presence beside her now would have dispelled the whole. And how was she to explain his absence?

And exclaimed finally and hotly: "S'life, I need a good gallop!" For if these vicissitudes had taught her anything, they had taught her to swear.

But as she, dressed for riding, descended the stairs some half an hour later to meet Curlee with Patroklos, so that she could have—not the gallop she craved—but the gentle tittup of a canter in the Park of which Society approved, she found that even this small thing was to be denied her.

"Beggin' your pardon my lady..." Curlee was standing in the front hall, his brown felt hat in hand. For all that he had put Myddelton on his first horse, *she* was a different matter and he was not looking forward to telling her where her prize stallion had got to.

"Yes?"

"I be sorry to disturb you, my lady, but the fact is, 'is lordship has taken tha' stallion o'yours wif 'im."

Jane paused. "I beg your pardon? His lordship did what?"

Curlee drew a breath. This was not going to be pretty. For all that young William was potty about her, he knew what he knew and *that* was a dangerous look in her eye. "'E took him. On account o' Macedon havin' thrown 'is rear shoe." He did not feel it appropriate to recount the whole of last evening's conversation.

She wanted to cry. But did not. Instead she drew a deep breath. "Ah...Of course." And said what she least felt: "How very wise of him..." *Oh Myddelton, where have you gone? Where has Castlereagh sent you?*

439

"In that case…I trust Macedon has been reshod?"

"Oh aye. First thing this mornin'. 'E's always tossin' that shoe, 'e is."

"Then tack him up for me," she declared.

The corners of Curlee's thin mouth twitched, and he emitted something between a cough and a chortle. "Yes, m'lady. I shall 'ave 'im round the front in five minutes."

"Thank you Curlee. I knew I could rely on you." And bestowed that perfect winning smile.

Mr. Hardy decided to take the long way from the Cowpers' to Myddelton House. Chose, in fact, to make several considerable diversions. For in his eagerness to rescue his beloved from the consequences of her passionate folly, he had not dreamt that Emily would insist he speak to Lady Myddelton. And he needed to consider how he might phrase such a difficult request as he must put to her.

Why he had been so shortsighted he could not say. Nor, were he honest, did he have an inkling of how he might even begin such a conversation. Though he believed she would understand hopeless love and the elation that he felt upon achieving that which he had dreamt of but never expected would be his. But could she, would she, forgive the distress, the unhappiness that Miss Wythenshaw had so wantonly—he wished he could think of a different word, but couldn't—brought upon her? That was a very different matter. And even were she willing to forgive, had he the right to ask such a thing? Was that not a matter solely between her and her confessor? Had he the right to ask her to forgive the young woman who had done so much to come between her and her husband? And how could she be asked to forget her dismay and distress at being made the object of poisonous gossip and malicious speculation? And would Myddelton even allow it? Would he permit her to maintain the acquaintance of one whom he had every cause to despise? Mr. Hardy did not know the answers to such questions. But he thought he could guess at Lady Myddelton's emotions this morning. And believed himself the unkindest man alive for making any such request of her. And though he saw the wisdom and foresight of Emily's demand—Lady Myddelton's continued friendship and support would indeed cast doubt on rumours of the identity of Miss Wythenshaw's paramour—he was convinced that this was asking too much and must mean the end of his friendship with Myddelton and Lady Myddelton. And that was very hard. For like Emily and Pam, he had known Myddelton since childhood.

Kettering asked him to wait in the Morning room. And as Lady Myddelton, unrefreshed from her ride, entered the room and he saw her in the unflattering light of late morning—sombre, as if she dwelt under some undefined pall—Mr. Hardy knew he should not have come. Knew he should never have intruded upon her.

"Lady Myddelton," he bowed. And found himself saying for the second time that day: "Forgive me. I should not have come." And would have made his bow to her at the door and departed.

"Mr. Hardy." Though she knew she appeared wan, unhappy even, still she was pleased he had come. He was always a delightful companion. And undemanding. "Stay. Do stay." She closed the door behind her. "What can it be?" And coming farther into the room and seating herself, said warmly and kindly, "Will you not sit?"

"No. No, thank you."

Quietly: "Myddelton is not here, you know. He has gone north, about a horse, I believe…" There she had said it. Had told the lie she dreaded, her first lie.

Thrown for a moment, Mr. Hardy smiled. "Oh! Oh yes, of course. I didn't know he'd gone off. But you know, he did that very thing three years ago when he was after those matched bays. Heard on the grapevine that they was for sale and was away on the instant to make his offer before they ever reached Tatt's."

Jane blinked. Were all deceptions this easy? And smiled faintly as if in assent.

Then, remembering the cause of this visit, Mr. Hardy stopped, drew himself up, and said in quite a different tone: "Ma'am. Lady Myddelton…I hope you will forgive the impertinence of my request, but I assure you I should never have come if I was not convinced that…that this favour, should you find it in your heart to grant it, will also be of

441

great benefit to you." Mr. Hardy paused to choose his next words.

Jane waited, curious, but with a certain misgiving or apprehension even—for this was very unlike Mr. Hardy.

Faltering, Mr. Hardy began again. "This morning, I paid my addresses to a young lady and had the good fortune to be accepted."

"Oh Mr. Hardy, I am so pleased for you." Even in her fatigue and sadness, this was happy news, and not at all what she had been led to expect, what she had feared—though she could not have said precisely what that was. "Please, do accept my wishes for your greatest happiness. But you must tell me, who is the young lady who has such great fortune as to be loved by you?"

He could hardly bear to face her. "Miss Wythenshaw."

Her smiles ceased. It was as if her stomach had dropped into her shoes. "I see." She averted her gaze from Mr. Hardy's earnest face—was it never to stop, this torture? Was there nowhere, even in her own house, where she might be free from this tormenting?

"I know what you must be thinking, Ma'am," Mr. Hardy burst out. "Indeed I do. You are thinking that I am the cruelest man of your acquaintance. And I confess, I think it too. But I swear to you, I should never have come had not Emily insisted that I do so. You must believe me, I would never have subjected you to such pain had she not insisted that it was the only way."

Jane was not crying, though her eyes were filled with tears. She would have preferred to have been in private. With Lotto or her cat—they neither of them gossiped or told tales. Her headache was returning and she felt ill. Dully, understanding little, she asked, "What is the only way, Mr. Hardy? Why should Lady Emily insist upon such a course?"

Mr. Hardy could look upon such unhappiness no longer. He turned and went to stand by a curio table, and only once he was looking away from her, upon the books and seashells and old miniatures on the table, did he say, "Last night, at the Castlereaghs' ball, Miss Wythenshaw caused…quite a scandal. I do not know the whole of it, but Emily told me that Miss Wythenshaw began a number of unsavoury rumours—about you, and your relations with Myddelton—all of which are a complete nonsense. Anyone can see that," he said dismissingly which, even in her distress, Jane found vaguely comforting. He heaved a sigh: "But it cannot have been pleasant for you. And later, later, I know she threw herself at him. And a number of people saw her do so." He hesitated. He found this recitation of events worse with each passing moment. And wished he might stop, but knew his only hope was in honesty. "When he rejected her overtures, she fell all to pieces. And that is how I found her. And it was sometime later that I took her home, but of course, the damage was already done."

As she had been listening, Lady Myddelton had been covering her face in her hands, but now she looked up. "No, it does not take long, does it?"

Mr. Hardy risked a glance at her and saw that she was crying. Silently. As if she were not aware of the tears running over her cheeks.

And coming to stand before her, he began again: "The thing is, Lady Myddelton...the thing is I have always loved her, you see. From the first time I saw her. Even though she never paid me the slightest heed or gave me any encouragement or any reason to hope. Until last night...last night when she'd been thoroughly rebuffed by the person she'd been single-mindedly pursuing all Season. And if I took advantage of her distress...well, that was wrong of me, but I cannot regret the outcome. Not for a moment." He swallowed. And determined to carry on. "The reason I am here though, as distressing as it must be to you, is to ask you not to cut her. Or me, now that she is my betrothed."

"I beg your pardon?" she whispered. Truly this was too much to ask, too much for her to bear, even though he loved his Miss Wythenshaw as he so patently did.

"Please, Lady Myddelton, please hear me out. It's just that...Emily said that was you, the injured party in this whole affair, was you seen to stand by her, then..."

"I should be very stupid indeed!" Abruptly she rose, but could not gain control of the unruly tears.

"No!" Mr. Hardy exclaimed. "No! Do you not see? I've said it was me in the antechamber with her. Me. Not Myddelton at all. I've said it was me she was embracing. Me she was with. Because it is true. But if you stand by us, then people will believe it. They'll be bound to, don't you see? Because we're engaged now. They'll fancy it was just the prelude to our becoming engaged…"

"Or that I am no better than Georgiana Devonshire, sharing my husband with Miss Wythenshaw, the way she shared Devonshire with Bess Foster!" she said tightly, with a hardness she did not recognise and did not like in herself.

"No!" Mr. Hardy protested, repulsed. "No one would ever think that." He blinked. Christ, this was awful! "For one thing, Myddelton's nothing like Devonshire was. Nothing. Devonshire was a…He was just a rum…Oh! 'Struth, it don't matter." He was silent for a long moment. This was hopeless. He should not, should never, have come. To have caused such anguish to one he held in the highest esteem. And she the wife of one even dearer than that…And to have persevered with this madness when she was awash with tears. S'life, what had come over him? Now appalled and deeply mortified by his own behaviour, Mr. Hardy stopped and bowed stiffly. "I am so deeply sorry, ma'am, I should not have troubled you…I accept that our friendship must now be at an end. Please accept my sincerest apologies for the grief…"

Ignoring him now, she had gone to the window and was staring at the windowsill, the pristine paint work of which she gently rubbed with one fingertip. She stood so still, except for the slight movement of her finger, that she appeared to have forgotten her visitor altogether. For in her head, she could hear her uncle saying in his mild way, 'Judge not that ye be not judged. Wasn't that the subject of the sermon a few weeks past?' She had been fourteen years old, an intelligent child, and prone to criticise. 'Perhaps,' her uncle had continued, filling the bowl of his pipe with tobacco. 'Perhaps Miss Ingram walks that way because she is ill or in pain.' There had been no rebuke in his speech, just a willingness to consider all things from another point of view. When Miss Ingram had died of a tumour on her leg some six months later, the effect upon Jane had been profound. How had he known, she had demanded? He hadn't, he said, but he did think that if one professed Christianity, one should make some effort to abide by its rules, that was all.

Mr. Hardy, always sensitive to any change in atmosphere or tension, felt he could bear the growing awkwardness, her terrible distress, no longer. "I shall take my leave now, ma'am. Please forget all that I have said and I pray that in time you can forgive me." He bowed to her back.

"No, wait!" Breathless, she spun to face him, holding her hands together at her breast. She should hate Miss Wythenshaw; she did hate Miss Wythenshaw. Loathed her—that manipulative and craven girl who had tried to steal and seduce Myddelton. The same Miss Wythenshaw who she now knew had—for whatever reason—begun the rumours and slanders which she had overheard in the ladies' withdrawing room, the slanders and lies which she knew from her ride in the Park were still fresh on everyone's tongue. And yet, Mr. Hardy—dear, kind, sweet-tempered Mr. Hardy—appeared to love this girl with all his being. Even as she loved Myddelton and wanted to be loved by him…And Christ had not stoned the woman caught in the act of adultery, had he? In the very act. But 'Thou shalt not bear false witness' was every bit as much one of the Ten Commandments as 'Thou shalt not commit adultery.' Though very few people opening their mouths in gossip consider it sin. Yet Christ had forgiven Peter his betrayal. So…so that was what she must essay to do, even though her very soul cried out against it. If she could have pressed herself against the wall, weeping, and so slipped unnoticed to the floor, she would have done. *Myddelton, where are you?*

"I…" She caught at the back of a chair, gripping it until her knuckles were white. "I…" She bit at her lip, forcing the words to come, the words that she must speak. "I do not know, Mr. Hardy, that I can stand your friend…But you have ever been very kind to me." She drew a deep breath; it did not steady her. "Therefore, I shall…I shall not…cut…either you, or her." There she had said it. Had spoken those hardest, those most heart-wrenching words, and her chest felt hollow in their wake. She bowed her head, to add softly, "You may have my word on it."

Then, beginning again: "I…" She faltered. "I cannot speak for Myddelton." Bleakly, wretchedly, she looked at him. It was the best she could do. It was so much less than the greatness her uncle expected of her. But it was all she could offer. And failing her dear uncle she now realised was perhaps the very worst, the most heart-crushing thing in all of this. And she did not know that she could bear it.

Mr. Hardy came to her, a brilliant smile of such gratitude lighting his face. "Thank you, ma'am, oh thank you so very much. You are all that is truly good." He reached for her hand to kiss it. "Thank you." He raised his head, earnest and no longer smiling. "I must go, and tell Emily and Miss Wythenshaw." He bowed and hurried from the room.

Bereft and silent, she sank into a chair to cover her face with her hands. "Oh Uncle..." she said aloud and to no one. "Oh Uncle...why did you send me here? Myddelton! Where are you?" she cried.

And in the kitchen below, the servants heard that my lady was weeping again.

❧

Lady Myddelton, finding that her chessboard offered little solace or diversion—for the white king so consistently swept all before him now and the black king mounted so little in the way of effective opposition to his ascendancy—went into the library, Myddelton's sanctuary, to read and to await Pemberton. And to wonder how much of last night's debacle she should reveal. For Pemberton had said he would call.

"Od's my life, what has you looking so blue-devilled?" he asked, masking his concern with flippancy as he ambled, unannounced, into the library, dropped a fraternal kiss onto her hair, and slouched into a wing chair.

"Oh, hallo" she exclaimed, looking up. "I did not expect you for another half hour," she observed, glancing at the mantel clock. And frowned. "And I do not look blue-devilled."

"Oh no, not a bit," Pemberton agreed dutifully—mendaciously to his mind. After a moment, he yawned and rose from the chair to wander over to where she sat upon Myddelton's sofa. "What are you reading in *La Belle Assemblée* that has you so engrossed? *Hymenæa in Search of a Husband?*" He peered over her shoulder. "Or is it *Zara; or the Adventures of an English Wife?*"

She slapped the magazine down onto the seat beside her. "No, addlepate. I have been reading about John Galt's travels in Sardinia, if you must know."

Pemberton grinned and returned to the wing chair. "Of course.

Nothing but edifying reading for the niece of Sir Charles Heron, classical scholar and magistrate," he teased.

Which at least made her chuckle. "Oh be quiet!"

Pemberton turned his attention to the draperies. "She laughed," he pronounced, addressing them. "Can you credit it? She really and truly laughed. Admittedly, not very loud nor for very long, but I heard her, and so did you."

She sobered. The anguish was too fresh for his silliness or further laughter.

"Angel, what is it? What is this all about?" Having coaxed that smile from her, his solicitude was unfeigned.

She sighed and shook her head. Where to begin—for such a convoluted tale as this made, where on earth should she start? And thinking, she rubbed Lotto's ear.

"Come along, tell Uncle Pem everything..." he pressed.

"Uncle Pem..." she chortled. "I'll 'Uncle Pem' you."

Then, as she hesitated, trying to find the right words or the right place to start, she said, "I don't suppose you have spoken to Mr. Hardy today, have you?"

"No. Can't say that I have. Why? What's he done now? No, don't tell me. Gone and bought another violin. I tell you, Dunphail's going to murder him some night."

Slowly she shook her head. "No. Nothing so uncomplicated...Lud, I don't even know where to start," she admitted, quelling the tell-tale quiver that was beginning again in her jaw and lower lip.

Pemberton eyed her with some misgiving. "I don't like this. What?"

She exhaled. "Mr. Hardy...has asked Georgina Wythenshaw to marry him."

"What?" he exclaimed, doubting his hearing, for this was both improbable and preposterous. Hardy loathed that chit—he would have sworn to that.

"And she has accepted him."

"What?" he screeched. "You're bamming me!"

"I'm not," she declared with a calm that stopped him short.

"Od's life, I don't believe this." He was on his feet and striding toward the mantel. "Has he taken leave of his senses? Gone completely starkers? What possessed him?" he demanded, rounding on her. "He's going to regret it—she's a devil's daughter, that girl. You mark my words."

"I don't think so, Pem," she said slowly. "He said he has always loved her."

"He told you that? Hardy told you that? Oh my life! When did all this happen?"

"This morning, I think." She drew a deep breath. "But perhaps I had better begin with last night." She bit her lip, and smoothed the fur on Lotto's head, and said with more hurt than she would have wished to reveal: "Pem, who is Ianthe Dacre?"

Had she searched for weeks for a question to rattle his equanimity, she could not have surpassed this, and this on top of the previous unforeseen corker. "What? Who the devil mentioned her to you?" Pemberton thundered. More shocked than he cared to admit, he turned from her and resting his elbow against the mantel, closed his eyes to hold his forehead against the heel of his hand. "I do not believe this. 'Struth, it's a plagued nightmare."

She shook her head to clear it. "No. Pem...Pem, I'm sorry. I'm sorry. Let me start again..." Gazing up at the ceiling in a futile attempt to compose herself, she began: "...Last night...last night, do you remember when I went upstairs to have the clip refixed in my hair?"

He turned and subjected her to a penetrating look. "Yes. I escorted you. Because Myddelton needed to see Castlereagh. Go on..."

The hardness of that intelligence which he generally sought to conceal calmed her. "Yes. Well..." She swallowed. "While the maid was attending to my hair, two other ladies came in—one, very large and older, and the other, her daughter, whom she called Dorothy or... Dee Dee..."

"Yes?" And suddenly, intuitively Pemberton believed he had a knacky idea where this might be leading. And did not like it. Disliked it intensely in fact. For he was acquainted with the females in question and knew their mode of conversation was likely to be gossip of the less than innocent variety.

"Well, they were exchanging gossip…"

"'Struth, I'm quite sure they were…"

"Rather loudly…"

"That too goes without saying…"

Suddenly, she frowned. "Pem, do you mean to tell me you know them?"

"The daughter—Dee Dee you said her name was—is I rather think a bosom friend of my Aunt Gateley," he admitted, and exhaled. "Go on…tell me…what was they saying?"

"Well, at first it was just the usual, you know. All those tedious on-dits about Byron and Caro Lamb. And the Prince Regent…They talked about him too. Endlessly. But it was all so tiresome and hyperbolic and I wasn't really paying attention or listening…But then they started talking about someone who had married beneath him. For money they said it was. And how *she* was perfectly vile. And how at last he had determined to gain an annulment, because he had not been able to bear the thought of…" She paused, needing to arrange her thoughts, to order them, to choose the most delicate and least offensive words. "…the thought of…bedding her." Still the admission made her feel sick with unhappiness. "And after the marriage had been dissolved he was going to marry Georgina Wythenshaw. With whom, apparently—according to the daughter—he had been 'intimate' for some time."

Pemberton who had been trying, but understandably failing, to follow the logic in her recitation, said warily: "Are we meant to be talking about Hardy here?"

"No." She shook her head. "I only wish we were."

"Then I confess, I am totally lost."

"Myddelton. The gentleman about whom they were speaking was Myddelton."

"What?" This on top of all the rest was too too much. "What? Myddelton?" Pemberton seemed dazed. "I need to sit down." And did so. And tried to work through the order of events again. "Now, let me understand this: According to these pathetically idiotish females, Myddelton married you for your money, but he finds you perfectly repulsive and can't bear to be in your company…Have I got this right?"

He paused. "Are they blind? He can hardly bear to be out of your company!"

He saw the haunted look come into her eyes and did not like it. She bit her lip. Hard. And maintained her equanimity. Then: "According to the daughter, all of that is...merely the show of a seasoned seducer and philanderer..." She found it nearly impossible to speak those words. "To throw me—and everyone—off the scent of his true intentions..." She tried to keep her voice steady. "Which is when they brought up Ianthe Dacre..."

Pemberton, hearing the break in her voice, gave her an intent look. And seeing the incipient tears, came and sat beside her, placing his arm about her shoulders. He shook his head. "That's a load of crock!" He sighed and leaned his head against her hair. "Oh Angel..." And though he knew he ought never to mention this, for this was so indiscreet as to be unforgivable, for a gentleman must never mention such topics to a lady, he said softly, truthfully, "Janey, his affaire with Ianthe is ancient history." (For surely it is better to be indiscreet and kind than correct and cruel—especially when that indiscretion may assuage another's misery.) "He broke with her ages ago." Then, bluntly: "Actually, she ran off. With a Frenchie, of all things...But you know, he had lost interest long before that, so I suspect he was relieved that she made it easy for him...As for him having any interest in marrying the Wythenshaw, I know for a fact he hadn't. And I know that, because he told me so not a week before he went up to Britwell Park and married you."

She looked up at him. Her vulnerability, her trust was a sting to him. "Truly?"

"My life on it," he said. But after a moment, he looked at her and saw the still clouded expression in her eyes. "But there's more, isn't there? Of course there is. Come on then, out with it."

She sighed deeply. "Well, as you will imagine, I was rather...overset...by what I had heard, so I left and went in search of Myddelton. Which is when I saw him with Miss Wythenshaw."

"Yes, I know that part...I still can't credit that she was that brazen." And kept his further reflections to himself.

She ignored his aside, drew breath and tried to marshal her thoughts to complete the story, only it wasn't as easy as all that. "Well, shortly after I saw them, Myddelton pushed her away and rejected her…"

"Yes, that's what Myddelton said."

"Well it was after that that Mr. Hardy found her—devastated, I believe he said—and saw his chance at last and took it. And went round there this morning to propose, and was accepted."

"I can't credit that part of it neither, you know. Upon my word, he's never given any indication of a preference for her…"

"No," she disagreed. "No. You are wrong, Pem. He has." She paused to ponder, then said with a passionate empathy which would have surprised many—though not Pemberton who knew her. "And I think it must have been terrible for him all those months, being so hopelessly in love with her, and watching as she pursued one of his dearest friends. It must have been awful for him, don't you think?" She looked up at him. "And then finally, suddenly, totally unexpectedly, he had his chance. And he took it."

Pemberton remained unmoved. "I still say he'll regret it."

"Perhaps," she agreed.

But now, wisely, pursuing another line of thought, Pemberton said, "But I still don't understand why he came here. 'Struth, I should have thought you would be the last person he'd be telling. Not the first." And he felt her flinch and tighten within the circle of his arm.

"He came here…he came here to ask me—and Myddelton too, I dare say, only of course he's not here—not to cut either of them. Not Miss Wythenshaw, nor him now that he's engaged to her."

He turned to look her fully in the face. "What?"

It was bitter hurt he saw there. And the tears had returned. "Emily advised him to."

"Emily? Emily Cowper? What in Heaven's name was she thinking?"

"According to Mr. Hardy, she believes that were I to stand their friend, it would cast doubt on both the identity of the gentleman Miss Wythenshaw was seen embracing and discount the truth of those rumours which she started."

He took her hand and gazed earnestly into her face, her sweet angelic face, full of fears and her eyes, full of unshed tears. "Janey…

Janey, are you telling me that it was the Wythenshaw who started those rumours—that whole pack of lies?"

Wordless, she could only nod.

"And knowing that, and that...that she had thrown herself at Myddelton, begged him to run off with her to some love nest, of all things...knowing what this must have done to you...how this must have hurt you, Hardy came here to ask you not to cut her? Them?" He shook his head in astonishment and utter disbelief, for it seemed as if all he had known of his friend had been proved wrong, and all courtesy or kindness had been abandoned. "I do not believe this!" And finally: "I hope you showed him the door."

She shook her head. "No."

"You certainly did not agree to it?"

She nodded.

"Sweet Christ, Janey..."

"No, Pem, don't you see? Emily is right. I wish with all my heart it were not so, but she is right. She is! If I give them the cut direct then the whole world will know that I have an injury. If I do not, then Mr. Hardy's story that it was he in the antechamber with Miss Wythenshaw, not Myddelton, may stand some chance of being believed. And those rumours, those horrible, vicious rumours will die for lack of evidence. If Myddelton had not gone away, it all might be different. But he is gone, and I must do what I can...No matter how much I wish I did not have to..."

"Janey, this is madness!" he pronounced, standing up to look down upon her. "That wretched female—she is a piece!" he pronounced, abandoning in his fury the polite niceties. "And she has been nothing but..."

"Pem, I know. I know. I know all too well. Believe me. But please don't make it worse. Please," she begged. "The things those women were saying were both wildly inaccurate...and frighteningly close to the truth. And if Myddelton were here..." *If Myddelton were here, I would be kissing him or being kissed by him and none of this would be necessary or even happening. My wedding night would be accomplished, I would be his wife and I would be in his arms and...* She blinked and the tears receded. "But since he is not, I must do what I can to prove that there was no injury. That all is well and has always been well between us. Even though both you and I know it has not been so. And if I am to do it, I shall need you to stand by me and help me..."

He caught at the hand she extended to him—to touch his sleeve—and held it firmly. "Angel, of course I shall help you. You know I shall do everything that is in my..."

A knock on the door caused him to stop. Kettering entered and bowed. "Sir Charles Heron, my lady."

Still close beside Pemberton, she rose from the sofa. "Uncle?" she exclaimed, but softly. And again in amazement: "Uncle? Can it really be you?" she asked, hurrying toward the door in astonishment and delight.

Sir Charles came to her. "Janey! Dearest girl." And was instantly hugging her to him, kissing the top of her head, her forehead, her cheeks. "Oh my dear girl, let me look at you." He hugged her again and lay his cheek against her hair, then held her away and his eyes kindled with paternal pride. "You have grown very fine, my Angel. I should not have recognised you." And with his arm still about her, said affably, "And young Pem. How do you do?"

The winds which sweep through the Solent and into the English Channel from the west have never been known for their zephyr-like gentleness. Quite the opposite—as sailors through the centuries might attest, including the unfortunates who manned the floating fortresses of the Spanish Armada. Indeed, such is the ferocity and delinquency of those winds and currents that even seasoned mariners know to go warily in the waters of the English Channel when the wind is from the west. Which is most of the time—or whenever the gales aren't sweeping down from the east or from off the North Sea.

A poor sailor at the best of times, Myddelton drew a deep breath and swilled down the last of the ale in his mug. 'Struth, if only he were not so infernally exhausted—to the point of dizziness. And, after riding all that way from London, he felt that all the sand, grit and chalk dust in England had settled in his throat and lungs and would never be washed clear. The boat lurched, jerking him back against the doubtful solace of a feather bolster in the captain's bunk. He clamped his teeth together against the threat of sea-sickness. And thought morosely on Jane, left at home and solitary. Which made his heart and mind and groin all ache with a fierce longing—an unwelcome companion to the dizziness.

Riding a wave and slamming down against the surface of the water, the boat pitched violently. Myddelton tumbled against the side of the berth and swallowed hard against the rising nausea. Everything had gone according to Castlereagh's word. Lieutenant Fiske had been awaiting him at Newhaven and had welcomed him aboard the Revenue Cutter. When the tide had turned, they had upped anchor and sailed for the dubious delights of open water.

When he had boarded, Myddelton assured himself that his sea-legs would come into their own. They must. But that was before they hit rough weather—or the winds in the Channel. Now, the combination and concentration of the Cutter's acrid odours (so infinitely worse than London even in high summer)—tar, salt water, decaying fish, and urine—together with the endless lurching as the boat bobbled over the choppy seas of the Channel made Myddelton wonder how long it would be before he was heaving his guts out over the side—no doubt to the unalloyed amusement of the crew.

He tried to pour more ale into the mug—if he could only drink himself legless—but, unable to focus, spilled as much as he poured. The boat lurched to the left and half the ale sloshed over of the side of the mug. Drawing deep breaths, he tried to steady himself: All he had to do was survive this week. He would be back in England, on dry land, by Friday. And Janey, bless her, would be waiting for him.

The Cutter rose as it mounted a white cap, then came down with a crash. Myddelton was flung off the bunk, landing with a thud on the floor of the cabin.

"Od's death!" He grabbed hold of the side of the bunk and heaved himself back onto the mattress. Victorious at last, waves of an implacable nausea engulfed him. Frantically he looked about for a basin. It was across the neat panelled cabin. He hauled himself off the bunk, and dove toward the large copper basin, staggering as the boat pitched this way and that. And reached it just in time. He retched. Violently. Relentlessly. Repeatedly. While sweat poured down his forehead and soaked his chest and back and legs.

Eventually, at last, his knees buckling and uncertain, his stomach settling—if only temporarily—Myddelton managed to stand upright. His head spun. 'Sdeath, this was worse than a hangover. Infinitely worse. His head pounded, the muscles in his chest and back ached as though he'd been beaten, and his stomach jumped and flinched with every movement of the boat. But grimly, weakly, cautiously, he made his way back to the bunk, hanging on to the rope along the cabin's wall as he went. Gingerly, he lowered himself onto the mattress and wiped the sweat from his forehead with his sleeve. And forced himself to think about breathing—gently, in, and out. In. And out. In. And out... Closed his eyes against the motion of the boat. And passed out.

28

Sir Charles Heron stood at the bedroom window, his hands clasped behind his back. And stood. And looked out upon the groat-sized patch of grass that was surrounded on four sides by brick and stone, pedimented and porticoed townhouses—the architectural jewel known to the world as St. James's Square—and stood. Already, at that hour of the morning, it was busy with tradesmen, curricles and carriages, horsemen, and footmen on errands, and no peace. And all of it, people and buildings and trees, all obscured by fog. The perpetual fog that London folk called fresh air. Disgruntled, he turned away.

And looked about his room, the drab painted wainscot, the papered walls, the chintz and lace-hung bed—a comfortable and pleasant bedchamber—but thought it little better. For Sir Charles found himself in the unpleasant position of being at a loss. Neither did he know how he came there. Nor precisely what he might do to right himself.

He went to empty his pipe into the grate, then returned to look upon the Square again. Two days ago, he had been certain that this visit to London to see Jane—this would clarify the awkward situation, would dictate what should be done in the face of the unwholesome allegations which Lady Choate had related to him. Well, that was a nonsense, wasn't it? For now, having seen his niece, Sir Charles knew less than before.

He sighed heavily. And meticulously filled his pipe and lit it.

There were so many questions, unanswered and indelicate even, which now nagged at him and yet must, it seemed, remain unvoiced. But as he had stood for that instant in the doorway to the Library—a fine room, he could not help but notice—observing as she stood hand in hand with young Pemberton, his first impression had been that his dear girl was looking tired. Which was unusual. It was not that he did not like what he saw—for what was there not to like or admire in her? No, it was more that he did not know what he saw, and it troubled him. Nor had he in the intervening hours between evening and midnight and morning come any closer to identifying it, though it had fretted at him, and kept him from sleep. Certainly he had detected no awkwardness between her and Pemberton, no hint of anything illicit. They seemed to him as they always had done—childhood friends and playmates, now grown. And while the delight and real pleasure—the laughter and smiles and tears—with which she had greeted him were unfeigned, his joy at seeing her had been tempered by the unhappy knowledge of the reason behind his visit.

But...but, gradually, over the course of the evening, Sir Charles had come to believe that something was indeed amiss. Though it obviously had nothing to do with young Pemberton. Still, he found its presence in so many little things: There was the small matter of Myddelton's absence. The which Janey had explained away so blithely, so charmingly. But as she had done so, an expression came over her features which he had never previously seen, only to be tucked away out of sight and replaced by the merest hint of bleakness. Or could it have been grief? Which was odder still. And searching her face—that dear face he'd looked upon since her infancy, learning its moods, observing her triumphs, perceiving her sentiments in the shadows that did or did not pass upon it—Sir Charles believed he saw a reticence or distrust or even fear (carefully, quickly concealed) that had never been there before. Though that made no sense to him...For what had she to grieve over? Could it have had to do with the assassination and his part in that terrible episode? Perhaps. But no. Sir Charles dismissed that thought the instant it occurred. But what other cause might there be?

It was in the music she played too—this indefinable, indefinite malaise. Gone were the contented, perfectly balanced certainties of her Haydn sonatas. And in their place...in their place was music he did not recognise—driven, compelling, bereft and unsatisfied, demanding answers with a melancholy passion, a rage even, which he found hard to associate with her. For he had never considered her a *passionate* child. Yet after listening to her practice—for her music filled the house—he felt uncomfortably that his perception of her may have been wrong.

And disquieted or harried by all that he had seen but could not identify, unable to dispel this perplexity, Sir Charles decided to take himself off to White's at the earliest opportunity, directly after breakfast and before his niece had come downstairs, with the intention of meeting up with whichever of his old acquaintances and friends were about. To take his mind off things. Or at least, that's what he told himself he was going there for. Had he been entirely truthful, he would also have admitted that he was going to his club (and Myddelton's), in the hope of encountering information. Any information at all that would throw some light onto the conundrum now confronting him.

However, the first person of his acquaintance with whom he met was the ancient General—James's mentor. And any hope of ducking aside or not being recognised was dispelled by the General's robust exclamation, "Well damn my eyes, if it ain't young Charlie Heron! Heh heh!" And he clapped him hard on the back. And coughed. "Damme, it's good to see you, lad. Good to see you. Been too long, been far too long, my boy. Step inside, step inside, we'll have a bottle to celebrate…"

Sir Charles, unlike his nephew-in-law, was more than able to follow the tortuous diversions of the General's discourse, though it was punctuated by the odd rheumy coughing fit and occasional references to his gouty foot. He knew the campaign where the General had first met and been impressed by James had occurred in India. He knew James' fellow officers by name; he knew the regimental highlights of the story, the skirmishes fought, the wounds and losses incurred, the battles and fortunes won there. However, he was not accustomed to drinking three bottles of claret directly after breakfast. Nor did brandy at that time of day suit him any better. And he thought, 'Why on earth am I sitting here listening to this…I could not be less interested…' and wondered how he might extract himself from the old man's tedious and wheezy perorations. And finally, he became first wary and then most definitively lost when the General started rambling about someone or other's Parliamentary duties. Sir Charles tried, in vain, to ascertain whose. But whoever had carried out these duties—whatever they were—of this person, the General was most assuredly in favour, and he related with inexplicable relish how he had told this someone, to whom he referred as 'the young scamp,' to 'Go to!' and 'Go to her, lad!' Which completely baffled Sir Charles as it made no sense at all. Unless Parliament was another name for some bawdy house or other these days. Nor, despite his patient questioning, could he guess at the identity of the recipient of these ribald admonitions.

At long last, he was able to escape from the General and his bewildering tales by pleading a luncheon engagement, for it was now gone one and Sir Charles was more than a little hungry. He fled to the Coffeeroom and found a quiet table in the corner, his interest in obtaining information about Myddelton long since quashed. And was grateful to find that the roast beef was neither tough nor undercooked and that the potatoes were nicely roasted too. And pointedly, studiously, kept his attention riveted to his plate. For he could not be sure that the General had not followed him, nor that some other senior member of the club whom he had known in days past would not light upon him as a new and receptive audience for his outworn and incomprehensible stories. And he was quite certain he could not bear an afternoon like the morning.

But it was pleasant to sit in the Coffeeroom, satisfied by a well-cooked meal and a last morsel of cheese. Though, of course, it was very different now than in the old days. It had been refurbished and repainted since then, since he'd last enjoyed a meal within these walls. For the last time he had sat here had been...had been with James. Which would have made it February 1799. Just before James had gone off to join the Austrians. Before he'd gone off to Italy, never to return. James, his fine, brilliant, beautiful younger brother.

'I say Dunphail...' A largish gentleman, a very pink of fashion, exclaimed as he greeted a gentleman at the near table. "Bit of a turn-up for the books, ain't it? Your cousin Hardy an' the Wythenshaw chit."

Sir Charles regarded them both with idle curiosity. The gentleman called Dunphail appeared severely hung-over.

Dunphail snorted. "It's none of my business who Ned chooses to marry, Alvanley." Definitely hung-over and stale drunk. "I don't give a tinker's damn."

Alvanley sat down. "Well it came as a complete surprise to me, dear boy, because I rather thought she was determined to have Myddelton,"

459

he said silkily.

Sir Charles sat up as though stung. And kept his attention firmly fixed upon his wineglass.

"What?" Dunphail, though hung-over and with a headache to match the size of the national debt, straightened. "What makes you say that? Myddelton's well and truly spliced. And Ned's been love-sick over her since the moment he clapped eyes on her. Believe me, I've had to listen to him," Dunphail finished, and stared dolefully into his tankard of ale.

Alvanley paused for a moment to assess, then said carefully, "Oh, I don't doubt you, Dunphail. But I heard she was in that antechamber with Myddelton, not Ned, you know…"

Dunphail squinted at Alvanley as though the light hurt his eyes or talking hurt his head—which it did, on both counts. "What antechamber? You don't mean that one at Castlereagh's, do you? Christ, I assure you, 'twas Ned. In there having an almighty snug with her, if the swelling of his tackle box is anything to go by…" S'life, his head hurt.

"What? Oh, ha! Oh yes, I see!" Alvanley burst out, then laughed. "Of course. Never mind…His tackle box…Ha ha…I'd heard she'd come out with her hair lookin' all no-how…But I say, fancy Ned gettin' up to it at the Castlereaghs', ha ha…But the thing is, you know, there were those rumours about the two of 'em an' then Myddelton left Town so suddenly, you know…"

"Aye, Pem told me he'd gone off…" admitted Dunphail, heartily bored by the whole conversation and thinking longingly of his bed. At home. Without the company of anyone in it. He waved a dismissive hand. "A horse. He heard about some horse he wishes to breed. You know what he's like…"

Suddenly alarmed and suspicious, Alvanley glanced about and lowered his voice significantly, "Not plannin' to challenge my team of chestnuts, is he?"

But Dunphail had had enough. "Alvanley, how should I know? I ain't been home in two days. And I hardly think that if Myddelton is plannin' to breed some youngsters to challenge your chestnuts…well, who the devil cares…by the time they're old enough to pose a challenge, your team will be well out to grass, won't they?"

"What? Oh! Oh, yes, I see what you mean…"

And Sir Charles had had enough too. What rumours? Were they the same as had been suggested to Lady Choate? And who was this—what was the name—Wythenshaw? 'Struth, was it worse than he had imagined? Was such a thing possible? Needing to digest, to ponder, to consider, he rose and, unnoticed, slipped from the Coffeeroom.

Cautiously, Myddelton, aching and stiff, but awake and able to stand, and to walk, had washed, had been shaved and had climbed the ladder to the main deck. And standing, keeping hold onto whatever was stationary and closest to hand, breathing the cool fresh air so different from the close and sour atmosphere below, had looked about him—first at the large square sails, then up the height of the Cutter's masts, and then at the guns. Very much at the guns. And finally at the water. Briefly. All around.

It was calmer today, and had he not been feeling as though he'd just endured the worst hangover since he and Pemberton had discovered the joys of Daffy's Club and Blue Ruin, he might have found pleasure in the experience. But as it was, he closed his eyes and thought on Jane. And how he would be back in London in another day and a half, all being well. And how he wanted nothing more than to hold her to him and hold her and feel the soft brush of her hair against his cheek. At least in the first moments…

"Good day to you, milord," said Lieutenant Fiske, coming to stand beside him. He was a tall man, with a narrow tanned face, a high smooth brow and an aquiline nose. "D'ye see just ahead there? That's St. Peter Port. Is that not a fine sight?" he asked with a nod, and handed Myddelton his spyglass.

Myddelton had not noticed the island. His attention had been focused on other things—like the simple tasks of staying upright, walking, breathing, not heaving. And now seeing, he closed his eyes briefly to savour the thought of its two chiefest, in his estimation, virtues: It was dry land; and his arrival there would mark the end of this mad foray into the realm of espionage—for there he would hand over the crucial papers and begin the voyage home. With rejoicing. He had managed to survive this far. Just. And surely the return journey would be kinder—Christ knew, it could hardly be worse. And finding solace in that, he peered through the glass. And thought instantly that it looked like so many other of the small ports which littered the coast of the mainland—a jumble of lime-washed houses hugging a hillside with lines of laundry flapping, billowing or taut in the breeze, while overlooking the harbour was a prominent and recently built grey stone fortress to protect it against French invasion. All of it dirty, smelly, full of sailors and fishwives. And all under the bright harsh light of the late May sun which shimmered, refracted and dazzled on the breaking, splintering, frothing surface of the water. And felt a swift intense returning nausea. Steady, m'lad, don't think about water...

Still, he did not return below deck as they came into port. But remained above, his intelligence if not his viscera engaged by the business of sailing and life at sea.

Debarkation was less troublesome, though not without its fraught moments. Unlike the Lieutenant, Myddelton did not climb down the ladder and step into the dinghy as if he were born to it—for he was not. But Jenkins, in his striped jersey and with an easy toothless grin, guided his steps down the ladder and into the rowboat. It tipped and juddered. Precariously, Myddelton thought. Dangerously. He clutched onto the last rung of the ladder and hoped that no one noticed how his jaw was clenched.

"Tha's fine now, my lord. Just you sit yourself down now, an' the boat'll not rock so. Tha's right. Easy does it. Tha's right..." Jenkins encouraged as, reluctantly, Myddelton released his hold on the Cutter's ladder and eased himself down onto the seat.

"Tha' be fine. I'll have both yourself an' the Cap'n to dry land in no time, jus' you think on tha'..." Jenkins said, as he and another took up the oars.

Myddelton did as he was bade and thought about dry land until they reached the quay, the great worn stone steps of which he found infinitely easier to negotiate than the Revenue Cutter's ladder. For unlike the ladder, the steps were stationary. And felt a flood of absurd relief surge over him. Dry land. Dry land! The static delight of it.

"Semple will be at the Duke's Head," Fiske had said with the authority of one who knew every inn, tavern, smuggler and intelligencer operating in the English Channel. He had changed his uniform coat for a plain civilian's coat.

As they walked up the quay toward the town, Myddelton noted at least three inns facing the harbour. How could one be so sure which Semple frequented?

"…'Tis the only one where they don't speak the local patois," Fiske continued. "It's run by an Englishman who married an island girl, which accounts for it. Semple's a fine shot and no doubt a brave lad, but he cannot make head nor tail out of the locals."

S'life, why had Castlereagh asked him to carry these papers? Surely there must have been someone, anyone, better suited to the job. He knew less than nothing—and every minute spent with Fiske underscored his appalling ignorance and civilian's naïvety.

He followed Fiske along the harbour wall, stepping over the ropes and around the nets and baskets of catch which littered the cobbles, avoiding the fishermen, sailors, and fishwives with their skirts hitched up above their knees. Two of the women stopped at their work as he passed to watch him furtively and to whisper. Then, Fiske turned to lead the way up a narrow street which became a steep hill, and finally paused, then entered a long white-washed building with a gabled roof and black shutters propped open: The Duke's Head.

After the glare of the harbour, the taproom was dark and pleasantly empty. Fiske took a seat at a corner table. Relieved, Myddelton followed suit. Too much standing, too much walking, too much sick, too much activity altogether and too little sleep or food had left him light-headed and weak as water. From the kitchen beyond came the mixed aromas of roasting ham and chicken and pork—the evening's supper—and with them, the sudden and surprising realisation that he was no longer engaged in the battle to keep a steady gut but was absurdly ravenous.

"'Struth, I've a long stomach!" he said, rueful, and reached into his pocket for his snuff-box. Dismally, he eyed the contents of the box before taking a few grains.

"Aye, you would have, my lord…" Fiske agreed cheerfully. "But Thomas keeps a good table here, so you'll not go wanting." Then, idly as he watched Myddelton inhaling, said, "Should you run short while you're aboard, you must help yourself to the Martinique in my cabin…we came upon it a few weeks past, but there wasn't enough to make it worth reporting…"

"Thank you," Myddelton said, returning the box to his pocket. "I'd not thought to provision myself…" And though the edginess which had settled somewhere between his heart and his stomach was not entirely dispelled, and the aching and dizziness of the past days plagued him sore, even sitting here, at this his final or nearly final destination, still…still, he knew a moment of pleasure, felt that indefinable blending of inward contentment, gratitude and pride which sometime accrues when one has discharged a difficult duty. In spite of the odds. The very long odds. And every vicissitude. And it would not be long now…Soon, he would have given the papers to Semple and be boarding the Revenue Cutter— this time to return home to the world with which he was comfortable and familiar. Home to his own bed and his wife. What felicity. And looked about at the beamed ceiling and lime-washed walls, the rush-strewn flag floor, the other tables and oak settles.

Eventually, a great tall bear of an individual, round-faced and florid, wearing a grease-spattered leather apron over his breeches came out of the back room and noted their presence. That is to say, he noted the presence of someone in his taproom. And approached.

"By God, Fiske!" he exclaimed. "What brings you here, my little man, in broad daylight? Come to ogle my Rozel, have ye?" he demanded, grinning. "When are ye going to make that little lass happy and name the day then, eh?" He nodded his greeting to Myddelton. "Sir."

"Ah Thomas, I'm too old for her. And she'd not fancy being a Revenue Officer's wife, I've told her that often and often," Fiske returned.

It was pleasant to listen to the good-natured banter of friends, Myddelton thought, and smiled to himself. Soothing. Restful. Like home. Though Fiske could hardly be called 'little'—to be sure he lacked the height and breadth of Thomas the mountain…And fancy him having a local sweetheart.

"I'll tell you what, she's not listening to ye," said the landlord, the young and lovely Rozel's father. "Ye'd best see her before you go or she'll not stop her cryin' for a week, you know that. Now, what can I get you gentlemen?"

Myddelton chuckled inwardly. And thought of Janey. And how she would smile and sparkle when he told her of this interchange. And that, and the certainty that this wretched business would soon be finished and done with, gave him such a sense of well-being and satisfaction—easily more restorative than any patent medicine.

"Two of your finest, Tom, and the whereabouts of Mr. Semple," Fiske said simply.

The landlord went and drew two tankards. And returned and placed them on the table, his expression having changed from easy to chary, and his voice now noticeably softer. "Young Semple, eh? Young Semple is upstairs in my second best chamber with the sawbones. Havin' his legs splinted. He fell down the stairs of some doss-house last night and broke both his legs. Or was pushed," he added carefully, and as an afterthought.

"What?" Myddelton whispered, stupefied. And caught his breath. And stunned, sat and listened, wordless. Sat motionless and stared. And his thoughts fragmenting, did not notice that he was hardly breathing.

"Surgeon reckons he cracked a rib or two as well..." continued Thomas the landlord. "He's lucky it wasn't his neck...So...So he'll not be much use to you today, Lieutenant. And Sawbones's given him a draught of laudanum, he were yellin' so, with the pain."

Overwhelmed, Myddelton barely heard the rest. This...this accident, this bloody catastrophe could not...could not have happened. It was not possible. It could not be. And recoiling from the cruelty of this blow, floundering, drowning in disbelief, he failed to notice that his mind had emptied of all coherent thought or emotion. Or indeed that his stomach had sunk into his boots. This one certainty, the fixèd point in this whole mad business—on Guernsey was William Semple and all he need do was hand the papers to him!—had been torn from him. There could be no simple delivery of the documents now. This whole unholy mission had been a waste and a folly. Dear blessèd God, what now?

Lieutenant Fiske risked a glance at Myddelton and saw that the colour—what there was of it after the last days—had drained entirely from his face. It was not good, this. Not at all. "Thank ye, Thomas. Thank ye. Bring us a bite of that chicken I smell roasting, now, would you? My companion here stands in need of a bit of feeding up."

"Aye, that I will," said Thomas, and with a nod and a shrewd look at Myddelton took himself off.

Myddelton said nothing. He couldn't. Nor could he think; could only sit. And all he could feel was the futility of his own efforts. And the rage, the stupid blind rage, building within. And could not imagine what he might do now. Semple was injured, crippled, and asleep. And God knew when he'd wake. Bloody death, what to do? And still, he sat, staring without seeing at the tankard. And would never know how long he remained so.

He shook his head to clear it. And grasped at the first straw. "Surely…surely, there is someone else here who can be trusted…" he said evenly, and with a measure of calm he was far from feeling.

Fiske had been sucking on the inside of his cheek, thoughtful. He drew a long breath and said quietly, firmly, "No. No. That's the difficulty, d'you see? That's why Lord Castlereagh sent you…Did you not know?" And with a second glance, affirmed for himself that indeed Myddelton had not known. Had known nothing. "There have been the odd things happening roundabout. Mostly in London, as you would expect. Like this with young Semple. Things have not been getting through as they ought. Lads going missing. Or falling down stairs when they wasn't drunk. Someone's been turned and is selling information to the Frenchies—a double agent, if you will. Like that poxy bastard Perlet a few years back. But Lord Castlereagh thought it must be at the London end of things. Though that would not appear to be the case…now."

The facts, and the ramifications of those facts were harshly, sternly sobering. No, he had not known. The workings of intelligencers— mostly the province of the Alien Office and the Irish Office anyway— was an aspect of Castlereagh's business about which he knew little. He knew only their names and translated their reports. He only guessed at what they actually did. Myddelton shook his head again. "But there must be someone…" he protested. There had to be.

Fiske only shook his head. "No."

Numb, Myddelton stared at his tankard. And took a long swill of brown ale. Now he knew why Castlereagh had chosen him. Small comfort.

Fiske eyed him furtively. "Will you go on then, my lord?"

Myddelton set down the tankard and drew a deep breath. And steeled himself. And though the thought which he was about to speak nearly crushed his heart, said, "I must." And would have sworn he felt it crack. And swallowed down the dread, the wretchedness and anger. "I have no choice…" And wanted, like so many other times now, to weep. "I must write to my wife."

Surprised, Fiske blurted out: "You have a wife, my lord? You're married?"

"Yes. I have a wife. A very beautiful wife." And Myddelton felt his heart and all hope withering within his breast. "We have been married almost a month now," he said quietly, and could not keep the aching bleakness out of his voice.

Lieutenant Fiske, paused to consider this new information, then said, "It need not be Spain or Portugal, you know. We could sail for France."

Myddelton looked up. "France," he repeated, disbelieving. "France?" France. To go into France? Enemy France. Death to all Englishmen. Quick, with a pistol shot. Or the quick drop of a lynching. Or slow, in chains on a prison hulk. Or slower yet, in La Force, at the hands of police torturers. Dear God. How would he withstand? He had not the courage of Sidney Smith. Oh dear God, to die. And without issue. Childless. And who would then inherit? Probably Anne's boy— he was the closest male heir, surely. But what of Jane? What would become of her? His bride and then his widow, never his wife. To die without ever having lain with her. To die like that. And he shut his eyes against the misery, the cruel unhappiness of it. Sweet Christ, why had he not husbanded her when he'd had the chance?

He shook his head. "I am no soldier."

"No," Fiske, thoughtful and considering, agreed. "No. But you do speak Frog, do you not? Well, then? It's a damned sight nearer than Portugal. And I know a fellow there. One of ours, my lord. One of the best. You could give those papers to him. He'd see them safe to old Hookey. He's on the coast, d'you see? Of Brittany. It's a short day's sailing from here. Easy in, easy out. We can have you back in London by Saturday, my lord."

And Myddelton knew that he lied. It would not be easy in, easy out. It would be fraught with danger, every minute, every second of it. And wished he did not know his duty. Or knowing it, wished he might turn from it. And knew it was all vain, all futile, this wishing —for he did know, and he must always obey. There was no other choice. Yet to obey his duty to his king, to his countrymen, he must now abandon that other duty—the duty he owed his family, his father, his wife. And all his father's tireless efforts to preserve his house and title, to pass it on unencumbered, the marriage to Jane, everything would be for naught— he had married but he had not performed that essential—he had not got an heir. Perhaps he now never would. And it would all be for naught. And wetting his top lip, he said with a lightness that was the antithesis of his sentiments, "Yes, that would be well. You see, I must be back in Town by Tuesday evening next. I must not be away so long as to arouse comment…And being absent from my own ball would."

Fiske, revising his opinion of this titled would-be intelligencer, giving him full marks for a courage he had not thought he possessed, said, "Aye, well, it would at that." And shrugged with the nonchalance of a master-seamen. "Still, it'll pose no difficulty, my lord. You have my word on it."

And the afternoon drawing to a close, the taproom began to fill, though few paid much heed to the silent couple in the corner who were finishing a meal. Then, their meal complete, Fiske went off to court with his Rozel, while Myddelton remained, composing on borrowed paper his letter to Janey:

> *My dearest Jane,*
> *Events have overtaken me once more. The gentleman I was to have met had sustained an injury the previous evening and I now find myself needing to continue my journey. I am assured however that I shall be back*

in London well before the opening of our ball. You did not truly believe that I would allow anyone else the great happiness of leading you out, did you? Will you inform our mutual acquaintance of these unforeseen circumstances?

My dearest, you fill my heart and mind. Every moment that I am parted from you is as the soul's winter night—joyless, frozen, lightless, desolate. I ache and long for you, and think only of you.

My darling wife, do not doubt me. Nor my love for you. I shall return to you.

Your loving husband,
M

And read and reread it. So much had been left unwritten and unsaid, yet he had not the time nor the serenity of mind to write all that he felt. Nor in this difficult and exposed situation could he commit to paper all that had occurred here. The barest essentials must suffice. Castlereagh would understand. And so he prayed would she. He paused and reread the letter, missing her so badly it pained him. Then, solemnly folded it, wrote the direction on the back, and using the wax from the candle sealed it. The Lieutenant had said it would go with the first boat sailing for England. And setting his face, Myddelton rose, left the inn and made his way down to the quayside where Jenkins was waiting to row him back to the Cutter.

29

Mr. Hardy was enjoying being betrothed. In truth, it delighted his every part. To have the pleasure of being with the object of his considerable affection as frequently as he might wish gave him such cause for happiness. Indeed, he had only to look upon Miss Wythenshaw—his Miss Wythenshaw, his Georgina—and his heart would warm with joyous passion. And then he would imagine their life together, their life of music-making and sweet laughter, and contentment would wash over him like a Mozart violin sonata.

And tonight, these sentiments had doubled or even tripled, for tonight they were at Almack's, that most exclusive of London clubs. Run by ladies of distinction for, primarily, ladies (although gentlemen were, of course, necessary)—to be seen, to gossip, to contract suitable marriages, to dance, to reign. To some, a stifling, static, artificial sort of place. To others, the pinnacle of civilisation, polite society, and power. Tonight, to Mr. Hardy, the scene of immeasurable triumph—for here he was with his betrothed, his against-all-the-odds future bride, she who had amazed all of Society with her beauty, she who had been coveted by many, she who was now promised to him. Ah, Almack's! Where the myriad colours of the women's gowns presented an English garden at the height of summer, beautiful against the soft pink of the assembly room walls. Which conceit made him smile. For indeed, how lovely, how beautiful *she* would look walking in just such a garden on a summer's day.

And as he watched her dancing with a young soldier in scarlet regimentals, the soon-to-sail Lord William Something-or-other, chatting, laughing, Mr. Hardy rejoiced that everything was going so very well. For Lady Emily's plan of campaign had worked to perfection. Lady

Myddelton, looking radiant and impossibly elegant, and escorted by Pemberton, had greeted and congratulated them most civilly—here, in front of everyone—and the gossip about his Georgina and Myddelton had been effectively and emphatically quashed. And now, now, really, it only remained to name the day.

Mr. Hardy was not, however, enjoying Miss Georgina's mother. Unfortunately for him, Mrs. Wythenshaw *was* enjoying being the mother of the affianced bride of the wealthy, the well-connected, the landed Hardy of St. Cross. And such pleasure as she found in this elevated position could hardly be kept to herself. But if her initial joy at her daughter's success had been half-hearted—for Mr. Hardy was not titled, was he? And that must be counted a detriment and a flaw—a cursory glance at the generous marriage settlement his solicitor had proposed had served to placate such reservations. And she was convinced that such wealth and property as he possessed must also include the accomplishment of several if not many noble connexions—and surely he must be in line to inherit a title from one of them—though she had not yet found the opportunity to study Debrett's in detail.

"Mr. Hardy," Mrs. Wythenshaw began, for she was sitting beside him, basking in the respect his future mother-in-law must command.

"Ma'am?" Mr. Hardy smiled. He did not like her tone—too shrill, too arch. And he did not like her spice-coloured turban headdress neither, even if it was a popular colour this Season, for it made her appear sallow, or worse, jaundiced.

"Was that not your cousin, the Earl Dunphail, I saw just now?"

Blankly Mr. Hardy shook his head. He had never kept tabs on his cousin. "I don't know. He rarely comes here though, you know...Not his sort of place, really." Though Mr. Hardy did not feel the need to elucidate what Dunphail's place was likely to be. Lud, that would shock her!

"How can that be? A gentleman in his position?" Mrs. Wythenshaw asked, fanning herself, wishing to appear disinterested or au fait. "Is he not the marrying kind? How excellent for you!"

"I beg your pardon?" said Mr. Hardy, undeniably at a loss.

"As his heir, of course," Mrs. Wythenshaw said, making the whole

471

clear.

But this did not make things clear. At least not for Mr. Hardy. He shook his head. "I think you must be mistaken, ma'am. I ain't Dunphail's heir."

Mrs. Wythenshaw seemed to freeze. "But I assumed...that is to say, you do share his house..."

"Yes," Mr. Hardy confirmed. Then shaking his head in denial: "But I ain't his heir." He thought for a moment. "I rather think it must be his nephew. His sister Margaret's boy...At least, I believe it may be he." He gave a deprecating smile. "I'm not absolutely certain. I confess, I've never paid much heed as it never concerned me. And no doubt, one of these days Dunphail'll marry and get a whole parcel of brats, with heirs aplenty..." he said cheerfully. "But I'm nothing more than a cousin," he said, without regret, and did not see the look of dismay, soon suppressed, which had come over Mrs. Wythenshaw's fine features, for he had been following the movements of her daughter. He stood and bowed. "Will you excuse me, ma'am? I see Miss Wythenshaw is about to finish this set. And she is promised to me for the next." And he could not help the beaming smile he bestowed upon her.

Pemberton waited until he and Jane were walking, her hand upon his arm, toward the centre of the dance floor to await the beginning of a waltz. And commented under his breath, "Never one to do things by half, was you?"

"What?" she replied absently. She was watching the gossips in the far corner of the room, their heads together...despicable loathsome creatures.

"That little tête à tête with the Wythenshaw and Hardy in the Park today, all wreathed in smiles and honeyed comfits...And never say you dressed like that on my account..." For she was perfection itself this evening, gowned in the expensive armour of perfume, pomade, graciousness and mousseline—beyond reproach, beyond speculation. It was a far cry from the rumpled apron and gown of a month ago.

"Ah, but of course I did," she objected with a measurable lack of sincerity. What easy pleasant company Pemberton was, to be sure.

"Ha! I cut my wisdoms years ago, Angel," he declared flatly. "You dressed like that so that the Wythenshaw—and every other female in the room—would know how infinitely beneath you she is. In which endeavour you have succeeded, m'dear. Rather beyond your wildest dreams, I suspect. Even Brummell noticed—with approbation, I might add."

Her smile was seraphic, then she chuckled. "How inconsiderate of you to say so. For I am not meant to care about such things, you know. Though I'm glad if Mr. Brummell did say so...But thank you." She paused, before continuing with airy sarcasm, "However, as important as Miss Wythenshaw is—and to you I will admit that it has all been for the calculated effect of giving the lie to the truth of the situation—*she* is not the sole reason that I have appeared 'la vrai comtesse' this evening, I do assure you."

He frowned and narrowed his eyes in speculation. "Well if it ain't for my benefit and it certainly ain't for Myddelton's, then who for?"

"Your aunts, if the truth be told," she said with an unmistakable edge, and took her place opposite him. As one whose personal life had suddenly become irrevocably un-private, she was learning to find her private moments in the most unexpected places—like the centre of Almack's assembly rooms.

Pemberton, taking her other hand for the opening steps, smiled. He had waited a very long time for the privilege of waltzing with her. "My aunts? By a stroke of good fortune, Angel, you don't even know my aunts."

"No," she agreed. "But they apparently know all about me." And returned the smile.

The music began. She was waltzing, albeit held at the strict distance required by the Almack's patronesses, with another man. Though it was only Pemberton...He waltzed very well.

"Oh, yes, like what?" he asked, unconvinced.

She waited until the steps and patterns of the dance brought them close together again. "Well...for example, they know about how you and Myddelton had fallen out and were to fight, because he believed you had

had an affaire with me."

She had his fullest attention now. "What?" Why had she waited until now to spring this upon him? Good God. "'Struth, I don't believe it. How can they have heard about that?" And narrowing his eyes, said in disgust, "That must have been Mary."

"Mary? The mother of your cousin, Lavinia? Why would she…"

His wickedest grin had appeared and he lowered his voice. "Because I turned up legless for one of Lavinia's do's. A ball, it was."

Jane bit her lips together and did not laugh. "Legless?"

"Aye." He nodded, grinning. "With Myddelton. Who was so nazy he kept sliding down the wall." He bent his head close to hers and laughing a little, recalled, "Actually, he wasn't the only one…" And stepped aside, holding her hand, while she executed a neat pirouette.

And those who were watching, those who were bent on observation, or gossip, noted that Lady Myddelton was not looking down-pin at all, not at all as one would have expected if it had been Myddelton in that ante-chamber. Or was wanting an annulment. She was laughing with delight as she waltzed with Pemberton. Lady Emily Cowper must have been telling the truth—it must have been Mr. Hardy in that ante-chamber, which if you watched the way he was dancing with Miss Wythenshaw seemed more than likely…

"Which caused no end of a dust-up as Mary had decided—off her own bat, this was—that I should have the very good fortune of marrying m'dear cousin."

Jane sparkled and laughed. "She didn't…"

"She did," he confirmed.

Mockingly, Jane sighed. "…And I suppose Myddelton had been pegged as a prospective suitor too?"

"Yes. If I didn't come up to scratch, I suspect he would have done almost as well…" Pemberton said with a trace of acid in his voice. He did not like the self-important and vacuous Lavinia. But then who did? "It was all for nought though…there was two young innocents, flats the pair of them, who looked as though one or t'other could be brought to the sticking point—but that was before they and their parents had the felicity of dining with my aunt and uncle, to make their acquaintance properly." His grin had become the insouciant. "However, the effusive sweetness, gushing charm and condescension of my aunt's manner, coupled with my uncle acting like a belligerent spaniel, proved too much for the prospective bridegrooms and they legged it, without ever having popped the vital question. According to Gussie."

"Poor Lavinia," she murmured without sympathy. "Hence your aunt..."

"Yes," agreed Pemberton. "Lud. Though how she got hold of that little nugget... Anyway, how do you know about it?"

"Because she, kindly, wrote to Lady Choate, who showed the letter to my uncle. Which is why he came to see me." There was a degree of anger behind the irony.

"What?" This was serious. And banished all happy thoughts of sliding down walls or Lavinia's well-merited spinsterhood. "Janey, what happened?" The joking was finished.

But their waltz too was finished. She swept him, her dear friend, her staunchest ally, a deep curtsy, and smiled. He took her arm. And with deceptive brightness she said, "He asked me about it, of course. I denied that there had been any such disagreement." And sparkled for all those who were looking on. "I said you were my dear friend, and Myddelton's, and that you enjoyed the run of the house as one would, and that that would hardly be the case had you and Myddelton fallen out or were you more to me than a friend."

"And?" There had to be more. He knew her perfect smile, her perfect manner far too well to be taken in by them, not to recognise they were a highly polished facade beyond which few were allowed to see.

She nodded her greeting at the Lady Jersey and Mr. Brummell.

There was more. "...And then it transpired that he had also been to White's, where apparently he heard any number of stories about Myddelton eloping with...another..." And waved and smiled at Anne. "And, he heard something about Myddelton wanting an annulment as well. So he wanted to know where Myddelton is...Lord Dunphail, how very pleasant to see you. But what can have brought you here? Pem has always assured me you do not like to come to Almack's...But of course, it is Mr. Hardy's first outing as a betrothed gentleman! He is looking very

475

well on it, do you not think?" The perfect smile from the perfect guest.

Or perhaps the centre of Almack's assembly rooms was not the best place for private speech, even between friends. So for the next hour as she danced first with Dunphail, then young Thurston, and finally with Sir Miles Northcote, Pemberton found himself keeping watch over her with a fraternal or paternal or avuncular eye—'struth, he hardly knew how to define their relationship or his sentiments toward her these days—always waiting for the moment when they might resume the conversation about her uncle and whatever misapprehensions he might be now harbouring.

Finally, the moment came. She had left the dancefloor and was unpartnered for the next set of country dances. "So what did you tell him?" he began without preamble as he came from behind to steer her toward an unoccupied settee.

She smiled, appreciating the familiarity, the comfortable quickness of his intelligence. Nor did she need to feign confusion at his question. And in replying, the facade came down for an instant. "I lied," she said simply. "Just as I have lied here tonight." She appeared serene. Or hard. "I have never lied to my uncle before, you know. Ever. I have not needed to." She shrugged and made a moué. "But I had no choice...I told him Myddelton had gone north...about a horse." She sat down and smoothed a wrinkle from her skirt.

Pemberton, listening intently, had taken to polishing his quizzing glass and giving the other guests the once over. "What did he say?"

"I do not think he believed me."

He paused. This was too puzzling. And more than a little unsettling. "Why wouldn't he believe you?"

And now, she smiled and turned her head away for an instant, as if he were flirting with her. "Because he believes Myddelton to be a gambler and a rakehell. Rather like his uncle, I believe."

"What uncle?" he asked, mystified and groping for sense. "Myddelton don't have an uncle."

"No. Not now. But he did. Until my father shot him. In a duel." She related the information as a recitation of facts, emotionless.

"What?" Pemberton demanded with repressed heat. "What?" he repeated, his voice rising. For this was the final straw. Each day since

Myddelton had left had brought some new difficulty, some new vicissitude to complicate what should have been a remarkably unremarkable exercise. And now, apparently, there were familial skeletons waiting to pop out of the cupboard to add to the mixture.

She shook her head to dispel his anger and anxiety. "It is ancient history. And does not bear repeating really. Sir Charles said he was a scoundrel, and it was to pay off his debts that my father lent Myddelton's father all that money. Which is when and why the contract for our marriage was drawn up..."

"What?" This bore no resemblance to Myddelton's version of events. And when had she become so blasé and imperturbable about these sorts of things?

But she ignored him. "...Anyway it does not matter—because Myddelton will be home by Friday, didn't you say? So, as long as I keep out of my uncle's way until then—and with the ball on Tuesday I have plenty to occupy me—it cannot matter what he believes..." she concluded, smiling, and did not notice his look of astonishment.

30

It was dusk when Lieutenant Fiske gave the order to drop anchor. The western sky was painted and streaked with madder, vermilion and mauve by the setting sun. Myddelton leaned over the ship's railing to watch the fragmenting mosaic of colour reflected on the surface of the grey-green water, and to listen to the heavy plosh of the anchor as it dropped. They were just beyond sight of the town of St. Pol. And tonight, he would be put ashore in a small cove not far from there. Pray the moon stayed out of sight.

He drew a deep breath and gazed at and into the water. The mirrored colours were deepening, merging, bleeding—violet, crimson and bronze against the now black depths. And thought on his duty, thinking and not thinking on the mission before him this night. He was no soldier. He had never been into battle. The closest he'd come to such a thing was riding to hounds, which Wellington's opinion notwithstanding, was a far cry from the assault on Ciudad Rodrigo or the hard-won victory at Talavera where the blood of five thousand Englishmen soaked the ground. He drew another breath, disliking such thoughts and their threat of imminent mortality. And wishing he could dispel them, knew the futility of such a wish.

All day he had noted a gradual sharpening of his senses, an increasing awareness of every sound and each movement, and a welling up of fear and pride, of duty and resolve. And wondered if this was what every soldier knows and feels in those waiting moments and hours before action. And thought too about all that was behind him—his wife, his home at Great Myddelton, summer afternoons spent lying on the bank of the River Itchen, ostensibly to fish, but in truth just watching the clouds and the endless flow of water rippling over the shallow stream bed. And observing the blackening water, he reflected that from the outset he had suspected that it would be he—and not some seasoned agent—who would deliver these letters, whatever they were, to mainland Europe. To France or Spain or Portugal. From the moment Castlereagh had asked him to undertake the journey, he had known. And it was this which had prompted his spectacularly unsuccessful attempt to tell Janey how he loved her. Stoically he accepted that now she might never be told. And frowned with discontent, for he had not left things as he ought.

He peered into the distance, wanting to gain some glimpse of France, but could see nothing beyond the dark blending of sky and sea. Lieutenant Fiske had been careful to anchor the Cutter well away from shore, out of sight of idle ship-watchers or *douaniers*. Yet in a few hours he would be landed there. Well before dawn he must find the house of the English agent, deliver the cyphered letters and return to the cove to be picked up. If he met with any officials or soldiers or guardsmen, if he were slow in finding the cottage of Fiske's intelligencer, if he had to speak to anyone, it would all be over for him. If he were caught he would be executed. Shot. With or without the prelude of torture, his body left by the roadside or in some ditch or field. And who would know? The French were remarkably cavalier about recording casualties, even their own.

And Jane? Would they just report him missing, leaving her to wait in a limbo of desperate uncertainty? To wait, for seven years?

'Struth, it did not bear thinking on...

Lieutenant Fiske, seeing him at the railing, came down from the upper deck to join him. "A fine night for a landing, my lord, is it not?"

Myddelton turned. If that comment was meant to encourage him, it signally failed. He returned a sardonic smile. "I shall have to take your word on that, Lieutenant. I am no judge of these things."

Fiske surveyed the sky, the cloud cover, the deepening blackness, and looked out in the direction of the coast. "Aye. It'll do. It'll do. But..." He broke off, searching for a diplomatic way to put the next. Then, for all that himself bore a great and ancient title, abandoned the effort. "But...well, as I was standing there admiring the cut of your coat, my lord, it came to me that you cannot go ashore dressed as you are. The

Frogs are as thick as pig turds, but they should recognise the work of an English tailor in a moment. I would."

Myddelton blinked. And murmured, "What?" without comprehension. He looked down at his cuff and saw only his oldest riding coat—drab, worn, remarkably undistinguished.

"It's in the cut," Lieutenant Fiske said finally, apologetically. "And it could give you away. Talking to them, you can avoid if you need to. But they're not blind. More's the pity..." He eyed Myddelton up and down. "Your boots may be a problem too...If you will come below, we'll see what we can do...See if we cannot find you a jersey. Or rig something up." He started toward the ladder to belowdecks. "The Frogs are a dirty people, you know. 'Tis a pity you shaved this morning."

Following—silently cursing his stupidity and what he considered his inadequacies—Myddelton shook his head. "Forgive me. None of this had occurred to me."

Fiske stopped at the foot of the ladder and turned. "Well no...Why should it? Frankly, it did not occur to me neither till just now as I was standing there admiring the cut of your lapel and thinking to myself 'I fancy Mr. Weston will have made that coat for him and a fine job he made of it—even as old as it is.'"

"Yes, he did," Myddelton confirmed, feeling discomfited—though why he felt so, he could not have said. 'Struth, why did Castlereagh send him here when there were so many more qualified, more suitable, more capable than him?

"Aye," Fiske said, his easy grin becoming a considering frown. "Aye...Well, it'll not look so well after we've finished. Still, it should buy your safety. And that's what matters."

Hours later, an education later, fed and filthied, Myddelton was sat in the Lieutenant's cabin. Waiting. His outer clothes Lieutenant Fiske had taken and had rubbed in grease from the galley pots and smeared with soot, for they had been unable to find anything else that was of his size. They had rubbed grease in his hair too and streaked his face with it, and soot had been worked into his hands and his fingernails. His boots had been used for a quick rough game of kickball on deck. Stamp would never recognise them now. Or him. At another time, in another place, in

Pemberton's company perhaps, he would have laughed to see himself thus disguised. But with the risks and perilous uncertainties of this night's work overshadowing him, he was not laughing. Instead, he felt the hard steady pulse of fear in his stomach. And did his best to ignore it.

Fiske inspected him, looking him over critically, up and down, front and back. And finally nodded his approval. "The lads have done well. I should not have known you for an Earl. Or an Englishman. That's good. That's very good.

"Now, my lord," he continued, suddenly more intent, at once the strategist and commander. "...The fellow you're wanting goes by the name of Dupont. Bernard Dupont. His house is just a mile or so to the west of the cove where Croggon will land you. To get there, you must stay to the track along the shoreline—the sea will be on your right—till you come to a fork. That will be the first fork. Continue on along the coastal path. Do not go off inland. Only at the second fork, do you head inland. The house—'struth, it's no more than a croft or a hovel—'tis on the left. 'Tis the only one you'll see. Bang on the door, and when Dupont answers, you must say to him, 'Est-ce que vous faites du miel pour les abeilles?'"

"Du miel pour les abeilles?" Myddelton repeated and translated, committing to memory each detail, everything he was told.

"Aye, that's it. Honey for the bees. And if it is your man, he will say, 'Mais non, je préfère chasser au nom des lions.'"

"'Mais non, je préfère chasser au nom des lions'. And if it is not the right man?" Myddelton asked, and wondered that he dared.

Fiske paused. And frowned. "Act the drunkard," he said firmly. "And the fool...sing la Marmotte loudly...Can you do that?" And narrowed his eyes as he considered the inherent dangers, the best possible means of escape. "And get yourself back to the cove quick as you can. We'll make for Spain with the tide."

Myddelton drew the deepest breath and closed his eyes against the fear of a failed mission. No, that luxury he could not, must not, allow himself. "Right." And rubbing his fingers together, he recited: "I am to follow the path to the west, along the coast. At the second fork, I head

481

inland and the house is on the left. When this Dupont answers the door, I ask him if he makes honey for the bees and he shall reply that he prefers to hunt on behalf of lions."

"Aye, that's it. Good." And his expression becoming even more serious, Fiske said, "You're well armed, are you?"

Awkward and stupid again. "I believe so," Myddelton said. "There's the knife in my boot. And my pistol is here." He opened his coat to reveal the small pistol stuck into the waistband of his breeches.

The Lieutenant grimaced and shook his head, murmuring, "You'll be wanting another knife at the very least." He went to the small chest at the foot of his bunk, opened it and took out a slim dagger and a leather sheath attached to a thin leather band. "If you'll just roll up your sleeve, my lord..."

Deftly, soberly, he fitted the sheath along the inside of Myddelton's left forearm and fastened it about his wrist, before sliding the knife in so that its handle rested against the heel of Myddelton's hand. And rolled down the sleeve before saying levelly: "There. Do not hesitate. If you need it, use it. 'Tis a good deal easier to slit a man's throat before he's seen you, than to silence him afterward, I do assure you. Take no chances. Remember, always remember, it's that simple. It's kill or be killed. And I promise you, they'll not think twice. So don't you."

Blinking, Myddelton felt a cold hardness or heartlessness settle over him. From civilian to combatant in one night, one lesson—most soldiers had at least the interval of several weeks' training. But the time was past for bemoaning his inadequacies, his naïvety, his ignorance of this business, this war. Now there was only onward. Now there was only the performance of duty. Whatever that might entail. Regardless of cost. He felt the blade rigid along his forearm. The steel handle was cold where it butted against the inside of his wrist. There had been those, he knew, who had ever objected to Admiral Nelson's views on waging war, his view that the only proper outcome was the annihilation of the enemy, those who thought such attitudes were not gentlemanly or honourable. Fiske was not of their number; he knew too much. "Yes."

Fiske nodded his approval. "Off you go then, my lord."

The upper deck was dark and quiet, the dark-lanterns shuttered, when Myddelton climbed over the railing and down the ladder to the dinghy where Croggon and another deckhand were waiting to row him ashore. Only Lieutenant Fiske was there to see him off. Cautiously, Myddelton stepped into the dinghy, placing one foot, then the other onto the boat's wooden floor. He leaned over, caught hold of the side and gently lowered himself onto a seat. Contemplation of this night's enterprise had overridden his habitual seasickness.

Fiske observed his debarkation with pleased mild amusement. He would have made a fine sailor, a sound intelligencer, this one. If he survived. Fiske leaned hard upon the railing in deliberation—it was a risky affair, this jaunt tonight. He did not like the odds. "Good luck to ye," he called, and waved, an indistinct motion against the gloom. A very risky affair.

Silently, Croggon and his mate pushed away from the Cutter and then, dipping their oars in time, the dinghy slid away, bobbling, cutting, lurching through the brackish water toward France. And with each stroke of the oarsmen, Myddelton felt an emotional numbness replace his previous fear, vanquishing all but the performance of duty, and the intellect, determination and daring needed to accomplish it.

The moon remained hidden behind the heavy clouds, the harbinger of more rain. Nothing could be seen in any direction. The only sounds were the lapping-slapping of the waves against the hull of the boat as it slid on toward the coast of Brittany. Myddelton was silent. As were the oarsmen.

Finally, even in the dark, the outline of land came into sight, approached, loomed close. And then, too soon, too quickly, unexpectedly the boat jerked forward as suddenly they hit the sand bottom of the Brittany beach.

Myddelton rose unsteadily to his feet, his throat tight with anticipated exertion and fear, and jumped over the side of the boat into the water. God's balls, it was cold. He shivered. And squinted into the darkness trying to make out the shape of the beach.

"The path be that-a-way, my lord," Croggon said with a nod and pointed toward an indistinct mound of something—gorse bushes perhaps. "Cap'n said we was to meet you back here in two hours. So

Tom an' me, we'll be waitin' offshore aways, just out o' sight. Then when we be comin' back in, I'll give a little whistle, so you know that we be comin' an' you can be ready for us. An' away we'll be then, right an' tidy."

"Yes," Myddelton agreed. 'Struth, Croggon made it sound easy. Like a pleasure outing to Brighton. "Thank you."

"Good luck to you, my lord," Croggon said, and Myddelton turned and waded to shore. He did not watch Croggon and the dinghy disappear into the night, but made his way over the pebbled beach toward the clumps of shrub and weed that Croggon had pointed out. The shingle and shell crunched underfoot. And he could see no path. In truth, he found it difficult to see anything that even resembled a path in the dark. But as his eyes began to focus more sharply, he noticed that the ground sloped slightly upward. He kept the sea on his right. And there, he noted a thin strip of packed soil between the quitch grass and weeds that grew unchecked. That must be it. The path. He hesitated. He did not dare get it wrong. And looked about for anything more definite, another possible path. And could see none. He searched the horizon in all directions for any sign that he had been observed or was being watched. Nothing moved. And listened. He could hear nothing above the surf. He drew a silent breath and started down the dirt path, heading west, with the sea on his right—as Fiske had said. Then…He stopped. There was a rustle in the grass ahead. Something…dashed across the path just a foot ahead of him. As one, his throat and gut constricted. Instantly. And his hand went to the knife hilt. A small animal turned and stared at him. A rabbit. It was a rabbit. His heart and head pounding together, a swell of relief flooded his veins, leaving him almost faint. He halted while he took great gulps of air before continuing on toward the house of Bernard Dupont.

He came to the first fork in the path. And still, his eyes combing the dark for anything, anything bright, any movement other than the stir of the grasses in the night breeze, he stayed to the seaside path. And then…s'life, was that the second fork? He retraced his steps and crouched down to examine the path. It was not much of a fork, if that's what it was. But…yes, a few steps ahead, the path inland widened out.

This must be it.

He reached inside his coat to rest his hand upon the pistol handle. For reassurance. For comfort. For courage. And went inland as instructed, walking, watching, listening. 'Fore God, this was a barren stretch of land—battered by the constant wind, houseless, unfarmed, ungrazed, deserted. But then, who was left to work the land now? For the past twenty years, the men of France had been drained off the land, like water off the Fens, forced to leave their farming for soldiering, all hostages to Napoleon's dreams of Empire and 'la gloire'. And now, who remained? A handful of boys? A few veterans too maimed to march in columns and shout 'Vive L'Empereur'? Even ten years ago, it had not been such a wasteland.

Then, in the distance, he saw a feeble glimmer of light—as from a poorly kept oil lamp. He kept walking. Yes, that was the outline in the dark. It was the cottage. He was nearly there. And thought he should have felt relieved, but did not.

And glancing about as he had done since landing, he halted, then started for the house.

The path continued on past the house, so he left it and crossed a dirt track to a narrow stone path leading to the door. Fiske had been right. It was a hovel, more byre than house. Even in the dark that was apparent. One window was boarded over. The other had a rag stuffed through a hole in its pane of grime-blackened glass. Within was the oil lamp.

Myddelton started up the stone pathway. Tussock grass and weed grew rampant between and beside the stones. He approached the door. Then stopped, his courage gone. He drew a great breath. *Dear God, let it be the right man. Please, let it be the right man. Let him be here. Let it not be a Frenchman and death.* And every muscle stiffening with fear, in expectation of the worst, of needing to draw the knife with its long double-sided blade, and to use it, he raised his fist and banged on the door. It rattled on its hinges. He waited. There was no answer. No sound at all from within. Or without. Beads of sweat, then a rivulet trickled from his temple. The skin on the back of his neck prickled and stung. Still, no answer. His stomach churned and contracted as if he were going to be sick. He clenched his jaw and swallowed hard. And raising his fist, banged again.

"Eh bien, eh bien, je viens…" came a voice from within. "Qu'est-ce que vous voulez, hein? Que je vienne ouvrir la porte sans mon pantalon? Hé hé…"

Through the plank door, Myddelton heard him grumbling and shuffling. He sounded old, peevish, menacing. Not what he expected. Then, the sound of bolts being slammed back and a cross bar being lifted. Myddelton held his breath. The door swung open. The owner of the house lifted the lamp high. "Oui?" he demanded. He reeked of soured wine. And garlic.

Myddelton gasped. Gaped. 'Struth, it wasn't…It was…It *was* Georgie Shuster. Thinner, sharper than he remembered. Unwashed and unshaven. But he would have sworn…

"Oui?" the man with the lamp demanded again. Without doubt it was a threat.

Myddelton felt the blood rush into his face. And felt his voice go. Shuster was filthy, grimy—and clothed like a labourer. Or a fisherman. A poor one. But it was surely he.

Myddelton caught his breath, suddenly inexplicably frightened. What was Shuster doing here? Like this? In France? "Bon soir, M'sieur. Est-ce que vous faites du miel pour les abeilles?" he asked, halting.

The agent eyed Myddelton silently. It was a hard, scrutinising glare. "Bon soir. Vous me demandez si je fais du miel pour les abeilles? Je vous dis mais non. Moi, je préfère chasser au nom des lions," he answered. He stood to one side, and held the door open.

Myddelton hesitated. Then, ducking his head, looking about, he stepped cautiously inside. Behind him, the agent shut the door and bolted it.

Within the thick-walled cottage, it was dim and squalid. And it stank. Sour, mildewed, damp…and acrid with the smoke from a pair of tallow candles. There was a table with a bench on either side. And in the near corner was a wooden bedstead, covered with a moth-eaten blanket, undoubtedly live with fleas. Within the open hearth, a heap of glowing embers gave off little light and less heat. And along the opposite wall was a sideboard with some cracked dishes, a collection of bottles and jugs and spoons and a round loaf of bread, half-eaten, upon it. 'Struth, it was a slum. A wretched heap. The dairy at Great Myddelton was a palace to it.

Myddelton turned to face the agent, Fiske's intelligencer, Harry's brother. "Georgie?" he said doubtfully.

The agent said nothing, but gave Myddelton an intent look, again scrutinising him, weighing him and perhaps finding him wanting. Or perhaps not. Then, after a pause he said softly with the merest trace of the lop-sided grin that was a Shuster family trait, "En français, mon vieux. Even the chairs have ears, here, you know," he continued in that language. And gestured to Myddelton to sit.

Fear melted. Myddelton sat and looked about. "Georgie, what in the name of God are you doing here? In a place like this?" Fiske may have prepared him for espionage, but not for this degree of privation.

"Me? I work for Wellington. As ever. And it's not so bad here..." He shrugged. "Better than some of the hell-holes I've been in, I assure you. But you..." He eyed Myddelton in frank speculation. "What are you doing here?" He went to the sideboard, inspected two of the tin mugs and set them with a jug of wine upon the table. "...you who likes to remain at home, what can have brought you here?"

Beneath the grime, the filth, the appearance of wretchedness, he was the same Georgie Shuster. And was completely changed. The easy physical grace and the candour were as Myddelton remembered, but measured now, tempered by an edginess, a tension. And the laughter, the daring, these were gone from his pale green eyes, displaced or overlaid by weariness or an instinct for survival perhaps, and a close acquaintance with physical pain. Myddelton felt some of the tension abate leaving a residue of uneasiness and chary awkwardness. For there was an alertness about Shuster now. As if he were always listening, always watching, never still...

"I've been with the Foreign Office since February, working for Castlereagh...Because of my languages..." Myddelton said, to explain, to establish his place in all of this.

"And the cyphers?" Georgie questioned, narrowing his eyes shrewdly. And filled the cups with wine.

"A little...Not much..." Myddelton admitted.

For which he received a disbelieving glance. "Hé hé! You know, I thought that last new one was too tortuous to have been invented by anyone but you! But then I thought, no, what would Myddelton be doing making up this stuff to addle the brains of the poor Frenchies…I don't suppose you've had much to do with any of those bizarre stories in the newspapers either, have you? Like that one about the Admiralty recalling all frigates to port for refitting or some such lunacy…"

"Well…not much…" Myddelton deflected. "I translate mostly. Honestly. For other people."

Georgie favoured him with a skeptical look and snorted.

And beginning again, Myddelton said, "But, I'm here, now, because I am carrying papers from Castlereagh for Wellington. I was meant to have given them to William Semple on Guernsey…"

"What happened?" Georgie cut in, razor-shrewd.

"When I arrived, he was in the upstairs room of the Duke's Head having his legs splinted. He'd fallen or was pushed down the stairs at some doss-house, the landlord said."

"Hunh," Georgie grunted. "Sounds like Semple…Lazy sod."

"So Lieutenant Fiske brought me here."

Immediately Georgie swilled down the wine in his cup. "Fiske? Really?" And shook his head. "Fiske! *Quel troyen*. He took a ball in the shoulder not six weeks ago. During a little contretemps with a French privateer, it was." He went to the sideboard. "So, what is it you have for me?" he asked as he sawed at the loaf of bread with a long partially rusted knife. "You want?" he gestured to the bread.

Myddelton declined, "No…I assure you, I don't know. Castlereagh gave me this packet…" He stood and began to struggle with the buttons of his ripped, ruined and soiled waistcoat. "…With the instruction that I leave for Newhaven immediately. That was on Monday night." He finished unbuttoning the waistcoat and reached in along the left side to free the packet from its hiding place. "But then we ran into that damned storm…"

Shuster grinned. Unsympathetically. "Yes, it hit us too. Badly. But I should think it must have been worse in the Channel, yes? You must have loved that…" he added, though his eyes did not sparkle with mischief or teasing laughter—not like at school.

Perhaps, after all, not everything had changed. Small comfort. "Here." Myddelton handed him the kidskin covered packet.

Shuster looked it over, then held it judiciously, first in one hand, then the other. "I'll leave at first light...And now, if you will be so kind as to close your eyes for a moment? What you do not know you cannot tell..."

Myddelton obliged, resting his forehead in the palm of his hand. And realised with a spurt of surprise that at that moment he had accomplished that improbable, impossible task which he been sent to do. He had not failed! S'life, what relief. What sheer blessèd relief. And listened to the grating of a stone or brick as Shuster prized it free and then returned it to seal the cache again.

"...So what news from home?" Georgie asked, wiping his hands on his shirt.

Myddelton paused and sucked his breath in. "The Government has fallen..." he said.

"What?" Georgie exclaimed. It had been idle, incidental, that question. "What happened?"

"Ehm..." he stalled. He closed his eyes. The grief, it was still fresh, still angry and far too potent. Still it unmanned him. "Ehm, the Prime Minister...Sir Spencer was assassinated. Shot. Just outside the Commons." And held his jaw stiff. No tears. Good. Excellent.

Listening in horror, stunned, Georgie sat down with a thump. "Good God." And drew several hard, measured, steadying breaths, and did not notice that Myddelton was struggling. "What happened?"

"It was a madman. Bellingham, his name was," Myddelton said, nodding. "He was mad. He blamed Perceval for the failure of his business. He confessed. I gave evidence at the trial. He was hanged. We thought...we thought it was a plot at first."

"When was this? When did all this happen?" Georgie demanded, grimacing.

"The 11th. Monday, the 11th...Then the Government fell on the 20th."

"The Government has fallen?" Georgie repeated, incredulous.

Myddelton nodded. "…And since then, Prinny's been nosing about for a Government among the Whigs—first he asked Wellesley, and now I've heard he asked Moira…all of which makes Castlereagh nervous…"

Georgie rubbed his face. "It would do…" He had seen a great deal, learned a great deal in his months as Wellington's aide. "Then you must tell him my news. He'll be glad of it. Napoleon left Paris for Dresden on the 9th, on his way to the Eastern Front, it's said."

"What?" Myddelton breathed, suddenly overcome and his shoulders weakened with relief. There was no threat of conspiracy. There had been no French threat! Their greatest nightmare had been nothing more than that—a dream without substance.

"That's right." Georgie gave a sardonic laugh. "Old Bony'd be kicking himself if he knew!" He shook his head at the irony. "Nom de Dieu!" And eventually: "Anything else?"

"I've got married."

"What?" Georgie exclaimed again, only this time with surprise and pleasure. "When?"

Myddelton smiled as he thought on it and how fine it felt to say so, how it banished all fear or trepidation. How soon he would be back home with her. "The end of April," he admitted.

And for the first time, there was a glimpse of the old Georgie as he smiled. "'Struth, Myddelton, look at you!" he declared. "Sacre bleu, you're in love, you old idiot! Utterly besotted, ain't you? Well, damn me!"

Abashed, and for no reason he understood, acutely embarrassed, Myddelton flushed beneath the grease and soot. 'Struth, was it that obvious? Were his affections that transparent? He himself had only just realised…

"…And Castlereagh had the tact to send you off when you're less than a month wed, did he?" Georgie continued, shaking his head. "They must be important, these letters. I shall take extra care."

Finally, still to his astonishment blushing, Myddelton drank his wine. It was cheap and raw. "But I cannot see how you come to be here without suspicion?"

Georgie shrugged, all twitchiness now at bay. "It's simple. A few months past I took a load of shrapnel. So now I'm not fit for much more than the odd bit of fishing." It was a statement, a declaration of fact, nothing more. "But Wellington, he thought I could do my fishing as well here as anywhere. So I keep my ear close to the ground. And if something comes up...well, it's quite usual for a fisherman to take his boat out for a few days at a time. It's not a bad journey from here to Oporto and back...And then, of course, the Bretons, they do not love the Emperor so much, you know. And when they think of one of their own young men, terribly wounded, with his back all scarred...well, you would be amazed at the things they tell me. All I have to do is show my scars and their tongues loosen...Still, I mean to return home soon..." His expression gentled, became wry and self-mocking. "There is a young lady...As soon as I am able to persuade her to come with me...If..." Then suddenly he stopped, straightened, and lifting his head to listen, held up his hand to hush.

Silenced, Myddelton heard nothing beyond the crackle and hiss from the dying fire.

"Tais-toi. We have visitors," Georgie said softly. And his eyes were alert, looking everywhere, measuring everything, examining everything. "One visitor," he clarified.

Still, Myddelton heard nothing, though his pulse had begun to race and his shoulders to tense.

Georgie waited, listening, wary, quiet. "It'll be Des Champs..." he muttered, shaking his head. "By God, I wish he'd rejoin his regiment...Say nothing, Myddelton. Act the mute. And slow too, yes? I'll get you out of this..." He smiled kindly. "...Or your bride, she'll not thank me, eh?"

Then Myddelton heard. The clip clop and snort noises of a horse. A large horse. Then someone dismounting. It was his worst fear. Steps and the clatter of exaggerated spurs upon the stone path. His greatest peril. And then the rumbling of the door as the visitor banged his fist upon it. Again, Georgie glanced sharply about the room, to check that everything was in place, everything was as normal and everything hidden.

Myddelton stared at the door. The banging continued. Sweat prickled on his neck and forehead and dread clutched at his lungs and stomach and throat. His heart thumped.

"I'm coming!" Georgie called out, exactly as he had done before. And added in an undertone, "Act the simpleton, all right?" His eyes kept straying to the door. "Let your mouth hang open if you can. Try to look vacant about the eyes. But do as I tell you, mon vieux." And anxiously: "For God's sake, you must do as I tell you."

Myddelton gave a sharp nod.

Georgie went swiftly to the door, dragging his shirt out and unbuttoning the top buttons on his trousers. "Eh, what is this that cannot wait while a man takes a piss, eh? I'm coming, I'm coming." He slid the bolts back, lifted the cross bar, and held the lamp high as he opened the door. "Oh, it's you, Des Champs. You had me worried. I thought you must be the customs officer...Hé hé. Come inside," he said, welcoming him. And rolling his eyes and spitting on the ground, added, "Come. Meet the family simpleton."

Myddelton felt his breath coming in short gasps, as if he'd been running, but could do nothing to steady it. Sweat broke out and trickled down his back and chest. He looked at the stranger and crossed into that region beyond fear.

"Parbleu, I did not know you had any relations, Dupont..." Des Champs declared, stamping his boots as he came inside.

Georgie laughed harshly and slammed the door. "But of course I have relations. With a surname like Dupont? I tell you, the whole of France is littered with my relations."

Myddelton risked a long glance and saw that the visitor, Des Champs, was dark and swarthy and wore the red and green jacket of a Chasseur à Cheval. Tall too. And like the officers of the Imperial Guard, he had a great moustache. Dear God, this was the worst of all possible encounters. This was mortal danger.

Georgie crossed to Myddelton and glared his unspoken warning. "Stand and greet our guest, little idiot," he growled.

And stepping into this uncharted chasm of espionage play-acting, Myddelton rose, clumsily knocking the bench over. He bent and carefully righted it. And praying desperately that he'd got it right, blinked stupidly.

Des Champs came and stood before him, regarding him, measuring him. "Why is he not in the army, Dupont? The Emperor has need of great tall lads like this."

Myddelton stared at his boots, even as he noted that like Georgie, Des Champs smelled of cheap wine and garlic, and added to this, the stench of the stables, and of sex, of immoderate coupling, like one who passed his nights in the seediest brothels.

Georgie shrugged dismissively, pretending disinterest. "Far too stupid...And terrified of strangers. Can you not see how he shakes? And he does not speak, you know. Him, he would be useless. Worse than useless...he would be a liability to his regiment..."

Des Champs took hold of Myddelton's face, and ignoring Myddelton's attempt to shrink back, jerked it up. "Do you not want to be a soldier and serve your Emperor, eh?"

Unblinking, unbreathing, unflinching, Myddelton stared ahead, striving to remain still. Not to tremble. To show no fear. And above all, no comprehension. A blank.

Des Champs looked him full in the face. "Do you not want the riches of plunder? The women? The glory? We shall be in Poland soon. Think of it! The Polish girls, they are plentiful...with great soft bubbies, hé hé. You'd like that, eh?"

And his life dependent on it, still Myddelton stared ahead, barely breathing, his eyes fixed on nothing.

"He does not know what to do with a girl, my friend," Georgie exclaimed. "You see, he does not understand! Leave him. It is of no use..." He shook his head with the shame of it. "Each year, my aunt, she has sent him to the recruiting officer. And each year, the recruiting officers, they send him back..." He shrugged eloquently. "Come, sit down...tell me why are you not riding south to join the others..."

With a final questioning look at Myddelton, a searching, intense look, Des Champs went to the table. "I know, I know." He slung his leg over the bench and sat. "There has been the trouble at home, you know...But first give me something to drink. I have been out for hours. Some fool thought he saw an English ship or something, and nothing would do but that we must ride out, up and down the coast, in search of it. I think he thought we could do a bit of wrecking. Fool. So off we ride, to the west, to the east. Nothing." He exhaled his exasperation and poured himself a cupful from the pitcher. And drank it down. "It was probably one of our own privateers, flying English colours to escape the naval blockade. Or those damned English Revenue Cutters...I tell you, they are everywhere." He poured himself another mugful and again drank it down. "Here, refill the jug, will you, Dupont?" He handed the empty jug to Georgie and turned to consider Myddelton. Then: "I tell you what, my friend. I shall do you a great favour. He is your cousin, but is afraid of strangers, yes?"

"The son of my uncle, yes," Georgie confirmed with apparent disinterest.

Myddelton remained still. Did he suspect? Or was it just in the nature of an officer?

"Well, this is what I will do for you, because you are my friend." Des Champs swung round to face Georgie and grinned. "I shall take him with me. There. How do you like that? And if he dies in battle, well, it will be a great honour for the family, non? And better than this..." He gestured at Myddelton standing, cringing, awkward and foolish against the wall.

Dear God. Myddelton's breath, and all emotion, caught in his throat. Dear God, he was caught. Trapped. Snared. Fiske was right. It was kill or be killed. And because he had not obeyed him, he was trapped. He risked a glance at Georgie as he laughed at Des Champs' suggestion. And tried to still the blind panic. Od's death, what now? How would he get out of this cottage and back to the cove, to England? And if he were not at the cove when Croggon returned for him, what then? He swallowed tightly; the ticking of his pulse rapid and relentless in his throat and wrists. The leather band about his arm felt tight and constrictive. Sweat dripped down his temple and over his cheek. Please heaven Des Champs didn't notice.

Georgie appeared to notice him not at all. As if he had forgotten him. And poured Des Champs more wine.

Myddelton crouched down and stared at the floor. His palms were wet. The sweat was dripping down his neck and back in rivulets. 'Struth, trapped. Snared, by God. No. No, he must escape. He must. But how?

"...I shall return to my regiment tomorrow, I think..." Des Champs was saying.

Myddelton blinked, flexing the muscles in his jaw. *Not with me, you won't, French bastard.*

Georgie said nothing, but crossed to the sideboard to fetch another bottle.

Des Champs told an extremely bawdy joke. And then another. Georgie laughed uproariously. And kept refilling Des Champs' cup. Brothel humour. 'Struth, not even Harry told jokes like that. Myddelton paid no attention. But the jokes kept coming—an apparently endless supply.

Christ, how long had it been? A quarter hour? An half hour? It seemed interminable. Myddelton's shirt and waistcoat were drenched now with nervous sweat. He must get away. Back to the cove. Croggon could only wait so long. Des Champs told yet another joke. S'life, they were foul. There was only one way. He must draw the skean d'hu from his boot. Must draw it and use it. It was a risk. To Georgie. To himself. But if he were slow and careful...Slow and careful, and no one would notice. He leaned back on his heels and wrapped his arms about his knees. And with his eyes fixed on the packed earth floor, felt for, and closed his fingers over the knife hilt. And slowly...as slow as if he were stalking deer downwind...slowly, patiently, incrementally, began to inch it out and free. First the hilt, then the blade.

"...But yes, I must rejoin my regiment. And I shall be glad to go, you know," Des Champs said and banged the cup down on the table. "This business with my sister, it has upset my mother, you know, but..."

"What business with your sister?" Georgie said, stopping. Then poured out more wine.

Des Champs drank it down. "Did you not know? She was courting with some Englishman!" And suddenly red with a drunken brutal rage, he threw the cup against the wall. "Whoring with some Englishman, the bitch!" he bellowed. "She said he wanted to take her to England. And I, I a hero of the Emperor's elite corps!" He spat on the floor. "Well I made sure this Englishman—whoever he is—will not want her. No one

495

will want her after this! Ha! Shall I tell you what I did, Dupont? Shall I tell you?" he thundered. "Ehn? I gave her to my men, that's what I did!" He nodded hard.

His hand on his knife, Myddelton stilled. As death. And drew no breath. Shocked, stupefied, sickened. Unable to comprehend what he heard. And closed his eyes against such evil. He did not look at Georgie. He did not see Georgie's face. In his horror, he could not move.

Beneath the grime, Georgie turned ashen. Ashen and still, like pale stone.

Des Champs noticed neither of them. He stared at the table, rehearsing in his mind the justice of his actions, the unquestionable righteousness of so saving his family name. "That is what I did. I gave her to the men to use as they wanted—like the whore she was. They enjoyed that! And when they were finished, I beat her. And threw her out. Ha! She went and hanged herself, the whore. Good riddance, I say." He gave a coarse vicious laugh.   "You should have come over, Dupont. You could have had her too. Just like on campaign, it was. At first she screamed, you know. They all do. But after a while, she stopped...And you know Jeannot? A big man is Jeannot. He was the first. And he had her four, maybe five..."

He had gone too far. Georgie, silent, murderous, avenging, came from behind. And in a single motion took hold of Des Champs' head and slammed it against the table. Hard. Savagely. With all his strength and purpose. Once. And again. And a third time.

Des Champs slumped onto the table. Blood trickled from his now slack mouth.

Georgie dropped his arm and stepped back.

Watching, Myddelton had not moved. Fear had become a remote emotion—a theory. Nothing to do with the present maelstrom of revulsion. His mouth dry, he swallowed hard on rising bile. And waited, transfixed.

They both waited. Des Champs twitched, then remained still, lifeless, his blood dripping onto the table.

Finally, blinking rapidly, panting, his hands limp at this sides, Georgie looked up to protest softly and in English, "I never touched her, you know. Never. Not even once."

And slowly, his leg muscles aching and cramped, Myddelton stood. Returned the skean d'hu to its sheath. And found that he was shaking. From civilian to combatant in one night. "Is he dead?"

31

From out the storm of rage that engulfed him, hard and battering like raining hail, shrieking and howling within, through the explosion of keening grief that tore at his insides as hemlock, Georgie Shuster heard nothing. Heard nothing but the fierce and desperate pounding of his own heart, the laboured intake of his breath. Felt nothing but the devastation of a savage hatred. And looking upon Des Champs, her terrible, lifeless, unnatural brother, and pulsing with loss, he roared, "Damn you, Des Champs! Damn you—and all your men! May you burn forever in hell for what you did to her!" And turning to look intently at Myddelton, he added with quiet passion, "I swear to you, Myddelton, I never touched her. Not once. I never laid a hand on her! Though my life on it, I longed to…For she was the swe…" And stopped. For the knowledge of her brutal rape and death defeated him. "Oh God," he cried, shaking and inarticulate upon a torrent of loss and despair.

Myddelton remained still. Motionless. Uncertain. His stomach churning, lurching, recoiling against the horror. Sweet Christ…"Is he dead?" he demanded, staving off the panic, his mind struggling for intelligent thought amidst the crowding nightmare images of pitiless barbarity. Of relentless inhuman violation. Of the final unquiet silence of suicide.

Georgie had not moved. For a battle-hardened soldier he was suddenly too close to weeping. And could not save himself.

"What?" he replied dully. And regarding Des Champs inanimate and bleeding on the table, said bitterly, "I don't know…Who cares? If he's not now, he soon will be." He shrugged—a routine gesture, nothing more. "I'll take him out with me and dump him at sea. Let the sharks finish him, the scum." Then, his eyes glittering and shining with unshed tears: "As God is my witness, I hope they may. And let him wake as he is ripped and tossed limb from limb for what he did to her."

It's war, Pem. Soldiers die. They fight, and they die. Myddelton swallowed hard. Swallowed down the bile and his own tears. For there was no time for this. Not here. Not in this place. Not now. Such emotion as had consumed Georgie led too often and too easily to folly. He knew that. Knew it led to unwarranted, uncalculated risks. To foolish risks. And stupid mistakes. To certain death. Dear God, what a mess.

In any other time or place, Myddelton would have left him. Left him alone to rage and lament. Left him to weep in disbelief and emptiness. But not now. And not here. For this was enemy France. And that, that was a Chasseur à Cheval of Napoleon's own Imperial Guard lying face down in his own blood on the table—dead or nearly dead. Neither sympathy nor mercy had a place here. Not kindness nor the comfort of prayer or Requiem. Only survival. For after all the distance he had travelled to reach this place, to fulfil his duty, Myddelton was not prepared to fail. Not now. And so, wiped hard at his eye, expunging the angry tears of fear and terror. And breathing hard, he remained silent. Considering. Ruthlessly severing those connections between heart and gut and head. He had to. He must close the door against befogging sentiment and grief. And instead, instead search out the implications and ramifications of each decision, the dangers, the possible pitfalls of each action. And how to avoid them. Or cheat them.

Bugger it all! He needed to be gone. He should go now. Already he had been far too long about this affair, far too long in France. And anxiously striving to decrease his rapidly increasing desperation, to gain some kind of a grip on the whole intolerable, impossible situation, he ran his hands fretfully through his grease and dirt-caked hair. Which oddly, in some peculiar detaching way, seemed to help. And clenched his jaw against the assailing waves of dismay and despair. And at last, his mind sharpening, focusing, and keen and shrewd as once Georgie had been, he said succinctly, "No. No, that won't do. There's his horse…And he said he came out with others."

"What?" It had a hollow, muted sound, Georgie's voice, as dead and vacant as his eyes.

"Des Champs' horse," Myddelton said. "The horse must be got rid of too."

"Sod it," Georgie muttered. And again furiously: "Sod it! Hobble the poxy brute!"

But perhaps Wellington was right in his assessment of the hunt—for it taught a cool head in the heat of the moment, if nothing else.

"No. No, he said he came out with others," Myddelton repeated. "They may guess he came here. They may even come looking." And frowning, still calculating, he forced his mind to work at this as he did cyphers. A game. Nothing more. A game of wits. A puzzle. Cunning against cunning. But quickly. The components: He had delivered the papers and now must away. Georgie must be protected. And Des Champs? Justice could not, could never, be served for his hellish crimes. But, alive or not, he must be disposed of that he could tell no tales. Not of Georgie, nor of whom he had seen at the house of Bernard Dupont.

And pondering the elements of escape, of accidents, of possible feints, and ignoring Georgie as he stood, wordless and brittle with pain, Myddelton narrowed his eyes. *Think, Myddelton, you ass! Think!* And rapped out, "D'you have any pepper? Or mustard?"

"What?" Georgie looked up, stupefied.

"Pepper. Or mustard," repeated Myddelton. And without waiting for Georgie's guidance or help, went silently to the dresser to open the drawers. To search.

Useless, Shuster watched him, too stricken even to comprehend. "What d'you want pepper for? We ain't goin' to cook him."

Myddelton ignored him. Ignored the petulant contempt and confusion in his voice. The condescension. Ignored the apathy, the emptiness of his gaze. And groping in the corner of a drawer, in the dust and dirt that gathered there, he felt for and found his answer: Four peppercorns. And exhaled his relief. Sweet Christ, it might work. "Here—it's not many, but it should do. Where's there a pestle? And mortar?"

Georgie looked on, his mouth ajar. But such urgency as was evident in Myddelton's razor alertness pierced for an instant the mindless void of his heart-ravaged thoughts. Even wounded soldiers must march on; must bury their dead companions in alien soil and march. It is a fact. Hesitantly, disjointedly, he joined Myddelton at the sideboard, and from a corner below drew forth the small pestle and mortar which he used for grinding salt.

"Here." He did not grasp Myddelton's purpose. But instinct—that instinct honed and refined over his years of army service—directed him to fall in, to obey. If nothing else, he had learned to serve. "There might be some mustard in the back there too. There was used to be." Obedience—the strength and salvation of Wellington's army. "Here. It's...It's here..."

"We must hurry," Myddelton said, determinedly mashing the spice into a fine powder. And nodded his head in Des Champs' direction. "His friends may come looking for him."

Georgie looked but did not see.

The pepper and mustard ground and mixed, Myddelton went outside. And found that the air had grown cooler and the wind had dropped. He could hear nothing of Des Champs' companions. Thank God. And the sky was still blacked with cloud.

And placing the mortar on the ground near the horse, he turned to face his accomplice for this feint. Od's life, it was a huge gelding—a dark chestnut, from what little he could see—and a bloody great bastard! In any other circumstance, Myddelton would have found it admirable. But not tonight. Tonight, it was the devil's own curse. And shaking his head—please God this would work—Myddelton untethered the reins and retied them close so that the horse's head was down. And went back inside.

"Georgie. Here! Help me get him outside. And up onto his horse."

"What? Why?" Georgie had remained by the sideboard.

Myddelton stopped for an instant. Then suddenly furious: "For Christ's sake, Georgie, just help me! It's our only hope."

Warily and reluctantly, pathetic, Georgie came to stand beside Myddelton, behind Des Champs. And following Myddelton's lead, slowly, resolutely placed Des Champs' limp arm about his shoulder. Just as Myddelton was doing…

"One, two, three…" Grunting with exertion, they shifted him backward, then lifted and hauled him up, up from the bench. His mashed face, his nose broken and awry, left a pool of blood on the table. A big man, Des Champs. And heavy. Riding 15 or 16 stone. And heavier now—dead-drunk or just dead. And with his arms still pinned about their shoulders, step by step, slowly, his booted feet dragging, trailing awkward and useless on the packed earth floor, they edged him away from the table, bumping and bruising their knees and ankles on the bench. And inched and staggered and dragged their way forward to bring Des Champs outside. Thank Christ it was a small cottage!

It was a slow business. Painfully slow. Too slow for Myddelton's liking. And with each minute, a riskier. Where were Des Champs' friends and companions now? Nearby? Or miles off in the opposite direction? When would they come looking? Any minute now. Any minute…

"Steady on, Georgie…Sideways through the door. That's it. Good, good…Now, whatever you do, don't let the horse smell him too closely."

As a somnambulist, Georgie blinked at the darkness, seeing little, understanding less. The horse snorted and stirred. Then stilled. War horses grow used to the stench of fear and death. They are trained for it.

Two more steps and they were beside the horse.

"Sod it, this had better work," Myddelton murmured. "Right. Georgie, stay where you are."

Grim and obedient, Georgie held on, bearing Des Champs' full fetid weight, while Myddelton lifted the arm he had about his shoulder and placed it across the horse.

"Hold him there," Myddelton ordered.

And obedient still, Georgie steadied him, while Myddelton reached down, took hold of Des Champs' great thigh and began to hoist him up and forward, across the saddle. The horse shifted slightly and pawed. Straining, Georgie grabbed at the saddle to hold the gelding close.

Determinedly, using all the strength he possessed, Myddelton lifted and shoved the dead weight of Des Champs up. Slowly, slowly up. Inch by inch, up. Then, surprisingly, Georgie followed suit, and gripped Des Champs' other thigh. And together, grunting, swearing like tinkers, they pushed and heaved Des Champs up—up and across the horse's back. Not collapsed against the horse's neck as Myddelton would have liked. But he was up, his head lolling, his arms hanging slack and heavy over the other side. It would have to do.

Sweating and gasping, Myddelton stopped to catch his breath, to rest his head briefly against the horse's broad shoulder and to pat him. "Good lad...Good lad," he soothed.

"Georgie, go to his head. And keep stroking his nose to keep him calm. Right?"

Georgie went. And stroked the long equine nose, all the while murmuring sounds more familiar to stable boys and gypsies than to intelligence men.

And Myddelton, the Melton man, the bruising rider in all fields, his eyes now adjusted to the dark, bent and let down the one near stirrup. And wedged it fast about Des Champ's boot. Then meticulously entangled the stirrup leather with his long spur. Then took the length of the near rein and wove it into the already tangled stirrup. And cautiously eyed the result. Would it work? He shook his head. God only knew...

And last, he found the bowl of powdered herbs, dumped them into his hand and went to stand beside Georgie.

"Lead him out into the lane. Away from the house."

And when they were in the lane, holding firmly on the gelding's halter, talking gently as a horse whisperer, Myddelton placed his hand, full of the ground pepper and mustard, over the animal's muzzle.

The effect was instant. The horse stirred, tried to back away, whinnied, and inhaled.

Myddelton released the halter. At once, his nose and mouth now filled with irritant spice, the horse snorted and sidled. And snorting hard, each breath taking the pepper farther and farther up his nose, the gelding whinnied in anger and distress. And reared up, throwing Des Champs to the ground. But it was not enough to satisfy. Neighing furiously, fully unnerved and irrational, spooked and wild, the gelding kicked out. And sidestepping frantically, he bolted, galloping, dragging Des Champs behind, his head bumping over the rock-strewn path, his body kicked and battered by flying hooves.

Watching, Myddelton exhaled with stunned relief. It had worked. Thank Christ! It had worked. And he would have turned to admonish Georgie to go inside, to spill wine over himself and the table, to eliminate all trace of Des Champs. But some thing, some sound heard in the distance perhaps, or the glow of a far away torch had without warning broken through the web of Georgie's grief, reminding him of who and what he was. His clouded eyes grew sharp with caution. And rubbing his forehead, he stopped cold, listening and hearing. "They're here, Myddelton. They're here! Just beyond that field. Des Champs' friends," he whispered, nodding to the north. And his expression intense and intelligent, he licked his lip. "Run, Myddelton. Run. Run like hell...I'll keep them here...Go on...I'll keep them..."

Myddelton hesitated and clasped Georgie's hand. It was too sudden, too unexpected.

"Go!" Shuster urged. "I'll get your papers safe away. Now go. I'll be all right."

He had no choice. Without a word, without farewell, without a glance behind, Myddelton left him and began to run. Toward the path. Toward the sea. Keeping low, always keeping low.

He ran and ran. Along the beaten dirt path as fast and as far as he could until he thought his lungs must burst. His throat ached. And the air scorched his nostrils and throat as he gulped it in. Blood drummed in his head. But still, he kept running, pounding at the dirt with his feet, putting distance between himself and the search party which must certainly be at Georgie's by now. Running as if his life depended on it. It did.

At last he came within sight of the cove. Relieved, he doubled over, and fell to his knees, catching at his sides. It was all he could do. Each breath ripped at his parched throat. Sweat poured down his face, his chest, his back and legs. He put a hand out to keep himself from toppling to the ground. And swallowed—an exercise in pain—then staggered back to his feet. He must keep on. His legs shook with exertion and his calves burned. Drawing himself up, he stumbled—knees buckling—toward the beach. He could see no one. Where the bloody hell was Croggon?

Gradually, his breathing slowed, allowing him to limp, to walk, to think beyond his hurts. And with that came the knowledge that there were men out looking for smugglers, English smugglers or seamen—looking for him. And again, his blood began to race feverishly. Willing his legs not to wobble but to obey, he crouched down and glanced in all directions. Oh Christ, what was that? Was it men calling to one another? Hell's teeth, it was. He froze and waited. The voices seemed to grow fainter—as if they were moving away from him. Still keeping close to the ground, ignoring the tingle and stab of agony in his legs and lungs, he quickened his pace to a run again. Beyond the impossible now, beyond to survival.

Ahead, the beach was empty. He ran forward and collapsed, panting, in the sand. Helpless, spent, defenceless, he lay there, clutching at handfuls of shingle and cold sand while he drew in great gulps of air, and the salt from his sweat stung his eyes.

The voices were approaching. Then, nothing. He raised himself to his knees and looked frantically about. There was nowhere to hide. No rocks. No dunes. Dear God in heaven, there was nowhere. Just salt encrusted tufts of grass, nothing more. Nowhere...Taut with anger and futility, with the inevitable blinding rage, he regarded the water, and in bitterness tried to compose himself, to prepare for that unavoidable. For death. Od's death, a pox on everything. To have come so far for this. Wretched and furious, he wiped his arm across his forehead. A plague take all Frenchmen in this God-forsaken country.

...The water. He could hide in the water. Urgent now, he dragged himself to his feet and scrambled over the sand to the bay. A cloud-mountain slid over the glimmer of a moon, darkening the sky and land to pitch. Myddelton strained to hear footsteps. Running footfalls. Or the patter of horses' hooves. Nothing. The white froth of a wave lapped, frivolous and playful, at the toe of his boot. He eyed it balefully. And drawing a deep, steadying, dread-quelling breath, he started into the chill shallows.

In three sloshing paces, he was up to his knees. And could feel the cold—the cold of the water encasing and penetrating the leather of his boots like strands of ivy about an old house. Another two steps and the water slid over the tops of his boots, slipping and trickling down his legs and feeling its way to his feet. It was biting as snow, a piercing ice-fire against the sweating heat of his calves.

The waves, rolling gently toward the beach, splashed against his buckskins and wetted his coat. A few more steps and he was in up to his waist. He clenched his teeth against crying out, and kept his hands close to his sides, resisting the impulse to raise them to keep them out of the water for as long as possible. He stopped for an instant, hoping to hear the sound of oars—Croggon's oars—slapping the water. Or his whistle, telling him that he was on his way in. Nothing. Nothing.

A shot exploded in the silence. *Hell.* Then another. And another.

Catching a mouthful of air, Myddelton sank down into the water. He must go deeper. But did not know how long he could stay under. Overhead, he thought he heard more shots. His lungs had begun to ache with the need for air. He turned his head to the side, exposing his ear and mouth. Air rushed into his lungs, gentle and soft like a spring rain. He heard nothing. He did not, would not look back to see them, to try to count how many of them there were. Whether they were on the headland or shore. Whether they had seen him, or drunk, were merely firing aimlessly.

Submerging his head once more, Myddelton made for deeper water—half walking, half-swimming. The shots exploded over his head again. Thank God his coat was of a dark colour—darker now with the water. The sodden leather of his boots and buckskins weighed him down, so that he could stand without bobbing to the surface. He began to see stars; his nose felt like it was collapsing.

He lifted his head for air. A wave splashed about his ears and over his head, filling his mouth and nose with salt water, choking him. Instinctively he raised his head, coughing. A shot rang out, whirred past, leaving a stripe of pain across his forehead. He flinched and cried out. A second shot nicked his ear. He stifled his cry, gulped at the air and pulled his head below the surface. The brine burned into the wounds. Tense

506

with pain and the necessity of silence, he reached up to feel his forehead, but everything was wet. He could tell nothing of the damage, nothing at all, nothing of how much or little he was bleeding.

He shifted his position so that he could roll his head to one side for a mouthful of air, while exposing the smallest target space. And waited. One breath. Two...Where the hell was Croggon? Christ, it was cold.

He could hear nothing. And wondered whether those on shore had gone. Or were they waiting for more of a target before they opened fire again? Were they waiting for Croggon? He inched farther away from the shore to accommodate the outgoing tide and prayed God the current didn't grow any stronger.

The waiting was terrible. And he was growing colder. Where the devil was Croggon anyway? Would he never come? Myddelton tried to wriggle his toes, but they were numb. His forehead and ear had been stinging for so long that they too were growing numb—numb with pain. But at least he was alive.

He tightened his jaw to keep his teeth from chattering. With his eyes closed against the salt water, anyone might creep up on him and he not know it. The powder in his pistol would be wet; his hands were too numb to hold a knife. He shook uncontrollably. From fear or cold? Did it matter? Was this what death was like? A cruel dull coldness blotting out all warmth, all life?

When he got back...he *would* get back...he wished he knew if he were bleeding or no. If he had to swim all the way back to that plagued Revenue Cutter, he would get back.

He did not know how long he had been in the water. It must have been nearly an hour. But he'd had to move farther out twice...or was it three times? Surely, the pissing bastards must have gone by now. Yes, he must have been waiting for at least an hour. So certainly they would have gone by now. Should he try to pull off his boots and start swimming in the direction of the boat? Wherever that was. Or were the damned French still there, still on shore and headland, waiting for him to move so that they could finish him off? Would Croggon find his body and take it back to England? To Janey? Sweet Christ, not that. Not after all this. Such injustice could not be. He *would* get back to her—alive. If only he were not so damnably cold, so bloody bloody cold. Shivering as he was made it difficult to keep his balance. A wave washed over his head, filling his mouth.

Through the water that filled his ears, he could hear the lapping of oars. With relief so sweet that he nearly fainted, Myddelton lifted his head and hissed softly. And waited, quaking with cold.

Minutes later, the dinghy was beside him, jiggling on the surface of small waves.

"Well now, there you be, my lord," Croggon said chattily, and steadied the boat with the oars. "I was planning to fetch you back sooner, but that were a bit too much busyness on the shore for my likin', so I stayed away. Need a hand up now, do ye?"

Myddelton grasped the side of the boat with both hands, but it was too much. He slid back into the water. Leaning over the side, Croggon's mate took hold of him under the arms and with a seaman's certainty, hauled him in.

Croggon frowned. It had begun to rain lightly. "Are ye hurt, then, my lord?"

Passively, faint with exhaustion, unable to feel his extremities, Myddelton sat hunched on the bottom of the dinghy, and leaned against the boat's wooden side. Croggon bending over him was blurred and watery. "I don't know," he admitted, through the chattering of his teeth and the shaking. And was conscious of the rough wood against his face. He was on his way home now. Home to Janey. *Du bist die Ruh...*

Croggon thrust a flask into his hand. "Here. This'ull warm ye."

"What? Oh. Thank you." His fingers were too cold to move, too numb to grip. The flask fell onto the floor beside him.

Croggon frowned again, reached for the flask and uncorked it, then put his arm about Myddelton's shoulders and tipped the flask to Myddelton's mouth. Brandy dribbled over his cheeks and chin. A trickle burned a warming path down his throat.

Silently, Croggon's mate picked up the oars and began rowing.

By the time they drew alongside the cutter, Myddelton was shuddering convulsively. Pain wracked every part of his body—the pain in his forehead and ear were indistinguishable to him from that in his legs.

Croggon bent near and shook his shoulder. "Can ye get yourself up that ladder, do you reckon, or will you be wantin' Batey's help?" he asked.

"Are we here?" Myddelton whispered.

"That's right. Back at the Cutter, all safe an' sound."

Myddelton opened his eyes and tried to focus on the ladder. It wove and retreated as in a dream. "Yes. Yes, I can do it. I shall be fine." He pulled himself to his knees and took hold of the ladder hanging beside the dinghy.

Croggon smiled reassuringly. He doubted that his lordship had the strength to make it even half the way up. And fishing a man out of the sea, particularly a man in Myddelton's condition, was a damnably mucky thing. "The lads are just up there, waitin' to haul ye in," he said cheerfully, and placed Myddelton's foot onto the first rung.

With his eyes closed against falling and his weight tugging and ripping at his arm muscles, and though he could barely grasp the rungs, Myddelton ascended the ladder, each rung a triumph of will against every odd. He felt as though he were flailing without direction. And he had no strength. Resting his face against the next rung, he lifted his foot to the next step. And again. And again. Nearly to the top. Nearly. He reached up to grasp the side of the ship and felt, through the cold awkward stiffness in his hands, his hold slipping.

A strong hand took hold of his, and then caught at his wrist and forearm. Two other hands grasped his other arm and pulled him up, wrenching his arms in their sockets, dragging him up over the side.

Completely spent, Myddelton sank down onto the deck, letting his eyes dwell on the Cutter's wooden deck. Safety. He had done it. He tried to savour the emotion, but it cost too much. Then, placing one hand before him, he tried to stand, but his legs refused to obey. He fell forward, broken as a crushed leaf. He blinked at the water streaming from his hair and into his eyes. Water...and something else. Something dark. He raised his hand to wipe at his eyes and hair and brought it away covered red. Blood. It was blood. His blood.

Someone held a lantern close. "Sweet Jesu, Cap'n, look at'im. 'e's turned blue, 'e 'as!"

Myddelton stirred at the voice. And looked at the blood on his hand for a moment, unable now to comprehend it. Then it blurred and went bright. *Du bist die Ruh, Der Friede mild*...And his head crashed insensibly onto the deck.

Perhaps it was best.

32

Sir Charles Heron had taken the indirect route home from White's Club. That is to say that by dint of several well-conceived excursions he had managed to make the short walk from White's Club on St. James's Street, down King Street and so to Myddelton House in St. James's Square last well over three hours. He stopped in at Locke's to place an order for two new hats, then at Hoby's for new boots—both errands he would normally eschew. And he called in at the booksellers and found three volumes he most particularly wished to examine and had placed an order for several more. For he had stopped off at White's on his way home from the City, where he had been consulting with Ruttridge & Chart and with his own man of business, Frobisher, of Frobisher, Fenton & Hayes, on a question of a most sensitive nature. The which had given him more than enough to chew over.

Hence his retreat to the security of White's. But his visit there proved less than restorative: In the Morning Room he overheard more unsettling talk about Myddelton, and his niece. As before, something about Myddelton seeking an annulment. Though the rather elegant gentleman seated in the wing chair by the bow window had laughingly discounted the whole as a figment of the Wythenshaw's—there was that name again—overwrought imagination. And by way of a rejoinder had quipped, "'Struth, I dare say you'll tell me next that Alvanley shall only win his race 'gainst Hurst by a whisker or Dunphail's taken a vow of chastity, ha ha…Not poss, dear chap, not poss. We're talkin' 'bout Myddelton here…"

Still, to his mind the innuendo only confounded the situation further and Sir Charles knew he must speak to his niece Jane again. And did not wish to. He wished not to. For his last discussion with her on these issues had been beyond distressing. To both of them. Thus the three hour walk.

But she was not about when finally he did return. And learned, eventually, from Kettering that she was unwell with the headache but hoped to come down later. And when at five, Lord Pemberton called to take her for a ride in the Park and was turned away by Kettering with the same excuse, Sir Charles knew he was right to anticipate the worst.

When she did emerge, he heard rather than saw her. Heard her at the fortepiano, playing—not the previous restlessly impassioned music (thank Heaven)—but something contrapuntal, ordered and precise though admittedly dark, which he had never heard before. And he came down quietly, and opening the door he saw her at the instrument, beautiful, washed in the yellow light of early evening. And saw too that she appeared pale or tired—which made him cross. For it must render his purpose all the more unkind, and therefore distasteful. That his dearest Angel should be brought to this...

"Janey?"

She turned. "Uncle." And rising from the bench, she closed the lid of the fortepiano.

"I have never heard that before," he remarked. "What was that?"

"It is an English Suite," she said with a certain frustration, regarding the music on the stand. "I found it in a stack of papers in the box room and liked the look of it. But the front cover is missing, so I do not even know who wrote it. It is very difficult though. At least for me." And she closed the sheaf of music, then smiled, as if in shutting away her music she had also shut away the melancholy which fed it.

"But where have you been, dearest of all uncles? Kettering tells me you were out for hours." And leaving the fortepiano, she came to him and kissed him as she always had done and tucked her hand through his arm. "Shall we not go through to the Morning Room? It is so very pleasant in there."

As ever, her smile and sweetness of disposition lifted his mood. And he was suddenly conscious of how very much he had missed her all these weeks. "Oh, I went to my Club, you know," he admitted, stalling. "And did a little shopping."

She chuckled low in her throat. And Sir Charles, hearing that dear familiar sound, wondered if he had not been mistook in his fears. And checked himself long enough to question whether his morning's interviews had not perhaps been rash?

"Shopping? You?" she teased, her spirits lifting in the company of her much loved uncle. "Soon you shall be telling me you have given up chess in favour of faro."

"Ha! Faro! That's a fool's game and you know it as well as I…"

"Yes, indeed," she agreed solemnly, pleased to find she retained her ability to ruffle him. "But I know you," she said. "You cannot fool me. This 'my Club' and 'shopping' was merely an elaborate ruse, was it not?" Her eyes sparkled. "…To cover your secret and true destination which was, of course, the infamous Minerva Press."

"The Minerva Press? The Minerva Press!" Though Sir Charles had often delighted in her quickness of wit, he had forgot her uncanny ability to surprise and to twit him when or where he was least expecting it. "My dear girl, I did no such thing, as you well know! I have no interest whatsoever in that melodramatic drivel and romantic muck."

Then, suddenly grave, but yet unwilling to reveal his earlier purpose, he said, "If you must know, I went to my Club…and heard such things there as disturbed me beyond measure. And I could not bring myself to come back to you in such a state, so I went instead and bought some hats and some new boots." It was almost the truth.

"It must have been disturbing indeed to drive you to such lengths as that," she observed drily even as the laughter fled her eyes. Unobtrusively, she disengaged her hand and went to sit by a vase of flowers—parrot tulips of brilliant red and white, columbine and lilac—and Lotto came to rest his head upon her knee. And had Sir Charles been as observant as he believed he was, he would have seen her guard go up. But he did not. For he knew her as she had been, not as she had become. So he did not even think to look.

Withdrawing into herself, she remained still, so still. For she could guess at what he might have heard. But really, she admonished herself, was it not just as possible that he had heard of some scandal at Horse Guards? Or of the latest casualty lists from Spain? Or indeed that Caro

513

Lamb was dressing herself as a page boy in her pursuit of Byron? (Which she found hard to credit.) But it was Saturday and Myddelton had not come. And though she had determinedly diverted all her energies into the many preparations for the ball, still, it was Saturday, and he had neither returned nor sent word. All day, a dull unshakable dread had been haunting her, hounding her—that somewhere, Myddelton lay wounded or dead, and she would never see him again. Ruthless, she dragged herself away from such fears. And castigated herself for growing maudlin.

Sir Charles had been watching her closely. Then, fidgeting, disliking the long silence, he took a turn about the room. "Janey, what is amiss? Why will you not tell me?" he said, searching her face.

Tell him what? That she had been gossiped about and maligned? That she had committed herself to helping the very creature who had started so many of those unsavoury rumours now in circulation? Or that Myddelton had gone abroad for the Foreign Office and might never return? Or that despite all, all the malicious rumours and misunderstandings and quarrels, she adored her husband? How could she? How could she tell him? What could she tell him? There was too much. For Sir Charles knew nothing and was not inclined to understand. And she was bound to silence.

So she took refuge in misunderstanding and shook her head a little. And deflected with a circumspection that Castlereagh, the master of such things, or her father would have commended. "It is the ball. There is far more to it than I should ever have imagined possible," she said lightly. "And though Lady Choate gave me endless instruction, and I consult with her instructions constantly, still..." It was a poor excuse. At least, she thought it a poor excuse. But it would have to do. Of course, if he had been Myddelton, she would assuredly have also told him about Chef Philippe's recent spate of catastrophes, including the alleged theft of a box of 'si belles, si precieuses, si douces' sugared flowers—and he would have laughed.

"Janey," Sir Charles began soberly, only to stop, and start again. "Jane, my dear, I have not been entirely honest with you about my reason for coming to visit."

"No?" She did not like this. His tone was too like that of a month ago, when he had broken the news of her impending marriage. And rubbing Lotto's ears, she bowed her head that he might not read the distrust in her expression. "And what have you not told me?"

"Well, you know I came because of some rumours which Lady Choate had been made privy to…" She did not look up. "But since I arrived, I confess I have grown more and more uneasy, for there are all these things being said about Myddelton and a young woman called Wythenshaw, I think it is."

"Gossip again, uncle? You never listen to gossip," she reminded him. And wished she believed it.

"No! No, I do not," he assured her. And himself. "But I have never before needed to rely on it for information—because you were unwilling to tell me what I wished to know," he countered.

Her hand stilled behind Lotto's ear. "What are you saying?" she asked, determined to hide her increasing wariness.

"Simply that it is Saturday and Myddelton is not returned. Nor is there word of his whereabouts. Which concerns me greatly. And which leads me to believe that you have not told me the truth of this business, if indeed you know it. And this afternoon, while I was at the Club, I again heard something about him seeking an annulment." There, he had said it.

She feigned surprise. "Really?" she said, feeling tired, and unhappily vulnerable. To be accused of lying. The thought made her ill. And when was that snaking little word, *annulment*, going to be expunged from her life? When first it had been used, she had been stung, certainly. But now, with it thrust constantly at her face, it had become an insidious torment. "How very industrious the gossip-mill has been. One would have thought they could find something else to talk about…" Agitated, she frowned. She detested all scenes of disharmony or dissension. But unless she was much mistaken that was where this was leading. But she could see no way to avoid nor avert it. She regarded the tulips, attempting to compose herself against the inevitable storm. Nor did Sir Charles notice that, in that instant, a further barrier of courtesy and due respect had been erected—for he did not even know she owned such barriers. Nor that she knew how to use them.

Sir Charles did not smile. "Yes, Janey, an annulment." He faced her. "They were still saying at White's that Myddelton was to seek an annulment!" He omitted to relate the way in which that particular rumour had been thoroughly quashed. But said instead, "Which was curious, do you see, because that is precisely what I was about this morning in the City. Consulting with Myddelton's man of business and Frobisher, my own man…"

Her breath caught in her throat. "I beg your pardon?" she said, caught off guard. For how can one prepare for the unimaginable and unthinkable? "An annulment?" she repeated. And covered her eyes with her hand. "I cannot believe this…" she whispered, more to herself than to him. "Why would you do such a thing? We were married. Myddelton is my husband, sir!" she protested. "I am his wife."

With a wave of his hand, Sir Charles discounted her. "Janey, you have been married for less than a month—what do you know of marriage? Yet in that short time, that time most couples would count their honeymoon, your fine husband has been careless of all appearance, and brazen in his infidelity." She loathed the sarcasm in his voice. The condescension. She made a desperate effort to control herself, to quell her panic and subdue that trepidation which would wreak havoc upon her.

"I have now heard countless rumours of it," Sir Charles exaggerated. "Already your good name has been vilely smirched by association! I would ask what can next befall you, but I am sorry to say I know the answer: he has abandoned you…"

He thought he saw a flash of outrage in her eyes, but continued nonetheless, for he would brook no argument: "Yes, abandoned you! And you know it to be true. You said he would return by Friday, did you not? And I believe you thought it to be the truth. But he is not here, is he? And you do not even know where he is, do you? Dearest child, gentlemen have always said they were off about a horse when what they actually meant was another woman. Believe me, you are not the first wife

516

to have been taken in by such a tale. I have seen it often and often, time out of mind…"

"That is your opinion, is it?" she said, breaking in at last, dismayed by his accusations and doubt. "Well perhaps it is true of your acquaintance, but I assure you, it is not true of Myddelton." Doubly dismayed that there was so much to be doubted which she could not answer. For such charges were unanswerable. Nor was she unaware that to anyone unacquainted with the facts of their situation that this was how it must appear—that Myddelton *was* careless of appearances and brazen in his infidelities.

Yet this was her uncle. Could he not see the spectre of despair which followed in her wake? Did he not recognise the unrequited longing or the worry and care which marked her? Was he blind, or merely blinkered? Was there no way to halt this tirade? And she wanted to protest and to shout: 'You do not know of what you speak. He is dead. He is dead. Killed in the service of his King and country! *He's gone, he's gone, his loss deplore…and I shall never never never see him more. O let me weep, for ever weep…*' There was an odd catch in her voice: "Is that all?"

In thrall to his own righteous convictions and sound conclusions, Sir Charles saw little, but her response had unnerved him and he took another turn about the room, digesting this. Had he so quickly forgotten the pride he had in her mien and bearing—her soldier's courage and bearing? Perhaps. Or perhaps he remembered and it made him uneasy. He prowled to the window and twitched at the curtain—the view the same as from his bedroom, both unsatisfactory—before rounding on her. "No, it is not. There is also the question of expenditure."

"I beg your pardon?" she asked warily, unprepared for this renewed assault, struggling still to cope with the torrent of wretchedness he had already unleashed. And she wished suddenly that all her training over the years to respect and honour, to treat all with grace and courtesy, had not made it impossible to speak or to contend as her sentiments bade. She sat up straighter—ramrod straight. "What do you know of our expenditure?"

"Not as much as I shall know on Monday!"

Her eyes widened in alarm and new fear. "What?"

Sir Charles, scandalised and angered by what he believed he knew, and proving that on occasion he could be just as pigheaded and irrational as the next man, went on heedless. "I did not approve of this match from the beginning, but I was prepared to stand by the arrangement as it had been your father's dearest wish." And disregarding the pallor that had extinguished all colour in her face, that now reached even into her eyes, he continued: "I knew, when eventually he did honour the engagement, that Myddelton was marrying you for money and to save his estates. Yes, I know he had no choice. But since that time, he has squandered those monies with a profligacy matched only by that of his dissolute of an uncle! And I will not have it! Frobisher was in the very act of writing to me on the subject when I called in this morning! He has been concerned with vast sums being withdrawn from the bank, allegedly by you. But I know better. And I will not have my niece ruined and reduced to penury by the recklessness and folly of a hardened gamester and libertine. Moreover one who has abandoned her less than a month after their wedding! I will not have it!"

Stunned, aghast, hardly able to breathe, she closed her eyes upon the threatening nausea and tears. She could not think. And could not think how to answer him. Not how to tell him that her mind was crippled with his unkindness. That his accusations were so wildly far removed from the truth or any accurate picture of her life or Myddelton's that she might have laughed—had her heart not been crushed with anguish.

She told herself Sir Charles' accusations were absurd and ridiculous and she must not heed them. Yet how such accusations taint and corrupt all they touch, blighting with an insidious doubt which unseen disfigures, growing by degrees into destruction and ruin. There was a corner in the box room, behind several trunks—she could go and sit there and no one would know to look. Not even Kettering. And she said as calmly as she could, blinking, "So what do you mean to do, Uncle?"

Sir Charles mistook her question for acquiescence. And drawing a deep breath, said, "I have spoken with Myddelton's man of business and with my own, as I told you. Naturally, I was deeply saddened by your admission that the marriage had not been consummated—that

Myddelton has not even had the decency to fulfil his duty to you as his wife! But as Frobisher pointed out…"

She could only stare now, open-mouthed, wordless and trembling, repelled and sickened—distraught that this confidence, bestowed in a moment of unguarded exhaustion, had been betrayed. Used. What in God's name had he done?

"…it does at least provide ample and indisputable grounds for gaining an annulment."

He could not have hurt her more. Her mind reeled and every feeling rebelled. That this most unguarded intimacy should have been discussed by him with his man of business. As if she were no more than a horse, or one of his bitches coming into season. And her breath coming in short gasps, she crossed her arms protectively over her chest and looked at the flowers, summoning all her courage and small wisdom to withstand the onslaught. Dear God in heaven, what was happening to her? First Myddelton was sent away…And now this? Now this…She was to lose him in this most public and humiliating fashion.

"…So I have given orders for the papers to be drawn up immediately so that it can be brought before Parliament at the earliest opportunity. And on Monday, I will convey Myddelton's books of account to my man so that he can assess how much may be recovered and may draw up a suit of reparation for that purpose. I shall have to tell that young secretary of his, Broke, to have the accounts ready…"

Dazed, deadened, she had ceased to hear, ceased to listen as the waves of furious sound, of specious argument, of invective and rage, washed over and past her. And instead, echoing, resounding through the corridors of her heart and mind: *I will lose him. I have lost him. He is gone…*

"…I would have liked to remove you from this house as soon as possible. But although I believe this ball you are so intent upon holding to be an unconscionable folly and will merely advertise Myddelton's abandonment, you would no doubt disagree with me, so I have decided that we shall leave for Britwell Park at first light on Wednesday."

She had never disputed Sir Charles' right to determine her future before and did not know how to begin. He had always held all her affection, all her loyalty. But this had been snuffed out. Wretched, unable to comprehend, she looked at him, her dearest uncle and friend, now a fallen idol and adversary. "Is that all?" she asked. And wanted to cry out, 'Can you not see what you have done? Can you not help me? My husband is gone, lost to me, dead or wounded, I know not where, and I miss him so desperately that I am broken in as many pieces. For I love him so dearly, so very dearly. Yet all you do is berate him and say such things of him and tell me you shall take me away—that I have been betrayed and abandoned and must have no hope of calling him husband again.' But she did not. For drilled in perfection as she was, she could not break that invincible iron-cladding of self-control and training. So she did not scream or cry, though from the dead ember of her struggling heart such a cry rose up. Instead, she stood, shook out her gown and went to quit the room—the perfect niece trained to be the perfect hostess. And glancing at the clock, she observed, her voice sounding foolish or thin in her ears, "I have just seen the time. If I do not return upstairs I shall not be dressed for the evening. And that would be impolite to my escort."

But then, at the door, she paused, and turning, said to him softly and bitterly, "You would not treat a dog so cruelly as you have treated me." And closed the door upon him. And went upstairs to the box room, to the corner, where she remained for more than an hour.

She found Myddelton's secretary as she had known she would, in his well-ordered estate office off the library. And standing in the doorway, she looked about her with interest, noting the many neat shelves of labelled account books and ledgers, the tidied piles of newspaper cuttings and political tracts and pamphlets which covered most surfaces, the pens and inkpot ready on the desk. Engrossed in copying a letter, Mr. Broke did not notice her there. She drew a preparatory breath and smiled. The perfect smile. "Mr. Broke?"

Mr. Broke looked up, startled, and instantly anxious. The house had become a devil's dance of madness with the preparations for the ball—in which fortunately he had little part. Yet. No doubt *she* was here to change all that. "Yes, my lady?"

"No, do not get up," she said, as he made to stand. "Mr. Broke..." She hesitated. She had known from the outset that this would not be easy, and she wondered that she had the audacity to even broach such a subject. Had there been another solution, she would surely have pursued it. But she could see none. And briefly considering the consequences of not asking, she squared her shoulders and began again: "Mr Broke, I know that you are entirely devoted to your cousin. And would do anything to spare him discomfort or embarrassment. Is that not so?"

"Y...yes," he stammered, perplexed already. "Lord Myddelton has always been exceeding kind to me. He is the best of good fellows—and employers."

"Yes. Yes, he is. Well...you will have perhaps been aware that there has been a certain degree of disappointment, or displeasure..." she continued, choosing her words with an unusual care. "...expressed by my uncle over Myddelton's continued absence from home..." She looked away for an instant. "Or perhaps you may have overheard some talk between Sir Charles and myself..."

Mr. Broke's habitually frayed expression increased. "I..." he began, determined to assure her that he did not and would never eavesdrop upon her conversations, but undermined by his own diffidence.

"No," she said firmly. "No, do not be afraid. I intend no rebuke. You could hardly have helped overhearing. Sir Charles speaks very loudly when roused. I know." She blinked rapidly, the first indication of her real embarrassment.

"But you see, the situation is this, my uncle has resolved to...to seek to have our marriage annulled. Or perhaps you already knew that." She did not, could not look to see the expression on his face. "Though that is not in any way my wish, nor do I believe it to be Myddelton's..." And she did not, would not answer his unasked question. She swallowed, intent upon going through with this, intrepid for Myddelton's sake. "He, my uncle that is, is also determined to press for financial restitution, for I have been spending a great deal of money recently, as you will have cause to know." She smiled briefly—a sombre, unhappy expression.

And as unfamiliar as he undoubtedly was with the opposite sex in general—and with her in particular—Mr. Broke knew he read dismay there.

"But Sir Charles believes Myddelton to have lost it all at the tables. As if anything so far from the truth could be imagined!" She regarded him from beneath her lashes hoping to gauge his reaction, but could tell little, though she could see he was bristling at the criticism of his revered cousin. And pressed on: "So...so he is going to come to you, to ask you to present Myddelton's accounts to his solicitor, one Mr. Frobisher."

"Is he?" said Mr. Broke, blanching, suddenly swamped with fear. These were the gravest accusations and insinuations. And grave demands. Mr. Broke remained still, silent. A deep furrow had appeared between his brows. "M...my lady?" he stammered.

"Yes," she confirmed. "Yes, he is. So I was wondering if you might do me a favour," she continued, subduing her many qualms, amazed at her own courage. "And Myddelton, too. Of course."

"My lady, you know I will do anything. Anything at all that is within my power. What is it?"

Quailing, she bit hard on her lip, then said it: "Would you...that is do you think that you might..." She swallowed and raised her chin. "Fiddle the books?"

"I beg your pardon?" Broke whispered, horrified though not outraged. She was pleading for her very life. Even he could see that.

"Falsify them! Add where you should subtract...Subtract where you should add. Cross-reference numbers from nowhere. Or stick the pages together. I don't know. Just make them so that they are incomprehensible to anyone but yourself..." she explained, growing desperate—for she had thought it all through. "So that my uncle can make neither head nor tail of them. So that it will take him and his solicitor months and months to decipher, to learn that they shall never have the least idea about Myddelton's financial affairs. Could you do that, do you think?" she pleaded.

Broke sat as though stunned. As shocked as if she'd asked him to commit a murder. All his beautiful neat columns, his perfect order, all the balancing to the last farthing. He blushed furiously and hesitated.

Hesitated while the tension grew and grew, and she began to fear, to be convinced even, that he would refuse—or worse, expose her to her uncle.

Finally: "Yes, my lady," he said with the same unexpected air of self-possession or self-assurance he brought to Myddelton's frequent and abrupt last minute requests for a speech on this or response to that. "You may rely on me. I shall see to it. By Monday, did you say?"

She nodded, breathless. Then exhaled and smiled gratefully, disarmingly and in profound relief, frankly astonished that he had agreed. "Thank you, Mr. Broke. Thank you. Myddelton shall thank you too, I promise you...And you will come to the ball on Tuesday?"

He had planned not to. But all that had changed. In five minutes. "Yes, my lady." Yes, I shall be there."

"Oh good. Thank you," she smiled again. And still smiling, she returned upstairs.

❧

Lord Pemberton did not have the reputation of being the most observant of young men. But then when has public perception been anything other than inaccurate? Yet as he stood in the anteroom off the foyer of Myddelton House, his chapeau-bras under his arm, running his eye over the newly repainted arabesque designs—Adam blue and pale gold against pristine white—waiting to escort Jane to the theatre, he was aware that things were not as they should be. And when he saw her descending the stairs, serene, remote, consciously and exquisitely gowned in pale satin with a demi-train, he observed that she had been crying, but noted too that she lacked that fragile or frail or hunted look which had marked her countenance at the Romford do. And he pretended not to see the strain between her and her uncle. But instead murmured all the appropriate pleasantries, asked Sir Charles if he was certain he did not wish to join them at the theatre, said how good it was to see him again, and only once they were seated in the town carriage and the door shut upon them did he say, "What? What now?"

So near to midsummer, it was still light. Jane affected to ignore his peremptory question and looked out the window. Then shook her head.

He eyed her with friendly patience, before saying affably, "That, whilst telling me a great deal, did not provide the requisite detail." And unperturbed by her reticence, he favoured her with a lazy smile.

She drew a deep breath. Regardless of her inclination toward reserve, these were matters which would never be permitted to remain private and she knew it. Indeed, as Sir Charles had proved, there was already talk. And she was now determined to fight to protect Myddelton, to save as much as might be saved, whatever else might befall her. So she did not pretend to misunderstand him, but said with that deceptive mildness which wisely he had come to distrust: "Pem, how much damage would a bill of annulment cause to someone?"

"What?" It was hardly what he had expected. "'Struth, I don't know. I've never been in the House when we've heard one. I should imagine it would depend on the circumstances. But a certain amount of damage—gossip—would be inevitable, I dare say. Why?" He added the last suspiciously.

"Well..." she began, uncomfortable. And resolutely quelled all mortification, all maiden modesty. It was possible he was her only friend. Certainly, he was the only one to whom she might turn for help. "Well...Well, because it so happens that Sir Charles has determined to bring such a bill before the House. On my behalf."

"What?" he snapped. She was gazing out the window, seemingly untouched and unfazed, but he was not fooled by her composed or perfect appearance. "An annulment? On what grounds?"

She turned her head to look at him. "He believes that Myddelton has abandoned me. He suspects that Miss Wythenshaw is involved, but does not know how. And he believes that all the money I have spent in refurbishing Myddelton House, was in fact lost at the tables—at faro, I imagine." Her prosaic recitation finished, she looked away, knowing it all sounded so foolish when put like that, like a plot from a summer play in the provinces. But she could not bear to tell him the whole, not yet.

"Well, you have been tossing the ready about pretty freely..." he observed, though without condemnation.

She smiled. "I know," she agreed. "But it was necessary."

"Not saying that it wasn't! That house was a bally mausoleum before you came. Hardy always said it gave him the glooms and wouldn't visit. But none of that gives Sir Charles a case. Abandonment might. But I rather think Myddelton would have to be gone for years—not a week."

She was silent, considering his terse dismissal of Sir Charles' allegations. And resigned herself to revealing the whole. Squaring her shoulders, she said levelly: "But he does have a case. For the moment."

Pemberton narrowed his eyes to regard her intently. "How's that?" he demanded. "Myddelton don't mistreat you. You wasn't damaged goods—sorry, don't mean to offend, but it's material evidence. And he ain't abandoned you! I'd go into the witness box to swear to that. So there is no case to be answered."

She could not bring herself to speak. And so remained silent, studying the pattern of embroidery on the gown. For she knew she could rely upon his fine intelligence to make the necessary connections and deductions

"Janey?" he said sharply, shrewdly. "Janey! No! No, do not tell me. No. I do not believe this!" he exploded. And exhaled fully before beginning again. "You cannot be serious! You're practising on me, ain't you? Janey, tell me this is all a lark."

Slowly she shook her head, denying him that hope.

"Janey!" Then, kindly, tenderly: "But why, in Christ's name? Why? I know it is none of my business, but why?" He shook his head in an attempt to clear it. "Myddelton's so deeply in love with you, he don't know his Greek from his Latin anymore. So I do not understand. I know things did not get off to the best start, but...But when I saw you at the Castlereaghs', I assumed...I was certain...I would have sworn... 'Struth, everyone there was certain...so how could this have happened?"

She drew a deep steadying breath and bit her lip. She had not realised this would be so difficult or painful. But there were no neat answers. And said finally, simply, in all earnestness and with no little shame: "Because...because I believe he meant to woo me. And to win me. Because he is honourable and good. And because he did not wish to force me to anything that I did not wish for. It was intended..." And the expression in her eyes grew bleaker as she remembered, as if she were pleading, pleading with him to understand, yet she smiled so sweetly. "I know he meant...on the night of the Castlereagh ball, only Lord Castlereagh asked him to go off for the Foreign Office. And of course, he obeyed." She had not meant to cry but could hold back the tears no longer. "So you see, because Myddelton is as he is, because he *is* honourable and good, Sir Charles may now pursue and destroy him. With impunity, do you see?"

He did see. Too clearly. "Oh Christ. Did you not tell him? Did you not tell Sir Charles this?"

Wretched and beautiful, she shook her head.

"Why not? Surely he would understand."

"No," she said succinctly. "No, he would not. I told you, he believes Myddelton to be just like his uncle. And how could I tell him without explaining all of it? All the various obstacles and misunderstandings that have littered our path—about Vauxhall or the rumours about us? Or without telling him where Myddelton is, even though I do not rightly know that myself."

Pemberton sat silent for a long while. The carriage bobbled over the cobblestone streets, in and out of potholes, through the mire left by other horses and thrown down from upper storey windows. It was unfortunate that Sir Charles had begun to believe all that he had heard, distrusting all that he should have known and knew. Terrible that he now saw her through this deceiving gossamer of lies and gossip, and not as she was. Based on such false premises as these, his conclusions must also prove false. "So what are you going to do?"

Again, she shook her head. "I do not know. I had considered asking you to..." She bit her lips together. "But I saw instantly that that would not answer."

"I should say not!" he snapped. "Anyway, I'd refuse. No offence meant."

Which statement she found oddly comforting. "I know." She gave him a watery smile.

"Damn Castlereagh!"

"Pem!" she reproved.

"Well, it was his stupid idea that landed you in all this mess in the first place!" He was quiet for a long time. She looked out the window. They were nearing Covent Garden and the street, on such a fine night as this, was thronged with gentlemen—young bloods, aging roués, town tulips and dandies—and the inevitable swarm of not-ladies.

"In the meantime," she said softly, picking up the thread of the conversation. "He means to remove me to Britwell Park—and to leave early on Wednesday. And, since he is convinced that Myddelton is a feckless wastrel, he has demanded to see the accounts, so that he can have his man draw up a suit of restitution."

Pemberton frowned. This at least he could counter. "I do not think he has the right to see Myddelton's accounts." He hesitated, pondering what he knew of the law. "No. No, that would come under an invasion or breach of privacy...or property...or something, I think..."

"Really?" she asked, brightening a little. Then matter of factly: "Well it does not matter, because I have already taken care of that."

He viewed her pleased expression with suspicion. "What have you done?"

Blithely: "Asked Mr. Broke to fiddle the books."

"You did what?" Pemberton gave an impious chuckle. "Tom Broke?" he laughed. "Tom Broke!"

"What?" She did not see the joke.

"Tom Broke? Od's my life, he is the most ordered, most precise body in the land." He laughed again. "Do you know, when first he came, he nearly drove Myddelton mad—because he was so dashed grateful to be away from those fiendish sisters of his that he instantly set about reorganising and cataloguing the whole library. He worked on it day and night. It took him, I don't know, something like a fortnight. Myddelton couldn't find a blessed thing. Then he went to work, beavering away on the accounts. Finally Avery got so exasperated, he sent him off to Great Myddelton to sort things out there—just to get some peace. Tom Broke fiddling the books? 'Struth, I'd like to see the job he makes of 'em." Then, doubtfully: "Did he agree?"

"He did," she said, sparkling. But reality and her fears intruded, bringing her back to earth and the present. And voicing her anxiety for the first time, she said quietly, "Pem, you don't think anything has happened, do you? To Myddelton? He said he would be home yesterday." She smoothed the first finger of her glove.

"Yes, I know." The carriage had stalled in traffic.

"Then where is he?"

He hesitated and frowned mightily, then took her hand in his own. "Angel, I do not know how to tell you this. The thing is, he did say he'd be back by yesterday at the latest. So when he didn't turn up, I popped round to have a quiet word with Castlereagh…"

"What did he say?" she asked, expecting the worst, despising her lack of faith.

His frown grew. "He said that Myddelton should have been back. Yesterday. Today at the very latest."

She digested this. "Did he say where he had sent him?"

"Guernsey." He pronounced it with a degree of contempt.

"Guernsey?"

"Aye. That's why he should have been back before now."

She was silent. Her fears had come to pass. A pounding of dread overtook her. He was dead. He was dead…She closed her eyes against the frightening jostling images of him, hurt, drowned, still and waxen. And at last, swallowing hard on her fear, she braced herself to ask the question she did not want answered. "Pem, you do not think, do you, that the boat has met with an accident?"

He risked a glance at her, hating the agony in her voice. "'Struth, I don't know."

She looked out the window, watched as a linkboy ran past the carriage window holding his torch aloft, watched as a pair of scarlet-coated officers out for an evening of pleasure accosted a pair of young ladies of unmistakably little virtue and were rewarded for their persistence. "If the boat had met with an accident, or with a French privateer for instance, how long would it be before we had news of it?" Her eyelashes were spiked with tears, but not one had fallen.

Pemberton bit his lip. "That would depend upon winds and tides, I think."

"He might be anywhere then, mightn't he? His body…" Her voice caught and broke. She squeezed her eyes shut against the picture forming in her head.

"Janey!" Pemberton reached over, catching hold of her hands. "Janey, don't."

When she spoke again, she seemed to have gained control of herself. "And if he was wounded, when finally he does come home, I shall not be there. And my uncle will not allow him access to me, I think. I had thought of running away—after the ball. But where would I go? To Great Myddelton? Would not my uncle look there first? And where would Avery know to look for me?" She found her handkerchief in her reticule and blew her nose. "So you see, I do not know what to do, what would be for the best. I should be here, waiting for him, when he returns. But…What if he is dead? What if it is his body they bring home to me? What shall I do then?" She finished on a cry.

Soberly, Pemberton listened. He took her hand in his own. "Upon my life, I don't know what, and I don't know how, but I give you my word, I shall think of something. There must be something. Perhaps you could go off to Anne's, if Myddelton don't get back right away. But he is coming back! He is. He said he would be back for the ball. And he will be…I'll have another word with Castlereagh…"

And more soberly still: "And the answer to your initial question is, yes, a bill of annulment would damage him. It would disgrace both him and you. It would destroy his political career—perhaps not permanently, but in the short term. He would be a laughing stock, not only in the Upper House, but at every club, and in every Drawing Room in London. And as for you…I should never put someone I cared for through the ordeal of the kind of questioning and, er, examination, that would be inevitable. The papers would be full of it…the Society columns, the cartoons…It would be a living nightmare. And it would not go away. Ever."

The carriage at last came to a halt. From behind, there came the noise of the footman leaving his perch. "Oh bother it, we're here. You don't really want to see this play, do you?"

"No," she admitted bleakly. "No, but I'd much prefer it to going home and being nagged by Sir Charles, I do assure you."

33

Myddelton heard noises. Sounds. Low murmuring sounds. Like the gentle lapping and smack of water against rocks or a sea wall. And the muted burble and mumble of lowered speech as a conversation heard from a room away.

He opened his eyes, then shut them on the ungodly brightness. Cautious and painful, he opened his eyes again. And tried to focus on the face leaning toward him. He could see the dark hair, but the features were indistinct in the fog and he could not make them out or connect them to make a face he recognised.

He tried to move his head, to look about. The room was hazy with a yellowish mist. Odd. Very odd. Rooms don't usually have mist in 'em. And it was moving, tilting from side to side. He did not think he was imagining or dreaming it, but his head throbbed. Dully, like a woodsman's axe against oak. There was no aftertaste of blue ruin in his mouth, so not drunk. No, not drunk.

"My lord? Can you hear me?"

Myddelton squinted at the face looming over his. "Yes, I can hear you," he answered. But the person only repeated the question as if he had said nothing. Myddelton squeezed his eyes shut and shook his head.

Someone was speaking again. Myddelton tried to listen, but drifted off…He wanted Jane so badly it ached, heart and groin together. And he was so thirsty.

The room lurched crazily from one side to another and he was thrown against the wall of the bunk. Pain sliced through his head. He reached to cradle his temple in his hand, but someone, something dragged his hand away from his head and held it to his chest. It was the

French! It was Des Champs. Des Champs had come back. Come back to catch him. To take him off to…

He opened his eyes to look frantically about. But it was all unfamiliar. He tried to focus and failed. Everything seemed to be moving—swaying and lunging for some reason. "Tell her!" he cried. "Tell her I love her…"

But no one answered.

He looked about him. It was all different. And it seemed smaller. And close. He should never have spoken to Janey so cruelly, never have rated her. His damnable temper. Damn, damn, damn. All damned. But where was she? Had she left him? No. Dear God, not that, not that…No, no, he could feel her touch…

Something soft, gentle, damp slid over his cheek and forehead. It was Jane. Janey, bathing his face with water. He opened his eyes to see her smile, the laughter in her eyes, but the cloth slid over his eyelids, soothing, easing his doubts. The cloth was cool and soft, like her skin when he had kissed it…

"Well, Mr. Hobson?" Lieutenant Fiske said, nodding toward Myddelton, and the plain-faced cabin boy who stood beside the bunk, bathing his face. "Will he do? Will he mend?"

Mr. Hobson, the ship's surgeon was a middle-aged, briefly spoken man, who had once been young and enthusiastic. Now he was older, and had seen a great deal of action, and was therefore more cautious. Like Fiske, he still wore his officer's pigtail. He regarded his patient for some time. "I believe so. It is not, however, the head wounds that are causing the fever and delirium, Lieutenant. Head wounds bleed like the very devil, but often they appear more serious than they are." He studied the unshaven face, thinner now and drawn under the faint tan, the beads of sweat forming on the forehead, the damp hair, the layers of blankets pinning him to the bunk.

"However, in this young man's case, it was the cold," he said flatly. "He was in the water for far too long. 'Pon my word, it is a wonder he survived at all. And we have had the very devil of a time getting him warm again, I can tell you. He's had hot bottles at his feet and sides for the last day and a half. But now fever has set in—which was my great concern—and he slips in and out of consciousness. I would bleed him, but I suspect he has already lost a good deal of blood."

"And that is the best you can tell me?" asked Fiske with an edge of temper.

"It is," said Mr. Hobson.

Lieutenant Fiske narrowed his eyes. "You must do better than that, Mr. Hobson," he declared. "This young man is a peer of the realm and belongs to the Foreign Secretary, Lord Castlereagh. And I am bound to have him back in London by the day after tomorrow. Do you hear?"

Mr. Hobson shook his head. Fiske had cowed him in the past, but not now. "I can promise nothing. Fever is no respecter of titles, Captain. He may never wake. And if he does, he will be in no case to travel, of that I can assure you."

Lieutenant Fiske scowled.

Mr. Hobson remained silent, weighing the possibilities, the odds, the various medical remedies at hand. He was a young man, this Lord Myddelton. And it would seem, strong as a horse. Eventually he said, "I could apply a blister."

The cabin boy looked up sharply in silent protest. Men woken by a blister woke in agony, woke screaming.

Mr. Hobson ignored the boy's unspoken panic and narrowed his eyes in concentration. There was a thin line in the application of blisters, a nearly invisible line between enough to wake and enough to kill.

Lieutenant Fiske took a long hard look at Myddelton. "Do it, Mr. Hobson," he commanded and turned to leave the sick bay.

Mr. Hobson pursed his lips. Captain's orders. Like the sailors on board, he was governed by the Articles of War. Disobedience was answered with death. "I shall need a man to hold him down," he said stonily.

"I'll send Croggon," Lieutenant Fiske said from the doorway.

Myddelton could feel the cloth again—soft on his eyelids, gentle on his forehead. And somewhere, he thought he heard her laughter spilling into the quiet…Why will she not kiss me? Does she not love me after all? No, there is Des Champs on the table bleeding, bleeding…they will find me. No, not Des Champs. Perceval. Bleeding, bleeding, the blood

533

running through my fingers, soaking my cuffs. Stop, damn it, stop! Jane, Jane, Jane, Jane, Jane, Jane, Jane.

He opened his eyes, but the walls, the wood-panelled walls were closing in upon him. And his thoughts, his dreams of his wife, fragile and fragmented, were shimmering, whirling, spinning like shards of broken mirror into a well of obsidian darkness, a darkness as black and liquid as ink spilt onto parchment, as dense as onyx...

❧

1 June 1812

Well knowing Dunphail's nocturnal habits of late—that after ten o'clock of any evening he was likely to be found at any one of several discreet nugging-houses—but less than eager to sample the delights of these establishments, nor to spend an evening trawling the various neighbourhoods in which they were found, Pemberton went round to the house on Mount Street well before Dunphail was likely to have gone to White's for his breakfast. And was shown by a bemused manservant to a small bookroom—a room devoid of musical interests—which Dunphail used as his own. Where he sat, content, in a wing chair that was showing signs of wear, and listened to the absence of music in the house, a sure sign that Hardy was still asleep. Or had gone out.

A short while later, Dunphail strode in, hastily dressed in shirt and waistcoat, his cravat gracelessly knotted, a tankard of ale in his hand. "What?" he demanded, expecting an emergency at least. Why else would Pemberton be here at this unholy hour?

Pemberton looked up but did not stir from his seat. And was pleased to note that Dunphail appeared abnormally clear-eyed. "I say, Dunphail, you're looking a little less debauched than usual. Are you sober?"

This drew a grudging morning-smile. "As it happens, yes." Obviously not an emergency. Dunphail sat down in the chair opposite. "Ned was off to dine with his future in-laws last night, so I had the unequalled luxury of staying home and going to bed." He took a swill of ale. "What do you want?"

534

Pemberton did not answer directly, but sat thinking. His fears deflated, Dunphail drank his ale.

Eventually, Pemberton said genially: "Upon my life, if you ever breathe a word of this, I'll shoot a hole through your privates."

Dunphail viewed him with friendly suspicion and without alarm. "Oh." He nodded. And pondering the direct threat, found it reasonable and even just. "All right," he agreed, mystified and unconcerned. "What is it?"

"Have you got the Jacobite coach here in Town or is it up North?" Pemberton said conversationally, his expression cool.

It took Dunphail by surprise. "What?" he snapped. It was too early in the day for this. He ran a hand through his hair. "A pox take you, is this some kind of an ill joke? In case you had forgot, harbouring a Jacobite is treason. It's a hanging offence..." he said with a rare touch of bitterness.

Pemberton was unmoved by what he considered the unnecessary display of dubious innocence. "'Struth, Dunphail, I couldn't give a tinker's damn whether you harbour Jacobites. And I ain't interested in seeing you swing neither," he added dismissively. "But the coach. Is it here or up North?"

Dunphail frowned and finished the ale. "How the devil d'you know about that?"

"I was at school with you, idiot. And as I recall we once drove halfway to Scotland in it with Ned tucked in the hidey hole."

Dunphail gave a laugh. "'Struth, I must have been drunk," he said by way of an adequate explanation.

"You were," Pemberton confirmed. "We all were." He chuckled, remembering.

Calmed, Dunphail flexed his shoulders. Lost causes, such as his antecedents' political intrigues, held little interest for him, particularly when they had been common knowledge, as this one clearly had, for well over a decade. "Aye, it's in the stable. Why?"

"Is it ready to go? Wheels checked, axles sound, seats brushed out, that sort of thing?" Pemberton said.

Dunphail eyed him with distrust. "It can be," he said cautiously.

"Good. Have More see to it. It may be needed tomorrow night."

"All right," Dunphail said, vaguely disconcerted by the whole tenor of the conversation. "For any reason in particular? An abduction? A race?"

Because he had promised to take care of her. To look after her. To protect her for his friend. Pemberton paused. "Because…it may be needed for a trip up North…Actually, you'll be going on a trip up North."

"I am?" Dunphail said doubtfully. "I will?"

"Yes," Pemberton said. "On an elopement. Of sorts."

"I am?" Dunphail said again, now dumbfounded. "With who?"

"Janey. The Countess of Myddelton."

"What? You don't mean Myddelton's wife, do you, because I bloody will not…" Dunphail exclaimed, jumping up from his chair. "He'd plant a bullet-hole in me the size of Edinburgh!"

"No, Dunphail!"

"And not just through my privates. And rightly so! I'd have to be mad…"

"Dunphail! It's not what you think! Dunphail! Shut up and listen!" Pemberton barked, roused. "Dunphail, no, just shut your gob and listen! You know Myddelton went off about that horse? Yes, well it wasn't about a horse! It was for the Foreign Office. And he was meant to be back by Friday. Only he wasn't."

Dunphail sat down, his expression wary. "Where is he? What's happened to him?"

Pemberton drew a deep, unhappy breath. "No one knows. Castlereagh thinks there may have been an accident, but he ain't heard anything. Janey's beside herself with worry. But that's not the problem. The problem is Sir Charles Heron. You've met him, I trust?"

Dunphail nodded. His grey eyes were alert now, sharp and canny— the eyes of one who stalked deer in all weather and fog. "Her uncle. Aye, I've met him." Idly, he rubbed his freshly shaven chin and jaw.

"Well, for reasons best known to himself, he has determined to bring a bill of annulment before the House on the grounds of non-

536

consummation. No, do not say anything! Just shut up and hear me out..."

This however was impossible. Dunphail shook his head. "You ain't going to try to pitch me some rum lay and tell me Myddelton ain't bedded her yet. Because I will not believe it!"

Pemberton rolled his eyes. "Believe it."

"What?" Dunphail exploded. This defied reason, logic, lust, experience, everything. And puffing out his cheeks, he stood staring blindly at the small still life of a hare, apples and a copper bowl over the mantel for a long moment. Finally: "Well, I'm damned."

"Probably," Pemberton agreed. "Now, shut up." He sighed. "Where was I? Oh yes, well, so Sir Charles has decided to run with this. He don't know that Myddelton's a Government man..."

"But, damme, everyone knows that," Dunphail interrupted. "Well, not this latest twist in the tale, but..."

"I know. But he don't know it and there's no telling him neither. And he's convinced that the story about a horse is actually a cover for Myddelton running off with some other female..."

"God's whirlygigs, why would he do that?" Dunphail demanded, breaking in again. Very little of this made sense to him, but that made even less. "Has her uncle never looked at her? No laddie in his right mind would run off with her in his bed..." Then, softly, almost to himself, "I wouldn't. Can't think why Myddelton..."

Pemberton shook his head. "You know what Avery's like." He shrugged. "He's in love. And he's not very good at it."

Dunphail shot him a derisive look, as if he were raving. "What can you mean?"

"Well, look at him. Anytime anyone so much as mentions her name off he goes, roaring about the countryside like some demented pagan warrior. S'life, anyone else in love with his own wife would just take her to bed." Pemberton sighed and repeated, "But you know what he's like..."

Dunphail sat back in his chair, stretched out his legs and gave him a hard, thoughtful look. "Aye. Stupid. With more guts than brain."

Pemberton ignored this. "Now will you listen? Sir Charles means to remove her to her former home on Wednesday, directly after the ball. I don't know much about annulments—they don't come up that often—but I doubt he'll be able to proceed without her in his care. He'd look a dashed fool, if nothing else. So she needs to go into hiding, to disappear. That is, if Myddelton ain't back by then—until we know what's happened to him."

"Why don't she just go to Great Myddelton?"

Pemberton hesitated. He thought he had considered all the options, but had he? "'Struth, that would be the first place her uncle would look for her, don't you think? And the thing is, I don't know precisely when she comes of legal age and I am concerned that in Myddelton's absence Sir Charles could still claim his rights over her. But in Scotland, he would have no claim, would he? If she had her marriage lines with her? You lot have a different set of laws. And anyway, he'll have to find her first." He shifted uneasily. "Then there's the delicate matter of my Grandfather Choate—he's Sir Charles' nearest neighbour."

Thoughtfully Dunphail stared into his empty tankard. He rubbed his eyes, his forehead. "What do you need me to do?"

"You will do it then?"

Dunphail frowned, before saying with a degree of exasperation: "A pox take you, you knew I would before you asked."

"That house we stayed at west of Inverness…I thought if you took her there. Your aunts are there, ain't they, to lend her countenance and bear her company?"

Dunphail nodded. "Aye. They're there. When do we leave?"

"Have the coach just beyond the mews at four. I shall tell her to have a bag packed for her and her maid—just a few days' worth—she can buy what she needs once you're across the border. If Myddelton don't return by the end of the ball, then she can go upstairs as if she's gone to bed, change, and come down the back stairs and out through the servants' entrance. If you put her in the secret compartment and her maid in the coach, with you riding alongside, anyone who sees you will only see you and one female and assume it's an elopement." He paused again. It would be a hard journey. And long. Janey would miss her dog too. But at least she would be safe. "Sir Charles will be searching for a lady and her maid. Though to be sure, I shouldn't imagine he'll think to look on the Great North Road. I fancy he'll look to the west and south—in the direction of Great Myddelton or the Northcotes' place. I shall remain in Town, because I'm damned certain he'll suspect me. But also so that I can tell Myddelton where to find her when he comes home."

Dunphail listened, blinked, and nodded. "Right. I'll have More check the wheels and brush out the Prince's box this morning..." He smiled softly. "How did you know?"

Pemberton regarded his friend. "What? That all your family are raving Jacobites? It don't happen often, but when you're drunk, and at home, you toast 'The Rightful King'. Then, there's the small matter of your ingenious coach with the false seat at the back leading to that rather well-padded false trunk. Anyway, I've known you since you was twelve. 'Struth, it would have been hard to miss. Was it really built for the Prince?"

"Who knows?" Dunphail grinned and shrugged. "My grandfather said it was. My grandmother said not."

Pemberton laughed. "How's Ned keeping? I ain't seen him recently..."

"Oblivious. Besotted. Stupefied with delight. "

"I take it you ain't pleased..."

"'Struth, it ain't for me to be pleased or not pleased. It's nothing to me whom he weds. He could make her happy, I dare say. But..." Uncharacteristically, he hesitated. Then: "...she'll not remain faithful to him," he said, shaking his head with certain regret.

34

For the benefit of onlookers—despite feeling suspended, robbed of will, vacillating between intemperate longing and an aching dread which like a canker nestled in the pit of her stomach, damning every hope, wasting every pleasure—Jane returned to the balanced harmony of her Haydn-days. And on this day of all days, all was precise, calm and effortlessly ordered—as she progressed from a discussion with the violinist conductor over the choice of dances, to Kettering and Philippe the chef (with his rich vocabulary of Gallic expletives) for a final approval of courses and removes, to the arrangement of the chairs and flowers in the several reception rooms. And had her uncle not been so preoccupied with his singular perception of things, he must have delighted to see her unruffled dominion and the procession of upper servants deferring to her—particularly in the prelude to such an Event as a Society Ball. It must have justified all his training of her, and the superiority of her breeding. It must have reminded him of his excellent brother. But absorbed as he was, discontented as he had become, he saw none of it. And what he did observe only caused his frown to deepen, his anger illogically and disproportionately exacerbated.

When Pemberton arrived, he found that two flowersellers' carts were taking up the entirety of the front walkway as their wares were unloaded into the house by a succession of maids and underfootmen under the direction of the unfazed and unfazable Kettering. Then he stood with his back to the doorframe in the hall for a full five minutes while two menservants manoeuvred a carpet down the stairs and across the foyer which was also banked with flowers. And finally, he made his own way through the house—each room a tableau of finely orchestrated upheaval performed by unsilent servants—in search of her. And found her, standing in a shaft of filtered light in the Dining Room, examining the table setting, a quiet solitary figure, wearing a gown of pale yellow and white stripe printed with sprigs and a fall of ruffles at the bodice. In her hand was a piece of paper with writing on both sides and a diagram, the seating plan. The which she kept consulting. And he thought she had never appeared lovelier, or sweeter. And thought too that Myddelton ought to be here with her. Not him.

Looking up, she saw him in the doorway and brightened, greeting him with a familiar lop-sided smile. "Thank goodness you are come! Things are in an awful mess…"

"Yes. I'd noticed." He waited until a manservant carrying an urn of pale flowers entered the room before him, deposited his burden on a side table, and left again. Then, he came across to her, and putting his arm about her shoulders, dropped a kiss upon her hair. And said softly, "It's all sorted."

She gave him a searching look, and reading assurance in his gaze, carried on as if he had said nothing, "Kettering tells me that he believes there has been a row…or a rupture. Or something between Mr. Brummell and the Prince Regent. Tell me it is not so."

With his arm still about her shoulder and his face close to her hair, he said, "Dunphail will have the carriage waiting just beyond the mews— at four—to take you to his aunts' house near Inverness. You'll be safe there." Then he chuckled and said louder, "I'm afraid it is. And it's makin' a pig's breakfast of everyone's dinner parties, I can tell you."

"Including mine! Is it serious?"

Pemberton grinned, the irreverence marked. "S'life, I should think so. Did you not hear what Brummell said? No? 'Who's your *fat friend*, Alvanley?'"

"He didn't dare!" She giggled. And tried to stop. "I should not be laughing. It is not at all funny…And they're both expected this evening. But the Prince is so very fat! What am I to do?" she asked, still smiling, and bit her lips together.

"'Struth, I don't know. It's making things dashed awkward though. Can't ask Prinny to a do that Brummell's sure to attend and can't invite Brummell if Prinny's going to be there. Either way, someone's offended." He left her to meander along the length of the table and peruse the setting, the fine porcelain in readiness, the polished silver, who she had seated next to whom. And more significantly, next to him. "Put Brummell next to Anne, here. 'Struth, Janey, as you love me, don't put me next to the Wythenshaw, I beg of you!"

She joined him midway down the table and twitched at the scripted name card. "Well I have to put her somewhere!" she said, mildly vexed. "I cannot seat her next to Dunphail, for I have seen the expression in his eyes whenever he looks at her. And I must make sure she is not near Sir Charles—that would be disaster. Or Myddelton."

Pemberton favoured her with a moody glare. Then: "No, no. No, no, look. Look, here. Put her beside the General." He moved farther down the length of the table. "Here! He'll love it!" And he came again to stand beside her, to say quietly, "Can your maid be trusted?"

She shook her head and responded equally softly, "I do not know. Indeed, I believe she would find it very hard to hold her tongue if my uncle spoke to her…"

Still quiet, he continued, "Then have Kettering pack a bag for you. I know, I know, he's your butler, but you know you can trust him. And your maid will need a bag as well…" He stepped away from her. "But you've not invited both Prinny and Brummell to dinner, have you?"

"No. Only Mr. Brummell."

"Well, that's all right, then. Brummell is sure to leave after the first couple of dances. He always does. And when's Prinny due? Not before midnight, is he? Takes him that long to get up from his chair. 'Struth, he'll need a hoist before long…"

She chuckled and shrugged. "Horrid creature…But again, I do not know. Although His Royal Highness has requested a waltz with me…"

"Ain't we the honoured one!" Pemberton teased, grinning. That grin had been absent of late. He pulled a face. "A bit like waltzing with a walrus, Anne says. In a corset. Creak, creak…But don't go into any empty rooms with him, whatever you do. 'Struth, Myddelton would go mad." He walked along the opposite side of the table, again eyeing the name card before each place. Dunphail was next to Emily. Good. And

Sir Charles on her other side! Well! Oh, there was Castlereagh...and Pam...

She smiled fondly. "Oh lud, so he would."

He wandered down to the far end of the room to admire the urn of flowers on the side table. She had worked wonders with this house. With the servants, with the appointments, with everything. Whoever would have believed it?

"There you are!" Sir Charles exclaimed sharply and strode into the room—the elegance of the aquamarine silk-hung walls, the flowers and laid table eluding him.

Pemberton saw Jane look up, her laughter stopped. Talking of things that would make Myddelton go mad, though not in that satisfyingly jealous way.

"Never have I seen such an appalling mess! Nor has Frobisher! Dear God in heaven, that secretary of Myddelton's is worse than useless! He is a fool! Worse than a fool!"

Pemberton watched as she paled, flinched, then drew herself up and squared her shoulders. "And why is that, Uncle?" she asked levelly.

Pemberton wondered at her audacity and new-found courage—he had never seen Sir Charles in such a rage—and stepped further back into the shadow of an open door. His presence, if known, would not improve this encounter.

"The accounts. The ledgers!" Sir Charles pronounced on a rising note. "Frobisher and I have spent the past two mornings trying to make sense of them. But it is impossible. Entries have been made with no regard whatever for the date, all higgledy-piggledy. The columns do not add. Nor do they subtract as far as I can tell! I dare say it might be possible to make some sense of them—eventually—if ever we could decipher them. But we cannot. The dolt blots his ink like a child. And mashes the quill tip. The pages have been stuck together where the idle fool has spilt his wine—and those entries have all but vanished—or more revolting still, where he slopped the gravy from his supper."

Pemberton gulped down a laugh, willing himself to stillness. Lud, Tom Broke had not done the thing by halves. No indeed. Rather, he had excelled himself. Janey was struggling to control herself. She had lowered her chin and was swallowing hard on the guilty smile, and biting even harder on her bottom lip. But to him, the look in her eyes gave her away—part intimidation, part triumph. Sir Charles did not notice. Fortunately.

"That Broke is an imbecile and deserves to be turned out into the street!"

"I believe he writes very good speeches," she ventured steadily, on Mr. Broke's behalf. Her eyes were opened very wide against her laughter and self-doubt. "That is, no doubt, why Myddelton is willing to overlook any other…"

"The whole of the last quarter of last year was obliterated by spilt coffee!" he retorted irascibly. "What we could make out of the pages we prised apart."

"Oh! Oh Uncle, I am sorry…truly, I had no idea…" she said in sympathy—still, after all that he had done, the dutiful niece, the perfect hostess.

"Hunh!" he snorted. "No wonder Myddelton's affairs are in such a state! The sooner I remove you from this house of want-wits and wastrels, the better. I should have done so last week!" he finished, and stormed from the room.

She waited, listening. Waited, unmoving and unmoved, until she was certain Sir Charles was out of earshot. Then looking up, she gave a tremulous half-smile. "Scotland, did you say?" she said with quiet determination. And Pemberton saw that she had set her chin. "It sounds a very pleasant place." She adjusted a name card. "And you will bring Myddelton?"

Her bravado fooled him not at all. Pemberton came and took her loosely within the circle of his arms. She did not look up. Tom Broke may have created an impenetrable wall of obfuscation, but he had not saved her from her uncle's displeasure. Soberly, she said, "He is still alive, isn't he? You do think he is still alive…"

"Yes. Yes, I do," Pemberton said from his heart. "And he said he would be here. He told me to tell you that. If he said it, he will be. For Christ's sake, he was only going as far as Guernsey! And though the Lord knows he will have been sick as a cat all the way there and back…"

She looked very young, very small, and very uncertain, but said fretfully, "I did not know he suffered from sea-sickness." As if she should have known, as if it were some failing in her that she had not.

"Lord, yes!" Pemberton laughed. "He was even sick in a punt once. Although, well, Dunphail was rocking it for the purpose…"

She grimaced and a laugh escaped her. "How horrible you all are!"

"Well, yes…" Pemberton conceded, unperturbed by her stricture. "I dare say we are. But look, Angel, he'll be here! Trust him. He said he would be back. He promised."

"Yes." She smiled bleakly, reluctantly, grateful for all his kindness. "Yes, he did."

He placed his arm about her shoulder. "I shall come round just after seven, so if he's not returned by then, you'll not have to greet the guests on your own. All right? Good? Till then." He dropped another kiss on her head. "He'll be back. He said he would. And no more crying!"

With growing frustration, Myddelton listened to the bells of the Newhaven church clanging out the hour. It was…It was…Hell and confound it! He closed his eyes and stood resting his head against a stone wall. He was too dizzy, too near fainting, to count. Still, it was dry land. And he was on it.

He placed his hand against his forehead. It ached like the very devil, but underneath the sticking plaster, the wound was healing. Or so the surgeon said.

His boots, all but destroyed by their prolonged soaking in seawater, were stiffly soft and made little sound on the cobblestones. He paused, looking about. It was cool in the shaded wynd. Was this right? Yes, it did look like the alley with the stable. Yes, there was the narrow blue house, leaning over the passage. And there, thank Christ, the stable.

Myddelton pushed open the door. "Patroklos?"

The stallion, black as a coal field, turned in his box and whinnied.

Myddelton felt a breath of laughter and joy stir in his lungs. "S'life, it's good to see you too." He fondled the horse's muzzle for an instant and let his hands be lipped and prodded and nuzzled, then let himself into the stall.

Excited by his visitor, by smells he recognised, Patroklos began to weave and to prance about the stall, to nudge at Myddelton's hands, to shoulder him. It was as life returning. And rubbing Patroklos' ears and chin, the horse pushing, pushing at his shoulder with his nose until he was backed against the wall, Myddelton found himself smiling with the familiarity of it, the pleasure of it, the comforting interplay of it—man and horse. Her horse. Life as he knew it. The scent of hay and horse and tack, the stiff horsehair against his fingers. "There, there...there, there..." And he felt an ebullient return of energy inconsistent with the surgeon's prognosis.

The saddle was over the stall's barrier and the other kit hung on various hooks on the wall. All had been oiled and polished.

"Come on...come on..." And sorely, Myddelton reached for the saddle—his arm where the blisters had been applied was stiff and ached like Beelzebub. But with grim determination, and ignoring the dizziness, the pain, the weakness, he lifted the saddle, and gritting his teeth and swearing, he heaved it onto Patroklos' back. And keeping a steadying hold on the gate, bent slowly down to fasten and tighten the girth.

Cheerfully: "Stand still, you bugger..." And nearly fell over as another wave of dizziness hit him. "Stand." Never mind. Never mind. Then the bridle. First the reins. Good, good. And standing close, laying his cheek against that of the horse, Myddelton slid his thumb into the side of Patroklos' mouth and slid the bit between his teeth...there, there. "Good lad." Excellent. And finally...gently up over the ears, the headpiece. Good, good. Well done, Myddelton, well done. And the buckles. Now the noseband. And throatlatch. Well done. He laid his cheek against the horse's neck and stopped to catch his breath. Well done.

"Christ's wounds," he murmured, rubbing the horse's bristly chin and stroking his cheek. Then: "Listen, Patty-lad, we must return to London as soon as we can—d'you understand? Good lad. We've got to get back home, back to Janey, and I do not know how much strength I have. So I need you to carry me. D'you understand? Good lad." And patted him. "Good lad."

Opening the stable door, he led him out, pausing only to leave two guineas on the small stool in the corner of the stable. "S'life, I hope no one thinks I've stolen you, looking as I do. I look like a beggar," he murmured—his shirt had been laundered and he was now clean-shaven, but as for the rest of him...He shook his head in resignation. "Stand." And gathering the reins into his hand, he stepped onto the near upping block, hauled himself into the saddle, and cautiously, his leg forward, bent—*stay on the horse, Avery, stay on the deuced horse*—to adjust the girth.

"Home, Patroklos. Home to your mistress..." He nudged the stallion with his heels.

Head up, full of oats, the horse snorted and stirred to a walk. Minutes later, they were out of Newhaven and into the open countryside of the Downs. A breeze ruffled Myddelton's hair and the horse's mane—the breath of the land, of ploughed earth baking in the sun, of hedgerows and wood, of England.

"Home, you bloody great brute. We are going home!" he said, ending with an almost laugh. "Home...And don't rip my arms out...you great pisser."

By three, there was nothing more for Jane to do: she had overseen the decoration of the ballroom with banks of fresh flowers and sprays of laurel, watched as chairs had been arranged at one end for the small orchestra, and more chairs lined up against the remaining walls. The Dining Room was ready, card tables had been set up in the Library, and there were three bedrooms set aside on the second floor for ladies' use. She walked through the house, inspecting it all. All was as perfect as she could make it. And so it must be. For Myddelton's sake, if for no other. Finally, she went upstairs to her rooms. Now to sleep for an hour or two—before she must rise, bathe and dress.

And standing in the centre of her sitting room, she looked aimlessly, drearily about her, her resolution buckling under a force of such emptiness. In just over four hours, the dinner guests would begin to arrive, whether Myddelton returned or no, and she would have to greet them as if nothing were amiss. At ten the ball would begin, whether he had returned to lead her out or no. And at four, if he did not return, she would be leaving this place, this house she had learned to call home, and flee. To Scotland. For safety. Where it was cold and wild and where she had never been. As an emigrée seeking refuge in an unknown land. Hollow, she pressed a hand against her eyes, then her mouth.

Then, hearing a tentative knock on the door, she pushed away her fear. For the moment. "Come."

The door opened. Hesitantly, as if he were uncertain of his welcome there, looking sheepishly about him and at her, Mr. Broke entered. He carried a large blue leather case in his arms. "M...my lady?"

She smiled. "Mr. Broke. Do come in. I have not thanked you for what you did for me. You have outdone yourself. And I cannot thank you enough."

Embarrassed, Mr. Broke shut the door with ostentatious care behind him. And even then, he did not look up, but appeared to be studying the pattern in the carpet. Then, blinking rapidly, he risked a glance at her face. And gathering his courage to speak to her, he drew a breath. "I am glad I was able to help, ma'am." He gave an awkward half-smile. "I believe the spilt gravy was the final straw. Sir Charles summoned me and asked me to explain myself..." Then, unable to quell his real anxiety, "My cousin, does he mean to return soon? That is, if he does not, I shall need to look for another position and I..."

"I do not know. He said he would be back by tonight." After all that he had done, she could offer him little but honesty. "But...if he is not and...and I have to go...then you must go to Great Myddelton until he returns. I know that is what he would wish."

Mr. Broke nodded. "Yes, my lady. Thank you. I shall take the genuine ledgers with me there then, shall I? I did not mar those, you see," he said in a rush. "I found that I could not do it. So I started from scratch! It took me both nights and all day Sunday, but I managed it. I've never seen such a mess in all my life as those books. I should never hold my head up again if they was the real ones..."

Her smile had grown. "Thank you, Mr. Broke. Thank you."

He stopped, surprised that he had said so much. And to her. Then, awkwardly he handed her the leather case. "Ehm, this arrived—fr…from Mr. Rundell—this afternoon. And I know his lordship meant for you to have it for this evening…"

It was terrible receiving something he had meant to give her himself. Terrible. As a body blow meant to fell. Holding the case, she tried to smile. And not to cry. "Thank you."

Mr. Broke hesitated. And would have said nothing more, but there was such a look on her face that he continued: "He drew up the designs himself. And wrote out the instructions too. It took him over an hour. He was very particular. And he told me to insist that it be finished for tonight. That is how I know he meant you to have it. Mr. Rundell complained about that. He said his lordship always wants everything 'On the instant!'" Then, surprised or undone by his own volubility, for he had never said so much to her before, he stopped, glanced at the floor, and said, "I'll leave you now. My lady." And bowing, quickly left the room.

For no reason she could say, she remained standing, still, distraught and overwhelmed by such emotion as she did not comprehend. She knew what the box contained—it was a parure—a parure of the Myddelton diamonds. The one set of gems that Myddelton's father had refused to sell. And he had given them to her, had meant for her to wear them tonight, as his bride, for all to see.

Reluctant, she went and sat and opened the clasp. And her breath caught in her throat. For there, on a velvet bed, lay a diamond tiara, necklet and earrings—composed of miniature wild roses, delicate pinks and laurel leaves, but all made up of tiny diamonds, winking, sparkling, shining. And several of the small flowers and leaves on the tiara were raised just above the rest and set upon the ends of tiny wires, so that they moved and trembled at her touch. *En tremblant* French jewellers called it.

"Oh Myddelton…" she whispered.

❧

Mr. Hardy drew his watch from out his waistcoat pocket to check the hour for the nth time. A quarter past seven. Four minutes later than when he had last checked. He returned the watch to his pocket and gave his waistcoat—palest yellow sprigs on a white background—a swift tug. Better. Still, it was unlike Miss Wythenshaw to keep him waiting this long. Though perhaps in the circumstances, he could understand. After all, tonight she would be seeing Myddelton for the first time since the Castlereagh ball. That would of course have made her nervous. One could appreciate her predicament, her need to fuss a little more than usual. And she always looked so beautiful, he thought. Exquisite even. And soon they would be married.

Idly he glanced about the small Drawing Room, at the collection of Meissen figures on the mantel. Or were they Sevres? His mama would know...Tonight, he would put it to Georgina that they should be wed in July. July at St. Cross. And honeymoon...Where should they honey-moon? Not the Continent—too dangerous. Although he would love to take her there once Wellington had driven Napoleon back to where he belonged. Paris—she would like Paris. And Vienna. And Italy, of course. Still, she had better hurry. They were due at Myddelton House at half past for dinner, and with the crush of carriages in St. James's Square, it was going to be...

Through the closed door, he heard a decisive knock at the front door. Mr. Hardy checked his watch again. Twenty minutes past seven. They were going to be late. He stood and paced to the mantel. In the hall, he could hear some commotion. And the sound of her mother, her viper's tongue as sharp as ever, as full of conceited pretension as ever...

The Drawing Room door opened. "Mr. Hardy? Mr. Edric Hardy?" a young man in uniform asked—navy or army, Hardy could not say. He carried a black bicorn—navy, then.

"Yes?"

"You are Mr. Edric Hardy of St. Cross Priory?" foundered the boy.

"Yes," Mr. Hardy confirmed

The young man approached and held out a letter. Then he bowed and stepped back. "By orders of the Captain, Sir."

Suddenly flustered and bemused, Mr. Hardy stepped back too. And abashed—for what could a Captain of His Majesty's Navy have to say to him? Had one of his cousins died?—he read the written direction, then turned the letter over to break the seal (he did not recognise the crest) and unfold the stiff paper.

Beyond the open door Mrs. Wythenshaw hovered, watching, pulling at a handkerchief, silent for once.

And finally, at last, slowly, as if in a dream, Mr. Hardy looked up from the letter. And said into the awful quiet, "She eloped with Lord William Manners." He frowned, his even features contorted with grief. "But then, you knew that, didn't you?

"She fell from the launch in Portsmouth Harbour...on their way to the transport that would take them to Spain."

And slowly, slowly, he walked past the midshipman, past the unsneering butler, and past Miss Wythenshaw's grasping, ruinous mother to the front door, where he paused.

"She is drowned," he said simply.

And leaving his hat, tearless and silent, Mr. Hardy, dear, kind Ned Hardy, went from the house, out into the evening, to walk and walk and walk—his life, as ever, cast in music: Sebben crudele, mi fai languir, sempre fedele, sempre fedele ti voglio amar...Con la lunghezza del mio servir la tua fierezza, la tua fierezza saprò stancar...Sebben crudele, mi fai languir, sempre fedele, sempre fedele ti voglio amar.

Although cruel, I languish for you. Always faithful, always faithful, I wish to love you. With the length of my devotion I will exhaust your pride.

35

It was upon her. Below, every candle was lit and the chaos had subsided to liveried perfection.

And in that final moment of stillness and silence before she would cross the threshold from private to public, Jane stood before the cheval mirror to give her appearance one last look. And found in her reflection an excitement which would not be crushed, a delight to leaven all other sentiment. For she…she whose vanity extended only so far as thinking, occasionally, that she looked quite pretty…she could not but see that tonight was different. That the ancient alchemic formula of tiara, ball gown, candlelight and long gloves had conferred upon her that aura of indefinable beauty—from workaday to shining. The gown, of white silk with an overdress of palest Maria Louisa blue was as Myddelton had requested. The diamonds in her hair and about her throat—his family signet upon her, vanquishing the uncertainties of her future and her uncle's threats—winkled and gleamed in the evening sunlight which streamed still through her window.

And hearing the first guest, Pemberton, arriving below, she stilled. But she did not go to the door and downstairs. Instead, she crossed to the connecting door and went through to Myddelton's room—to gaze upon his bed, his chair, his books—a last moment of reflection and reverence in his sanctuary. On the small table beside his dressing table lay his collection of snuffboxes, neatly arranged, ready for his use— carved sardonyx, cloisonné, the chased gold which was his favourite. By now she knew his poetry by heart. And his final words to her: *My heart, I shall return to you as soon as ever I may.* He would return. When, she did not know. But he would come.

And passing back through her room, she crossed to the door and went out. It had begun.

"Janey!" Pemberton exclaimed as she came down the stairs. And with him another—standing as tall and broad-shouldered as Myddelton himself, handsome, though his nose did lean slightly to the left having been long-broken by an intimate encounter with an unyielding paving stone. For Pemberton had brought Brummell. Mr. Brummell, always last to arrive and first to leave, clever, witty, an artist of deft repartee—his presence alone so early in the evening would cement her social standing. Pemberton smiled seraphically, indicating by not so much as a glance that he understood the social coup he had initiated.

"Pem. And Mr. Brummell. You are most welcome," she said, stretching forth her hands to them both.

Mr. Brummell had raised his quizzing glass to survey the foyer and all its fitments before turning to her to clasp her fingertips and kiss the air above her hand. "'Pon my soul, ma'am, you are a sight to refresh the most fatigued. I do trust Myddelton will continue to mangle his neckcloths so that we may enjoy your company without the awkward impediment of his jealous glances..." Gracefully, he placed her hand upon his arm that he might escort her to her own Drawing Room. And as they walked, he continued his examination of the antechamber and its appointments through his quizzing glass.

She risked a glance at Pemberton. He was laughing silently.

"In truth, Mr. Brummell," she began without hesitation. "...you need not fear his glances, jealous or no, for he is still in the north. He did say he would be here, but I expect he came upon a mill, or something of that nature..." It all sounded astonishingly lame to her. But at least on one occasion Pemberton had used the very same excuse with his grandfather, who had found it perfectly believable.

"Depend upon it, Pemberton," Mr. Brummell said, half turning to face Pemberton, his eyes laughing. "He got *himself* involved in a mill."

"Dash it, Beau, don't tell her that. She'll fret all evening..."

As if struck by inspiration, Mr. Brummell faced her. "Dearest Lady Myddelton, a thousand pardons. Pay me no heed. 'Pon my honour, Myddelton is a man of his word. If he has said he will be at a place by a

553

certain hour, you may depend upon it, he will be there. And Ned Hardy must needs remember that the next time he's placin' a wager on Myddelton's drivin' skills, eh, Pem?"

And from behind, Kettering began to announce the arrivals: "The Viscount Castlereagh. The Viscount Palmerston. The Lady Emily Cowper. The Earl of Liverpool...the Lady Anne and Sir Miles Northcote..."

"'Pon my soul, Ma'am, is this a dinner party or a meetin' of the next Cabinet?" Mr. Brummell, yet in possession of her arm, and his eyes teasing still, asked.

And suddenly quite certain that the evening would be a resounding success, Jane laughed. "It does appear that way, does it not? But I assure you, I had no intention of such a thing. May I depend upon you to keep them from brangling? Because you know, sir..." Her eyes were bright as she caught Pemberton's eye. "More of this ilk are expected."

She went to the doorway to greet and to welcome.

"You have heard our hostess, gentlemen!" Mr. Brummell wagged his quizzing glass at the assembled guests, his wry smile in place. "We shan't have any branglin' this evenin'."

"Positively you cow me into silence, Beau," Palmerston retorted, and bowed to his hostess.

That slight smile, the smile of impertinence and superiority of wit, appeared on Mr. Brummell's mouth. "That last was especially for you, Pam. There shall be no mention of those unpleasantnesses such as politicks...Frenchies...Mushroom Corsicans...or 'pon my soul, m'dear boy, I shall compose a verse upon the travesty that is your cravat. And perform it as a post-prandial treat." He peered through his quizzing glass at the starched linen knotted about Palmerston's throat. "Now let me think..." He raised one eyebrow. "An elegant column thou art not. Thou hast more in common with a cha..." His eyelids flickered. "...imney pot..."

With his friends, Palmerston laughed, and blushed.

And amid the general amusement, Lord Castlereagh took Jane's hand, kissed it and held it. "It is a great pleasure to be here this evening, ma'am. My dear wife will be along in a moment. I preferred to walk; she is bringing the carriage, you know. But will you not present me to your uncle, for young Pemberton told me that he is come to pay you a visit. I was presented to him long ago, by my dear friend Pitt, you know, when I was newly arrived to the Commons." And he gave her his arm, that she might lead him to Sir Charles.

"The Earl of Dunphail...The Countess of Jersey...General..."

Her uncle, she saw, had entered unannounced and already had been cornered by Lord Liverpool. Good. "Lord Liverpool, you are most welcome. I see you have found Sir Charles. You know he has been longing for the comforts of Britwell Park and does not like Town, but I do believe, with you here, he may leave such thoughts behind—for this evening at least...Lord Castlereagh, I take great pleasure in naming my uncle, Sir Charles Heron, to you..." And smiling, Jane disengaged her hand and went to greet her other guests.

"Sir Miles, have I named my uncle to you, Sir Charles Heron..."

"But my dear..." Lady Emily Cowper said, slipping her arm through Jane's. "Where is Myddelton? He cannot spend all evening wrestling with his cravat, just because Brummell is to be here."

"Emily, dearest Emily," drawled Mr. Brummell, once again taking centre stage. "Myddelton is not such a savage that he must needs wrestle with his cravat..."

"But where is he?" Emily reiterated.

"Still in the north," Jane repeated. "He promised to be here but I expect..."

"Lud, how like a man!" Emily exclaimed. "I should read him a curtain lecture for this if I were you. Though, certainly, Cowper has forgotten more than one soirée of mine," she admitted, puckering her brow and mouth in mock vexation. "And usually, he don't recall it until the next day, when I tell him it was a dreadful crush and he should have been there!"

Everyone laughed. And the crowd broke again into little groups of twos, threes and fours, with Jane moving from guest to guest, clique to clique, putting all at their ease, all amiability and graciousness—once the perfect guest, now the perfect hostess. And Pemberton, looking upon her brightness in the midst of this assemblage of the socially great and politically powerful, upon her grace and unequalled composure, longed for his friend.

Quietly, Kettering entered the room and leaned his head close to his mistress's. "My lady, it is now five minutes before the hour and two of the guests—Mr. Hardy and Miss Wythenshaw—are not arrived. Did you wish me to hold dinner back or remove the table settings?"

Her smile in place, Jane glanced about the Drawing Room at those assembled—ladies in pale silk gowns and gentlemen in sombre evening coats—but saw neither Mr. Hardy's musician's hair nor a coloured and patterned waistcoat among them. How odd. "Oh. Is there much traffic in the Square now? No? Then, I suppose wait another five minutes and if they are not arrived by then, remove their places and adjust the table."

"Yes, my lady. And his lordship's place?"

"No." She paused delicately, but did not frown and barely faltered. "No, leave that." Though Kettering did not like to see that shadow of fleeting sadness in her smile. "Thank you, Kettering."

꩜

Myddelton heaved a great sigh as he turned Patroklos into St. James's Square. Though the sight of his home had sent an ungoverned rush of energy and something else surging through him. A trickle of sweat slid down over his temple and cheek. He had made it.

Slumping in the saddle for a moment, he rested. Then with a dragging clip-clop on the cobbles, Patroklos took the last dozen steps, coming to a halt before Myddelton House, where great torches blazed on either side of the open front door and a red carpet had been rolled out over the front steps and onto the street.

"Groom!" Myddelton's voice came out as a breathless croak.

"Sir?" an undergroom replied, coming forward. "Sir, you shall have to move on. This is...Milor'!" he exclaimed, and rushed to take hold of Patroklos' bridle.

Leaning heavily on the pommel, Myddelton dismounted. "Take him to the stable and have Curlee see to him." Uniformly wearied, hot, his shoulders and arm aching, he climbed the front steps. Sweet heaven, he had made it! He wiped at his cheek and forehead with his sleeve.

"Sir?" William (in powdered wig and livery) questioned, before suddenly his eyes grew round. He swallowed. "My lord!"

Myddelton glanced about—all the candles were lit in the sconces and ceiling lantern and the flowers were lovely. "Yes, William, yes." Home. He was home! And he wanted to laugh and cry together. Mercifully, there were no guests present. "Where's Kettering? Oh, there you are." He started for the stairs, a peal of triumph ringing in his head. "Send Stamp up with hot water, will you?" Od's truth, he had done it. Sweet blessed Christ, he was home.

Kettering took in my lord's appearance with a flicker of his eye—torn shirt and coat, stained buckskins, ruined boots and all coated with grime and filth. "Yes, my lord. At once, my lord." No need to pack a bag for her ladyship then, thank all the powers in heaven. "And welcome home, my lord." And my lord will want ale too, to wash the dust from his throat.

"Thank you, Kettering. Thank you." He did not add what pleasure it was to be there, to have returned. He did not need to. "How far along are they?" Myddelton nodded in the direction of the Dining Room. "Have they gone through yet?"

"I was about to announce dinner, my lord. Shall I hold it back?"

"Yes, but only for a few minutes. And drag out the first course too, will you? And do not tell Lady Myddelton. I shall be down as quick as I can. Now get Stamp. Oh, and send up a pot of strong coffee too, will you?" He turned and trudged up the stairs, pulling at his stained neckerchief as he vanished from sight.

Stamp arrived, bringing to the fulfilment of his duties a certain suspicious alacrity. He bustled into Myddelton's chamber looking decidedly cheerful, followed by three footmen carrying canisters of hot water which had been on the boil for use in the skullery. And went on to bathe and shave his master with a disconcerting air of bonhomie, applying himself with an alarming rigour to the cleaning of Myddelton's hands and nails and hair, and clucking like a doleful hen over Myddelton's head wound—which he considered too conspicuous for a gentleman of Myddelton's rank and position. ("Don't touch it, Stamp. It's healing nicely.") At which, his sensibilities lacerated, Stamp sniffed meaningfully.

Still, some half-hour later, now scrubbed and jolted alert by the ingestion of strong black coffee, Myddelton stood in front of his mirror whistling tunelessly while he knotted and arranged the ends of his neckcloth. Minutes later, having been shovelled into his evening clothes by the still too-jaunty-by-half Stamp, he slipped a snuffbox into his pocket, put on his signet ring and quizzing glass and went downstairs.

And paused at the doors of the Dining Room to gather his thoughts, to prepare himself for the sight of her, to gain some control over those unruly and unequivocal emotions as now ran rampant through his head and everywhere else. Then with a nod to the footman, who threw open the door, he stepped inside.

Slowly, as guests and servants alike became aware of his presence, the chatter, eating and service all came to a halt. One by one, the guests turned in their seats to face him—Castlereagh, Liverpool, Pemberton, Miles, the ancient General—they were all there. And there, there at the far end of the table, there she was. There. Startled and entranced, the colour falling and rising in her cheeks, radiant, perfect, breathtakingly beautiful. His wife. His own dear girl. To have and to hold. Sweet Christ, yes, to hold. His own. And felt a gutful of joy, tight and ecstatic. He smiled and saw how the answering smile grew from within her, transforming her surprise to wonder and breathless elation, riotous and subdued.

And coming to the foot of the table, he took her extended hand— the hand with which she had reached out to touch him, to brush his sleeve, to prove to herself that he was indeed here. He had returned! And she wanted to throw herself into his arms and cleave to him. Surely her heart had stopped and in that same instant accelerated to a frenzied gallop.

He bowed, and still holding her hand, he kissed it—a profoundly mundane gesture transmuted into an electric charge by the intensity of affection, and felt by all. "My dearest." *My beloved, blessèd girl, I will hold you until…*"I was unavoidably and inexcusably detained. Will you forgive me?" And read in her face such joy and pleasure.

Her voice was lost, tangled in the rush of affection that raced from her heart to every extremity. "I…" She looked up at him, upon his dear face, thinner, so much thinner, tired, and victorious, and felt the tears pricking at her eyelids. He was home. He had returned. *Oh my love*...Stifling a sob, she held her breath and her smile grew as his tangibility became reality. Still, he gripped her hand. "Please..." She gestured that he should be seated.

He could have taken her upstairs there and then. And felt a painful throbbing at the cruel knowledge that he might not. Not now. Not with this company.

Then suddenly, she became aware of all the guests, each watching this reunion, and a wild blush rose in her cheeks. And her smile grew more joyful still. "Please, will you not sit, sir?" Laughter and jubilation filled her eyes. "We have only just begun the first course."

"Thank you. My dear." *My life, my heart, my very dear.* He released her hand and bowed. *Dies Augenzelt, von deinem Glanz allein erhellt, O füll es ganz!* And regretting that he must go so far from her, he went to the head of the table where Kettering waited behind his chair.

"A very forgiving wife you have, Myddelton," observed Lady Jersey as he passed her.

"I know it," Myddelton said, still smiling. "I know it."

He took his place. Jane gave the nod. Service resumed, and conversation.

Sir Charles sat and stared at his soup. With the rest of the company, he had felt that current snap through the atmosphere. And he had been shocked. For he had seen such a transformation once before—that loveliness which flowed from his niece like a spring stream, swelling and surging like a tide into Myddelton. In just such a way had Sophie loved his brother. And just so had she been loved by him. *Coram populo.* He had been startled too by the sight of the Myddelton diamonds in his niece's hair and about her neck and wrist. Newly reset, of course, but he had recognised them nonetheless. And now this. Now this. And Sir Charles would happily have left the table and hid himself for the devastation he would have, and had already unwittingly, blindly, self-righteously caused.

"I expect you mean to gammon us with some tale of an overturned Mail coach, Myddelton?" Emily teased as Myddelton settled in his chair.

"No. No, I assure you, not this time." Two servants stepped forward to fill his soup bowl. "But you must tell me all the latest...I've been away for, 'struth, above a sennight. What have I missed?"

Lady Emily Cowper leaned forward, her eyes very bright, and toyed with her spoon. "Mmn, where shall I begin? I suppose you are most interested in the Government...Yes, well, Prinny has still not found anyone who can hold a Cabinet together, which is vexing, but not, I think you'll agree, unexpected. I believe Wellesley is out of the running now...Though no one has actually said so. Canning is, of course, still desperate for office, but that again seems most unlikely." She rolled her eyes and slid a glance in Castlereagh's direction; while he lived, Canning would always be a poor second choice. "I fancy there has been some talk of a coalition with the Whigs, but as to that...it will never happen— though do not, I beg you, tell my mama I said so. She would count it disloyal above all things..."

Dinner continued. The second remove of meat and fish, of whipped syllabub, pastry and jellies was brought, carefully laid out and served, the guests all laughing and conversing. And Myddelton, looking about upon them all, and upon the room, knew such a sense of happiness. And yet...yet, he would infinitely have preferred to be away from there, away with her—somewhere, anywhere, their life together and as one begun, lying in a meadow with her perhaps, or on the banks of the Itchen— every sense enfolded in the fragrance of her sweetness.

Wishing only to gaze upon him, to reassure herself that of a certainty he had returned, Jane glanced up and saw him. And she blushed and smiled—for she thought she knew his thoughts, could read them in his face. And he must know they were reciprocated.

"...I think, ladies, if we have all finished..." Jane said, dipping her fingers in the finger bowl and drying them. "...That we must leave the gentlemen to their wine."

There was an outburst of chatter as the ladies gave their assent. The gentlemen stood. Jane rose and went to lead the way to the Drawing Room.

Mr. Brummell waited until the doors were shut on them and the servants had removed the covers and cleared the table. Then standing and lifting his glass as the decanter of port was passed from one gentleman to the next, the corners of his mouth quirking up, he said, "Gentlemen, I give you a toast. To our host, Myddelton, the Benedick. In all my life, I never thought to see such a bad case of it as he has got!"

"To Myddelton, the Benedick!" In gleeful solemnity, the men lifted their glasses and drank the toast. And laughed.

Hesitantly, for it was a hard thing to do, Sir Charles raised his glass and drank.

Then Liverpool, that unlikely advocate of marriage, rose. "To Myddelton and his beautiful bride. May they enjoy every happiness—health, long life, the felicity of children, and the comfort and joy of mutual companionship."

Their glasses refilled, the company again stood. "To Myddelton and his beautiful bride."

This was harder still, yet Sir Charles again stood with the company to drink the toast.

"I had heard, Brummell, that you was going to treat us to a verse on the travesty of...what was it?" Castlereagh asked genially. "Palmerston's cravat?"

"I was," Brummell admitted. "But he has been behavin' himself. Truly the joy is goin' out of my life. Hardy ain't here with his panoply of waistcoats to dazzle the eye—or do I mean 'blind'? And now this..." He sighed melodramatically and sipped his port.

"'Struth, there's always Prinny," consoled Dunphail.

"Ah yes. Our beloved Prince George, Regent extra-ordinaire, patron of leeches and hyperbolic architects. S'life, I was just thinkin' of him. It was this fine mahogany table that put me in mind of his..." Brummell tapped on the wood with his finger. "...ah, corsets."

"Thought you was goin' to say his brains..." quipped Dunphail.

"No." Brummell chuckled. "For unlike mahogany, his brains is neither useful, nor strong. Whereas his corsets do at least serve a necessary function."

"Brummell, you are too hard on him..." someone spluttered.

"M'dear fellow, that ain't possible!"

561

Still chuckling, Myddelton finished his port. And checked his watch. "Gentlemen, I do believe we should be joining the ladies..." He stood, then crossed to the door to wait for the others to precede him out of the Dining Room.

Lord Castlereagh stepped aside and fell behind to linger beside Myddelton. He, and no other, appreciated the full significance of Myddelton's belated appearance, the pallor, the healing head wound. "Am I correct in thinking that all did not go according to plan?"

"No, sir. It did not," Myddelton confirmed, and lowered his voice: "William Semple has broke both his legs—the landlord of the Duke's Head thought he had been pushed down some stairs...But, ehm, I saw your letters delivered. At least as far as the Continent."

Castlereagh paused, digesting this. "Did you? The Continent? Ah. I see. Bless me, the Continent? To France? Well, I am very glad to see you. Your dear wife was, I know, most concerned. As were we all...Perhaps you shall find a moment to tell me about it later."

"Yes," Myddelton said, following Castlereagh out and into the Drawing Room. Which surprisingly was empty. "'Struth, it's later than I thought." He smiled. "We had best be getting upstairs..."

"Or we may be testin' Lady Myddelton's spirit of forgiveness too far," continued Mr. Brummell, overhearing from the stairs.

Laughter broke out. Acknowledging the hit, Myddelton grinned.

"S'life, I didn't know you read minds, Brummell," someone said.

"Only our dear Myddelton's," replied Brummell over his shoulder. "But then, with his heart in such plain sight..." he added with a wry glance at the fall of Myddelton's formal white breeches. "And such a pretty heart as it is, do not you agree—it would be difficult not to..."

"Don't you mean his leg, Beau? His well-turned leg?" came a teasing voice from behind.

A slow smile pulled at the corners of Myddelton's mouth as he followed the others up the stairs. Nearing the top, he paused. "Doing it too brown by half, you know, Beau."

"M'dear fellow, it ain't even warmed yet," drawled Brummell. "Though I daresay it will be, you know, before the night's out."

Pemberton gave a shout of laughter and clapped Myddelton on the shoulder. "He is right, you know, Avery. By God, he's right." Then, more quietly, "But, upon my life, it ain't a bad thing. Tisn't a bad thing at all."

Jane was already standing at the head of the stairs, prepared to welcome their guests to the ball. And a smile, so private, so intimate that it made Pemberton feel like an intruder, appeared on her mouth and in her eyes when she saw Myddelton.

Myddelton took hold of her hand, and clasping it, raised it to his lips. "My heart, I have missed you...How are you?" He searched her face, studying it, relearning it, rejoicing in her.

"Very well," she whispered. "Very well, indeed." And standing so close beside him, dwarfed by his great height and breadth of shoulder, she caught a breath of him, of his much-missed familiar smell. His scent of orange blossom (musty and sharp) and cloves and snuff. And she drew it in deep, as the scent of fresh air after a long illness. "And you? Your head, you have been hurt."

He could not take his eyes from her face—he had dreamt of it on the boat. *Je ne vis onques la pareille de vous ma gracieuse dame...* "Yes. But I'm on the mend. I promise. I shall tell you about it...later." And such passion, desperate and craving, bolted through him. Not now. Not here. Christ, all he wanted was to gather her to himself and kiss her and kiss her until they melted together.

She smiled, certain of his thoughts. The sound of guests arriving for the ball echoed through the stairwell. He drew a deep breath and tried to stamp out all desire for the moment. In this, he failed. "Lady Derham, you are very welcome...Verdon, how d'you do? Have you been named to m'dear wife...Princess Esterhazy, how very kind of you to honour us...Mrs. Arbuthnot, it is a great pleasure..."

The ballroom began to fill. Few, it seemed, who had received an invitation chose to decline, for among other interests this was the first time Myddelton House had been open to receive guests in over a dozen years. Nearing eleven, the stream of new arrivals became a throng and all but the elderly widows seemed set for dancing. And finally, after a brief glance at his watch, Myddelton bent low to Jane's ear: "May I have the great pleasure and honour of this dance?"

She turned to look at him and found his face so close that she might have brushed his mouth with hers. For an instant, she contemplated his mouth, so alluringly near—and knew what Tantalus must have felt—then looked tenderly up at him. "Yes. Please."

He straightened, and catching hold of her hand, slipped his other hand about her waist to lead her into the centre of the ballroom. Others, seeing them, found their partners and came out to join them. And the leader of the small orchestra, observing Myddelton leading his bride out, turned to his musicians. Then marking the air with his bow, he played the first resonant chords of Mr. Beveridge's Maggot, before taking up the melody and variations.

It was sweet torment to dance—to bow and to touch, to weave and to part, to smile, to look, to yearn—all formality and patent longing. It went on too long and was over too soon.

But Pemberton was waiting for her when they had finished. And Myddelton lost sight of her after that, his attention monopolised by one after another of the guests who crowded in each room. "...Yes, it is wonderful to have the house open again," and "I am delighted you could come..." Downstairs and up, in the Drawing Room, Ballroom, Library and antechambers. "...'Struth, I believe m'wife is dancing...I did not know my parents held a ball then, no..." and "Did you try the cardroom? Yes, there are tables set up in the Library, downstairs..." Trial by affability. If nothing else.

Eventually—even as he castigated himself for such a rum idea as holding this ball when like any sensible couple they should have gone away to honeymoon in private, though it was very fine to receive the felicitations of so many—Myddelton could bear it no longer. And he disengaged himself and returned to the Ballroom to find her. And taking her hand, begged that her partner would permit him a few moments. A few moments, that was all—if only to gaze upon her and know that she was his. And guiding her, stopping every few steps to be congratulated upon his recent marriage to her, to smile, to endure tired witticisms, he achieved his aim—the corner balcony which opened onto the rear garden—and slipping through the opening in the curtain, drew her out behind the voluminous draperies.

"My dearest girl. Dear heaven, how I have missed you." He was determined to be gentle—but out here, in this place, and with the look in her eyes of such trust and delight, that resolve foundered. For smiling, glowing, she came to his arms, and without hesitation lifted her face to be kissed. He held her to him, cradling her head, his arm tight about her, and kissed her. Gently and not gently. In patience and in passion. And he discovered too that his possible loss had purged her of caution; she had lived for his return and this moment.

They had been there, away from their guests, too long, and he knew it. They would be missed. And struggling to locate some vestige of equilibrium once more, he held her against him, savouring her slightness, the perfume of her hair, the curve of her throat and shoulders and waist. And laying his cheek against her hair, his breathing erratic still, he said softly, "All that time I was on that tub of a boat I promised myself that if I should return alive, I would apologise for the abominable hash I have made of everything, and say, please, please, my dearest girl, can we start this again? Can we expunge the past month's horrors?"

Smiling, she drew back to hold his face between both her hands, to allow her gaze to rest upon his dear dear face. "How can you think I would need that? How can you think..."

He bowed his head, then mirrored her smile. And risked all. "No. No. You must let me say this. Please, will you let me start again?"

He could see the answer to his questions already written in her eyes, the answer, and a hint of tolerant laughter. She would grant him anything he might ask.

He took her hand and kissed it, then pressed both her hands against his chest and held them there. "So let me begin again and say what I should have said when first I saw you on the lawn at Britwell Park, playing with Lotto: 'I am Myddelton. I love you madly, and with all my heart. And I always shall. Please, will you marry me?' And I want you to say, 'yes.' But not because I'm telling you to or because you must, or your father arranged it, but because you want to. Because you wish to be my wife. Because you love me, and wish to be beside me every day and

565

every night for as long as we both shall live. And I will show you all my life how much I love you."

Her response took him by surprise. For she hugged him to her with a strength he had not known she possessed. And pressing her face hard against his chest, she whispered, "I love you so desperately, so dearly. I thought I had lost you. I thought I should die when you did not return."

Sudden tears crowded his eyes. "Did you not have my letter? No? Oh Christ..." And the blood and relief and urgent desire all whistled through his veins like a torrent. And his gratitude and exultation were so great that he knew of nothing to do but kiss her, softly, tenderly, as a pledge and a promise. For he was here with her. And had not died. But was here. "We must return to our guests...though I do believe the next waltz is mine."

Some time later, the Prince Regent's favour-conferring visit, a waltz and a fond and public kiss later, Myddelton found Pemberton just emerging from the library where he'd been playing piquet with Dunphail. "I've been looking for you...I have a question."

"Oh yes?" Pemberton grinned. "What happened to your ear?"

"I was shot. By a Frenchie." With a sniff, Myddelton drew out his snuffbox.

"Where's Hardy tonight?"

"I don't know," Pemberton shrugged. "He was meant to be here. Something must have come up. Probably one of those deuced violins he's forever after. And your head?"

"The same."

Pemberton nodded. "So this Froggie, he wasn't aiming for anything vital then?"

Reluctantly, Myddelton began to laugh. And rolled his eyes. He should have expected that. He took a pinch of snuff. "Ehm, can I ask you something? It's about Sir Charles—Janey's uncle?"

"Oh yes..." Pemberton said warily, darting a glance at Myddelton in a futile attempt to read him. "What?" This was one conversation he did not wish to have. At least, not if it was the conversation he thought it might be.

"Well, I don't know him particularly well, having only just met him the once, but, is it my imagination, or is he acting very oddly toward me? I'll swear he ain't said two words to me all evening."

It was the conversation he did not wish to have. "Your imagination's good, Avery, but it ain't that good." Ah well. Nothing for it. Pemberton scowled, hesitating, carefully choosing the route in. "I suppose you could put it all down to my aunt's doing. My Aunt Gateley, that is…"

Myddelton eyed him with suspicion. "This ain't still about that ball of Lavinia's, when we turned up three sheets to the wind, is it?"

Pemberton winced. Why did Myddelton have to have such a fine memory? "Sort of." He blinked and studied the ceiling for a moment. "The thing is, she got hold of that story about you rowing with me over an alleged affair with Janey—God knows who told her. So naturally she wrote to m'grandmother, who confided the whole to Sir Charles. Who came haring up here, thinking you was mistreating Janey. Only you wasn't here."

Myddelton remained silent. Good God, his appalling temper. What a mess. What a right mess he'd made of it.

"And the thing you don't know is that before she threw herself at you at the Castlereaghs' last week, la Wythenshaw had been inventing stories about you too. Well, mostly about Janey." Myddelton wasn't going to like this. He hated gossip. But he was going to hate this more. Pemberton braced himself for the inevitable reaction. "Saying that you had refused to bed Janey because you was wanting an annulment so you could…"

"What?" Myddelton exploded. "She said what? I never…That was…that was not the reason at all…" he spluttered. "I had meant…" Overcome with astonishment and mortification, defeated by his own admission of failure, he looked away, then studied the lid of his snuffbox. Hell's bells.

It could have been worse. Pemberton waited, and decided against repeating the full gamut of the allegations. He waved it away. "I know," he said gently. "But the thing is, Sir Charles got hold of that little nugget too. And what with one thing and another—like he assumed you had deserted Jane, and she refused to say where you was—he concluded that an annulment was just what was wanted..." He gave Myddelton a searching look. And felt that 'dumbfounded' was the word that best described him at that moment. And knew there was nothing to do but carry on. "So, he and his lawyer got the papers all set to go to bring a bill before the House, and he was planning on taking her back to Britwell Park in the morning. Which, I should imagine, accounts for his odd behaviour." There, that ought to cover it.

Stunned, stupefied, winded, Myddelton remained silent, shaking his head in disbelief. At last, in an attempt at calmness or wry humour: "I daresay he wants her to marry you."

"Me?" Pemberton burst out, suddenly furious after all that he had done on Myddelton's behalf. He did not see the joke nor, after the past week, was it likely that he would. "Me? Upon my life, I don't want her." He turned to face his friend. "I'll tell you what I do want though!" His look was intent as if he were taking aim. "What I want...What I want...is for you to get yourself upstairs and bed her soundly, you great idiot. Upon my life, what I want is for you to get yourself between her legs and stay there. For at least a fortnight!" Unexpectedly and suddenly, he grinned: "So that the rest of us can have some peace. For a change."

Myddelton blinked. Chagrin, anger, resentment, outraged pride, all dissipated. And drawing a long steadying breath, he smiled and admitted, "Od's truth, that sounds perfect to me."

36

His eyes closed, his back to the wall, Myddelton remained alone in the hallway in a futile attempt to recover himself or at the very least to bring himself under control before he returned to the ballroom—bracing himself for the rush of desire that would likely fell him when next he saw her. For the thought and wish and act having been articulated by Pemberton, he found it impossible to think of anything else, for his mind and all his senses were now united in yearning and would not be diverted.

Where was she now? Perhaps he should find her and say, 'The devil take it all, I'm taking you upstairs. Let the guests do as they will.' And had it been their wedding breakfast, he might have done so with impunity, though not without a measure of ribald amusement—initiated no doubt by Pemberton. Still…

And then there was the matter of Sir Charles' machinations and his attempt to rob him of his bride. Which had fair levelled him—rather like Jackson's right hook.

"My dear Myddelton, you appear perplexed," Lord Castlereagh said, finding him thus. "Is this a convenient moment?"

No and no and no. "Yes. Yes, of course."

"Is there some place…"

No. "Yes, absolutely. We can go into Broke's office, sir—just off the library. We may be private there." And his mind and heart resisting, protesting, Myddelton led the way through the library full of card tables and guests at play to that one room which he knew would be untouched by the provision for guests and the rearrangement of furniture. But found instead of the orderly stacks of files and newspapers, a desk cluttered with empty ink pots, pens and broken nibs, quills and quill shavings, a muddle of books and ledgers on the floor, and papers strewn everywhere. What on earth? It made his desk at the Foreign Office appear a paradigm of ordered symmetry.

"Forgive me...'Struth, I...I cannot think what has happened... generally Tom is a paragon of tidiness and all that's proper..."

"Do not regard it," Lord Castlereagh said, dismissing the whole. "You shall sit down in that chair in the corner—for you rather look in need of a sit-down—and tell me the whole of what has happened to you in the past week."

It wasn't just a sit-down he needed. It was a lie-down. A lie-down with...Shut up, Myddelton. And determining to leave out the sea-sickness where possible, he began: "Well, sir, I left as you instructed and reached the coast at dawn..."

And sitting at Broke's desk—having pushed the detritus out of his way—leaning on his left elbow, cupping his chin in his hand, Castlereagh listened. And listened. Without interruption or question to the entirety of Myddelton's recounting—the events and speculation about Semple, the near disaster in France, the death of the Imperial guardsman, and Myddelton's risky and cold escape. And sat, considering and pensive for some time too after Myddelton had finished. Then: "But your head, you will be all right, will you? And the effects of the cold, they will pass?"

Myddelton smiled. Always, always Castlereagh was solicitous as to the well-being of his staff and friends. "Yes. The surgeon was unimpressed by the head wound—despite the accompanying headache. And he said that while I would feel the cold extremely for a time and may find it difficult to get warm again if I become very cold, that too should pass."

"Good. Good! For I certainly had not meant to put your person at such great risk, I do assure you. It is true that I have been concerned by the number of attacks on those carrying or collecting information. But had I even an inkling of the peril in which you would be placed, I should never have asked you to act as my courier. Never. Please, accept my most sincere apology for that...

"Now, you must tell me truthfully, is it your opinion that Shuster should perhaps be recalled? Though, to be sure, I would be loth to do so, I admit. He is exceeding valuable where he is. But has he been too marked by this, do you think?"

"I do not know," Myddelton said. "I cannot say." He stopped, remembering and reliving his revulsion, his horror, then said gravely: "Upon my life, I was as unprepared for the brutality and savagery of that French officer as any civilised Englishman must be. Though, of course, I have translated and read reports of just such events...But knowing—as in a written account—and seeing and hearing for myself, such as I did in France—these are two very different things, I now see."

Castlereagh nodded, the compassion evident in his dark eyes. "Yes. Yes, the Irish Uprising in '98 taught me that. The one in no way prepares one's mind for the other. And yet, it is only when we witness first-hand the direct personal loss that such violence inaugurates and engenders, only then do we comprehend how tirelessly we must work to defeat it. I must think on this..."

"But, sir, you'll not credit it, though Shuster was certain of it. He said I must tell you that Napoleon left Paris, left Saint Cloud, on the 9th of May. For Dresden. For an Eastern Front."

Lord Castlereagh gasped, sucking in his breath. "Thank God! Oh thank God for that!" He placed his hand over his mouth and jaw as the anxiety of the last days dissolved. There would be no invasion. There was no French plot. They were safe. Tchernishev was right after all. "Oh, thank God...I shall have to tell Liverpool. Oh, that is excellent news."

He rose and went to stand by a bookcase, ostensibly to peer at a shelf full of ledgers, then turned. "I cannot thank you enough for all you have done this past week. Your journey to France was a sacrifice well beyond the call of duty. And without your ingenuity and care, I cannot think what would have happened to Shuster, or to the papers you carried. And if it were possible for me to do so, had the King not been ill, you may be sure I would have told him."

Myddelton opened his mouth to speak, but undone by such praise, by every thing, found that he could not. Then: "I am no hero, sir," he protested. "I am a code breaker. Nothing more."

"Nonsense! Had you or Shuster been taken, I dare not think what the consequences would have been. You have saved not only Shuster's life by your actions, but our entire French network. And I shall not forget it."

Then, as delicately and diplomatically as if he were opening negotiations with the Russians over the further partition of Poland, Castlereagh hesitated, then said: "But, if I'm not mistaken...that is, I understand from young Pemberton that your absence over the past sennight has caused certain difficulties and a degree of misunderstanding...in some quarters."

Incredulous and disconcerted, Myddelton felt his eyes widen. No. Pemberton had not told him...He could not have. It was not possible that he had gone to his Governor.

"...That my sending you off when and as I did prevented you from putting your marriage on a proper footing, as it were..."

But he had, damn him. And like a schoolboy, Myddelton found himself blushing furiously. God in heaven, did the whole Town know? Lud, it was one thing for his oldest friend to know what he had and had not done. Quite another for the Foreign Secretary to be in possession of such details. Chagrin, embarrassment, mortification—was tonight meant to be an infernal medley of these emotions? Apparently so.

"Which has, I have learned, led to Sir Charles taking the unhappy and highly inflammatory step of preparing a bill of annulment to bring before the House. Forgive me, I can see I am causing you the greatest discomfort. But, my dear Myddelton, I must ask, is this indeed the case?"

"Yes," Myddelton admitted. "That is to say...ehm...I believe so. You would appear to be better informed than I, sir. For I did not know of the bill of annulment myself. Until this evening, that is."

"But, forgive me, I must ask, the grounds exist as stated, do they?" the Foreign Secretary probed as gently as he might.

Flushing wildly, Myddelton sat as frozen, then nodded, rueful. "Yes."

"I see. And this unresolved issue has been hanging over your head for more than a month now. And in all that time, I have been commanding your services at the Foreign Office, day after day requiring your presence there, relying on you for all my translations and code-breaking. And you have not said one word in protest, bless you. It was badly done of me and I must apologise unreservedly." He frowned. "I certainly did not stop to think when I asked you to travel to Guernsey, and I most assuredly did not intend to cause you any familial discord." He hesitated. "This is most unfortunate. Alas, sexual scandals, as you know, are the one thing that can irredeemably blight the most promising of political careers. So..." He drew a pensive breath. "Upon my word, we must prevent such a scenario from developing. Hmnph. And since it is I who have kept you from your lovely bride...Then, since that is the case, I must do all in my power to set things right." He frowned and flexed his shoulders, then obviously came upon a solution, for he brightened. "Yes, to clear the field for you, insofar as it is in my power so to do...Yes...that will do. That will do.

"Thank you for a wonderful evening, my dear Myddelton. And now, if you will excuse me, I must seek out Lady Castlereagh," he said and departed, leaving Myddelton, not for the first time this evening, bewildered and amazed.

Sir Charles Heron had passed a most remarkable evening. Most remarkable indeed. For from the moment he had come downstairs for dinner, he had been the recipient of the fullest barrage of the Foreign Secretary's amiability, urbanity, gentility, wit, and formidable intellect. And in the company of his friend, Liverpool, and the Foreign Secretary, as well as others of Myddelton's circle like Northcote, Sir Charles had found himself discussing the latest developments on the Continent, the overtures being made by those disaffected Frenchmen such as Talleyrand and Fouché, the critical economic situation caused by the Continental Blockade—whether the revocation of the Orders in Council would in fact satisfy the Americans—and had heard too a subtle but continuous panegyric on Myddelton's many talents, his judgment and devotion, and his indispensability to the Foreign Office and the Government. All of which might have proved a welcome and gratifying escape from such thoughts as must now plague him about his behaviour toward his niece and Myddelton—had not the evening also provided indisputable evidence that those whom Myddelton considered friends, like Northcote, were not the reckless gamblers and foppish fools Sir Charles had convinced himself they must be. And despite all this, despite the certain knowledge that he must apologise to Myddelton for his unwarranted interference, he found he was having as fine an evening as ever he could remember.

With Liverpool at his side, he now strolled from the Drawing Room into the Dining Room, where a supper buffet had been laid out.

"I do believe Napoleon will find he has more than underestimated the stolid temperament of the Russians," Liverpool was saying. "I tell you, I am convinced of it."

"Ah, supper!" the Foreign Secretary declared, coming to stand beside Sir Charles; clapping his hands, he rubbed them together. "Now this is pleasant. Good gracious, what have we here? Lobster patties, quails' eggs, and jellies...And caviar...Myddelton has a particular fondness for that, I do believe...Now, Heron, what do you say to coming across the Square with me after supper? Liverpool, you must come too. Are you speaking of the intended French campaign of Russia? There are some maps I would desire to have you look at...Heavens, yes. Heron, I should very much like you to see the scale of the war, but also the scale of our successes...Wellington's command of the situation in Spain is so very competent and far-sighted...But I'm afraid we shall have to look to our Allies in the east if Napoleon is indeed planning an invasion of Russia as we believe he must be...Say you will come? My dear Lady Castlereagh has already returned home to ensure the candles are lit and the house ready for guests..."

"Well yes. Yes, thank you. I should be most pleased..." Sir Charles said, flattered and flattened.

Castlereagh's keen eyes sharpened. "Good, good. Now if you will excuse me, there are just a few others I would wish to include in this..." And humming softly to himself, he went off.

Thus it was that a little before two, well before anyone with experience of Society balls would have believed possible (unless of course the food had been inferior or the champagne had run out) that

Myddelton House had grown surprisingly thin of company—that is to say, any male company that might be reckoned to have political leanings. All had decamped to Number 18, St. James's Square. Which had left a good many ladies partnerless, so that they too began to depart.

Myddelton wandered through the half-empty ballroom and out. Was it possible that the ball would not go on all night? 'Struth, it was too much to hope for, was it not? And found Pemberton on the vestibule landing, standing on the lower of the two steps to that hallway which led to their private chambers, sipping contentedly at a glass of champagne. Myddelton stretched his shoulders beneath his black evening coat and yawned. "'Struth, this is peculiar…"

"What is?" Pemberton said, gratingly cheerful.

Myddelton shrugged. "This is. Suddenly, for no reason I can understand, more than half the guests have just gone. Vanished. There's only a handful in there now," he said nodding toward the ballroom. "'Struth, I've never seen anything like it…" But it had been an evening of confoundedness, so perhaps this was no odder than Sir Charles' behaviour, or that of Castlereagh…

Pemberton smiled. Serenely, cheekily, like a smug putto. "Yes, that worked rather well, didn't it?"

"What did?" Myddelton asked shortly.

"Castlereagh's little plan. He said he meant to clear the field for you, didn't he?"

Now truly confounded. "What?" Myddelton murmured, his eyelids flickering.

A smile of such friendship, such warmth, replaced the insouciant grin. "Clear the house for you. So you could get yourself to bed. Where you belong." Pemberton gestured in the direction of the bedchambers with his head. "Go to her, lad."

Myddelton was now well and truly lost. "What?" he spluttered. "I can't go to bed. There are still guests here and…"

"Never mind them. I'll look after 'em. Give you m'word, no one'll even notice you're missing." Pemberton nodded toward the bedroom again. "Now, go on. Go to her…"

Bemused, uncertain, torn, but such an opportunity as took his breath away was before him. Myddelton smiled and shook his head confusedly. "What? Now?"

"Aye. Go on. What are you waiting for? She's been in there, waiting for nearly a quarter of an hour."

Stupidly, for this was beyond his comprehension, it was too wonderful, too unlooked for...

"Go on," Pemberton urged. "Go to her."

Myddelton's breath quickened and caught in his throat. "She has? Right." And his expression softened even as a rush of urgency took hold. "Thank you. Bless you. Thank you." And grinning widely, his exhaustion forgot, he took the two steps in one and disappeared down the hall.

Coming up the main staircase was another guest—one obviously lacking in political inclinations. "I say, ain't that Myddelton?" he asked.

Pemberton recognised the voice. "No, Simmons, it ain't," he said firmly. "Try the library. Last time I saw him he was playing piquet in there."

Simmons laughed. "Oh. Right you are. Jolly good." And returned down the stairs whence he had come.

She had danced as his bride; she had been fêted. It had been the bridal party she had not had. And throughout the evening, whenever he had passed her, he had touched her fingers or rested his hand briefly— fleeting as the lighting of a wagtail—about her waist, wooing her, courting her. Briefly, all too briefly, until she ached with an unquiet yearning that would not be still. Until consumed with longing, she wished for the guests to all be gone and the night to be upon them. And with a fervent anticipation that would not be tempered nor suppressed, she had come to her bedchamber. And now...now, she had been here for more than a quarter of an hour, undressing in the haloed glow of a single candle.

She had removed the diamonds from her hair, from about her throat and her wrists, and returned them to their case. With great care, Haseley had removed her gown and would have unlaced her too, but she had sent her away. She had washed. And now she waited, uncertain, reaching round her back to catch hold of the laces of her small corset, fearing that she had been precipitate and it would be some time before he came.

She did not hear him open the door.

And for that moment, Myddelton remained on the threshold, just to take in the sight of her, seeing nothing but her standing patient and still, wearing only her chemise and stays. And his blood had gone racing with such thumping desire that he nearly crumbled with the force of it.

"Jane." Her name was a word of love in his mouth.

Her breath caught upon the first sound of his voice. And she halted, and her hand stilled, then fell to her side. And smiling, she looked up. He was here. Standing in the doorway, filling it, his coat and his waistcoat removed, his cravat unknotted and loosed about his neck. And that smile, that smile of breathless, wild rejoicing grew from within her as she gazed upon him.

And then he was beside her, standing with his head bent to hers, his hands reaching about her back, his face against hers, his mouth upon her cheek. "Let me…" he said, reaching around her, encircling her in his arms. *Unlace yourself, for that harmonious chime tells me from you that now 'tis your bedtime…*And his eyes closing, he found her mouth, and kissing it, kissing her, he sought out the laces, untying the ribbons and pulling them free— first with the fingers of his right hand, then with his left, until the two sides came apart. And kissing her, kissing her still, he lifted it from off her shoulders and flung it away.

He stepped almost away from her, for an instant no more, just to gaze upon her, soft and exposed and beautiful, and to know before God she was his. For it had been the thought of her, the hope of this moment which had dragged him back to life from death by exposure and all those other pains.

Then he bent to kiss her again. Tenderly, softly, deeply. For now and for always. To feel her joy and return it tenfold. To look upon her and see in her eyes such love.

She placed a trembling hand upon his chest, which he caught up and brought to his mouth so that he might kiss her palm. *License my roving hands and let them go Before, behind, between, above, below.* And gathering her hard against his chest, he held her close and kissed her and kissed her, his arm about her pressing her to him, his hand travelling the length of her back, moulding her to him, touching and savouring, and finally, coming to rest upon her breast. And he heard her love-sigh against his mouth.

Reverently, her newfound passion transporting her, clinging to him, she kissed his face, his throat, his mouth. For she would never have enough of his presence, of that which she had nearly forfeited, nor were there kisses enough in all the world to tell him of her love for him.

And though he wanted to gather her up and carry her through to his own chamber, he would not. But catching her in his arms, he set her upon the edge of her own bed. Weak with the urgency of a month's yearning, he dropped to his knees before her. And caressing her ankle, holding it, he slid his hands up along the length of her calf. *O my America, my new found land, my kingdom...*

Slowly, slowly, she lifted the hem of her chemise until it revealed her beribboned garters, tied with rosettes just above her knees, there for his pleasure and possession. Straining for control, he carefully untied the first. And pulled it away from her thigh, then slipped her stocking down over her knee to reveal her leg and the soft skin of her inner thigh, of palest pristine pink, *cuisse de nymphe*, untouched and perfect. And he bent to kiss her gently there. Then resting his head upon her knee, he untied the second of her garters, drawing on the ribbon until it loosened and fell away. *My mine of precious stones, my empery...* And raising his eyes to her, he caught sight of her smile, and closing his hand about the ribboned garter, he held it, then tucked it into his pocket. *How blessed am I in this discovering thee!*

And the smile she gave him was her lover's smile, as delicately she smoothed the back of her hand across his cheek.

And now, conquering and conquered, he stood and drew her chemise up and over her head and dropped it to the floor. She loved and had confessed it; she was his triumph. He could hold back no longer. And with her naked beauty before him, he buried his face against her throat, against her breast, filling his nose and mouth with the feminine scent of her, and touching her, her breast, her thigh, laid his hand across the flat of her stomach to span it. And felt too the gentle swell of her breast against his chest, the tender softness and exquisite warmth of her thigh next to his.

Delighted and delighting, awash with his touch, his smell, his pleasurings, his kisses, she whispered against the kindness of his mouth, "Take me…now. Please."

And some time later, or much later, for who was counting any longer, he knitted himself into the fabric of her being. To take and be taken. To want and to know. To have and to hold. From this day forward. "Te amo."

๛

She awoke to the familiar sensation of Lotto's wet nose and warmer tongue on her outstretched hand, indicating the urgent necessity of his wish to go downstairs. And turning her face from him, she looked upon Myddelton, asleep beside her, breathing deeply, peaceful in the pale light. For it was the morning and she was his wife. And could not now be sundered.

She reached for the negligee laying across a nearby chair and rising from the bed, quietly, so as not to disturb his rest, she wrapped it round her to let Lotto out. And discovered in her dressing room that at some time, hot water had been brought to her washstand, which was still warm. And there on her dressing table, a letter on a silver tray:

> *My dearest Jane,*
>
> *Events have overtaken me once again. The gentleman I was to have met had sustained an injury the previous evening and I now find myself needing to continue my journey. I am assured however that I shall be back in London well before the opening of our ball. You did not truly believe that I would allow anyone else the great happiness of leading you out, did you? Will you inform our mutual acquaintance of these unforeseen circumstances?*
>
> *My dearest, you fill my heart and mind. Every moment that I am parted from you is as the soul's winter night—joyless, frozen, lightless, desolate. I ache and long for you, and think only of you.*

My darling wife, do not doubt me. Nor my love for you. I shall return to you.

> *Your loving husband,*
> *M*

"Oh my dear...my very dear..." she murmured, clutching the paper to her, glancing through the open door to where he slept. And, washing herself, she returned to the bedchamber to slide once more into the bed beside him.

And it was later still, the sun high overhead and penetrating through even the thickly padded curtains, that she felt him stir. His eyes were still closed and his breathing even. He reached out, pulling her to him. And half-smiling, feeling her warmth, her softness at his side, he said contentedly, *"Busy old fool, unruly sun, Why dost thou thus, Through windows and through curtains call on us...Saucy pedantic wretch, go chide late school-boys..."* And he opened his eyes to look upon her, his wife, his heart, his life. And rolling onto his side, exultant, he bent to kiss her awake, to brush the fair curls back from her forehead, to rejoice over her and kiss her again.

"What happened to your head?"

"I was shot. In France."

"You went to France?" she questioned, fearful in retrospect. "Lord Castlereagh only said Guernsey..." Carefully and gently, she touched his ear. "And this?"

"The same." Her touch removed the sting of it.

"And this?" She ran her finger along his bandaged arm.

"I became delirious...so they applied a blister to wake me."

"Oh...Oh, my dear..." she fretted, and leaned over to kiss, as one does to a child, his hurts.

As ever, her sweetness, her tenderness infused him with such tranquillity and contentment, and a new, unexpected burgeoning of deeper affection than even that of a moment ago. And she found herself fully embraced, kissed, and touched as only he had touched her. "I am sorry if I hurt you...But I swear it will never happen again. Upon my life..." And he bent himself to please her and to teach her all rapture.

And between their happiness and discoveries of each, entwined still together, languorous, he gave her a highly expurgated version of his voyage to France; and learned, finally, who the General was and what he was doing dining at their table: "He is my mother's cousin, and was my father's mentor in India. Did you not know? I have known him all my life as a sort of godparent...or great uncle, I suppose." And when she explained how she scuppered Sir Charles' intention to learn of Myddelton's finances (which made him sit up in anger), he fell back against the pillows, roaring with unstoppable laughter, jiggling the bed, and murmuring, "Tom? Tom? Dear God in heaven, I wish I might have seen his face..."

And later still: "We should no doubt get up," he said, waking slowly, his arm about her, cradling her to him. It seemed like a very poor idea to him. The worst. "I must and should speak to your uncle..."

"Leave it," she pleaded, tracing a shy pattern on his bare shoulder. "There will be time for that." Her touch, though tentative still, was more persuasive than her words, her smile, dozy, replete, radiant, and imperfect. "Let it keep. Leave him. Leave it all. Until tomorrow...or another day."

And looking down upon her, he returned the smile. For she was here and he was home. *"She is all states, and all princes, I, Nothing else is...Thou sun art half as happy as we...Shine here to us, and thou art everywhere; this bed thy centre is, these walls, thy sphere."*

Also from Dragon International Independent Arts

Harbour
Paul House

They came down out of the mountains with the flat plain of Kwantung stretching away before them to the horizon, unaltering and immense.

Three cultures collide — the end of an Empire.

Half a world away from the Nazi menace, Hong Kong stands at the crossroads of East and West — proud colony of the Tai-Pan and the triad, of Tao-ism and traders, of the outsider and the half-caste.

But just as Britain and Europe are threatened by Hitler, so Japan is advancing relentlessly on Hong Kong. As war is declared and hostilities gather pace, this flawed, glittering society, forgotten and abandoned by its colonial masters, is turned upside down. Privilege and power, honour and chicanery, self-interest, fatalism and opportunism all collide.

As these worlds fragment, a love story emerges to defy convention and culture.

www.diiarts.com